Las Palomitas
(The Little Doves)

A Story of El Salvador

Laura L. Valenti

ISBN 978-1-9701-0920-7
Library of Congress Catalog Card Number: 0000-0000

Published June 2021

PUBLISHER
LOGO

Dedication

Dedicated in loving memory to
Dorothy K. and Dorothy L.
two incredibly special women,
one my friend, the other
my friend and my mother,
both of whom loved Latin America,
especially El Salvador;
and to the great love of
Our Father in Heaven
with whom they both now live,
along with Jesus and His Angels.

*"I have told you these things,
so that in me you may have peace.
In this world you will have trouble. But take heart!
I have overcome the world."
John 16:33*

Author's Preface

Almost thirty years ago, I wrote *Las Palomitas* as the peace accords to end El Salvador's Civil War were signed in January 1992. By God's grace, I was in the country then, for the first time since that war began. It was a deadly dangerous time for so many—people of faith, poor people, anyone who had the audacity and courage to stand up to those who had run the country to their own advantage for generations. Unfortunately, as in other Latin American countries, the US response was that anything was better than a Communist or even a Socialist based government. And once again, just as they had done in Guatemala in the 1950s, in Chile in the early 1970s and in Nicaragua in the late 1970s, the US supported right-wing dictators who would rather kill hundreds and then thousands of their fellow citizens rather than do anything to improve living conditions for the majority of those living in these impoverished countries. Make no mistake. I am not a Communist, Socialist or supporter of any particular form of government in its pure form. I am what I have always been—a freelance writer as well as a novelist—simply a reporter of that which has already transpired.

While this story is a novel, the news clips that open each chapter are real, taken from the headlines of the time. The experiences shared by the characters are based on my experiences, living for several years in a Salvadoran fishing village and on the experiences of several of my Salvadoran friends and associates, including other American technicians, teachers, and missionaries, including Father Denis and Father Bill, Catholic volunteer Rose Mary, and our martyred friend Sister Dorothy Kazel.

Although it was written almost three decades ago, life has now reached a point where it could be published, or perhaps, another way to put it, is that God would no longer allow me to live in peace with this manuscript lying quietly in a box on a shelf in a closet. This war, like all civil wars, was a tragedy that marred so many lives, and it would be easy to try to forget and pretend it never happened. Yet, to do so endangers future generations. We must remember, even the saddest of times, so that we can learn and grow and do our very best to never let people's hatred and distrust reach such a catastrophic point again. If we are to ever progress in this world, we must do so by reaching out to one another with love and compassion despite our differences. That is my prayer. I hope with all my heart that it is yours as well.

PROLOGUE

The heavy telephone receiver struck its dull black cradle with such force that nine-year old Ricky stopped open-mouthed in front of his uncle's scoffed packing crate of a desk.

"Those fool jackasses couldn't find a well with both hands and a road map if they was sittin' on it!" Dallas Mercy finished the statement with an oath as he hunched over his desk, shoveling through towering mounds of papers. The boy, who had come into the room to ask if he and his cousin David might go fishing in a nearby pond, thought better of it and turned to go, grateful at this point, to remain unnoticed.

"Ana Luisa!" Dallas' heavy drawl spilled the first name across the second. The thunder in his voice made the wooden floor shiver beneath the boy's feet, bringing him to a sudden stop.

"Oh, hey, Ricky." The voice as well as the manner, softened abruptly, as he caught sight of the bright blue eyes and tousled blond hair in the doorway. "You doin' okay, young 'un?"

The boy answered with a shy smile, wondering what happened to all the fury from the moment before.

"*Sí, don Dallas*." The lithe and lovely Ana Luisa darted into the room, still catching her breath. Barely twenty years old, she served as Dallas' housekeeper and caretaker for David whenever his father was not at home.

"Ana Luisa! Good, look, girl. I gotta light out of here for a couple of days and I don't know when I'll get back. Those jack—, sorry, them fools up north have got things so screwed up what with the drilling rig, as well as something wrong in the rights statement that they're tellin' me now. I dunno. All I know for sure is I gotta get up there before the whole thing comes undone. It's too good a deal to let go."

The crestfallen look on her face said more than any words.

"I know. I know. I told ya you could go home to San Antonio to your sister's place this weekend, but this here's an emergency, and it just can't be helped. It ain't my idea of how to spend Easter Sunday neither, believe me. Don't imagine I'll be back before then. Now go pack me some duds, clean shirt or two, ya know what I need. I got to go now!" He gave a small clap of his huge hands to emphasize the last word, and the girl scurried from the room. Ricky lingered, peeking around the door frame, before scampering off to tell David the news of his father's immediate departure.

In less than half an hour, the three of them, Ricky, David, and Ana Luisa stood assembled in front of the low frame house, as Dallas hoisted himself into the driver's seat of a battered white pickup truck. The thinly upholstered springs complained beneath his weight. He goosed the engine to life, threw it into reverse, and waved as he hollered above the roar.

"I should be back by Monday, kids. Don't give her no trouble now. Sorry, Ana Luisa." He shrugged the last words. "I'll make it up to you. I promise."

She waved with a bright smile, like the boys, and wrapped her thin arms protectively around Ricky as he took a step or two back to avoid the turning nose of the truck.

The spring Texas wind that tugged at his jacket still carried winter's edge despite the bright sunshine that made them squint to watch the truck pass out of sight. Ricky snuggled against her, enjoying the extra measure of warmth and was surprised by the drops that splashed first on her arms and then into the dust at his feet.

Despite the falling tears no sound escaped her. "What's wrong?" he asked in innocence, trying to fathom the source of raindrops on a sunny day. Ana Luisa was the most beautiful woman in his small protected world, with the sole exception of his own mother. He could not comprehend a problem so serious that it might reduce her to tears.

She shook her head, refusing to explain, dabbing at her eyes with a tiny white handkerchief.

"Come on in the house." David herded them both toward the front door. "It's bad, huh?" He looked from one to the other, once Ana Luisa was inside, seated on the living room sofa.

"You was supposed to go be with your family this weekend. I know that much."

Ricky perched beside her, his short legs sticking straight out on the overstuffed couch cushions. He never ceased to be amazed by his cousin's grasp of what was going on in his own household. Whether here or in his father's house in the Midwest, Ricky felt totally divorced from the discussions of the world of grown-ups. David, two years his senior, was a marvel in his eyes, having learned to decipher the language of adults at an unusually early age. He regularly impressed his younger cousin by having at least an idea, if not necessarily the right one, about what was happening.

"Did somebody die?" David asked bluntly. "Is that why you need to go?"

The sunshine of her laughter broke through her tears for the moment. "No," she spoke in heavily accented syllables that even Ricky could hear were different from the local Mexican farm workers.

"No one dies." She chose to offer her own explanation, a safer option at this point than depending on the extrapolations of the boys. "It is *Semana Santa*. Easter, you call it."

"And that's why you're crying?" David eyed her in a sideways measure of disbelief, his arms folded across his chest, in a miniature replica of his father. "'Cause ya won't get to pick up Easter eggs, and you won't get no chocolate bunny in a basket?"

"Oh, no!" Ana Luisa's eyes widened in surprise as she realized how little he understood of her intent.

"*Semana Santa* is much more than that. It is the holiest of days, the greatest of the year, even more than Christmas. Today is Wednesday, yes? Day after tomorrow is Holy Friday, the day of the *alfombra*, and then three days later..." her voice trailed off. "It is not gifts in a basket, but it is *la resurrección de Cristo*, all the beauty and celebration. And for me this time, it is my whole family together for many years now. Even *mis abuelos*, my grandfathers are coming to the Texas home of my sister from El Salvador."

"I thought you told me your grandparents were from Guatemala." David corrected her English as he made the statement.

"Those are the grandparents of my mother," she endeavored to say it correctly and still mixed up the words. "*Mamá y papá de mi mamá.*"

"Your grandparents," David sorted it out for her. "Your mother's mom and dad."

"*Sí*," she nodded. "The fathers of my father come from El Salvador."

"Did my dad know they were comin'? Are they gonna live in San Antonio now like you used to?"

She shook her head. "I do not think he knows. They are here just these few days and then no more." Her hands flew to her face, and her tears began again with no hint of stopping any time soon. She retreated to her room at the back of the house.

"Okay, we got stuff to do," David announced as he headed down the hall over the matted green shag carpet.

"Like what?" Ricky trailed along behind. "She feels so bad. What can we do?" David climbed on a chair to pull a small savings bank in the form on a metallic bucking bronco off the high shelf. "We'll go to San Antonio, that's what." The matter-of-fact answer both amused and startled his cousin.

"We can't do that," Ricky laughed, albeit somewhat apprehensively at the ridiculous suggestion.

"Ana Luisa can't drive, and there's no car or truck." David spilled the contents of the bank across the thin chenille bedspread. "That's why we take the bus. It stops right out there on the highway. That's how Ana Luisa went before." He proceeded to organize the different coins and flatten the crumpled paper bills. "There's $37.52. Some saved from my birthday and some from other things. It's enough."

"But what happens if....?" The younger boy stopped, not even certain what the next question should be.

"Just go get Ana Luisa and tell her to come here." David took charge of the situation. "You want to make her feel better, don't cha?" He continued speaking as his head and shoulders disappeared under the bed. He re-emerged tugging a bedraggled leather suitcase after him. Ricky remained rooted to the floor. "Well, don't cha?" David repeated.

"Yeah, but...."

"No problem then. Go get her and try to look happy about it, will ya? She won't want to take you along if you look that scared about the whole thing."

It took some convincing on David's part to persuade Ana Luisa that such a venture would not result in some sort of disaster, but Ricky had long been aware that his cousin was an expert in that field. Nor was the desirous fire that burned in Ana Luisa's soul to be with her own people on this particular holiday easily quenched.

When he looked back on it years later, certain parts of that journey, what was to become for Ricky and David the first of many adventures, remained crystal clear in memory while other portions faded mercifully with time.

Ricky remembered following behind the tiny funnel clouds of dust that arose from David's cowboy boots as they trekked up the quarter-mile to the highway and the strain that showed on Ana Luisa's face as she paid the bus driver in handfuls of pennies, nickels, and dimes for their tickets. The driver asked if she was certain she was supposed to be taking these two white boys with her, and she paled as she assured the driver it was perfectly all right. Even David had to get into the act as he guffawed and told the driver, he must be new as the three of them went places together all the time. The man leaned over the huge steering wheel with a dubious expression on his face before handing Ana Luisa the three tickets. Ricky held his breath certain he would be caught in the biggest lie of his young life.

Watching out the large gray-green tinted bus window over the next many hours, the boys saw the hills of northeast Texas covered in towering dark green pines change into plains dotted by small struggling ranches like the one that had just left.

The Ft. Worth area behind them still spoke as clearly of the past of cowboys, horses, and longhorns as nearby Dallas led toward a future based on oil, modern investment, and commerce. Then came the dry prairie lands of brambles and brush which burst forth into the busy city of San Antonio, a stunning inseparable blend of two cultures, Anglo and Hispanic.

The glittering mass of advertisements and store windows in English shifted gradually to English and Spanish, and as they entered the *barrios*, home of the city's Latin community, they switched to one flavor only, *español*.

"We are almost there," Ana Luisa whispered to them both as she pointed to what looked like just another upcoming intersection of stoplights swinging in the wind. Ricky had been studying the ribbed rubber mats of the bus floor when everything caught up to him at once. The thrill of mischief and the fear of discovery added to what might have been a simple case of motion sickness on any other day. Everything he had eaten earlier in the day was on the floor of the bus, a mere few blocks from their final destination. David was as disgusted as Ricky was humiliated. Ana Luisa was, as ever, simply forgiving.

"*Ay, pobrecito*," she crooned. "Why did you not say you are sick?" There was no accusation, only genuine concern. "Come. It is time. We get off. Too much bus for you today."

The driver scowled at the three of them as the woman bustled the two boys up to the front and asked for the doors to be opened at the next intersection, blocks from the proper station.

"Can't do it, Missy," he croaked at her like a large self-satisfied frog. "This ain't no city bus that drops people all over town, you know."

"But the little boy, he sick." She cocked her head toward the back of the bus as she gestured with her hand in a running motion up her body that clearly indicated what was coming. In an unusual model of good timing, the stench of Ricky's last meal wafted to the front of the bus as she made her explanation.

Ricky did his best imitation of a hound dog slinking out of the room after creating a mess as the driver threw open the bus door, cursing all small children under his breath. Ana Luisa and David followed happily after him.

The coursing rhythm of a Latin city flowed over, around, and even through them as fast as their country boots hit the sidewalk. "*Ven acá*". Ana Luisa converted to her native language as she, too, experienced the palpable taste and feel that was as close as she had known to home in a very long time. She grabbed Ricky's hand and struggled with a large old-fashioned valise in her other. With a happy grin plastered across her face, she headed down the broken sidewalk, admonishing David to stay close by.

The streets were brightly decorated with colors, banners, streamers, all manners of things that glittered in the late afternoon sunshine, especially so in comparison to the grime, grit, and graffiti that seemed to cover nearly every other vertical and horizontal surface in sight. Ricky struggled to keep up. David carried the suitcase the boys shared, and a quick glance at his face said he was almost as happy as Ana Luisa, enjoying everything he laid eyes on.

The younger boy was not sure how many blocks they trundled along before Ana Luisa pulled up short in front of an ugly gray door with what looked to be no less twenty coats of paint chipping off of it.

She pounded on it with her fist.

"*Halo, Mima!*"

A scurrying sound behind the door was the only immediate answer, and then a heavy lock turned, and the door swung inward.

"*Mira, Ana Luisa! Mami, ya viene.*" The wide woman behind the door jumped onto the sidewalk and hugged Ana Luisa so tightly, Ricky was afraid she would not be able to continue breathing. She grabbed for David next, but he dodged out of the way. Ricky, however, was not so agile. They were swept through the narrow doorway and down a long, cramped hallway that was more alley than indoor room, by the woman and half a dozen of her squealing, hugging, kissing relatives, on a wave of welcome and adoration the like of which Ricky had never seen upon anyone's arrival.

At the end of the alley, they burst into a room with no ceiling, a huge patio, concrete surrounded by gardens of flowering plants, and a second-story balcony that encompassed all four sides, topped off by the crowning warmth of the sunshine and white fluffy clouds. He wondered if this was how Alice must have felt at the bottom of the rabbit's hole. It appeared as if out of a dream, this place of life, love and laughter, that reverberated from music with a beat and incomprehensible words, and the shrill chatter of excited Spanish. The dirt of the city was locked outside of the polished premises by that great gray door as securely as were the ghetto thieves.

Ricky was hugged, squeezed, winked at, and teased in two languages by Ana Luisa's huge family who gathered en masse in the courtyard as they poured forth from rooms and apartments on two levels. The sweet perfume of bougainvillea, sweet pea blossoms, and a half dozen other flowering plants mixed with the steamy aroma of rice, beans, fresh tortillas, spices, stewing tomatoes, and peppers. Despite his recent mishap on the bus, Ricky arrived ravenous as did his two companions, and *la familia* was quick to respond to the needs of the hungry travelers. He only half-heard, as Ana Luisa explained their status to her family.

"*No mamá?*" Ana Luisa's own mother shook her head in disbelief as she pointed to the two boys while they attacked a meal of some kind of boiled fish, rice, and vegetables.

"No," Ana Luisa nodded emphatically, gesturing toward David but explained further in Spanish that Ricky was from *el norte* and was just *visitando*.

They met dozens of people that weekend, only a few of whom could Ricky remember when he tried to think about it later. Mima, the fat sister, who seemed as much as anyone to be in charge of the entire household and her skinny husband, whose name he could never remember. There were dozens of children, younger, older, some his own age, but he could not remember any of their names, only some of their faces. Ana Luisa's grandfather was a joy—*Tío Pío*, many in the family called him, a name Ana Luisa explained that he acquired because he raised chickens and liked to mimic their clucking and chirping and could do so expertly.

"What is the noise baby chickens make?" Ana Luisa asked David and Ricky halfway through the explanation.

"Peep, peep, peep," Ricky answered immediately.

"*Pues, en español, es pío, pío, pío,*" Ana Luisa laughed. "The children of our village in El Salvador called him *Tío Pío*. I guess that makes him Uncle Peep in English. *Tío Pío* sounds better, yes? Go ask him to make his chicken noises for you. He will if you ask him."

Shyness overcame Ricky, but he was more than willing to listen when David boldly stepped forward to ask the gray-haired old man with the calloused hands to cluck like a mother hen. Ana Luisa translated the request, and a wide grin spread across the old man's lined face under the drooping gray mustache.

Ricky had never heard a human being make a sound that so imitated a feathered beast. He soon discovered that *Tío Pío* could mimic wild birds as well, and he whistled, chirped, and sang like a whole flock of different birds, much to the delight of most of the children present.

Ricky and David shared a small cot that squatted at the end of the squeaky bed that Ana Luisa shared with one of her sister's daughters. No one else slept on anything much better, but sleeping was the least important of their activities that long weekend.

The pageantry of the holiday—from the carrying of Christ's cross through the streets on Good Friday by a man who looked as though he were truly about to suffer his Savior's same fate, to a miniature version of the famous walk over rainbow-colored streets to the great Mass on Easter Sunday—brought the celebration of new life home to his heart in a way that Ricky had never before envisioned. He could certainly never have imagined it all, reading the Easter story in colored leaflets each year in his father's church.

When he recalled it all later he realized, it was in the streets, the beautifully decorated streets that he enjoyed the many disconnected kaleidoscope moments that formed a huge stained glass window, organized yet separate pieces, big and small, that graced his dreams for months and years afterward. And it was in the streets as well that he observed the one true ugliness, lurking in the shadows.

They spent most of their day, Friday, making an *alfombra*, as they called it, the Spanish word for carpet, Ana Luisa told the boys. The entire family, in cooperation with their neighbors, turned out to decorate the surface of a side street with tiny mounds of colored sawdust. Only a couple blocks from Mima's house, Ricky understood little of what was being done but was content to do as he was asked, which was carrying small paper sacks full of the sawmill crumbs to different members of the family as they bent over their back-breaking task. They were busy creating a mosaic that covered all of the pavement. It was a mystery to him, and yet a fascination, so much effort put into a work of art that would soon be destroyed.

"Why?" Ricky could contain himself no longer. "Why do you do it?" His upturned face was irresistible, and Ana Luisa laughed at his wrinkled-nose puzzled expression.

"It is a matter of *respeto*," she attempted to answer his question. "When Jesus rode into the streets of Jerusalem that last time, the people threw down their coats for his little horse to walk over, yes? They had so much love and respect for him, they did not want even the feet of his horse to touch the ground. But in just a few days, it was all gone. All their respect, all their adoration...the people were fools, and he was crucified."

She frowned and took a deep breath. "Now he comes through the streets again, this last time as a man and we do this to show, we still care for all that he is, all that he offers us. With these colors, we tell him, we do not forget. We still love and respect him...always." She stopped and searched the small, freckled face before hers. "Does that explain it better?"

He nodded without a word, soberly considering all that she had said. As they finished, people began to line both sides of the street, the street that looked to Ricky as if it had been painted with the tiny mounds of colored sawdust, laid out in the intricate patterns that Ana Luisa and her family had so painstakingly arranged.

Adorned in his finest vestments, the crowd was led by the local priest who carried forth a golden cross of Christ, high above their heads. The parade of the faithful followed carrying statues of the Virgin Mary and Mary Magdalene as well as an effigy of the interred body of Christ. As the crowd approached from the far end of the street, Ricky's first thought was to protect the sanctity of the precious *alfombra* he had helped in his small way to create. As he broke free from Ana Luisa's grip, the masses surged forth, nearly knocking her and several others off their feet. He dove immediately beneath a nearby bakery cart rather than be trampled by the swelling human tide.

Safely nestled between the wheels of the cart set across an alleyway, he watched the swirling sawdust, once so neatly organized, turn into a rainbow-hued dust storm only inches off the ground. He glanced backward to discover the way behind him, empty, except for three half-grown boys. His first thought that he knew one of the boys, one of Ana Luisa's nephews, also staying at the house, was quickly dispensed as he recognized the scene—not the players nor the particulars of this conversation— just the drama, re-enacted in all cultures, of two stronger entities standing unfairly against a third weaker one.

He watched while the fragrance of baked sugar and cinnamon sifted down from overhead as the taller boys leaned in a menacing fashion over the shorter one. The older ones wore clean clothes and had on shiny polished shoes while their cowering victim who looked like any one of the many street kids he had noticed on their sojourns outside Mima's house. He sported grayish cotton clothes, the very colors worn out of them, and a pair of ragged tennis shoes. The smaller boy was further hampered by the stack of newspapers he had stuffed under his arm, his hands blackened with their ink. As he continued to resist the demands made upon him, he gripped his papers even tighter, until one of the older boys kicked him. The shiny leather shoes kicked again and again until the younger boy was on the ground, still suffering blow after blow and the newspapers scattered around him in a brightly colored ring of comic pages and advertisements. He held up his small hands in defeat and heaved himself to his knees, one arm holding his ribs. Digging into his pocket, he offered up the money they demanded, and they snatched it all. The other non-kicker slapped the smaller boy beside his ear as they walked toward the end of the alley and the vendor's cart, counting their loot.

Paralyzed with fear, Ricky watched their approach of what was certain to be a similar fate. In near panic, he realized he had nothing to offer. He shifted his position in hopes of spying David, but the small movement was enough to attract the would-be assailants' attention.

"*Gringo!* What you doin' there?" The kicker shouted at him and laughed as he kicked the wheel in front of Ricky, causing the boy to jump violently.

"No!" The older boy shoved his companion. "*Dejalo!*" he called over his shoulder, but his eyes never left the blue ones staring out from beneath the bakery cart. Ricky's first impression had not been wrong. He swallowed hard as his tears welled up. He glanced once more at the poor boy at the end of the alley as he tried to salvage the remains of his business.

Ana Luisa found him there not long afterward. She assumed his tears were those of a lost child, and in a way, she was not wrong. They went home to the house he had learned to love in such a short time, but now although none of its charms had changed in any way, it was also a place to be fearful. He anxiously watched for the mysterious unnamed relative, terrified he would come around a corner to extract some further measure of ransom.

On Sunday morning, they had their bags packed at Ana Luisa's insistence as soon as they were roused from their beds. "We go this morning to *la misa*," she told them as they complained about the early hour.

As the sun's first rays chased the last of the night's gloom from the nearly empty avenue, they scurried out the door.

Ricky remembered that Mass was long but far from boring as he listened first to the priest chanting in Spanish and then the parishioners' response, first in words, then in song. The people fell on their knees, a phrase he had often heard in his own church, but here, they actually did so, with much clunking and thumping as kneeling rails were dropped to the floor, and then tucked back into place when no longer needed. There was a pot of strange-smelling smoke, swung around in arcs, bells which sounded in the midst of everything and even here, the people paraded, up to the front this time, to receive that cracker that served the purpose of the miniature ones passed along the pews in the church back home. It was much like the church he attended on rare occasion with his mother and grandparents, when his father was not around. And here, like there, each one wished the others, *la paz de Díos*, the peace of God.

Afterward, they returned to Mima's house just long enough to enjoy a huge breakfast of tortillas, fried rice, refried beans, *huevos rancheros*, and *leche con café*.

His mother would never have permitted him to drink coffee at home, but here he was allowed, even encouraged to drink the strange combination of hot milk with a heavy hint of instant coffee and a serious amount of sugar stirred in.

Their leaving was a constrained version of their arrival, with kisses and tears, too, as Ricky was sure they were hugged by nearly everyone in the entire household. The bus ride home was shorter somehow and uneventful, a time to drift off into dreams of both the waking and sleeping variety.

As they trudged down the thinly graveled road, Ana Luisa suddenly dropped her valise and crossed herself.

Dallas' pickup truck was parked in the front yard.

"*Madre de Díos!*" She prayed in a whisper rough with emotion.

"Sweet Jesus, here we go." David, too, was muttering under his breath.

Ricky looked from one to the other, trying to determine if he should also be fearful of what was to come. He had forgotten all about Uncle Dallas, his own parents, almost everything outside the *barrio*, the entire time they were there. Perhaps it was the same for Ana Luisa, he thought idly.

"Just remember," David was instructing the trembling woman who walked as if to her own execution. "This was MY idea. It was MY money. Don't worry. He'll yell a lot, but it won't mean anything. You'll see. Come on." The taller boy led the way in as Dallas barreled out of the front door.

"Where in the name of Jesus, Joseph, and Mary, have you three been?"

This wouldn't be as easy as David made it sound just now, Ricky decided.

There were tears and accusations, shouting and recriminations, most of it between David and Dallas. Ricky, whose own father only rarely had anything to say to him, good or bad, had never seriously considered crossing him. Listening to the full-blown storm as it raged through the house, he was aghast at the way twelve-year-old David talked back to his father as if he were an equal.

When it was over, Ana Luisa was, as she must have known in her heart coming down the road, the big loser. Dallas fired her and told her she was lucky he did not beat her senseless for taking the boys into such a terrible part of the city.

"What if somethin' had happened to one of 'em? Did you ever give that a single thought? B.J. would have my head and my ass, too, if he knew his boy had been down in the barry-os. What in the hell's a-matter with you, woman?"

David continued to defend her but to no avail.

"You can do as good a job takin' care of yourself if this is the kinda thing that's gonna go on when I ain't here' was Dallas' last sour comment on the matter.

On Monday morning, he took command and ordered the boys into the pickup truck for the long drive back to Fort Worth, where they would meet Ricky's parents later in the day. Ana Luisa was told curtly to pack her things and catch the bus to wherever she cared to go. Ricky noticed that Dallas laid out the bus fare and some extra cash on the kitchen counter before going outside to finish the necessary chores.

"What will you do?" David asked as she stoically re-packed her valise and a large shopping bag with her meager possessions.

"Back to San Antonio, to Mima's house," she sighed. "Then, I find other job."

Ricky secretly longed to go with her, only partly because he envied her destination. His small heart ached for her, for some way to ease the overwhelming loneliness that emanated from her.

"Ana Luisa, I'm sorry. I guess this wasn't such a hot idea. I never thought of it turning out like this." It was a rare moment when David apologized for anything, Ricky thought.

"*O Corazon*," Ana Luisa cooed as she took his face in her hands, the way her sister, Mima, had done to all of them in her big house. "It is not you who said yes. Anyone can have an idea, but I said yes, and I would say yes, again. It was worth the pain. We did have a good time, no?"

"Well, yeah." Both the boys brightened as they nodded. "It was great, but it looks like you're the one that's got to pay for it, big time."

"Because I was the oldest. I cannot tell your father he is wrong. I was responsible. It is true. I did what I wanted. Now, I pay." She shrugged as the tears welled up in her eyes. "But I am not sorry we did it. Are you?"

They both shook their heads.

"Then we will never forget."

Dallas leaned on the pickup truck horn outside, and David gave her a clumsy farewell hug, embarrassed by more than the situation. The younger boy clung to her, afraid in some ineffable way, to let her go.

The ride to northern Texas was silent, almost sullen, and although no instructions were given, Ricky noticed as he was handed back to his own father that nothing was said about their weekend escapade.

As he sat in the back seat of his father's Buick for the long drive back to the rolling hills of southern Missouri, he vowed silently to keep that secret accord. He treasured every stolen moment the three of them had spent together, mulling it over, daydreaming about the events, harking back to that long weekend, whenever life as he knew it, became too boring or difficult.

Ricky never saw Ana Luisa again. He never even knew her last name, but it did not matter. She had left her mark, deep within him—a delicate name, a tender spirit, an introduction to another way of life, imbued with love, laughter, and a people who speak and act from the heart. He would never forget.

CHAPTER 1

*J*uly 1975, San Salvador, El Salvador. Unarmed students from the National University, marching to protest the government's million-dollar expenditure on the Miss Universe Competition to be held here later this month, were surrounded by government troops and tanks and fired upon. At least twelve students were killed, and others were critically injured. More than a dozen others have been reported missing since the incident. The government has moved to close the National University and deport forty professors accused of alleged subversive activities.

March 1977, El Paisnal, El Salvador. Father P. Rutilio Grande, a native of this rural village, located north of the capital, was murdered on his way to conduct Saturday Mass. Ambushed by unknown gunmen, he was accompanied by a teenager and a seventy-two-year-old peasant, both of whom were also killed.

Monsignor Oscar A. Romero, El Salvador's newly ordained archbishop and a personal friend of Father Grande's, is demanding an investigation. El Salvador's president, Colonel Arturo Molina, has stated that the priest's death is part of an international communist conspiracy.

March 1977, San Salvador. Several thousand gathered in the Plaza La Libertad to demonstrate against the results of the recent elections. Reminiscent of the last presidential election here in 1972, in which the winning candidate, José Napoleon Duarte was exiled to Venezuela, this year's contest was also marred by violence and charges of fraud as yet another military man, Colonel Carols Humberto Romero, has been installed in the Presidential Palace.

The demonstrators fled when government troops opened fire from armored personnel carriers. A government spokesman put the number killed at less than ten. José Moroles Ehrlich, the losing vice-presidential contender for the opposition, stated he saw "many people fall from bullet wounds." Outside observers estimate more than 200 demonstrators were killed.

May 1979, San Salvador. Soldiers fired on political demonstrators who were seated in and around El Divino Salvador, the city's metropolitan cathedral, killing at least 22. A spokesman for the army claimed the demonstrators fired first; however, several foreign correspondents at the scene reported that the attack was unprovoked.

Violence against private citizens in all sectors is on the increase, in this, the smallest of the Central American nations. According to recent reports by the Inter-American Human Rights Commission of the Organization of American States (OAS), during this month alone, 115 persons have been killed and 30 more seized off of the streets or dragged from their

homes in the capital by various organizations within
the military. These figures reflect only cases within the
city of San Salvador. It is feared that many more such
murders and kidnappings are taking place outside the
capital but go unreported by the peasant population.

The rising sun poured out its brilliance, first
across the sea, then over the land as it climbed into
an azure sky, from the deep blue-green Pacific. The
transfiguration of the gently rolling surface of the
water to liquid gold ensued as the heaving waves
reflected the light from above.

A band of native fishermen, scantily clad, nets
in hand, moved in silhouette against the radiant
background, wading in the frothy shallows. With the
skill of the many generations behind them, they cast
their *atarrayas*, hand-woven nets, over the schools
of sardines slipping through the waves. Like great
woven butterflies, the nets floated then hesitated
in mid-air, before landing with a definitive smack.

Beyond them, the brown volcanic sand lay empty
and pristine. In the thick grove of emerald splendor
that lined the beach, towering palms grew side by side
with evergreen *caserinos*, tropical cousins of northern
pines. Already a thin layer of pallid blue wood smoke
hung in the upper reaches of their branches, mute
testimony to the morning fires providing a hot breakfast
of corn tortillas, rice, and beans in the various thatch
huts scattered along the tree line and adjacent road.

Resting so quietly beneath the tallest palm that he
appeared to become a part of the natural landscape,

Rick Mercy watched the day begin. The first light of many days found him awaiting the darkened beach's sunrise transformation in *Las Palomitas*.

He drew a deep breath of the salty air, savoring the flavors before his eyes as well as those he could only taste and smell. Overhead, a few small doves flitted from tree to tree, and higher yet, the distinctive black outline of a frigate bird glided by, in search of another's meal to steal.

Rising to his feet, Rick strolled down to the water. The bubbly edge of the latest wave ran toward his sandaled feet, like cream pouring forth to the kitten's waiting tongue. He wriggled his toes, relishing the wet tickle as the shifting sands trickled around and between his toes with the receding waters. He fished out a tiny clam and rinsed it off, holding it up for a closer look. Happy as a clam, he smiled to himself, remembering one of his mother's favorite phrases, and tossed the tiny mollusk back into the gentle waves.

The morning sun, blindingly strong now, warmed him even at this early hour. He gazed out to sea, once more, across the gulf to the island mountain peaks and the misty distant coasts of Honduras and Nicaragua.

One of the fishermen glanced up from his nets to call out a greeting and wave. Rick answered in kind before turning away. His long stride carried him across the sand and the thick cushion of dead pine needles, long collected under the trees, to a solitary one-room wooden shack nestled in their midst.

Opposite the lone door stood a miniature kitchen, made up of a long wooden table supporting a tiny two-burner kerosene stove, a few jars and bottles, and a wooden rack with a handful of mismatched dishes and utensils. An extra-long canvas and wood frame cot, which held a knot of unmade bedclothes, was flanked by an old wooden crate, a large backpack, and a duffel bag, to make up a corner bedroom. A second small table and a chair beside the door and a cotton string hammock slung across the near corner, along with a miniature bookcase of planks and bricks, completed his home. All he needed for what had become the longest camping trip of his life.

He jammed a straw hat, like those worn by the local fishermen, over his longish straight blond hair and picked up an under-ripe mango from a bowl that had been fashioned from the husk of a large gourd.

Back outside, strolling toward the main road, he found the villagers were already bustling about, occupied with their daily tasks. Women and girls in faded cotton dresses carried heavy jugs of water balanced on their heads. A local farmer drove a cumbersome ox cart past two barefoot boys who switched at a few thin cattle, moving them along, ever in search of a morsel of green grass. A miniature pickup truck bumped over the washboard track, its blaring radio and staccato horn sending animals and children scurrying out of its path. Smaller children chased one another, giggling and shrieking about the huts, while their mothers admonished them to chase the scrawny chickens from their doorways instead.

"*Buenos días, don Ricardo*," a man bent nearly in half by the load of firewood strapped to his back, called out as Rick crossed the road. At Rick's approach, two young girls giggled, covering their shy smiles with one hand, while balancing their water carriers, with the other.

"*Don Julio*," Rick waved, and with a silent nod to the girls, continued on his way.

On the other side of the road, Rick cut between the huts. The raucous strains of a *ranchera* melody, the Spanish equivalent of old-time country music, wafted from a radio perched in a window. He continued through a long-abandoned mango and coconut plantation before emerging on yet another shore, this one vastly different from the one he had just left behind.

The dark sand of the river's edge was covered with a thin layer of heavily scented mud. Leaves and other natural debris washed down from the mangrove swamps above were deposited on the sand by both the incoming tide and the coastal estuary flowing to the sea.

The ocean sands on the far side of the road lay tranquil and untouched, but the river sands before him were alive with a noisy yet loosely organized chaos.

Barefoot fishermen scrambled in and around wooden *cayucos*, dugout canoes, as they unloaded huge, corded and nylon nets, and the small and medium-sized sharks and fish they had caught with them. While the men straightened and refolded the nets, women and children carried the catch high up onto the drier sands away from the mud and brine, to begin carving it into manageable portions.

The sharks were skinned, the hides salted and preserved for foreign processing into sharkskin leather. The fins were cut away next, dried and sold to an elderly gentleman who visited on occasion from the capital's Chinese restaurants. The shark livers were cooked down for their valuable store of shark liver oil, which often brought more than the meat itself. The meat was butchered last and sold to the local fishermen's cooperative. Half of it would be shipped and resold as frozen shark steaks while the rest would be salted, dried, and sold for local consumption, a veritable necessity for the coming days of Lent. Finally, even the teeth and jaws would be saved, painted, and sold to tourists, both foreign and local.

A great deal of good-natured chatter and scolding directed mostly at the children and wandering animals accompanied this morning routine. Deathly thin dogs and small pigs had to be chased off as they tried to steal any unguarded tidbit.

Rick stepped gingerly around the busy women and children as well as the pesky four-footed thieves. The distinctive aroma of marine fuel mixed with saltwater filled his nostrils as he congratulated several of the fishermen, his neighbors, on their day's catch.

Halfway down the beach, Rick stopped just short of the canoe of a barrel-chested man who was so engrossed in his own work that it took several seconds before he noticed he was under observation.

"*Don Ricardo!*" The fisherman's jovial salute echoed down the beach once he caught sight of Rick. "*Buenos días. ¿Qué tal?*" He shot his chin forward and threw his head back in lieu of a handshake as his hands remained fully occupied with the enormous nylon net he was struggling to fold.

"You have done well today, *don Miguel.*" Rick stepped forward for a closer look at the gleaming *curvina*, their silver scales sparkling like shiny new dimes in the morning sunlight as they lay in the bottom of Miguel's long narrow canoe. "They should bring a nice price."

Miguel's beaming face was its own answer. "You two were a lazy pair this morning." Miguel teased as he gestured toward his nephew, a young teen who was busy carrying the rest of Miguel's fishing equipment toward his hut, further up the beach. "You should have been out there this morning, and then, *si Díos quiere*, you would have something to show for it also." He grinned, robbing his words of any offense.

Rick smiled in response and watched as the boy headed back toward the boat. The youth's dogged pace changed when he saw his friend waiting for him.

José de la Paz Flores, known simply as Paz, had been Rick's fishing partner for the past several weeks. Miguel had taught Rick much of what he needed to know to fish these waters using local methods, but it was in fishing each day with Paz that he had gleaned most of what he knew about the sea and life in the fishing village of *Las Palomitas*.

Unlike the *tiburoneros*, or shark fishermen who left their heavy cord nets and *simbras*, hook-strewn lines, the night before and collected them the next day, Rick and Paz usually set out before the first light of day and drifted their net near the rocky shoreline of the bay and collected it a few hours later. They could do the same, leaving late in the afternoon and coming back before dark. Like Miguel, they fished for *curvina*, red snapper, and other quality white fish, using lightweight nylon gill nets that would become hopelessly tangled if left overnight.

The night before Rick and Paz had decided to take this day off, yet both were drawn, like every other fisherman in town, back to this beach, even on days when they did not fish.

"Have you seen don Paco's catch yet?" Paz asked, his voice laced with excitement. "It is truly a monster. He caught it on one of the long lines, a giant tiger shark, nearly six meters long! He said he went out very early today because he knew that the tide and moon would make this a very good time. He always fishes with his sons, and it took them hours to bring it in. They say—"

"*Ya!*" Rick laughed, taking hold of the boy's shoulders to bring him to a standstill. "Slow down."

"Can we go now, Uncle?" Paz turned to Miguel. "I can show *don Ricardo*, the great shark. If we do not hurry, it will be all cut up before we even get there."

"There is no way," Miguel barked, and his nephew's face fell.

"No, no," he added with a chuckle, noting the boy's expression. "There is no way Paco is going to begin to cut that fish before noon. Not until the whole town has seen it. You have not been yet?" He raised an eyebrow in Rick's direction.

Rick shook his head.

"Well, neither have I. I have just this moment come in myself. He is on down below with it. I saw the crowd when I floated past and wondered what all the excitement was about. Someone called from shore to say no one had drowned, so I decided it was nothing too serious. Just Paco and another of his monster sharks. Now the question is...." He dropped his voice and leaned forward as if to share a confidence.

Rick and Paz drew closer to better hear the juicy bit of gossip.

Miguel continued, "how many fingers does the man have now?"

Miguel laughed loud and hard at his own joke. Rick continued to shake his head with a grin this time. Pablo was well-known for having only seven fingers. The others had been lost, two from one hand, one from the other, catching sharks on long lines. While the results could be dramatic, like today's profitable prize, the risks were not small either.

Paz teasingly grabbed the edge of the *cayuco* and rocked it, keeping a careful gauge on the older man's balance as he threatened to dump him into the shallow water.

"Get away from here with you now." Miguel made a half-hearted swipe at the boy who dodged out of reach with ease. "Go see Paco's latest trophy, and while you are there, count his fingers!"

The two ambled along the water's edge toward the point of the peninsula on which the entire village was built. Clustered tightly together, the thatch huts and few permanent buildings that constituted the entire village were perched between the estuary and the sea on a tongue of land, split by the road that stretched only a few hundred yards between the two shores.

They made their way through the gathering of onlookers who had come to admire the great fish, pulled only partway out of the water onto the sand like some great beached craft. Paco and his sons trudged like zombies, exhausted by their struggle with the prehistoric fish as they prepared for the large job of butchering their catch.

They had found the animal alive on a *simbra*, an anchored line that they had left to drift between buoys, trimmed with huge, baited hooks. They had killed it with knives and clubs, pulling it up beside the boat, attacking it, and then releasing the animal to race wildly away, spurred by the pain and terror, before they pulled it in again to repeat the process. Eventually, the men had won but not without a long and laborious fight.

Rick walked around the shark, contemplating the once-powerful beast at his feet. Except for its size, it seemed unworthy of its fearful reputation.

The gray sandpaper exterior, with all the sheen of a new battleship, was rough to the touch. It didn't look much like a buffalo, Rick's thoughts meandered back to an explanation his cousin, David had once given him, comparing sharks to the American bison's importance to the Native Americans of North America. While the mystic reverence was missing, there was respect, and the economic realities were similar in that the Salvadoran fishermen were as dependent upon the shark and its many components as the plains Indians had once been on the buffalo for food and trade.

Paz poked at its nose with a damp, bare foot.

"*Cuidado!*" Rick spoke sharply, causing the boy to jump. "It's not been dead that long. What if it reaches out and clamps down on your foot as a last act of revenge?"

The surrounding fishermen chuckled and began to share their own well-worn stories about the dangers of shark fishing. Paco's smile was tired by this point, but he held up his hands, showing he had lost no more fingers to this particular battle.

"*Chiflado.*" Paz dismissed Rick's joke with the name and sauntered on, but he moved back ever so slightly from the shark's snout.

The last of the fishing boats had returned for the morning. The sun was climbing past the treetops, and the heat of the day would soon be upon them.

Rick and Paz retraced their steps, passing now empty overturned canoes, beached high above the water's edge in preparation for the incoming tide.

"Oh, I nearly forgot!" Paz dashed into his uncle's house as they came abreast of it. He returned with a pale pink envelope. "Arturo, the postman, brought this for you late yesterday. He asked if I would give it to you. It is from your family, yes?"

The look of consternation that crossed Rick's face was not what the boy had expected. "I'll look at it later" was all that the American said as he stuffed it into his back pocket.

As they walked on, crossing through the same coconut palm and mango trees Rick had passed earlier that morning, they skirted one of the original plantation's caretaker cottages. Rick and his cousin David had shared the little two-room house during Rick's first weeks in the village. But as his need for solitude grew and their differences became more strident, Rick had sought out his own individual abode.

The awkward silence was interrupted by the scampering of a two-foot-long black lizard that had been sunning itself on a rock in front of the house before their appearance.

"*Por Díos!*" Paz jumped at the rustling in the grass. "I thought it was a snake."

"Only a *garrobo*," Rick squinted in Paz's direction. "Is somebody still fretting about monster sharks? Now who is the *chiflado*? I always thought those things looked like they could be a miniature relative of Godzilla."

"Who is Godzilla?"

"A Japanese lizard," Rick stated, deciding not to elaborate further.

Rick left the door standing open behind them as they entered his cabin. He unlatched two of the window shutters on the walls away from the sun's burning rays and swung them to the inside. He had fashioned and attached the shutters himself, copying others he had seen in the village. While they did little against the seasonal swarm of flies and mosquitoes, they did an adequate job of discouraging larger intruders.

The cabin had long been abandoned and in danger of falling in on itself when Rick first discovered it. After much hard work and a minimum of materials, he had made it livable. Although he still was not certain who owned it, he had discovered that squatting on another's abandoned property was a time-worn tradition in *Las Palomitas*.

Rick pulled two large green coconuts from under the kitchen table. He positioned the first one as he crouched on the hard pack dirt floor and began to hack at its top with a short machete.

Paz dropped contentedly into the empty hammock, contemplating the man before him. Taller than anyone else in the village, blond and blue-eyed, it was obvious he did not fit in here, and yet in other ways, he did. Some days, he seemed almost like a boy his own age, but other days, he took on the long, thoughtful silences of a troubled man. He came from what Paz believed to be the richest country in the world. Therefore, he, too, must be a very rich man. If that was so, why, then, would he leave all that he must have there in such a fine rich

country, to come and live here in such a desperately
poor one like El Salvador? Why did he work so hard
to learn simple things like opening a *coco* with a
machete or taking fish from the sea? Surely he must
have servants or even machinery that could do these
things for him in his own country. Only one thing
he was sure of, Paz thought. Americans are a puzzle.

He had seen a few American tourists. Some were
rich and rude, apparently disgusted with most of
what they found here in El Salvador. Others were
sweet, sometimes in a patronizing, pat-you-on-the-
head sort of way. That did not particularly bother
Paz, since at his age, half of the village still regarded
him in much the same manner. It was not the same,
however, when they treated his father or his uncle
like that. It was condescending and insulting, and he
had seen it infuriate his cousin Franco.

Franco had his own opinions about Americans,
especially the businessmen and the government
types. Paz had never actually seen one as they had
bypassed the village for the most part, finding little
that could be converted into any kind of profitable
industry. He listened to his father, his uncle, and his
cousin argue late into the night about Americans,
their government, their people.

According to Franco, they came only to exploit and
rob them all of what little they have; to put people to
work in factories, turning out cheap goods for sale in
their own country. He called them *imperialistas* and
said they worked hand in hand with the government
types who Paz had heard on the radio, talking of

arms and helicopters for their own government's struggle against the *guerrilleros*, also known as the *muchachos*, the boys fighting in the hills. Franco said all Americans were alike, and none of them could be trusted.

Paz admired his cousin in many ways, but he also knew Americans like Rick, his cousin David, and the American priests who lived up the highway in Chirilagua, Padre Dionisio, Padre Guillermo, and the sisters who served the people there. They were all Americans, but even those few were not alike. These last ones came with open hearts and a warm honesty. Try as he might, Paz could find no wrong in any of them. They lived alongside the people and called them friends. Paz couldn't see what harm they did or discern any secrets they might be keeping. The only certainty was that Americans were a confusing and illogical people. Still, there were at least a few amongst them who were worth getting to know better.

With a sheepish grin, Rick handed Paz one of the coconuts that now had a paper straw protruding from its flattened though somewhat minced top. He shrugged. "I'm getting a little better with the machete, and Emelina gave me a few straws," was all he said.

Paz grimaced, remembering when he had first tried to show Rick how to slice off just enough of coconut's outer green husk at the top, to slip in a straw and sip out the sweet water inside. Rick's aim had been poor, and he'd split the coconut down the middle with one whack, like any Midwesterner chopping firewood, spilling the refreshing contents into the sand.

Paz took a long drink and leaned back in the hammock. "You can read your letter now?"

Rick sat on the floor, his long legs stretched out in front of him as he leaned against the cot. The sunlight spilled through the cracks of the far wall, making jagged stripes across the floor. From where he sat, he could see just a tiny portion of the beach as the clouds began to move in. He watched the glittering waves, gaining in strength with the incoming tide.

He reached back and pulled the now crumpled letter from his pocket and tossed it to Paz. "You read it," he answered, not unkindly. "You'll probably get as much out of it as I will."

"You know what it says, without reading it?"

"Probably, more or less. There's two more over there in the crate by the bed that read about like that one will."

Paz mistook his friend's curious reaction for a strange sort of homesickness. "You must at least be glad to hear from them, yes?" Paz opened the letter and studied the foreign script. "Here is the word *father*. I know this word in English. It is the word for *bank*, I think. Here is the word for *family* and *school*. The rest I do not know." He looked up to find an amused yet painful little smile, tugging at his friend's face. He had never seen Rick look so unhappy the entire time he had been in the village.

"I do not understand" was all that Paz could think to say.

"Neither do I," Rick answered and wished he could leave it at that. He listened to the pounding surf a moment more before attempting a better response to his friend's inquiries.

"The letter is from my sister, Amy. She writes about my father, his work at the bank, how all my family is embarrassed because of what I've done and that I should come home and go back to school. So, see? You did a pretty fair job of reading the letter after all."

"What did you do to embarrass your family?" Paz was nothing if not persistent.

"I came here."

"They did not want you to come?"

"Amy and my father did not know until after I was already gone. She says my father needs me."

"Do you not believe her?"

Rick sighed. "My father may think he needs me, but only because by being gone, I'm embarrassing him."

"How can that cause shame? Your father thinks it is a bad thing to come to El Salvador?"

"Oh, Pazito. It is not that simple. Nothing is the world that I come from is simple." Rick's gaze drifted back to the beach as he sought the words that could provide the bridge between the idyllic life he had found here and the world he left behind.

"Do you remember when I first came, and you asked me what I did? What my father does? I told you my father works at a bank and I was studying at a university. Well, my father is president of the bank. He works out loans, big business deals, that sort of thing. I was studying to go into business with him. That's what he said he wanted, to have his only son working with him."

Rick took a deep breath and continued. "It seemed fair enough, and since I didn't have a better idea of what I wanted, I agreed. I guess I should have known better, or at least sooner than I did, that it would never work out. I am not like him. I just didn't realize how different we really are. I mean, my father likes to spend his time at the country club, playing golf, making deals on the golf course as likely as not and I'd rather spend mine working with a bunch of—"

How could he ever make a boy from a Salvadoran fishing village understand why he didn't want to work in high finance and American banking?

Rick cleared his throat. "I would rather spend my time working with a bunch of young men who needed some help. That's all."

"Help? What kind of help?"

"It's pretty complicated sometimes, but there are young men and women in America who find themselves in trouble for all kinds of reasons. Some don't have good families, others are in trouble with the law or in school. I worked in a place where we helped them. It doesn't make much money, but it's something I was good at. Working with boys like you!" Rick whipped around and kicked the hammock, nearly pitching the youth onto the floor.

"*Puchica!*" the boy yelped as he caught himself.

"Now you've got school in a little while and then—"

"I'd rather go fishing."

"Of course. What boy wouldn't? In your country or mine!"

"But school is such a waste of time."

Rick knew Paz attended afternoon classes because there were not enough teachers, books, desks, or even space for all of the village children to attend the tiny school for a full day. Instead, the day was split, with half going to class in the morning and half in the afternoon.

Paz added. "Your father sent you to school, but now you do not go?"

Rick was accustomed to Paz's quick deductions and not particularly surprised by his response.

"Yes, he did, and I went every day through the twelfth grade. Sometimes, college is different, though."

"Twelfth grade?" Paz yelped like a dog that had been kicked. "*Gracías a Díos*, the school here only goes to the eighth grade. Twelve years! I would be going to school for all the rest of my life!"

He let out a heavy sigh. "*Vaya pues.*" The teen dragged himself to his feet. "Then I must go." He stepped outside as the rain-swollen clouds raced across the sun in advance of the afternoon showers. The rainy season in El Salvador was ever faithful, ever predictable.

"So we will go fishing later today, after the rain? And tomorrow?" Paz turned back toward Rick, who was now moving toward the comfort of the hammock.

"Yes, this afternoon, but tomorrow I have to meet David in San Miguel."

"And what will you do there?"

"I really don't know. He just told me to meet him there at a certain cantina. You know how he is."

Paz laughed as he walked away. "Yes, don David is the way he is."

Rick called after the departing figure. "I'll be at Emelina's later, and we'll go fishing after that."

* * * * *

In the center of the village, a small, wiry man squatted beside the church of *Las Palomitas*. It was a new structure, one room, the walls covered inside and out in light gray stucco. Of all the buildings in the village, it was the one of which Imanuel Flores was most proud. As the local catechist, he was the church's resident lay leader, the one who had helped to convince others in the area that a church building was needed. At the moment, he struggled to plant delicate pink and white flowers, evenly spaced around the outside perimeter. The ground here was more sand than soil and not as supportive of his efforts as he would have liked.

He could not help but think how the flowers were like some in the village, desperately in need of more support than he could give. There was Niña Ana, the frail little grandmother who lived near the end of the peninsula. She was ravaged by bouts of malaria, which threatened to shake her thin little body apart with the raging fever and chills. Niña Sonia was another who worried him. A young woman with too many mouths to feed and a husband, Andres, who tried hard but could not keep up with the constant needs of his growing family. They had already buried two of their babies, the results of malnutrition and poor sanitation, he was certain. Imanuel prayed that their other three young children would survive. No more baby funerals, please Lord, he pleaded with his head bowed in an extra moment of devotion for all the village children. There were also the angry young men, the kind who went off to join up with *los muchachos*, leaving their women and babies in the care of relatives at best or worse yet, on their own.

He had to find more ways to teach them all that he had learned from the priests over the years. How to be proud of who you are, not pride like in the Bible, the kind that destroys, but simple pride, to know you are a person of worth. How to stand up for yourself without going to war with someone else. How to put your family's needs first, before your own, and to realize that your community is a part of your family, many families coming together. Still, the Archbishop's words on the radio this morning were of little comfort. Once again, Monsignor Romero sounded as if his own heart might break as he spoke of the disappeared and murdered souls, nearly 600 people killed for political reasons during the first months of this year, he said. How could that be? What was this country, named for the savior himself, coming to?

"*Buenas tardes, don Imanuel.*" Rick's call startled him from his reverie. He turned to greet the

American who had become a devoted friend in the
few short weeks he had been here.

"Flowers?" Rick seemed surprised. In a place
where so many people struggled daily with the
basics of survival, he had not seen much interest
paid to amenities. Still, the colorful blossoms were
a nice touch.

"Emelina bought them in the market in San Miguel
yesterday, for the church," the older man explained.
"It is good to have living things here close to the
church, yes? There are more inside, too, in pots.
Come. I will show you."

As Imanuel pushed on the unadorned heavy
wooden door to the little church, Rick was once
again unprepared for the full impact of the simple yet
poignant scene that opened before him. A full-sized
cross on the front wall, fashioned from the mother-
of-pearl interiors of oyster shells, provided the only
permanent ornamentation. The open windows along
the side walls spilled light across the homemade brick
floor. The reflections from a thousand tiny rainbow-
hued surfaces of the shells produced a natural,
unpretentious radiance that was far removed from
the ornate churches and cathedrals Rick remembered
as a child. He had been here before, yet each time,
this scene took his breath away. While bits of Catholic
prayers his mother taught him over the years swirled
through the mists of memory, it was a line from a
hymn in his father's church, the one about God being
hidden only by the splendor of light that he recalled
each time he crossed this threshold.

Imanuel and Paz had both invited him to attend Mass, but he preferred to listen from the beach, at a safe distance even though a part of him longed to take in this scene, christened in candlelight. Still, too many conflicts held him at a distance, except when he came alone, like this, with Imanuel.

If only he had learned to worship first in a simple place, to be of a basic faith, uncomplicated by doctrine, priestly instruction, and his parent's own religious conflicts. Maybe then his own path would be clearer now.

Imanuel had already walked past a homemade wooden rack of votive candles in the back corner and the few wooden benches that served as pews. They were never enough when the circuit priest came through, and although they were supposed to be available on a first-come, first-served basis, Paz told Rick they were really a place of honor, reserved for the oldest and most frail in the community, for those who needed them.

Near the cross, Imanuel was looking at still more flowers in two small buckets. "There is enough to go all the way around the church."

Rick tried to pick up on what his friend was saying without admitting he had not been listening. Double entendres were quite popular with the villagers, and although he could usually understand them, Rick's grasp of the language was not often strong enough for him to make them.

"Then, *don Imanuel*," Rick spoke slowly, "we will have flowers all around the outside and *flores* inside the church as well."

"*Flores* outside? *Flores* inside? It took a moment for the strange-sounding joke to sink home, but when it did, a large grin followed.

"So, Emelina is buying you *flores* now?" Rick continued to tease. "Maybe she likes you more than you think."

"Not you, too?" Imanuel feigned annoyance. "You listen too much to Pazito, I think. Emelina was my wife's sister. She is a sweet person, but she is no Guadalupe." He looked around as if to make certain they were truly alone. "She is twice as much woman as 'Lupe. She was thin. *Dios mío*, a woman like Emelina, and a man would have to be careful. If she fell...I mean, I am not very big."

He thoroughly enjoyed his own joke before he continued. "Besides, she already has a man, Candelario. I do not think she needs another one."

Rick shrugged. "I don't know. I only know what I hear and what I see." He looked down at the flowers one last time.

"What you hear is what Paz tells you. He would simply like to see two of his favorite people together. That is understandable, but it is a child's wish, nothing more. And what do you see? These are for the church, no more."

"If you say so." Rick changed the subject. "You were deep in thought when I came up just now. Is everything all right?"

"Right here, right now, when compared to other parts of this country, I suppose the answer is yes. They are all right." The enigmatic response followed by a huge sigh was hardly what Rick had expected from this busy little man who always had a smile and a little time for everyone.

"I'm not sure I understand," Rick hesitated. "Is it the work with the church? You know I would be glad to do more. Is there something I can help you with? We make a pretty good team when I help with deliveries, don't we? I can see that something is troubling you."

"It is just the musings of a foolish old man with a pain in his back," Imanuel smiled deceptively and bent backward as if the plantings had taken a strain on him. "What can I do for you this afternoon is a better question. You did not come into town because of an old man and his flowers, surely."

"No, I promised Paz we would go fishing tonight," Rick let go of the previous conversation with reluctance. "I'm going for a little dinner first at Emelina's. I don't suppose you would like to join me?"

Imanuel's face brightened at the invitation. Still, he declined but not without a glint of mischief in his eye. A remarkable resemblance to his son, Rick thought.

"No, I have to go take care of the store now," Imanuel chirped. "Then, Emelina can go to the restaurant and cook for hungry troublesome types like you." He began closing windows as he walked toward the front door. "I'll tell Paz to meet you there when I see him."

Comedor Emelina was the largest, and in Rick's opinion, the best of the tiny 'dining rooms' as the local restaurants were called. In the smallest ones, a person simply entered the front porch or the front room inside the door of the home and announced his presence with a question. "*Hay comida?*" Is there food?

If the answer was yes, then the meal of the day was brought to the table, whatever it might happen to be.

At Emelina's, the huge open-sided porch held no less than four picnic-style tables, with benches running down each side, a large eating establishment in a hamlet this size. More importantly to Rick's taste, there was a menu of sorts. The large proprietor, who wore her heavy black hair pulled back in a tight ponytail, served as both cook and waitress. When asked, she would meander out of the kitchen wearing a huge coverall apron that had once been white. With a welcoming smile, she would rattle off half a dozen available meals, ticking them off on her fingers.

They were nearly always the same—stewed chicken with vegetables, fried fish, beef steak with onions, *huevos rancheros*, and fried chicken. On occasion, a meal of black-market shrimp or fried squid might be added to the day's offerings. No such luck today. Rick chose the stewed chicken.

It arrived at the table accompanied by a large side order of rice, which lay in the thin, oily tomato sauce covering the chicken. The requisite stack of steaming tortillas was also delivered to the table, wrapped in a dishtowel.

"Why do you always sit on that side?" Paz arrived at the table just as the food did. He plunked down opposite Rick and promptly found the answer to his own question.

"*A la gran puchica! Chancho!*" It sounded like an oath, but Rick had learned upon his arrival that *puchica* was the Salvadoran's own special word, inoffensive and used for a great many exclamations, both good and bad by small children and their grandmothers alike.

"Aunt of mine!" Paz continued to fuss. "I cannot believe you still allow this pig in here under the table!" Paz gave the large sow a swift kick, and the animal climbed to its feet, ambling out the open doorway.

"Do not hurt my pig, Pazito!" she called out from the kitchen where she was busy patting out more tortillas in anticipation of those who would soon be coming to dinner.

"Do not hurt *mi chancho*, indeed!" Paz snorted. "Why did you not make that thing move?" He turned to Rick. "I bet you do not have these kinds of problems in the restaurants of America, do you?"

Rick nearly choked, laughing.

"No, pigs under the table are not a problem in most restaurants in the US." He found it impossible to take Paz's concern seriously. "She wasn't hurting anything, Paz. I mean, she's under this table all the time, but she stays on her side, and I stay on mine. We do just fine together."

Paz shook his head. Only an American, he thought, would eat at a table with his feet resting on a sow.

"Well, it is disgusting." Paz shook his head one last time. "And you should not let her get away with it."

"Who? She?" Rick leaned forward with a whisper.

"The pig, of course." Paz straightened up and then quickly covered the giggle behind his hand. "Or my aunt either for that matter. You should not let either one of them get by you so easily."

* * * * *

Within the hour, the two were ensconced in a dugout canoe as it skimmed across the light, choppy waves headed out to sea. Rick sat in the stern with his hand on the tiller of the small outboard motor while Paz kept watch, perched in the bow. Between them, in the bottom of the boat, lay their nets, anchors, and other fishing equipment.

The estuary was emptying now as the outbound tide flowed the same direction they were heading. Over the centuries, the fresh water pouring down from the hills had deposited its load of silt and sand, building the peninsula that supported the entire village. They had already rounded the point, leaving the brackish water behind. Rick glanced over his shoulder. Just a few hundred yards offshore and already the hamlet blended so well into the trees as to be almost invisible. Only the occasional white or colored beach house, owned by city dwellers, who came to *Las Palomitas* for holidays and weekends, could be seen further up the beach.

Below the thick wooden sides of the *cayuco*, blue sea water swirled as their passing further disturbed the low breakers. Rick's attention turned back to the front of the canoe as Paz began to signal the zigzag course necessary to get them past the multitude of small sand bars that posed a natural barrier to the area at low tide.

A man in the front of the canoe could see the way or, as was the case with most of the local fishermen, they knew the way by heart and could guide their boats through as easily as Rick could drive a car along the road to his own home. Even in the short time he had been there, he had seen a tourist from the capital beach a large, expensive cabin cruiser with powerful inboard motors because he did not want 'an Indian on his boat.' The result had been an embarrassing six-hour wait for the tidal shift to float the craft free.

As they passed the last sandbar, Rick gunned the small outboard motor to its top speed. It was here at sea that he felt the most free from troubles at home and even the few concerns he had come across in village life. He had gone fishing alone a few times when the tide was most favorable, but he found Paz's presence was rarely a hindrance to his need to simply take in the vastness of the sea and sky and little else as it helped him put his own difficulties into perspective.

When he needed quiet, the boy seemed to sense it and would sit looking out to sea. He too was troubled from time to time, by the past, the present, or the future, Rick could not tell. He had asked once or twice, but Paz had only grinned sheepishly as if caught doing something he should not. Sometimes, the youth slept curled up on the fishing nets in the bottom of the boat.

Rick slowed the engine, and Paz tossed out an *araña*, a homemade anchor, shaped a little like the spider it was named for. Then he began to throw out the cork line from the front of the boat. Rick tended the weight line, watching to make certain the small chunks of lead, spinning out over the back edge, did not become tangled in the motor or propeller as they trolled along, stretching the net long and full above the rocks. With the last anchor in place and the buoys marking the spot, Rick turned the canoe back toward the sand bars.

Once before, he and Paz had gone walking on these short sandy stretches after they set their net. While Rick had discovered an eerie sense of power, walking on land that was usually beneath the sea, Paz had seemed particularly uneasy. He admitted that walking on land that habitually rose and sank again made him nervous. Rick laughed at first until he realized his friend did not see much humor in the situation.

"It is different for you," Paz pouted. "You can swim. More than a few men have drowned here and at the change of tide, too. The water is very powerful."

"Are you telling me you don't know how to swim?" Rick was more than a little taken aback.

Paz hesitated. No man in the village talked readily of what he could not do.

"What are you doing out here with me in a boat then? There are no such things as life jackets here, and I realize nobody thinks much about safety, but I thought surely you know how to swim."

Paz only shrugged his answer. "Nobody here knows. Only a very few. I think my Uncle Miguel can but not many others."

Rick was incredulous and set out at once to correct that particular gap in Paz's education. It was not as easy as it sounded that day on the sand bars, for either of them. The lessons had dissolved, as often as not, into much laughter and splashing, but gradually the teen learned the fundamentals of keeping himself afloat. Now he would even follow Rick out into water over his head, although he still paddled at a beginner's rate of nervous high speed.

As they stepped out of their canoe, Rick turned to watch Paz's reaction. "Do you feel any better about being here now?"

Paz seemed puzzled by the question.

"Now that you can swim? I thought you might feel safer walking out here."

Paz's face brightened, but there was still a wariness about his eyes as if he was trying to look everywhere at once. "Yes, it is better," he lied unconvincingly. "Now I *can* swim. Still, the ground. It does not feel too strong here." He stamped his foot on the mushy surface, sending sand-laden drops flying. Rick laughed out loud.

The American turned to stroll the forty feet of wet sand, one end to the other. At the far end, the water rushed past in the short deep channel they had just come through twice in the *cayuco*. Just a

few tantalizing feet across the water, another sand
bar beckoned. Rick had also heard the stories of
fishermen who had drowned, walking here, but
according to David, the men had also had too much
to drink before setting out. A bit too much *chicha*,
the local homemade liquor, and a man could believe
he could walk on water out here, Rick thought
as he watched the water's hypnotic charge through
the narrow channel.

As he turned back toward Paz, still waiting
patiently where he had left him at the other end
of the longest sand bar visible at the moment, he
bent down to examine the only spot that broke the
smooth surface of the sand and picked up a sand
dollar the size of a small apple. Paz still stood next
to the canoe, holding tight to the halyard.

Ignorance can be cured with knowledge, Rick let
his thoughts wander as he glanced at his nervous
friend, but what is the cure for superstition?

Their catch for the evening was one of their best.
As they hauled in the heavy net, hand over hand as
fishermen had done for centuries before them, silver-
scaled *curvinas* flopped into the bottom of the boat.
Paz had to move quickly more than once to keep them
from hurling themselves back into the sea.

The sun was hanging low in the trees, ready to set,
as they pulled up in front of Miguel's small, thatched
house. He stood outside before a gill net stretched
between the house and a pole stuck in the sand, a
net shuttle in his hand. He paused in his repair work
to help the two bring in their catch and equipment.

The canoe, motor, and fishing equipment all belonged to Miguel. Like the fishermen's cooperative, he leased equipment to several local fishermen who could not afford to buy their own. It was a profitable arrangement for all concerned. As always, Paz took the entire catch to the cooperative, and he, Rick, and Miguel divided the proceeds. It was enough to keep Rick in spending money, the little he needed for life in *Las Palomitas*.

Rick finished beaching the boat and stowing the last of the equipment as Paz returned from the cooperative. "They said ours was the best catch today," he announced with obvious pride. "Amongst the fishermen, of course," he added as an afterthought to distinguish their take from that of the *tiburoneros* like Paco.

"How much?" Rick asked.

"Twenty-five kilos. That is, uh—" he struggled for a moment with the figures in his head. "Fifty, fifty-five pounds, yes?"

"That's right," Rick answered as he glanced upwards, noting the rosy underside given to every cloud overhead as the sun slipped from sight behind the mangrove swamps at the far end of the estuary.

"Well done," Miguel complimented the two of them. "Maybe you two are not such a lazy pair after all, just slow to get started with your day."

"That could be." Rick was amiable. "But tomorrow, I will have to start earlier." A few moments more and Rick bid them good night and walked back to his own hut.

Nightfall comes quickly in this part of the world, Rick thought. He wondered if it had something to do with being closer to the Equator. He thought about lighting a lamp but decided not to waste the kerosene. He returned to the same place where he had started the day and leaned against the same palm tree as early this morning.

The lights of *Las Palomitas* twinkled down the beach just a short distance away like a string of tiny diamonds strung around the merrily lapping waters. Far out to sea, the winking lights of the shrimp boats dotted the dark ocean before him. He remembered that Paz had told him once that when the shrimp boats' lights blinked, it was really a secret code between someone on the boat and black marketers on shore, who often bought shrimp illegally. It sounded pretty funny and melodramatic to him. Probably just boats, like everything else here, with weak electrical systems, Rick mused. He listened to the mild breakers, although at the moment, it was so dark, he could barely make out where the land ended and the water began.

He wondered what was on David's mind and what he had planned for them tomorrow. Lately, some of David's plans made him more than a little nervous. He was enjoying his time here in *Las Palomitas* but not for the reasons he thought he would when he left Texas. He came here, thinking life would be again like it was when he and David were boys, but all of that had changed. He and David seemed to find less and less in common, not more.

What he found was the peace and serenity of this place, and he did not care to mar that with being anyone's version of an 'ugly American.' That idea never seemed to enter David's mind. He hoped tomorrow's trip would not be a wasted effort.

Ever so slowly, the silhouette of the two islands far out to sea began to glow. A bright orange-yellow line appeared above the top of the taller peak as if the mountain's edge had turned to fire and blackened ash. The full moon eased out of its hiding place, changing from gold to white as it rose higher in the sky, casting its silver luminescence across the sea and the land, catching and revealing all in its ethereal light.

Rick savored the deserted beach, the quiet, broken only by an occasional peal of laughter from the brothel located far down the beach at the edge of the village proper. The satin-soft breeze was kinder than a lover's caress against his cheek.

His thoughts drifted back to his conversation with Paz earlier in the day. "William Joseph Mercy," he whispered his father's name aloud. He wondered how his mother was handling things at home, like his father's anger and Amy's whining. A slight shudder passed over him with the cool breeze.

He had found peace here, a peacefulness of the soul, he never knew existed before. For once in his life, it did not matter what Amy or his father or even David wanted. Until he could find a way to capture and hold unto that kind of peace and take it with him, wherever he might go, he was determined to stay.

CHAPTER 2

Billy Joe Mercy, like his older brother Dallas, was a by-product of the Texas oilfields. The brothers were raised as much as not, by an alcoholic father, the three of them abandoned by a wife and mother who never adapted to the harsh reality of life in a succession of impoverished trailer parks. By the time they were teenagers, the two husky boys who always appeared older than their years were working side by side with their father, a roughneck in the glory days of the wildcatter oil industry.

After a short stint in the army during the Korean War, Billy Joe returned to the oilfields. His father had died in an explosive accident during the ensuing years, convincing a young Billy Joe there must be a better to make his way in the world. He was soon spending much of his time studying, beginning with business and economics at night school. Then on to the fulltime college level as he came to the realization that true control of the oil industry lay in the hands of the money handlers as power brokers.

He changed his name from the Billy Joe Mercy listed on his birth certificate to William Joseph Mercy. Only his brother pretended not to notice and continued to call him B.J.

William met Doris Wilson, the daughter of a Midwestern college president, through an acquaintance and married her after a six-month courtship. They stayed 'in her part of the country' as big brother Dallas referred to it while William continued his education. Settling down in any single location, however, was never part of William's strategy.

His ultimate ambition was always the same, a triumphant return to Texas and entrance there into the wealthy social circles that had always been closed to him and his kind. A wife, the birth of a daughter, Amy Renee, and then a son, Richard Francis, slowed his plans but never truly curtailed them.

Instead, he began work at smaller Midwestern financial institutions and worked his way up the administrative ladder. While his dreams turned him into a workaholic, his wife Doris shunned the public life her husband loved to devote herself to her children.

Amy, four years older than her brother, grew up enamored of the man she called Father. As a toddler, she mimicked his movements and mannerisms and waited patiently for him to come home for dinner, an occasion he missed as often as not. Rick, however, was most devoted to his mother as she was to him. His father's absence rarely perturbed him except when it bothered her. Rick's cousin, David, often came to visit, especially during the summer when the two boys seemed to spend the entire school vacation, out of doors—camping, fishing, and hunting, first with slingshots, and later with more serious weapons.

When Rick was very young, his Uncle Dallas brought David for those extended summer visits, and he too often stayed longer. Both boys enjoyed Dallas' gruff manner and Texas drawl, which was closer to their world and was a sharp contrast to William's more reserved carriage and refined speech. William had worked long and hard to scrub all signs of his oil field upbringing from his life, yet when Dallas was around, William would relax, and the country boy Billy Joe would return for a brief moment. Dallas could always tease William out of his 'cityfied businessman' personality, at least for a short time, and he took great pleasure in doing so, finding William's assumption of a different lifestyle more amusing than offensive. And it was during these times that Rick could feel close to his father as they enjoyed a brief afternoon of fishing or a day of hunting. As the years passed, Dallas did not come as often or stay as long. And as the years passed, Rick found the only common ground he and his father shared was the occasional discussion on issues of business.

Each time the family moved throughout the Midwest as William sought higher positions, Doris managed to find a comfortable home for them in the countryside, outside of the nearby town or city where William worked and each time, Rick was grateful. At every new location, Rick and soon afterward, Rick and David together, would explore the nearby fields, woods, and streams.

By the time the boys were in their teens, Dallas, who now owned some of the original oil sites he and his brother had once worked on, began to push William to return home. The time was right, he encouraged.

Twenty-four years after he left, William Mercy and his family returned to Texas as William claimed the presidency of Texas Financial International, TFI, the banking giant, based in Houston.

While his father's dream was becoming a reality, Rick felt as if he had been cut adrift. There was no country home at the end of this move. William insisted the family live closer to the heart of the city, to his business interests. While Amy adapted quickly to the social life afforded by a large city university, Rick wandered through his last years of high school. Unlike many his age, he was not rebellious, nor did his boredom lead him into any serious trouble. He simply became quieter and more introverted.

As his father lectured him about taking a more serious approach to school and classes, he also began to speak of his son following his lead into business. Rick rarely voiced opposition.

He graduated high school and immediately enrolled at the University of Houston's School of Business. While he continued his studies, he corresponded with David, who had opted out of formal education at his earliest opportunity, a choice Rick secretly admired yet felt obligated to forego.

Like the previous generation, David began with work in the oilfields. Nothing lasted too long with him during those years, however, as he also worked for the railroad, on an Arizona truck farm, and briefly, as a long-haul trucker. Finally, as Rick finished his third year of college, the letters from David quit coming. One rumor said he had become a soldier of fortune in Central America, and while Rick did not exactly believe it, he could not find any information to the contrary. Even Dallas seemed uncertain as to his son's whereabouts.

Rick spent his last summer before graduation working at one of TFI's smaller partners, a far cry from the summers of his youth, running the Ozark hills with his cousin. And then working with troubled youth at the local Boys Club, he found his calling. Working at the bank was not what he wanted, and he knew a decision was being forced upon him. The life his father planned for him—one of business suits, board meetings, money-handling, and paperwork pursuits—was not one he could ever make his own.

Two months into the summer job, he broached the subject with his father after a rare Sunday family barbecue. Rick had rehearsed the conversation in his head at least a hundred times, but nothing went the way he had hoped.

"So, what is this you are telling me?" His father exploded after Rick explained his reasons for considering a change in his college classes. "That you don't want to work in business. Then what? As a social worker? A teacher? You can't be serious! You'd be starving in a year's time. What kind of future is that?"

"It's the kind of thing I already do, to a certain extent. I like helping people, especially kids. I need to work with people, not just with money, figures, computers, and paperwork."

"You want to help people? Fine. Lend them money to build what they want. That's helping, but it's helping yourself, too. Who do you think is going to do that? There's no future in this other drivel, I tell you." The man went back to reading his newspaper as if he had dispatched an annoying insect.

"This is different. As for the future, the world will always need social workers, just like it needs teachers as well as bankers and lots of others. It's what I want to do." Rick continued with quiet dignity, struggling to hold onto his own temper.

"Do you think I went into banking because it's what I wanted to do?" William thundered, lumbering to his feet. "I took a good look around and knew I couldn't spend the rest of my life eeking out a living on somebody else's ground. I did this because without it, you and your mother and your sister wouldn't have anything."

Nor would you, the thought occurred to Rick, but he chose not to give voice to it. The veins stood out on the sides of his father's neck, and for the first time in his life, Rick thought about what he might have looked like in another life, one that did not include a daily diet of suits, ties, and button-down collars. A vision of an old man, a Texas field hand, ranting and raving out in a field all alone, went through his mind and helped him maintain control of his own voice and expressions.

"I'm sorry if it's a disappointment to you," he began in a conciliatory fashion, "but—"

"Good God!" his father raged on. "A disappointment is when it rains on the day of a golf tournament. This is a hell of a lot more than that! Now I know how Dallas must have felt when that idiot son of his decided not to go to college! What the hell's the matter with you? You were always interested enough in what I was doing. You kept up with the stock figures and knew how to follow the economic indicators."

"That's the only way you would talk to me!" Rick dropped the polite pretense. "I learned what I needed to, to be able to share something with you. When you wouldn't come into my world anymore, I had to learn something about yours, but it doesn't mean I can move in and live there forever. I'm not like you. Maybe I'm more like Dallas and David than you know. I only know I can't be what you want me to be!"

William threw down the newspaper and stormed from the room. A terrible silence followed the tumult's end as Doris and Amy had come to stand in the doorway to the ornate living room. Neither said a word. Amy glared at Rick as she turned on her heel and walked out. Doris only watched without a word.

The silence continued for the rest of the summer. Rick finished his internship and returned to his classwork in the fall, but William did not speak to him again.

The college work provided a respite from the tense situation at home, but days filled with marketing strategies and economic statistics were simply one more reminder of the life that awaited him upon graduation. It was an unexpected letter from David, postmarked El Salvador, that provided Rick with an answer to his dilemma.

Rick,

Figure you've about given up on me by now, but think again! I've found as close to Paradise as a man can expect to see. I've got a government contract that's paying me to eat, drink and be merry—and all that is cheap down here. There's five miles of beach out the front door, an ocean full of fish, and the only trouble is I can't party enough for both of us.

As kids, this is what we always talked about. Don't know how much longer it's going to last, though, so I suggest you get your butt down here PDQ. So far, it's still safe enough for gringos—so get out of whatever you're doing and head south. This may be our last chance for anything this good!

David

Rick had thought for some time that all he needed was a few weeks away in a place with time on his hands to clear his head and find the right answers for himself. With David's letter, he knew his opportunity was at hand.

There was no point in trying to open up the discussion with his father again, but Rick thought his mother might be a different case. The look on her face was one Rick had seen many times in the past, a saccharine smile with a hint of sadness behind it, but it was only now that he began to understand.

"I wondered how long it was going to take you," she said, surprising him with her forthrightness. "I've watched for years as William insisted that you take this course or study that, but I've also known for a long time that your heart wasn't in it."

"But you never said anything." Rick wasn't sure if he should be insulted or complimented. He was mostly grateful at this point that she was willing to listen and allow him to make his own choices.

"Neither did you," she countered in a gentle fashion. "You never complained or said this wasn't what you wanted. What should I have said? Richard, you don't really want to be a financial advisor. I can see it in your eyes?"

A weak smile crossed his face, but relief flowed through him as he contemplated how much he was not going to have to explain.

"So what are you waiting for? You are going, one way or another, to join David. Whatever you do, your father will be furious when he finds out. Amy will undoubtedly join him." She sighed, and the sadness that had only been in her smile threatened to engulf her. "It may not seem right, but I think it might be best if you just leave without telling them."

Rick was caught off-guard, but the idea grew in appeal as his mother went on.

"Yes, that would be best." Her decision buoyed her spirits as her enthusiasm grew. "This is a ridiculous situation, but it's one of William's own making.

Why shouldn't he get a big surprise? You will be all right with David, I'm sure. When you come back, maybe you will have a better idea of what you want to do with yourself.

"It'll be our secret," she continued. "In that way, it will almost feel like I'm going along on your adventure. You don't mind that, do you? I mean, if I pretend and share in some of your excitement?"

Looking at her face, lit by the prospect of doing something out-of-line, he realized she had been no happier in this city than he. He had always known his mother as a beautiful woman, but she was a shy beauty with dark auburn hair and flawless milky-white skin. She could not stand the scrutiny of public life her husband craved and was becoming a near hermit, locked behind the doors of her city home. How he wished he could take her with him, if only to see a genuine look of happiness on her face.

"Of course you can share it with me," he laughed at her little-girl response to the entire situation and scooped her up in an impromptu hug. "I might not even have the courage to do this at all if it weren't for your response right now. I'll write to you and tell you all about where I am and what I'm doing. But are you certain this is the way you want it? Surely, he'll be angry with you, too."

"No, it's all right, really. He never stays angry with me for long. I'll be fine. Write him a note, if you like and tell him. I'll see to it that he finds it after you're gone, and that way, at least, he can't say you just ran out. You told him. First, in person, and when he didn't want to listen, you wrote it down. He can't ask for more than that."

Her mood turned back to somber as she reached out to cup the side of his face the way she often did when he was a child. The fit was no longer the same. "Whatever you do, learn to follow your own heart from now on. You don't need either of us to tell you what to do. I rather think you know even now what you want. You just haven't figured out how to do it."

He shot her a startled look.

"I never thought you spent all that time at the Boys Club because you were lazy and liked to play basketball." Her penetrating gaze and the evenness of her voice made him uncomfortable as if he had been caught naked.

"You need to take this time for yourself. Don't be afraid to take what you need from the world, Richard, because you always give back so much more."

* * * * *

Within the week, he was on a plane that stopped in Mexico, Guatemala, and was scheduled to continue to El Salvador.

"There are mechanical problems with the plane." The official's voice echoed down the stone, cold halls of the Guatemalan airport as he spoke to those gathered at the far gate, waiting for their flight. "We hope to fix it today, but—" He shrugged in a gesture of helplessness. "We will have another flight early tomorrow morning." The man turned to walk away but not before Rick caught up to him, firing questions as they both walked back toward the main airline desks.

"It's early yet today." Rick was surprised by his own impatience. "Is there another flight, maybe on another airline?"

"*No, Señor*," the airline employee replied with a weary smile and tried once again to walk away.

"But it's not that far to San Salvador from here, right?" Rick had studied his map well when at one point, he had considered making it an overland trip. "If I caught a bus, I could still get to San Salvador tonight?"

"Well, I do not have a bus schedule," the man began, "but perhaps, it is possible—"

It took him a couple of hours, struggling in the Tex-Mex Spanish he had learned in and out of school, to wrangle his luggage away from the airline and catch a taxi across the city to meet a bus that was leaving for San Salvador.

As he settled back in the comfortable seat of a first-class tourist coach, Rick began to congratulate himself on his quick thinking. He had even managed to whip off a telegram to David's government-affiliated office before leaving the airport, informing David he would still be in San Salvador before nightfall.

The bus wound its way up into the mountains as it curled out of Guatemala City. A postcard-worthy view of the entire city laid out behind him on the last curve before majestic deep green pines with nearly perfect straight black trunks lined the highway as Black Angus cattle grazed leisurely beneath their high-flying limbs. On the far side of the first mountains outside the city, Irish green hillsides, interspersed with rocky patches of ground, gave away the secret that the soil here was little more than a thin layer stretched over solid rock. More mountains, half-hidden in distant blue shadows, lay ahead.

The countryside more than made up for his change in plans as Rick enjoyed the unexpected opportunity to see more of it. The mountains so close together on such a short hop would have made for a rough plane ride, anyway, he mused. A couple of hours later, however, as the bus pulled into the miniature military installation that is the Guatemalan-Salvadoran border crossing, recent history repeated itself.

The coach driver tried to start the engine multiple times but to no avail. Leaning out of his driver's window, he complained to the Salvadoran border guard who stood closest to the bus as if he could be of some help.

"There are no repair parts anywhere anymore," he whined. "Not in your country or mine, for these American-made vehicles. Soon we will all be sitting by the roadside."

The border guard shrugged and turned to the business of checking out the passengers on the bus.

"Why do you come to El Salvador?" he asked Rick in heavily accented but structurally perfect English. He looked over Rick's few possessions with little interest, which included only a duffel bag and a large overstuffed blue backpack stretched over an aluminum frame.

"To visit a friend."

"American or *salvadoreño*?"

"I'm sorry. I don't understand." Rick's attention was totally absorbed by the large number of soldiers who loitered about the area. None of them seemed to have any specific tasks. They simply stood, talking and telling jokes to one another, their M-16's hanging casually at their sides. A closer look at their faces revealed that in another time and place, these teenagers would have been found hanging around outside of a dance hall or a soda shop.

I've never seen so much military hardware in a civilian zone, Rick's thoughts whirled in alarm. So much firepower. How well can they use it? As fast as the thought came to him, he decided he really did not want to know. Their presence alone was enough to make him more than a little uncomfortable.

"Your friend. Is he American or *salvadoreño?*" The official repeated.

"Oh, American." Rick jerked his meandering thoughts back to the business at hand. "He works for the Developmental Assistance Agency."

"*Técnicos de Desarrollo.*" The man's smile was genuine. "I have heard very good things about them. It is a government program, yes?"

Rick nodded.

"And you? You are part of this program?"

"No, I'm his cousin. I've just come for a visit. He told me El Salvador is a beautiful country."

Rick struggled to find something to say that made sense, as moment by moment, he was beginning to feel as if this whole situation made very little.

The man's ceaseless questions, coupled with the rifle-toting teens, gave the whole place more than a touch of the surreal.

"Then your cousin likes it here? *Vaya*...I hope you do, too." He finished his inspection of Rick's things. "You do not plan to stay long? You have so little luggage for an American." It was a statement of fact. Nothing more, or was it? Rick couldn't tell.

"I tend to travel light." Rick felt compelled to give some sort of answer, even a meaningless one.

"And where will you go while you are here? Where does your friend live?"

"In a village called *Las Palomitas*."

"You are going to the beach then. It is a beautiful place. All of El Salvador knows and loves *Las Palomitas*."

Rick sincerely hoped this man did not. Why was he making him so nervous?

"For now, however, you are not going very far, my friend." The official was no longer smiling. "Come this way."

Had he done something wrong? Was he being detained? Arrested? He glanced at the soldiers to see if they were coming his way. His mind was racing, nearly out of control. Should he run? This was insane. The soldiers did not appear to be interested in him, but the official continued talking.

"Your bus is not working. I am afraid it is not going any further today."

Rick's knees nearly gave way with relief as he realized what the man was referring to. He hoped he did not look as foolish as he felt. The man took no apparent notice as he continued in his casual, chatty tone.

"If you hurry, you can still catch *La Miranda*." He pointed to a brightly decorated blue bus parked at the head of the line of vehicles about to leave the area. "José is ready to go. *La Miranda* is smaller than this." He gestured toward the huge silver coach that was partially blocking the narrow highway, "but *rápido*." He slapped his hands together, and Rick jumped involuntarily at the sound.

Rapid transit, Rick came to discover in short order, means different things in different cultures. To José, *rápido* meant tearing through the countryside, blaring the horn at all who were foolhardy enough to cross his path as well as frequent and proficient use of a magnificent braking system.

La Miranda. The name was painted in bright yellow script along all four sides of the azure mini-bus that carried nearly as many passengers as the large touring coach, even though it was only a third of the size. Rick was unaccustomed to so much humanity crammed into such a small place. Live chickens, fish, baskets of fruits and vegetables, and a variety of other items that would soon be turned into a tasty meal were also welcomed aboard. Even the original 'pig in a poke,' a live squealing piglet, bound tight in a twine bag was tossed on top of the bus with other luggage and bundles for a short but ear-splitting ride.

Rick leaned against the rough bus seat, exhausted by his recent encounter with local law enforcement, while trying less successfully than not to find space for legs that supported his six-foot frame. Salvadoran buses were not built for men of his height, and his knees banged painfully against the seat in front of him, no matter how he shifted his weight. He thought about standing as many of the passengers did, but a quick glance at the low ceiling told him he'd be no better off with his head banging there than where he was, and once this seat was lost, it would surely be gone forever.

While the earlier encounter had left him shaken, he was also strangely intrigued. Why had he reacted that way? What had really happened there to make him feel so panicked? He didn't think of himself as a prejudiced person, but maybe he wasn't as open-minded as he liked to think. Was it too many old movies where the Spanish-speaking officials with guns always turn out to be the 'bad guys'? He did not know, but it was certainly something to ponder and to try to make certain the next encounter was less gut-wrenching.

La Miranda followed the narrow, winding ribbon of blacktop that cut through the rocky mountain passages and across the lush green valleys in between. Cascades of tropical flowers that had never known the controlling touch of a gardener's hand wandered freely over all. The countryside jouncing past the open bus window felt closer now than it had on the closed, air-conditioned bus.

Tiny huts and grimy stucco shacks dotted the landscape. The speeding bus sent the occasional herd of bony cattle or goats scampering off the highway while young barefoot cowboys cursed and scurried after their charges, long herding sticks carried high over their heads as they ran.

The beauty of the land and the poverty of the people. It was a strange combination in which neither diminished the other, Rick noticed as he watched it all fly past his window.

As the bus pulled to a stop at a major crossroads, several new passengers jostled on while others attempted to squeeze out the back door. Country women and young girls in polyester and cotton dresses and stained white aprons surrounded the bus, loudly hawking their wares as Rick was introduced to fast food, Salvadoran-style.

"Naranjas!"

"Tortillas y carne!"

"Mangos! Sandia!"

"Quesadilla!"

One cried out in a shrill twang, and the others echoed her call.

Rick surveyed the tattered mob, offering peeled oranges, sliced mangos, and homemade soft drinks. The aroma of the charbroiled pork wrapped in steaming white corn tortillas and his own hunger eventually overcame any precautionary tendencies. His mad dash across the Guatemalan capital had not left any time for food. Willing himself not to consider the source nor the manner of preparation,

Rick passed an American dollar out the bus window and received tortillas, wrapped around small pieces of pork and a paper napkin full of squares of what appeared to be a sort of oily cornbread. The bus rolled on, and his initial worries about the quality of the food were quickly forgotten as the taste of the small meal measured up to the promise carried in the aroma of the cooked pork and the sweet smell of the Salvadoran *quesadilla*, a local specialty, a sort of white cake baked with cheese.

The narrow asphalt highway gave way to a modern four-lane concrete thoroughfare as the countryside flattened into cultivated fields and poultry farms on their approach into San Salvador. There were no more stops now, and with the better highway conditions, José's speed noticeably increased as they cruised into El Salvador's only major city, San Salvador.

* * * * *

Slouched low in the driver's seat of a battered gray topless Jeep, David Mercy looked like a man who could wait forever. In the midst of the near rictous activity that characterized the *Terminal Occidental de Buses*, he sat, unmoving, his feet perched on the base of the windshield, his arms folded, and a straw cowboy hat pulled low over his eyes.

The terminal's regular sellers quickly surrounded the latest arrival, one of the last buses of the evening. David was waiting for a leisure coach and took little interest in the unloading of just another local bus until an unusually tall, yet familiar form stepped down onto the oil-packed dirt. David was on his feet in an instant, peering through the growing dusk as he pushed his hat back to reveal an expression of mischievous delight.

"Hey, *Primo!* Rick!" He clapped his equally surprised cousin on the back. "Are you traveling in style or what?"

Rick smiled wanly and promised an explanation as he grabbed his belongings and attempted to follow David's retreating form through the crowd. He was not altogether successful. The place was alive with travelers, drivers and their helpers, the ubiquitous vendors, children—half of whom were begging or working as vendors, the other half, running, playing, shrieking, and hiding amongst the buses. This was referred to as a terminal. Rick had heard that much, but he could see no terminal building, only a huge tin-walled packed earth yard, filled with buses, people, and too many of both. The smell was equally intimidating—a combination of diesel fumes, exotic cooking odors, urine, and the stench of too many beings in too small a space.

"Holy smoke, what is this place?" Rick gasped as he unceremoniously dumped his two bundles onto the rear floor of the already purring Jeep and scrambled into the passenger seat. Despite the chaos, David had the Jeep gliding backward as smoothly as if he were in a perfectly striped shopping mall parking lot in his own country. He eased the vehicle out into the mostly two-footed traffic, heading for the narrow opening that served as a gate in the corrugated metal fence. A sharp right turn onto a one-way street of bustling traffic, and they lurched off into the darkness.

Rick soon discovered David's driving bore a marked resemblance to that of the bus driver, José, as did that of all the drivers in the erratic Latin traffic pattern. They sped past a dazzling array of small shops, brightly lit stores, and homes where doorways and windows were thrown wide open to the tropical evening air. Solid blocks of homes and shops, each individually painted yet sharing common walls with no alleys in a single block, were fronted by a wide sidewalk and separated by narrow streets.

At one point, they zipped through an area that was easy to recognize, no matter the nationality, as scantily clad women lounged provocatively in doorways and on street corners, not bothering to conceal what they hoped to sell.

The downtown area was filled with all manner of blazing neon signs, advertising everything to be found in any other modern city in the world. A few blocks past the commercial district, David pulled to a stop in front of a row of large older homes that had belonged in another era to a wealthier set than most of what Rick had seen on their wild ride across town. These houses were protected by thick walls and gardens with tall trees. Still, there was a dejected look about them that plainly stated their best days were behind them. Outside the pale brown walls that lay before them, hung a single bare bulb and a small sign, *Casa San Cristobal*.

"Come on." David was already out of the vehicle, snatching up Rick's things.

Rick followed more slowly as the day's events began to take their toll. David pulled on a rope near the door, and a heavy bell echoed deep within the house walls.

"*Buenas noches, don David*," the white-haired woman who opened the door welcomed the two Americans inside.

"*Buenas noches, Señora*." David's voice was honey-sweet, and Rick remembered all too well the beguiling smile that had maneuvered them out of some tight spots and into difficulties of another kind in years past.

Ushered into an open-air living room of unblemished white stucco walls that reflected the yellow glow of wall-mounted iron lamps at this hour, stiff, uncomfortable-looking furniture from the last century formed a border between the walls and the large shiny terra-cotta floor tiles. White cloths covered dark wood tables, which were encircled by caned chairs to create a tiny dining room in the back half of the room before it gave way into a miniature garden. A banana tree and various short palms graced the patio garden, all still within the confines of the same room. A large balcony supported by graceful arches that blended into square supports stood opposite the dining area. Doorways lead off the balcony and also lined the hallway created underneath.

David's line of flattery to the older woman slowed as they followed her to one of the lower doorways where she handed him a single key. Inside, they found two twin beds, which reminded Rick once again that few things in this country were designed for anyone much over five feet tall. David tossed Rick's bundles onto the nearest bed as his own belongings were already neatly stacked on a low chest on the far side of the room. A large wooden rocking chair graced the corner and exhausted as he was, Rick accepted its silent invitation.

He heard the squealing complaint of ancient water pipes and much splashing before David emerged shirtless from the tiny bathroom while toweling his hair.

"Don't just sit there!" He tossed the wet towel at his cousin. "A few of the guys said they'd wait for us over at Yani's. It's a *pupusa* place a couple of blocks from here. You want to eat, don't you? Let's see. Where is...yeah, here they are."

He walked over to the tidy arrangement on the chest. "I was running late when I got into town, so I just dropped my things at the door and *Señora Altafe* there, put 'em in a room for me. She's a sweetheart, that one."

"The old lady?"

"Yeah. This is a classier place than the *pensión* where I usually stay, but I thought you might be tired and need a little peace and quiet, not to mention a hot shower. The other, well, it's cheaper, but you're likely to deal with drunks or a party crowd a good part of the night and man, those showers are cold. This is still cheaper than a hotel, and *Señora Altafe* runs a tight ship. No nonsense in her boarding house." David's laugh said more than his words, but Rick was too tired to chase that particular rabbit tonight.

David had slipped into a clean shirt and combed his hair while he was making his explanations.

Rick looked with longing at the bed despite its short construction and dragged himself to his feet.

Back out on the sidewalk in front of the place, they walked through the quiet streets of the once-stately neighborhood. Rick glanced back at the entrance of *La Casa*, as David called it and noted how the dingy walls outside gave no hint of the exquisite interior and wondered if every house on the block held the same sort of interior treasure.

A handful of young girls, dressed in colors too bright for an ordinary weekday evening, stood out like exotic birds in the aged neighborhood. They giggled and called out after them as they crossed the street a half a block below.

"What are they up to?" Rick muttered under his breath.

David grinned with a wicked glance over his shoulder. "You really don't know?"

Rick took another look at the girls, some no more than young teens. They began to bid with their fingers as to the amount they wanted from would-be passing customers who drove slowly past in small cars. Always young men, alone in their cars.

"You've got to be kidding? They are just babies." Rick was incredulous.

"Welcome to a whole new world," David chuckled as his feet kept moving.

The warm fragrant air, heavy laden with the aroma of evening meals and tropical blossoms, wrapped around Rick like a favorite comforter from childhood, and he began to revive as if from an afternoon nap. David's pace quickened, and they neared a busy corner restaurant, fashioned from the open-air stone porch of another old home. Dimly lit and filled with the pungent odors of frying pork, hot cheese, and steamy tortillas, the place was filled with the noise of a Latin dance party supplied by a small radio in the far corner.

They passed by the large woman in charge where she tended a huge grill, filled with what looked to be greasy pancakes, cooking over a tiled firebox. David called out over the racket as he moved toward a group of four other Americans gathered at the corner table, furthest from the radio.

He ordered two beers and two dozen *pupuas* 'to begin.' He and David pulled up cast iron black chairs covered with worn-out red plastic upholstery that reminded Rick of those that might have once graced an American ice cream parlor a quarter of a century before.

David made the introductions and Rick, the obligatory greeting to John, a redhead from Seattle, Todd, a mustachioed blond from California, Michael, a strikingly thin New Yorker with clear blue eyes and a headful of black curls and Tim, a tall, lanky baby-faced youth who looked like a runaway from a high school basketball team.

"Looks like I'm no longer the newest kid in town," Tim drawled, further explaining he had arrived only a month before from South Carolina. "How do you like it so far?"

David hooted before Rick could make an answer. "He's had a real introduction, I can tell you. I was down at the Terminal waiting, figuring he'd come in on one of those Greyhound look-alikes and here he comes on—"

"It's been quite a day." Rick decided he had best tell his own story. "Mostly one of things breaking down along the way, like the plane which got as far as Guatemala City and the big bus I was supposed to be able to take from there to here, but instead it only made it as far as the border. Then the choice was to stay there for who knows how long or try this smaller local bus. And it wasn't so bad really, just very different." He noted sympathetic smiles around the table.

"Welcome to El Salvador, the land of the eternal breakdown and the never-ending screwup," Michael stated flatly. "Don't worry. If you stay here very long, you'll get used to it. That's when you should really start to worry."

Rick was unsure of how to respond, but the edgy silence that followed said he was not the only one. "Excuse me?" he answered noncommittally.

"You should begin to worry when it no longer bothers you that everything you touch is royally screwed over before you ever get started." Michael finished his beer and ordered another as he carefully set the empty long neck bottle on the window ledge beside three others.

"It's not that bad," David laughed, giving the New Yorker sitting next to him a playful shove.

"Unless you have to work here and try to get something accomplished on a daily basis."

"But Rick's not here to work. He's just down here for a little R & R, taking a break from those tough college courses in Houston."

"Another Texas boy?" Todd groaned. "We all know," he overemphasized his last word, "that David is from Texas where everything is bigger and better than everywhere else in the US."

"Well, I'm not really from Texas," Rick began to explain. "That's where my family lives now, but I grew up in Kansas and Missouri."

"Kansas?" The laughter exploded. "And you admit to that? Dorothy and Toto, too?"

"All right." David made an attempt to quell the laughter. "I should have warned you about these guys. A little free time, a few beers, and they just can't handle it."

Their food arrived, and in short order, they were all busy splitting open the hot *pupusas*, white corn tortillas filled with a steaming stuffing of spiced ground pork the boys called *chicharrón* or a heavy layer of white cheese. Rick watched as the others pulled the two sides apart while trying not to burn their fingers and then rolled each half around a thick layer of *curtido*, a spicy blend of pickled cabbage and shredded carrots, which they scooped from a large glass jar at the center of the table. It was a strange taste—tangy and exotic, but one Rick thought he could enjoy getting used to. The two dozen *pupusas* David had ordered when they sat down did not last long.

Despite the earlier teasing from David's friends, Rick had not felt uncomfortable. He envied their easy camaraderie with one another. He realized, too, after the day's experiences, it was also relaxing just to hear English spoken in a group again.

"So, you remember these?" David's question caught Rick by surprise.

"Remember what?"

"*Pupusas*," David replied. "We ate 'em when we were with Ana Luisa. I didn't think about it until I had 'em here for the first time."

Rick shook his head. "I don't remember. All I remember was lots of fish."

"That's because it was *Semana Santa*."

"You fellas have been to El Salvador before?" John raised an eyebrow in their direction.

"No, it was a long time ago. A crazy little trip we went on years ago as kids," David answered.

"You know," John observed. "This really isn't a bad place once you get used to it."

"I hear the same is true of hell." Michael's tone of voice was the same as earlier, but John ignored him.

"There are a lot of things that are wrong here, too, too much poverty, too many people and not enough resources, but the people, most of them anyway, are good-hearted. They mean well."

Michael interrupted again. "You've got a Salvadoran girlfriend, John, and it's ruined your whole perspective."

"I don't think so. I've lived with different families here, and I've seen it in a lot of ways. The people are the best thing this country has going for it."

Michael just shook his head.

"I don't think he's wrong," Tim stepped into the conversation. "I know I haven't been here very long, but the family I board with is really great."

"They try to marry you off to their daughter yet?" Michael's point of view was consistent if growing ever more irritating.

Tim seemed confused. "They don't have any daughters," he answered. "Just five sons."

Rick attempted to turn the conversation a bit while he tried to open one of the newest *pupusas* to arrive at the table. Instead, he dropped it on the paper-covered rattan paper plate holder that served as a plate and stuck his burned fingertips in his mouth. "So what do each of you do here? For work, I mean?"

He soon discovered that Todd, a tool and die maker was helping in the local industry in the capital while Tim was an agricultural advisor. John worked for the Ministry of Education, helping to develop some of the country's first special education programs. Michael was also involved in agriculture, working in a village a few miles outside of San Salvador. David worked the farthest from the capital city, as a business advisor to a fishermen's cooperative in *Las Palomitas*.

Rick nearly choked on that last job description. "Business advisor?"

David grinned. "Hey, business is business. I help the fishermen's cooperative get a few new markets here or there, make a loan at the bank, buy a new truck—sounds like business advice to me!"

Rick was unconvinced.

"You have to understand," John explained. "A great deal of the work done here is just acquainting unsophisticated people with the resources and government programs available to them. Many people who have simply lived and worked in a developed country and have the ability and patience to deal with government red tape and bureaucracy can do what needs to be done. The majority of the population is uneducated when it comes to those kinds of systems. Plus, the government has a rotten record with the people. They don't have any faith in anything that bears a government label, and you can't blame them when you know something of their history. So we're really coming in at the ground level, trying to connect grassroots programs with the people in need and sometimes even with government resources. It's not easy. You can't change 150 years of history overnight, but there are small successes."

Michael stretched and yawned. "Thank you, Mr. PR man. It sounds really good. Too bad it doesn't work so well in practice. Face it. I can't even get the people in the village I'm supposed to be helping to follow basic agriculture practices. When they don't make a mess of some new project, the animals and the insects do."

John was growing weary of Michael's constant harping. "Why don't you face it, Mike? Half your

problem is that you want everything to work here
the way it does at home, and it just isn't that way.
This isn't the good ol' USA. So what? They've got
their own way of doing things, and just because it's
different than what you're used to, you've decided
it can't possibly work. How do you know unless you
try? Maybe a better question is if you hate it so, why
do you stay?"

Michael stared across the table for a few moments,
shrugged, and took a long pull on yet another beer.

David loudly called for more beer and chattered
nervously, trying to ease the tension.

"So you speak Spanish, Rick?" Todd asked.

"Some," came the answer. "I've lived in Houston
for a few years now and work part-time in the *barrios*
there at a Boys Club. Might be better to say I speak
Tex-Mex."

"Well, you'll need it where David is taking you.
No English spoken down there on the beach. Hey,
David, what do you hear from your friend Herbie
these days?" Todd asked with a malicious twinkle
in his eye.

"Who's Herbie?" Rick inquired, when David, his
mouth full, did not answer immediately.

"Yeah, well," David stalled. "You know he wasn't
exactly my friend. I just felt sorry for the guy. Okay,
Herbie was a guy who..." he stopped. "How do
I explain him?"

"Herbie just never fit in here. He tried, but he
couldn't quite figure this place out, and things really
got to him, bad," John interjected. "Things like the

poverty, the strangeness. He got so homesick as fast as he got here, he basically couldn't function."

"Sounds kind of sad," Rick said.

"It was," Todd laughed sympathetically.

"He did get off to a bad start," David explained. "He spoke a little Spanish, and as fast as he got here, he had to try it out. He went down to a local *tienda*, a corner store, you know, and tried to buy a comb. Well, the word, of course, for that is *peine*, but Herbie mispronounced it. Instead of asking for a *peine*, he ended up asking for a *pene*, a local word for prick. I guess the little girl behind the counter about laughed herself silly, trying to figure out what it was this *gringo* really wanted. Herbie just kept saying it, louder and louder as he got more frustrated, and pretty soon, she dragged half a dozen people out of the back of the store to hear what it was this crazy *gringo* was saying.

Finally, she asks him, well, what happened to yours and he just goes on real casual like, telling her 'he lost it on the plane.' That, of course, sent her and everybody else off on another round of giggles. After he makes combing motions over his hair with his hands, she figures it out and sells him a comb. Then once back at the hotel, he asks one of the other guys who spoke more Spanish than he did, and when he finds out what he had been saying, he claps his hand over his mouth. His next words are '*Estoy tan embarazado*,' but that's no help either. He got caught by a false cognate."

"What's a cognate?" Rick looked from one face to another.

"It's a grammatical term, and most of them are true cognates and no big deal. True cognates are words like *comercial* for commercial or *televisor* or *televisión* for television, and they translate straight across. Others are not so clear, like *principal* in Spanish doesn't exactly mean principal like in English but more like main. For instance, Main Street is literally, *Calle Principal* for the main drag through town, close but not exactly the same thing. You don't talk about Mr. Main Street at the local school. See what I mean? But false cognates come completely out of left field. You hear English speakers try to make English words into Spanish, like *el fisho* for fish or something stupid like that. But some...." He hesitated a moment longer. "*Embarazado* is not the word for embarrassed. It actually means pregnant."

"Poor Herbie, screwed again." David was still tickled by the story even though he had obviously heard it many times. "Herbie told me he never went back into that particular *tienda* again," he finished, covering his mouth to keep from spraying beer and *pupusas* over his companions in one last afterthought of Herbie and his troubles. The others also broke into a round of laughter at the now-familiar tale, but it was new to Rick. He smiled at the not uncommon tale of English speakers getting themselves into trouble in another language and wondered if a similar fate awaited him in the not-so-distant future in a beach community where no one spoke English except himself and David.

"He never did learn much more Spanish after that, and the truth is he didn't stay more than a few weeks. I took him down to the beach for a few days at one point, but it didn't seem to help much. It was like everything around here made him crazy. The language was the start of it, but it was things like the way the people all pack in close together in places like the bus. You know what I mean.

"I do?" Rick wasn't following.

John added. "After your bus ride today, you know. You get packed in there like sardines, and when you get off, your bare arm is wet with sweat. Then after a few more seconds, you realize it ain't even your sweat but somebody else's. Herbie told me once it was like his private space was being invaded."

Rick laughingly asked, "Where was this guy from, anyway?"

The others looked to one another, but no one seemed to have a clue.

"Well, maybe he was the smart one," Michael added. "He got out. He's back in the US, eating hamburgers that taste like real burger meat while I'm going back to the village tomorrow where they raise beef but can't make a hamburger that tastes like anything you'd want to eat. I've lost twenty pounds since I got here a year ago," he grumbled as much to himself as to the others.

"I told you before," John began, not unkindly. "I think you've got parasites. You ought to go see the doctor."

"Oh, right," Michael snorted and sat up straight. "And carry in a little teeny cup of your own shit for some lab guy to go digging around in. No way, man." His last words came out with a definitive slur.

John shrugged and let the matter drop.

The others did their best to ignore him.

"No matter how you got here," David turned back to his cousin, "at least, it was this week and not last. I was beginning to think I'd given you lousy advice to come at all. Things were more than a bit tense, militarily speaking."

"What was last week?" Rick asked.

"Independence Day here is September 15," John explained. "They celebrate, mostly with parades of school kids, carrying the flag, that sort of thing. Marchers in the street have gotten to be a real touchy issue with the government, though. Parades have turned into *manifestaciones*—protests against the government because of political repression, lack of freedom at the ballot box or anywhere else and the government's attitude is it's a free for all. Of course, they have the guns, the protestors don't."

Involuntarily, they had all dropped their voices as they discussed the forbidden subject.

"The military is pretty jumpy these days is all I know," David continued. "Coming into town today, they stopped the Jeep and had more questions than ever." He turned to Rick. "It belongs to the government, and has their license plates on it so every soldier with a gun figures he needs to ask why a *gringo* is driving it."

Rick began to feel less paranoid about his experience at the border.

"You're lucky you live out where you do," John added. "Some of the people here in the city are really running into trouble. A number of the Salvadoran teachers are being harassed, really ugly stuff—phone calls threatening their children, deadly threats left on their doorstep, a letter, a warning spray-painted on their front door. If they say anything supportive of those who are against the government or just those who are trying to make a difference like the union organizers, those who support free speech, or are even supportive of the church, their name is suddenly on a list and look out. None of the Americans have been bothered yet, but I wonder if it isn't just a matter of time."

David refused to let the somber mood continue. "Hey, boys, enough of politics. Not a wise topic of conversation in public places anyway. Lighten up and drink up. Tomorrow we're heading home, back to peace, quiet, the beach, and nobody bothering anybody except the fish in the sea. We bother them a lot."

The rest of the group pounced on him in a similar spirit, especially since they were not headed out to such idyllic circumstances.

Michael, however, now with a slur to his words and a bit of a stagger when he stood up. "I don't care where you're going in this country. You better keep your eyes open and your wits about you 'cause anything could happen here at any moment."

CHAPTER 3

O ctober 15, 1979, San Salvador – It was announced late today that the government of General Carlos Romero has been overthrown in a bloodless coup and replaced by a junta, a panel made up of younger military, civilian politicians, and business leaders. Colonel Romero has been exiled to Guatemala, and the military has stated they will stand by the new government.

Boarding the bus for the return trip to *Las Palomitas*, Rick could see it was already full, and he cursed the luck that was not running with him. After spending most of the afternoon in San Miguel's *Cantina El Gallo*, waiting for David, he was in no mood for a long ride with his head banging the ceiling. His spirits lifted momentarily as he caught a glimpse of Candelario, Emelina's *marido*, her common-law husband. Rick started to raise his hand in greeting to the only other person he knew in this packed can of humanity, but then the face he thought he knew disappeared in the crowd at the back of the bus. Thinking he'd made a mistake, his dark mood returned, his contemplations went back to the fact that David had never shown up at the bar.

The day had not begun so badly. He had found the cantina David described without any problem upon his arrival in San Miguel. After the cramped bus, it was good to be out walking again. The second-largest city in the country, San Miguel seemed no more than an overgrown village. It was larger with a main market and a charming little park at its center, but it was nothing a man could not walk across in short order and unremarkable except for the gleaming white stucco shops and the colonial arches that fronted many of them. This was not a modern city like San Salvador, which could compete with any other metropolis in the world in terms of goods and services provided. San Miguel was a provincial capital, little more than a trading center for area farmers.

The longer Rick sat in the back corner of the cantina, however, the more sorely out of place he began to feel. It was more than just being the only foreigner in the place, although being the only six-foot-tall blond foreigner didn't help. It was the unnerving whispers of *déjà vu*, his mind surely playing tricks on him because he had never been here before.

A handful of well-armed soldiers ran down the street past the wide-open door while two others came inside and spoke nervously with the bartender and a few of the patrons sitting nearby. The longer he stayed, the stronger the sensation that something ominous was about to happen, he just could not tell what. After his third beer, he simply sat and waited. He wanted a clear head for whatever was coming next.

His mind wandered back to the day he had first crossed the border into the country. The guns had made him nervous that day, but nothing came of it. *Malicia*. He had learned the locals even had a name for this feeling of unidentifiable dread. A friend of David's told him once, listening to it can be the difference that it makes, in getting out of a tight situation, alive or not. At the time, sitting on the beach in the bright sunlight, he thought the man was exaggerating. At the moment, he was no longer so sure.

He remembered the large volcano, just outside the city of San Miguel, that the bus had passed this morning. He and David had driven by it on the other side in the Jeep the day after he arrived. Although David told him the black volcano had not erupted since 1917, he had seen a tiny white cloud over the top of it early this morning and wondered if it might not be a puff of smoke. Maybe this was that strange sensation he read about, the one that said animals and even certain people could sense an impending earthquake or volcanic eruption. It was something about the air—intangible, untouchable, unidentifiable, with more than a hint of urgency, a need to do something, but what?

Eventually, it was too much, even for Rick's patient nature. He left the cantina and concentrated on the bus, the last one for the day, returning to *Las Palomitas*. Wherever David was, he would surely find him there.

The *cobrador*, the boy who punched tickets, stowed luggage up top and generally acted as a train conductor might, called to the driver from the roof that they were ready to go. Rick wriggled his way past several passengers and their goods—some live, some not—who were already standing in the aisle.

A young man sitting next to where Rick stopped in his struggle to advance past the others apparently changed his mind, picked up his small bag, and slipped out the back door as the bus was preparing to pull away from the curb.

Rick had assumed the man was traveling with the woman sitting next to the window, but she took no notice of his departure.

"May I sit here?" Rick asked her in Spanish.

She cast a withering glance in his direction, but said nothing, only shrugged and turned her attention back to the window.

Rick fell into the seat as the bus stopped with a jerk, throwing several of the standing passengers off balance. Half a dozen soldiers were in front of the vehicle, their rifles at the ready. The officer in charge was halfway up the steps when a shout from behind the bus captured the attention of passengers and soldiers alike.

Rick caught only a glimpse of them as they dragged off the unfortunate man who had been in his seat only a few moments before, beating and prodding him with their rifles as they went. The soldiers turned the corner with their unwilling quarry and disappeared out of sight, but Rick continued to stare after them. With a shudder, he realized he was no longer angry with David, only concerned about where he might be.

Once outside the city, the weighty sense of dread he had been carrying since the cantina began to lift. He would soon be back in his own niche. Just thinking of it helped him to breathe easier.

As he relaxed, his attention drifted toward his traveling companion. She stared out the window, her face turned away from him, yet he had seen enough to discern that she was strikingly attractive. Her thick shoulder-length black hair was smoothed back from a classically sculpted indigenous face. Her large dark eyes, high cheekbones, and flawless complexion bore only the barest trace of make-up. Her clothes were not the bright polyesters or faded cottons of most women her age, out here in the countryside. He guessed her to be about the same age as himself. As he watched her from the corner of his eye, he thought she could walk down any cosmopolitan avenue in the world and command respect in her fitted blue and white linen suit and high heels. Here, on the bus bound for the outer villages, however, her understated elegance was even more prominent.

Initial attempts at conversation had proven unsuccessful. With her attention focused on the passing scenery, Rick tried a different tack. "I didn't expect this country to be so beautiful." He spoke in Spanish, not expecting a response but hoping for one just the same. "It is so green with so many flowers. What is that yellow field out there?" He pointed to an area below the volcano, an out of place stretch of maize-colored grass, tucked in amongst bright green fields of corn and sorghum.

"Rice." She spoke without turning around.

"There are rice fields in Texas, but I guess I haven't seen any for a long time."

"Is that where you are from? Texas?" She glanced in his direction.

"Yes. Have you ever been there?"

"Hmm," was her only response. The window once again claimed her full attention.

Rick continued. "There is a pretty little spring just a short distance up the highway. A friend of mine took me there once."

"*Capulin.*"

"That's it. I couldn't remember the name."

Rick was finding it more difficult than he had expected to talk to this woman. Maybe he should just forget the whole thing. "I'm sorry." He tried one last time. "I don't mean to *molestar*—" He choked on the word. He knew in Spanish it only meant 'to bother,' but under the circumstances, it sounded even worse than usual.

She turned to him with a genuine smile this time, albeit a small one. It was ample reward for his efforts. "You are not *bothering* me," she responded, stressing the verb in amusement at his discomfiture. Her English was charmingly accented.

"You speak English." He breathed a sigh of relief and immediately blushed.

"Many people in the world do." She met his gaze with a level one of her own.

Rick introduced himself and waited for her to do the same.

"Rishard Mercy," she repeated, pronouncing his first name differently than anyone else he had ever met. "Mariana," she added after a moment's hesitation.

Rick scrambled for something else to say, not wanting the conversation to end. "When I came by this volcano this morning on the bus, it looked as if it might be acting up. When I came through with my friend a few weeks ago, I saw the other side, the damage a volcanic eruption can inflict on the land for decades to come."

She nodded as if considering his words. For a stretch of two miles on the southern side of the volcano of San Miguel, once-fertile farmland lay buried under a layer of thick black rock as if an out-of-control asphalt maker had been turned loose to pour the stuff in all directions, destroying everything in its path. The hot sun, beating down on the blackness, created a daily reminder of the heat that must have attended the original issue of the rock as the air temperature soared as one crossed the lava-covered ground.

Rick and David had buzzed through the area in a Jeep, but not before Rick noticed even there, the barren landscape was dotted by tiny huts thrown up on the charred, now-worthless earth. "This is where the poorest of the poor live," David explained. "When they have no place else to go, they come here. No one will fight them for this land."

No one fights for a place in hell, Rick remained silent despite his thoughts and was thankful they had speedy transportation and were not cursed like the ones he saw who were walking across the blazing hot ground.

"El Salvador has 22 volcanoes. Did you know that?" Mariana almost sounded like a tour guide now, but at least she was talking to him, and for that Rick was most thankful. "Although it is more than 60 years since *Chapárastique's* last great eruption, she likes to remind us all that she can still be dangerous when she wants to be."

"*Chapra*—?" Rick tried to pronounce the unfamiliar name.

"*Chapárastique.*" She said it for him again, a bit more slowly this time. "That is her Indian name. It means *jardín de carbón*, Garden of—" she hesitated, looking for the right word in English, "Garden of Ashes." The bittersweet name for the black mountain overlooking the fertile green plain on this opposite side from where he and David had passed weeks before, did not make sense until seen from the other side, Rick mused.

"With so many volcanoes, it makes for even less usable land and with so many people—." Her voice took on a wistful tone, and she left the statement unfinished. "As anyone can see, we have more serious problems here than the threat that comes from an ancient volcano." She stopped speaking and turned back to the window.

Rick waited for several minutes, wondering what had caused the change. The bus shifted gears noisily as they climbed into the mountains, leaving the plain and the volcano behind. They traveled on in silence, but as they neared the spring waters of *Capulin*, the bus slowed to a stop.

A rockslide had narrowed the road to a single lane, but a huge boulder blocked even that passage. A man approached the bus as if to give directions or explain about the conditions. With no warning, the boy on the roof of the bus screamed as a bullet whizzed past his head. He dropped, spread eagle over the boxes and suitcases. A half dozen men, armed and dressed in tatters, sprung out of hiding from behind the rocks and surrounded the bus. The leader shouted at the driver, who turned off the engine and began to frantically scream for everyone to get out.

"*Los muchachos*," she muttered as she followed Rick off the bus. He tried to question her, but she only shook her head and said nothing more.

One of the guerrillas stood on a rock, making a political statement at the top of his lungs, the same noise Rick had heard spew from loudspeakers in the capital and in San Miguel. He had blamed his inability to understand on the distortion caused by the poor equipment, but he found the personal delivery was equally unintelligible. Something about the people, the good of the society—how is it all politicians, no matter the language, sound so much alike, Rick wondered as his mind proceeded to operate in a kaleidoscope fashion, bits and pieces falling together in a nonsensical fashion.

Another man was passing in front of the crowd, starting at the rear of the bus, working his way forward. He carried a burlap bag, collecting money and valuables, Jesse James' style, from the passengers. He was accompanied by a short heavyset man who carried a rifle, apparently to encourage the donations. Good God, Rick thought, as he watched the progress of the two bandits. If this was their idea of how to finance a revolution, they are in serious trouble.

The rest of the *muchachos* stood about casually, watching, their guns trained carelessly on the crowd, while another kept the only true vigil high up on the ridge, where he could observe approaching traffic for a half-mile in either direction.

Rick began to mentally prepare for his turn. He had no rings, no watch, and very little money on him. Lined up, standing along the shoulder in front of the side of the bus amongst approximately fifty Salvadoran peasants, Rick stood out like a lone albino ram in a flock of brown lambs. The disparity was not lost on his captors.

As they approached, the enforcer leveled his gun straight at Rick. Looking down the cold barrel of a World War II vintage rifle, Rick felt his blood run the same way. The mindless grin on the scraggily-bearded face behind it did nothing to calm his mounting fear. When the man spoke, however, it was not to him but to Mariana.

"So you have found a friend, have you?" He leered at her. "You are friends with the *gringos* now and their government, too?"

The color drained from her face as the allegation became clear. Despite her best effort to maintain her composure, her voice cracked when she spoke. "I do not know what you are talking about!" she snapped.

"You have been talking to him, no? It is plain enough for everyone to see what you are!" The man jerked his head in Rick's direction.

"Him?" Mariana shrieked back. "I do not even know him."

"He is traveling with you, is he not?" The accusation was too calm, too self-assured. The warm afternoon air, a bit cooler here in the mountains, was suddenly oppressive.

"I tell you I do not know him," Mariana repeated, panic rising in her voice.

"Elio!" The bearded face shouted for a higher authority, but his gun never wavered. "If you do not know him..." his words were meant for Mariana, although his attention was focused on the gun and its target. "Then you will not mind if I kill him right here." Even the other rebels seemed startled by this boast, and they gathered closer to see if their companion would make good on his threat. Mariana crossed herself, her lips moving involuntarily.

I can't die like this, Rick's thoughts continued to cartwheel. Who would know? Who would care? This isn't real. He fought off a sudden desire to laugh out loud, a suicidal impulse at this point, he feared. Was he losing his mind, or only more frightened than he was willing to admit? He didn't know. If I close my eyes, maybe it will all go away, like a bad dream. But Rick couldn't close his eyes, couldn't pull them away from the barrel of that gun. While the propaganda man began launching into a tirade about *yanquí imperialistas*, a few small rocks fell from high above as the man on the ridge shifted his position.

"Lito, no!" The cry came from the back of the pack of human jackals. A square-shouldered curly-haired man made his way through the throng of rebels and displaced bus passengers.

"She was with him." In animated tones, Lito proceeded to explain the situation to the newest arrival. "*Elio, lo mato!* He concluded. "We will send a message to the *gringos*."

"Lito," came the surprisingly gentle yet firm response. "What do you care about sending messages, especially to *gringos*? If you kill him, we will only have more *gringos* looking for him and looking for you. It is not worth it. Besides, you will make a terrible mess of the side of the bus. There is no reason." The joke went unappreciated.

A voice of logic, at last, Rick thought, yet just as quickly Elio was also speaking harshly to Mariana. "And what are you doing with him?"

Rick thought he caught a flicker of surprised recognition in the man's eyes, but he could not be sure.

"I do not know him, I tell you. He is only a tourist. I do not know who you think he is but of this much I am certain. You have made a mistake." The panic was gone from her voice now, replaced only by weariness and the sudden onset of tears. Even so, Rick found himself thinking there was a sense of refinement about her that put her above everyone else in the God-forsaken place, including himself.

Lito tried once more. "I kill him, and we take her with us."

The image of a man slinking off the back of the bus, and this woman's all too present tears whirled through Rick's colliding thoughts. It was too much. More rocks, a few larger ones this time, dislodged by the fidgety lookout man sent the propaganda man and two of the gunmen scrambling out of harm's way. The brief distraction was enough. Rick seized the barrel of the gun, thrusting it skyward as he dropped almost to his knees. The discharge reverberated through the hills, showering the bus passengers with bits of window glass. The boy conductor shrieked and jumped from his resting place, scampering off the back end of the bus.

Rick Mercy slowly rose to his feet. He stared steadily down into the eyes of the Salvadoran rebel who held the butt and trigger of the gun while he maintained his own double-fisted grip on the barrel.

Lito's deep belly laugh began as a low rumble and then burst forth almost as explosively as the gunfire. "*Vaya!*" He cried out as he slapped the shaken American on the back. Rick released his hold on the weapon, and Lito dropped it carelessly to his side.

The game over and the rest of the passengers' valuables collected, the driver began easing his charges back onto the bus. Elio had pulled Mariana toward the front of the bus and was speaking quietly with her. She stepped back on to the bus in front of Rick.

The rebels' bag man had accepted Rick's meager offerings earlier without question but stopped him at the door of the bus once more. "Your *pasaporte, gringo*." He made the casual request, one businessman to another. It was the one item Rick had hoped to salvage from the situation. He had heard that American passports were worth several hundred dollars on the black market. Unwilling to risk yet another confrontation, however, he sighed and reached inside his shirt to the small leather pouch he carried on a cord around his neck.

"Wait!" Elio stepped forward, and Rick's hand froze. "I see no *pasaporte*." He shifted his gaze back to Mariana for only the briefest of moments. "I have seen a brave man today, nothing more." He patted Rick's hand, still inside his shirt, before pushing him toward the open bus door where the American scrambled to safety.

"You should come with us and learn to fight, like a man, instead of taking care of a bunch of old women and crying babies." One of the rebels called out to the boy *contador* as he was once again riding carefree on top of his packages.

"Maybe, someday," he returned their call, which echoed off the nearby rock walls.

"I am sorry," she began speaking as soon as they returned to their seats. "I am sorry for—"

"For what?" Rick snapped. "For telling the truth?" He knew it was not fair, but he did not seem to be able to help taking his frustration out on her. "You weren't lying. You don't know me."

"You are angry. I am sorry," she repeated.

"Hell, yes, I'm angry. I don't need this, people pointing guns up my nose and for what? I don't know what was going on back there, but I think you do."

She looked away with an evasive answer. "I forgot how hard it can be here."

"What does that mean?" It suddenly occurred to him she could be as much of a foreigner here as he was. "Where are you from anyway?"

She had turned back to the window. Other passengers now settled back into the routine of the bus' regular starts and stops, reached out and patted Rick on the shoulder and complimented him on his courage as they left the bus. Even the boy from the roof, slid through one of the open windows of a now nearly empty bus, to stop and have a word with the 'courageous *gringo*.'

"You are very brave," the young *contador* began, "to challenge *los muchachos*. Even the *guardia* are afraid of them, and well they should be. You are lucky, Lady," he spoke to Mariana, "to be traveling with such a brave man." He scooted off down the aisle to confer with the driver.

As the last of the passengers departed the bus at the few remaining stops, Rick expected that she too would be getting off the bus at any moment. He was not prepared for her to walk away and leave things as they were.

"Look," he tried again. "I'm sorry I spoke to you the way I did. Maybe it wasn't your fault. I just want to know what it's all about, okay?"

"I do not have answers for you." She finally spoke after several long minutes of silence. "I told them the truth. I think they mistook you and me for someone else. Someone on this bus line told them I was talking to you. That is obvious. Now my question, who are you? They seemed to think you were someone threatening. I was in trouble because I was speaking to you, or have you not figured that out yet?" There was a cold edge to her voice.

Rick shook his head. "I'm down here visiting my cousin, nothing more. I told you that. What you haven't told me is anything about you."

"For someone who put me in harm's way, you ask a great many questions." She turned back to look at him, without smiling this time. "I am returning home, not that it is your business, but it is the first time to see my family in a very long time. That is all."

Her face pivoted back to the window, and Rick knew there would be no more conversation. The bus turned off of the highway onto the long dirt track leading to *Las Palomitas*. It seemed like much more than a day had passed since he had bounced over this washboard route, as dawn was breaking this morning. Exhaustion threatened to set in, and he looked forward to the end of this long day's journey. He stole one more appreciative look at Mariana.

The bus pulled up under the large tree in the center of the village that served as a bus stop. Paz was waiting there just as Rick thought he might be, but the expression of awe and wonder that lit his face was completely unexpected.

"Mariana," the boy whispered the name like a prayer as he watched her step down in front of Rick. He turned toward his friend with a wide grin.

"Don Ricardo!" he shouted. "You have found her and brought her home to us!" He threw his arms around the woman who dropped her belongings in the dust and hugged him in return.

"Pazito." She sounded as if she wanted to cry, but her composure held even as she hid her face in the boy's hair. "How did you grow to be so tall?"

Rick tried to watch the curious reunion without appearing to do so. He caught Mariana's bags as they were thrown down off the top of the bus.

Paz scampered over to retrieve them. Mariana picked up her things and followed Paz.

"Where did you find her? How did you get her to come home?" Paz was full of questions. "This is wonderful! My father will be so happy to see her. And Emelina, too."

"It looks as if *los muchachos* are not the only ones ready to credit you with things you have not done." Mariana no longer spoke in English, but her tone was icy.

"*Los muchachos?*" Paz' questions increased. "You have been with *los muchachos?*"

"It is a long story." Rick's sense of weariness was growing. "Paz, I didn't bring Mariana. She came on her own. We sat on the bus together, that is all. She is your—?"

He waited for an answer from one of them.

"She did not tell you?" Paz continued with his questions. "This is my sister. I thought she would have told you." He hesitated, sensing things were not as they should be between the two of them. "You do not know one another?"

Mariana glanced at Rick. "Right now, I just want to go home, Pazito, to see Imanuel and Emelina. We cannot conduct family business here in the middle of the street, please."

Rick had not noticed until she mentioned it, but other villagers were stopping to stare. A few greeted Mariana but with hesitation, as if they were not quite certain who she was.

"Goodbye." She offered Rick a formal handshake, and he noticed she looked as pale as she did with their earlier encounter with the rebels on the bus. He watched her walk away, the air of eloquence, a bit battered in the foray with the rebels, was once again back in place. The entire village could hear the scream of delight as Emelina caught sight of her at the restaurant door.

"I have to go." Paz danced in front of Rick, not wanting to leave his friend nor miss the family reunion. "I will see you tomorrow. What a day this has been, yes? A new government, and now my sister is home for the first time in so many years!"

"What do you mean, a new government?"

"Don Ricardo, you do not know? It has been all over the radio this evening, which means, of course, it happened this morning. There is a new government in San Salvador this day. I do not really know what it means, but everyone is happy about it. Some of the young officers took over and put out *el Presidente Romero*. This is good. He was a very bad man."

A number of the day's events began to fall into place a bit more clearly.

"Wait, Paz. Have you seen or heard anything from David?"

Paz was taken aback by the question. "I thought you went to meet him. Did you not find him?"

"No, he didn't show up."

"This is not good." Paz frowned, but his enthusiasm was not easily quelled. "But you know how don David is. It is most likely nothing at all. The roads are not always so safe on days when there is much trouble with the government. We were a little worried about you today, too."

Rick smiled faintly. All he wanted at the moment was to walk up the beach and collapse in a weary heap in his own cabin.

"Don David would know this, and he will stay wherever he is for a day or two longer. He will come home soon. He always does." Paz scampered off to the restaurant to join in the family celebration.

Watching him go, Rick wished for some of that same childlike faith.

CHAPTER 4

*O*ctober 16, 1979, San Salvador – Monsignor
Oscar A. Romero, Archbishop of El Salvador,
*addressed his nation today in a special radio message,
calling on the Salvadoran elite to listen to the needs
of the poor. He admonished the new government
to keep their promises of economic and political
liberty, justice, and equality, announced yesterday
as a part of the Proclamation of October 15th. He
called upon the Revolutionary Governing Junta, as
the new government is calling itself, to prove that
their "beautiful promises are not just dead letters."*

The next morning Rick was once again up with the
sun, but not by choice. Unable to sleep well, a first-
time occurrence since his arrival in *Las Palomitas*,
his dreams had been laced with visions of raggedly-
dressed guerrillas, his missing cousin, and a crying
woman. Most disturbing was the vision of the man
who left the bus in San Miguel. Rick had not seen
his face clearly, but in his dreams, the scene replayed
itself time after time, and each time, it was David
being dragged away.

He bought a few hot tortillas from one of Julio's
daughters from the hut across the road. Coupled

with a banana he already had and some hot coffee, it made an acceptable breakfast.

While it was already too late to go this morning, Rick decided to walk into the village to arrange an afternoon fishing trip. Along the way, he realized he would probably be going alone. Surprisingly, he found *La Tienda Guadalupe* standing open and unattended.

Imanuel regularly divided his time between the store and the church and its projects, but he never left the store without first making certain someone else was taking care of business.

Rick called out and looked around. His voice echoed back from the plaster walls, piled high with merchandise, most of which might have been found in an American general store a century ago.

Rope, tin pails, lanterns, candles, eggs, dried beans, and rice were crammed between barrels of cooking oil, vinegar, and kerosene—all of which were sold to the individual according to the size of the jar or bottle brought in to be re-filled. A large wooden box held a variety of empty liquor bottles, sold to those who forgot their own vessel.

A few items from more recent decades were also interspersed among the basic necessities, including rainbows of brightly colored plastic water jugs, small tubs, and rubber sandals, all of which hung suspended on ropes tied to the rafters.

Wooden crates of bottled beer and soda pop were stacked beside the lone modern convenience in the place, an avocado-colored home refrigerator, which was filled with cold drinks and homemade frozen ice treats.

Rick grew impatient, and after calling out again, stepped behind the counter to the curtains that separated the living quarters from the store. Trailing after Paz on various occasions, this was far from the first time he had passed through the dark green drapes, yet he hesitated momentarily this time.

Pushing aside his own reluctance, he took a step inside. Everything in the well-worn little living room was as he remembered it—the wooden sofa and a matching chair that held overstuffed vinyl cushions, a bent reed rocking chair, the pre-requisite hammock strung cattycorner across the back part of the room, the tiny triangular desk in the near corner, piled high with business receipts and Imanuel's Bible. The door at the back was closed and the curtains drawn over the back window, making the room darker than usual. Maybe that was why he did not see the figure standing so near to him until it was too late.

A quick movement caught his eye but not in time to avoid the crashing blow to the right side of his head. There was a bright flash, and the pain crumpled him to his knees. Then, mercifully, there was only darkness.

"You did not have to do that!" The woman's voice was sharp but familiar as it sifted through the agonizing fog that enveloped his brain. As he drifted back to consciousness, Rick tried to move but gave up the effort almost immediately. He could not feel his feet, and it was easier to lie still and listen. A cool, wet cloth was gently laid across his forehead.

"How was I supposed to know who or what he is?" A man's voice answered in defense. "What is he doing, poking his nose in here anyway?"

"Apparently, he has been back here before." Her voice was frigid. "A better question might be, what are you doing here?"

"*Puta!*" he cursed, letting his temper go. "I get word last night that my dearly beloved cousin is back in town for the first time in five years, so I risk everything to come and see her. And this is my welcome! I accidentally hit your *gringo* boyfriend in the head and—"

"I do not need your smart-ass assumptions, Franco. If you must know, he has been a good friend to Paz and Imanuel. They were busy telling me all about him last night." She paused for a moment, moving the cloth. The light scent of her perfume drifted closer as she leaned over him. It did nothing to make him feel any less dizzy.

"Oh, he is going to live. Quit fussing over him. I did not hit him that hard."

"So, you know the ones who stopped the bus yesterday?" Her tone was accusatory.

"Maybe." He shrugged.

"Well, if that is their idea of how to win the people over to their side, they have a long hard fight ahead of them, and I am not talking about the one they already have going with the government. They nearly scared me to death, not to mention stealing what little people have. *Por el amor de Díos!* What was that supposed to accomplish anyway?"

"*Puta*," he repeated, throwing up his hands in mock surrender. "I was not the one in charge yesterday. I was not even with them. I heard Lito got a little, uh, out of hand—"

"Is that what they called it? He was threatening to kill this man and drag me off, I do not even know where. *Díos mío!* It made me sorry I ever decided to come home!"

"Oh, stop being so melodramatic! You've known Lito since we were children. He would not have hurt anyone without cause, and he would not have kept you long," he chuckled. "He knows the moment he closed his eyes to sleep a little, you would have chucked him up alongside the head with the first thing you found, like a big rock. He still has that scar across his forehead where you hit him with a big stick that one time."

She giggled in spite of her irritation. "Oh, yes, there was that. Well, it was his own fault. I told him at the time I did not know how to play baseball, but he wanted us all to play, saying there were not enough players to make two teams. To be honest, it has been so long, and we have all changed so over the years, I was not sure that was him, and then he was pretty scary with that old gun. *Puchica!* By that time, I was sure it was him, he was acting pretty crazy with that gun, and I was not certain he wasn't going to shoot someone."

"Yeah, well, I did not know they were going to do anything like that yesterday. I was at a meeting of some of the leaders, trying to figure out our best response to this crisis in San Salvador. The next thing I hear, they are out robbing a bus, and they find you on the bus, all cozy with some *gringo*. Made for quite the day," he continued while dropping his full weight into the nearby hammock.

"So why did you come back?" He switched gears on her as his voice softened with the new question. "You know it is no safer for you now than it ever was. You will worry your poor father to death."

"I am tired, Franco," she sighed. "Tired of everything. I just decided it was time. That is all."

"Tired of living, are you?" He had asked a sincere question and apparently did not appreciate the less-than-candid answer.

"Look who scolds me for being reckless, yet here you are and in the light of day, no less. Who dares to sneak into town in the middle of the day? At least I am not a known *guerrillero*, only the lowly relative of one." She began to tend once again to her patient, who realized he was not going to be able to feign unconsciousness much longer. She shook his shoulder gently.

"Rishard," she called. "Wake up." She threw a quick glance backward. "Well, are going to stand there and answer his questions, or are you going to disappear. Which is it?"

Franco lost his chance to decide as the back door opened, and Imanuel scurried inside, apparently on his way back from the church. The curious sight in his living room—the tall blond foreigner stretched over a too-short sofa, being tended by his daughter as his rarely seen nephew looked on, was too much even for Imanuel's patient nature.

"*A la gran pu—*" the words began, but he cut them off quickly.

"Careful, *Tío*," Franco admonished. "Saints don't swear."

Imanuel glared at him but said nothing more as a shuffling noise on the other side of the curtain reminded them all that customers in the store also needed attention. Imanuel passed through the front curtains.

"Now see what you've done?" Mariana hissed at Franco. "I did not come back here to upset him."

Rick opened his eyes. His feet were asleep, a direct result of his knees hanging over the armrest at the end of the couch. Slowly, he sat up, dragging his wooden legs around to rest on the floor in front of him.

"Are you all right?" Mariana asked.

"I will be." Rick looked across at Franco, who sat with one foot on each side of the hammock, watching Rick like a cat watches an unsuspecting dove as it bathes itself in the dust. "As long as nobody else decides to hit me in the head." He looked at Mariana. "What is it with the men you know?" He felt a little guilty dumping his aggravation all on her, but his head and his legs both hurt, none of which was improving his mood.

A strained silence hung in the air, but it did not last as Imanuel came back into the room.

"What has happened here?" He demanded in an imperious tone that, before this moment, Rick would never have imagined coming from the gentle diminutive catechist.

Rick said nothing, and Mariana looked down at the floor like a little girl caught in mischief not of her own making.

"It was my fault, *Tío*," Franco finally spoke. "I did not know this man was a friend. I made a mistake. I am sorry, friend." He looked hard at Rick.

Rick was surprised to feel the apology was genuine and nodded silently in the other's direction.

"I came down to see Mariana. Nothing more. I heard she was back but feared she might not stay long, so I came right away and—"

Imanuel visibly relaxed. "And now we have another situation," he continued. He stepped back near the curtain so that he could continue to listen in case anyone else came into the store. When he spoke again, it was the voice of the friend Rick had come to know.

"It was a dangerous thing to do." His chastisement of his nephew began softly but grew in intensity. "To come at night is one thing, but to come in the day is quite another. Do you not realize, it is not only yourself you put in danger but also your cousins, both of them? Paz is still quite young. I take it you are not armed?"

"*Tío*," the younger man hesitated. "I did not carry my rifle into your house, out of respect, but only a fool travels unarmed in this country as things stand now."

Imanuel's eyebrows shot up in silence, and Franco babbled on, defending himself against shadows. "You know what I mean. Even the lowliest *campesino* carries his *cuma* or machete when he walks alone, day or night."

"Some travel on faith." The voice was gentle but the words, commanding.

"That may work for you, *Tío*, but not all of us are so lucky," the younger man shot back. "I should go."

"No," Imanuel continued. "If you were seen this morning, then the damage is already done. If not, you will be safe here for the day, and you can leave tonight. Now that you are here, you might just as well enjoy your visit."

He disappeared through the curtain, leaving the three sitting in confused silence. When he returned, a moment later, it was with three cold long neck bottles of beer which he handed to them silently. He crossed the room and locked the back door.

"I am not sure where Paz is, so if he comes to this door, just leave it. He will come around to the front. I will keep him busy for a while. He can see you later tonight, once he comes home to stay for the evening.

"He is already most excited that his sister is home, and I know he will be happy to see you, too. But it is not good for him to be seen in the streets too happy, yes? He is not so good at keeping some secrets." Imanuel disappeared back into the front of the store.

The three traded glances briefly, each feeling foolish for his or her own reasons.

"I came looking for Paz," Rick stammered. "Since he's not here, I really should go." He tried to stand, but his head and feet simultaneously refused to cooperate, and he sank back onto the sofa. He smiled self-consciously. "On second thought," he sighed and took a draught from the bottle in his hand.

Franco, relieved to no longer be the object of Imanuel's displeasure, spoke up. "I am sorry about your head," he repeated. "Can I ask you a question?"

Rick nodded.

"What the hell are you doing here, really? If you are not the troublemaker you were mistaken for yesterday, then, who are you?"

Rick laughed and leaned his head back gently against the wall. "Is it so hard difficult to believe that I am just someone who came here for a little sun and sand, rest and relaxation, as they say?"

"Why not try Acapulco or Mazatlan if that is what you are after? Most people do not choose a civil war zone for that kind of thing." His tone was direct. His uncle might speak to him like an errant schoolboy, but Rick guessed few others could get by with that.

He returned Franco's level gaze. "I honestly didn't think of it as that when I arrived and certainly not before I left Texas. I came here because I needed some time away from where I was. My cousin's been here for over a year, and he invited me to join him. Until yesterday, there were no problems. I'd just been fishing with Paz and helping out Imanuel on occasion—"

"*A la gran puta!*" Franco exploded again, returning to his original derisive tone of voice. "He does not know anything, does he?" He glanced at Mariana. "Just helping out a friend, is that it? Do you expect me to believe you are that naïve?"

Rick was confused. Why did such a simple thing as a conversation have to take such roller-coaster twists and turns? His head throbbed. He looked at Mariana, not daring to hope for any true help from that quarter.

"Do you not know what Imanuel does?" she asked matter-of-factly, handing him back the wet cloth as she saw him wince from the too sudden movement.

Oh, God, here it comes. Rick felt the bottom was about to drop out from under him. She's going to tell me he's the head of some large spy ring or guerrilla gang. The personality shifts he had just observed in the man, barking like a general one minute, plotting how to disguise his nephew's visit the next, had left his faith in his friend more than a bit shaken. Still, his pride demanded he try to salvage at least a few shreds of his dignity.

"Well, yeah. I know what I've helped him do," Rick began slowly. "He dispenses medicine at the clinic behind the church and delivers extra food and clothing which he gets through some of the missionary programs. He's helping some people to build latrines further down the road, and there is talk of getting some sort of drinking water brought in, water piped from the other side of the estuary. He's started a literacy program. He also got hold of some simple print versions of the New Testament, and now one of the teachers is giving evening classes for some of the kids and adults who have to work during the day. I heard that last year he organized some fund-raising to buy more school desks, and he also teaches some religion classes."

She nodded to everything he listed.

"I can't remember the rest right now, but it was all along those lines as I recall. So?"

"So!? He helps people, poor people!" Franco was on his feet. "Do you not know anything, *gringo*? Don't you know that to help the poor is a crime in this country, in certain people's eyes?"

Rick was startled. "That's it?"

"That is enough!" Franco hissed, glancing sideways, half-remembering the store just the other side of the curtain. "You think you have to pick up a gun or distribute communist literature to get into trouble here. It is much simpler than that!" He whirled on Mariana. "You better educate this one quick before he gets himself killed through sheer stupidity!" Franco finished in disgust. "I need something to eat." He stalked out to the pantry that served as the kitchen.

Mariana watched him go, and Rick leaned his head back against the wall again. "Is it just me," he asked after a minute, "or does everybody bring out his best the way I seem to?"

"He is very committed to what he believes in." She frowned, trying to determine just where to begin in explaining her cousin's intolerance.

"Sounds to me like maybe he needs to be committed," Rick muttered to himself in English.

"I am sorry. I do not understand," Mariana was still trying to bring some sense of civility to the entire situation.

Rick shook his head and suppressed a grin. It would take too much explaining to make that one clear, he thought. "Nothing."

"Franco just does not have much patience with those who are not as clear about what they are doing and why."

"Oh, now what? You, too?" Rick sat up straight. "You want to know what I'm doing here, too? Weren't you listening three minutes ago?"

"Oh, I know what you are doing here. My brother and Imanuel told me enough about that last night. I think you have been a good friend to them, especially to Pazito. He needs that right now, I am sure." She stopped before continuing. "What I do not know is why?"

"Why what?" He knew her acceptance of who and what he was had been too good to be true.

"Why are you here, and why do you help them?"

"Oh, for the love of heaven. Enough! They are, how do you say, *buena gente*—good people, all right? I came here with time on my hands. Paz helps me with the fishing, so I help his family in return. That's all!" He put his head in his hands, his elbows resting on his knees.

"All right." It was as if with that out of the way, she was ready to move on to more urgent matters.

"What Franco said is true, you know. There are those who would harm you just for helping the poor. You should be careful."

"I'm sorry. Call me stupid. I really don't understand. What about Imanuel?"

"He knows it, too, but somehow he refuses to believe it. Or worse, he thinks he is exempt from it."

She began to explain, and like Imanuel's frequent explanations of situations here, he found hers to be to the point with no condescension involved. "In your own history, in the US, it was once against the law to teach slaves to read, is that right?"

Rick struggled to follow her logic. "Yeah, I think so."

"Well, here it is not a written law, but there are many people like those plantation owners of your old South who are afraid. They are afraid of the poor, of how many there are and that a slave revolt is coming, so they do not want the poor to receive any help at all. For them, change means they will have to give up something, so they refuse to give up anything. The changes are coming, though, and the longer they fight, the harder it will be for everyone. I suppose they are afraid that if they give up a little, it will start something they can no longer control. And they have controlled everything for so very long." Her voice took on a wistful bitterness.

He watched her closely as she spoke. "You make it all sound so simple, so cut and dried, as they say in English."

"Do not be misled," she smiled, her more typical cool demeanor back in place. "Remember your history lessons and what it has taken to resolve such a simple state of unbalanced affairs in your own country. There are parts of the US that still have not recovered, yes?"

Rick felt woefully undereducated. He started to ask about the new government that Paz had mentioned last night, but thought better of it. Franco came back in from the pantry with a hard bread roll in his hand, spread sticky with homemade sorghum syrup.

"So did Emelina welcome you home with open arms?" he asked with his mouth full. "I imagine she screamed loud enough for *los muchachos* to hear her over on *Conchagua*, yes?"

Mariana's smile was broad at her aunt's reaction to her arrival the night before. "They were all glad to see me, I think."

"And where is Carlos?" The question was casual, but Rick couldn't help but notice a slight stiffness on Mariana's part.

"He is in the capital."

"And he let you ride all the way down here on the big dangerous bus all by yourself?" Sarcasm was obviously one of Franco's favorite sports.

Mariana stifled an urge to snap and instead answered him in kind. "And in your opinion, a private car would have been so much safer, I suppose. Let me see, a fancy one with a chauffeur in uniform, yes? That way, I could be kidnapped and held for ransom by some of your friends. That would probably make more money than stopping buses and taking the change out of the pockets of old men and women. That is a really good idea, Franco."

Her smile could give him frostbite, Rick thought as he watched the exchange that he guessed had been going on for a couple of decades now.

"Who is Carlos?" Rick dared to ask.

"Oh, she has not told you?" Franco feigned surprise. "I thought you two were such good friends. He is her husband, of course."

"I see." Like Mariana, Rick felt a sudden determination not to give Franco the kind of reaction he was seeking.

"I wanted to come home, and Carlos has business to attend to in the capital," she continued the battle to keep the conversation on some sort of polite plain. "At the time, the bus seemed the most logical choice, not that I owe you any kind of explanation."

"Yes, well, Carlos and his business." Franco cleared his throat. "What is it this week? Plastics? A new factory? Shrimp boats? Maybe he has a deal going with another one of the American clothing companies by now. That sounds important and is always worth at least a couple hundred jobs for the poor."

"Franco, you have a smart mouth." Mariana gave up the pretense of courtesy. "Why did you come, anyway? I thought you said you wanted to see me, not pester the hell out of me. Men! They are all the same. They live *solo para joder a las mujeres*."

Rick was unfamiliar with the phrase, but it did not take a lot of imagination to figure out what it was she was accusing all men of doing to all women.

"What did Carlos ever do to you?"

"Calm down." Franco strolled over to the hammock. "Nobody is accusing your precious Carlos of doing anything. He is just one more big fish up there in San Salvador, yes? I mean, one rich guy is the same as the next as best as I can tell. They are all the enemy, just like all the *gringos* are *imperialistas*, yes?" He grinned at Rick. "It is much too complicated to contemplate at the moment. Uncle does not want me going anywhere until after dark, so I might as well get a little rest. God knows it is not something I get much of any other time.

"Mariana, will you bring me back some dinner from the restaurant a little later? There is not a damned thing worth eating in that poor excuse for a kitchen back there. I could find more to eat in camp, I swear." He closed his eyes as he settled deeper into the woven net that enveloped him.

"Well, what do you expect? Imanuel and Paz eat at the *comedor* or from the store. They do not keep much here. Why would they need to except for marauding pests like you?"

Franco grinned, his eyes already closed.

Rick struggled to get up, feeling somewhat steadier on his feet than earlier. "I'd better go find Paz," he began. "I can keep him out of here for a while if that is what Imanuel would prefer and—"

"Yeah, you take care of that kid, *gringo*. He is a good one. I do not imagine he will be around here too much longer." He opened his eyes one last time and gave Mariana a wink.

"Do not even think of talking to him about that!" She spit out the words. "Imanuel is a brave and, in some ways, a foolish soul to continue to welcome you as warmly as he does into his home. I doubt that you get such from your own father. But if you steal his son away to the *guerrilleros*, I do believe he would kill you." She glared at him.

She brightened as she turned back to Rick. "I will go with you. At the moment, there is certainly no reason to stay here."

Franco chuckled and settled down for a *siesta* as the two pushed through the curtain into the store.

They passed through the store, giving Emelina a wave as she helped a little girl pick out a new pair of rubber sandals on the far side of the doorway. They walked along the fishing beach behind the house and store. Most of the regular morning activity was long past.

"Is he always like that?" Rick asked after a short silence.

She smiled in a half-apologetic fashion and nodded. "Ever since we were small. Our houses were always next door to one another, and Franco was always the bravest and the smartest. 'Impudent,' the teachers called him, each time they threw him out of class. It was such a waste. Men like Franco should be scholars or business leaders or someone who is, in some way, showing the rest of us to a better life. But the way things are here, there is little chance for the ones like him. The ones with faith as well as the energy that comes with the anger become leaders in the church. Others join the army and become a part of the problem, although I do believe some of them think in the beginning they can help turn things around. Sadly, by the time they learn the truth, they find themselves just trying to survive. They join the oppressors, and they, too, leave more victims behind them as they go. The ones like Franco go off to the hills.... And I am afraid the time he has spent there with his new friends has made him even more bitter." She ended with a sigh.

"New friends?"

She shook her head and pulled a cigarette and a tiny box of the locally rolled wax matches from the pocket of her skirt.

"You look just like Imanuel would if he saw me right now." She appeared to be reading his mind, a skill Rick found more than a little disconcerting. "I am trying to quit, honestly."

"And in the meantime, you smoke out here on the beach where your father won't see you?"

She shrugged. "Imanuel said he had not seen Pazito this morning, which means he could be eating to his heart's content at Emelina's or working with my *Tío* Miguel or... he does not have school in the mornings this term, does he?"

"Paz? Working or going to school if he doesn't have to?" Rick looked skeptical.

She laughed. "You are right. You do know him well."

"Frankly, he is not so different than any other boy his age, no matter the country or the culture.

I expected to find him home this morning as happy as he was to see you yesterday. I felt pretty foolish about the whole thing. I did not even know he had a sister."

She continued to stroll along the muddy sand toward the point. "There is no reason you would know. It has been a long time, and I did not leave under the best of circumstances. It is not something he can talk about freely, and he knows it."

There were a thousand questions burning in Rick's mind, but he had already learned asking any of them might put a quick end to an otherwise pleasant conversation.

They walked on, away from any possible place Paz might be found.

"How is your head?" she asked.

"Bruised." He gave an honest answer. "But Franco is right. I'll live."

"You were awake then?" Mariana's gaze shot in his direction, and he was sorry he had let that slip.

"Just coming around, really," he stammered. "I mean, I don't remember much, just him saying something like that."

"Uh-huh." She gave him a dubious glance but let the matter drop.

"So the name Franco? Where does that come from?" Rick shifted gears, hoping to direct her attention elsewhere.

"Oh," she giggled. "That is one more of his inventions. Miguel named his son Juan Francisco, and like so many here, he goes by the second name, but when he was little, even before he became a *revolucionario*, as Paz likes to call him, he re-named himself Franco. Miguel had gone to California when he was young, like so many from here, part adventure, part money-making trip. He fell in love with the city of San Francisco, so when he came back and married and had a son, he wanted to name him after the city he loved. Of course, with it being a city in America, Franco was not going to have any of it. I think he did it to irritate Miguel. That is what young men do, no? Live to aggravate the older ones. And then, of course, being Franco, he did not want a name that made him think of an American anything."

They stopped at the point. It was covered with huge rocks the villagers had piled there. After years of depositing sand, silt, and soil onto the peninsula that supported the village of *Las Palomitas*, the river and the sea, for unknown reasons, had reversed themselves. The constant movement of the water past the point was now carrying away more than it left behind. Little by little, the very land on which they stood was being washed from beneath their feet into the ocean.

Mariana flipped the cigarette butt into the wet sand and looked out to sea, past the point and the breakers washing over the sand bars. "He wanted to know why I came back." She spoke as if she were as far away as the horizon that lay beyond the churning waters.

Rick watched as the wind whipped at her hair, blowing it straight back from her face. The thin cotton dress, a finer version of the ones most women used here, pressed against her, revealing her form, the firm full breasts, trim waist, and thin, smooth hips, in innocent provocation.

"I told him I came because it was time to come home. I missed my family, but I also missed all of this. How long can a palm tree exist when you plant it in a forest? How does a desert cactus bloom when you take it to the snow country? It is not that those places are wrong or bad, but it is not where those living things belong. I could not continue as I was, so far from what I needed. Is that so difficult to understand?"

For a moment, Rick was certain she had forgotten he was even there. He shook his head, although he was certain his was not the answer she sought. "No, it's not hard to understand at all."

They found Paz happily strolling down the beach, once they turned back and had passed the village again. His bare feet were covered with thick, dried mud, as were those of his companion, a boy about his age who carried a string bag, filled with heavy dripping clams.

"We have been digging for *curriles*." Paz was as enthusiastic over this day's catch as he was over anything they regularly brought in by *cayuco*.

"You have been up in the *mangle*?" Mariana's eyes were wide with shock as she pointed up the river toward the mangrove swamp that shrouded the head of the estuary.

"Of course," Paz laughed. "And look at all we got for it. We will take a few to have tonight before dinner, but I told Gilberto he could have the rest. He came by this morning early before you were even awake. Gilberto goes into the *mangle* every day, *verdad?*"

The other boy's shy smile darted across his face as he nodded. Digging upriver in the nutrient-rich mud was not the adventure for him that it was for Paz. It was a part of the daily routine necessary to help feed his six younger brothers and sisters.

"Paz, are you crazy? You know how dangerous it is up there! What possessed you to do a thing like that? Does Imanuel know? I cannot imagine that he would allow it—"

Unprepared for her reaction, Paz backed away, his face reflecting his hurt and confusion. Gilberto, like a deer ready to run in panic at the first sign of danger, edged around her, his bag of clams still gripped in his hand.

"*Adíos,* Paz," he called back over his shoulder as he began to lope through the trees toward the village. "I will leave yours with your father at the store."

"What is wrong with you?" Angry at being embarrassed in front of his friend, Paz turned on his sister. "How could you do that? I was not doing anything wrong. I went with him because I remembered that you always liked the *coctel de conchas*. I thought it would be a nice surprise for you." He started to follow his friend, but then he stopped.

"You have been gone a long time, my sister, and many things have changed. I am not a little boy anymore. *Mí papá* does not tell me what to do.

He talks to me, and he has never screamed at me on a public beach."

Rick watched him stalk away, and his heart hurt for both of them. It also occurred to him how easily he could have been the recipient of that little speech on a different day. He, too, still saw more of the boy who was the past than the man who was the future, and like Mariana, he was not yet prepared for the transition in between.

"He just does not realize—" Marina spoke half to herself.

"What? He doesn't realize what?" Rick asked. "What scares you so up there? I've never been there, but Paz keeps promising to take me one day. He says it's beautiful."

"Do not go there." She shifted her attention from Paz's retreating figure to look directly at him. She had to shade her eyes with her hand as Rick stood with his back to the sun. "It has never been a safe place for anyone."

Rick did not argue the point. "He is right about one thing. He is not a little boy anymore."

Mariana shook her head and made no response. She left Rick on the beach, and he watched her every graceful step as she made her way back to her father's house.

* * * * *

The sun hung low in the afternoon sky by the time Rick directed one of Miguel's *cayucos* toward the open waters of the bay. After carefully negotiating the labyrinth of sand bars, he gunned the tiny outboard but quickly cut his speed as he discovered a strong wind was whipping the waves higher than usual. As he trolled along to his favorite fishing area near the rocks, he found he could not keep his thoughts from returning to the troublesome scene of yesterday's bus trip as well as that at the house earlier in the day.

Without a partner, he could not set the large net. He pulled off a short distance from where they usually left their net, set an anchor, and dropped a line over the side of the boat, fishing native-style, without a pole.

How had his tiny paradise suddenly become such a complicated place? He had come here to escape from one set of troubles and now found himself worrying instead about David's whereabouts, a woman he barely knew, and her lunatic cousin. How much truth was there to what they had said about Imanuel? Everyone he had met through the church work was simply grateful for whatever was delivered to them. It was true that even in the short time he had been there, it seemed the programs Imanuel had begun were growing at a rapid rate, but surely that was only because the need was so great. David was also there to help with the fishing cooperative program. Did that also put him in danger? Who could be angry over providing such a small amount of aid to a group of subsistence fishermen? How could they be seen as a threat to anyone?

The waves continued to grow, interrupting his reverie. Off in the distance, a shrimp boat bobbed along as it turned back toward El Triunfo, the big shrimping port further up the coast. In the face of the growing wind, Rick realized it was time for him to head back to shore. He gathered in his line. Heading home was not as easy as coming out. The wind beat the boat. While Rick struggled to keep it on course, the gusts pushed the craft crosswise, forcing it across the sand bars at dangerous cockeyed angles. As a wave washed over the bow, Rick feared the whole thing might capsize at any moment.

Until today, his only experiences in these waters had been pleasant ones. For the first time, he discovered that the sea here, like everywhere, could be a terrifying adversary as well as a welcome companion to the lonely. He struggled on, making progress at a sluggish pace. By the time he rounded the point into calmer waters, he was exhausted.

As he pulled up onto the nearby dark beach, he was startled by a figure that stepped out of the shadows.

"*Por el amor de Díos!* You scared me half to death!"

"I was worried about you," Paz spoke in an uncharacteristically serious tone.

"I'm sorry," Rick answered. "I had no idea the wind would come up like that when I left. It was really tough getting back in here in one piece. It's probably no surprise to you that I didn't catch a thing."

Paz smiled. "No, it is not good fishing weather. It is still hurricane season on the other side toward Honduras."

"The other side?" Rick frowned and then made sense of it, "Oh, you mean in the Gulf of Mexico. But they don't come here, surely?"

"Not the hurricane itself but the rain sometimes."

The wind was starting to pick up now, even along the protected shore of the estuary. They walked toward Emelina's, where Rick hoped it was not too late to still find a little dinner. After he finished eating, Paz began to coax. "Come back to the house. The store will soon be closed, and we can sit in the back for a while. I will even play a game of cards with you."

Rick agreed without thinking. As they walked, huge drops, like Rick remembered from Midwestern thunderstorms, began to fall around them. It was not until they started in the door that he remembered what, or rather who, was waiting inside. "Paz, maybe this isn't a good night. I should just go on home—"

"What are you going to do in that cabin all alone tonight?" Paz chided. "You cannot go sit on the beach tonight; that is for certain. Come on before we are both all wet." He pulled Rick inside through the back door.

Mariana looked up from where she was counting the day's receipts from the store. Imanuel sat at his desk, going over an account book. He pulled off his reading glasses as the two came in.

"*Buenas noches*," he greeted them with a surprised look at Rick. "Somehow, I did not expect you back today." He warmth of his voice said he was glad he was mistaken.

"*Buenas noches.*" Mariana echoed her father's words without interrupting her count.

"*Buenas noches.*" A third voice came from the pantry as Franco stepped out of his hiding place.

"*Primo!*" As his father had predicted, Paz was delighted to see his cousin.

"How long have you been here? I would have come sooner if I had known. Are you all right? Why have you come? Oh, this is my friend, Ricardo." Paz's elation bubbled over as he made the introduction.

"We've met," Rick stated without enthusiasm.

"You know each other? You knew he was here, and you did not tell me?"

"I found out accidentally earlier today," Rick admitted. "But I didn't have a say—"

"I did not think it was a good idea for Franco to go as he had come in the daylight," Imanuel explained. "I told him to wait until tonight, Paz, and I did not want you coming and going with him here either. That would not have been a very safe thing for Franco, would it?"

Rick admired the man's gift for explanations. How could he be in any serious trouble with anyone? He wondered to himself again.

Franco and Mariana exchanged a look that Rick could not quite read.

Paz shrugged, leaving the explanations behind in his enjoyment of the moment. "So tell me, how is it in the camp now? Are all of you doing better? Are you fighting regularly? More importantly, are you winning? How many men have you shot?"

"Paz!" Imanuel barked.

"I am sorry, *Papá*. It is just a question. He is a soldier in the liberation army, yes? I just wanted to know."

'Well, remember who you are and to have some respect for all who are involved in this struggle. Killing men at random is not an honorable part of any fight."

Franco looked at his feet, trying unsuccessfully to hide his amusement with the whole situation. "Come here, little one." He guided Paz over to the far side of the room. "I will tell you all the latest news from the front lines."

"You be careful what you tell him." Imanuel's warning did not go unheeded.

Rick sat down next to where Mariana had finished her tally for the evening. Bundling up everything in an expert manner, she carried the drawer over to Imanuel. She picked up an embroidery hoop with stitch work already in progress.

"I found this in the back of the closet in my room. It must have been one *Tía* Angelica started. You do not mind if I work on it—"

At the mention of the name, Franco stopped speaking to Paz and stared at Mariana. She hesitated and looked down at the handiwork in her lap as she directed her question to Imanuel.

"You do not mind if I work on it?" she repeated.

"Of course not," came the reply.

Slowly, his eyes never leaving Mariana, Franco continued his account to Paz.

"I heard you went out fishing. Any luck?" She looked across at Rick as her fingers deftly slipped the embroidery needle through the white cotton cloth.

"No," he answered, his eyes flitting between the woman before him and her cousin. "Only bad. The wind came up so strong that it was a fight just to get the canoe back across the breakers."

Imanuel finished his bookkeeping chores and slapped the ledger shut. He moved to the rocking chair next to where Rick was sitting and reached over to turn on the old-fashioned cabinet radio. As Rick looked around the room, wondering if he really belonged here at all, a scene from a movie danced through his head, of an American family from the 1940s gathered in the evening in their living room in front of their radio. Somehow this was not exactly the way Norman Rockwell had depicted it.

As the radio crackled to life, the man's voice droned loud in the quiet of the evening. Rick's Spanish was not good enough to follow the speech that was being given, but an occasional phrase was recognizable. In this case, *politica* and *el pueblo* were enough to tell him they were tuned into another of the never-ending series of political diatribes. Imanuel stopped his searching for only a moment before changing to another channel, but on every station, it was the same.

"Paz said yesterday that there has been a change in the government. Is that what all of this is about?" Rick finally dared to voice one of the many questions that had been ricocheting around in his head for more than a day.

"What change?" Franco asked from across the room. He came closer to where they were seated and stretched out on the floor. Rick noted how Paz followed and did the same, nonchalantly, as if he were not trying to copy his cousin's every movement.

"Uh, yesterday, there was some kind of takeover or something. I'm not sure exactly what."

"You and the rest of the world. It is not a change, really. It is only the younger military men taking some of the power away from the older ones. Nothing will change in the end. The *Yanquí* government is all excited, of course, but what difference does it make? *Militar es militar.*"

"But didn't you lose a president out of it?" Rick couldn't help but wonder out aloud. "If that happened in the US—"

"But it has never happened there, has it?" The bitterness in Franco's voice was thinly veiled. "And it probably never will. I will say this, *gringo*, to be president in the United States means something. Who is the president here? Who knows? Who cares? It means nothing. You have had your presidents assassinated, yes? But if you notice that does not happen here. What would be the point? If you cut the strings of the puppet, it is true that the wooden thing lies there, dead, but the puppeteer, he continues. All he needs is a new puppet. Killing the puppet has very little effect. The puppeteers will simply buy a new one tomorrow."

"Oh, Franco. You have the whole thing figured out." Mariana was laughing despite her less than pleasant words. "If you are so smart about all of this, why are you still out there running around in the bushes, living on the mountainside?"

"It is only a beginning, Mariana," he sighed as if explaining life to a small child. "We do not have the money that the rich ones do, but we will. We have to wear them down, just like the *Sandinistas* did in Nicaragua. But we can do it. It will take time, but eventually the people will see the light and join us in greater numbers. Then, nobody will stop us, not even the *norteamericanos*."

"I think you are forgetting a few things, Franco." Imanuel switched off the radio and spoke as he usually did, with the gentleness Rick always thought a father should have. "In Nicaragua, the president was no puppet. He pulled his own strings, and it gave the people an enemy, one single person, one single family to rally against. Here, as you yourself say, there is no single person on which the people can declare war. That makes the effort much more difficult."

"The Sandinistas are being portrayed as liberators one place and communists in another." Rick knew he should probably stay out of this conversation, but an unexpected preoccupation with Franco's curious political orientation made that impossible. "Which is it?"

"Communist. That is the first word the United States likes to scream about any revolution that threatens to upset any regime that is profitable to them. Who cares in the long run, whether they are *comunista* or if we are? Ask yourself what the former president of Nicaragua believed in. When he was asked why there was no education in his country for poor children, he said he did not want educated people. He wanted oxen! It is not much different here. The people are starving the way things have been for the past fifty years or more. Are you telling me it would be worse under a different system of government? I will not tell you we are or are not *comunista* simply because, as a *gringo*, you probably do not even know what the word means anyway."

He continued. "How many Russians have you ever known? How many Cubans? Me, too—*nada*. But for the man on the *burro* in our countries, far right is as bad as far left. Either way, you are told to shut up, do as you are told, or you will be shot. In the long run, if you take a good look at Cuba—not what your government teaches you in school, but what really is—you will find that most of the people eat some, get some education, and some medicine under the system they are under now in Cuba. It is not perfect, and Russia pays for most of it, but we are not trying to duplicate that here. We are trying to make a change which is made even more difficult when a rich country, which was itself established by a pack of *revolucionarios* two hundred years ago, stands against us. It will not stop us. Like some of those men and women in your history books, we will choose death over nothing. And nothing is what we have to go back to if we cannot make that change."

Silence filled the room following Franco's speech, which, while impassioned, was not nearly as offensive as Rick feared it might be. He pondered the forces that had driven Franco, the son of a local fisherman, to join *los muchachos* in the mountains.

"The other part is you forget our history is different than that of Nicaragua," Imanuel added to his earlier comments as if Franco had never said a word. "They had no *matanza*. I am not saying they have not had their problems, but they are different. There are too many here who have not forgotten. I do not think you will find many willing to go against the soldiers with their machetes and *cumas*."

"*Matanza*?" Rick raised an eyebrow at the mention of the new word and was instantly sorry. The response was more silence, but this time with an icy edge to it as all eyes in the room sought the floor.

"*Matanza* means massacre," Mariana began to speak after a few moments. She hesitated, organizing her thoughts as her fingers continued to whip the needle through the fabric in her lap. "It was a peasant uprising in 1932. Most of it was concentrated around the capital and the coffee plantations in that area. The people thought the time was right for them to take back some of their land from the rich, the oligarchy who had stolen it over the years from the Indian workers. They thought they would have leadership, but the true leaders were already in jail, captured by the government the day before. The workers came at the landowners with their machetes and a few old guns, but the government soldiers had something the peasants did not: machine guns. The battle and the taking of some of the coffee farms lasted only a few days, and less than 100 of those fighting with the rich and the soldiers died."

Her voice had started to quaver as she continued, but she took a deep breath.

"You do not have to do this." Imanuel reached over and patted her arm. "It can be done later."

"No." A new resolve came into her voice. "He asked now, and he needs to know now. Maybe it will help all of this to make a little more sense to him."

"Very well," her father sat back, and she continued.

"Afterward, the government rounded up everyone—men, boys, even some women and children and claimed they were all guilty, just because they were *campesinos*, country farmworkers. They tied the *campesinos* together, thumb to thumb, stood them against the walls of the churches, and shot them. In some places, they made them dig their own graves first, just like the Jews in World War II years later. When it was all over, there were more than 30,000 peasants killed, to make certain no one would ever go up against the government again."

Throughout the explanation, her voice had remained steady, but she clenched her teeth as she spat out the last words. Tears spilled down her cheeks as she finished, and her fingers lay still in her lap.

Rick lifted a hand toward her and then stopped, realizing he had no right, no matter how he longed to reach out and wipe away her tears.

"So you see, *gringo*? Revolution is an old pastime here." Franco tried to make it all sound like a game as he stretched lazily. "Something we learn about early, although God knows you will never learn about *la matanza* in the history books. According to the official version, it was a terrible Indian uprising, all the work of communists!"

"It is true," Paz added, his usual exuberance quelled by the mood and the story. "That is exactly what they teach us. Also that anything that has to do with a major change in the ways things are, is *comunista* and very dangerous."

Franco turned back toward Imanuel, and his voice hardened. "When we do it this time, we will do it right. We will make them pay for each one they killed then and every single man, woman, and child they have killed since."

Rick thought to himself that he would not want to be opposite Franco in this or any other conflict.

Mariana had found a handkerchief and her dignity once again. "Imanuel is right, Franco. Too many people still remember, and if they do not, then they lost a father, a brother, an uncle, a cousin, or someone they know. I was not alive then, and neither were you, but even we remember in a way. All the deaths since, only make it worse. While more deaths now may make a few more committed to the cause," she hesitated, looking straight at him, "they only make others more frightened."

Imanuel rocked softly in his chair for a few moments, listening more to the storm outside than the one going on inside the room. The wind howled, and the rain beat against the windows. "Too many have tried your way for too long, Franco." Imanuel finally spoke. "And the only result has been more dead on both sides, but mostly on the side of the poor."

"And what is your answer?" Franco raised himself up on one elbow. "To stand and pray while the oligarchy starves us to death or the government forces kill any who dares to complain? In the capital, they kill the demonstrators in the streets. In the country, they drag people from their beds in the dead of the night. What is the difference in the long run—dead is dead. We need more than prayers, *Tío*."

"Prayer is a powerful weapon, Franco, but we have more than that. We finally have a leader, a true leader who cares. *Monseñor* spoke earlier today on the radio, and it is obvious he is standing with us, even at very great risk to himself. He is urging us all to stand together in faith against evil. Violence is not the answer on either side. A revolution is one thing. But I agree with *Monseñor* when he says he is against 'a revolution that looks only for vengeance and with violence tries to make things right.' That is what it sounds as if you are after now—only vengeance."

"*Monseñor Romero, Presidente Romero*. Two old men in the capital who have been fighting with each other for two years now, and what do you have to show for it?" Franco pulled himself to a sitting position and leaned against the wall opposite his uncle, his cousin, and their guest.

"*Cuidado*, Franco. Do not compare the two men in the same sentence in my house, please."

Once again, Rick was surprised by the no-nonsense tone in Imanuel's voice that he had heard earlier in the day for the very first time.

The catechist continued. "They may have the same last name, but you know as well as I that they are not related in any way and that includes their approach to our many problems here.

"It does not matter if you agree with *Monseñor* or not. The people of El Salvador must convince the world that we are not all angry *revolucionarios*, bent only on taking our revenge on those who have ruled over us in the past. It is in quietly demonstrating on a daily basis who and what we are—common people who only want to feed and care for our families, have decent medical care and schools for our children— that we can convince anyone, including ourselves, that we are worthy of those things for which we ask. Is that not how it was done in your country?"

Imanuel's sudden shift with a new question toward Rick startled him.

"Was it not through peaceful, non-violent meetings, based in the churches, with a churchman as their leader, that the black people of your country reclaimed their rights? They were once slaves, then they were only servants, and now they are doing better than before. Is that not correct?"

"Well, yeah. It's all true, I guess," Rick stammered. "But it's taken over one hundred years, and things are still not as they should be. I'm not trying to join either side here, but there was still much violence, and people died, even though it was supposed to be a non-violent movement."

"I understand that," Imanuel continued. "But Franco is right that people here are dying every day, regardless. The children die of disease and malnutrition. The *politicos* are killed or exiled. But in this way, all standing together, every person can say how they feel—men, women, and children working together. If we are attacked, then it will focus the world's attention on the government leaders and hold them accountable."

"Tell it to Rutilio Grande, *Tío*, or to Alfonso Navarro or Ernesto Barrera or to the children or old people who were with them. What did any of your world leaders do about their deaths? Nothing!" There was no longer any attempt to disguise the bitterness in his voice. "Tell it to the people of *Santa Maria de las Aguas*." He hesitated, barely in control. "Tell it to my mother and my sister," he finished in a deadly whisper.

"Franco!" Mariana broke in. "*Un poco de respeto* in this house."

"Well, it is the truth. They were all priests, and now they are dead, and so are those who were unlucky enough to be with them at the time. Their churches sacked and destroyed, people in their villages, shot at random, even those who were just there for a visit. You have been lucky here in *Las Palomitas* thus far, but it cannot last. The whole country is being invaded by our own government forces and standing around in church is not going to help anybody!"

The back door flew open with such ferocity that everyone in the room jumped, certain the *Guardia Nacional* was at the door. Franco was on his feet first, closing the door against the wind and the pouring rain.

He stood at the window for several moments, staring out at the storm, with his back, ramrod straight. When he turned back toward the others, he was calmer, his customary arrogance restored.

"The weather does not look any too pretty for an evening stroll, but I suppose it will suit my purposes quite well. Besides, if I wait too long, I may not be able to get back across the *estero*. At least that fool of a Marine will not be out in this weather, checking to see who is crossing in the middle of the night."

"You say you are not on either side, *gringo*?" He spun, his attention now focused on Rick. "Why is that? I thought Americans were always on the side of good and the American way. What if they would have caught some of those *revolucionarios* that founded your country, halfway through the battle? Would they not have hung or shot them as subversives, as enemies of the state?"

"That's one way of looking at it, I suppose." Rick squirmed, his head reeling from the whirlwind history lessons of the evening.

"Your government has been busy propping up this government for years, you know. Maybe you would like a chance to see how this one really works."

"Excuse me?"

"Maybe you ought to come and see how real *revolucionarios* live."

"Franco, what are you suggesting?" Mariana glared at him and sat up straight.

"Nothing so shocking. Not tonight or tomorrow but one day. I will be back, and if you are still here, maybe you would like to take a little trip and visit our camp." There was more than a hint of a dare in his voice.

Rick hesitated, wishing for more time for a contemplative answer.

"Could I not go?" Paz did not wait to be asked as he scrambled to his feet. "I would go with you, Franco. You know I would. I could—"

"Paz!" The sharpness in Imanuel's voice caught all of them off guard. He immediately softened his next words. "It is out of the question, *hijo*. It may sound like an adventure, but it is a very dangerous one at best. This is not the time to be discussing it, regardless." He winked at his crestfallen son. "I do not believe the invitation was extended to you."

He turned his attention back to Rick as did everyone else in the room.

"Well," the American replied with obvious reluctance. "I might be willing to go with you. As long as I was certain you would offer me some kind of protection."

"Protection? Like what? You want a gun?"

"No," Rick switched to English. "I would have to be certain you keep guys like Lito on a short leash."

Mariana burst out laughing, and Franco turned to her for an answer he could understand. She gave him a quick translation.

"If you were with me, you would not have to worry. I would be your protector. We will plan it, then, for another day. *Nos vemos*."

With a quick salute to all, he whirled and was gone, out into the pouring rain before any further comment could be made.

CHAPTER 5

*O*ctober 20, 1979. The National Weather Service reports that Hurricane Erica continues to wreak havoc along the gulf coast of Central America. Honduras has been hit particularly hard with over a thousand believed to be dead. Food, medical supplies, and blankets are pouring into the area through international relief organizations as rescue personnel work around the clock to bring people out of the ravaged areas.

Another day of rain. It made Rick tired, just thinking about it. Everything he owned was damp, soaked, or mildewing. There would be no fishing again today. For three days, it had rained day and night. They had heard news on Imanuel's radio about the hurricane in the Gulf and the damage done in Honduras and Guatemala. Here, there were no hurricane winds, just rain. He had tried to call David's office in San Salvador two days ago to see if they knew where he was but all the phone lines were down. He left word to be notified whenever the lines were restored, but at this rate, there was no telling how long that might be. He rolled over and tried to go back to sleep.

"Don Ricardo! Don Ricardo!" Paz burst through the door, startling his friend awake. "Are you all right?" Paz was surprised to find the American still in bed, in the middle of the morning.

"I'm fine. What's all the yelling about?"

"The water. It is everywhere. Have you not seen?"

Yeah, I've looked outside, Rick thought about the surly reply he could make. He had been up several times during the night, checking on David's house. The water run off the back by the river continued to cut new channels throughout the night and threatened to collapse the house from beneath as the sandy soil was washed away from its foundation. A vague childhood memory of a song from Sunday School, the one about the fool builds his house upon the sand while the wise man builds on the rock wafted through his head.

"We need everyone to come." Paz was out of breath, and Rick was chagrined that he had not been listening to the boy's explanations.

Rick snatched on his clothes and followed Paz out the door. The landscape had changed remarkably since he had last seen it in the full light of day. The road he had so blithely walked down a few hours before was now a full-fledged river. No vehicles bumped along it today. Rather in the distance, closer to the village, he could see a *cayuco* gliding along where cars and cattle usually disputed the right of way. During the night, it was as if the landmass had actually grown narrow, for now the dark waves of the sea were breaking considerably closer to the

caserinos and more significantly, closer to his house.
As he stepped gingerly into the six-inch-deep water
that was the road, he heard a distant roar.

"What's that noise?"

"It is the water in the *estero*," Paz answered, as he
led them in that direction. "With the tide changing
and all the water running off the ground, it is racing
now. It sounds like a great river, yes?"

A quick look in the direction of David's house
assured Rick that it was still standing, at least for
the moment.

The sound, Rick soon discovered, was not the only
similarity to the wide and mighty Midwestern rivers
that he knew so well. The chocolate-colored water
tumbled past the shoreline, on its mad dash to the
sea. All the fishermen's *cayucos* had been moved
during the night to higher ground, and even there,
they were tied tightly to nearby trees.

"*Mí Tío* Miguel says we must keep the boats safe
now because if this rain continues, we might all have
to cross to higher ground on the other side and leave
the village to the water."

So it was not his imagination. They really were
sinking. Rick looked across at the raging water before
him. He did not relish the idea of trying to cross it
with a *cayuco* filled with women and children.

Paz continued down the fishermen's beach, and
Rick scurried after him. On the point, men were
gathered around a short flatbed truck, unloading
huge slabs of black rock, piling them carelessly along
the water's edge at the worst erosion points. Beyond

them, women were scooping sand into burlap sacks with plastic pails. Quickly, they tied each one closed and let it fall, just above the waterline.

"The truck came in late last night," Paz explained in short bursts. "Before the road flooded and was closed. The driver said closer to the highway, the road was nearly closed when he came through. With this rock, maybe, we can save some of the point. If we do not, before long, houses will begin to fall."

Rick noted that the nearest home was already within fifty feet of the water. After that, the huts were stacked next to one another, ready to fall like so many dominoes. It would be only a matter of time.

He followed Paz to the truck and heaved a slab of the unwieldy stone onto his shoulder, like several of the other villagers were doing. His hands slipped on the smooth wet surface. Following the others, he dropped it onto the growing mound. The stones he had seen here with Mariana, just days ago, were now barely visible below the surface of the churning water. He shivered as he looked down and turned back toward the truck.

As they worked, the stone dike grew taller and gradually began to look as if it might prove to be a true barrier to the encroaching waters.

"When we finish with the rocks," Paz pointed toward the women. "We can begin to put the sandbags on top."

Rick had shoveled his shoulder under another piece of rock when he heard the shout. He spun around in time to see Paz reel wildly as he lost his footing on the slick pile of stones. The large one he was carrying slid sideways, crashing and bouncing out of control. Paz struck the bottom of the pile, still struggling to regain his balance, and plunged headfirst into the water.

"Stand up!" Rick shrieked above the roar of the water and the rain, beating down. If he can only get his feet under him...

But the boy, now frightened by his predicament and perhaps even injured by the fall, began to thrash wildly in the water, as he was pulled past the point and the retreating waters.

"Swim, Paz! Swim!" Rick yelled, hoping the few lessons he'd taught him would somehow help.

"He does not know how," a voice screamed at Rick's elbow. He turned to see Mariana, standing beside him, clutching a drenched shawl over her long dark hair.

"Yes, he does! Now he does! Swim!" He yelled again and began running up the beach toward the *cayucos*. As he began to fumble with one of the ropes, he realized it would take too long to get the heavy craft into the water. Besides, he would never be able to handle the thing in such rough water. He glanced over his shoulder again, noting the location of the boy's fleeting face. He grabbed one of Paco's anchor lines, and with the heavy knife he often carried as a fisherman, he slashed madly at the concrete weight the *tiburoneros* used to hold their heavy nets in place on the sandy ocean floor. He ran to another boat, jerking anchor lines free, cutting and tying the ends together. Others who stood helplessly by, as the tragedy unfolded, came over to watch the man's curious reaction.

"What are you doing?" Marina ran to his side. "How can I help?"

"More rope!" Rick told her in English. "Get me more rope!"

He tossed the knife to her and looked forlornly at the meager 150 feet of cord he had managed to free. He tied the free end around his waist and cinched it tight.

"Tell them to hurry!" He yelled in her direction as she screamed directions to the others, who now began to move in a frenzy of activity, tugging at other lines, freeing them from the fishing equipment. A burly fisherman tied the opposite end of Rick's rope to another rope as fast as it was freed.

"Swim, Paz! Swim!" Rick yelled once more. He dove off the lower edge of the rock pile, stretching his six-foot torso farther than he ever had in any swimming pool dive. A chorus of admiring curses and whispered prayers followed him into the water.

Bits and pieces of lifeguard training from nearly a decade ago whipped through his mind. Always keep your eyes on the victim. Never go after him yourself. Take a towel or a pole. At least I've got part of it right, he comforted himself in the mental chaos as he breast-stroked swiftly, his head out of the water keeping Paz's tiny face in view. Running with the current gave him a momentary advantage until he was struck in the ribs, a blow that took his

breath away. Half a tree trunk whizzed past in the
swirling floodwaters. Flood debris was a threat he
hadn't even considered until now.

The heavy line around his waist tugged hard and
slowed his progress. He turned back and grabbed it
with both hands, giving it a mighty jerk. He felt it
loosen ever so slightly as many hands at the other
end began to make sense of the desperate plan and
truly help in the physical effort.

He called to Paz again, getting a mouthful of
saltwater that nearly choked him in return. This
time, however, Paz seemed to hear. Ever so slowly,
the boy began to swim against the current and
toward a possible rescue. At first, Rick was uncertain,
afraid he was seeing only what he hoped to see. He
shouted again, and now he was certain. One little
stroke followed the next as Paz's arms made one
round and then another in a windmill style crawl
stroke. Confirmation came from behind him as he
heard faint cheers from the beach.

Then just as quickly, the rope around his waist
caught and held him fast. Not yet, his brain screamed
at one more delay. Not yet! He swung around toward
the beach and gave a fierce tug on the line. He saw a
couple of fishermen scurry to work on the snarl and
was relieved when he felt the line go slack, but when
he turned back to look, Paz was gone. Only empty
ocean lay before him.

No! No! No! The word was beating in his brain.
Not now, it can't be happening. I saw him swim.
We were so close. Where is he? God, where is he?

Rick searched frantically. Did he sink? If I have to start diving, I'll never find him. He gave a quick kick up, trying to rise even an extra couple of inches, as he reached what he thought was the last place he had seen him. Nothing. He kicked again with the same result.

Twisting around in a full turn was tangling the rope around his own feet and legs. God, not like this! Please! Another vicious kick and this time, Rick caught a glimpse of the red T-shirt fifty feet away. He fought to rise again on the next wave, without letting it send him in the wrong direction. Yes, it was him. Thank God. Just a short stretch away. In the same moment, his spirits soared, buoyed by the sight of Paz, Rick noted grimly that the youth was now floating face down. Rick put his head down and swam straight ahead with all his strength.

He reached out to touch him, half afraid, again remembering the lessons taught to a sixteen-year-old lifeguard in the safety of an Olympic swimming pool. Rescuer beware—always be wary of your victim. They can wrap themselves around you and drown you, too.

Rick caught hold of the back of Paz's shirt and pulled the boy backward to his chest. There was no reaction. He stretched his left arm across Paz' chest, keeping the boy's head above the water, roughly balanced on his own shoulder as he swam on his side. Kicking constantly, he jerked on the rope three times. He dropped it and waved as high as he could reach. Now nearly exhausted, he turned his attention to just holding on, hoping those on the beach had noted his signal.

At first, nothing happened, and he continued to tread water, fighting the current and holding up both of them as well as the long heavy dangling rope. Thoughts as dark as the waters around them began to engulf him. *This won't last long if they don't start reeling us in soon.* And then he felt it, a slow but steady tightening around his waist and then the pull toward shore.

"Hang on, *amigo*," Rick talked a steady stream to Paz, hoping to keep him from sinking any further into unconsciousness. "Talk to me, my friend. Come on. You are always talking. I could use a little of that right now."

Rick remembered that they had tried to teach him and the others a way to give artificial respiration while still in the water, but under the circumstances, he did not think he could manage that, too. Pushing more saltwater into Paz's lungs would not be of much help at this point.

As they neared the shore, Rick looked over his shoulder to see the fishermen pulling them in, hand-over-hand, like one more big fish. He noticed with great relief that the men had managed to maneuver around the point, pulling them up on the ocean side, avoiding the rocks. As his feet found the sand, he attempted to stand, pulling Paz with him. His own weight felt as if it had tripled since he entered the water. Using what felt like the last of his strength, he forced his leaden limbs to function as others pulled Paz from his grasp.

Still unconscious, the boy was ashen, with bluish shadows around his mouth and eyes.

"Pazito!" Mariana screamed as she stumbled through the crowd, with Imanuel close behind her. She clutched at him, then at her own chest as she fell unconscious beside him. Imanuel caught her before she hit the sand.

"Get back!" Rick screamed at them all as they pushed and pulled at the deathly still boy. He grabbed at his motionless friend, practically throwing him flat on his back on the wet sand. The one thing he had learned well in lifesaving classes and had even used once before on a lifeless boy on the basketball court was CPR.

Despite his own fatigue, he went to work. Tipping Paz's head back, Rick breathed for him. Pumping his chest, he continued the breathing. The fishermen stood tense and silent in a circle around the two of them.

Mariana, still lying in Imanuel's arms as the pair sat on the sand beside where Rick worked, opened her eyes watching without making a sound.

"Why is he kissing him?" one of the younger men asked.

"Shut up, you fool!" Mariana hissed through her tears. "I have seen this before. It is his only hope now. *Por el amor de Díos.*"

Imanuel said nothing, only crossed himself as his lips moved soundlessly and his eyes never left his son.

Now I know what forever feels like, Rick's thoughts leap-frogged one over the other as he watched for even the tiniest glimmer that what he was doing was making a difference. The blue color faded first as a tinge of Paz's natural bronze complexion returned to his pallid face.

Paz jerked involuntarily and began to cough. He rolled sideways and began to spit up water interspersed with more coughing. Rick gave in to his own exhaustion as he dropped onto the sand, laughing and hooting through his own tears.

"*Esta vivo!*" Someone in the crowd shouted, and they exploded in a frenzy of joyous shouts, whistles, and conversation as it became apparent that the young man had certainly come back from the dead. They pounded each other on the back as if each had made the dramatic rescue all by himself. On his knees, Paz continued to vomit saltwater as Mariana leaned over him, hugging him so tightly Rick feared he might lose his ability to breathe once again.

Rick continued to lay on his side, watching with true contentment, in no particular hurry to do anything. Imanuel untied the rope still around his waist.

"Come," he said, as strong hands half-lifted Rick to his feet. He was mildly surprised to see Miguel at his side. The older fisherman pulled Rick's long arm across his own shoulders and started toward Emelina's café. Imanuel and Mariana helped Paz, one on each side of him as they followed Miguel and Rick.

"You have done an incredible thing today." Miguel was the first to speak. "No one who saw this will ever forget it. You were truly sent here to be with us. Of that, there can be no doubt now." Rick had never heard him sound so much like his brother.

As they made their way, step by step to the restaurant, several of the fishermen trailed along behind. They were still voicing their approval, giggling like schoolboys and calling out after the departing figures.

"You are a lucky devil, Paz," someone cried out. "Everyone should have such good fortune as you."

"Everyone should have such a good *gringo* friend as you!" another echoed back.

"Enough with the rocks!" someone else shouted. "Load on the bags! We do not need any more swimmers today!" The crowd headed back to finish their task.

Seated in Emelina's kitchen on a pair of high wooden stools, Paz and Rick huddled as close as they could to the cook fire, which was waist-high, supported on a huge concrete slab. Imanuel brought out light blankets and pulled one around each of them, first Paz, and then Rick.

"It does not get cold here like in your country," he said, looking at Rick. "But you both look pretty chilled to me." Mariana handed each of them a steaming cup of soup.

A weak smile crossed Rick's face. "I can't say I ever thought being cold here would be a problem."

Paz, who had not yet uttered a word since the ordeal, sat sipping his soup, watching his friend.

"I have never seen anyone do anything like that before." He finally spoke. "To risk your life for me—" he stopped and swallowed hard. "As the water pulled me past all of you, by the rocks, I remember thinking, *Ya estuvo*, Paz—it is finished, your life. I could see it on their faces, too. There is nothing anyone can do. All of the men, they looked so sick, so sad. I thought to myself, you will not wiggle your way out of this tight spot. But you—"

"Now wait," Rick cut him off in embarrassment. "Don't do this. Don't make me into anything I'm not. I just couldn't stand by, that's all. I spent a couple of summers as a lifeguard years ago, so that gave me something of an advantage today. Besides, you know how to swim, right? We worked on that. That's what saved you as much as anything."

"Paz is right," Imanuel's voice was low and soft but thick with emotion. "You did something when no one else knew what to do. And what you did is save the life of my son, my only son. A man lays a heavy burden on his only son. I used to wish that I had more than just one. And now," he laid his hand meaningfully on Rick's shoulder as he looked at him. "Now, I feel as if I do." His eyes sparkled with tears as he turned away.

A happy, if wan smile rested on Paz's face. Half the soup gone, he set the bowl down and nearly fell from his perch on the stool while doing so.

"Come, Pazito," Imanuel shepherded the boy toward the door of their living quarters. "To bed with you for a little while. You need a good long rest."

"For once, *Papá*. I will not argue with you."

Mariana silently took Rick's empty cup and started to re-fill it.

"No, that was enough, really." He sipped the coffee instead, keeping his eyes on her.

"Are you all right?" he asked with genuine concern. "I remember you were not doing so well out there on the beach yourself, at one point."

Mariana shrugged. "It is nothing. It happens sometimes, you know, to women when they get too emotional."

"To women, huh? Are you trying to make me think you believe that stuff about the weaker sex? It hardly seems your style."

She made no reply and busied herself, stoking the fire. "Lucky for you two that Emelina made soup yesterday."

Rick continued, this time with less confidence. "I don't mean to say anything against your father. You know that he speaks of having only one son. It's not as if he doesn't have more than one child. He has you, and surely he is proud of your accomplishments, too."

He wanted to attribute her feeble smile to the immediate situation and not their conversation. "What accomplishments? I have done well in my life, not to have gotten him killed."

Rick was confused and wondered if fatigue was interfering with his ability to comprehend her Spanish.

"Besides." She took a lighter note. "This is El Salvador, not America, where sons and daughters both count for something. In this country, a man's sons count for everything. I know Imanuel loves me as I do him, but it is not the same. I did not take everything I learned in the United States about women's liberation to heart. You need not worry. I am not offended by anything he said, so you need not be either."

Rick decided to let it rest and pulled the light blanket a little tighter around his shoulders.

She continued, but in English. "They were very grateful to you as am I. You can pass it off if you want, to them, or even to yourself, that you saved him only because you knew how and they did not, but it is more than that. It is something I have seen before."

He looked at her. "I'm not sure I understand."

She took a deep breath. "Americans many times get into trouble around the world for jumping in where they do not belong, but one thing I have admired often is the way, how do you say, you do not accept that so many things are impossible."

Rick frowned.

"Today, on that beach, when Paz fell into the water, his fate was already a fact with most of those fishermen. They cannot swim, and they knew that if it had been any of them, the end would be the same. No one could manage a *cayuco* in those waters, so it was accepted. The boy would drown. They would console themselves later saying it was his own clumsy fault or even a more kindly, 'it was God's will for him to die young,' but just the same, it was already a fact." She choked for a moment, cleared her throat, and went on.

"But you said, no. He would not, or at least not without a fight." A frown knitted her brow. "Maybe if more of us were like you, in that way, not so easily defeated, things would be different here in our country now.

"We are more like *las palomitas*, the little doves that fly overhead. Maybe that is why our village bears their name. We accept what life deals us. We make a few sweet cooing sounds, but we do not fight back. No one knows the reasons. It is simply the way it is. Like the Bible tells us, God takes care of the little birds which neither plant nor harvest nor build barns. We know he loves us, but I sometimes wonder if we have come to rely on that and nothing else, for too long now." A deep sigh escaped her. "Still, to be able to do what you do—" she stopped speaking.

He studied her carefully, almost wondering if, like Franco, there wasn't a bit of mocking to her tone with that last, but he found only sincerity in her face this day.

"Still your way is not without risk, is it?" She pointed to a gaping hole torn in his shirt and reached down to pull it away, revealing a nasty gash beneath.

"*Por el amor de los cielos*," she exclaimed. "None of us saw that before. Not even you, yes?"

"Well, now that you mention it—"

He slipped out of his button-up shirt as she disappeared around the corner into the store and returned momentarily, her hands full of gauze, tape, and disinfectant.

"Where is Emelina, anyway?" Rick tried not to notice as she dabbed painfully at his ribs with a wad of gauze dipped in something that smelled vile.

"She was taking care of the store first thing this morning but at the moment, more likely, fussing over Paz. Between her and Imanuel, he will be well taken care of. He will be lucky if she ever lets him near the beach or the *estero* again." Mariana laughed, and Rick considered the lovely melodic sound as she did.

"You should do that more often."

"What?" She concentrated on her first aid measures as she answered.

She gave him a serious look. "Too often, there is nothing to laugh about."

Chagrined, Rick kept silent while she finished. Lines like that sound great in the movies, he chided himself, but rarely come off so well in real life.

Still, he continued to struggle to make conversation, if only to ease his own embarrassment at having her tend to his needs in such a personal way. "You said you have been living in the United States. Where?"

"Oh, lots of places."

"Such as?" He pressed.

"Oh, Miami, Los Angeles, Washington, D.C., Houston, to name a few."

"Houston? You lived in Houston?"

"For a while," she nodded. "Also in San Salvador."

"Why so much moving around?"

"We go wherever Carlos' business takes him. He has a home in Miami and, of course, one in San Salvador, but I prefer to travel when he does, rather than sit at home, alone."

Rick sat, contemplating her answer. *He* has a home in Miami, rather than *we*. What an odd way to phrase it, he thought. He rose to his feet, more painfully now after the short rest and the new bandage on his side.

"Now it is my turn to say thank you to you." He spoke in Spanish a bit too formally as he put his shirt back on, and Emelina scurried in from the store.

"Don Ricardo, injured! Saving our dear Pazito!" Emelina frowned at the bandage. "*Gracias, mil gracias, por el amor de Dios. Bendito sea Dios* that you were there today to save him!" She reached up and grabbed the sides of Rick's face, pulling him down as she stood on tiptoe and kissed him on both cheeks.

Mortified by her own impulsiveness, she just as quickly covered her own face with her hands and scampered back toward the store, still prattling about his bravery, poor Pazito, and other things Rick could not quite understand.

"No one can say Emelina does not know how to welcome a hero," Mariana's English now carried a mocking tone but not one that Rick found to be unpleasant, simply once again a fact of life.

After making his goodbyes, Rick slowly made his way back to his own home, at first wading through the shallow water on the road and then moving to the beach. Walking in soft sand or wading in shallow water. There did not seem to be much difference. Now more than ever, he had every intention of spending the day in his hammock or on the cot, and he was thankful when he remembered the last time he had been in the capital he had bought a couple of new paperback novels. The rain had stopped, and he hoped it was the start of brighter days to come, including finding his cousin, David.

* * * * *

It was two more days before the bright sunshine and warm breezes that Rick had come to regard as normal in *Las Palomitas* returned. Sitting on the beach of a morning was a bit different now, as the powerful waves of the flood had carved a high bank from the sand in front of the tree line.

Even so, the warm sun was most welcome, and although they had yet to return to fishing, Rick felt the strong urge to get out and do something. He settled for a walk up the long stretch of deserted beach as it curled around the bay, away from the village.

The large beach houses owned by wealthy city dwellers held the dominant position along the route, each one accompanied by a smaller shack or hut which sat on the same property, some distance from the main house. They came in all colors and styles. Some of the two-story ones looked like classic well-to-do homes one might see along beaches in the United States, with huge gates and impressive fences surrounding them. Others were simple affairs, little more than one-story bungalows with a few strands of barbed wire in front to discourage the wandering animals from invading their private space.

Rick was unable to concentrate on the scenery, either the manmade or the natural variety. A return telegram had come early this morning, brought by a runner from the telephone office in the village.

NO WORD ON WHEREABOUTS OF DAVID MERCY. IF YOU DO NOT HEAR FROM HIM WITHIN NEXT 48 HOURS PLEASE NOTIFY IMMEDIATELY. EMERGENCY PROCEDURES WILL BE INVOKED.

He would need to be ready to leave for the capital by late tomorrow. It meant packing it all up, he mused and heading for what? A long, heart-breaking search? He did not even know where to begin. Would he be returning to the United States alone? What would he tell Dallas and the rest of the family? That David just up and disappeared one day? It had been a full week now since the missed rendezvous in San Miguel and while one part of him was frantic with worry, another portion, albeit weaker with each passing day, continued to hang on to Paz's words. "He will just stay wherever he is. He will come home soon. He always does." God, how he hoped that kid was right, but with each passing day, that wish seemed less likely to come true.

Whatever the outcome, it certainly meant leaving all this behind. Rick slipped off his sandals and walked barefoot in the sand. He would miss it all, he realized. He took a deep breath of the fragrant salt air and tried to concentrate on just enjoying the basics of the morning—sun, sand, surf.

Far down the beach, a small square dot was moving close along the waterline, accompanied by a steady hum. Rick could not quite make it out at first, but he kept his eye trained on the spot as he walked. Slowly, all the tension he had known this last week began to drain away.

"Hey, *Primo!*" Rick heard the shout above the roar of the engine, as the Jeep came into clear sight, yet he stiffened as he realized the three men with David were fully armed uniformed soldiers.

"*Que tal?*" David's flat Texas accent came through in his Spanish. He brought the vehicle to such a sharp stop beside Rick, he almost tossed one of his passengers out onto the wet sand.

"I'm fine," Rick's grin was wide and genuine as he gave silent thanks for Paz's intuition. "Where the hell have you been? I've been just a little worried about you."

"Oh, well, you know how it is in this part of the world. First, there was that government business. Definitely not a good day to travel, and then there was the hurricane thing and all that rain. How'd you make out?" He did not wait for an answer. "Did you know there are three major highway bridges washed out between here and the capital, not to mention the road to the highway is still completely impassable up above? Makes traveling a little complicated.

The only way in and out is over the beach at low tide, like now. Hop in, and I'll give you a ride back to town."

Rick gave him a dubious look and then took in the M-16s and the young faces in charge of them who already crowded the Jeep. "It looks a little cramped in there. Maybe I'll just walk back."

"*No problema*." David motioned to one of the men in the back. "Alfredo here, will move over, *sí?* David smiled without guile. "Climb in."

Rick slipped in directly behind David, watching the gunmen while trying to appear not to do so. Before David could shift gears, however, one of the soldiers let loose with a series of rounds that snapped even David's usual unflappable composure.

A string of coconuts and several huge palm fronds crashed to the ground a short distance away. The shooter ran over to retrieve the *cocos*.

"What the hell's the matter with you?" David whirled on the soldier who was now reloading his weapon. "Are you crazy in the head or something?"

The soldier stared back at him, like a boy who studies a bug on the sidewalk as he decides whether or not to squash it.

"It has been a long ride," the man finally spoke. "I wanted a drink."

He offered one of the streaming coconuts to David, whose only response was to continue to stare at him. The full metal jacket rounds had cut near perfect holes in the green husk. The soldier dropped the second coconut with a shrug, plugged a couple of the holes with his fingers in the one he still held, and slurped the sweet liquid that dribbled off his chin and down the front of his shirt.

David gave a furtive glance in Rick's direction, who also could think of nothing to say or do. "Well, hey," David gave a nervous laugh, his mind racing. "Whatever makes your day, I guess. Listen, just uh, tell the driver the next time you decide to use that thing, okay? I mean, you scared the hell out of me, and you wouldn't want to smash into a tree because you gave your driver a heart attack, right?"

The soldier, his thirst assuaged, looked at David a moment longer. A smirk appeared as he dropped the now empty coconut. "*Vaya pues*," he responded. "The next time I want a drink, I will tell you first." He patted his weapon as he climbed back into the Jeep. David drove on.

"How many more *gringos* are there living in *Las Palomitas?*" Another soldier directed his question toward Rick as they rolled over the smooth cushiony surface of the wet sand.

"Only the two of us, no more." Rick wondered if telling him the truth was such a good idea, but he felt he had little choice. After a moment or two, he ventured a question of his own.

"Why do you come to *Las Palomitas*, Captain?"

"*Capitán!*" The soldier began to laugh. "He called me *capitán*," he called out to his companions. "I am no *capitán*," he told Rick, leaning forward as if to share a secret, "only a sergeant. *Cabo de estes burros*, though." He cuffed Alfredo playfully. "The *teniente*, he is coming in a few days with many men. They are transferring a whole platoon to this area. There has been some guerrilla activity here lately, no doubt troublemakers, invading from Nicaragua, so the lieutenant says we will put a stop to it." He rubbed his M16 as he spoke.

Rick knew the wise course would be to remain silent, but somehow he could not resist a dance with the devil. "That's very strange. I have been here for several weeks now, and I find *Las Palomitas* to be a very quiet place. That's why I like it. Isn't that true, *Primo*?"

Rick patted David on the shoulder, and his cousin shot him a backward look that said plainer than any words that he was playing with fire.

David nodded his head. "Very quiet, very quiet."

The vehicle continued all the way to the end of the point where the soldiers tumbled out and walked toward the village. In their black leather knee-high boots and green uniforms, trimmed with hard helmets, black nightsticks, and accompanying weaponry, they looked shockingly out of place, walking across the soft brown sand, between the thatch huts.

"Are you in the mood for a little Russian roulette today?" David's tone was acidic as he spun the Jeep around to head back the way they had just come. "Don't play cat and mouse with these guys, Rick. You don't ask them questions, and you sure don't need to offer your opinion of the situation at the moment, not the weather, not politics, nothing."

He mimicked Rick's earlier tone. "Very quiet, that's why I like it. Who cares? I'm telling you, if they don't like your answers, they cut your balls off or worse." He frowned. "Well, I guess there isn't anything worse, but hell, you know what I mean."

Rick just laughed, enjoying the fact that David had returned and all in one piece. "I think you've been gone too long, that's what you mean."

"Yeah, well, maybe. Having those guys in here the last thirty miles hasn't exactly added years to my life. Geez, I'm glad they are outta here." He gave a shake like a dog fresh out of the water. "It's a bitch when the hitchhikers have more rights than the guy driving the car. I mean, when soldiers stick out their thumb here, you don't pass them by. You stop and politely give them a ride, whether you want to or not. What a pain!"

Rick's laughter continued. "I really was worried about you. Why didn't you call? I got a telegram from your office today, saying they didn't know where you were either, so I figured—"

"Oh, man, you didn't tell those guys, did you? Holy Mother of God, now I'll have to call in and listen to the old man bitch about the fact that I haven't been on the job. What did you do that for?"

Rick did not want to argue. He felt too good, like a tremendous weight had just been lifted from his shoulders. He spoke deliberately, trying hard to avoid any further offense. "Like I said, I was worried about you. I'm sorry. I didn't do it to complicate your life. I hoped they'd have some idea as to where you were, that's all. When you didn't show up in San Miguel, I couldn't imagine—"

"You went to San Miguel?"

"Well, yeah. You told me to meet you there, so I went, but you never—" Rick stopped speaking and instead began to pound on David's shoulder as the driver burst into his own peals of laughter.

"Man, the capital was full of rumors over the weekend. Everybody and their dog seemed to know there was going to be an overthrow, except Romero. Even the Archbishop knew. You could hear it in his Sunday homily if you listened and apparently just about everybody did. Of course, the president probably never listened to the Archbishop anyway. That caught up with him, huh? Anyway, with all that, I had the good sense to stay put, and I thought you would, too."

"I can't follow that political stuff on the radio. You know that!" Rick spat out, not sure if he should be angry or just amused and frustrated. "I left here on the first bus of the day. What is that, about 5 am? So how would I know? I didn't know anything about it until I got back here that night."

"Which I see you managed to do—and all in one piece, too. Nice work!"

"No thanks to you." Rick grinned, since now a week later, the situation didn't seem nearly so serious as it did back then. "The bus was stopped on the way back here by a pack of rebels who unloaded us all at gunpoint, took everybody's money, threatened a few people, including yours truly. It was not a Sunday picnic, thank you very much."

David's face took on a somber look despite his tone of voice. "Did they burn the bus?"

"No, after the fun and games, they let us back on, and we came on home but—"

"You keep saying, 'we.' Did Paz go with you?"

"No, I met Paz's sister on the bus, and we talked on the way, although at the time, I didn't know who she was."

David let out a long low whistle. "You mean Mariana is back here?"

"You know her?"

"Not exactly. I know who she is and, more importantly, what she is. Somebody pointed her out once in the coffee shop at the Sheraton Hotel, but no, I can't say I know her. Not sure I'd want to either. She's a real looker. There's no doubt about that, but she's also a real hot political property, if you know what I mean."

"No, I don't think I do." A part of him didn't want to know whatever unpleasantness David was about to share, but his own instinct for self-preservation told him he needed to hear it, just the same.

David turned the Jeep sharply and goosed the accelerator as they topped the sharp bank with an air-borne hop, before crossing under the pines and onto the road in front of Rick's cabin.

"Looks like the tide got a little rough while I was gone." David looked back at the beach. "You want out here or coming on with me?"

"Keep going," Rick answered quietly. "I want to hear the rest of what you have to tell me."

At David's, they opened the door, and Rick dropped into the hammock as David stood and stretched, trying to undo the knots that more than a hundred miles of rough road had put in his muscles. He rummaged around in the near-empty rust-coated refrigerator and came up with two cold beers. He snapped the lid off of one, then the other with a sharp downward smack on the concrete ledge of the window frame.

"Stop stalling." Rick finally told him. "What do you know about Mariana that I don't?"

"Better question." David shot back. "Why are you so interested?"

"Just a general interest in the family." Rick tried to sound nonchalant. "I go fishing with Paz and occasionally, Miguel. I enjoy visiting with Imanuel. If there is something more I should know—"

"I really don't know that much." David exaggerated his natural Texas drawl, savoring the effect his delaying tactics were having on his cousin. "She's from here originally. You know that much already, and she's Imanuel's daughter, who nobody in the family talks about."

"Yeah, yeah, all old news, go on."

"You know that beach house way up the way about three-quarters of a mile? The big pink two-story job with the gold R and G on the black wrought iron gate. You can't miss it, gaudy as hell. Well, that one belongs to Raúl Gomez, one of the wealthier members of the Famous Fourteen Families, the oligarchy, you know, from San Salvador."

Rick nodded silently.

David continued. "I hear he can be a real bastard when he wants to be except that here in *Las Palomitas*, he does seem to try to make nice, as best as I've been able to tell. He comes down from the city from time to time, especially on the regular vacation days, you know—Easter, August holidays, first week of November, like that. I've seen him a few times, no big deal as far as I can tell, just a little shriveled up old man."

"So what's this got to with anything? I thought we were talking about Mariana."

"We are, or at least, I am. Give me a minute. This guy Gomez had a son, Roberto, who used to come here, too. He wasn't as smart as his father. He was a real jerk all over town. Lorded it over everybody. They say Roberto always had a bottle in one hand and a pistol in the other. You could say nobody in *Las Palomitas* exactly looked forward to his visits."

David plunked down, straddling a wooden chair, crossing his arms over the back while facing the hammock. "One day he and a buddy took a little trip in one of Daddy's fancy fiberglass boats up into the mangrove swamps, probably to hunt or fish a little. Mariana was just a teenager then, but she was up there, too, looking for firewood. A lot of the women look for driftwood up there. Anyway, nobody's exactly sure what happened but the best they can figure, the guys found her and had their own little party. The end result was that Roberto came floating down from the mangrove swamps in his boat, alone late that afternoon, and never said a word to anyone. Mariana didn't turn up until late the next day, not until a search party—her father, her uncle, and her cousin went up and found her. And the buddy, he came floating down about three days later, with the high tide, shot through the heart."

"My God, who shot him?"

"Well, that's what everybody would like to know. Roberto refused to say anything, and of course, he had rich Daddy Gomez to protect him, so no problem. He didn't have to. And Mariana, well, the truth is she couldn't say anything. They found her, just sitting alongside the water. The fishermen say she'd look at you all wide-eyed like a little girl but never say a word. The ones that went looking for her had called and called, and when they found her, it was as if she'd never heard them or even knew her own name. They just sort of stumbled across her."

He watched Rick, trying to figure the exact effect the story was having on him. "You've not been up there yet, have you? The *mangle*, as they call it, is beautiful but more than a little spooky. I don't think I'd care to spend a night up there alone, and I can't imagine what that could do to a young girl's mind, that and whatever Roberto and his friend had managed to get away with.

"At any rate, things sort of settled down after a bit. Roberto went back to being a jerk, and Mariana was sent home to Imanuel's where they took care of her the best they could, I suppose, not knowing exactly what was wrong with her. After a couple more months, Mariana was to the point where she could walk around and understand what was said to her. She still didn't speak.

"One day, Emelina sent her to carry lunch to her Uncle Miguel, who was helping friends put a new roof on their house up the road. It was broad daylight, and she just had to walk up the road a mile or so, but she had to walk past Gomez's place. No one knew Roberto was even there at the time. He was supposed to be in San Salvador. No one heard anything, but before the day was over, Roberto's body was found inside the courtyard of the Gomez house, shot through the heart with his own *pistola*."

David took a deep breath, no longer jovial about relating a painful story that was having a significant influence on his cousin, but he just couldn't quite read exactly what or why.

"Nobody's sure exactly what happened. He might have seen her alone and thought he could continue where he had left off all those weeks before. Or maybe she had vengeance on her mind for some time, although no one seemed to think she had much of a mind left. Maybe somebody else took advantage of the situation and grabbed the chance to get rid of Roberto. Who knows?"

Rick said nothing.

"So," David heaved a sigh of relief as he neared the end of his story. "It was shortly after that, don Raúl was running around swearing vengeance on Imanuel's daughter for the murder of his son, although he had no proof. That's when Carlos showed up here. No one seemed to know much about him, but before you know it, he left with Mariana, apparently with Imanuel's blessing. And that is pretty much the whole story. She's been with him ever since, and they are always on the move. Carlos has his fingers in a lot of business pies, if you will, all different kinds. Don Raúl swore if she ever set foot in *Las Palomitas* again, he'd see her dead. He could do the same in San Salvador, I suppose, but I hear she's spent much of her time in the US since leaving here. She makes the occasional stop in San Salvador or even San Miguel. As far as I know, this is the first time she's ever come back to her home village."

He hesitated but continued when there was no response. Rick sat, swaying gently in the hammock, his feet brushing the floor as he stared off into space.

David added. "She's either awfully brave or awfully stupid, depending on how you want to look at it. Gomez certainly has the ability to make good on his threat. He's not somebody I'd want to tangle with."

"So this Carlos took her out of here when she was what? Still just a kid?"

David was at least glad to know Rich had been listening to a part of the story.

"Yeah, that's what the fishermen said. Couple of them told me the whole story one night when we got drunk together. I mean, it's not something anybody here talks about regularly. Carlos showed up to visit Imanuel one evening, and I asked them who he was, and we just sort of got into the whole thing from there."

"So you've met him?"

"Well, sort of. Saw him actually. He's an older guy, older than Imanuel, and drives a big English Land Rover. Guess he saw his chance to get him a sweet young thing and took it. I heard he sent her to finishing school and the whole bit. The day I saw her—well, she doesn't exactly look like a village girl, does she?"

A small smile broke through Rick's somber reflections. "No, she doesn't look like any of the others here."

"But hey, partner, what's been happening here since I've been gone? I sure hope you haven't been getting mixed up with her in any way. Best advice there is to stay far, far away."

"No, really. I've spoken to her a few times, and I was curious, that's all." Rick shrugged and let a lazy smile cross his face. "It's been the same old stuff here. A lot of rain actually but not much else."

David would hear about the incident with Paz soon enough, he decided, and in his current state of mind, if he told him anything of Franco's visit—well, suffice it to say, he wasn't in the mood for another lecture from his older cousin.

"Still just sitting around on the beach and fishing, huh? Well, hey, I've got this really sweet deal set up, that's why I told you to meet me in San Miguel. I was supposed to be there with a couple of guys from

San Salvador. Actually, they live in San Benito if that tells you anything—we're talking major money here. They want to go hunting, and they want to hire us as guides.

"The whole deal has been temporarily postponed because of this government overhaul and the weather, but that will all settle down in a couple of more weeks, and then they're going to meet us down here. They're going to pay us to take them dove hunting out here. Can you believe it?" David chortled.

"Dove hunting?"

"Yeah, over on the hills across the *estero*, there's some great hunting. And you know this isn't like in the States. We're talking no limits, no hassles. We can hunt and shoot to our hearts' content. I haven't taken you over there yet, huh? But you'll see. This is gonna be great!"

CHAPTER 6

Washington, D.C., October 30, 1979—The US government announced that military aid to the government of El Salvador, which was officially suspended in 1977 due to human rights abuses, will resume with a new shipment of significant military assistance. The State Department's own human rights bureau opposes the aid which comes with no conditions and was not requested by the Salvadoran government. It includes $300,000 worth of tear gas, gas masks, chest protectors, and other military supplies, characterized by both the US and Salvadoran governments as "non-lethal" assistance.

Second Lieutenant Hector Antonio Hernandez was not a happy man. As the Jeep in which he was riding pulled up short in front of his new headquarters, Hernandez glared at the driver. The sweating young recruit stared straight ahead, apparently unaware that he had nearly thrown his new commanding officer through the windshield of his own vehicle. The lieutenant surveyed the two-story hovel that was to serve as his command post. The original blue painted stucco had faded to a pale gray, and along the roofline, large, washed-out letters still identified the original tenant, *Tienda San Juda*.

He looked back at the main highway, a rock's throw from where he stood, on the outskirts of the town of San Marcos. The highway continued west to the Pacific port city of La Union. The dirt track that turned off across from his new post meandered for several more kilometers before terminating at the village of *Las Palomitas*.

Hernandez turned back to the building confronting him. He barked at the driver who scrambled from his seat and began unloading some of the files and supplies that filled the back of the Jeep. The lieutenant's National Guard boots echoed on the wooden floor of the empty shell of a building. As he climbed the staircase to the second floor, he noted its dilapidated condition and skipped several of the weaker steps. The living quarters of the previous tenants would adequately serve his purposes, he decided after a cursory examination. He stopped to stare out of one of the two southern windows. From here, he could not quite glimpse the ocean, but he could smell it.

He raged silently as he had done for the entire four-hour Jeep ride from San Salvador. In truth, as he had done for days ever since he had been informed of his transfer. He knew why those bastards in the capital had stuck him out here. Did they really think him such a fool that he would believe all their bullshit? They could jabber all they wanted about this being his part of the country, the cradle of his birth, and that no one would know better than he how to pursue the local *guerrilleros*. He was not impressed.

Everyone is this country with a brain and half an education knew the truth. Only those who could not make it one way or another worked out in the countryside. It did not matter if you were a doctor, a teacher, or a professional soldier. If you were any good at all, you were working in or near the capital. Only the alcoholics and the truly incompetent settled for a position out here in no man's land.

If they only knew how hard he had worked to get away from here. Maybe they did and just did not care. He pulled off his hat and ran his fingers through his thick black hair. He hated having it shaved short the way it was when he had first joined the army. Now, as an officer, he had grown it as long as convention would allow.

Some of his superiors still considered him little more than an ignorant *campesino* despite his grades at the military school. He knew for some it would never make any difference. Station in life was forever determined by the place and person you were at birth, but he would continue to be relentless. He would show them. Let them stick him out here in hell again, if they thought they could break him. He was determined to make this the best damn rural command in the country and rout every cursed *guerrillero* in the countryside while doing it. He would prove himself, and then they would have to admit they were seriously mistaken. He replaced his hat and strutted across the floor with new resolve.

Downstairs, the driver was making a mess of everything. "Not here, you fool," Hernandez snapped.

He surveyed the heavy wooden desk, shoved sideways in a corner of the main room. The dust on top, churned up from the road outside, looked to be at least a centimeter deep. In the anteroom behind it, leading to the back door, he caught a glimpse of a military issue iron cot and a single chair.

"Get something and clean up this mess," he ordered. He strolled back outside and looked around at the nearby houses of San Marcos and back down the long road toward *Las Palomitas*. He was supposed to have a full platoon, two squads coming in short order, transfers from other areas. Some had undoubtedly already arrived. With no one in charge, they were probably drunk on the beach or giving the local girls a hard time in some back alley. He would have his work cut out for him, kicking their butts into line. It did not matter. He would make them work for every *centavo*, every *colón* they stole as representatives of the government.

* * * * *

Life was back to normal in the village. Rick and Paz were fishing regularly, and in another few days, with Paz out of school, they had plans to do even more of the same. David had made peace with his superiors and was back to spending a sizeable portion of his time sitting around with the other fishermen, swapping stories and drinking beer, alternating between the local pool hall and the beach brothel.

Imanuel's workload had not been made any easier by the ravages of the hurricane's rains. At least two dozen local families had been left homeless as their huts collapsed under the weight of sodden thatch roofs or due to shifting sands beneath. While most had found at least temporary shelter with relatives or neighbors, three or four families had left town. Imanuel suspected for at least two, this had been the final blow, and they had gone to join Franco and the others in the mountains. Meanwhile, Imanuel struggled on, searching for new sources of aid for extra food and clothing. Despite the fact that he had been warned away, Rick continued to help his friend whenever he could.

It was a particularly gorgeous afternoon of clear blue skies, white fluffy clouds, and silky sea breezes. As Rick strolled toward town, he noticed Mariana sitting alone at one of the three tiny wooden tables that made up *Mariscos Marielos*, an open-air oyster and clam café located across from the bus stop.

"*Buenas tardes*," Rick spoke first, telling himself he could hardly walk past in silence, without appearing to be rude.

"*Buenas tardes*," she returned his greeting. "Are you and Paz fishing tomorrow morning as usual?"

"We're planning on it. The fishing has been extraordinarily good since the hurricane. Maybe all that rain got the fish up and moving."

"It happens that way sometimes," she mused. "A change in the weather seems to make things very good or very bad, yes?"

"I suppose so." He approached her table. "You're eating alone?"

"Just waiting for a *coctel de concha*. Would you like to join me? Nobody makes them better than Marielos."

Rick pulled out the chair on the opposite side of the table. The diminutive young woman who ran the place came over to take his order.

"*Conchas y cerveza*," Mariana ordered with the question on her face. He nodded.

Rick watched Marielos at the small table that served as a full kitchen. He had noticed her before in town, a sober-faced tiny woman who always seemed to be nervously busy, with an anxiety that deemed it necessary for her to watch everything around her at once. With the dexterity that comes only from much practice, she quickly chopped open a dozen large clams with a device designed specifically for the job, an evil-looking meld of a hatchet and an old-fashioned pump handle. She minced the still quivering clams with onions and tomatoes and dished them up in their own dark liquid, adding a plentiful shot of Worcestshire sauce—*salsa inglesa*, English sauce, as they called it here.

She delivered two small bowls of the hashed cocktails in their black liquor and two cold bottles of beer to the table without saying a word.

"Stay and sit with us for a minute." Rick was surprised at Mariana's invitation to the other woman. As she put down the refreshments, Mariana caught her by the hand, but Marielos pulled away, although not too quickly, Rick noticed.

"That would not be right. You know that."

"Marielos, how could it not be right? We were friends all through school. We are the same."

"No, Niña Mariana," Marielos corrected her, not unkindly, invoking the local term of respect most of the villagers used for women here with the exception of their own relatives and closest friends. "We were the same once, but it is no longer true."

"Marielos—"

"I mean no disrespect, Niña Mariana, but we are not the same, and I cannot sit at your table. You should know better than to ask."

Rick was having a difficult time following exactly what was going on, but he could not help but see the heavy sadness that had now been added to the woman's usual resolute expression as she turned away. She began to scoop up the empty seashells and tidy up her work area.

Mariana's attention returned to the food before her. Rick held his silence, hoping for an explanation. She did not keep him waiting long.

"She was my best friend when I was growing up here," she began, glancing sideways at Marielos, apparently concerned she might understand even though she was now speaking in English. Mariana picked at the food before her as if the anticipated enjoyment was now gone from it.

"We walked to school together every day, told each other all the dreams and secrets young girls share. It is incredible that now she feels she cannot even sit at the same table with me, no?" The strain in her voice was obvious as she tried to cover the pain that her eyes could not hide.

"Maybe a great many things have changed in her life, as well as in yours, in the time you've been gone." Rick chose his words carefully, not wishing to reveal just how much he already knew of her history.

"Perhaps." Mariana frowned. "You know, she has not spoken to me since I returned. I do not know if she is angry or hurt or both. I just thought, maybe if I came over here—" She left the thought unfinished. "Maria de los Cielos, that's her real name, you know." Mariana dared to speak it as she saw her friend walk out on the beach to throw out the empty shells. "I shortened it to Marielos years ago, that was my special nickname for her. I guess I should be pleased that she decided to keep it." She looked up at the sign overhead. A tiny smile crept across her face.

"Emelina will have a fit if she sees me over here. It does not matter that she does not serve *conchas* or oysters. She still thinks of Marielos's place as competition." Her smile grew, although the sadness behind it remained.

Rick struggled to find something to say to keep the sorrow for taking possession of her again. He glanced around, only to discover that someone else was watching them, and he felt himself flush unexpectedly as their eyes met.

In the doorway of the brothel a short distance away, David's unmistakable shadow loomed large. He stared menacingly at Rick and shook his head before disappearing inside. Rick had never before noted any similarity between his cousin and his father, but suddenly, it was quite plain to see—the hardness in the eyes, the stiffness in the neck— leaving him wondering how it had gone unnoticed all these years.

"Well," Rick let a nervous laugh escape. "You are not the only one who is likely to be in trouble with the rest of your family after this afternoon."

"Excuse me?" Mariana raised an eyebrow in his direction. "I do not understand."

"Neither do I." Rick laughed at the absurdity of the whole situation. "But it doesn't matter. These were very good. *Coctel de conchas*. I'll have to remember that."

He leaned back precariously in the simple wooden chair. Despite the late afternoon hour, the sun still burned hot on his shoulders and back. He watched half-hypnotically as a fly climbed down into the sparkling beer bottle, lured by the half-inch of sweet liquor warming at the bottom. What had begun as an easy conquest turned swiftly into a transparent trap. The fly buzzed momentarily in frustration until the intoxicating fumes landed him in the dregs, where he soon drowned.

For a change, she broke the silence between them. "What is that strange phrase in English? A penny for your thoughts?"

"Uh, oh," he stammered, startled from his musings. "I don't think you'd find them worth even that much," he admitted with a sheepish grin. "How's your father today? That's really where I was heading just now when I saw you. I promised to lend him a hand this afternoon." He stood up. "Can I walk you to—where? Back to the store?" He fished in his pocket for a few *colones* to cover the cost of the afternoon snack.

"I invited you," Mariana corrected him, handing him back his money as she stood up. They stepped onto the dirt road together as a military Jeep rattled into town.

"Stop here!" The command echoed above the dust churned up by the sudden halt. "Mariana, is that really you?" The same voice softened with the question.

The handsome military officer hopped agilely from the vehicle almost before it had come to a complete stop.

"Hector?" Mariana's face brightened as she recognized an old friend, but as she glanced over the military uniform before her, a tautness could be seen in her as well, as she sidestepped in Rick's direction.

"I am very surprised to see you here." His voice was friendly, as was his manner. A look of amusement played across his features.

"Why should you be?" Her tone reminded Rick of the way she put Franco in his place whenever she felt disposed to do so. "I live here, after all, as does my entire family."

"Well, of course, they do." The warmth was quickly changing to condescension. "But, after all, you have not been here for some time now."

"Things change, Hector. Things always change. You of all people should be aware of that."

He frowned, unsure of how to respond. "So you are home in your father's house to stay now?"

"Not exactly." Her response continued to be cool. She casually took hold of Rick's arm. A stirring within surprised him, and he moved closer to her as well.

"This is a friend, Rick Mercy." She completed the introductions. "And what are you doing here, Hector? Are you not stationed in the capital these days? Did you come all the way to *Las Palomitas* to ask about me?"

"I have been assigned here temporarily." Hector's lips parted to reveal straight white teeth, but it would have been dishonest, Rick thought, to call his expression a smile. "We have some problems in the hills. *La situación*, people in the capital like to call it. You understand. I doubt that it will take very long for professional soldiers like ours to clean it up."

Rick admired the way Mariana's face gave nothing away. "Well, then I am sure I will see you from time to time, in the street, if nowhere else." With that icy comment, she turned to Rick as if to leave but then seemed to remember a last detail. "Oh, by the way, Hector. You will find some of your professionals over there." She pointed to the doorway where David had appeared earlier. "I believe you will find them engaged with other professionals at the moment."

Rick was glad they left quickly after that. He had never met any soldiers who did not like to be taken seriously.

Outside the restaurant, he glanced around for Imanuel, and although his mind told him escape was the wiser choice, no other part of his being was listening. Her hand still rested lightly on his arm.

"So I have been elevated to your friend now?" He could not help but ask, once they were out of the hearing of others.

"Is that what I said?" The question sounded innocent enough. "I meant to say a friend of my brother, of course."

"Of course. Do you always treat the military so respectfully?"

"The military? Oh, Hector. Well, that was a bit of a surprise. We grew up together, and I guess I always knew he would end up as a *militar*, but it is still hard to accept. His uncle is the local Marine who supposedly watches out for contraband shipments of any kind here, illegal immigrants, that sort of thing. It has always been a local joke. Partly because Don Cristobal is such a—what is the word in English? A clown? A wimp? He would not hurt anyone. And also because who would want to sneak into this country illegally? I mean, the United States has this problem, and it is understandable there, but here? Now with *los muchachos* and the new government of Nicaragua, I suppose that they think the boys in the hills are receiving daily arms shipments."

"They are receiving some, or something, aren't they? That's what the US government believes from what I've read at home."

"Then they are fools. My cousin would laugh to hear such talk. They struggle daily just to have anything at all to fight with, let alone to eat." Her voice had dropped perceptibly, and Rick noticed she never called Franco by name, although she continued with the confidence of one who speaks a foreign tongue, incomprehensible to others within earshot. "They make homemade bombs and re-work fifty-year-old arms to keep them going. Do you not remember? What did Lito push at you that day? Was it some new fancy Russian gun?"

Rick thought back, remembering how he had worried about embarrassing himself publicly with a failure of bodily function as opposed to noting the make and model of any particular weapon. Still, when the memory of that particular gun barrel came back to mind, he had to admit she was right. It was similar to those he had seen in World War II displays in museums back home.

"If someone like Lito had such a gun, do you think anyone, even Elio could convince him to leave it at home and out of sight? You know he would insist on carrying it with him everywhere, even to the outhouse."

Rick could not argue her point.

Paz was waiting for them impatiently inside the store. "*Por fin, hermana mía!*" he complained. "Where have you been? Do you think I want to spend my life back here doing homework?" He sat perched on a high stool, a school notebook spread open before him on the old-fashioned battered glass countertop. The notebook was snapped shut quickly when Paz saw his chance to escape.

"*Mí papá* says that when you come back, I can leave." There was almost a challenge in his voice.

"*Vaya pues*," she laughed good-naturedly. "Who am I to stand in the way of a boy and his freedom? It is so nice to know you are such a devoted student."

Paz followed Rick, who touched the brim of his hat in lieu of a goodbye to Mariana before ducking out of the door.

"And what have you been up to today?" Paz tossed off the comment as he munched a handful of some sort of snack that he carried in a paper cone.

Rick heard more mischief in his friend's tone of voice than he cared for. "What's that supposed to mean?"

"Oh, nothing. You just looked kind of happy when you came walking in the door with my sister, that is all. It is the same way Gilberto looks every time he looks at Silvia. She is this new girl at school, and you should see—" He made the appropriate curving motions with his free hand and the cone.

"Hey, Paz. I'm not doing anything except minding my own business. Don't start something that doesn't even exist, okay?" His voice sounded more defensive than he intended.

"*Vaya pues*." Paz backed off quickly.

"What are these?" Rick asked as he took a closer look at what Paz was eating.

"Try some. Gilberto's mother makes them when he has a good catch."

Rick picked hesitantly as the greasy, gray crisps. Crunchy, salty, but definitely fishy, he decided. Still, he tried a few more.

"They are fried sardines. Pretty good, yes?"

"*Así, así,*" Rick answered honestly, as the idea of French-fried sardines took hold. He decided the French fry industry had nothing to fear. "Not bad, but not great."

Paz laughed at his tentative approach.

They found Imanuel struggling to put the top crates on a triple stack in the clinic, a tiny one-room building that was two doors behind the store. Rick bowed his head to pass the low doorway. After the indispensable polite greetings, Imanuel proclaimed, "You are just in time. I need some tall help."

Rick cheerfully complied and noted the crates were stamped from *CARITAS*, the Catholic relief fund. According to the labels, the boxes were filled with bandages, tape, and antiseptic.

"My apologies for arriving so late," Rick began to explain after finishing the simple task.

"*No hay problema,*" Imanuel said. "The truck that brought these was supposed to bring several other things as well, but they did not arrive today, so I did not really need much help." He finished with a sigh. "*Así es, verdad?* It is the way it always is, yes? Very little arrives when it should."

"I suppose." Rick was unsure how to answer. "What are you going to do now?"

"Oh, just the accounting remains. You know, writing it all down, what we received, where it is going. I will have to do that."

An anxious young woman appeared at the door. Her husband Andres was deathly ill, she told

Imanuel. Could he come at once? Imanuel agreed and motioned for Rick and Paz to follow.

They found the man lying on a cot in his dark one-room shack near the point. He was pale, sweaty, and twitching uncontrollably. A memory from childhood, stories of Jesus visiting the sick and the demon-possessed filtered through Rick's mind as the sunshine sifted through the cracks in the walls, throwing tiny bands of sunlight across the floor.

"Where has he been?" was Imanuel's first question to his wife, Sonia, as he set about opening the door and the windows.

"Working in the fields the last few days, out by the highway. Fishing is not so good for us, and in the cotton fields, he sometimes earns better." She sounded almost apologetic.

"And they have been spraying?"

"Yes. I am sorry that he is so dirty. He said the truck he was riding in this morning slid off the road and several workers fell out of the back. No one was hurt, but some, like Andres, rolled down a muddy hill by the roadside. He said he was covered with mud by the time he got to work."

"Do not apologize. It may be what saves his life, Niña Sonia." Imanuel tossed the words over his shoulder as his hands felt over the prone figure, probing for broken bones. "Andres, can you sit up? Can you look at me?"

The man pulled himself to a sitting position with difficulty, and the thin blanket fell from his shoulders. Sonia was right. He was covered with dirt but also with some sort of milky white spray. Despite his best efforts, Imanuel had brought only a small amount of light into the room. Still, the man's pupils were tiny dots in his dark eyes, as if he was standing in the brightest sunshine. Imanuel steadied him with a hand on his shoulder.

"Paz, go tell Niña Ana, I need some of her charcoal and *beleño* tea, as quickly as she can make it." Paz trotted off in the direction of the old medicine woman's hut.

"Charcoal tea?" Andres began to come alive although he was still having difficulty with his own muscle control. "Who do you think I am? *El Cipitio?* I am not drinking anything made from ashes." He pushed at Imanuel and nearly fell off of the bed, like a drunk. Saliva ran from the corner of his mouth as he stood up and promptly urinated on himself.

"*Por Díos, Sonia!*" He looked helplessly at his wife and sat down on the floor, with his head in his hands as if he might cry.

"Listen to me, man," Imanuel began to explain. "They sprayed today in the cotton fields while you were there. Is that right?"

Andres nodded without looking up. "I held a flag."

"You have been poisoned just like the bugs they are spraying. We are going to the well, and I am going to give you a good bath. Then I want you to drink all the water you can hold. Have you been throwing up yet?"

He nodded without saying anything more.

"That is a good sign. You might do that some more, but it will not hurt you. That is part of what you need right now. How are your lungs?"

Andres looked up at Imanuel for the first time, as if he did not understand.

"Your breathing. How well can you breathe?" Imanuel thumped his own chest for emphasis.

"It is not bad. The stuff that they spray smells bad, so every time the plane comes by, I hold my breath. You cannot do it forever, but it keeps you from smelling so much of it."

"Good for you," Imanuel laughed. "Come on. Let's get you up."

Rick and Imanuel lifted the man to his feet and guided him outside to a nearby well. Imanuel helped Andres out of his clothes down to his undershorts. Then Imanuel began to pour bowlfuls of water over Andres' head, bathing him and washing his hair as if he were a child.

"Sonia," Imanuel called. "Have you got some laundry soap?"

"Sí, don Imanuel," she answered as she appeared with a bowl filled with the remnants of a ball of soap and the scraps of some sort of plant fiber, used to distribute the soap over the laundry as it was washed by hand. Rick had seen the local women using it to wash clothes and tried it himself a couple of times. The skin peeled off of the palms of his hands afterward, and he wondered if it might not be the original lye soap. After that, he also found it much more convenient to pay one Julio's daughters to wash his clothes than do it himself.

"Where are the children, Niña Sonia?" Imanuel asked.

"I sent them to my sister's house across the way when Andres came home sick. I was not sure what was wrong. I did not think having them underfoot would help." Embarrassed by the sight of her husband being bathed, she went back inside, but Rick could see her watching their every move from the open window. Andres, meanwhile, was surprising in his acquiescence.

As the water barrel ran low, Rick drew more water from the well, trying in some small way to be helpful. "This man has been in the cotton fields where they spray poison for the insects," Imanuel explained as he continued to scrub Andres' hair, neck, and arms with the wad of fibers. "Sadly, sometimes it poisons the people, too, and his job, holding the markers to guide the plane, is the worst."

An ironic little smile slipped across Imanuel's face. "The funny part is how dirty he got on the way to work today, falling from the truck. That will be the thing that keeps him from getting as sick as he might have. The spray soaks in through the skin and is also breathed in, but since he was covered with mud, it actually protected him. God does work in mysterious ways!"

"Imanuel, do they not know about this?" Rick interrupted without thinking. "Surely, the landowners must know that this makes the workers sick—" He stopped speaking, not sure what to say next.

"Yes, they know," came the quiet response.

"Then why—why do the landowners not stop it? Why do the people still go to work there?"

"Why, indeed." Imanuel shrugged and answered in a tone that sounded more like Mariana's or Franco's sarcasm than the usually optimistic catechist. "The easy answer is that the people go because the money is there. Right-now-money for work done today means your children eat today. As to why does it continue, that is not an answer I like to think about. It continues because the field workers are seen as—what is the word that Franco uses?—expendable."

Andres interrupted the lesson when he turned sharply and vomited onto the sand at their feet.

"That is good," Imanuel said with a small smile as he guided Andres back to the stump he had been sitting on. He began to pour more water over the now shivering man.

"We need a towel, Niña Sonia," Imanuel called out. "Where is that, Pazito?"

No sooner had he spoken the words, his son came around the corner of the house, carrying a two-handled earthenware pitcher. "Here is the tea from Niña Ana, *Papá*. She says there is enough here for tonight and also for tomorrow, so he should drink just a little at a time, not all at once, or it will also make him sick."

"Oh, yes." Imanuel toweled his patient dry and then wrapped the towel around him before turning him over to his wife, who had come back outside. "Clean clothes and a clean bed," Imanuel instructed.

"*Sí*, don Imanuel," Sonia answered. "The bed is ready."

"Why does Niña Ana always say that, as if we will forget each time." Paz gave an exasperated sigh. "Like I am a little child or even you, *Papá*. She tells you the same every time."

Imanuel grinned, now that his work was finished. "Maybe because she is so old, we all seem like little children to her. It is not a serious problem. I am happy to listen to her instructions each time as long as she keeps making her tea for those who need it."

"You are probably right." Paz rolled his eyes in response.

Back inside the house, Imanuel instructed Sonia on the judicious use of the medicinal tea. "It is made from a plant that is poisonous all on its own," he warned. "But when used like this, along with the charcoal that is in it, it will work against the poison already in him. Just a little several times a day. What you have here should last, tonight, tomorrow, and into the next day. After that, he should be better. You can add a little sugar to it if he does not like the taste.

"And you," he turned to Andres, who lay with the covers clutched under his chin. "You drink all that she gives you. Do you understand? It may taste bad, but it will help. And stay out of the fields for a few days. When do go back, if they are spraying, wear a big hat, put a handkerchief over your face, like a *bandito*, and cover yourself with mud. I know it sounds crazy and nobody likes to do it, but it is the best protection. You must keep that white stuff off of your skin and out of your lungs."

"*Muchas gracias*, don Imanuel," Sonia said as she handed her husband a small cup of the black foul-looking liquid.

After drinking, Andres wrinkled his nose in disgust but also thanked Imanuel profusely. "We do appreciate all that you do. I know it is not easy for you." He reached from beneath the covers and clasped his neighbor's hand. "Take care of yourself, *amigo*. May God bless you."

Imanuel's hand slipped over Andres' for a brief moment. "He does, my friend, he does. Everyday. Sleep well."

Back outside in the sunshine, the three walked toward the clinic.

"Will he be all right?" Rick asked. "Pesticide poisoning is no small thing."

"He should be fine in a few days," Imanuel sighed. "Until he goes back to work, then who knows? Now, you understand why there are strikes in the fields, yes? The workers are always looking for more, more, more, the government claims, in terms of money and better working conditions but with such as this, who should be surprised? I hear stories about those who live along the fields, when their houses are sprayed. It is terrible." He shook his head forlornly.

"What do you mean?"

"When they spray the workers' homes, their children and babies get covered with the stuff, too, and often, there is no saving them."

"My Lord," Rick could think of nothing else to say. "What did he mean when he said it is not easy for you? Are you in trouble?"

"Me? No. It means nothing." Imanuel smiled and turned away. "Just the ravings of a man half out of his mind with sickness and now worry, too, I suppose. If he cannot work—" He left the thought unfinished. "I'm going by to see Niña Ana and thank her for the tea."

"Do I know her?"

"Oh, I do not think so. Once you meet Niña Ana, you are not likely to forget."

"It is true," Paz chimed in, laughing. "She is not forgettable. We will see you later, *Papá*. We have plans."

"We do?" Rick followed but with misgivings. Imanuel looked tired, and it seemed to Rick that it was more than a man sick from pesticide that bowed his shoulders as he walked away. "Is there something more I can help with?"

"No, my son," Imanuel answered.

My Lord, he even sounds like a priest today, was Rick's next thought, and for some reason, the reflection alarmed him more than he liked to admit.

"Come on. I want to show you something. I finally got it all arranged." Paz was the picture of impatience, but as they turned the corner, Paz stopped abruptly, throwing a protective arm up to stop Rick as well.

"*A la gran puta!*

A large blue Land Rover was parked in front of Emelina's restaurant, and at the sight of it, Paz seemed to have lost all reason. Rick had never heard him swear before, but he was even more startled when Paz grabbed his arm and ducked down, dragging him along.

"Come on!" The boy hissed as he crept back the way they had come, tucked close to the building.

Paz hurried around the corner of the store, diving down a tiny back alley Rick had never noticed before collapsing melodramatically in the dust.

"What's this all about?" Rick was losing patience with the whole thing.

"That is don Carlos Panameño's car out there. *Puta!*" Paz let fly again. "I cannot believe he is here. I mean, she never talks about him. I thought maybe she finally left him. I cannot believe he followed her."

"So that's it?" He did not have the chance to say anything more. Paz scooted down to the closed end of the alley and was piling up plastic buckets one on top of the next.

"Now what are you doing?"

With a finger to his lips, he pointed wordlessly to a small window halfway up the wall. Climbing quietly on top of three buckets, he pushed his nose up over the edge. He motioned to Rick to do the same. Despite feeling ridiculous, Rick did as he was told, although he needed only one bucket to boost himself to the window ledge.

Carlos had apparently stopped first in the restaurant since their surveillance through the grimy glass revealed a corpulent gentleman with iron-gray hair and a thick mustache, who was just coming into the store.

Marina was also caught by surprise. "Carlos!" She did not move from her station behind the counter where she was counting out cigarettes, breaking packs of twenty into banded bunches of four.

"*Buenas tardes*, my dear." He leaned over the counter, not without difficulty, and kissed her on the cheek. "I see that being home is agreeing with you. You look well."

"Thank you." She recovered quickly. "Why did you not call and let me know you were coming? I would have told Emelina so we could clean the big house for you. She will be most upset that there was no chance to tidy up before your arrival."

"I know what a bother the local telephone is. It was not that important. I can only stay tonight. I will sleep up there, but I am not concerned about whether there is a layer of sand on everything or not. How are you, really?"

"I am fine, Carlos. Much better than I was. It is good to be home, really home. Just like it is good to see you." She reached out and patted one of the small hams that rested on the counter and served him as hands. "Are you sleeping better these days? I will worry about you up there tonight."

"Please do not," he replied with a smile. "I always rest well at the beach. I only came to see for myself how you are and looking at you now, it was worth the trip. Is Niña Ana making tea for you every day?"

She nodded, but Rick had already stepped down from his perch. He'd had enough of eavesdropping on a private conversation.

Paz remained at his post until Rick finally reached up and jerked on his pant leg. "Get down."

Paz obeyed with reluctance. "I still cannot believe he is here. At least, he is only staying one night."

"What did your sister mean about the big house? Carlos does not stay in your father's house?"

"Why should he?" Paz shrugged. "He has his own, one of the big *ranchos* up on the beach. The one made of sand-colored bricks, two stories, a kilometer or so past don Raúl's place. You know which is his?"

"Yes," Rick replied thoughtfully. "But then why does she stay here, and he stays there—"

Paz made a gesture of impatience. "What is the difference who stays where? She stays with us. I thought it was because she was finally home again, but now, who knows? And for how long? I hate this!"

"What is it you expected anyway? She never denied he was her husband, did she?" Rick was surprised to hear his own voice sound so reasonable. "What is it that has you so upset?" He wondered the same about himself.

"I do not know." Paz gave him one of those sullen-what-do-you-want-from-me shrugs known best to thirteen-year-old boys around the world. "I just did not want him back here."

"You never said anything about him before."

"Well, you cannot exactly go around this town saying you hate your brother-in-law even if it is true. My father would not like it." He gave a little shudder. "I do not like to admit he is my anything. He and my father, they are old friends. My father likes him, but that does not mean I have to."

"What do you dislike about him so much?" Rick found the conversation distasteful but irresistible.

"I do not know really. He is just old, much too old for her. An old fat, rich man. It is like he stole her when she was sick before. Do you know about that?"

Rick nodded.

"It is like he is the one who stole her away from us."

They stood in morose silence. A shadow passed as someone walked across the open end of the alley, and Rick realized he did not want to try to explain why they were back there. He looked once again at the white plastic buckets. *Manteca*, they read in large green letters. Lard.

"What were you going to show me earlier?" He asked as he headed out of their hiding place. "You were pretty happy about something."

"Oh, that." Paz's pace was not what it had been, but he led the way to the fishermen's beach, stopping at Miguel's door. "*Ya nos vamos.*" He called inside as he scooped up a plastic jug of drinking water and a fat dish towel bundle that Rick recognized as having come from Emelina's restaurant.

Paz placed the items high up on the bow of their *cayuco*, away from the dampness of the floor. No explanations were forthcoming, so Rick simply followed Paz as they launched their craft, hopping in as it released its grip on the sandy shore.

There was no fishing equipment in the canoe this day, only an anchor. Paz, as always in the bow, pointed the way, not toward the open sea, but toward the mysterious *mangle*, the mangrove swamps on a calm afternoon's high tide.

They rode along quietly for some time. Rick guided the boat through the twisting turns of the wide smooth river. He watched the landscape change, from trees with open land and huts beneath to close-packed mangrove trees, their long finger-like roots clutching, almost obscuring the banks. The heavy aroma of mud, made thick with wet, rotting natural matter—fertile, exotic, saturating—hung in the still air. *A little Spanish moss*, Rick thought, *and I'd feel just like I was in the Louisiana bayou.*

The surrounding forest and undergrowth looked impenetrable. It was as if they were the first to ever have come this way. Rick slowed the engine to a virtual crawl, allowing himself more time to look around.

"This is the easiest time to come." Paz finally spoke. "Before the tide change when the water is high. It is like the pictures I have seen of your rivers, no? Wide and flat."

"Sort of," Rick smiled. "So who comes here, Paz? It looks so, so—untouched."

"Those who dig for clams and some who look for crabs." Paz leaned back and begin to loosen the knot on Emelina's dishtowel. He handed Rick a large fresh tortilla from the middle of the stack. It was still warm. "Sometimes, the girls and women looking for firewood but not too many really. The fish do not come here. My uncle says they do not like to be pulled by the changing of the waters at the tides. They prefer down below, closer to the ocean."

Maybe they don't like the brackish water, either, Rick thought as the water here, fed by the land drainage and smaller tributaries above, was fresh as much as salt, a deep velvety green, rather than the blue-green of the sea.

"The only others who come here are the shrimp," Paz continued, leaning back lazily in the bow, dangling thin strips of torn tortilla into his mouth. "Gilberto can tell you. He is very skilled with the little *attarraya*, the hand net, you know. And he comes at certain times and catches many shrimp with it. Of course, this is a dangerous business."

"Catching shrimp?"

"No, selling them afterward. It is illegal. Shrimp is a business protected by the government. Everybody knows that. If you catch them on your own and eat them, that is one thing, but if you sell them, you can get into trouble. Of course, they are worth more to sell than to eat, so—people do it all the time. But it is risky. Gilberto's cousin, he died from it."

"They killed someone for selling shrimp?" Rick was aghast. His raised voice echoed eerily off the encircling trees.

"He was into it in a bigger way. Remember when I told you how the shrimp boats signal to people at night with their lights? Gilberto's cousin Mauricio was one who would go out in a *cayuco* and pull up beside the shrimp boat *en secreto* in the dark. Then someone on board would make like he was dumping a bucket load of shrimp heads over the side, but they would really have a load of good shrimp, with just some heads on top. They lower it to the ones below where they take the shrimp and send up the money and then disappear quietly. Gilberto says his cousin made a great deal of money that way. One night when Mauricio went out with another friend, the shrimp boat turned and ran over their *cayuco*. They never found Mauricio, but they found his friend the next day. He spent the night in the ocean, holding onto a piece of the boat. He was pretty crazy by then and nearly dead. He said Mauricio drowned, but we never found him. They put the other man in jail after he got out of the hospital. It is a dangerous business."

The macabre story told here in the swamps gave Rick goose flesh. "I'm sure I'll think of this the next time I order shrimp somewhere."

Paz laughed in delight and passed along another tortilla. Those produced by Emelina's griddle were huge and round, heavier yet similar to plate-sized country flapjacks. The tortillas Rick had encountered in San Salvador were much smaller, thick creations that nearly broke when folded in half. These could be wrapped around an entire meal of rice, beans, a little cheese, pork, or fish, and often were.

Around the next bend, a great *ceiba* tree loomed large on the far bank, like a tropical oak, the top of it covered with delicate long-necked pink birds. Rick instantly cut the engine, feeling like some sort of obscene intruder in this ethereal tropical marshland. He wondered if they were flamingos, the only pink birds he could think of, but the birds' familiar long legs were nowhere to be seen. As they drifted closer, he decided he was mistaken. They were white, their feathers tinged with the color of the setting sun. Neither he nor Paz spoke a word as the boat coasted soundlessly under the spreading arms of the roosting tree. When the first one lifted its great wings, all the rest followed at once, in an alarmed explosive flight.

"Aren't they beautiful?" Rick exclaimed as they passed overhead. "What are they?"

One single pink feather floated down to Rick's outstretched hand as the birds disappeared from sight. His first impression had not been wrong.

"I do not know." Paz watched in amazement. "In all the times I have been up here I have never seen anything like them. But then, that is the way it is in the *mangle*. Always different than the time before."

As the sun slipped lower in the sky, the lengthening shadows seemed both sheltering and ominous, as if they could almost shut out the rest of the world. A kingfisher swept past them, and Rick tried to imagine the terror that might have seized a young girl, abandoned here overnight.

"It is time to go." Paz signaled to Rick to turn the boat around. "The tide will soon be headed out and—" He turned back with a grin. "It will soon be dark."

"I don't think I'd want to be here at night," Rick commented as he set a new course for them.

"No?" Paz feigned surprise. "You do not want to watch the owls swoop down, and other things jump from tree to tree?" He snatched at empty air in his imitation of an owl attacking its prey.

"No, thanks," Rick replied. "You were right, though. It is a beautiful place. I see now why you and Gilberto like to come here. I'm glad you brought me, too."

Paz leaned back with a smile of satisfaction.

* * * * *

Rick made dinner for the two of them that evening in his cabin, a special treat for Paz who made it clear he was in no hurry to go home and face Mariana and Carlos. After placing two different-sized pots of water on his tiny stove—one for rice and one for the two fresh lobsters they had bought in town after their trip to the *mangle*—Rick stepped outside to see what was keeping Paz so busy.

"What are you doing with those?" He was more surprised than disgusted, but Rick realized after he spoke, it did not sound that way.

"You know what these are?"

"Yes, I know." Rick nodded.

"But you do not know what to do with them?"

"They have only two uses in my country. You can break them up and put them in the garden to make the tomatoes and flowers grow better, or in some places, they have contests to see how far you can throw them."

"Really? I never thought of that." Paz dropped the stack of dried cow chips outside Rick's door and tossed one as far as he could toward the beach. He shrugged. "It is all right, but I think I like throwing a *beísbol* better." He busied himself, arranging several of the others in a tidy pyramid, pausing only to slap at an occasional mosquito.

"You are not making a cow patty campfire out here?" Rick's lack of enthusiasm left Paz unfazed.

"It will not smell. Wait and see. They are very dry. This kind of fire makes a lot of smoke, but it is not bad, and it keeps the mosquitoes away."

Rick learned something new about pest control that night, as they enjoyed their lobsters and rice in a nearly-mosquito free cabin.

"That works surprisingly well," Rick acknowledged as they finished. "Will you be all right, walking home in the dark, or do you want to stay here tonight?"

Paz grinned. "I would love to stay here, but it has nothing to do with the dark. I did not tell my father that I was staying the night, so I will walk down the beach in only a few minutes."

"I know. Want some more rice?"

"*No, ya no.* Too much food now. You like lobster, yes? You eat it in the United States, too?"

"No, hardly ever," Rick chuckled. "In a restaurant in the US, the dinner we just ate would cost ten times what it cost us tonight."

Paz's eyes widened in surprise. "Why so much?"

"It really is very funny. Here, you can buy lobster, stone crabs, oysters, red snapper, even black-market shrimp for much less than they cost in the US but—" He hesitated, "nowhere in this town can you buy meat."

"Sure you can." Paz countered. "There is Niña Alicia. She comes once a week with her bucket of meat. She will even come right to your house."

"Oh, yes, Niña Alicia," Rick repeated, remembering a day when he was at Julio's house, his next-door neighbor, when Alicia arrived. She carried in a large plastic bucket, the size of a large laundry basket balanced on her head, and lowered it onto Julio's table. It appeared to be filled with banana leaves, but as she began to unfold them, Rick was able to see there were pieces of raw meat—beef, pork, and even liver, wrapped up inside each bundle. As he watched in fascinated horror, Alicia and Juana, Julio's daughter, unwrapped bundle after bundle which they handled, flipped, and examined with their bare hands. After much debate and bargaining, Juana chose a pound of raw liver and paid for her purchase. Alicia expertly re-folded her wares, hefted the heavy load back on her head, and proceeded on to the next house. At that point, Rick made a mental note, no meat available for sale in *Las Palomitas*.

"So I will see you tomorrow?" Paz asked as he stopped at the door. "We will go fishing?"

"Sure, probably. Tomorrow afternoon. After you finish with classes."

"Classes, school." Paz let his shoulders droop.

"It'll be all right," Rick added as an amused look came across his face. "Honest! School is not fatal."

"Sometimes, that is hard to believe." Paz stepped outside. "*Buenas noches*, don Ricardo."

"*Buenas noches*, Paz," he called back.

The boy sauntered down the silvered beach, lit in pale moonlight. Rick stepped outside to watch him go, envying his innocence. He tossed the last cow

chip on the smoldering heap and enjoyed a final
cup of coffee as his dessert, watching the moon sail
higher into the black velvet night.

He had rarely felt so satisfied—good food, good
friends, good weather. For the moment, there
seemed to be little more that he could ask for. It was
not, however, his current situation that continued to
nag at the back of his mind. It was that ever-present
trepidation, the future that refused to grant him any
prolonged serenity, despite his yearning search.

Chapter 7

*M*onday, November 5, 1979 – Yesterday, Monsignor Oscar A. Romero of El Salvador, the country's archbishop, denounced the American offer of military aid from the pulpit during his regular Sunday homily. He urged the US to limit its military assistance to purification of the security forces, and true resolution of the problem of the disappeared as well as punishment for those responsible. Supplies to Salvadoran security forces such as those promised by the US government "will mean more confident repression of the people," the Archbishop warned.

It had been a strange week. True to his word, Carlos has only remained in town overnight. As fast as he was gone, it was as if he had never come. No one spoke of his visit, and Rick found he was content to leave it at that. He and David continued to spar verbally on occasion, but mostly, they avoided one another, except in public. It was not a good situation, but not one Rick felt inclined to do anything about, at least not for the moment.

School had been dismissed in time for the November holidays. *Día de los Muertos*, known as Day of the Dead, November 2, and *Día del Primer Grito de Independencia* on November 5—holidays observed throughout the whole country. Having grown up around his mother's church, Rick found he understood a great deal about the first, although it was observed here much differently than he was accustomed to, but the second was a more difficult concept.

Paz was convinced he was explaining it easily enough, however. "It is the day of the first shout of independence, the war that freed all of Central America from Spain."

"I understand that part," Rick responded. "But why is Independence Day in September? September 15, right?"

"Sure. But that was years later."

"Years later, after the first shout?"

"*Sí, como no*. The first shout came, but that did not make the war. The war did not start until years later. The first shout came during one of the *manifestaciones*, a demonstration that was put down by the army. They did not get around to the war for independence until a few years later." He frowned. "How is it in the United States? You celebrate on July 4th, yes? That is what we study."

"That's correct. When they signed the Declaration of Independence, but the war came right afterward."

Paz persisted. "But it lasted a long time, like many years, this war?"

"Well, yes. I think so."

"And do you not celebrate the last day of that war, like the day England said, 'We give up. You can have your own country if you want?'"

Rick chuckled at the simple description. "Well, come to think of it, I guess we don't. I don't even know what day that is."

"You should know these things. Do you not study your history? That is one thing I really like at school. It is important to know what came before, to be able to make sense of what is happening now."

Rick leaned back in the canoe that afternoon, fishing line in hand, and contemplated his young friend with new respect. "I did not know you were such a history scholar."

Paz shrugged, slightly embarrassed at the realization that his reputation as a mediocre student was in jeopardy. "I just like the history of every place. It is like reading a storybook except that it is real. And it helps me to better understand why things are the way they are now."

"Don't apologize for that. It is a good thing. God knows the world needs more people who understand how the world got to be the way it is and what we should be doing about it."

Rick fell silent, his thoughts flying back to an afternoon on the fishermen's beach, the day he met Franco. It was the echo of Mariana's words that came to mind now. "Men like him should be scholars... someone who is leading the rest of us to a better life." It seems the same could be said of her own brother.

Thinking of her in any way sent his thoughts skittering down a half dozen different paths. One day she appeared to emulate Franco's contempt for him as... what? A beach bum? An educated fool who knew little of the real world? And the next, they could share a bite of food and a pleasant conversation, and it was as she had told the lieutenant that day, they were friends. The problem was it kept changing, day by day. While Paz gave him a history lesson, it was Mariana who taught him about the true meaning of devotion, even after death.

Early the next morning, Rick saw her walking past his hut and the pine trees, headed away from the village, carrying a large bundle of flowers in a string sack of what looked to be wire, twine, rolled newspapers, and other assorted supplies. Crafts like in Sunday school were all that came to his mind, but that made no sense out here. Without an invitation, he fell in beside her, curious about her destination.

"You do not know what today is?" She responded in Spanish.

"Uh, let me think. It's Friday. I know that much. Date? Well, I won't claim to be too good with those these days. It's about two days past Halloween so it must be—"

"Halloween?"

"Yeah, Halloween. I know you don't celebrate it here. I tried to explain it to Paz the other day. That was very funny. I'm sure he thinks I made it all up. He couldn't quite get the idea. I think it had some original religious significance, but I couldn't remember what it was, and that made the explanation more difficult. It didn't come out so well."

"It is the day before All Saints Day, November 1." She proceeded to explain. "The last chance for evil spirits to run about freely and do bad things just before the day of the saints and so many prayers. Evil cannot stand so much of a chance after that."

"You know about it." He was surprised, which only added to her amusement.

"Of course, I know Halloween. I told you I lived in the United States. They do not celebrate it here, although it is coming more to the capital now. I really do not understand what it has become in either place, all that candy and dressing up. But you asked me about today, no?"

"Well, if today is the day after that, that makes it November 2, but that doesn't help me much."

"Today is *el Día de los Muertos*, Day of the Dead. You probably hear about it in Mexico where it is a big celebration but very different than here. Did you not see the bus when it came in today?"

"No," he answered slowly, not following the conversation very well. "Day of the Dead and the bus?"

He took a couple of quick steps to catch up to her. Despite the fact that his legs were longer, her pace was brisk, and he tended to slow down as he concentrated on the Spanish conversation.

Noting his difficulties, she switched to English, but her steps never slowed. "The bus was full of flowers this morning as well as people. It is the day people go to decorate the graves of those they love, to honor them. Something like your Memorial Day, only that is more military. This is more of the church."

"So how far are you going? A better question, where are you going?"

"The cemetery here is a little further yet, where the land is more solid and the water is not so close."

"The sea?"

"No, the water under the ground." She sounded impatient. "You cannot dig graves when there is water just a few feet below the surface."

He had never given it much thought. He knew that digging wells was not a problem locally, although the water was slightly salinized and not drinkable. People used the local wells for washing and laundry only. A few people bought their drinking water as he did at the store in bottles, but most hauled it from the other side of the estuary by *cayuco*. He had not thought about the difficulties raised by a high water table when it came to burying the dead.

"Can I help you carry some of what you have there?"

"No, I can manage."

"Do you mind if I come along?"

"I suppose it does not make much difference because we are here." Her tone was warmer than her words. As they rounded a curve in the road, she turned off onto a rocky trail barely wide enough for a small vehicle and climbed a short distance to a large green meadow that set up just about the level of the road.

A white hand-woven wire fence surrounded the ornately decorated graves that dotted the lush green field before them. As she stopped, Rick stepped forward to open the gate and lift the sack from her arm. Still, she hesitated, and then he noticed the paleness of her face and reached out again, this time to catch her as she nearly fainted. Beads of perspiration stood out on her brow despite the cool ocean breeze that he had found cooler than usual this particular morning.

He eased her down to sit on the sweet thick grass as still, she leaned heavily against him. "I am all right," she protested despite all physical evidence to the contrary.

"Oh, I don't think so." Rick laughed at her stubbornness in spite of what he feared might be a serious situation. "Maybe you should have let me carry something after all."

"No, it is not that. It is just—" She pulled both her fists to her chest and pressed them tightly against her as she struggled to catch her breath.

"It's just what?" His concern was growing. "Who are the flowers for today, anyway? Is that what's upset you?"

She smiled in surprised relief as at an unexpected gift. "After so much time, you would not think that would be a problem." Her voice sounded far off, yet stronger. "I will be all right if I can sit here for a few minutes. It really is what I came to do anyway, sit and put flowers together for my mother's grave. I also brought flowers for Angelica and Cristina, since no one else in the family will."

"They are all buried here?"

"Yes, my mother and Franco's mother and little sister."

Rick hesitated, aware he was treading on perilous ground. "They are the ones he spoke of that other night, at your house, just before he left? I've wondered and wanted to ask but—"

"It is all right." Her voice was still unnaturally light.

"Can I get you something, some water to drink?" He interrupted and looked around helplessly as he realized there were no nearby houses, no *tiendas*.

"No, really. I will be fine if I can just rest and talk freely about them." She looked over her shoulder at the brightly flowered wooden crosses and other tiny memorials.

Rick took her at her word. The color was returning to her face. As he glanced around, he realized there were no buildings of any kind in sight, an uncommon occurrence in El Salvador, a country with ten times the population density of his own country. The road ran below them, just barely out of sight, and from where they sat, one could look out to sea, just as he could from his own cabin.

It would have been the perfect location for a house with a gorgeous view, he found himself thinking. But as she spoke, he appreciated it was equally well-suited to what it had become, a place for those with broken hearts to come and contemplate in solitude, surrounded only by their memories.

"*Mi mamá* is there." She pointed to a weather-worn board with the name and dates cut deep into it. "My father used to be a sort of woodcarver, and he cut and trimmed the marker for her grave himself. I remember watching him do it," she sighed. "I was nine years old. When he finished, he put the carving tools in a box and put them on a high shelf in the store. I do not think he has ever touched them again since that day. It took away all of the *gusto* in the wood for him after that."

"I can appreciate that," Rick replied, lowering his voice as if afraid he might wake the sleeping spirits nearby. "How did your mother die?"

"Oh, like many here who die of one sickness or another," she shrugged. "She died of many things. She was never a strong woman, physically. My father said she was like a little bird, always too thin, very pretty to look at, very sweet to listen to, but no great strength, just the opposite of her sister, Emelina, yes? It took her a long time to recover after Paz was born, and the truth is, maybe she never really did. I remember vaguely when he was born, and after that, she never was out of bed much. I helped around the house as much as I could, but then she got malaria, and after that, it was just too much."

She was quiet for a moment. "Mostly, I remember how much I missed her love. She was a person who loved a great deal, and as a child, it was very difficult to live without that, once she was gone. Emelina helped as much as she could afterward, but it was not the same. Imanuel changed, too, after she was gone. He certainly became more loving toward his children, thinking, I suppose that we would need that since we had no mother. Or maybe we gave him a place to spend all the love he had inside, once his beloved 'Lupe was gone."

"Lupe?"

"My mother was Ana Guadalupe, but he always called her just 'Lupe. It took me a long time to realize that even after someone you love is gone, the love is not. It goes on forever."

She pulled the newspapers out of her string bag and began to shape them, wrapping them with the wire, into a large ring. Rick watched as she selected the flowers and gently tied each one in place. He stretched out on the grass beside her. Except for an occasional glance over his shoulder, he found it difficult to remember exactly where he was. The air was soft, the sun warm but not hot, and the sea breeze was just enough to blow her hair gently into her face from time to time.

He thought about the fact that he would never consider doing this sort of thing in a cemetery at home. They were, after all, places of cold gray and pink stones, a duty to be attended to, a brief visit to be made, and a place to flee from as quickly as possible.

She continued on a more somber note. "The tragic ones here, the ones who drive men to fight against their own, either with the rebels or the army, are the ones like Angelica and Cristina. It is one thing, if those you love die of disease or an accident, but it is completely different when they are murdered. It leaves a burning anger in your soul, a fire that nothing seems to be able to put out."

"Is it what happened to Franco?"

"I think so, as much as anything else. He was always headstrong and difficult. He was often angry at the many injustices he saw and our own inability to do anything about it, but I am not sure he would have done what he did if they had not murdered his mother and his sister.

"They went to visit a cousin of his mother in another village a couple of years ago. No one knows for sure what happened, but sometime after Angelica and Cristina arrived, the army came in and killed his mother. They shot them all, and then they burned the village to the ground. I was not here then, but as I understand it, Franco was one of the first ones to go there, once the story was out. He had to sneak in because the army also blocked the roads in. He found his mother and his sister, who was only ten years old and shot in the back. They were behind where the cousin's house had been. He also found the cousin. She was six months pregnant. He secretly buried the cousin there but brought his mother and his sister back here. And then Paz and Imanuel say, after that, he just left for the hills to join *los muchachos*. After what he had been through, I cannot be angry with him for that."

"I guess not." Rick shook his head in wonder at man's inhumanity to man and woman. He could think of nothing to say under the circumstances. He climbed to his feet to take a closer look at the graves in question. One for the mother and a smaller one for the child.

"Miguel is the one who I really feel the deepest sadness for," she added. "Imagine having your whole family one day, and within a very short time, your wife and your daughter are dead, and your son leaves you and your way of life forever."

"Still," Rick countered, "he seems to be doing okay now, yes? What are these?" He reached down and picked up a tiny clay dish of corn. There were two, one each in front of the wooden crosses, marking Angelica and Cristina's graves. He carried one back to where Mariana still sat.

"*Por Díos*," she whispered, shaking her head. "It looks as if Franco was here, maybe during the night."

"He left corn at their graves?" Rick was puzzled.

"It is an old Indian custom. Sometimes the Indian beliefs and the Catholic ones get a little mixed together here. You have studied the Egyptians, no? They buried their dead with many things and foods for use in the journey to the next life. Well, the Indians offered food for the use of the spirits of the dead. It is a token of respect, something simple, but it means these persons are not forgotten, and the one who left it here still believes in some of the old ways. The question is who left it—Franco or Miguel?"

"Which do you think?"

"It is hard to know. They do not say much, either of them. I do not think *mi tio* even lets Franco into his house now, but then, things were not great between them even when we were little. Franco would never listen, so Miguel would just yell louder." She laughed at the memory as she shuddered a bit. "Very different than our house."

With two wreaths formed, the newspapers completely covered with the flowers now, and the remaining flowers pulled into a small but lovely bouquet, she stood up slowly. Rick leaped to her side.

"I am fine now," she announced proudly. "This part," she stooped to pick up the wreaths and flowers, "I need to do alone."

Rick stepped aside, quickly replaced the corn offering, and uncertain of how much privacy was needed, threw his long legs over the makeshift fence. He stood close to where they had entered, looking out to sea.

At the moment, however, he found the scene behind him much more captivating than the view of the ocean. He watched her place the flowers, kneel, pray and cross herself three times in succession. He made certain that he was out of her sight when she turned back to gather the leftover papers and flowers into her bag.

They walked along the road, saying little. For the first time, he found himself comfortable in her presence, with no spoken words. Judging by the look on her face, Rick decided that her thoughts, as well as her heart, still lay in the meadow behind them, overlooking the sea. He watched his sandals make tiny clouds appear on the dusty road with each step and reflected on the difference a few short weeks can make, remembering the river that this road had become during the last of the heavy seasonal rains.

"Would you like to come in?" He dared to ask as they neared his cabin. "It is not much as houses go, but I promise to leave the door open."

She smiled in appreciation, although the smile did not quite reach her eyes, he noticed. "For a few moments," she nodded. "I cannot stay as Imanuel will be expecting me to work in the store."

Rick nodded. She seated herself at the small table. Rick was thankful he had talked Julio into selling him a couple of extra coconuts, thinking he and Paz would enjoy them one day after fishing. He pulled two from beneath the table that held his kitchen and wondered if he would be able to top them without amputating a finger, with her watching. He glanced in her direction and was delighted to see she was busy studying the rest of the cabin, paying scant attention to his efforts. She spied the collection of paperback books he had borrowed from David's house.

"Would you lend me one or two of these?" She asked as she walked over to the tiny makeshift bookshelf while he swiftly and almost expertly cut off the coconut stems.

"Sure." He handed her one of the *cocos* in triumph as he slipped a paper straw into the now open top.

"*Muchas gracias*." She took a long deep drink of the natural cooler. "You do that rather well."

Rick tried not to look as pleased as he felt.

She picked up two of the books. "I do not have many books and reading practice in English, it is good, yes?"

Rick nodded. 'You can borrow any of these you like."

She chose two. "I am also glad to get the chance to practice my English with you and sometimes, with David, although I do not see too much of him. Where is he?"

"Well," Rick wondered how evasive he could be without arousing her suspicion. "I don't see much of him myself. He's just sort of around, working with his agency, you know."

"And which agency would that be?" she asked, still perusing the back of one of the paperbacks. "The one which sent him here or the local brothel? Are you two fighting, as Paz says?

"Sorry," she responded with a giggle at his startled expression. "It is a small village and forget *fútbol* or soccer as you call it or even *beísbol*. Gossip is truly the number one sport here."

He grinned in response. "I'm not sure you'd call it fighting. We just see things differently."

"What things?"

Lord, I'm going to remember this, the next time I hesitate to ask her a personal question, he thought but left the sentiment unspoken. She certainly doesn't hold back when she wants to know something.

"Things, things, all kinds of things, everything really. We just have different views of the world, I guess."

"You mean, the fact that he spends his days with beer and prostitutes, and you fish with the locals and help the church catechist in his work on a regular basis?"

His head jerked around as she now had his full attention.

"Like I said, it is a small village, Rishard." She pronounced his name in that funny way of hers again. He rather liked it. "Everybody talks. They say that don David came here to work, and he plays all day, but that don Ricardo came here to rest, and he works. Of course, I guess that depends on if you consider fishing work. Here, for most, it is a living, so that makes it work. I gather in the United States, fishing is seen more as sport, so it is play, yes?"

"Yes, I mean, no. I mean—" Hell, he hated it when she made him feel like such an idiot. He took a drink of the coconut and tried again. "Yes, most Americans consider fishing to be a form of relaxation, except professional fishermen, I imagine, but in the US, they are mostly in big boats like the shrimp boats. But no, I don't know what to tell you about David. If you know how it is with him, why do you ask me?"

"Oh, I never said that I know. I only repeat what I hear in the store. It is fine. Do not worry. It is not important. I really must go. Thank you for the *coco* and the company today. It was good to practice my English."

She disappeared out the door before Rick had a chance to say another word. He stepped to the bookcase to see which books she had taken with her. Only two were missing, Boris Pasternak's *Doctor Zhivago* and Harold Bell Wright's *The Shepherd of the Hills*. What a stretch, he thought, from Moscow to the Ozarks. He shook his head with a slight smile. I hope she doesn't try to read them simultaneously.

* * * * *

It was still early in the day, and after a few housekeeping chores, Rick also headed to the village. He had noticed more traffic than usual on the road, and he found *Las Palomitas* surprisingly crowded with what were apparently out of town tourists from the cities of San Salvador and San Miguel. Holidays, Rick remembered, people off work.

Near the bus stop tree, as he thought of it, a couple of soldiers lounged in the shade as they watched the comings and goings. Rick recognized Alfredo from the Jeep ride they had shared. The tourists were easy to spot. Both the men and women wore beach clothes—the men with their paler-than-everything-else legs sticking out of their shorts and the women in bathing suits and stylish cover-ups or fashionable shorts sets. It occurred to Rick for the first time that he had never seen a village girl or woman in a pair of shorts. The visitors ambled about buying fish and other seafood from the locals. At the restaurant, a man from the city was arguing loudly with Emelina, who looked more embarrassed than angry, as Rick walked in.

"*Buenos días*, Niña Emelina," Rick greeted her, hoping to give her the break she needed.

The stranger gave Rick a perplexed look. "You are an American?" he asked in accented English.

"Yes," Rick answered without elaboration.

"And you are staying here? How do you stand it, dealing with these people every day?"

"Excuse me?" Rick raised an eyebrow. Emelina slipped unnoticed back into the kitchen.

"They try to cheat us because they think we do not know what they are doing. They are the ones who are stupid. This Indian, arguing with me about the price of the oysters we just ate here."

"You ate oysters here?" Rick was surprised.

"Yes, we ate a full meal, with tortillas, cooked pork, and rice, but my son and I also wanted oysters, so we told her to get us some. And then, she tries to overcharge me. Right over there, we can see the sign from here." He pointed across the way to Marielos' café. "Oysters it says, and there is the price. And we saw her go over there to get them. Now everybody knows she gets a good price from her friend across the road, but still, she thinks she can overcharge us as if we are fools. And I simply told her I won't pay it."

"Let me get this right," Rick began. "You sent Emelina across to that place to get oysters from Marielos. How many?"

"Two dozen."

"And then she brought them back and served them to you and charged you... let's see, how much?"

The man told him.

"I guess what you don't understand is that first of all, Emelina and Marielos are not very good friends. I imagine Marielos charged her the full price for them as she would anyone else. Secondly, the price you see there is for the way Marielos prepares and serves them, half a dozen at a time. The *media* from *media docena*, or half dozen, is covered up by another sign. Do you see that?" He urged the man to take a step sideways.

Rick let him mull that over before continuing. "What I don't understand is, if you wanted to eat oysters, why don't you just walk over to Marielos' seafood bar in the first place?"

"You cannot be serious. It is out in the sun. You expect us to sit there, without any shade for my wife?" He indicated a diminutive auburn-haired woman with light skin, who had been sitting so quietly at one of Emelina's tables, Rick had not even noticed her.

"*Ay, dejalo.*" The man spat out the words and threw the disputed amount on the table. "*Vengase,*" he barked at the woman who bolted out of the door ahead of him.

"You should be careful." He left Rick with a final warning. "You stay here too long, and you'll begin to believe these people and their cheap lies. You'll start to believe they are like everybody else." With that, he huffed his way across the road to a shiny late model import car. Rick watched him go, thankful the man had spoken his last in English, minimizing the chances of causing more upset to anyone within hearing distance.

"*Muchas gracias*, don Ricardo." Emelina hustled out of the kitchen as the car churned up a small cloud of dust on its way out of town. "I tried to explain, but he would not listen. He just kept saying I was cheating him, but it was not true."

"I know. Don't worry about him." Rick tried to soothe her ruffled feelings. "You know how tourists are sometimes. They get away from home, and they just fuss and feel out of place and can't get anything right."

She laughed at that. "I am glad you came along when you did. You are not really a tourist anymore, you know. You are more like don David, like one of us, who lives here."

Out in the street, a new scuffle was underway. A local man, staggered drunkenly, calling out while two of his friends tried unsuccessfully to quiet him.

"I have seen them before, I tell you. They are the ones who pulled poor Chepe Perez from his bed, never to be seen again. *Dios mío*, we have to hide! They are dangerous people. Poor Chepe never did a thing to anyone in his life. It is not his fault that his crazy brother went off to join *los muchachos*."

The soldiers were now beginning to focus their attention on the man as well. "Get him out of here!" one of them yelled at his two *compañeros*. "We do not need any trouble in town today."

"*Sí, Señor,*" one answered back as best he could manage under the circumstances.

"Poor Chepe," the drunk began to cry. "He never hurt anybody. He was my best friend. Why did he have to die? He lives in Los Llanos in Morozan. You know where that is? We buried him after they cut out his tongue and cut off his—" One of his friends managed to get his hand over his mouth to cut off the drunken speech while they dragged him away. Others like Rick, who heard what was being said, traded nervous glances and anxious smiles, but most of the out-of-towners simply ignored the entire episode.

Imanuel came out of the store as the three men disappeared around the corner of the store building. "What is going on?" he asked.

"Somebody with too much to drink," Rick answered. "He didn't have very nice things to stay about the military, I'm afraid."

"It was Augustín Rivas," Emelina stated quietly.

"*Por Díos*." Imanuel let out the quiet exclamation. "He just came here from another village to stay with relatives, but I understand from what he has come to pray about in church that he has suffered through a great tragedy at their hands recently, as you say. I hope he did not say too much."

"Oh, surely it was just drunken chatter." Rick tried to sound hopeful. "Nothing anybody would take seriously."

He spent the rest of the afternoon helping Imanuel make deliveries to families along the point. "It is a good thing to give food and clothing to the living on the day of the dead, yes?" Imanuel observed in an almost jovial mood.

Rick found his perspective of the entire village changing as they were welcomed into one shanty after another. People with so little, yet willing to share the few scraps of food they could claim as their own with the two who brought them a blanket, some extra beans and rice, and a few items of clothing.

"*Pase adelante*," a weak voice called from inside as Imanuel called out at the door of their last stop. Three children, a boy and two little girls, played on the floor beneath the hammock where a thin, aged woman reclined.

"*Niño*," she called. The boy scrambled to his feet. Thin, barefoot, and wearing only a pair of colorless shorts, he looked to be about ten or twelve years old, Rick thought.

She slipped her hand into the pocket of her dress, handed him a few coins, and whispered something in his ear. He nodded in understanding and slipped out the door.

"Niña Ana, that is not necessary," Imanuel protested. "Please. We bring these things from the church."

"Church?" He made a snorting noise. "Some of it, maybe, but I know where these came from." A broad smile creased her narrow face, crinkling her thin skin into a thousand tiny wrinkles as she held up a child-sized pair of new rubber sandals, the kind Rick had seen hanging in the store.

Imanuel grinned and shrugged like a boy caught in mischief.

"And we thank you for it. I thank you from my heart." She laid a bony hand across her chest as she sat up in the hammock.

"*Por el amor de Díos*, don Imanuel. I do not know how we would have managed if it had not been for your kindness. Marielos works all day, and I watch over her daughters because, of course, you know their father is..." She made some vague motion in the air with her hand. "But I also have my grandson, Fabiano. He lives with me now, but he is Marielos's brother, not her child, and she cannot take care of him, too. He is fourteen now, a little older than your Pazito, yes? I sell *curas* still, but many others have no money. How can I charge them much of anything when I know they are in as much need as we are? Besides, the young people are losing faith in the old ways. Now the ones with a few *fichas* in their pocket." She rattled the coins in her dress pocket. "They only want what they can buy at the *farmacia*. I swear, don Imanuel, half of what they sell in that place is nothing but sugar and water and something to give it color. They sell it to those who are ignorant enough to believe it works. Now my *curas*, they come from the true plants and herbs. They work. You know that." She snorted again. "I guess Andres Parada knows that now, too, yes?"

"I imagine he does," Imanuel chuckled.

Rick's original impression had been of a weary old lady lying in a hammock, but as he listened, he realized there was still plenty of spirit left in this tiny, wizened woman. The boy returned with two cold bottled drinks, which he handed to Rick and Imanuel.

"This life is a puzzle, not easily understood by mortals like us, yes?" she continued.

Imanuel nodded sympathetically. "This life is sometimes very difficult to understand, it is true."

Ana sighed. "Don Imanuel, in my lifetime, I have been poor. I have been poor in the country and poor in the city and now in the country once again. We may be poor, but I have learned it is better to be poor in the country."

Imanuel gave her an encouraging look without interrupting the flow of her litany. "When you are poor in the country, there are always people of true faith and good heart, like yourself, who are willing to share. You can bathe at a neighbor's well, find fruit on a wild tree, even steal a little food now and then, if you have to, and no one seems to mind. In the city, there is only dirt and greed, and everyone trying to grab their share and little more besides. There is nowhere to bathe, you have to beg just for water to drink, and God help you if you steal anything, even to feed your babies. The police do not care what you stole or why you did it, only that you are, in their eyes, a thief and away you go to jail with all the other black-hearted thieves. It is definitely better to be poor in the country."

Imanuel smiled broadly and nodded.

"And besides, in the city—" There was more than a hint of mischief behind her eyes now. "There is no good place to grow my curing plants. Let me show you the newest ones." She led Imanuel to a shelf perched beneath the far window. "A lady who sells *curas* on the road to San Marcos told me this one could—" She continued, but Rick's attention was drawn to the children who were fascinated with the exotic foreign visitor in their midst. The girls had giggled as he ducked his head to enter their tiny house and now they seemed to be most amused at how long his legs were and the curly blond hair that covered them, as he sat cross-legged before them.

Rick motioned for them to come closer. The girls scooted across the floor, bringing the tiny rubber ball and metal jacks they had been playing with earlier. Their eyes widened in astonishment when Rick scooped up the ball and showed them he could play as well. Never had any village child seen a grown man stoop to play jacks before. The wide veranda on his grandparents' farmhouse where Amy taught him to play the game, despite his occasional protests, on many a rainy afternoon was a far cry from where he sat now. The basic rules of the game, however, remained unchanged.

While Rick played the girls' game, he learned their names, Isabel and Anita. He also tried to watch Fabiano from the corner of his eye, who, unlike the girls, had not come forward. The boy hung back in the shadows, seemingly keeping an eye on both Rick and Imanuel.

Imanuel downed the last swallow of his soft drink and set the bottle down firmly, marking the end to the visit. Rick gulped his quickly, remembering one of the few cultural lessons David had given him shortly after his arrival in the country.

"It's a real insult to refuse anything offered to you in someone's home. Sometimes it's tough, and you've got to be quick to keep 'em from giving you stuff made with water or ice since God only knows where it came from. If they give you something to eat or drink, you better eat it, and that means all of it."

As he got close to the end of the bottle, however, Rick could not help but notice the small eyes fastened on him. He offered it to the girls, and they gave a furtive look in their grandmother's direction, noting she was still in conversation with Imanuel. Isabel and Anita accepted and dispatched the last of it with wide grins to their co-conspirator.

Rick and Imanuel walked on, leaving one last delivery inside the unlocked door of an empty hut. As Imanuel put down an armful of used clothing, a T-shirt fell from the pile. Rick picked it up and was amused to notice three identical triangles across the front of it.

"Where do you get this stuff?" he asked.

"From the church relief services," Imanuel replied casually, without looking up. "Much of it comes from your country, I think. Why?"

"Oh, just curious. I recognized a college club's trademark, I guess you would call it. It just made me wonder." Somewhere a former Tri-Delta sorority member is missing a shirt, Rick chuckled to himself.

Later that evening, they were back at a table in Emelina's restaurant. The tourists had all scampered back to their respective cities, and the only commotion came from an occasional peal of laughter and the loud music of the jukebox from the only business still open at this hour, the house on the beach.

Emelina fried some special seven-to-the-pound shrimp she had managed to finagle from one of the shrimp boats. "These are deep water shrimp," she announced with pride as she set what looked to be small lobsters before Rick. "You cannot catch these out in the *estero* with an *atarraya*," she added with a wink.

"All I know," Rick told Paz as he speared one of the tender morsels with his fork, "is that seafood doesn't get any fresher than this."

After dinner, Paz pulled out his deck of cards and kept Rick busy playing *casino*, a local game vaguely akin to blackjack.

"Mariana says you went with her to the cemetery today," Paz commented. "I asked her after I saw the flowers."

"You were there today?"

"Yes, I went with my father in the morning. We usually go, although no one has truly decorated the graves in a long time. It was really nice to see that again."

"And did you see the corn there?" Rick asked. "Do you know who brought that?"

"Oh, probably my cousin. I think that is the sort of thing he would do."

Imanuel joined them after he closed the store and even shared in the card game for a short time. Emelina closed down her kitchen and left them with instructions to turn out the lights as they left. It was an enjoyable quiet evening. Not wanting it to end, Rick stayed later than he had intended.

Watching the door of the brothel, Rick had hoped to catch sight of David on his way out, but he had seen no one leave. Walking home alone in the dark without a light of any kind at such an hour was not high on his list of favorite activities.

As he walked as quickly as the dark would allow, he found himself wishing he had asked Imanuel to lend him a flashlight for the evening. Footsteps were all but silent on the soft sandy surface of the road. Still, Rick had the feeling that someone was close by. When he whirled around to check, however, he came face to face with only more inky blackness and a feeling of overwhelming foolishness.

He looked down the side road that led to David's house and saw no lights. Rather than continue on, he decided to turn in and take a quick bath at the well behind David's house.

Bathing, for the most part in this country, was done at wells or in the rivers, out in the open. Women wore their skirts or slips while they bathed, bare-chested, at a well during the late afternoon hours. But Rick had found with the cover of darkness, he could enjoy a hand-dipped shower the way bathing was meant to be done as far as he was concerned, in the nude. After dark, he could pour bowlfuls of water over himself, dipped from a larger tub beside the well, without disturbing any of the local conventions.

A thin sliver of moon moved from behind the clouds, putting out barely enough light to allow him to find the half-metal barrel that served as the top of the well without falling in. The bucket beside was already filled, saving him the trouble of drawing water and a *moro* shell, a bowl fashioned from a fruit husk, floated on top. He stripped and reached for the soap which David kept in a tiny string bag, hung on a nail by the door. The cool water was refreshing despite the light breeze. He had no towel, but his T-shirt served the purpose almost as well. As he slipped on his shoes, he heard a scuffling noise in the field and instinctively ducked down beside the well.

Most of the area villagers were already in bed by this hour, particularly those without electricity. Poor people could ill afford to spend money on such luxuries as lamp oil and candles when they could just as easily arise early and go to bed the same way, thus saving a few pennies each day.

Rick moved silently toward the disturbance. There were no houses out where the noises were coming from, only coconut palms and mango trees. Rick's first thoughts were of some sort of animals, fighting, but as he listened, voices were also a definitive part of the struggle.

"What do you know of these activities?" a gruff voice demanded.

There was no answer, simply scuffling noises as if something or someone was being dragged across the ground.

The question was repeated, and although a part of his brain was silently screaming about the danger, Rick, dressed only in his shorts and sandals, crept closer.

"What do you know of these activities?"

"I told you." The answer was barely audible as the speaker seemed to struggle to breathe. "I know nothing."

"We know you were involved in this business in Morozan. You may have gotten away with it there, but it is not going to happen here."

As Rick got closer, he could make out three figures standing around a tree. Two of them proceeded to beat on the tree while the other stood by and smoked a cigarette. It was not until the tree moved, or rather the man tied to the tree did so that Rick realized what was happening.

"You were a friend of Chepe Perez, were you not? Everyone heard you say so today. You must have known of his anti-government activities. We want to know who in this area is involved. We know you came here for a reason. We know there are others, like Perez, working in this region. All you have to do is name them, and then we will let you go. It is that simple."

"You are all dogs!" The tree spoke back, coughing out the words. "You will never let me go. How stupid do you think I am?"

He was silenced by a rifle butt to the mouth.,

Rick had seen enough. He retraced his steps, moving as quickly as he dared. My God, but what to do now? His heart was racing, and his legs felt weak as he scrambled as fast as he could. He fell hard more than once, but despite the jarring, he was thankful the road was covered more with sand than rocks.

He ran first to the brothel. David would know what to do. His eyes struggled to adjust to the lighting, which though low, seemed bright compared to the dark road. He found David, sitting at a table in the corner with several others, playing cards. He blundered into the table as much as sat down beside his cousin.

"David, you've got to come quick!" He tried to calm himself and speak in a rational manner, although what he had seen made it nearly impossible to do so. "There are men, up behind your house, beating some poor guy to death. I'm not sure what it's all about, but I really need your help."

"Hey, Cuz, you look like you've had a rough night." It was as if David had not heard a word he said. "How long have you been here? Wouldn't those girls in the back room give you back your shirt?" His speech was slurred worse than Rick had ever heard it before.

"David, did you hear what I said?" Rick raised his voice to be heard over the jukebox. Rick snatched the cards from his cousin's hand and threw them against the wall.

"Hey," David frowned and appeared to be thinking and moving in slow motion. "That was a good hand."

Rick looked directly into David's face. "My God, you're drunk!" he shouted in disgust as he realized he could expect no help from this quarter. "Somebody is getting killed in your back yard and—" Rick jumped to his feet and upended the table in front of him in angry frustration.

"Hey, take it easy. I heard you, but why do you want to get yourself mixed up in somebody else's squabble? It's probably just over one guy messing with another guy's woman. They do that all the time here. They won't like it much if you stick your nose in that."

Rick was out the door as David bent over to retrieve his playing cards. The only other source of help he could imagine was Imanuel, and yet, the truth was he could not conceive of a single thing the little church catechist would be able to do. Still, he could not simply go back to his own bed as if nothing had happened.

He knocked on the heavy wooden door of the store. It took several moments for someone to respond, but finally Imanuel called out to ask who it was and opened the door immediately upon hearing Rick's voice.

"Don Imanuel, *gracias a Díos*. I am so sorry to bother you, but I didn't know where else to go." He rushed inside and began to try to pull his decimated thoughts together in Spanish, at least, enough to make some small amount of sense.

Imanuel's eyes shot open wide, and then his brow took on the deep furrows of a troubled man.

"Come." He pulled on long pants over his shorts and slipped his feet into a pair of rubber sandals. He handed Rick a flashlight and followed him out of the door, still buttoning his shirt as they hurried up the road.

"What will we do when we get there?" Rick dared to ask.

"I really do not know." His friend answered honestly. "But I'm praying that by the time we reach the place, God will have an answer for us."

Rick asked nothing more.

Once past David's house, they crept in silence to the tree where Rick had seen the man tied and beaten, but now all was empty and quiet.

"They were right here, I swear." Rick's voice rose in frustrated desperation.

"I see." Imanuel took the flashlight and began to examine the ground around the tree.

"I know it sounds fantastic and that I was scared, but I don't think I heard wrong, don Imanuel. It sounds crazy in one way, but I'm sure I heard—"

"Calm down, my friend." Imanuel stood up straight from his examination of the dirt at his feet. "Look." He pointed to the ground. "Here is the blood of someone or something who was hurt. And here on the tree, it has been cut with something sharp and also maybe, scraped by something. I do not think you are crazy."

Rick relaxed a bit as his friend was speaking. "What I do not know is what we can do now. They have taken him away, and there is no way to know where or even who, for certain. Did you see well enough to tell if they were soldiers or civilians?"

Rick stopped short. "I don't know." He answered slowly. "I have no idea. I was so shocked by what I did see and hear. They had guns, and it was as if one was the boss, telling the others what to do. But I saw no faces, no uniforms, nothing that would identify anyone, except for what I heard. I think the man they were beating was the one who was drunk in town today."

"Augustín?"

"Yes, I think so."

"Wait—" Imanuel cast the flashlight over the ground once more.

"What is it?" Rick asked.

"May God be with him." Imanuel crossed himself. "Look here. Those are boot prints in the sand. Who wears boots at the beach, except soldiers? There is nothing more we can do tonight. Perhaps in the morning—" He stopped speaking, but Rick did not need to see his friend's face to comprehend the seriousness of the situation.

"Don Ricardo," Imanuel continued, his voice lowered to a point where Rick had to strain to hear what he said next. "Be very careful from now on. Tell no one else of what you have seen and heard here tonight. You have told me, and you know I will do what I can, but I know of what has happened in other places. We have been fortunate here, so far but you can see what happened to this man on the same night, he gets drunk and says too much in town. Please be very careful. Do you understand?"

Rick nodded in the dark as unexpected tears filled his eyes. He managed to utter a barely audible, "*Sí*, don Imanuel." He swallowed hard and asked once again. "Is there really nothing else we can do? There are no police? Nowhere else we can go for help?"

"I am sorry, my son." The older man's shoulders drooped visibly. "This is not like your country. Here, the police—the soldiers, it is all the same, and many times, they are the ones who are committing the crimes, not stopping them."

* * * * *

Rick finally fell asleep as he watched the first streaks of dawn burn their way across the sky. It seemed only a few moments later that Paz was shaking him by the shoulder. He was surprised to discover it was nearly noon.

"I thought we were going fishing this morning." Rick could not tell if he was asking or telling. "I waited for you, but—what happened to you?" Paz caught sight of Rick's dirty chest, face, and scrapes from the falls of the night before.

"Uh, nothing, really. I mean, I took a bath over at David's house last night, and it was dark, and I fell walking back. That's all."

"How many times?" Paz began to giggle. "Are you sure you took a bath at all? You look terrible." He shook his head, still grinning, not sure if he believed Rick's story or not.

"Well, an incredible thing happened in town this morning, and you've already missed it," Paz continued while poking about Rick's kitchen table, looking for a snack to munch. He found a small, locally packaged handful of nuts and opened the cellophane bag. "Gilberto and another boy went looking for *curriles*, the black clams early this morning in the *mangle*, and they found someone."

"Someone? Like someone else fishing or digging for clams?

"No." An expression of horror crossed Paz's face. "A dead man."

Rick, who was still lying on the cot, waking up slowly, was now completely attentive. "Who?"

"He was half-buried in the mud, like up to his waist, as if he had been walking or maybe digging for clams, too, but had stepped in the wrong place. There are pockets of sinking mud up there, the kind where if you step in, you cannot step back out. Mostly they are small, and you can usually pull yourself out easily, using the trees, but this man did not do that."

"Why? What do you mean? What is sinking mud? And why didn't this man get out?"

"Well, no one is sure." Paz frowned as he dropped himself into the hammock while still concentrating on the nuts in his hand. "Somebody said they saw him in town yesterday and he was drunk, so maybe that is why. If he wandered up there while he was too drunk, I suppose he could not pull himself out. One of his arms was broken, and he was really beat up, so they are thinking he went through the high tide. High tides, you know, if a body was stuck in the sinking mud and couldn't get out, it would get beat up by the debris that comes with the high tide that would hit against it. You know, the worst part would be, if he fell in and couldn't get out, he would have to watch the tide come in and get deeper and deeper and not be able to get out. I mean, he would know what was coming, little by little—"

Tangled in the sheet, Rick scrambled from the cot, nearly falling as he tumbled out the door, trying to make it to the sand before he vomited.

Paz followed him slowly, not aware until that moment that his friend wasn't feeling well but still more fascinated by the grisly tale than by his friend's condition.

"No wonder you are still in bed. They said don David got sick at the brothel last night, too, but I figure he just drank too much. He does that sometimes, but you don't. Did you go drinking with him last night? Someone said you were there." He finished the last of the nuts and threw the cellophane package on the sand. He looked at Rick, who was still on his knees, and remembered the lesson he had taught him as fast as he moved over to this side of the beach. Paz retrieved the scrap of paper and stuffed it in his pocket.

"I'm sorry you are sick. Can I get you something?"

"No," Rick croaked, as he rose to his feet.

Rick dropped himself onto a nearby tree stump but said nothing more for the moment.

"The only thing that is still so strange—" Paz's mind was still on the tragedy in the *mangle*, "is that Gilberto said that this man was not in sinking mud, so no one is quite sure what happened to him."

Rick leaned forward, his elbows on his knees, his head resting in his hands. "Paz, what does your father say about all of this?"

"Not much. He looked very serious, and he knew the man's name. He was not a tourist but more like a field worker from up north somewhere. Do you know something more about all of this?"

Rick looked hard at his young friend. "Maybe, maybe not. I'm really not sure, but I do want to ask you a favor, a very important one."

"*Sí, como no*," came Paz's instant response.

"No, don't agree until you know what it is," Rick cautioned. "It may not be so easy, but I think it is really important. Don't discuss this anymore with anyone. Will you promise me that? Not even with Gilberto. It may be nothing, and if that is the way it is, then you have lost nothing, just spread a little less gossip than usual. But if there is more here, if this man was somehow mixed up in something dangerous and then killed for it, then you may be protecting yourself and many others."

Paz eyed his friend, taking his measure anew.

"You are very much like my father. He said something very similar this morning. I do not always like or understand what he says, but when you both talk this way, so serious, it is almost frightening. I will do as you both ask. I will not speak of this man again."

CHAPTER 8

November 19, 1979, San Salvador – While the US government's answer to recent problems in El Salvador includes the sending of six military advisors to the troubled Central American republic, cracks appear to be developing in the new government's ruling junta as they struggle to determine how to best control the escalating violence that is gripping the country.

Current reports indicate that while some members of the government, labeled as leftists by one CIA source, argue that demonstrations from both the right and the left are a natural consequence of a society long repressed by right-wing dictators, others are not so tolerant.

Colonel Vides Casanova, commander of the National Guard, was credited with the following statement during a recent stormy session. "In 1932, the government killed 30,000 peasants to keep that government in place. Today, the armed forces are prepared to kill 200,000 or 300,000, if that is what it takes to prevent a Communist takeover."

Rick leaned back contentedly in the new hammock he had just tied between two palm trees outside the door of his hut and gazed at the sapphire sky of late morning. He had a cold Coke, a good book, and the rest of the day to call his own. The soft, ever-present cooing of the doves in the trees overhead added to the sweetness of the morning. Still, a slight frown tugged at his forehead. Life could be so good here, and yet there were nagging problems at the back of his mind, reminders that every place, no matter how beautiful, held its own kind of troubles.

He had been awakened early this morning before first light by what sounded like rifle fire. Maybe the troubles Franco and Imanuel had alluded to had finally come to *Las Palomitas*. He could not be sure, and somehow, not knowing made it worse.

They had gone fishing early, he and Paz, and they had brought in a hefty catch. It was one of those rare days when Paz had appeared more asleep than awake, as if he were simply going through the motions, and Rick had decided not to ask him about the dawn gunfire.

Paz had already hauled their catch to the fishermen's cooperative and promised to come by later to drop off Rick's portion of the earnings.

The sudden crack of small arms fire close at hand threw him face-first into the sandy soil. Paz's mischievous laughter followed immediately as Rick climbed slowly to his feet. "What the he—" He looked down at the spent firecrackers as he dusted sand off his bare chest and arms. "Wait until I get hold of you!" He recovered quickly as he started after the boy who darted away.

"It is *el Día de San Rafael*," Paz called over his shoulder, laughing. "Everyone celebrates today. I went fishing with you this morning, but I forgot that the cooperative would be closed today. They are busy dressing it all up for the big *fiesta* tonight."

Rick stopped. "So what did you do with the fish?"

"Oh, it is all right." Paz pulled a fistful of cash from his pocket and held it high over his head. "I sold them to some tourists instead and got much more."

"Come here," Rick called him. "Put that away. Didn't anybody ever teach you anything? Like don't wave your money around in public?"

Paz obeyed and came toward Rick to show him how they had nearly doubled their money. "Of course," Rick continued in a serious tone, despite the relief that was spreading over him. "The other thing someone should have taught you is never trust your friends after you throw firecrackers at them!"

He grabbed Paz and tossed him, kicking and screaming onto his shoulder and ran straight toward the open ocean. They tumbled into the surf together, although Rick was careful that neither Paz nor his pockets were turned upside down.

"*Loco! Chiflado!*" Paz continued to sputter as Rick danced about on the beach, hooting and pointing his finger at the dripping Paz. "The money is wet, too."

"It was worth it," Rick laughed. "Besides, it will dry and be as good as before. We used to get ours wet all the time at home, on canoeing trips."

"That is American money. Dollars. *Colones* are not made so well. This stuff might turn into toilet paper when it gets wet if you are not careful."

"Oh," Rick looked concerned. "I didn't know. Well, come on. Let's see what we can do."

Paz's dire predictions turned out to be unfounded. The money dried, hanging like tiny dingy dish towels on a short clothesline inside Rick's cabin.

"*Día de San Rafael*, heh?" Rick asked after they had settled down, Rick now in the outside hammock and Paz on a chair he had pulled from inside the cabin.

"*O sí*," Paz's initial enthusiasm returned. "He is the patron saint of fishermen, so of course, that makes for a great celebration here. Today, many will come for the parade in the afternoon, and they will pick a queen for tonight. Then even more will come for the *música* and the dancing. The boys in town will shoot off fireworks all through the day. It is a party all day long."

As if on cue, Paz's explanation was punctuated with the echoes of distant firecrackers. Rick wondered if they were rendering as much havoc as the ones he had so recently experienced.

"What did I tell you?"

"And what time did this celebrating start, with the fireworks, I mean?"

A sheepish grin brought a renewed wave of relief flooding over Rick.

"So you heard us early this morning, yes? Gilberto found a great bargain on fireworks yesterday, and we had already waited as long as we could. I tiptoed out of the house early today, and he and I were just making sure everyone knew it was a *día de fiesta*."

"I see." Rick kept his earlier misgivings to himself. "It sounds great. I'm surprised you agreed to go fishing this morning. You never said anything about it before."

"Oh, nobody does anything in the morning, except of course Emelina, who is already cooking for all the extra people who will be eating in town tonight. She makes the dinner for the *músicos*, the ones who will play tonight. I saw Marielos, who is also busy shelling oysters and *curriles*. Both of them will have a long day, but they will make a little money, too, no?" He chuckled to himself, and Rick asked to be let in on the joke.

"Even Candelario is working this morning. I saw him at the restaurant, and Emelina was bossing him around, making him move in extra tables and chairs. It was very funny. He was actually sweating."

"What's so funny about that?" The truth was Rick had never found anything about the skinny, sour-faced man to be the least bit humorous. Rick had assumed he just did not like foreigners as the man rarely spoke to him. As far as Rick could see, his long drooping mustache not only took over his whole face, it characterized his entire personality.

"Candelario never works." Paz was still laughing. "He is very lazy and passes his time, drinking and trying to figure out how to get out of work. He is don Carlos's *cuidandero*, the one who lives in the little house behind Carlos' big house and looks after it for him when he is gone. A number of people here do this kind of thing as an extra job. Candelario thinks it is his only job and is always walking around like—" Paz puffed out his chest and drew back his shoulders, in a caricature of the man living with his aunt.

"He thinks he is superior to everyone else, yes? Because he works for don Carlos. *Mi tía* must have caught him early today, to get him to work so hard. So, I think it is very funny."

"I think I'm glad I'm a friend of yours and not some poor guy like Candelario," Rick smirked. "You're heartless."

"No. Candelario is the one with no heart." Paz sobered quickly and changed the subject.

"I have to go to school a little later. First, I guess I have to go home and change my clothes." He made a face at his friend.

"School?" Rick frowned in confusion.

"They are making a float there, and I promised to help. It is for the girls to ride on, the ones who are the candidates for queen later today. They wear fancy dresses, so it is not good that they are walking in the dirt."

"I suppose that makes sense."

"The only other one that needs any help, of course, is my father."

"What's he doing today?"

"Well, the store is full, but Mariana is running that. He is also busy decorating the church. We do not have the saints in our church, like the big cathedrals, but you know how he is. He managed to find one that needed a little fixing up for the parade in the afternoon."

He stood up to leave, but first, he carried the chair back inside. "Take your part of the money off the line," Rick called from the hammock. "That sounds pretty silly, doesn't it?"

"Yes, it does, but then only silly people throw money into the ocean." Paz gave the hammock a playful push as he walked by, carefully folding the dry *colones* before tucking them into his pocket. "I will see you later, yes?"

"Oh, I wouldn't miss a *fiesta*," Rick called after his departing figure.

* * * * *

As he walked toward town later that afternoon, Rick thought of the last procession he had seen on this road a couple of weeks before. It was the funeral for Augustín Rivas. The people had trudged past his house carrying their heavy load, and Rick had stepped outside to watch. Although he had never seen a funeral cortege without vehicles, just as in his country, all traffic, even those on foot, came to a momentary rest, out of respect. He had glanced around at the others and watched them stare, hollow-eyed at the pathetic little clump of mourners.

First, came the pallbearers, shouldering their unwanted burden. Rick recognized a couple of the fishermen, but their stoic expressions acknowledged no one as they journeyed on. The man's family followed, and Rick was surprised to see Marielos and her daughters amongst that group. He had asked Paz about her later and learned that Rivas was a distant cousin of hers. Then came a few friends. Imanuel walked with this group, his Bible in hand, representing the closest thing *Las Palomitas* had to a local priest. He said the few words there were to be said. Finally, the professional mourners brought up the rear of the tiny procession. Paz had explained on another occasion about them, and Rick was glad as he listened to their wailing and sobbing, to know that at the end of the day they would be paid for their services as professional mourners.

Imanuel had said little to Rick since the night they had gone in search of Augustín Rivas. Rick did not like what they shared, such an evil secret, the truth about the man's death, and yet, what did they really know? Did they know definitively who or why? He had asked himself more than once. The army made a great suspect, but Rick now regretted not waiting a few moments longer that fateful night, long enough to hear or see something that would reveal the true identity of those involved.

When he had tried to express his frustration to don Imanuel, however, the older man had been almost curt. "A double funeral would have been better than one?" was all he said. Rick tried to comprehend his friend's distress, but more than anything, as he watched that day, he was saddened to think he was part of anything that added to the churchman's troubles.

Maybe a *fiesta* day would help to ease some of the tension between them, Rick mused. Maybe it would at least be a day when don Imanuel could forget his troubles for a time.

Rick found him, not at the church like he expected but rather in the store, helping an overworked Mariana. Standing room only did not fully describe the crowd that crammed into the small amount of floor space that was not already filled with merchandise. They bought everything from cigarettes to homemade candies to cold beer and soda.

Both the proprietor and his daughter raised a hand in greeting in Rick's direction when they saw him, but they had no time for anything more. He strolled back outside and sat down on an empty nail keg beside the door and waited. After several customers trickled out with their various purchases in hand, Imanuel finally emerged mopping his brow with a handkerchief.

"Where do they all come from on days like this?" Rick shrugged his answer with a smile. "Come and see what we have ready for today." Imanuel led the way around to the church. As he opened the doors, the sunlight fell across the skillfully painted face of a meter-tall statue of the Archangel, Rafael. Rick smiled as he noted a golden-brown complexion and darker hair and eyes than might have been seen on the same figure in the United States.

"It is really beautiful." Rick was sincere.

"Mariana painted it for us. I tried but—" He stuck his thick stubby fingers out in front of him. "I do not have that kind of talent. I was afraid the colors were wrong, you know. They are not exactly as we see in the books, but Mariana insisted that children in a country of brown people should not have to look at a saint with pure white skin and blond hair."

"I think she may be right."

"I told her it was fine with me as long as the priest in La Union does not know until it is all over. Then, what will it matter?" He laughed heartily, and it was good to hear that sound again, Rick thought.

"So now what?"

"Well, that is why I wanted your help." Imanuel grinned sheepishly. "Paz and Gilberto are going to carry *el santo* in the processional. The problem is that they are at the school and that is where the parade starts. We need to get San Rafael up there soon so that they can begin."

"I think I understand." Rick walked over and gingerly lifted the statue, half-expecting it to be hollow. No such luck.

"Wait." Imanuel hurried over to the corner and picked up an old blanket, which he wrapped around the solid plaster saint, as if it were a living child, painstakingly hooding the face. "We cannot have everyone seeing you carry a saint through town."

Rick gathered the extra blanket onto one side and used it as padding as he hefted the heavy figure onto his shoulder. "*Vaya pues*," he told his friend. "Let's go."

They walked at a brisk pace toward the little school, located on the edge of town, well past Rick's cabin. He tried a bit of conversation on the way but discovered it was enough to concentrate on carrying the weight. He did not envy the boys their task.

The schoolyard was filled with a startling array of persons from the village as well as several outsiders. Rick recognized the schoolteachers and the officers of the local fishermen's cooperative. Imanuel pointed out the *alcalde de* La Union, the mayor of the nearest large city.

A handful of uniformed boys clutched battered brass instruments at the ready, while another practiced on a small drum. The most impressive group, however, was a bevy of five young ladies, all dressed in party dresses that would have made any girl proud, Rick thought. How and where do they manage to look like that? That was all he could think when he knew full well they lived the rest of the year in thatched huts or one- or two-room shacks. Just like at home, he thought, parents of an honored child would go far out of their way to see to it that their daughter never forgot her special day.

Gradually, the director of the school, seen as the person in town with the most education, began to form the chaos into a more organized confusion and then into the line-up he was after. Imanuel pulled two clean white shirts from the string bag he carried, one for Paz and one for himself. Gilberto also appeared in a clear, light blue *guayabera*, the popular Latin American dress shirt that requires no tie.

Rick stepped over to Imanuel, who was helping the boys secure the statue to a tiny platform. "I think I'll walk back to town if you don't mind. I'd like to see the parade there as it moves along."

Imanuel smiled. "That would be a good idea, yes? Who needs to see all of this *relajo* first." He waved an arm at the general confusion that continued as different persons argued with the director as to who should come first, second and third in the parade.

"Will you do me a favor? See how Mariana is doing by herself. I told her to close the store when it is time for the parade, but I do not know if she will do it."

"I'll remind her," Rick assured him.

He stopped at his own house and at breakneck speed, changed into a clean shirt and jeans—the best clothes he had with him—and continued on his way. He arrived at the store just as Mariana was locking the front door.

"Did you need something?" she asked as she saw him coming up behind her. "Something from the store?"

"Oh, no," he stammered, feeling foolish. What would he tell her now? That her father had sent him to check up on her?

"I just came back to town to watch the parade, and I wondered if you could tell me the best place to stand," he adlibbed quickly.

She frowned as if she were not quite convinced by his words. Instead, however, she unlocked the door and invited him inside. As she re-locked the door behind them, something inside Rick turned over, and he knew he could not have spoken a word. Fortunately, she did the talking as she led the way through the curtain to the living area behind.

"The best place for the parade is where I used to watch when I was a little girl." Near the corner behind the hammock, she opened a narrow door that Rick had assumed was a closet. Mariana stepped inside through the collection of stored items that littered the floor and lined the walls. She kicked the back wall hard, and it swung open to reveal a cramped set of wooden stairs.

"Pretty tricky," he whispered.

"Franco designed it when we were still teens. I guess even then he knew he would need a hiding place or two one day."

He followed her as they climbed to a landing at the top, with a low ceiling and a trap door cut directly overhead. She pushed the door up and over and climbed out. Rick followed and discovered they were standing on the roof of Emelina's restaurant. A four-foot wall trimmed all four sides of the building. From the ground looking up, it was not apparent that this building was put together in such a unique fashion. From here, however, the village was laid out before them, yet they were all but invisible to those in the street.

Directly below was the colossal bus stop tree and beyond, the cooperative, the building with three open sides which was now festively decked out in blue and white bunting and crepe paper. Behind and to the right stood the brothel, with the beach lying just beyond that. Across the wide street was Marielos' seafood café, and off to the left, the church and the rest of the village meandered toward the point. To the right, lay the empty road, the sides of which were filling with spectators, and in the distance, they could hear and see the coming parade.

"Come and see." Mariana rested her arms on the upper edge of the wall, closest to the street.

In the front came four boys, all in light brown uniforms with bright orange trim from a school in La Union. Two played trumpets while the third pounded a regular march beat on the drum that hung from his belt. The fourth carried the blue and white flag of El Salvador. At least the drummer hits no sour notes, Rick thought as he winced at some of the trumpeters' efforts.

Imanuel came next, carrying a cross on a high pole above all. Paz and Gilberto followed, along with two others, carrying San Rafael on their shoulders on the tiny platform Rick had seen Imanuel working on when he left the school. Unlike the pallbearers from what seemed like only days before who had also carried a heavy load, the boys struggled to cover their smiles, barely restraining themselves from waving to all of their friends as they passed by.

Rick noticed Paz watching the crowd when suddenly his eyes were cast upward. A wide grin followed as he spied his sister and his friend in her favorite observation point. Rick waved, yet no one else seemed to notice their presence.

"Did you and Paz come up here often when you were little?"

"Paz? Here?" Mariana laughed. "Not Pazito. He does not like the high places. He would come to the top of the steps and talk to me, but that is all."

"It's as if no one even sees us up here."

"No one does. There is a song about that in your country, *Up on the Roof*, no? No one ever thinks to look up. I used to come up here for hours when I was younger, and rarely did anyone see." She turned back to the parade, but Rick continued to watch her, trying to imagine her as a little girl.

Down below, the director of the school strutted past with the other teachers following along with some of the best students. Mariana explained who was who. Afterward came the important officials from the town and surrounding communities. Finally, the ones everyone waited for, the young ladies on their float, decorated with paper bunting, palm branches, and armloads of delicate blossoms, came into view.

A few yards behind another group marched, this one made up of men in faded forest green uniforms. Second Lt. Hernandez marched one of his squads of the *Guardia Nacional* into *Las Palomitas*, directly behind the *Día de San Rafael Fiesta* day parade. A chilled hush fell over the crowd as they filed by.

"*Pendejo*." The word that escaped her lips was little more than a whisper. "What a jackass he is sometimes. That was unnecessary on such a day as today. Well, at least, Hector has no doubt now as to how everyone in this town feels about him and his men."

She turned to climb through the door in the roof when they heard a shout and the crack of a single gunshot. "*Por Díos*, now what? she muttered as she jumped back toward the wall around the roof.

They peered over the nearby rooftops, and behind them, they could see the local marine in his dress whites standing in the bow of one of the largest *cayucos*. He still held his smoking pistol over his head.

"The race of the *cayucos* is about to begin," he shouted through a battery-operated bull horn.

"We must hurry, or we will miss it." The delight in Mariana's voice was completely childlike. This festival must have been a high point in her life when she was younger, Rick thought. How he suddenly hated anyone or anything that had caused her to lose so much of what had once been hers.

Before ducking down toward the door, he looked back once more over his shoulder and watched the crowd move as a wave toward the *estero*, leaving the soldiers standing alone in the empty street. Following her lead down the steps, he stopped only to pull the rooftop door closed behind them.

Out the back door, they stood on the porch and watched as just over a half dozen dugout canoes gathered before the watching crowd, waiting for the signal to begin. Another pistol crack and the race was on. The paddling was fast, furious but surprisingly controlled, Rick observed. Don Cristobal stood poker straight at the finish line, in his dress Navy uniform. He flagged the winners, the two smallest boys in the entire race, both about Paz's age, thin and wiry. "No extra weight in that canoe," Mariana noted with a smile.

Back at the church, the parade had broken up, and the saint was now safely ensconced on a pedestal beside the cross. After a short prayer for the continued blessing and protection of *San Rafael*, the crowd moved back to the fishermen's cooperative, where four smaller chairs and one large one awaited the queen and her court.

With a drumroll and more fanfare, pomp, and ceremony than Rick would have imagined possible in this small fishing village, *la reina de los pescadores* was announced, Silvia Vasquez. Paz slid up beside Rick and Mariana just as her name echoed over the cheap public address system.

"Gilberto will go crazy for sure now that his girl Silvia has been crowned Queen of the Fishermen," Paz laughed as he stood on tiptoe to look for his friend in the crowd. He was not difficult to locate. Gilberto stood as close as he dared to the newly crowned queen, grinning foolishly as she rewarded his attention with a honeyed smile.

"Who chooses her?" Rick asked Mariana

"Oh, the director of the school and the teachers, make up the list of candidates and then, some of the other men in the town vote also. They made a good choice this year. Silvia is a pretty girl, and Paz says she is sweet, too. Some years, it is based more on who her father is or who is trying to gain favor with who. Like these things are done everywhere, yes?" There was more than a hint of mischief in her smile.

"That's the sad truth." Rick nodded. "And were you ever one of them? The candidates? The queen?"

A nostalgic expression, a sweet smile with sad eyes, crossed her face in the moment. "Once. A very long time ago," was all she said.

The ceremonies completed, the crowd was drifting away as two large trucks pulled into town and began spilling out equipment, which was loaded onto the cooperative's wide, open concrete floor.

"*Y eso?*" Rick echoed the question he so often heard in town for 'what's this?'

"*La Marimba Nacional*," Mariana told him as her eyes lit up. "The National Marimba is playing here tonight. Did no one tell you? Tonight you will hear truly beautiful Latin music, the way it was meant to be."

Paz walked up just as she finished and wrinkled his nose as he imitated his sister's words and tone. "Tonight, you will hear old people's old-fashioned music. Better you should listen to the radio if you want to hear beautiful music."

Mariana made a playful swipe at him, and he dodged easily out of her reach.

"Nothing like a difference of opinion in the family," Rick noted aloud, glancing from one to another.

"It does not matter," she stated in her best matter-of-fact tone. "You'll be able to hear for yourself in short order."

While the workmen busied themselves with the setup, Rick noticed that the musicians themselves walked directly to Emelina's, where a long table was reserved for them.

Mariana moved swiftly across the street toward the restaurant, calling back over her shoulder in English. "I have work to do, but you two better eat soon unless you want to be left waiting outside."

"Shall we?" Rick made an exaggerated bow and gesture toward Paz. As they stepped inside, Rick realized even the extra tables set up earlier in the day by Candelario were not going to be enough.

Mariana, working as a waitress for Emelina who never got out of the kitchen on this particular evening, served them both a dinner of fish and rice with clams, tortillas, and salty white cheese.

"And don David?" Paz asked halfway through dinner. "He so enjoyed *el Día de San Rafael* last year, I am surprised he is not here."

"I guess he is not back from the capital yet," Rick explained. "He had some sort of meetings to attend. He did ask me if I wanted to go, but it didn't sound like he would have much free time, and I'm not that crazy about big cities. Now I'm glad I didn't go."

"*Por supuesto*," Paz agreed.

They finished their meal in silence, and Imanuel joined them as Rick enjoyed a cup of coffee and a piece of *quesadilla*, cheesecake that Emelina had baked specially for this day.

"Well, are you ready for more celebration?" He was interrupted by another series of exploding firecrackers outside in the street.

Lt. Hernandez and his second in command swaggered into the restaurant, a man who liked to drink the water from coconuts, Rick remembered. The lieutenant nodded to the three of them as he passed by them and seated himself at the next table.

"Is this not charming? Just like the old days when we were children," Hernandez began with what he apparently perceived to be engaging conversation.

Mariana looked down at him and his companion without a word, her order pad at the ready.

"You on this side of the street and your best friend, Marielos, waiting tables across the road, and I get to be the one in the middle who chooses."

"Fine." Mariana turned to leave. "Go eat across the street then. I don't have time for your games tonight, Hector."

"Wait," he called after her. "That is hardly the way to attract customers to your aunt's place of business. And besides, you should call me lieutenant now."

"I do not care about your business, and I can assure you, *mi tía* does not either. Where you eat or even for that matter, if you eat, is hardly a concern of ours."

"Maybe it should be." He spread his lips in that cold way of his that resembled a smile. "After all, if the *guardia* will not eat here and we make it known to people that they should not eat here either—" He left the threat hanging in the air.

"Is this the way the military operates under the new government?" Mariana's irritation was not quelled in the least.

"The military does what it has to, to keep the subversive elements of society under control."

"Is that what we are now, subversives? Because I do not want to listen to your ridiculous drivel about the good old days of you, me, and Marielos?" A mirthless smile crossed her face. "I left town, Hector, but I see she would not have you either."

"Oh, I think it is much more serious than that. Don Imanuel?" He raised his voice slightly as he called over to the next table. "I think you should be careful in the planning of these events, like the parade this afternoon. Surely, it was inappropriate for you to carry the cross higher than the flag of our nation. I realize the church carries some significance for you and some of the others here, but you should be careful to keep your priorities in the proper order." His attention returned to Mariana.

"As for you and your friend, it is not my fault if foolish country girls do not recognize the very best when it is offered. Marielos prefers to work her fingers to the bone, shelling oysters for a living while her no-account husband is off, who knows where and you—" He hesitated for the briefest moment, weighing his last comment but he never got the chance to deliver it.

The sergeant who was grinning, enjoying the game, blundered in. "Oh, do you know about her? She prefers to play games with the sons of the rich, like Roberto Gomez."

The slamming of Rick's chair against the wall as he jumped to his feet brought an instant halt to all conversation in the restaurant. Imanuel grabbed Rick's arm.

"*Sientase*, Ricardo," he cautioned as he tugged at him in a futile attempt to get him back into his chair.

Hernandez gave his second in command a harsh look but could not bring himself to publicly rebuke him. Mariana dismissed both Hector and Rick with a withering glance and gave the still seated sergeant an icy stare.

"Eat across the street, or anywhere else you like, but do not come back here. I would rather give the food to the *aquacateros*, the ditch dogs in the back alley." She spun on her heel and disappeared into the kitchen.

A red-faced Hernandez stalked out of the restaurant, his second in command scrambling behind him, still trying to comprehend the damage he had done. The rush of many whispered conversations filled the room. Imanuel scurried into the kitchen to confer with his daughter.

"What's with that guy?" Rick hissed at Paz as he sat back down. "Why would anyone say a thing like that?"

"I do not know. Hector was around a lot when I was little, but I thought he just had a thing for Marielos. I guess he liked both my sister and her friend, and now, the truth is," Paz shrugged, "he has neither. That was a stupid thing to say to my sister, but for a *militar*, it is not surprising. That is their problem. They think they can tell everybody what to do, and the worst part is, they usually do." His attention returned to the last of the warm tortillas.

Imanuel returned to their table. "She is all right, upset mostly that she may have cost Emelina more business than it was worth, but I think he was just making noise tonight. I do not think he will really try to shut us down over this. Emelina is making Mariana some tea to calm her nerves."

The older man shook his head in wonderment. "I guess even the *guardia* have to learn a man cannot force a woman's affections. That must be a particularly difficult lesson for those who are accustomed to always getting their own way."

The *músicos* trooped en masse across the street to their waiting instruments. Within moments, an exquisite melodic roll up the scale burst forth from the fishermen's cooperative building, as the men of the National Marimba, dressed in matching white *guayaberas*, took their places and tested the tone of their instruments. Another man stepped to the microphone and announced that the music would begin in a few minutes.

Imanuel and Paz took over for Mariana in serving the remaining customers, and Rick, at Imanuel's suggestion, stepped into the kitchen. She was sitting in the same spot where he had rested the day he had pulled Paz from the raging *estero*.

"Are you okay?" He asked in English. She looked pale and tired, not at all like the spirited young woman who had just told the local commander and his sergeant what they could do with their business.

"I will be all right," she assured him, trying to convince herself as much as him, he thought, as she sipped from a steaming cup.

"What is that stuff?" He looked at the greenish-colored water in her cup.

"Just some tea that Emelina makes for me. She experiments a little with herbs, things she gets from Niña Ana. She is the real expert on natural medicines here. I do not know exactly what it is, but it always makes me feel better."

"They had no right to say those things to you."

"Hector always knew how to make me angry, even when we were little, and he still enjoys it. That is why a few minutes together and still, we fight. It means nothing. As for the other one, he is not from here. They will probably be back in here tomorrow, looking for breakfast and Emelina, no doubt, will serve it to them." She smiled weakly. "Hector was angry when he left and not just at me. I would not want to be his sergeant right now." She stood up and swayed like a reed in a strong breeze.

"Hold on there." Rick slipped an arm around her for balance, but he was startled by his own response when her dark eyes met his.

"I think maybe I will lie down for a little while," she smiled wanly. "I just need a little rest, and then I will come over to listen to the music. Go find Paz and have a good time." He watched her disappear through the doorway that led to the store.

The music was everything he had been promised and more. Their hands moved deftly across the eight different sets of highly polished wooden xylophones, the most sophisticated of a once primitive African instrument. It was as if they could play anything, everything—traditional Latin rhythms, popular show tunes, the latest melodies. What surprised him was the number of young people who shared Paz's opinion of the music—it was all right, they said, not bad for old people's music but what they really wanted to hear was rock and roll.

The human condition is always the same, Rick mused. You want what you don't have, can't appreciate what you do have. He watched local couples and those who had come from neighboring areas as they danced and swayed to the romantic rhythms.

Rick saw Paco, his sons, and various other fishermen he knew with their wives and girlfriends, dancing or standing alongside the dance floor as he was, finding enjoyment, simply in watching and listening. Even shy Gilberto whirled past, with the smiling Queen Silvia as his partner. This is an evening that boy will never forget, Rick thought as he watched them.

At the back of the building, Miguel and a few other fishermen were actively engaged in selling beer and cold drinks. With every break in the music, a crowd converged on the tiny window through which drinks were passed as quickly as possible for as long as the quiet lasted.

The lights flickered and then went out at the restaurant behind him, and shortly afterward, Paz joined him.

"I heard even Gilberto is dancing tonight." Paz laughed out loud at the thought. "I cannot imagine how Silvia managed that."

"And you? Who is the little girl who will steal your heart and have you out there on the dance floor?" Rick teased.

"Not me," came the embarrassed answer. "You will not see me making a fool of myself like that."

"You don't dance? Is that like, you don't swim?"

"No, not exactly. I could learn to dance in this town easier than learn to swim, but—" He gave an exaggerated shudder. "Who would want to?"

Now it was Rick's turn to laugh at the view his young friend held of the world.

"You will change your mind one day. Wait and see."

The music began again, and as it did, Imanuel stepped on the concrete floor with a ravishing young woman on his arm. She wore a simple yet elegant crimson dress that fit her petite figure and complimented her golden-brown complexion and wide dark eyes. Golden chain earrings sparkled, surrounded by a cloud of ebony hair that fell freely to her shoulders. A little rest, Rick remembered, is what Mariana had said she wanted when she left the restaurant, and it had worked wonders. They stopped not far from where Rick stood, and it was obvious he was not the only one who had noticed her. A few of the brasher younger men came forward, but none asked her to dance.

"Really, I only came to listen." Rick heard her say to Imanuel as he came closer.

"I see you are feeling better," Rick spoke as he nodded a greeting to Imanuel.

"Yes, I am fine now. They are wonderful, yes?" Her eyes never left the skilled musicians as she spoke as if to look at him might give away some secret she was not ready to share.

"Don Imanuel," the voice of a young boy, Rick had often seen about town, made all three of them turn around. "Niña Emelina says she needs you to come to the restaurant for a few minutes."

Imanuel frowned. "*Vaya pues*," he answered. "Will you be here for a little while?" He asked Rick. "I am sure I won't be long."

"Of course." Rick took a step closer. As they continued to watch the dancers, he noticed that the beer sales were going a little too well, as a few of the men along the fringes of the dance floor seemed to be more than a little intoxicated. Emboldened perhaps by the alcohol, a couple of the men approached them and asked Mariana to dance. She shook her head, but another one followed.

"You know," Rick gave her a sideways glance. "There is a way to get them to stop asking."

"I do not want to dance with any of them, if that is what you mean," she answered a bit sharper than she intended. She switched to English, and her words now carried more than a slight hint of an apology. "I suppose I should not have dressed up so, but somehow I just could not help it. This was always such a special time.

"It feels like when they look at me, they think everything has been easy for me, and that is not true. I know it would have looked that way to me when I lived here before. Money solves everything, right? Instead, I struggle with the memories every day of how things were before and how I wish my life could be simple again, but I am learning, it never can be that way. Still, when I started to get ready tonight, all I could think of was how exciting the night of the dance always was for me in the past. I guess I just got carried away."

"Don't ever apologize for looking the way you do tonight." Rick leaned in close to be heard over the music.

She smiled almost shyly.

"Well, are you interested in stopping the dance requests?"

"Yes," she answered, her head held high. "What is your idea?"

"There is really only one way." He reached out and caught her around the waist. "Perhaps they won't ask you if you are already dancing."

He pulled her firmly onto the dance floor, and despite a look of apprehension, she did not resist. Within moments, Rick realized she danced every bit as well as she dressed.

The heady combination of the sweet rolling melodies, her perfume, and above all else, her very presence in his arms, was almost beyond belief. The music, the moment, or was it all this woman? As they whisked gracefully across the floor, it all touched a part of his soul as nothing else ever before.

A tiny chill passed over him as he caught her watching his face intently. He considered the consequences if she were to discern all that was in his heart at this moment.

"You realize, we are probably going to cause a scandal, just by dancing this way in front of the whole of *Las Palomitas*?" she asked in a serious tone.

It was the first time since she had come into his arms that he was reminded that there were others still in the area.

"Do you care very much if we do?" His voice was equally solemn.

"Not too much, if it is only dancing." A small anxious smile followed.

"Then it is not worth worrying about." He stated emphatically.

She gave him a genuine smile as the dance floor emptied around them, and the others stopped to watch. Yet the musicians, also watching, made no attempt to slow their haunting melodies as one song melded into another. Rick almost laughed at the fleeting thought that occurred to him, of how angry he used to get with his mother for forcing him to attend dance classes with his sister.

He caught glimpses of faces he knew, including those of Paz and Imanuel, but he could not bring himself to look beyond those glances to determine the thoughts behind their stoic expressions. For once, it did not matter. Nobody else's opinion of what he and she were doing at this moment, could stop him. His attention was focused on the beauty in his arms. As long as she was happy, he knew he was.

After what seemed both a lifetime and yet, only moments, the music reached a final crescendo, and with one last dramatic roll up the eight separate sets of marimba, he swept her ever so briefly off of her feet before they both came to a standstill. She covered her cheeks with her hands as she felt herself blush, and the crowd began to applaud. Rick looked down as he walked her back to her father, but he could not bring himself to meet the eyes of his friend.

"Now you want to ask me again, why I do not dance?" Paz looked almost as happy as Rick felt. "How could I, with people out there, like you? I would look like a *burro* next to you—next to both of you." He laughed again as he patted Rick on the back after handing them both a cold bottled soft drink.

Imanuel was characteristically more reserved, but not angry, Rick was relieved to see.

"You dance very well together." There was a twinkle in his eye that Rick could not read. "I thought you were tired?" He asked Mariana with true concern.

"I was, but Rishard said the only way to stop them from asking me to dance was to—" She stopped and asked him. "What did you say exactly?"

"I guess it doesn't matter now." He shared a self-conscious smile.

Another voice answered. "No, I suppose not." David stepped out of the shadows.

"Don David!" Paz welcomed him warmly. "I told don Ricardo you would not want to miss *el Día de San Rafael*." He was off to the back of the building for another cold bottle.

"That was quite a performance," David remarked, raising an eyebrow in Rick's direction.

"It was just a dance, a little longer than usual, but just a dance," Rick commented, but his eyes met Mariana's as he spoke and belied his every word.

David looked over to the musicians who were nearly ready to play again.

"So, how was San Salvador?" Rick asked.

"Same as always." David slipped into the pattern the two of them had been following for weeks. "Still there. Not much changes. A bunch of stupid meetings. They don't mean much. Justify a number of bureaucrats in their jobs, that's about all I could tell."

"Sorry it didn't go well."

"It wasn't that bad. It's just that I would have preferred to be here, dancing with pretty girls and—" he held the beer bottle high as Paz handed it to him, "enjoying the party!"

He stepped to the center of the dance floor, not worrying about whether or not he had a partner, a matter that quickly resolved itself as one of the girls who worked in the house on the beach, stepped forward to fill the vacancy.

Strong headlights swept over the crowd as a large white Mercedes pulled up to the open side of the building. "What's this about?" Rick asked as a uniformed chauffeur who looked like his day job might easily be that of a professional wrestler, stepped out and opened the back door of the car.

"My worst nightmare since the day she returned home," Imanuel stated flatly.

An ancient white-haired gentleman slid out of the car. He wore a white suit, a white impeccably crafted straw hat, and carried a black lacquer cane. Rick's first impression was of an aged heroin king or wealthy pimp.

"*Jesús!* It is don Raúl," Paz whispered.

Mariana said nothing. Her earlier glow had faded to the pale shade Rick had seen when they were in the kitchen earlier. He took a protective step closer to her.

The old man made his way into the cooperative. Candelario scooted up with a chair, respectfully backing away almost immediately. He didn't quite bow and kiss his feet, Rick thought, as he, like all the others, stood and watched the drama unfolding before them.

Once seated, the old man's hands rested on the cane before him as he took a long look around the hushed room. His eyes came to rest on Mariana, and it was to her that he spoke.

"They told me you were back, but I did not believe it. So I came to see for myself." He coughed as if the effort of speaking was almost too much for his dried-up wrinkled body.

Mariana stood as if transfixed. She had the look Rick thought that he had seen on occasion on David's face when he first spies a snake, half terrified, half murderous.

"And now you can see," was all she said.

"Now I see you wear the red dress of the harlot I always knew you to be, and you come to dance at a party named for a saint." He chuckled, but there was no humor in it as the whispers of the crowd rose around them.

The color returned to Mariana's face as her anger seethed. Her voice was low but intense. "A long time ago, a little village girl ran away from this town because she was afraid of you. Some things have changed since then. I see you have not. You still like to pick on those weaker than you. But that little girl is all grown up now, and she has no intention of running away again."

"Running away?" Afraid of me? You still talk like a child." He snorted.

"Have it any way you want, don Raúl, but I am done with the past and with you. There is nothing you can do to me anymore." She turned sharply and left for the restaurant. With a few quick strides, Rick was walking beside her.

"Not too fast," he whispered in English. "That was good, but don't walk too fast."

She threw him an angry look, which quickly melted into a smile when her eyes met his. "What do you know of all of this, anyway?"

"Not a lot," he lied, as they reached Emelina's "but probably enough."

Once inside, they sat down at a table on the darkened porch. They could easily observe the activity across the road in the brightly lit dance area. Gomez remained only a few moments longer. As he stood to leave, the music softly began again.

"If I had stayed, he would have been there all night," she began to explain needlessly. "I did not want to ruin the dance for everyone else."

"I think I understand. It was a wise move. What I want to know is how much danger are you really in?"

"From who or from what?" She laughed mirthlessly, and Rick wished he could see her eyes better. "So far, this evening, I have insulted the *guardia*, and don Raúl has come to announce that nothing has changed from years ago." She sniffed with contempt. "Not such a good record, yes?" She stole a sideways glance at him. "The truth is, though, that I am not really worried. Both of these men have—what is the phrase in English? They have bigger fish to fry than me. They will make a lot of noise, but it means nothing. Truly, they cannot hurt me."

Another set of headlights, higher and closer together than those of don Raúl's Mercedes, cut off Rick's chance to ask for a fuller explanation. They pulled up in front of the empty restaurant, and Rick's heart sank as he recognized Carlos' blue Land Rover.

"I think you have a visitor and it would probably be better if I was not here—"

"What are you going to do?" she chided with a tease in her voice. "Slip out the back door? I would never have thought that to be your style." Her face, lit by the car lights, was quite serious and fastened by her gaze, Rick found he had no desire to go anywhere.

Paz and Imanuel walked in from the back before Rick had a chance to say more.

Imanuel strode purposefully out the front door. "Good to see you, my friend." He greeted Carlos as the larger man struggled out of the driver's seat.

"Emelina told me that Candelario had been called to your home earlier to attend to your needs."

"Is everything calmed down over there now?" Rick asked Paz in a quiet voice as he dipped his head in the direction of the cooperative.

"As soon as you two left, don Raúl turned to the rest of the people and chatted with them like we were all old friends. Then he left. I guess he just came to give my sister a bad time. I am worried about her."

"You are not alone, my friend," Rick answered honestly without thinking.

Carlos lumbered into the restaurant, and Paz, trying to be helpful, quickly found a light switch and nearly blinded them all.

"Pazito, that is too much," Mariana complained as she shielded her eyes with her hand.

"It is fine," Imanuel announced. "Leave it on, son."

Carlos made his way over to Mariana, who offered a cheek, which he kissed dutifully. He shook Rick's hand as they were introduced before he sat down beside her, covering one of her hands with one of his. Rick felt something turn over sharply inside.

The attempts at conversation were brief and stilted, with Imanuel, Carlos, and Mariana seated at the table. Paz and Rick stood awkwardly in the doorway, and while Paz was barely concealing his irritation, Rick hoped his was not nearly so easy to read.

"It has been a long day and night," Imanuel stated as he stood up. "So if you will excuse me—"

He turned and looked fully at Paz, who quickly cleared his throat and made a similar excuse.

"*Buenas noches*," Rick told all of them and stepped outside into the street. He looked toward the *fiesta*, which was still in full swing, but he knew he had no heart for it anymore. He walked in the dark, willing himself not to remember his last experience of walking up this road, alone at night.

Tonight, however, although the road was dark with the long shadows of too many trees, the beach was wide open, faintly illuminated by the pale moon that had come out from behind the clouds. He stopped in the shadow of Marielos' café and looked back at the two figures still seated beneath the flicking fluorescent lights of the restaurant.

Rick strolled along the shore, trying to take comfort in the beauty of the beach, the soft waves lapping gently over the dark wet sand. Why had he ever come here in the first place? David had been right, and that, in addition to all the rest was almost too much to bear. Was it really just this morning that he had felt so good about life in general?

He stopped inside his own little house, dark and lonely, and came back outside into the moonlit night, where he leaned against his favorite tall palm. He contemplated the few stars strong enough to be seen despite the weak moonlight. Lonely strains of the *marimba* still echoed faintly in the distance, further haunting his thoughts. The gentle sea, shimmering despite the darkness, set off by the islands and distant hulking shores of Nicaragua and Honduras, should have been of great comfort to him, as had always been the case in the past, but not tonight. There was no peace in this for him. Maybe there would never be for a restless soul like his. He turned back to the little shack, undressed, and fell mercifully into a deep sleep.

CHAPTER 9

D *ecember 5, 1979, Washington D.C. – Despite the contention of various Administration officials that the coup of October 15 ushered in a new era in Salvadoran politics, others claim the US government is allowing the new junta there "to die of neglect."*

No response, other than the reinstatement of military aid shipments, has been forthcoming from the US government administration, which is apparently overwhelmed by the current hostage crisis in Iran. The only Latin American nation receiving any attention from Washington at this time is the new revolutionary government of Nicaragua.

Thanksgiving had come and gone, and although it was not a traditional holiday in Latin America, it provided an opportunity for the only two Americans in *Las Palomitas* to lay aside their differences for a time.

"It ain't exactly turkey and stuffing," David drawled as he surveyed the meal of stewed chicken, rice, yucca, fried plantains and tortillas he had paid the neighbor, Juana, to make for them. "And there's no football games, but hey, it's as close to Thanksgiving as you and me are gonna see this year."

"It's fine." Rick was appreciative of the simple invitation to share a meal in David's house again.

Their attempts at conversation, though stilted at first, became more natural, particularly when their thoughts turned to Thanksgivings past.

"Remember all those years we'd go hunting in the mornings at Gramps' place while your mother and Gram would cook?" David began. "Dallas would always fuss about how we really shouldn't be there because your Mom's folks weren't really ours, but it never bothered your mother's people, did it? I thought of them as my grandparents for years, despite what he said, and every year we'd go back again."

"Her folks were like that. They'd take in just about anybody. I mean—" he hesitated, ready to apologize, but David was concentrating on the food. "The only one who ever seemed to feel uncomfortable there was my father."

"I remember that," David replied. "I never really understood why, though. He'd hunt and fish with us and be just fine as long as we were outside, but once in the house, he'd get real quiet, like he was nervous or something. Seems like they did everything they knew how to make him feel welcome, but he was always kinda edgy."

"The only thing I could ever come up with was something leftover from when he and my mother were first married. I think my grandparents were against the marriage, at least initially. I think it also had to do with the fact that Gramps used to be with the university." He stopped speaking long enough to savor a mouthful of fried *platano* dipped in sorghum syrup. "It's funny the things that impress you as a kid."

David nodded. "It's hard for me to think of him, like that. Gramps, I mean. I remember seeing him in a suit a few times when I was little, but what I remember most about him was after he retired to the farm. I think about the horses, the hay, you and me helping to bale it in those fields, the woods at the back of the farm. I just do not think of him as a university professor."

"It's true," Rick agreed. "He seemed more like a farmer to me, too, after he retired."

"Well, I've been thinking." David sucked a drumstick clean as he spoke. "About hunting, I mean. I thought you and I ought to get back to that."

"Here?"

"Yeah, you remember the guys I told you about before who are wanting to go dove hunting. Well, they're all set to come down. They're kind of funny in a way because—"

"David, we're not exactly equipped for that here. I'm not sure it would be a good idea anyway. It seems like a good many of the wrong people here carry guns if you know what I mean."

"Who? The *guardia*? Where we'll be, they'll never see us, and it doesn't matter. These guys have everything we need, guns, ammo, all of it. That's what I started to tell you. They've got everything they need except a place to go and a way to get there. It's their country, but I swear, you get some of these fellas outside of San Salvador or off their family-owned *fincas*, the big ranches, and they don't know their way around at all."

"And you do?"

"Yeah, for what they want. I met these guys when they came down here fishing with some friends of theirs who own a beach house up the way. I think they're all right. Their friend is the one who owns that big inboard-outboard that's always tied up down by the gas station. I told you about him. He's the guy who after he bought that thing and discovered how much gas it took, he bought the gas station, too. Pretty funny, don't you think?"

Rick said nothing. He remembered the high-speed pleasure craft, with its twin 270 inboard engines. It was the one he'd seen stuck on the sand bars for hours one day because the driver didn't know the way in or out of the *estero*. It was the one he'd seen pass by in front of the dugout *cayucos*, going too fast, cutting too close, throwing a wake that sent the local fishermen scrambling to keep their boats from being swamped.

"Come on, you need to get out and do something just for the hell of it. You can't take life so seriously all of the time," David continued. "Say you'll go with us. They'll be here tomorrow. It'll be a great time, you'll see."

* * * * *

They picked up the three men at their beach house early the next morning, under a starlit sky. Rick, who

was accustomed to traveling light, was more than a
little aghast at the number of leather pouches, gun
cases, coolers, and other paraphernalia that filled
the Jeep.

"Where are we going anyway?" Rick asked as they
bounced along in David's Jeep.

"Below *Conchagua*, the mountain over there."
David attempted to point at the hulking shadow
that loomed at the far side of the bay.

A certain uneasiness gripped Rick at the mention
of the name, and yet he could not place where or
how he had heard it before.

"There are some good fields over that way, and
there's a guy who is the caretaker over there, along
with his family, who will help."

"Help?" Rick was confused. "I thought we were the
guides."

"We are," David laughed. "You'll see."

The things they had brought littered the floor of
the large flat-bottomed boat David had borrowed
from the fishing cooperative. Good thing we aren't
all trying to cram into a *cayuco*, Rick thought to
himself.

He studied the three men as best as he could.
He had caught first names only. The leader, a man
perhaps fifteen years older than David and himself,
was 'Neto. Tall and well-built, he moved with the
ease and confidence of someone who rarely makes
errors in judgment. Felipe, also tall but thin, almost
gaunt, had a hunted look of his own as if life for him
had always been something of a struggle, and he was

not necessarily winning the battle. Victor, was the quiet one of the three, a chubby city boy who did not belong out here at all.

The boat ride was longer and rougher than expected. The wind was up, whipping the waves so that they were all thoroughly soaked by the time they made land a half-hour later.

David moored the boat to a tree, and they walked through a short band of trees, carrying the guns.

"*Buenos días*, don Pedro," David called out to no one in particular. A short, rotund figure, dressed only in trousers and sandals appeared from the shadow of a low house at the edge of the trees. He greeted David and was introduced to Rick and nodded respectfully to the others. David explained their situation briefly, and Pedro began barking out orders as his children tumbled out of the house in the early morning light.

He sent one boy to watch the boat and its contents, and he told the rest to stay with him. Each carried a string sack.

They proceeded to the field ahead, which was flanked on both sides by dense woods. They stopped and unsheathed the guns, dropping the cases to the ground. Rick's was a double-barrelled 20 gauge, not unlike the ones he had used in years past. It felt good in his hands, and although he was no longer sure what he expected, the familiar gun was somehow vaguely comforting, as was this place, an empty field, surrounded by woods in the early morning hours.

Like many Americans, he had heard so often
of South American jungles, he just assumed that
Central American vegetation would be the same,
but it was not. The land here was thickly wooded,
and the plants and trees, while different from those
in the Midwest where he had grown up, made up
a forest not unlike those he had frequented all of
his life.

He glanced sideways as one of the men from the
capital slipped the case off of a Browning Superposed
12 gauge. Even here in the half-light of the early
dawn, the Belgian workmanship of the exquisite
over and under he had seen only in catalogs, was
evident. These men may not know where to hunt,
Rick thought fleetingly, but they certainly knew
what to hunt with. His time for reflection was cut
short as the dawn's light brought with it the first
flight of the morning.

As the initial shots rang out, Rick remembered
the dog, his grandfather's dog, and how he would
miss—He glanced involuntarily over his shoulder at
Pedro and his children, crouching behind them in
the grass, and suddenly, everything that had been
clouded earlier was crystal clear. As the hunters
moved forward, firing repeatedly, the man and his
children scurried forth to retrieve the birds that
rained down onto the empty field.

Rick put the gun to his shoulder to join the
others, but he found it was not possible for him to
fire above, with human beings moving about below.
He thought of a neighbor from years past who had

accidentally shot his own dog on a morning hunt, and how the man had grieved for that animal like he might for his own child.

The firing continued. They filled the air with so much shot, nothing could have flown through the hail of steel and survived. And still, they kept coming, more and more birds. Where did they all come from? And then he realized he knew the answer to that one, too. "Birds fly south for the winter," he could hear his kindergarten teacher repeating in a sweet, lyrical tone.

"There are no limits here, no game laws." The memory of the first time David proposed this little trip came back to him at almost the same moment.

Rick lowered the gun. There was no point. He could not fire, not like this. As hundreds of birds continued to fall, he found the entire spectacle more than he could bear. He stepped into the woods, past the point where they had waited, hoping his absence would not be noticed by David and the others as they advanced into the field. The children and Pedro continued to scurry through the stubble, gathering up their feathered bounty.

Rick eased backward, watching the hunters, longing now only for a bit of solitude. The metallic click behind him, of a gun as its safety was taken off, stopped him cold. His thoughts raced, trying to determine who or what was behind him. Another hunter? *La guardia?* He was not left wondering long.

"So you did not even wait for my invitation?"

Rick whirled at the familiar taunting voice. Franco slipped from behind a tree, as the man with an M-16 still trained on Rick stood up from the dense underbrush.

"*Esta bien,*" Franco told the gunman.

"But he is armed." The other man did not immediately lower his weapon.

"I do not think he plans to use it." Franco pushed the barrel of the M-16 toward the ground and then gently took it from the man, before motioning for him to join the small group that Rick saw gathered a few hundred feet away.

"You do not like to hunt?" Franco maneuvered them quickly to a point where he could keep an eye on the hunters without being seen.

"I'm not sure what they're doing is hunting." Rick immediately regretted the remark, realizing a discussion of semantics with Franco would only lead to a different kind of battle.

"That is what they call it, no?" Franco's wide-eyed act might have been convincing had they not met before.

"Yeah, well, there's a phrase in English—shooting fish in a barrel. That describes this better."

"I see. And they do not even own the barrel." Franco laughed unexpectedly. "Well, *gringo*, we could kidnap you here as you stand and take you with us. That would get you out of your little hunting trip and make your explanations easy, yes?"

Startled, Rick said nothing, as Franco continued to think out loud.

"That would improve our reputation as very fierce *guerrilleros*—kidnapping Americans. Of course, it would bring far too many *guardia* and God-knows-what-kind of *norteamericanos* down here to look for you," he finished with a sigh. "Besides, it would also get me into a lot of trouble with my cousins and my uncle.

"I could also," his speech slowed as he raised and trained the M-16 on one of the hunters, "do a little hunting of my own. '*Guerrilleros* kill Felipe Damas—that would make a very big headline in tomorrow's newspapers.'"

"You know these men?" Rick was surprised.

"You do not? You should be more careful who you associate with. Did your mother never tell you that when you were growing up? What do American mothers tell their little boys, anyway?"

Rick tried again, ignoring Franco's chatter. "How do you know them?"

"This is a very small country," Franco explained with overstated patience. "He is one of the Fourteen, or did you not know that?"

"Fourteen? Fourteen what?"

"You really do now know, do you?" He heaved an exasperated sigh. "I do not have time for these kinds of explanations. Ask Mariana. She can tell you." He laughed as if he had made a joke. "God knows she knows more about them than I do anyway."

Rick was still at a loss.

"*A la gran puta*," Franco was losing patience. "Would you recognize Mr. Ted Kennedy if you saw him?"

Rick nodded.

"Well, we recognize our rich men's sons, too." He lifted a small pair of binoculars to his face. "Yes, that is Felipe Damas and his friend, Victor Guevara. Also, Ernesto Benavidez, Felipe's brother-in-law, he is the only one I would be sorry to shoot. He tries a little, it seems. At any rate, their fathers are all very rich men, and they are nothing more than, how should I say, very rich playboys. Maybe we should just snatch one and hold him for ransom, but—" He dropped his binoculars. "But not today.

"You are lucky, *gringo*. We were close by and came down to see what all the noise was about. We are not prepared for 'guests' at the moment." He smiled in a way that reminded Rick of Lt. Hernandez.

"You should be more careful. Careful who you choose for friends and where you go walking."

Rick shrugged as it became obvious he had little to fear, at least for the moment. "What can I say? My cousin chose both the friends and the place."

"Hmm, that is a problem. One cannot choose their relatives, yes? Still—" Franco began to studiously inspect the weapon in his hands.

"I'm sure Mariana would agree."

Franco shot him a sharp look before breaking into a grin. "*Touché, gringo*. You are probably right."

"I see you've improved your quality of weapons since last I saw your—" Rick hesitated, looking for the right word, "troops." He took note of Lito, standing in the group, well behind Franco.

"*Pues*, somewhere there is a division of *guardia* who are missing a number of arms. It is very kind of the United States to ship them such fine weaponry. It is the easiest way to increase our own supplies, steal them from the *chafa*." A malicious grin crossed his countenance briefly.

"*Saludos* to my cousins and my uncle, *por favor*. We will see each other another day, I am sure. You had better think of a good story."

"For what?"

"To explain what you have been doing over here in the woods, the whole time they have been out shooting the fishes in the barrels. *Buena suerte, gringo,*" he called back over his shoulder as he rejoined the others.

They disappeared so quickly it left Rick wondering for a brief moment if they had really been there at all. He started at a yell from the edge of the field that echoed through the trees.

"Rick, what the hell are you doing?" The impatience in David's voice was unmistakable.

He walked out to them in silence. "I didn't feel well," he began to craft what he hoped would be a believable explanation. "I walked over here to sit down and rest for a few minutes." It was not a total lie, he told himself, as he watched the children empty their sacks into one of the large coolers that the boy had brought up from the boat. The whole thing made him feel more than a little ill as he watched the mound of blood-soaked feathers grow ever higher.

"*Mariado,*" the one Franco had identified as Victor stated matter-of-factly. He broke the Browning in the middle and peered down the barrel. His friend Felipe started to snicker.

Rick grinned sheepishly and shrugged. Let them think he was seasick and a wimp. That would be a great deal easier to live with than the truth.

David, who knew better, looked at him sideways but said nothing.

The one identified earlier as 'Neto Benavidez spoke up. "You had best be careful in these areas, wandering off by yourself. From what I have heard lately, there are guerrillas in the hills to the north of here."

David laughed out loud, but the other two traded furtive glances in silence. "I've lived here nearly two years now, 'Neto. *Los muchachos* know where they belong, and they don't bother us down here. That is the truth, heh, Pedro?"

The little farmer's face bore an instant yet classic dispassionate expression. "*Pues*, don David, I know nothing of their activities here or anywhere. We are not the kind of people to mix ourselves up in that sort of thing."

A silent rage flared in Rick as he realized the uncomfortable if not downright dangerous position into which he had just pushed the young *campesino*, particularly in front of such powerful men from outside the area. David could be almost unbelievably ignorant at times, he thought. Then he remembered his own most recent conversation with Franco and the kind of havoc that revelation would also bring.

The others took no notice of his quandary. "It does not matter," Felipe Damas countered. "With these," he raised his shotgun to scan the woods, "nobody is going to bother us, *verdad*?" He chuckled with self-satisfaction, and Victor joined him.

"Just the same, if we are done here," Ernesto turned to David. "It would be best if we returned. There is no point in standing around, making a target of ourselves."

Rick was impressed with Ernesto Benavidez's unhurried efficiency. The children had finished their packing job and were now struggling to carry the cooler to the shore. David handed Pedro a few bills for his morning's efforts, as the men paraded after their catch.

Great White Hunters, Rick snorted to himself as he shook his head and stopped to unload his gun. He watched the procession wind its way back to the boat.

"Oh, I brought this to show you." Felipe reached into the boat and brought out a gun case that was shorter than all of the others. He motioned for one of the children to hold it as he whipped out his latest acquisition.

Everyone in the group from Ernesto Benavidez to Pedro's smallest child jumped as Felipe's long fingers unleashed thirty rounds of ammunition from the Uzi. In an instant, it cut coconuts from a nearby tree at the water's edge and then proceeded to hash them to bits as they floated away from the shore. The youngest of the children, a little girl standing behind Felipe, ran in terror to wrap her arms around her father's leg.

Felipe chortled as the last round slipped past the open bolt. He snapped off the empty magazine. "You do not have to worry about *los muchachos*, 'Neto, when you have this kind of power!" David and Victor stepped closer to examine the new prize.

Despite his best effort, Rick could not disguise his own agitation. Ernesto studied him as the American stalked up the trail toward Pedro and the children who were now gathered tightly around him.

"Felipe," Ernest's voice seemed even quieter after the burst of gunfire. "What are you going to do with that? What purpose does it serve?"

"For protection. What else?" His exuberance remained unabated. "In these times, a man needs to protect himself. Now with this—" He brandished it over his head. The laughter that followed had a maniacal ring to it.

"Protection?" Ernesto snorted at the idea. "If you ever did need it, by the time you got it out of the case, the chance to use it would be long past."

"No, you can wear it, too. Like this." He clipped it to his belt on the hip, where it made a strange modern replacement for a six-shooter.

"That's very good. I'm sure that will be helpful and comfortable right there." Ernesto busied himself with replacing his own gun in its tooled leather sleeve as he shook his head.

Pedro assured Rick that he and the children were fine. As they returned to their house, Rick walked past Ernesto for the second time.

While the waters were calmer on the boat ride back, the deep silence in the boat was more difficult to bridge than that of the earlier trip. David and Felipe chatted at the back, but Rick stayed hunched in the bow, his face turned into the wind, as he tried to avoid contact with the rest.

"It is difficult for you to understand, isn't it?" Rick whirled at the smooth, barely accented English. He hadn't thought about it today, yet he knew a great many well-educated Salvadorans spoke fluent English.

Rick looked at Ernesto Benavidez for a long moment, trying to take his measure. "What do you mean?" he stammered, uncertain if he even wanted an answer to the question.

"Felipe and his passion for the guns." Ernesto glanced over his shoulder, noting that the other three men were in the stern, engrossed in conversation. "You seemed distressed to some extent by his little show earlier."

Rick knew he should proceed with caution, but for some reason, he didn't seem to be able to stop. "It didn't seem to me that you were too impressed with it, either."

Ernesto shrugged, but his face remained open. "Many people here are afraid. There is much to be afraid of in a country at war with itself. Some people, like Felipe, buy bigger and better guns. Some, like your friend Pedro take refuge in claiming they know nothing. Others—"

"He's not my friend," Rick interrupted. "I never met him before today. He's someone David knows, but I thought he treated him pretty shabbily today.

I didn't like the kids being scared in that way. It was just—" he groped for the right word. "Just stupid, that's all." He'd have to be more careful, he chided himself. Don't let your anger take over and have you saying too much.

A half-smile crossed Ernesto's face, the kind of expression Rick remembered on his father's face in years gone by when his father knew he was not being honest with him.

"As I said, many are scared, and they react in different ways. Yourself, for example?"

"Me?" A fleeting thought had Rick wondering if Ernesto had been watching more than doves in the sky earlier.

"You are a quiet man, who does not bother to deny knowledge of anyone or anything, yes? You simply watch and listen. But I think there is more to it than that."

Rick turned his face back to the wind for a moment before answering. "You can think what you want. I have nothing to fear. After all, just like David, whenever I decide I've had enough here, I have somewhere else to go." It sounded harsher than he intended.

"That may be true," Ernesto nodded solemnly, "but perhaps there are things there you fear worse than anything you may encounter here."

Rick tried to maintain his composure, but he grinned widely in spite of himself. Ernesto Benavidez was a difficult man not to like.

"*Touché*. And what is it you fear, don 'Neto?" He employed the term of respect he'd heard the other villagers use when speaking to the wealthy landowners who came to *Las Palomitas*.

Benavidez smiled at the familiar yet quaint name, coming from this foreigner, as he contemplated his answer. "Like any man of means and power in El Salvador today, I fear for my life to some extent. I fear for the lives of my family and my closest friends, as any of them could be used to extract a ransom and then killed and tossed aside, with no more thought than say—"

"Than a dove?"

"Exactly," he continued. "But on a larger scale, I fear for my country. It is not only for my way of life, because I am one of those who already realizes that change must come, but I am also afraid of the great and terrible suffering that will come for so many before any amount of real change can ever take place."

Rick continued to watch him even after he stopped speaking. The sincerity was genuine, and yet, it was clear even to him, a foreigner, that there was still much the man did not know or realize in terms of what was coming in the near future.

David yelled above the roar of the engine, and the wind and Rick shifted his position to begin to guide the boat through the sandbars.

It was nearly noon by the time David pulled the Jeep up in front of the men's beach house.

"Come in, gentlemen," Ernesto Benavidez insisted. "We will share a cold drink."

Rick looked to David for support. If it had been at any anyone else's urging, he would have found it so much easier to resist. David did not even make the effort.

Behind the weathered brick wall that partially concealed the house from the road, they found a spacious open-air home, centered around a large veranda that faced the beach.

Ernesto motioned them to a round glass-topped table and disappeared for a moment. When he returned, he was followed by a local woman Rick vaguely recognized who brought them cold beer and appetizers.

Rick passed on the turtle eggs, a delicacy that, like the shelled oysters also on the table, were supposed to endow those who ate them with an extra measure of virility. He watched the others suck down the still runny eggs, which, although cooked, never lost their soft centers.

They sat late into the afternoon. More than once, Rick was ready to leave, but he could not find a tactful way to do so, and David was not the least disposed to going anywhere. Perhaps it was *pena*, the local term for life's little embarrassing moments, as well as frustration that had him eating more oysters than he normally would have.

The conversation ricocheted around the table, about guns and hunting, and as ever in El Salvador, of people and politics.

"Were you serious when you said there were *guerrilleros* this close?" Victor asked in a grave tone.

"They are in Morozan. There is no doubt of it," Ernesto answered evenly. "I doubt if they are particularly close to us here, but who knows? They are the kind of people who are always moving, so it pays to be cautious."

"It is too bad Felipe did not find a few out there today with his new Uzi. He might have taught some of them a lesson," Victor continued. "God knows they are destroying the country, blowing up electrical stations here and bridges there. Did Felipe tell you that Rosa Maria gave us all kinds of hell about even coming on this trip?"

Ernesto shook his head.

Felipe grinned. "*Pues sí*, it is true, but what man lets his wife make his decisions for him? I told her we would be with you, and we would be fine."

"I am certain she found that very comforting." Ernesto's fine features creased in a small smile.

"Well, at least she left me alone after that. Sometimes, that woman—"

"I do not want to hear it." Ernesto held up his hand good-naturedly, like a policeman directing traffic.

"I know. I know." Felipe sighed.

"She is afraid for you." Ernesto shot a knowing look in his brother-in-law's direction. "I should think you would find some comfort in that."

Felipe snorted and reached for another turtle egg.

"Well, there's nothing for her to worry about," David added. "Things are nice and quiet here in *Las Palomitas*."

"It is certainly not like that everywhere," Victor continued. "The capital has been full of stories and rumors about how bad things are here in the countryside. Things have been better in the city since October, but life was pretty tense for a time."

"I know. I was there." David grinned broadly.

"Then you do know." Victor raised his beer in a semi-salute. "And you?" He turned his attention to Rick. "You were there, too?"

"Oh, no," Rick corrected him immediately. "I was in San Miguel, waiting on this one." He nodded his head toward David.

"Don't let him kid you," David teased with abandon as the alcohol and the heat of the day hit him. "He was out discussing mass transit with *los muchachos*."

All eyes focused on Rick as another oyster slid down his throat. "Oh, thanks, Davey boy." Rick invoked his uncle's nickname for his cousin, one he knew his cousin hated. "I'll remember this one."

"You have actually spoken to these men? You know some of them?" Victor was completely taken aback.

Ernesto looked at him with new interest, and it was to this man alone that Rick found he had any desire to explain himself.

"David's jokes are not always so funny." He looked pointedly at Victor. "I was in San Miguel on the 15th, it is true. I was busy trying to get back here after David didn't show up to meet me. I just happened to be on a bus that was stopped by a group of rebels. We didn't discuss much of anything. I spent most of my time looking down the barrel of a gun."

Victor's laughter began as a nervous twitter and then broke into peals of unmitigated glee. "I really thought you knew—" He could not continue speaking. Rick fidgeted in what had previously been a pretty comfortable chair.

"Not one of your best days?" Ernesto raised an eyebrow in his direction. Rick was not sure if he was referring to the day of the coup or today, but he readily agreed, regardless.

"It is good that you are not friendly with them." Victor's tone turned serious as he regained his composure. "They are dangerous people. Outlaws. If the army had any sense at all, they would hunt them down and kill them like the wild animals they are. We would then be done with the whole problem."

"Which problem?" Rick could not help but ask. "The coup? That was military officers, wasn't it? The poverty, babies that go hungry, kids with no education? The threat of change? Which problem would eliminating the rebels take care of?"

Victor's eyes narrowed, and Rick was abruptly aware that despite his pudgy appearance, this man might prove to be a vicious adversary in a real contest.

"Obviously, you do not know much about this country. There is not going to be any major changes, military officers aside. We—the people who know what is going on, the people of stature—have run this country for more than fifty years now. There is no reason for that to change. The people you speak of are only the ones who do not want to work. Those who are willing to work are well taken care of. You are talking of the people who live here in this village, yes? Indians, like the one who helped with the hunt today. There are people who need to be cared for. They cannot take care of themselves. Even if they had an education, what good would it do? You cannot educate a burro. It is, in the end, still what it is, a dumb animal."

Rick was too shocked to respond. He opened his mouth but glanced first at David, who was making a careful study of the beer bottle in his hand, and then at Ernesto. His attention, however, was focused on the woman who had served them earlier and her daughter as they carried in one of the coolers that had been in the boat.

The others gathered quickly around as it was opened. Hundreds of heart-shaped deep pink bird breasts lay packed in ice. The first to look inside, Rick turned quickly away when he saw the contents.

"*Casi cuatro cientos*," he heard the young girl, tell Ernesto. Almost four hundred birds in one morning of shooting.

"Time to get you out of here," David half-whispered in Rick's ear. "Hey, it's been great." David turned to the others. "You want to go again tomorrow?"

"No!" It came out louder and more vehement than he meant. David gave Rick a sharp look at his outburst. Rick's thoughts were no longer on the hundreds of dead doves in the cooler or even another slaughter of the same, but rather on who might be waiting in the woods tomorrow upon their return.

"We appreciate the offer," Ernesto answered for all of them as he kept a concerned eye on Rick. "But we have to get back to San Salvador by noon tomorrow.

We may go out later today yet, for a little fishing, but then our holiday must end."

"I understand." David gently pushed Rick toward the door. "We've got to get going. I've got some work to check on yet today," he lied convincingly. "Rick does, too. It was good to see all of you again. Come by the next time you are in town. Have a safe trip back. *Que les vaya bien.*"

"Are you just looking for trouble or what?" David asked after a few minutes in the Jeep.

"What specifically are we talking about?" Rick was in no mood to play games at this point.

"You don't argue with a guy like Victor Guevara."

"I didn't start it. You're the one that brought up the bus trip."

"Hey, it was just a joke. I didn't figure it'd turn into a major political debate."

"Well, the guy's obviously an ass. Did you listen to him? The way he talks about people. 'They need to be taken care of' 'hunt the animals down,'" Rick mimicked Victor's heavy tone.

"A lot of 'em feel like that here." David stared straight ahead as he spoke. "And it's their country, after all."

"Great, it's their country, so if a small elite group of them want to annihilate or just merely enslave a major chunk of the population, that's okay by us. I bet that attitude played well in Germany about 1939, too." Rick no longer tried to disguise his bitterness. "The whole thing this morning was a travesty. I thought you said we were going hunting. That was a massacre."

"I never realized you were such a great bird lover. Next time take your binoculars and leave the guns at home."

Binoculars brought back the image of Franco, silently observing everything that went on this morning.

"There's one thing you should know." Rick's tone was now deadly serious. He described his encounter with Franco and his men, finishing as David pulled the Jeep to a stop in front of Rick's cabin.

"One of them had Felipe in his sites and could have squeezed off the trigger as easily as you shot those birds this morning. Now, what kind of political mess would that make for you and your friends? They're not the only ones in this country ready to solve their problems by shooting those they disagree with."

He walked away, leaving David to draw his own conclusions.

"What the hell are you talking about? How do you know? You talked to them? You know them?" His voice rose to such a high pitch as David scrambled from the Jeep that Rick winced.

"Relax." Rick sighed in resignation, wondering why he trusted David with the information in the first place. He leaned against his favorite palm tree and looked out to sea. "I met one of them a while ago. It was an accident, but he was there today, along with several others."

Agitated to the point of nearly jumping up and down, David continued to babble. "What do you know about them? They're dangerous people. Revolutionaries living in the hills, like the Sandanistas and the Cubans, before them. That's where they get their support, you know. There's supposed to be Cubans living among them, training them."

"And where did you get that? From your very reliable friends up the beach, or are you talking to US government agents now? How many Cubans and Nicaraguans have you seen since you've been here? I'm no expert in Spanish, but even I can hear the difference. I've met a few Nicaraguan fishermen. You figure they're bringing in guns in their *cayucos*? That sounds like a real reliable way to get supplies. The only thing I've heard about the Nicaraguans here is that they make quite a few of the *cayucos*. And they talk funny."

"So will you, if you start hanging out with communists in this part of the world, I tell you." David hissed in disgust. "I can't believe you. I bring you down here and—"

"And what? Go ahead and finish it." Rick's patience was exhausted. "You bring me down here, and what? Introduce me to all the local customs, getting drunk every chance you get, whoring all night long, hunting birds, like shooting fish in a barrel." He started to laugh, remembering the way Franco had repeated the phrase.

"What's so funny? I taught you to fish here." David's arguments were more whine than substance.

"*A la puchica!* Paz and Miguel taught me to fish here. You were always too busy hanging out with the guys. I bet you haven't been in a boat half a dozen times since I've been here."

"I—I can't." he stammered, and Rick was genuinely surprised. "No matter how hard I try, I go out to sea in a boat, and I get... sick."

"Seasick?"

"Yeah. It doesn't go down well with the guys, so I just stay out of the boats. It's easier." He finished completely crestfallen.

"I'm sorry. I didn't know."

"Well, now you do." His gaze followed Rick's. "What do you see out there, anyway?"

"Nothing... and everything."

"Come again?"

"I'm not sure I can explain it."

"It's okay. I'm not sure I'd understand it if you did." They stood in an awkward silence for a few moments more. David stuffed his hands in his back pockets. "I gotta go." He climbed into the Jeep and drove slowly away.

* * * * *

The cramps began innocently enough. Trying to ignore the pain, Rick thought he must have caught a chill from the drenching in the early morning boat ride. It came on quickly, though, and soon the alternating waves of nausea and diarrhea had him outside in the weeds as much as lying on the cot inside the hut. He remembered Tim, one of David's friends in the city, talking about being sick shortly after his arrival. "It's the kind of thing, where you're afraid you'll die, but then again, you're afraid you won't."

He watched the last streaks of daylight disappear and hoped a good night's sleep would bring the relief he sought. He heard the door open and saw Paz standing in the doorway.

"Don Ricardo, don Ricardo." The concern in the boy's voice told Rick he must have looked as near death as he felt.

"What did you eat today?" Paz asked.

Rick gave him a brief recounting of the day's events. The grave look and the boy's tone disturbed Rick as much as what he was suffering at the moment.

Paz found a rag, wrung it out with fresh water from a plastic jug on the floor by the kitchen table, and found a small bucket which he placed beside the cot.

"I will come back," he told Rick. "Stay here and I will see you soon."

"Oh, I'm not planning on going anywhere." Rick gave him a weak smile.

Consciousness came and went and it seemed that Paz was gone a very long time. He pondered in an emotionless state if a person as sick as he was could actually recover. At one point, he was certain he was awake, but when he opened his eyes, it was so dark, he could not tell if they were open or not. He tried to lift his arm, to put his fingers in front of his eyes, but it was as if there was a great weight tied to his arm. He could barely move it and only with great effort.

A light began to float to him out of the darkness. Or was he floating toward the light? He couldn't tell. He heard a voice, a woman's voice, but he could not make out what it was she was saying. Hands lifted him halfway to a sitting position, and a cup was at his lips.

"Drink," was all she said. "Drink this now."

The bitter concoction was down before he realized how dreadful it was. He shuddered as Mariana and Paz eased him back down onto the cot. The night's sleep he longed for came at last.

She was the first thing he saw the next morning as the first streaks of dawn filtered through the sidewall of his hut. She was sitting next to the open door, reading one of his books. As the waves moved rhythmically behind her, he watched without moving at first, enjoying the beauty before him, grateful to have survived the night.

"*Buenos días*." The expression on her face told him she had caught him in his reverie.

"I'm sorry," were the first words he spoke, although he was not quite certain what he was apologizing for. "For you to have to come here in the night and—"

"And it's a good thing I did. You are lucky Paz came to see you when he did." She put the book down and came over to perch on the edge of the cot. "Bad seafood, especially oysters, can be very serious." She shook her head. "Niña Ana taught me how to make a lime seed cure for that when I was a little girl."

"That's what you gave me last night? Lime seeds?" He sat up on one elbow and ran a hand through his bed-rumpled hair.

"I know. After you have been in the world of modern medicine, it doesn't sound like much, but it works, yes? How do you feel?"

"Well," he said as he tentatively swung his legs over the wooden edge of the bed. "Better, much better. Like I'm empty, but like I could eat. Last night, I wasn't sure I'd ever want to eat again."

"It is pretty amazing, yes? How much power those little seeds can carry."

He tossed back the sheet and found he was still wearing his blue jeans from the day before. His shirt was gone, and the jeans were undone. He moved quickly to button the fly.

"It is all right." Mariana busied herself at the kerosene stove as she began to scramble some eggs. "I did that. You did not need anything tight around your middle last night. I took off your shirt, too. It was too wet from sweat, and I was afraid it would make you chilled. As sick as you already were, that was not needed."

"How long have you been here?"

"Since Paz came to get me last night." She grinned mischievously at his discomfiture. "It was all right. Pazito came back with me. He was here until just a little while ago. I sent him to Emelina's to bring us some hot tortillas. I knew your stomach would be very empty this morning. If not, I thought Paz and I would eat them."

He smiled but said nothing more. He was simply happy to have her here, talking to him. Life looked so much better than just a few short hours ago.

She continued. "I slept in the hammock and Paz, over there." She pointed to an open place on the floor, piled with some of Rick's dirty clothes that had not yet made it to Julio's daughter's laundry *pila*.

"Well, uh, thank you," was all he could think to say. "Thank you so much for everything. For saving my life, I do believe."

"It was my pleasure," came the simple reply.

"Where did you get the eggs?" He suddenly thought to ask.

"From Juana. *Huevos de amor*."

"Eggs of what?" Rick was once again feeling foolish in front of her for some reason.

"Eggs of love. You know, not *huevos de la tierra*." She looked at him innocently enough, but he remained completely lost.

"No, I don't know," he answered with the truth, trying not to laugh. "Eggs of love, eggs of the earth. It doesn't make any sense to me at all."

"Eggs of love are from when the rooster and the chicken, they are together, yes? They make love. Eggs of the earth are just that. They come from inside the chicken, but they do not do anything except go back into the ground. They will never make into little chickens one day."

"Fertilized eggs, got it." Rick nodded.

"These are better eggs," she announced. "They will make you stronger."

Fresh tortillas in hand, Paz appeared in the doorway. "What will make you stronger?"

Rick answered before she could. "Mariana was just explaining something about eggs and making love on the earth." The words tumbled out in the wrong order, and Paz blushed accordingly.

"I am sorry I asked," he said with a shy smile.

"What did I say?" Rick asked.

"Oh, never mind," Mariana told them both. "Men are all the same, with their minds only on one thing."

"What?" Rick tried to appear wounded by the turn in the conversation.

Mariana took the tortillas. "There is breakfast for the two of you now."

"And you?" Rick sat upright, taking the plate she offered that now held a fragrant tortilla piled high with yellow scrambled eggs. Sitting cross-legged in the middle of the cot, he was astonished at how hungry he felt after the previous night's ordeal. The tantalizing aromas were not to be denied.

"Oh, I cannot stay," she explained. "Even now, Imanuel is probably looking for me. I promised to watch the store for him this morning. I think he said he had work to do at the *clínica* today."

She was nearly out of the door before Rick could gather his thoughts.

"Hey, wait a minute. Do you need some help?" He tried to untangle his feet too quickly and nearly pitched face-first onto the dirt floor.

"Wait, wait, you wait," she responded, laughing at his ungainly exit from the bed. "You are not too steady on your feet today. *Ostras*. Remember?"

"I feel much better already. Really."

"Well, rest anyway. Come and see me later, if you like. And please explain to my brother what we were really talking about, will you?"

CHAPTER 10

*D*ecember 26, 1979. San Salvador. The latest figures released by Amnesty International and the Catholic Office of Human Rights Concerns of this city indicate than more Salvadoran civilians were murdered or 'disappeared' during the first three weeks after the change in government than during any three week period under the regime of Colonel Romero.

While the military hierarchy disputes those figures, insiders claim the armed forces have taken it upon themselves to rid the country of all undesirables or, as they call them, subversives, using any means necessary.

Colonel Mojano, a member of the junta, however, stated recently that the 'gates of the country's jails will be opened for them [families] to look where they want.'

According to the latest release from the American Ambassador to El Salvador, Frank Devine, the US will continue to support the current government, in the belief that they will bring the violence under control as soon as they can determine who is responsible.

It was a Christmas tree, Rick decided, as he cocked his head sideways to look at the limb cut from a *caserino* tree. Propped up, slightly askew, on a small table inside the Flores store, the branch had a dried starfish wired to the top.

"You do not like my tree?" Mariana surprised him as she stepped from behind the curtains.

"It's unique." Rick scrambled for an inoffensive comment.

"My mother used to put one up in here when I was little, and then she would invite everyone in the village to add their own ornaments. The only rule is it has to be something you make or find." She tied a few small seashells to one of the lower branches as she spoke. "She always said she did not want anyone to feel they could not afford something for the tree. And this way, too, it is more for the children as they make their own things. See?" She held up a paper ornament obviously crafted by very small hands. "Niña Ana's granddaughters made this one.

"Besides," she continued, "Imanuel's idea of Christmas decorations is, well—" She grimaced at the foil garlands that were strung around the store, close to the ceiling. "But do not tell him I said anything." She pressed a finger to her lips.

"Not me. I like your tree, especially the idea behind it. Christmas. It is hard to believe it is nearly here."

"It is very different than in the United States, yes? No snow, no cold."

"Christmas in Texas is cold, rainy, and gray. I'll take sunny skies, shorts, and sandals compared to that. Still, Christmases with snow and sledding, the

ones I knew as a kid further north, they are the best.
I'll always miss those."

"Sledding?"

"On the snow, you know." He made a swishing
motion with his hands together. "Kids mostly, on
little flat wooden carts with metal runners."

"*Tobogán!*"

"Toboggan," Rick repeated in English this time.
"Of course."

"Well, there is no snow, but maybe you could try
it on sand. Still, it feels cold at this time of year,
with the wind blowing all of the time. No one has
been able to go out fishing for days now because
of the *nortes*. It makes the men edgy just sitting
around, yes?"

Rick nodded. "Yeah, we don't know until each new
day whether we will be able to go fish or not. How
long do they last, these north winds?"

"Oh, usually just a few days but sometimes for
weeks."

David walked in the door as she stepped back from
the tree to survey the new decorations.

"So, what are you two planning for Christmas,
anyway?" Mariana asked them both. It was an
innocent enough question, but Rick was caught off
guard nonetheless.

The two men eyed each other, neither willing to
be the first to answer.

"I don't know," Rick finally spoke up. "I guess
I hadn't thought about it much. It kinda snuck up
on me, to be honest."

"Carlos called yesterday and said he is hosting a party in the capital on Christmas. Of course, he wants me to come, and he encouraged me to bring along anyone I like. I thought about Paz, but it might be too much for him, a party in San Benito. I thought maybe the two of you would want to get out of the village for a change."

Rick looked at the floor, completely taken aback by the unexpected invitation, but David was quick to respond.

"Now I could go for that. Sounds like fun. Are you sure it would be okay?"

"And why not?" Mariana challenged him gently. "It is probably not his party anyway. He is doing it at someone else's urging, I am sure, so I warn you, there will be a great many boring people there I do not even know. But there will also be plenty of very good food, lots to drink and music. So that is always good."

David shrugged with a grin. "Sounds good to me. Count me in. Come on, Cuz, it's not like you have a lot of other great offers for that day, right?"

"Don't count on me." Rick turned quickly as if he had suddenly remembered something important.

"Rishard." She said his name in that funny lilting way of hers that made his heart feel like it had somehow gotten tangled in his vocal cords. "Are you all right?"

"Yeah," he muttered the lie as he stumbled out the door. "I've got to go."

He headed quickly down one of the alleys, not at all sure of which direction he wanted, except that he had to get out of the store, out of the situation. He tried to imagine himself at a party—with David, with Carlos, and most of all, with Mariana. The thought of her again, all dressed up the way she was for the *Fiesta de San Rafael*. He was not at all certain he could handle that again.

He wandered around until he found himself at the back of the church, where he found Imanuel working in the makeshift clinic. He was stocking shelves with bandages and other first aid supplies from a large carton.

"Do you need help?" Rick so startled the older man he nearly dropped the pack of bandages in his hand.

Rick apologized.

"The nurse is coming next week to give government immunizations, so I was straightening up in here a little. Here." He tossed a rag in Rick's direction. "You want to dust things off a little?"

The one-room clinic included a wooden exam table in the center, four wooden chairs by the door for waiting patients, and a long table that held a half a dozen jars and bottles. Shelves above the table held a few other supplies, and a fold-up cot leaned against the far wall. Everything was covered with a thin layer of light sand, courtesy of the strong and constant seasonal winds.

"Look at this." Imanuel turned toward a large armoire. "Miguel found it in La Union for us and had it brought over on a truck. Paz and I painted it and now..." He undid the clasp and swung the doors open to reveal a large empty closet space. "I only have to build some shelves, and we will have a better place to store everything, out of the wind and dust."

Painted the same light yellow as the wall, it almost disappeared into it, Rick thought but said nothing.

"My brother likes to pretend he does not think much of the work I do with the church, but every now and then, he does something like this. Then I know the truth." A melancholy little smile crossed his face.

"I even have a lock for it." He held up an old padlock, complete with a key. "We will be able to keep a few much-needed drugs, like antibiotics here, too. We need so many things, but I have been afraid to keep much here." He made the local hand sign for *mañosos*, thieves who picked up anything that was not tied down or locked up. Rick had learned early on about such hazards, having left a few of David's tools outside the first week he was in *Las Palomitas*. They disappeared overnight.

Rick started to carry the empty carton outside, but Imanuel motioned for him to leave it.

"I will take care of it later." The little catechist sighed as he took one last look around before closing the doors. "It is not much, is it?"

"It is a great deal more than was here before," Rick said in his most comforting tone. "What is it that is really troubling you?"

Imanuel looked up with a wry smile. "You know me too well. It is nothing that telling and then involving you would help. There are so many people here who are in trouble, and I know too many of them. Sometimes, it is a heavy burden, knowing all I can do is pray for them."

They walked back to Emelina's in silence, where Paz was waiting. "Where have you been all day?" Rick asked.

"Working," Paz answered in disgust as his father looked in his direction. "*Mi Tío* Miguel says if we cannot fish, we can still make a new net, so we have been weaving the whole day, and I am sick of it."

Rick laughed at his expression. "Come on, it can't be that bad. We will have something to eat, and I will beat you at cards. That ought to cheer you up."

The small joke brought a wide smile. "You never beat me at cards. I always beat you."

"See? I'm making you feel better already, just thinking about it. But the truth is, I think you win because you cheat."

Paz laughed out loud and shook his head in denial.

They had to play in the room behind the store as the strengthening *nortes* swept across Emelina's porch, closing the restaurant and making it inhospitable for all purposes this particular evening.

After a few hands, Paz stretched out in the hammock, and Rick realized he should be headed home. He was about to say as much when a slight tapping on the back door alerted the three of them—Imanuel, Mariana, and Rick. Paz was already sound asleep.

Imanuel opened the door to find Niña Ana, shivering on his back porch. "Please, can you come?"

she pleaded. "It is Fabiano. He is in terrible trouble." She said more, but Rick could not catch the words over the howl of the wind.

Imanuel pulled his head back inside and spoke to Mariana. "Meet me at the clinic" and disappeared after the old woman. Rick scrambled to his feet after him.

He discovered that the elderly woman and Imanuel could both move quickly when the need arose. Inside her one-room shack, they found Fabiano in the hammock where she had been the day he and Imanuel had visited. He was barely conscious and bleeding heavily.

"It was *la guardia*." Niña Ana began to cry as she tried to explain. "He was taking some food to my sister. She lives on the other side of the *estero*, and they must have thought he was going to see someone else. I do not know. What can we do, don Imanuel?" The sobs threatened to overwhelm her. "He is not a bad boy involved in things he should not be. He was only taking some pork to his aunt."

"We will take him with us," Imanuel told her in a voice that sounded so much calmer than Rick felt right now. "We cannot help him here. Clean up after we leave, and if anyone asks, he did not come back here tonight. You have not seen him. Do you understand?"

She did not answer.

"This is important, Ana." Once again, Rick was caught by surprise at the authoritative tone his friend could invoke whenever it suited him. "You have two tiny girls and Marielos to protect. Do you understand? He did not come back here."

"*Sí*, don Imanuel," she replied in a whisper. "I understand."

Rick had not realized there was another adult present until her name was mentioned. A shadow that had blended into the back wall until that moment stepped closer to the hammock, just as Fabiano himself had done the day he had played jacks with Niña Ana's granddaughters.

He turned his attention to the injured boy in the hammock and knelt beside him. As he prepared to lift him, Imanuel's hands grasped Rick's arms at the wrists. "If you do this, you are crossing a line you may not be able to undo later. This could put you in a seriously dangerous position."

"I appreciate the warning." Rick swallowed hard. "But I cannot turn away now. It's too late for second thoughts."

Niña Ana's sobs subsided, but Rick was certain her tears had not. He scooped up the frail youth and whisked him down the dark alleys to the clinic, following Imanuel. Mariana already had the door open, the light on, water and clean cloth at the ready.

Once in the light, they could see he had caught bullets in the leg and the shoulder. It was the leg wounds that had produced the most blood. Mariana wordlessly went to work, cleaning and tending the wounds. Imanuel stepped outside, and Rick watched helplessly at first, and then found himself busy, holding down the boy as he began to come around. He moaned loudly.

"Keep him quiet," Mariana hissed, and Rick tried to figure out how to comply.

Imanuel came back inside. "I dusted away all the blood I could find, from here to Ana's house and around there. Still, you know it will not be long before they will come."

Mariana nodded silently. Fabiano squirmed from Rick's grasp.

"Here." Imanuel moved to the supply table and soaked a cloth with a clear liquid. He held it over the boy's face briefly, and he quit struggling. "Be careful with it," Imanuel admonished as he handed the cloth to Rick. "Just what he needs, no more."

He handed Mariana a bottle of alcohol, which she poured over the leg wound she was working on and then moved on to the next one. Even in his comatose state, the boy heaved in pain.

She kneaded each area, feeling for bullets that had not passed through. She bound up the leg wounds with gauze and tape and then began working on his shoulder, where she found one more slug. She poured alcohol over a long pair of tweezers, catching the excess in the large bowl that held the water and now bloodied cloth. As she dug into the torn flesh, Rick marveled at the way she performed under pressure. He tried to imagine any woman he had ever known who could do what she was doing under these conditions, but he could not think of a single one.

Imanuel, who had gone back outside earlier, now came in swiftly and turned out the lights. "They are coming."

Mariana had found her quarry, and after rinsing it off, dropped in into her skirt pocket. In the half-light provided by the outside streetlight, it was if they were all moving in some sort of bizarre dream.

She stepped to the large wardrobe against the wall, threw open the doors, and looked at Rick.

"Can you stand it in there for a few minutes with him?" She asked in English. "I cannot put him in there alone, and we certainly cannot have him out here. I mean, you are not—what is the word? Claustrophobic or anything, are you?"

He shook his head.

"Then come, be quick. There will be too many questions if you are seen here."

He picked up the boy once again, who was still mercifully unconscious. He angled his six-foot frame into the interior of the armoire with Fabiano resting across his chest, his head tucked against Rick's shoulder. Mariana pushed the doors partway closed.

Imanuel stepped to the shelves above the side table and raked most of the items—bandages, cotton, and the like, down into the cardboard carton from where he had emptied them earlier in the day. Mariana dumped the water from the bowl into a can and set it inside the armoire at Rick's feet. She grabbed the rags, wiped up the last of the blood that had dripped on the floor, and dumped the rags beside the can. She placed the bowl under the matching metal pitcher on the long table, as if it had never been used. Imanuel turned the lights back on and began slowly replacing the items on the shelves.

"I am sorry," Mariana whispered as she handed Rick the ether-soaked cloth. She closed Rick and Fabiano in the darkness of the wooden closet and dropped the padlock over the hasp.

"*Buenas noches, Teniente,*" Imanuel greeted Lt. Hernandez as he opened the clinic door. "What a surprise to see you and your men out on such a disagreeable night."

"Disagreeable?" Hernandez stepped inside alone, leaving the others in the alley.

"I meant so much wind. It cannot be comfortable to be out on such a night."

"Comfort is rarely a soldier's lot," Hernandez quipped. "Unfortunately, we are not out for pleasure. We are looking for a young man. We came very close to catching him earlier on the far side of the estuary. We have reason to believe he is working as a liaison to the *guerrilleros* in this area."

Mariana's eyes widened in surprise. "And do you know this man's name?"

"There was no time for exchanging such pleasantries," Hernandez continued, "but he should not be difficult to find. One of our sentries shot him, so I am certain we will find the wounded cur soon enough. I thought maybe he was here since this is serving as a makeshift medical station."

"It is a day clinic," Imanuel replied casually. "We make a place for the visiting nurses to give immunizations, for instance."

"And what are you doing here at this hour?"

"We are simply putting out some supplies we just received and tidying up for the next nurse visit in just a couple of days."

Mariana held up the dusting rag from earlier in the day. Lt. Hernandez walked around the center exam table where Fabiano had been lying just a few moments before.

Inside the wardrobe, Rick's heart beat so loudly he was certain that alone would alert the soldier to their presence. He held his breath, listening to Hernandez's heels strike the wooden floor as he moved about the room. Fabiano began to stir, but as Rick moved to put the cloth back over his face, it dropped to the floor. There was no way to retrieve it in the cramped space. He slid his hand over the boy's mouth in an attempt to block any sound. What was it David said yesterday? That he would talk funny. He wondered if they still used firing squads in this part of the world. Something told him Hernandez would not bother with such amenities.

"And what is that?" was Lt. Hernandez's next question.

"Oh, it is a cabinet that we just received," Imanuel continued in a smooth, unconcerned tone. "It is all messed up on the inside, so I have to work on it. Clean it out, build some shelves, that sort of thing."

"Messed up?" Rick knew any moment Lt. Hernandez would rip open the doors and then—

"Bugs, you know." Imanuel wrinkled his nose. "*Cucarachas.*"

The lieutenant turned his attention elsewhere, but Mariana's eye caught sight of the single crimson streak, slipping from beneath the door.

"I smell something medicinal. Have you been treating someone here tonight?"

"That was me," Mariana spoke up, causing him to turn toward her as she moved to dust the waiting chairs by the outside door. "I turned over a bottle of alcohol when I was putting things on the shelf. The lid was not on tight, and it spilled all over the shelf."

The lieutenant took a couple more thoughtful steps toward the front door and then turned back toward Imanuel. "I suggest you finish your work and get home early." He looked directly at Mariana. "The streets are no longer safe at night with these rebel types running around," he stated with all the sincerity of the wolf that has already slaughtered the lamb.

"*Buenas noches*," he added brusquely as he stepped out the door to rejoin his men, leaving the door open behind him.

Imanuel crossed the floor and also slipped outside. Mariana waited the long moments before Imanuel returned and closed the door before turning off the lights and rushing to the armoire.

Fabiano was struggling and starting to moan as she opened the door.

"Good Lord, is he gone?" Rivulets of sweat were running down the sides of Rick's face and down his spine as Imanuel retrieved the ethered cloth and applied it to Fabiano's face before moving him off of Rick. Together, they eased him back onto the center table, where Mariana began to redress his bleeding leg.

"I couldn't believe it when I dropped that cloth," Rick breathed his relief. Fabiano lay still once again, under Imanuel's careful ministration of the ether.

"I thought it was all over for all us when I saw this." Mariana reached over with one of the wet cloths and wiped the blood drips off of the bottom of the pale yellow cabinet.

"Oh, my Lord!" Rick barely breathed the words aloud. "And Hernandez did not see that?"

"No," she smiled at him in silent gratitude and wiped a tear from the corner of her eye. "God was definitely watching tonight—watching out for Fabiano as well as for all of us. Hector lost interest in the wardrobe once Imanuel told him it was full of *cucas*." She laughed in delighted relief.

"Full of what?"

"*Cucas*. Cockroaches," she giggled again. "Now what?" She finished tying up Fabiano's bleeding leg once again.

"What, indeed." Imanuel was deep in thought. "First, we clean up a bit more." He picked up a rag and allowed himself a little chuckle. "I am so glad Hector did not turn back around. I could not think of a good reason why the *cucarachas* inside this cabinet would be bleeding."

"He felt awfully close," Rick admitted as he rubbed the back of his neck and flexed his shoulders. "I just kept thinking if he opens the door—"

"If he had opened that door," Mariana stated flatly, "we would all be on our way to Hector's headquarters right now, and God only knows where this boy would be. A man, he called him. Consorting with the rebels." She sniffed in contempt. "What did Ana say?"

"Oh, she told me yesterday that a neighbor had killed a pig, and he let her have some of it. I think she was sending part of it to her sister when the army decided it was something else altogether," Imanuel explained. "Only God knows what the truth is here, but he has always been a good boy. Of that I am certain.

"Right now, the question is how to protect him until he is well enough to travel. He must stay here for now. I can stay with him for a while and then about three in the morning or so, we can move him to the house. He will be safe there for a day or two, and then we will figure out after that, where to send him."

"That is fine, except that I think I should stay here. Excuse me, old man," Mariana teased him fondly, "but if he wakes up or needs more medical help, I do not remember you being much of a nurse."

His eyes smiled first, and then the rest of his face followed suit. "That may be true, but you cannot stay here alone. What if the *guardia* comes back? And someone must go home to Paz. He is probably wondering even now what has become of us."

"I can stay, too," Rick volunteered, without thinking.

A grave solemnity crept across Imanuel's usually open countenance. "Already we have gotten you more deeply involved in all of this than we had any right to do. It is too dangerous. You do not know what can happen."

"Oh, I think I have a pretty good idea of what happens when the *guardia* has one idea of what someone is doing, even if it has little to do with the truth." His gaze fell across Fabiano, who still lay unconscious on the table in the center of the room. "They have already been here. Why should they come back? If the lights are off, they will surely have every reason to think we are gone. Mariana will watch him, and I'll look out for both of them. I won't claim to be as good at it as you are, but I'll do my best."

"What do you think?"

"I think he makes sense, but he must make up his own mind."

* * * * *

They sat quietly in the darkness on the waiting chairs for a long while, neither saying a word.

"Are you awake?" she asked after a time.

"Yes," he answered. "After what I saw tonight, I'm not sure I'll ever sleep again."

"What? What the *guardia* does to those whom they judge to be guilty?" she asked bitterly.

"No, what I saw you and your father do tonight," he replied with genuine admiration. "I've never seen anyone handle a crisis like that. You were so quick, so efficient. Like you'd done it a hundred times before."

She laughed softly. "Is that what you think?"

"Sometimes, I don't know what to think. Imanuel strikes me so much like a quiet little priest who missed the seminary, a simple man of God, but when he wants to, he can sound like a general. You should have seen him there tonight at Niña Ana's."

"Oh, I can imagine it. I have heard that general's voice, as you call it, more times than I care to recall, especially when I was little. People who do not know him well think he is soft and easy, but he can be tough when he needs to be. The amazing thing to me is that with all that he has seen and all that he has lived with here for so long, he has never become bitter or resentful. It could happen so easily, I think, to *buena gente*, like him."

"*Buena gente*. Good people. That describes him well."

Once again, the darkness overwhelmed them, leaving each with their own private thoughts. Rick harked back to the first day they met, and how he had come to realize since then that silence was simply a part of who she was.

The wind grew louder outside, and Fabiano moved slightly on the table.

"There is a blanket inside that cot," Mariana spoke up.

Inside the folded *tijera*, the scissor cot, as the locals called them, Rick found two blankets. He stretched one lightly over the sleeping boy.

"Should I set this up? Are you tired?" He asked her.

In the half-light, he could barely see her shake her head. He brought the other blanket to her, and she allowed him to drape it around her shoulders.

"I am trying to think what else we have for him," she spoke, without taking her eyes off of Fabiano. "When he wakes up, he is going to be in so much pain. I hope Imanuel has something." She smiled wanly. "He probably does." She slid her hand into her pocket and brought out the misshapen slug.

"Fabiano is lucky, you know." She continued, almost absent-mindedly.

"That's not what I was thinking."

An amused look came to rest on her face. "I mean, in that this is the only bullet that stayed with him. And the fact that they hit high and low. I am no doctor, and I could never have helped him if he had been hit elsewhere. Of course, what it amounts to, also, is that Hector's men are not great marksmen, either."

"Somehow, that does not surprise me." He settled on one of the chairs by the door.

She studied the chunk of metal as she turned it over in her fingers. "It is a strange thing. The United States that is built upon the ideals of freedom and justice, more than any other country, is also the one who supplies bullets to that bunch so they can shoot a boy on his way home from his aunt's house. Does that make sense?"

For once, she sounded more pensive than angry.

"No, it doesn't, but the longer I stay here, the more things I find that don't make any sense.

Things in your country, things that my country is also involved in. It makes me want to drag some of those high and mighty lawmakers down here and let them see for themselves. I guess it will never happen, though."

She laughed, but there was no joy in it. "Not very likely. Men like that, whether they are the mighty lawmakers from your country or mine, only come to places like *Las Palomitas* for a little rest and relaxation during the daylight hours. They do not want to know what people really do here the rest of the time." She sighed. "Maybe it is just as well in the long run. After all, whose side would they line up on? Would they ever stand with this boy and his grandmother? I doubt it. They are much more used to semi-educated bastards like Hector, who wear a uniform and can speak to them in military terms. They do not want to know the truth."

"Stop, please. Don't say anymore."

"Why?"

"Because...." He hesitated. He had no right. What should he say? That it was like a knife twisting inside of him when she spoke of life in such bitter terms as if it never was and never could be any better for her. How could such a beautiful vibrant creature allow herself to be tied to an old man who obviously appreciated none of what she had to offer? How could he continue to be near her, especially at times like this, and never do anything about it? Even he was afraid to answer that one.

"Why?" She repeated.

"Because you make it all sound so hopeless." The silence returned for a few moments, and then he turned the conversation in a different direction.

"When I ran across Franco over there on the mountain, the day of the dove hunt—"

"You found Franco on *Conchagua*? That must have been something with 'Neto and the others. How did you ever...?" She stopped, not even certain as to how to finish the question.

"Oh, he only popped out of the woods when I was alone. The others didn't even know the rebels were there, thank heavens. That would have been a mess. But that is not what I wanted to know. Franco said something about The Fourteen and was irritated when I didn't know who they were. He said to ask you."

She covered her mouth with her hand to stifle her laughter. "That would be Franco. Oh my, well, let me see. He probably mentioned them because, of course, 'Neto is one of them. The other two, not so much, they just like to think so."

"So, who are they?"

"The Fourteen Families. They would be the Salvadoran form of royalty, you might say. The British royals really do come from kings and queens. Ours are maybe more like the American ones, all of it based on their money, the banks, and here, their land. In the US, you have Rockefellers, Vanderbilts, Carnegies, even Kennedys, yes? They are families who made their money from oil and railroads. The number fourteen comes from the fourteen departments of El Salvador, sort of like your 50 states. You are, for instance, right now in the Department of La Union.

"The oligarchy, the other name for those who rule here, their money comes from the coffee and the land. It started back in the 1700s and 1800s. In the beginning, they were cultivating indigo, a crop that was used for dying cloth blue but when the market for that fell apart, they turned to coffee. For the first many years here, the land belonged to the communities, literally to the locals, the indigenous people but around the turn of the century in the early 1900s, the government along with some of the Famous Fourteen passed laws and took the land away from the peasants. Not unlike your government did to the Indians there, no? They promised them much of what is now the Dakotas but when gold was discovered there, the white people took back the land. Once the elite of El Salvador, especially the people of the west like those near Santa Ana and Santa Tecla, found that the land there could grow coffee, they took the land away from the poor people."

A heavy sigh escaped her. "Remember *la matanza* of 1932, that we spoke of the one night in Imanuel's living room? Much of that was the people's attempt to retrieve their land from the ones who had taken it from them. The Fourteen Families as they are called, made certain no one would go up against them again. That is who they are, the people who run the country because they control the banks

and the money and own so much of the land.
They are the ones who think they are above the
rest us and they have owned and run everything
for so long."

"Good grief." He shook his head and then dropped
his forehead against his open palm. "Why did you
come back here, after so many years in other places,
if you knew it would be like this?"

"And who says that I knew?"

"Didn't you?"

Now she hesitated before answering. "I thought
I did. I knew what it was like before. But it is different
now. Life here has always been difficult in one sense
or another, and a person had to be careful. But this—"
She waved an arm from under the blanket toward
Fabiano. "This was not a daily occurrence. I came
back here because—" Her answer was cut short as
the door soundlessly swung open. Rick rose to stand
behind it, ready to pounce on whoever might enter.

"*Vaya pues*," Imanuel's quiet voice broke the
tension as the light from outside fell across Fabiano,
and both Rick and Mariana sagged visibly with relief.

"*Papá*," she chastised him gently. "You gave us
such a fright."

"I was not certain how to come back in here.
I mean, if you three were not here, I did not want to
think about who might be waiting."

"*Díos mio*. Do not even speak about such things!
Are you ready to move him?"

"Yes, I think so. Paz and I made up an extra bed in
Paz's room. How is he doing?"

"He has been quiet, but when he wakes up, you may not be able to keep him that way if you do not have some heavy painkillers."

"I have that at the house. I did not think it would be wise to keep that here."

Mariana traded a knowing look with Rick.

"Have you talked to Ana again?"

"No, I will go around and see her later this morning. I'll take some clothes for the girls from the church. That should look natural enough since I am sure they are watching her house."

"And here? Do you think they are not watching this place, too?" The American could not help but ask.

"It is possible," Imanuel shrugged, "but not too likely. Hector seemed calm enough when he left. He cannot watch too many places and still have enough men to patrol. These *guardia* like to travel in larger numbers, especially at night. They have much to fear also if they go off alone."

"I hadn't thought of that." A vision of Franco hiding in the trees leaped to mind. "Are we ready?" Rick lifted Fabiano once again, and the trio whisked their charge to a safer haven.

* * * * *

Rick spent what little was left of the night in the hammock behind the store. Mariana washed the blood from his shirt, which he carried home, wet, walking up the fishermen's beach as if he had come from the *cayucos*, in case anyone was more interested in his activities than they should be.

He found David waiting for him when he opened the door to his own cabin.

"Nice day for fishing," David spoke first, noting the winds of the night before had finally died down. "Surprised you ain't out there. Or did you get up and go early?"

Without answering, Rick set a small coffee pot on the stove and lit the kerosene burner beneath it. "Want some?"

David shook his head. "You spent the night with her, didn't you?"

A wistful smile slipped across Rick's face as he considered the tumult that would ensue if he told David the true extent of his activities of the night before.

"If I did, that's my business. No one else's," was all he could think to say.

"Jesus, Joseph, and Mary!" David exploded, employing one of Dallas' favorite expressions as Rick remembered the familiar phrase in his uncle's Texas twang.

With his back to his ranting cousin, Rick tried to steel himself against the inevitable. David was going to misread everything he said and did this morning, so what was the point?

"You are crazy! I can go whorin' all night and so could you for that matter and nobody in this town would care, but you can't go messing around with another man's wife. Not here! This is like Texas 150 years ago, only worse. They'll kill you, and nobody will even have time to miss you before you're cut up and buried on a lonesome stretch of beach or fed to the sharks. Can't you get that?"

"Oh, I think I've gotten the message quite clearly, thank you." Rick calmly spooned sugar into an empty coffee cup and waited patiently for the water to boil.

"Oh, I don't think you get it at all." Utter disbelief was splashed across David's face as he sat straight up, straddling the hammock where he had been lounging. "What is it with you? She's a village girl for crying out loud. A classy one, no doubt, these days, after having lived in some fancy places and gotten some education, but she started out here, no different than any of these others. She can't be worth what you're risking! How good could she be anyway?"

The cool composure fell at once as Rick reached out and grabbed his cousin by the shirt front, lifting the shorter man to a standing position. "That's something I don't want to ever hear you ask about again, you got that?! You don't know it, but you're about as far off the mark as you could be right now, but I don't have the time or the patience to explain it to you. Wouldn't make any difference if I did, I'm sure." He finished in disgust and turned him loose with a shove.

He picked up the steaming coffee pot. "As far as you're concerned, I don't want to hear you ever mention her name again."

"Damn, Cuz." David made an attempt to pull his shirt down from around his ears. "I didn't mean anything by it. I'm just worried about you, that's all.

You are cruising on some mighty thin ice, is all. As for not saying her name, that's likely to be kind of difficult. Guess I'll just have to call her 'Hey, you' when we go to San Salvador for Christmas in a couple of days."

"Good God," It slipped out under his breath.

"Good thing you're not coming, though. Can't say this attitude of yours would go over well in the capital." David stood up. "You take care now. Go fishing or something, will ya? You need to relax a little."

* * * * *

He held out two hollowed eggs, decorated with school coloring pens he had borrowed from Paz. "I thought maybe they'd look nice on your tree."

A bright smile lit her face, despite her last-minute attempt to conceal it. "We have never had any like these before," was all she said. She picked them up by the strings run through the tiny holes at the tops where the contents had been blown out.

"Well, you said they had to be something you make," he shrugged. "My mother used to make these."

She had no sooner hung them on the tree when two little girls came into the store to buy a small amount of cooking oil. They gave Mariana their bottle to be filled from a barrel in the corner then held up dried sand dollars, collected off the beach, as their Christmas tree contribution.

"You can put them on the tree," Mariana told them.

Both Rick and Mariana watched as the girls hung their ornaments. The two then spent several moments talking over the other contributions already dangling from the branches of the community tree. The colored eggs proved to be an immediate source of fascination, as two other girls about their age entered the store.

"Who brought these?" one of them asked Mariana.

"Don Ricardo." Mariana gestured in his direction. He turned away, feigning interest in a collection of galvanized buckets hanging from a wire attached to the ceiling.

The four girls conferred, with much giggling and whispering, before the oldest, a child of no more than ten years old, was pushed forward by the others.

"Please, don Ricardo," she asked in a voice barely loud enough to be heard. "We want to see the magic chicken."

"The what?" He looked at Mariana in confusion.

"The magic chicken," the child repeated, her eyes wide with apprehension. "We want to see the magic chicken that lays the hollow eggs."

Mariana turned her head, doing a poor job of suppressing her own soft laughter. She watched the slightly embarrassed American as he struggled to explain.

Most days, these little girls were too shy to even return his greeting on the beach, but today they were brave enough to ask the impossible. He cleared his throat and pulled one of the eggs off the tree.

"I'm sorry," he began, the sad look on his face further disarming his audience as he knelt before them. "There is no magic chicken. Look here." He showed them the little holes, one in each end of the egg that he had made with his pocketknife, to blow the contents out of the egg.

They watched closely, listening, and then said a polite thank you before snatching their bottle of oil and scurrying out the door.

"So, you are raising magic chickens now?" Mariana asked with a giggle. "That was certainly unexpected."

He just shook his head as she continued. "They still surprise me sometimes. You never know what they are thinking. They know so much of the hard things of life, like the business the other night at the clinic. Too many of them already know about dying and just the struggle to live. Girls their age can already keep house, cook, do laundry, and yet somehow, in their hearts, they still believe in magic, like magic chickens. How can that be?"

"You tell me," he replied. "I actually came by here with a surprise of a different kind. I'd like to change my mind and go to San Salvador with you, if the invitation to Christmas is still open, that is."

"Certainly," she answered without hesitation. "What changed your mind?"

He shrugged. "Nothing special. Just a little talk I had with David and—" he hesitated. "The other night."

"And what about the other night has anything to do with a party?" She frowned, unable to make the connection.

"I don't really know," he lied. "Maybe just what you said originally, it's a change, a chance to get out of the village for a while."

"*Vaya pues.*" His explanation seemed to satisfy her. "We leave the day after tomorrow. Carlos is sending his Land Rover and a driver for us. No bus this time," she added with a wink.

Rick grimaced at the thought of the bus as well as riding with a driver sent by Carlos. "How is he doing?" He changed the subject so abruptly it took her a moment to follow.

"Much better. He is young and strong. He will be gone in another day at most."

"Then where?"

"That is one of those things, as Imanuel likes to say, it is better if you do not know." A honeyed smile lit her face, all the way to her eyes for a change.

* * * * *

It was a busy two days that followed. Packing, fishing with Paz, and making explanations to both Paz and Imanuel took time, but in the long run, the last was easier than he had dared to hope.

After the *nortes,* they had an especially good catch the day before he was to leave for San Salvador. Paz had said little about the fact that he was leaving for a few days.

"I am sorry I won't be here for Christmas," Rick broached the subject as they neared the shore, fishing for some sort of response from Paz who seemed to be lost in thoughts of his own.

"The *misa* at the church is pretty, and the fireworks are fun," Paz mused. "Truly, the celebration that you do not want to miss is *Semana Santa* in a couple more months."

"Easter." Rick nodded. "I'll remember that. You don't mind that I'm going then?"

Paz threw him an unexpected bright smile. "You have a good time in the city. One day I will be going off to things like that so come back and tell me what it is really all about so I will be ready."

"I can do that," Rick agreed.

"I am glad you are making the trip with her," Imanuel told him, a little later the same day, standing on the back porch of the house, watching the sunset over the estuary. "It will be easier for me if I know she is safe." Something in his voice did not ring true, but Rick could not fathom exactly what it was.

"What?" he asked.

"Life." Imanuel's answer was too quick. "What else?"

'I never know anymore," Rick responded in total honesty.

"Do not worry," the older man replied. "Everything will be fine here for a while. Our visitor will be on his way soon, and things will be quiet again."

"For how long?"

"Only God knows the answer to that one." Imanuel's smile was disarming as he walked through the store with Rick trailing behind him.

"I was hoping you would be through here again before we leave," Mariana called to him as he came through the curtain. "Look."

Her Christmas tree now held no less than half a dozen egg ornaments, the newest ones decorated with pencil drawings and bits of colored paper glued over the outside shell.

"You made quite an impression. Each of those little girls went home and made their own eggs."

Rick was not sure what to say as a rush of emotion welled up inside of him.

Mariana continued. "You added a lot of color to this tree this year." She turned to look him full in the face. "You add a lot to the lives of this whole village, whether you know it or not."

Rick shifted his gaze back to the tree and the young artists' endeavors and swallowed hard. With a heart full of Christmas spirit completely different from any he had ever known as well as a love he dare not acknowledge, there was nothing he could say, in English or Spanish, and he did not try.

* * * * *

The road trip was not the tension-filled ordeal Rick had been dreading. David immediately chose the front seat beside the driver, leaving him and Mariana to share the back. Despite his previous protests about Mariana, Rick was appreciative that David treated her with total respect. They spoke in English, seemingly ignoring the Salvadoran driver, which made Rick uncomfortable after a time.

"How are you doing, Rutilio?" Mariana asked in Spanish after a while. The man, who was easily large enough to serve as a bodyguard as well as a driver, smiled and nodded amiably to her in the rearview mirror.

"He does not speak," Mariana returned to English. "He has worked for Carlos for several years now. Before that, however, he was accused of talking to the wrong people. For that, they cut out his tongue."

"What?" Rick was stunned. "Who?"

David said nothing but cast an I-told-you-so glance at Rick in the mirror on his sunshade.

"Who? What? Who knows?" Mariana answered with impatience. "People like those who stopped the bus we rode together one day are undoubtedly the ones he was accused of talking to, people like my cousin. As for who did it? Those who claim they are protecting the government. He is from Chalatenango, north of the capital. I think the particular group responsible there calls themselves the White Hand of Death. Or at least, that is their name at night. As likely, their name during the day is *ORDEN*. And that is what they give to anyone that does not go by their rules."

"*ORDEN?*" Rick frowned. "Why does that name sound familiar?"

"Because they really are a group sanctioned by the government. They are supposed to be regular citizens, helping to keep law and order and keep the peace. Of course, the way they do that is to spy on their neighbors and report anything suspicious. Sounds like Russia, yes? And yet, they claim they are fighting communism. The other part of the problem is that sometimes, the army lets some of them have weapons as well, so in the night, they can go out and take care of the problem themselves." She shuddered.

While it was not clear whether or not the driver understood English, he was comprehending enough of the conversation to give Mariana a stern cautionary look.

"*Vaya pues*, Rutilio," she laughed gently at his reflection in the mirror. "I will be good. No more politics, yes?"

He nodded with satisfaction.

Rutilio drove the way his size suggested he might move down a football field, with plenty of power and speed, Rick thought. They barreled up the coastal highway through Usulatan, Zacatecoluca, Santo Tomas without even the hint of a stop to be made.

Winding through the narrow traffic-laden streets of San Salvador at dusk, David directed the driver to leave them outside the *Casa San Cristobal*.

"*Y mañana*?" Mariana asked as they climbed out.

"I don't know," Rick answered.

"Do you want to go to the market with me?" she asked.

David said he had other things to take care of, and Rick sensed even this evening he would not see much of his cousin. Rick, however, accepted her invitation for the next day.

The car pulled away, and David came inside long enough to drop off his bag in the room before making an excuse and taking his leave.

Left on his own, Rick wandered around the exquisite little guest house before going back outside. He walked aimlessly toward the bright lights of the commercial district, down Calle Arce taking in everything from the rough sidewalks and cobblestone side streets to the assorted collection of goods available in the thinly lit shop windows. So many familiar appliances, washing machines, clothes dryers, and tabletop ovens, manufactured in miniature versions, yet still carrying full-sized price tags. Other items like treadle sewing machines, long-abandoned items in his own country, sat here in brand new versions, ready to operate anywhere, without the benefit of electricity. Still other things, available only in multiple packages in his country, were sold singly here, from rubber bands to envelopes and pencils—one, two, three or four, like the cigarettes Mariana banded together in the store from a regular-sized pack of twenty, making tiny affordable bundles for the country's majority population, the poor.

The shops' Christmas decorations, winking lights and plastic bits of holly and evergreen, clashed with the warm night air, heavy with the scent of flowers, yet always undergirded with the stench of diesel fumes. Mingled with the smell of the recently steaming pavement, it made for a slightly intoxicating mix of its own.

Rick entered one of the clothing shops, and after much searching, found what he was after. He walked back outside, carrying a small paper bundle.

After a time, he took a position, as he had seen so many others do in this city, leaning against the wall, arms folded, and simply watched the steady streams of people and vehicles pass by. It was not an unpleasant way to unwind after a long trip. The ancient phrases—Peace on Earth and Good Will to Men—lingered in the back of his mind as he felt the Christmas spirit of human kindness to be as alive on these streets, as any other place in the world, at this time of year.

He bought a few *pupusas* from a woman who was grilling them over a makeshift portable stove on a street corner and walked back to the *Casa*, as David called it, ready for a long, restful sleep.

* * * * *

David was up surprisingly early the next morning, and they shared a hearty breakfast of fried rice, beans, *huevos revueltos*, and tortillas in the great house's small dining room. Rick wondered privately just how much sleep David had managed to get since he never heard him come in the night before.

"I've got a meeting at the office this morning, but I'll catch up with you all in time for the party tonight," David explained. "I'm not sure what's going on, but I don't like much of what I'm hearing."

"About what?" Rick asked as he ladled a spoonful of sour cream onto the beans on his plate.

"I'm not sure," David frowned, uncharacteristically concerned over a matter involving his work. "We keep hearing about people worrying about rebel activity around *Las Palomitas*, and the truth is, I guess, there is that kind of trouble everywhere. Things are to a point that it sounds like they may be considering closing down several of the different projects."

"It's that serious?" After what he had seen the past few days, Rick knew he should not be surprised, but somehow he never thought of David's work being threatened.

"I guess so. I really don't know much, just rumors at the moment. Maybe I can find out more today."

He left, and shortly afterward, Mariana arrived in the Land Rover with Rutilio. He dropped them off in a part of the downtown district Rick had not seen before. Following Mariana through an arched door in a once-white stucco wall, Rick found himself in a world of vendors and stalls, piled high with fruits, vegetables, spices, and foodstuffs he could not begin to name. It was as if they had passed through a wall made, not only of wood and stone, but equally comprised of overwhelming humidity and exotic aromas, not all of them pleasant.

"Where are we?" He gasped after several moments.

"*El Mercado Central*, the downtown market." She glanced over her shoulder as she reached out to squeeze a honeydew melon. She stopped to look closer at his face. "You do not like it?" She seemed surprised. "You are not like those American ladies who live in Colonia Campestre or San Benito and brag how they never come here. They say it makes them sick because it is too dirty and too smelly.

They only send their maids." Her derogatory tone cleared his head immediately.

"I do not understand them, really. They claim they love El Salvador, but the truth is, all they love is life in a tropical country club. They do not know El Salvador," she chatted on while moving along in front of the various tables and stalls, oblivious to the vendors' chants and calls to buy or make an offer. She smiled meaninglessly at some and waved away others like pesky flies.

"How can they say they love my country when they turn up their nose at a place like this? This is some of the best this country has to offer."

Rick took a deep breath and tried hard not to laugh out loud. Fancy places and educated talk, David had denounced her. If only he could see her now, Rick thought as he followed contentedly along behind her.

Bananas piled higher than his head, melons of all sizes, colors and descriptions, including watermelons with a bright golden interior instead of the familiar red, coconuts, both new and fresh and full of liquid and small round older hairy ones full of pulp, huge mangos and avocados that dwarfed their tiny northern cousins displayed in American supermarkets, *guayabas*, *sapotes*, *marañones*—exotic tropical fruits, with stranger sounding names—the place was overrun with produce of all kinds.

"Look, Rishard." The excitement in her voice as she said his name took his breath away. "*Manzanas y uvas*, these mean Christmas here."

Apples and grapes. Rick did not follow her logic.

"Look at the boxes," she told him as she began selecting apples, one by one.

"Washington's Finest." He read aloud in English. "California Red."

"*Lo major.*" The heavy-set woman behind the table told them. The very best.

"They are imported. You can only get apples and grapes in El Salvador at Christmastime," Mariana explained. "Sort of like tangerines in America."

Rick noted the imported prices as well as she paid over three dollars a pound for table grapes.

Delving deeper amongst the stalls, they came to the herb and spice vendors where Mariana stopped and bought a few small plastic envelopes of a brown powder that looked like light-colored cocoa.

"*Y eso?*" Rick asked the common question he heard so often in the village.

"Mix for *horchata*," she told him proudly as she handed him one. "It is a drink made with rice, milk, and ground seeds, like pumpkin and sesame seeds."

Rick made a face.

"You probably would not like it," she said, laughing. "I have never met an American who did, but we love it. But then," she looked at him sideways. "I bet you like peanut butter, yes?"

"Well, sure," he answered with a confused expression. "Is this like peanut butter?" He held it up to the light but could not make the connection.

"No, *loco*," she giggled again and snatched the packet from his hand. "It is not. But I think peanut

butter is terrible stuff, and so do most people
that I know. It smells so strange and looks bad,
like something you find in a baby's diaper. But
Americans love it. They eat it from the time they are
little children. Their mothers give it to them, and
they think it is wonderful. I never even saw the stuff
until I was in the United States for the first time,
gracias a Dios.

"My mother made *horchata* when I was little, and
so it is with most people here. We like our *horchata*
because, for us, it is like your peanut butter. Precious,
all mixed up with childhood memories, yes?"

"I can't say as I ever thought about it like that, but
it makes sense," Rick agreed. "So how did you ever
survive in the US, if you don't like peanut butter?"

"It was not easy," she added, moving on to the
next table.

They drifted through other sections of the
market—baskets and straw mats, not the kind the
tourists buy but those made for durable daily use;
rubber and plastic goods, from shoes to washtubs,
metal buckets, bowls, and jugs. A vision of Mariana
tending Fabiano's wounds darted through his mind
and tugged at his heart at the sight of the metal
pitchers and washbasins.

The meat market was grisly as swarms of black
flies buzzed over and around the various offerings,
most of which Rick knew had been on the hoof, be
it pork or beef, the day before. Aged meat was not
a readily available commodity in this country. The
chorizos, strings of cured sausages, nearly as long

as Rick was tall, hung from the sides of the vendors' stalls and were the only meat product not besieged by winged insects.

At the entrance to the flower market, a tiny old man squatted on a three-legged stool, bending over a pile of squares of white cardboard he held on his lap. With a common pocketknife, he cut tiny images of Christmas bells, pines, garlands, and birds, set against mountain peaks. He finished each with the words, *Feliz Navidad, Prospero Año Nuevo*. Each white on white homemade Christmas card took on its own unique character, coaxed from the common paperboard, by the gnarled bony hands. He offered Rick a toothless grin, in return for a compliment on his handiwork.

Rick bought three of the tiny works of art. "Complete with *palomitas*," Mariana noted as she pointed out the tiny doves at the corners of the cards. What will you do with these?"

"I'll take one back to Imanuel and Paz and send one to my mother."

"It is rather late to be mailing Christmas cards, yes?"

"Yes, except that it's sort of a tradition between us. I always give her my Christmas gift late. When I was little, I used to say it was so that I could make sure mine was different than what everyone else had given her. I'm sure that will still be the case with this."

"And the other?"

"I think I'll save that one for a bit, for something special."

The adjacent flower market was a welcome relief in more ways than one as they were surrounded by the fragrant rainbow of roses, carnations, and exotic blossoms. Bougainvillea blooms trailed from hanging pots and bright-colored newspaper-wrapped bundles of all the rest, spilled into the aisles and around the stalls. Rick could not resist the age-old temptation to bestow at least one bouquet of loveliness on the lady at his side.

"For the party tonight," he told her as he laid them in her arms. "I'd bring them then, but they might be misunderstood."

"That is always a possibility," she told him as she returned his steady gaze. "They will look lovely tonight."

I'm certain they won't be alone in that regard. Rick kept the thought to himself as they retraced their steps and headed toward the waiting car.

* * * * *

True to his word, David was waiting at the *Casa San Cristobal*. After a shower, Rick put on clean blue jeans and the pale blue embroidered *guayabera* shirt that he had purchased the night before.

"Very nice," David teased. "Where did you find that?"

"It wasn't easy," Rick answered. He held out the sides. "I think it was designed for someone a great deal rounder than me, but it was the only one that was nearly long enough."

"It looks great." This time David was sincere. He compared his own image in the mirror, dressed in an open-collared shirt and jeans. "I wish I'd thought of it."

The car returned for them at twilight. Climbing a long hill into a well-to-do section of the city, they soon found themselves amongst sprawling cream-colored brick homes that graced wide well-tended streets, far removed from those Rick and David had come to know well.

At the top of a long drive, Rutilio pulled up in front of a huge tan two-story house, trimmed with decorative yet practical wrought iron window and door protection. Fronted by a large green exquisitely manicured lawn, the lights and music flowing from the house said the party was well underway on the second floor. Mariana met them at the door.

Her dress was simple this time, a shimmering white fabric pulled tight at the waist with a red sash. As he watched her every movement, while trying to appear not to, Rick realized how little it mattered what she wore. She was the one who made the clothes look so appealing, not the other way around.

They followed her upstairs to a wide room that opened onto a large balcony, overlooking the entire city. A buffet table and a portable bar, complete with a bartender, took up one end of the room while a small combo played on the opposite side. In between, the room was crowded with well-dressed guests, most of whom were standing, drinking, and chatting with one another. Rick and David's assumption that they would not know anyone was quickly put to the test as the threesome from the hunt at *Las Palomitas* stood out in the crowd.

"*Feliz Navidad.*" Ernesto Benavidez raised a glass in salutation toward the two of them as Mariana introduced them to a few of the other guests.

Ernesto stood alone, but the other two men were accompanied by their wives. Dolores, the small mousy woman who stood beside Victor, acknowledged them with a nod of her head and a shy smile. Her diminutive nature only served to emphasize her husband's rotund shape and size.

The tall, stately woman beside Felipe greeted them with a firm handshake and a perfect English introduction.

"Gentlemen." Ernesto took over the introductions from Mariana, who seemed to almost shrink in the presence of these particular guests. "Allow me to introduce my sister, Rose Maria Benavidez de Damas. You remember, of course, her husband Felipe from our day at the beach."

"And how is the hunting these days?" Felipe asked.

"We haven't done much since you were there," David made a quick answer while giving Rick a cautionary glance. "Just fishing. That's all we seem to find time for."

"I cannot imagine two Americans, like yourselves, finding much to do in a place like *Las Palomitas,*" Rose Maria commented as she set her empty glass on a passing maid's tray and retrieved a full one. Rick was certain that was not her first refill of the evening.

"We fish, we work, we stay busy," David answered blandly.

"Work at what?"

"With the fishermen's cooperative," he continued. "It's a real business these days, getting the fish to market, keeping up with the demand here in the city."

"And you?" she asked Rick. "Do you work with the same project?"

"No, not exactly. I've only been here a couple of months, really. And I'm not a member of David's organization."

"Then what do you do there?"

Felipe had drifted off, deep in conversation with Victor and Rosa Maria took a step closer to him. Rick glanced around, looking for Mariana. All he found were Ernesto's eyes resting steadily upon him.

"I fish, and I help out where I can, with the local church, helping to make deliveries of needed things, like food, clothing, like that." He knew it was probably the wrong thing to say, even as he said it.

"You work with the church? Are you a missionary?" She seemed slightly taken aback. "Carlos," she called out. "Are you entertaining missionaries in your house these days?"

All conversation came to a halt as Rick felt many of the eyes in the room were now focused on him.

"I'm not a missionary," he stated quietly, looking at the floor and then shifting his gaze to the woman who seemed determined to misconstrue everything he said. "Although I'm not sure what the difference would be if I was. I'm a tourist if you really must know. I've made a few friends there in the village of

Las Palomitas, and I help them out whenever I can. That's all."

"Friends? There? What could you, an American, possibly have in common with anyone there?" She took a healthy sip of the drink in her hand. "That is the trouble so often here. Americans meddling in business they know nothing about. What do you know of the people there?"

"I don't claim to know anything about anyone." Rick wondered why he was even attempting an answer under the circumstances. "They are just some people who have been kind to me, and I wanted to return the favor."

"I imagine you feel sorry for them, don't you? You think they need all your help, all kinds of charity."

"I never said that."

"Well, they do not. They need to be left alone. If it was up to you Americans, you would be putting a dishwasher and an air conditioner in every one of their huts. Now what good would that do? They do not feel the cold or the heat the way you do, you know. They really do not. They work hard, but that is what they were meant to do. And they do not miss what they never had. If Americans would just stay out of things they know nothing about, the world would be a less complicated place. That is for certain."

"Rose Maria, that is enough." His voice was not loud, but the power behind Ernesto's words was unmistakable.

Mariana was suddenly beside him, and for that reason alone, Rick could not leave Rose Maria's charges unanswered.

"It may be true," he spoke softly, yet all who heard were riveted where they stood. "That the people of *Las Palomitas* don't miss dishwashers and other modern conveniences they've never had. They are a talented people who adapt well to whatever their lot may be. But you will never convince me that they do not suffer. Oh, not in the heat, perhaps, the way you would if you worked as hard as they do. But more importantly, when their children are sick or suffering from malnutrition or their men are sick from ingesting poison in the nearby cotton fields and can't work. Then they suffer, and they agonize over their health, and just like anyone else, they worry how they will pay their bills and put food on the table for their children. And when their children die for lack of a few dollars' worth of penicillin or malaria medication as often as not, and they bury their babies, their tears are no less painful, their hearts no less broken than yours." He turned and walked, unseeing, out to the balcony with Mariana still walking beside him.

"How do you stand it?" When he finally spoke after leaning against the railing for several moments. It was all he could think to ask.

It was a sad smile that drifted across her face as she looked out over the city that lay before them. "I warned you, yes? All kinds of boring people I said that day in the store."

"That's not exactly what I would call her," Rick answered sharply, and Mariana giggled and put a finger to her lips. She was smoking again tonight, he noticed.

"Did you get a drink?" she asked, holding hers up to him.

He shook his head. "Not now. Maybe later."

"Sometimes, it helps. It is not easy to listen to people with ideas like hers, but unfortunately, she is one of many amongst her class, who think that way. Others are kinder, like her brother, don 'Neto, but even he is afraid."

"Afraid? Of what? What kind of threat do Imanuel, Miguel, Paz, and all the others present to people like this?" He waved his arm in a wide arc of frustration that took in the entire hillside of expensive homes.

Below, the city seemed to erupt with homemade fireworks, the standard fare of Christmas Eve in San Salvador. He watched the arcs of bottle rockets, firecrackers, and other handmade fireworks that streaked across the city blocks, creating a colorful patchwork of lights, punctuated by explosions, big and small.

"Do you remember that day in the store when we talked of such things, and I reminded you of your own country's civil war? This is more of the same. What do you remember of your own history lessons? The plantation owners were afraid of the slaves, yes? Of revolution and change but also of revenge. They were afraid the black people would come for their revenge for the way they had been treated for so long. People like Rosa Maria are not only afraid of what they will have to give up but that they will have to pay for their sins as well."

Her voice, so empty of the bitterness that might have been there—should have been there as far as Rick could see—had a calming effect on him. "And so you think she will?"

"Oh, no," she sighed. "How often do you hear Imanuel, Niña Ana, Miguel, or any of the villagers speak of such things? Even Franco, for all his big talk, is not interested in that, not really. All they want is to live, to live free from fear, and to raise their children to have a better chance than they did. Is that not what all people, all parents want, no matter who they are or where they live—a better chance for their children. Nothing more than that."

She took a little breath and then continued. "Some, like don 'Neto really do try to do something to change things. That is what makes him so different from her."

"What are you talking about?"

"Oh, just that it is funny how two people can be from the same family and be so different. Their whole family is very wealthy, from coffee, *por supuesto*, of course. You heard Rose Maria and what she thinks of the people from the country. We are all like dogs and *burros* and should be happy we have food given to us and a dry place to sleep with a little fresh straw at night." She laughed with more than a touch of sarcasm.

"Don 'Neto, her own brother, is different. He has always treated us with respect. He is not married and has no children, no heirs. A few years ago, he converted one of his big *ranchos* into an agricultural cooperative. He sold his land to the eighty people who have worked it all these years, and now they own it. I always like seeing him here at the parties that Carlos gives because many of his friends, the others of his social class, will not even invite him to their homes. They consider him a traitor to his own."

"And Rose Maria? What does she say about her brother's generosity?"

The music of Mariana's laughter filled the night air. "Well, she is not strong enough to say much directly to him, but you heard what she thinks in general. She is bitter. I usually try to stay away from her."

"Because of her views?"

"That and the fact that she has a crush on Carlos. She has for years, although he has no interest in her. I think she only married Felipe to make her parents happy. She is not a happy woman, and I certainly do not make her any happier when I am around. I can see that."

"And you, Mariana?" Are you a happy woman?" Rick leaned against the balcony railing, wondering what her answer might be.

"Happiness is a fleeting thing, no? It comes, it goes." She shrugged and looked past him at the continuing fireworks show below. "There are days when I know how blessed I am simply to be alive.

Other days—" she shrugged. "Other days are more of a struggle, yes?

"Don Neto looks happy tonight." She shifted the conversation away from herself. "For him, I am glad. He deserves it."

"From what you say, he is, no doubt, a courageous man," Rick stated. "There has been something about him that I liked from the beginning, even though I didn't like anything about the hunting trip that day."

"Oh, yes, he is very brave, I think. Like my cousin told you, it is often a dangerous thing here to be kind to the poor." She frowned at him. "You did not enjoy your day hunting? I thought it was only the bad *ostras* that ruined the day for you."

"Food poisoning by bad oysters was the perfect ending to that day, believe me."

Others were joining them now on the balcony to watch the city come alive with the ongoing pyrotechnics. As the night wore on, more and more fireworks exploded across the city, a major part of the capital city's Christmas celebration.

"It is beautiful," Rick noted. "We do fireworks for July 4th, Independence Day, but not for Christmas. Of course, in much of the US, it's too cold or wet to be shooting them off outside like this in December."

"Oh, not here," Mariana replied as she watched the twinkling lights laid out before them, further accented by the streaming rockets and crackling firecrackers. "The night air is perfect, not too cool, not too warm, and no rain."

"Yes, no rain," he repeated. "A lot of Texas is rainy about now."

"That is the worst curse here for it to rain in December," she added.

"What is so bad about rain at Christmas?" he asked.

"It's not about Christmas," Mariana explained. "It's harvest time. Do you not remember all those trucks, heavy with cotton that we saw on the way here yesterday?"

"I'm not likely to forget them." Rick had tried not to think about how many times Rutilio dodged the trailers of cotton that seemed barely attached to the trucks that hauled them. They zipped around them on blind curves at a speed that would have been about right for flying but was perilous at best for passing traffic on a narrow two-lane highway.

"The cotton is harvested and baled on the eastern side of the country, and the coffee, here in the west, is also picked at this time. Rain in December means wet cotton and wet coffee and many tears for all. The cotton cannot be put in the warehouse if it is wet—it makes its own fire like the hay in your country, yes? If it is put away wet."

"Yep, you can't bale wet hay or put up wet bales, that's for sure."

"And the coffee, when it is wet, it molds. So much can be lost in El Salvador if it rains at the wrong time of year."

He looked beyond the exploding city at the mountains beyond, contemplating the tenuous hold so many held over their own destiny. As more people drifted toward the balcony, he and Mariana stepped back inside. They found David, close to the huge buffet of meats, vegetables, and other party foods.

"Nice work, cousin," David cracked wise. "I can't take you anywhere, can I?" he began to laugh at Rick's expression. "I'm only kidding. I'd heard from Rafael and Victor, she's a hard one to handle, but I'd never actually met her before tonight." He looked at Mariana. "This is quite a layout. Thanks for including us. This is your house?"

Mariana nodded. "This is Carlos' house, yes. We stay here when we are in San Salvador, which is not so often, really."

David shook his head in mock wonder and exchanged a look with Rick.

Their host approached as they spoke, and watching him, Rick stiffened at the exchange he assumed was coming.

"My most sincere apologies," Carlos spoke in Spanish. "For one of my guests' outrageous behavior. The lady had too much to drink, but of course, that is no excuse."

"It's all right," Rick stammered, caught by surprise. Somehow an apology from this man was more disturbing than the confrontation he had been expecting.

"My dear, are you enjoying yourself this evening?" Carlos inquired of Mariana. "I hope the earlier conversations did not upset you."

"I'm fine, Carlos," she reassured him. "I do not let Rose Maria upset me anymore. You know that."

A rare smile crossed his face. "Yes, I do." An expression of true affection passed between the two of them, a look Rick wished he had not seen. "This party was her idea, you know. Sometimes I truly do not understand her."

"Who does?" Mariana laughed. "Maybe she just needed the distraction of the party. Everyone else seems to be enjoying it. That is the important part, yes?"

Carlos lumbered off in the direction of the relaxing musicians as don 'Neto joined them.

"Do you have brothers or sisters?" He asked Rick and David as they stood together.

David shook his head, but a smile spread across Rick's face as he nodded and answered. "Yes, one older sister."

"And does she do or say things that are sometimes completely impossible to comprehend?"

Rick nodded again.

"Then I suppose you know to some extent how I feel right now." Ernesto's voice remained serious, although a smile played around his eyes. "Not only does she insult an invited guest, but she talks about things she knows nothing about and acts as if she does. It is a mystery."

"I've been there, many times, with my sister," Rick agreed.

"I do hope you know I share none of her opinions."

"I'd already guessed as much," Rick replied, trying to keep his guard up but finding it difficult to do with this man. "But why do you care that I know that?"

Ernesto regarded him for a moment before attempting an answer. "I really do not know, but for some reason, it is important, just the same. You are a person whose opinion matters to me.

"Tell me, do you really work with the church in *Las Palomitas*?"

Rick was instantly wary, but the moment was short-lived. David walked up and handed Rick a drink from the bar.

"I help out the local catechist a little, that's all. His son and I fish together often, so it just seemed like a natural thing."

"And what does the church do and say, really, about all that goes on in the *campo*, the countryside, these days?"

"Truly? I find that the church says little but does much. Those who work through the church are looking for ways to help the people make a difficult life a little easier. Isn't that part of what the church was designed to do, no matter where it is? That is all I have seen in *Las Palomitas*. Attempts to ease people's pain—with blankets, food, shelter, clothing, shoes, medicine, in addition to prayer and a deepening of their faith. The catechists are taught to minister to the whole person, the body and mind, as well as the soul. That's all. Surely there is no crime in that."

"No, no crime at all. As you say, that is what the church was designed to do. Here in the capital and in many areas, the issues have become much more clouded than that. There are those who cry that the church is meddling in politics, and indeed it would seem to be true. I do not know. There are many of us who want to know, who want to do the right thing, the best thing, yet it is not clear just what that may be."

Rick replied. "The purpose of the church is to make people's lives better. Stated simply, that should also be the job of the government. Maybe the question is, which is doing a better job? And if they are in conflict, could it be that the government is not doing its job, yet resents the intrusion of the church?"

He took a deep breath and wondered where he found the courage to continue talking this way to a man he barely knew.

"I know what I see is a small piece of a much larger puzzle, yet it is a revealing piece just the same. The people shrink at the presence of the soldiers in *Las Palomitas*. They are afraid of them, afraid they will come in the night and accuse them of things they did not do. In my country, people are more likely to stand a little straighter with pride when the soldiers pass by, and shrink from the presence of the local priest, for fear he knows their unconfessed sins."

Ernesto laughed out loud at the thought.

"At the very least, no one ever crosses the street there, to avoid the presence of a few soldiers, like they do here. Men in uniform are respected. Here, they are feared. Those who work for the church here are respected and beloved. The only fear associated with them is FOR them and what they might suffer because they dared to help others."

Ernesto regarded him for several more moments. "All of what you say is true, my friend. Perhaps we, who have long feared the power of the church, have been looking at things in a reversed manner. It is not the church interfering in politics as much as it is the government interfering in the lives of the people, people who have always belonged first to the church, and secondly, to the government. It is a matter worthy of much thought and study."

Ernesto excused himself to check on his sister, who was, he said, lying down in a back bedroom. Rick found Mariana near the front door. She had a shawl over her head and was preparing to leave.

"Where are you going?"

"It is nearly midnight and no one here will care, but I told Carlos I was going to Christmas Mass. It's held at midnight."

"Wait, and I'll go with you."

"It is not necessary."

"I know, but I'd like to if you don't mind."

She nodded.

Outside, they rode across the city, with Rutilio at the wheel, and they were nearly as silent as their driver. Rick watched out the window at the activity in the streets, children and youth still actively engaged in their fireworks celebration. Others were walking, chatting in groups, and like them, many were headed toward the large cathedral in the downtown area. It was as if every window in the city was lit this evening, while most of the city's residents seemed to be outside on the city streets.

"Stop here," Mariana spoke after they passed a small park on the right. "We will walk the rest of the way. We will find a taxi for the ride home. *Buenas noches, Rutilio. Feliz Navidad.*" She patted his large hand as it rested on the driver's side window ledge as she sent him on his way.

He smiled his answer back to her as he drove away.

The sidewalks were covered with layers of shredded newspapers, the remains of hundreds of firecrackers. It reminded Rick of walking through piles of leaves in the fall near his own home as a child. A few more firecrackers exploded above as they passed beneath the windows of apartments and balconies built over the shops along *Calle Rubén Dario*. A shower of shredded newspaper floated down around them.

"I love to walk at Christmas, even if only for a few blocks," she laughed at the startled look on his face as she took his arm. "Christmas in your country is almost sad to me. It is so serious and of course, so cold. Here, everyone is outside in the street. It is a big party, and we have all been invited."

As they walked, the last of the firecrackers died away, almost as if on cue, as the bells of the city's main cathedral began to ring. They joined the standing room only crowd that overflowed the cathedral. Rick listened and watched as hundreds came together to celebrate the night of the Christ child's birth. While a few like Mariana were well-dressed, coming from this or that secular party, most were the vendors and street people, like the ones he had seen earlier in the day, in the marketplace.

As Monsignor Romero, El Salvador's Archbishop, celebrated the Mass, Rick listened to the intensity that poured forth from the small-statured man. He began to comprehend the effect he was having on both the poor, who had found a true friend at the head of the church for the first time in recent history, and the rich as he struck fear in their hearts that their days of power and prestige might indeed be numbered.

Walking down the cathedral steps after the *misa*, Mariana bent over and clutched at her chest.

"What is it?" Rick reached an arm around her and felt her entire body tremble.

"Nothing, really." Her breath was coming in tiny gasps. "It will pass quickly, really."

He guided her to an iron bench near one of the ornate concrete barriers that led up to the church. "Can I get you something?"

"No, really. Just let me rest here a moment, and then I will be fine. I think I just ate, maybe drank a little too much earlier." The paleness of her skin, poorly illuminated by the city street lights, further alarmed him. "I don't usually drink alcohol, so—" She gave him a little smile.

Rick looked up, taking in the full magnitude of the three-story church. "Are they working to renovate the building?" He asked, as his eyes climbed over the unfinished brick exterior, where construction seemed to have stopped in mid-project.

"The cathedral here was never finished," Mariana stated with a touch of pride in her still thin voice. "Monsignor ordered that it should not be until the needs of the people are met. I guess you could say that the church is being renovated, but it is from the inside out."

Her color returned, and she was breathing easier now. He handed her a white envelope.

Inside, she found the third Christmas card he had bought earlier in the day. Her face held a question as she looked at him after reading the inscription.

"I told you I needed to save it for something special." He shrugged with a smile. "I'm glad I came with you tonight. To the party and especially, to Mass. It made my Christmas in El Salvador very special."

"They will be eating dinner when we get back," she told him as they rode in the back of a taxi he had flagged down. "They probably will not even have missed us."

"Dinner? Now?"

"Always. Fireworks, Mass, and then dinner. Christmas lasts from the 24th all the way to the 25th here."

"And on the 25th?" He asked.

"That is mostly for recovering." The return of her laughter was a welcome sound. "From all that you did on the 24th!"

The dining room on the lower floor was full when they arrived, the guests all seated around a couple of long tables. Carlos and David, however, were anxiously waiting for them when they stepped through the front door.

In a serious manner, Carlos whisked her off to the next room, closing the door and leaving David and Rick, standing alone in the vestibule. Still, Rick could just catch a glimpse of the pair behind the crystal window pane in the door.

"What's going on?" Rick's conscience, filled with thoughts of what he would like to do, worried him more than anything he had actually done. "Is he angry with her? It's not her fault. She told him she was going to Mass and I asked at the last minute if I could go with her. She didn't know, so I'm sure he didn't either but—" He started toward the closed door, but David pulled him back.

"What are you babbling about? He's not mad at her."

Rick tried to listen but still wasn't comprehending the full scope of what was going on around him.

"While you were gone, a messenger showed up with a telegram for her, from Paz as best as we could figure. And the news isn't good."

Mariana's scream captured everyone's attention as Carlos caught her in his arms when she fainted. Rick struck out on his own, but David stepped into the dining room and announced that they had received a bit of startling news from the village of *Las Palomitas*. Everything would be fine, he assured the guests. They just had to figure out a couple of things and make some hasty arrangements.

Caught in an awkward position, Carlos couldn't move. Rick reached around and eased Mariana out of Carlos' arms and onto a nearby couch up against the wall.

"What the hell is going on?" Rick muttered under his breath as David handed him a cloth napkin that he had soaked in ice water. Carlos laid it across her forehead.

"Here." David thrust a yellow telegram slip into Rick's hands.

Please come soon. Imanuel disappeared. Do not know who to ask for help. With Peace.

"Looks like the operator did not understand that Paz is his name, so he or she signed the message, with Peace, which is why we are not quite sure who it's from." David startled him, re-reading the message over his shoulder. "Maybe she thought with it being the Christmas season and all, that was the way he meant to sign. Who knows? That's the only thing we could think of."

David continued to jabber. "The bottom line is that it sounds like the kid is down there, pretty much on his own, which means somebody needs to get back there quick." David shook his head, uncertain of what the next move should be. For the first time in quite a while, Rick began to feel like David cared about their friends in *Las Palomitas* as much as he did.

Mariana stirred and opened her eyes. "*Díos mio,* Carlos," she began through her tears. "Tell me it is not true. Tell me, I did not do this. You know I have to go home now."

"*Vaya pues.* In the morning. We will go. *Calmate, Niña.* None of this is your fault. Imanuel does what he does, and you did not have anything to do with it."

He continued to speak to her, like a little child, as he slid behind her and held her in his arms. "We will go and be with Paz. He needs you now. Tomorrow."

David guided Rick toward the door. "Come on. We should go. Carlos already told me, you'll be leaving before dawn, and he'll be driving. That means you'll make it down there in the fastest time possible if I remember right."

"What do you mean—me? Aren't you coming?"

"Not this time. Remember I told you there's trouble here with my agency. I found out more about that today, and I'd hoped for a few more days to get it all worked out, but no such luck. I'll be along in a few days, but in the meantime, I can't leave the city right now."

"But what about—" He realized he didn't even know what to ask. Was it just a moment ago, David had sounded so concerned about Paz?

"There's nothing I can do for them that you can't. The truth be told, you'll probably be more help than me anyway."

Nothing he had heard in the past several minutes made any sense. David continued speaking as he opened the front door.

"Come on. We'll go pack and get a little sleep. To be honest, you don't look much better than she does right now." He tossed his head back toward the weeping Mariana.

Probably because I feel about the same way, Rick thought as he followed his cousin down the street.

CHAPTER 11

January 14, 1980. San Salvador. – Ten days have passed since the resignation of the last of the original members of the junta, named immediately after the coup of October 15 of last year.

Despite an attempt by El Salvador's Archbishop Monsignor Romero to mediate a settlement between the civilian and military members, those resigning cited the military's flagrant violations of the law and all attempts toward reform, and respect for basic human rights. Only Colonel José Guillermo Garcia, Minister of Defense, and believed by many to be the source of much of the controversy within the new government, remains, after the resignation of Mario Antonio Andino, a Salvadoran businessman, Guillermo Manuel Ungo, a former vice presidential candidate, three younger military officers, and at least 40 other members of the new government.

Meanwhile, the number of dead and disappeared persons continues to increase, as tortured bodies are found along the roadsides on a daily basis. On New Year's Eve, in separate attacks, soldiers and members of ORDEN seized peasants in several rural villages. Josefina Guardado of Conacaste was found the next day, tortured, raped, with her throat cut.

An unnamed man taken in El Jicaro was found hanged and shot in nearby El Terreno. Yesterday, in La Joya, Chalatenango, three Recino brothers, ages 12, 16, and 18, and a 14-year-old friend, were all killed by the National Guard and ORDEN.

When he thought about it later, Rick always remembered the return trip to *Las Palomitas* as one of the worst experiences of his life in an automobile. True to his word, Carlos was outside the boarding house before dawn. Rick was ready but ill at ease from the moment he scrambled into the back seat of the large blue Land Rover. A glance at the mute, hollow-eyed Mariana in the front passenger seat was enough to know she had spent a sleepless night of tears and self-recrimination.

Carlos was also quiet, but his silence was marked by a grim determination as he gripped the steering wheel. He drove the narrow, unmarked pavement that wove its way across the countryside of mountain ranges and valley plains in a brutal manner that made the trip two days before with Rutilio look like a kindergarten excursion. The so-called highway that crossed the open range and was punctuated by the occasional mini-herd of cattle or wandering pigs was especially hazardous as it wound through hamlets, villages, and a couple of fair-sized cities since at no time did Carlos ever slow his speed. Rick drew more than one sharp breath at near misses, collisions avoided only by Carlos' deft steering, constant use of the horn, and a rare application of the brakes.

José, the bus driver from Rick's initial foray into the country, would have been impressed, he thought, as he remembered that first day in Salvadoran traffic.

He tried to focus his attention on the rising sun and the spectacular colors spreading across the eastern sky, silhouetting the distant mountains. At any other time and place, it would have provided a welcome distraction. His most fervent desire at the moment, however, was to say or do anything that might prove a comfort to the woman riding in the front seat, but he could think of nothing that might not be misinterpreted either by her or the man riding at her side. And so he, too, remained silent. He felt like a caged animal, unable to do anything, yet seething within. He concentrated on the journey's end, willing it to happen more quickly, yet wondering and dreading what might await them when it did.

The crunch of gravel and the bone-jarring rattle of the final track that led to *Las Palomitas* from the highway was a welcome change from the high-pitched whine of the tires on pavement. Mariana, who had drifted to sleep minutes before awoke with a start.

"*Esta bien*," Carlos told her. "We are almost there."

Rounding the curve below the cemetery, they caught their first glimpse of the sea. The tranquility of the blue-green water, heaving gently as the waves neared the sand, was far removed from his reeling thoughts and emotions. This is a place of peace and beauty, Rick found himself thinking.

The Land Rover sped on, past the large vacation homes, the thatch huts, the battered shacks and waving children, to pull up sharply in front of Emelina's restaurant.

Emelina was out the front door, wringing her hands in her apron as she began to pour out her sad tale.

"Please," Carlos admonished gently as he helped Mariana from the car. "Not here, in the street. Come inside. Find us something cool to drink and then tell us everything."

"*Sí, como no.*" The distraught woman made half a curtsy toward Carlos and threw her arms around Mariana before whirling back toward the store. "I am so sorry, don Carlos." She prattled on as she opened the store's refrigerator and began to pull out cold bottles of Coca-cola. It is not possible for me to think anymore. This is such a terrible fright for all of us."

Mariana sat down at one of the tables inside the restaurant, and Emelina set the cold bottles in front of them. Carlos turned to Rick before he took a seat at the table where Emelina looked at him in expectation.

He caught Rick by surprise when he spoke in English. "American, you might want to think about it before you go any further. This is not going to get any easier from here, and it is likely going to become more dangerous. It may be time for you to simply catch a plane home."

The man had not spoken a word to him in Spanish or English for the last hundred miles in the car. Now, he left Rick at a loss for words.

"Don Ricardo!" Paz had his own answer as he rushed in from the store and threw his arms around Rick's waist. "We have been so worried."

Rick looked at Carlos over the top of the boy's head. "That decision was made some time ago," was all he could think to say. Paz released his hold and, sensing a conflict between the two men, turned to glare at Carlos.

"Whatever you decide is fine with me. Just be certain you understand the consequences." Carlos' voice was cool and even.

"I think I do." Rick put his arm around Paz's shoulders, and they moved toward the door of the family's living quarters. Mariana and Emelina were now moving in that direction as well. "Thank you for the ride back here."

Carlos shrugged with a nod of acceptance and followed the others inside.

They sat, all eyes fastened on Emelina as she told them what little she and Paz knew. Imanuel had gone to the church, two nights before, to clean and prepare for the Christmas Eve *misa* to be held there the next night. He never came back. When she and Paz went to look for him, an old fisherman down by the beach told them he had seen someone led away by soldiers. At first, they had dismissed the story because the old man was a drunk, and it did not seem to make any sense. But when they found a boy who said he had seen a scuffle at the back of the church and a man with a black bag over his head being led away by two other men, they feared the worst. The boy further reported that one of the men had hit their captive on the side of the head and that they had dragged him away as much as led him. He was stuffed in a *cayuco* and taken to the other side of the *estero*, a faster, less conspicuous way out of town than the road. It was also a route where they could easily have taken him to the main highway in a truck or other vehicle.

"*Madre de Díos*." Emelina ended her story as she crossed herself and wiped the tears from her eyes. "I do not know what to say or what to do. I wanted to send Paz to the telephone to call you, but the telephone is at the marines' station, and I was afraid they would not let him call."

"They let me, finally," Paz added, "but there were several soldiers there, and they all had calls to make first. And you know how it is. It takes so long for a call to the capital to go through. I sent the telegram the next morning, the 24th, but I did not know if or when you would get it."

"We got it, *hermanito*." They were the first words Rick had heard from Mariana since the night before when they were coming back from Midnight Mass. She reached an arm around her younger brother and hugged him close. "We came home as soon as we heard."

What should we do now? The words were practically screaming inside his head, and yet it seemed to Rick, no one could even begin to form the question, let alone the answer.

"I was afraid to say anything to anyone," Emelina continued, explaining to Carlos now, as much as anyone else. "I knew we could not ask the soldiers. What if they are the ones who took him? The boy on the beach said the two men wore no uniforms, but when we asked don Talo, the drunk, once again, he said they wore soldier boots. We have been pretending everything is just fine, but we cannot do that for much longer. People asked about him last night at the *misa*, and it was terrible, having to lie."

"Did you hold the Christmas service without him?" Carlos asked a little too sharply, Rick thought.

"*O, sí*. Paz and his friend Gilberto did it. They lit all the candles and read from the Bible and led the songs. We told people that Imanuel was home sick but of course, before long, people will want to come and see him. Niña Ana has already brought some of her *curas* for him today. What shall we do?"

"So far, you are doing fine," Carlos encouraged her. "If there is a chance for Imanuel to find his way out of this alive, he will do it in the next couple of days. That is all the longer you will have to keep pretending. It is the very best help you can give him right now. That and your prayers," he added softly.

"Of course, we have already been doing that," she added with a sniffle. The little bit of strength she had mustered so far seemed to drain from Mariana as he spoke. The words grated harshly on Rick's ears as well.

If he can find his way out alive...

"I think I want to lie down awhile." Mariana moved to stand up but did not make it all the way to her feet. Rick jumped to her side as she tried again.

He steadied her by her arm this time, and Emelina escorted her to the back.

"Now what?" Rick turned to Carlos without further ceremony.

"There are several courses of action open to us now," the older man began. "The difficult part is knowing which is the right one, the one that will bring about the desired result." Rick did his best not to squirm under the older man's scrutiny.

"And how are we supposed to know what that is?" was all Rick could think to say.

"First, we have to know, for certain, who took him, which is directly related to why he was taken. What do you know of Imanuel's recent activities?"

Rick closed his eyes for a moment, remembering the dark interior of the musty wardrobe, the heavy heartbeat of a bleeding youth lying on top of him, and Hernandez's boots echoing against the wooden floor, just inches away from the two of them.

Carlos's eyes roamed over Rick's face before falling to his fingers, whitely wrapped around the bottle of Coca-cola, resting in his lap. Rick tipped the bottle up and downed the last of its contents.

"Why do you ask me? Wouldn't Paz or Emelina or even Mariana have a better chance of giving you the information you need?" He looked at the floor, wishing he was somewhere else. Had he helped land Imanuel in whatever kind of trouble he was in now? He wondered. Riding in silence with this man had been relatively comfortable compared to the direction this conversation was taking. He listened to the outside street noises as the local bus pulled away from its shady tree stop and trundled past the outside door.

"Perhaps, but they are too upset right now to give any truly helpful information. Besides, I think you know as much as anyone as to what he really does here."

"He helps people," Rick answered quietly, still staring at the concrete floor. "That's probably the best answer I can give you. He helps people with deliveries of food and clothing, seeing to it that their children get the medical care they need, that those who need it get a chance to learn to read and write. It can be as simple a thing as helping the community to build a church or delivering food to those in need. That's what he does—he helps people."

"And only that?"

"Yeah, that's about it. He teaches religion classes, he is a catechist, after all, but all the other, I guess you could say, is his way of practicing what he preaches." Rick was starting to feel like a suspect in a criminal investigation. "So, you tell me, what kind of crime is that anyway? Does any of that come under subversive activity, organizing to overthrow the government, high treason, what?"

Carlos regarded him gravely. "You may be speaking in English, but you need to lower your voice, under the circumstances. And whether you like it or not, yes, some of that is enough to get him into some pretty serious trouble right now, depending especially on who he helps."

The man's calm exterior in the face of the desperate situation, as well as his ability to ask such questions, was infuriating.

"I don't want to lower my voice," Rick spat out the words. "I'd like to go shouting through the streets to find out who kidnapped a harmless little man with a heart of gold. If I thought it would bring him back, that's exactly what I'd do, in English or Spanish or Hebrew, if I knew it!"

A small smile crossed Carlos's broad countenance. "You really do care for him, don't you?" He seemed surprised.

"Yes, I really do. Imanuel, Paz, Miguel—the whole family," he finished lamely with a shrug of his shoulders.

"Well, if the church work is the reason they are after him, then it is most likely—"

Emelina scurried in from the store, a look of panic on her face. "Is she here?"

"Who? Mariana?" Carlos shook his head. "She left with you—"

"She went to her father's room. To rest, she said, but it is empty, and Paz has not seen her. He is with Miguel, and she is not at his house either. I do not understand. Where could she have gone? Why would she leave—" She wrapped her frantically fluttering hands in her apron as tears filled her old eyes once again.

Both men were on their feet, although Rick was at as much of a loss as Emelina as to where to begin looking.

While the others walked out toward the restaurant and began to search outside, Rick turned toward the tiny closet door that led to the roof. He felt light-headed while remembering the last time he had climbed this narrow staircase, following her to the roof. It seemed a lifetime ago.

He pulled himself up through the trap door, and once on the roof, he leaned on the retaining wall to look over the town. It had been a day of joy and celebration, the last time he had stood here. His gaze came to rest on Marielos' seafood café across the street. He was startled when she came out of the back and her eyes met his directly, despite his elevated position. She motioned for him to come down, which he did at once.

In the heat of the afternoon, there were no customers at her tables, but despite her earlier signal, she did not seem overly eager to talk to him. She glanced about nervously as she motioned him to a table and prepared to serve him a *coctel de concha*.

"I can't sit here and relax," he protested.

"You are looking for Mariana, true?" She savagely whacked open the clams, speaking over her shoulder. Rick had to struggle to catch what she said next. "What is going on over there, anyway?"

"I'm not sure I can tell you that."

"You better tell me something and do it quickly, if you want to know where Mariana is."

"What do you know about it? God, they didn't take her, too!" His worst fear came to life as he said it aloud.

"Nobody took her anywhere. What do you mean? Is that it? They 'disappeared' don Imanuel, didn't they? *Por Díos!*" Her hand lifted from the clams as she crossed herself. "Now I understand."

"Understand what?"

"Why. Why Emelina has been such a nervous wreck. I do not think that woman has ever been nervous about anything in her life until the last two days. Why Paz looks like he has already been through a funeral. Why the old man was not at the Christmas *misa*. Nobody understood that. We all knew there was no sickness that could keep him from it, not unless—" Her voice trailed off.

"Unless what?"

"I talk too much. We did not know."

"Didn't know what?"

"We knew something was wrong. We just did not know what it was. I guess we should have figured it out. *Santisima Maria.* The man risked his life to save my brother and now, this."

"And your brother? Is he well?"

"Yes, he is safe now." She crossed herself once more.

"Please, you were going to tell me about Mariana. Where is she?"

She stood up straight. "I do not know where she was going, but she left on the bus."

"On the bus? That doesn't make any sense."

She sighed. "It does if she thinks don Raúl had anything to do with what happened to Imanuel."

"Is that where you think she is? With don Raúl?" Rick was already on his feet.

"I cannot think where else she might go without telling someone like you first."

He leaped toward the street.

"Don Ricardo," she called after him. "Mariana and I are not the same kind of friends we once were, but that does not mean I do not care what happens to her."

Rick stopped for a brief moment. "I'll tell her that. Thank you very much." He turned back to slip a couple of *colones* under the dish of untouched *conchas*. "I wouldn't want anyone to think I came here for anything more than a *coctel*."

She nodded in solemn gratitude as she watched him go.

They tore up the road together in the Land Rover, with Carlos once again in the driver's seat.

"Is this something she was planning?" Carlos gave voice to his suspicions.

"If it was, she didn't share it with me," was all Rick could think to say. "Maybe like us, she is just trying to determine who took her father, only she came up with a different answer than we did."

Carlos gave him a sideways glance. "What do you know about her and Gomez?"

"What is there to know?" Rick was tired of being interrogated. "All I know is what people say in town, that he holds a grudge against her because of something that happened a long time ago with his son. Is there more?"

Carlos stared straight down the road. "There is always more to every story in El Salvador. Have you not learned that yet?"

As they scrambled out of the vehicle in front of the gaudy gates of Raúl Gomez's beachfront home, they could see the bus in the far distance. Repeated shouts and rattling of the gate brought no response.

"She must be inside already." Rick gasped in exasperation, surveying the eight-foot high gate and the accompanying brick wall, neatly topped with two strands of barbed wire.

"She probably is." Carlos was more pensive as he looked over the obstacles before them. "And now that the old spider has what he wants, he has no plans to allow anyone else in." He pulled open the back of the Land Rover and tossed a heavy canvas tarpaulin at Rick. "Fold it and throw it over that wire up there. That will get you over, and I will wait for you here. You best hurry because if she is not in there, we still have a bus to catch."

Rick did not take time to marvel at the older man's unconventional methods. He quickly shinnied to the top of the wall and landed on the soft sand on the other side. He loped up the drive and then walked brazenly inside the open-air house, willing himself not to consider the Salvadoran penalty for trespassing in the home of someone like Raúl Gomez.

A long hallway led to a large outer room that faced the beach, much like the home he had been in with Ernesto and his friends. Voices echoed down the passage as he flattened himself against the decorative brick wall. He edged forward until he could barely glimpse Mariana standing before don Raúl, who sat in a huge rattan chair.

Like a king on his throne looking down on a lowly subject, Rick thought, as he took in Mariana, dressed in her plain cotton house frock, standing poker straight before the little old man in his great chair. She must have changed when she told them she was going to rest, he thought. Now, like Carlos, he wondered how long she had been planning to confront Raúl Gomez. She did not keep him in suspense.

"I have come for what is mine, don Raúl," she announced without hesitation. "And to offer what you have wanted all these years."

Gomez squinted at her. "And what is it that you think I have?" He asked with obvious irritation at the disturbance.

"The old man the soldiers took from the church. He is of no real interest to you. You have harassed him over the years, but he is not the one you want. We both know that."

"What makes you so certain?"

"Because he is not the one who killed your son."

"And are you admitting that you did?" He seemed genuinely surprised.

"I admit nothing," she shot back, her head held even higher than before. "But I know it is me that you blame, and I am here for whatever reason you desire. I will give you no trouble, only let him go. Let Imanuel go. He means nothing to you."

"And you think that you do?"

It was all Rick could do not to run screaming into the room, to stop her and tell this old man what he could do with his bitter craving for revenge. Still, he hesitated, wanting first to see the end of that which was being played out before him.

Mariana did not falter. "I know I do."

Gomez studied her for a few moments more before speaking. Rick listened to his own heart beat, growing louder by the minute.

"You have more courage than I would have expected from any peasant, especially a woman." He snorted before turning almost coy. "I thought you told me the last time we spoke that you were done with the past and with me."

"I did not think you could hurt me anymore. And in one way, you cannot. In the end, whatever you decide to do, it changes nothing for me."

Rick frowned and leaned forward, thinking he had not heard correctly, but he never got the chance to hear anything more. The maid, who had come up behind him, screamed and dropped the pitcher of water she was carrying.

Mariana whirled, regarding Rick with a scorching gaze as he stepped out of the hallway.

"What is it you want?" don Raúl demanded. "Is he a friend of yours?" He turned on Mariana.

"I know him," she answered, "but he did not come with me if that is what you are asking."

"We were worried when we could not find you," Rick spoke to Mariana as if they were the only two in the room. "I only wanted to make sure you were all right. Why don't you let me take you home now?"

"That is a good idea," don Raúl barked as if he had thought of it himself. "Get out of my house!"

Mariana turned angrily on Rick but seemed unable to think of anything to say. He eased her gently toward the hallway, where the weeping maid was cleaning up the broken glass.

"Don Raúl." Mariana turned back at the last moment. "Never before did you stoop so low as to hurt any of my family because of what you thought of me."

"Get out! Get out! Jorge, get them out of here!" The old man's high-pitched screams echoed down the corridor as Rick pulled her quickly from the house.

The maid followed them out. "*Ya estuvo*," she called to the man who came running at the sound of don Raúl's screams. He looked different without his chauffer's uniform, Rick thought about the night Raúl Gomez had put in an appearance at the dance at the fishermen's cooperative.

"You are lucky," the maid muttered under her breath as she unlocked the gate for them. "Do not let her come back here. I was very scared for her. She will not be so lucky here a second time."

The woman gasped as she finished. Rick's gaze followed hers to rest on the green Jeep that pulled up beside the Land Rover. The two soldiers remained in their vehicle and were in conversation with Carlos, who climbed out of the driver's seat of the Land Rover to speak with them.

Rick looked back to see the maid scurrying away and was surprised to see her already halfway up the drive. He tried to convince Mariana to get into the front passenger seat, but she would have none of it. Instead, she stalked around Carlos' car to confront Lt. Hernandez and his new second in command, Sergeant Fidel Fuentes. Carlos made the appropriate introductions.

"Mariana, I am so sorry to hear about your father," Hector sounded almost sincere. "Don Carlos Panameño was just telling us—"

"I cannot imagine that Carlos would be telling you anything, Hector," Mariana snapped. "I came here to find out what has happened to Imanuel, it is true. I do not suppose you would know anything about that?"

"*Señora*," Fuentes answered first. "You are not accusing the army of any involvement in these matters, surely?"

Mariana glared at him but refused to acknowledge his presence beyond that. "Hector, I only asked you, not your trained parrot here."

"*Cuidado*, Mariana, you cannot call army officers animals, even if—" he hesitated as he glanced at the sergeant, "they are not as polite as they should be. Of course, I have no idea what has happened to don Imanuel. The man is a catechist at the church, is he not?"

"You know he is, Hector," she replied impatiently.

"That is enough to get him into trouble with some people. He must know that and surely you do, too, but I cannot imagine here in *Las Palomitas*, that we are having that kind of trouble. Whatever it is,

I assure you, I will look into it at once. Try not to worry." He reached out to pat her hand that was resting on the side of the Jeep, but she drew it back abruptly.

"Drive on, Sergeant," Hector commanded. "*Buenas tardes*." He touched the brim of his hat. "I will keep my hopes up for your father's quick return."

Mariana did not move as their tires rolled within inches of her feet.

In the car, all three seemed determined to speak at once, as both men turned on the woman.

"What kind of crazy idea was that?" Rick asked. "Even the maid says we were lucky to get out in one piece."

"Truly, my dear." Carlos' tone was conciliatory, but the message was the same. "That was very dangerous."

"Do neither of you understand?" Her voice was high and agitated, on the verge of tears. "He is the one who must have done this. Gomez is the one—"

"Carlos and I were trying to figure out just exactly who or what when we discovered you were gone. Why didn't you talk to us first?"

"And if I had, what would your answer have been? You see, it is on your face. Why would I talk to you when you would say, don't go!"

"Mariana," Rick leaned forward from the back seat. "What makes you so certain Gomez is behind this? The ones who saw what happened to Imanuel said the men who took him looked like soldiers, dressed like civilians. If they are military, Raúl Gomez is no soldier. Isn't Hernandez more likely the one we want?"

"Augh," she exploded, whirling toward him. "You are an American, and you think like an American! This is not the United States. Where do you think the soldiers here, the ones like Hector, receive their orders?

"Hector and I grew up together. We may have fallen to different sides for the most part in all of this, but—" She let out a heavy sigh. "The army here is not like yours, with real order and chain of command. Hector may have sent the men, but Hector gets his orders from somewhere else, and believe me, they do not all come from some general in San Salvador."

Rick sat back, uncertain of how to answer.

"*Por el amor de Díos!* Sometimes I think Franco is right. Americans understand nothing of what we live with!" She threw up her hands in exasperation and fell back against her own car seat.

Rick appealed to Carlos, who seemed content to let the two of them fight it out. "What do you think?"

The big man shrugged. "She is probably right about the orders, but it still does not make going there any less dangerous. What if Gomez had decided to simply keep or 'disappear' you or even both of you, for that matter?"

"Which two? Imanuel and me or Rishard?"

He shrugged again. "Whichever. I do not know that he would be willing to get involved with an American, so it is good that we followed. You did not give us much of an opportunity to do that." He gave her a look that reminded Rick of his grandfather whenever he had been caught as a child in some sort of minor mischief. Mariana looked down, folding her arms tightly across her chest and said nothing more.

Carlos continued, and Rick leaned forward again to better hear what he was saying. "On the other hand, if you are wrong and Gomez is not behind this, you really have not lost anything. Confronting Hernandez probably would not get us anywhere. Does he have any reason that you know of to be after or against Imanuel?"

Mariana's eyes met Rick's for the briefest moment before she turned away, shaking her head. "Just a lot of history," was all she said.

Rick leaned back in his seat, but his eyes never left her. She sat staring out the car window, silent tears slipping down her cheeks.

* * * * *

Emelina fixed full plates for all of them as the sun set, but no one was interested in eating despite the tantalizing aromas. After picking at his food for several minutes, Paz remembered something he had left at Miguel's and went out the back door. They were all startled, moments later, by his cry.

"*Es mi papí!*"

Rick's long legs took him out the door first, where he found Paz crouched beside a *cayuco*, resting at the water's edge. On the floor of the craft, Imanuel lay wrapped in a dirty sheet, a band of material still tied tightly across his mouth.

Rick waded into the shallow water and untied the gag. He eased the frail man to a sitting position. Imanuel's face, covered with welts and bloody scrapes, was distorted beyond recognition. The sheet was wrapped around him like a straight jacket, pinning his arms to his sides, making it impossible for him to move.

He tried to speak, but no sound came from his swollen, quivering lips. As Paz reached forward to loosen the sheet from this father's shoulders, Rick realized the man was naked beneath it. He reached out to stop Paz's hands and then gently slipped his arms under him to lift him from the boat, like a child. Behind him, he could hear another villager telling Paz how he had seen two men across the river push what looked to be an empty canoe into the water and how he had watched it float across the sluggish water of the end of the ebb tide.

Rick could not concentrate on the story, however. His own eyes were clouded with tears, and he had to watch his step as Mariana, Emelina, and Miguel crowded around him. Only Carlos stood a respectful distance away as he kept an eye on the entire proceeding.

Once inside, Rick eased Imanuel onto his own bed. His friend moaned piteously, and Rick winced as he felt the swollen knots in the injured man's torso. Rick slipped from the room as the women began to clean his wounds and care for him.

"God, he looks awful." Rick ran his fingers roughly through his long blond hair as he spoke to Carlos, who stood alone in the restaurant. The curious onlookers had stopped at the outside door. "They insisted I put him down in there, but shouldn't we be taking him to a doctor or hospital? Or could we go get a doctor and bring him here?" His own sense of helplessness added an unintended note of desperation to his voice.

Carlos chewed on the stem of a rarely smoked pipe and raised an eyebrow in Rick's direction. "I think he is lucky to be alive." He spoke in English. "The military here is not known for their humanity in questioning people. As for a doctor, I doubt that you could find one within a hundred miles who would touch him. Doctors fear for their lives, too, and helping those that the military or the White Hand of Death or whatever they call themselves at the moment, has questioned is not a good way to stay healthy. He is receiving the very best medicine available right now, in his own house, from his own people."

Rich shivered. "You think it was Hernandez then, who did this? Not Gomez?"

Carlos shrugged, a gesture that was wearing thin with Rick. "Who knows? The army is not known for giving their victims back alive, yet just hours after Mariana makes a big noise at don Raúl's house, here he is. There certainly are a number of wealthy people in this country who 'buy' themselves a few soldiers as protection, someone to do whatever they want done. Raúl Gomez is the type who would enjoy that, I suppose."

"Still, you don't believe it, do you?"

Carlos' shoulders sagged. "I never thought the man was stupid. And I wonder at his timing. Truly, it is impossible to know for certain. That is why they do it the way that they do."

"Do what?"

"Strike terror in the peasant population. Simply kidnap or kill a few of their leaders, like their priest or catechist, and the rest will quickly fall into line. At least that is the way their thinking works, and most of the time, it seems to serve their purposes."

"And you?" The man's coolness in the face of this kind of suffering touched an angry nerve. "What do you think?"

Carlos let out a great sigh. "I am one of the few who hears and perhaps understands both sides. Some in the capital of this country are terrified that if they give up a little, they will have to give up much, too much. They do not want to see their world change, the world of their fathers and grandfathers who ruled the peasants with an iron hand to get what they wanted from what was and still is, basically a population of slaves.

"On the other side, I understand the people of the *campo*, too, places like *Las Palomitas*. They have been patient a long time. It cannot last forever. The world is changing, and no one can stop what is coming. Of that I am certain and acts like this," he waved his hand toward the room where Imanuel lay in pain, "will only make the day of judgment when

it comes that much worse for everyone. Just like in
the mountains—" his voice trailed off.

"What happened in the mountains? What do
you mean?"

A startled look crossed Carlos' face as if he had
unintentionally spoken his thoughts aloud. He
glanced at Rick and turned away to light his pipe.

"You know something about what is happening
in the mountains here, do you not?" Carlos spoke
casually.

This time Rick was determined not to tell
everything he knew. "I don't know what you are
talking about."

"Then do not worry about it. It does not concern
you." He walked toward the door to gently disperse
those who stood waiting in the doorway.

* * * * *

Rick spent the next two nights in the hammock in
the living room. Carlos returned to his own beach
house, apparently convinced that any immediate
danger had now passed. Rick was not so certain.
He was more than a little uneasy at the thought
of leaving Mariana and Paz to sleep alone in the
house with Imanuel so seriously injured. He was
thankful that David remained in the capital when
he thought about the issue his cousin might make of
him sleeping under the same roof as Mariana.

Equally surprising was the fact that Carlos was
gone again within another few days. More business
in San Salvador and as Paz overheard him explaining

to Mariana and Emelina before he left, he had a long business trip to Europe coming up soon. He assured them he would be back to *Las Palomitas* before he left. Paz related all of this on the first day he and Rick went fishing, not quite a week after Imanuel's return.

"Does it seem strange to you, the kind of marriage your sister has with this man?" Rick blurted out the question and immediately regretted the bold remark. Paz did not seem to notice, however.

"Everything about the man is strange." The youth sniffed in disdain. "I do not know why she wastes her time with him. He is an old man, fat and ugly. He is older than our own father. I would not mind if he never came back."

Rick did not get the chance to say more. The wind came up as the season of the *nortes* was still upon them. They gathered their empty net in as quickly as possible and sat instead, hand fishing from reels over the side, as they both kept a cautious eye on the size of the growing swells.

"How is your father today?"

Paz wavered his hand like a small boat on the ocean. "*Así así*," he sighed. "I think his body is mending. Mariana and Emelina are good nurses, but his spirit, that is another thing."

Rick nodded in silence. Staying in their house the first days after Imanuel's return, Rick had gone to sit with his friend in the evenings, but Imanuel was still incapable of speech. He had been beaten methodically around the head, which caused much

of the swelling they had seen the first night. One of
Rick's first concerns was that the man's jaw might
be broken. Mariana told him later, however, that he
had apparently been forced to breathe something
that had burned his nose, mouth, and throat,
further complicating his condition. Rick watched,
heartbroken and with a growing anger, as Mariana
patiently spoon-fed him soup and rice water. The
only choice then, as now, was to wait and allow
nature's healing to do its work.

They caught no fish that day, and the high winds
prevented their return to the sea for several more
days. Rick returned to his own house as life came
close to the normal pattern they had enjoyed before
Thanksgiving and Christmas.

He deliberately stayed away from the Flores home
and store for a few days, hoping to erase the painful
picture of Imanuel and Mariana from his mind. He
took long walks along the beach up to the great
rocks, as Paz called them, and did a little swimming
and diving among the rocks at high tide.

In the tide pools, sculpted by nature along the
beach in front of the rocks, he found a plethora of
colorful anemones, tiny sapphire-colored jewel fish,
and the richness of the sea laid out in a few inches
of crystal-clear water. He scooped up soft and spiny
creatures he could not name and shook hundreds
of tiny snails from curly ocean foliage he had never
seen before. Just as the shallow waters began to warm
in the mid-afternoon sun to the point of cooking
the many tiny inhabitants, the tide returned with

cooling relief to whisk this particular population away and bring in a new one.

As he sat and watched the change, he found himself longing for David's return, although he suspected that would lead only to more disagreements. Much as he hated to admit it, maybe it was time. He began to mentally pack his bags and consider what he would do with his few acquired possessions. He made the long walk back to his cabin, once again in silence, resolving to begin the process in earnest the next morning.

The door stood open behind him, but he turned quickly when a shadow appeared there.

"May I come in?" Mariana stood in the doorway, her body silhouetted in her thin cotton dress, with the light spilling around her. She stepped inside and collapsed as much as sat down at the table as the door swung shut behind her.

"Are you all right?"

"Of course. I just came by for—" she hesitated. "For a little conversation. A little practice in English. We have not seen you for a few days."

Her composure was as cool as ever, and Rick made up his mind to meet her on the same ground.

"I had some things to catch up on around here," he lied, while he busied himself at his kitchen-on-a-table. He concentrated on stacking two metal plates, a bowl, and a couple of plastic cups together and moved them to the far end. "There wasn't anything more I could do at your house."

"My father has been asking for you," she stated flatly.

"He's talking?"

"A little. Nothing much yet, but he is saying a few things. He still gets too excited when he talks very much, and it causes problems with his breathing."

"I had no idea." He was finding it more difficult to play the disinterested party than he had anticipated. "I'll come tomorrow, first thing, and see him. I'd be anxious to hear anything he has to say. What has he said exactly? Anything about what happened to him?"

She shook her head. "No, not really. What good will it do anyway? I think it is better not to know."

"Are you serious?"

"Yes!" She practically spat out the word as she stood up. "Do I really want to know that this one or that one of my neighbors is spying on us? Telling Raúl Gomez our every move or informing on us about the night we helped Marielos' brother? I know you have thought about that, too. I have seen it on your face when people ask why."

Her near frantic accusatory tone caught him by surprise. "Or is someone counting how much Imanuel has given to the poor ones, some of them with relatives in the hills? Your government screams we must not be taken over by the communists, but what I read says it is the same in those places. Neighbor and relative informing one on another. What is the difference? What does it matter?" She fell heavily back into the chair, her hands over her face.

He crossed the room swiftly and knelt beside her, gathering her tenderly into his arms like a delicate bouquet of flowers. He could bear her tirades but not her tears. She cried there on his shoulder for a brief few moments while he stroked her raven thick hair and buried his face in it. Its light natural perfume made him dizzy with desire. She sat bolt upright.

"I am sorry." The chill was back in her voice. "I had no right."

"To turn to a friend for comfort?"

"It is all so pointless. I mean, crying over the whole situation. I have learned to live with worse."

"I don't understand." He backed away, fighting against his own impulses, trying to give her whatever it was she needed.

"It is like so many other things in this life. There is nothing I can do about it, so I must learn to live with it. I worry about Pazito and what will happen to him in all of this. If Franco has his way, he will take him away to live God knows where or how, but the life Imanuel chooses is no safer."

"Don't you think Paz should have a say in all of this?" Rick was reeling at the speed with which she was shifting gears, but this last was one area he was all too familiar with.

"What does he know of life? How can he choose? There are forces at work here much stronger than he can understand. The question is, how can he best survive? Maybe just remaining a fisherman at Miguel's side, but I fear he will not be satisfied with that, and if he strays too far, the results could be disastrous." A weariness descended upon her, and she leaned back against the chair, her head resting against the wall behind her.

"Where is David?" She shifted things on him again.

"David? He's never come back from San Salvador after Christmas. I was thinking of him today, too. He should be back soon. Why?"

"I was just wondering."

He watched her, unobserved for a moment, as she sat with her eyes closed. She seemed to relax, and he wondered what she was thinking of now.

"Why do you stay here?" he asked softly.

Her eyes flew open at the question, her wariness instantly returned.

"What a question." She snorted as if it were not worth answering.

"It should not be a surprise. You were gone for years, Paz tells me, and then you suddenly return. We can all see it is dangerous now. Why don't you take your father and your brother and go?

"Surely you can go back to the United States or even San Salvador, somewhere you and they would be safer."

She stared at him for a moment before speaking. "I came home to be with them. I need to be here. And could you see Paz in an American city or even San Salvador, where he would have to wear shoes all the time and not go fishing every other day? And if you think Imanuel would ever leave here, even after what has happened, then you don't know him at all."

"Even if staying is going to get one of you killed? Your father has already been seriously hurt. I heard the offer you made to don Raúl, remember? Does Imanuel know about that? What happens when

Gomez comes calling or sends his henchman to collect what he wants?"

She shrugged as if it was of no importance.

"Don't act like that! Like it's nothing! It's hard enough to watch Imanuel in the condition he's in, but I swear if it was you—" He swung wildly and sent the stack at the end of the table flying with a crash across the cabin floor.

She smiled and shook her head as if she were explaining life to a child. "If it was me, Rishard," she spoke with careful deliberation, "then no one would have been hurt. If it was me, then an old debt would have been paid. That is all."

He kept his back turned toward her.

"I should go." She reached for the door latch, but his hand quickly covered hers.

"Don't go. Not yet." He nearly choked on the words.

She whirled, and his arms encircled her.

"Rishard, this is not possible."

His heart leaped again, the way it always did, at the delicate way she mispronounced his name. As her lips whispered one thing, her body answered differently. His lips nuzzled and kissed the length of her neck. Her skin was like honeyed satin, and the touch of it sent waves of ineffable joy flowing through him.

"Why? Because you don't want it?" he whispered in her ear. "Tell me then. Tell me you came here just to practice English. Make me believe it."

"No, no." Her words were barely audible, more a protest against her own reaction than to anything he was doing.

His mouth covered hers as they both responded to what had been growing between them since that first day on the bus. For the first time in a long time, he knew exactly what he wanted and why. Still, he sensed a resistance within her. He released her and took a step back.

"Impossible." His voice was low, clouded with emotion, but it carried no accusation. "You once told me how much you admired those who do not accept that word."

She sagged against the door, watching, assessing his motives. Her silence lent courage to his pounding heart.

"You must know I would never hurt you, Mariana. What I feel for you makes THAT impossible. But you've got to want it, too. I won't take anything you cannot offer freely." He held out his open hand to her, surprising even himself at its rock-steady appearance.

She turned away from him, clutching the top of her dress as if she feared her heart might leap out of it, without her full consent. She reached for the door handle once more and hesitated for only a brief moment before twisting back and flinging herself into his waiting arms.

All the passion he had held within these last months, afraid to let it be known, more afraid to leave without ever telling her, coursed through him as he wrapped his long sun-tanned arms around her, holding her closer than close. He kissed her deeply over her mouth, her face, her neck, and shoulders, his hands locked in her thick black hair.

Most astonishing was the way she returned all of his passion, all the love he had ever dared to dream of. Her hands reached out to him, slipping deliciously over his body, in scintillating moves that more than suggested that she, too, had dreamed of this time more than once.

He lifted her to the cot, and there were no longer barriers of any kind between them, as the last light of the sun slipped from the evening sky.

The waves of the incoming tide thundered against the sand in the daily ritual that brings these two disparate powers together, neither dominating nor diminishing the other. Over the centuries, their union has inspired the deep thinkers, the lovers, and the poets, yet not one truly understands the attraction, the hold that these two very different forces have on one another.

Without the sea, the beach is only a desert, and without the shore, the sea is only heaving mounds, blue, green, or gray, deep and foreboding, with nowhere to demonstrate their incredible faithfulness. Together, they rise and fall, the frothy drenching waves caressing the waiting coastal heart, providing a vital rhythm for all that lives. Without their rich union, the rest of life would be much poorer indeed. And so it is when two of different worlds with the same empty longing in their souls come together. Their union blesses the rest of life and the lives of others around them, with a richness they might otherwise never know.

Their lovemaking exhausted momentarily, they lay in each other's arms without speaking at first, and then softly telling one another bits and pieces of unfulfilled dreams.

"I never knew it could be like this," she whispered, her breath tickling his chest.

"Like what?" He dared to ask.

"Like this." A contented sigh escaped her. "In many ways, I know my life has been different from others and that there are many things I have learned to live without, but it is like that phrase in your country... 'you don't know what you have been missing.' I feel like now I know, and I have truly missed something wonderful."

He stroked her hair and cupped his hand around her face, his heart too full to dare to say anything.

They listened to the mesmerizing love song of the waves, and before long, he pulled her close once again.

He awoke naked and slightly chilled the next morning, the sheet having slipped off the end of the bed. He reached for the one who had spent the night at his side and was instantly awake when he discovered her gone.

A note on the table by the door quelled his fear. "Come and see my father today. I will wait for you there. M."

* * * * *

He found her cooking in Emelina's stead at the restaurant. He had left home without eating, and she promptly laid out a breakfast of tortillas, rice with clams, refried beans, fried *platanos*, and steaming hot coffee.

"You must have gotten up early to be working in Emelina's place," he teased with a smile.

"I was up early to make a quick run down the beach before sunrise." She hissed in his ear as she leaned over, coffee pot in hand, to fill his cup to near overflowing. She straightened up and answered more seriously *en español* for the benefit of those at the next table. "I am only watching the restaurant for my aunt while she takes my father his breakfast." The sparkle behind her eyes said, regardless of how or why she was there, she was happy to see him.

Rick watched her graceful movements with a new respect this morning as she moved to the other table to check on the customers there. Her natural rhythm, her understated elegance, the way she smoothed her hair back from her face, seemingly unaware of the casual gesture—these were but a few of the moments he had learned to savor from a distance in the past few months. Now, for at least one night, he had held them all in his own two hands, loving and being loved, in a way more satisfying than anything he had ever imagined.

"*Mas café?*" She slid past his table, interrupting his reverie, on her way back to the kitchen. The other men were preparing to leave.

He shook his head and watched contentedly as she drifted away. Emelina returned, and Mariana came to sit across from him. "Good breakfast?"

"The best," he answered honestly. He watched the men amble across the road, toward the sea, passing by Marielos' café.

"I haven't seen her lately," Rick spoke his thoughts aloud. "Not since the day we came back from San Salvador. Is she sick?"

"Oh, I do not think so, but I do not know. It is true that she has not been there in recent days. I had not thought about it."

Rick's thoughts jumped from Marielos to Niña Ana and the pang of guilt that followed, thinking he should have checked on her since Imanuel was not able to do so right now.

"You will go to see Imanuel this morning, yes?" she changed the subject. "Emelina says he looks better this morning and seems a little stronger."

He followed her lead to the back bedroom where the older man sat, propped up against pillows, his bony legs making twiggy humps in the smoothness of the worn sheet that lay over him.

"*Pase, pase,*" he croaked at the sight of Rick, motioning him into the room.

Mariana stopped at the door. "You go. This is a time for just the two of you. I know him. He will say nothing important if I am there, too. He does not want to worry me. You understand?"

Rick nodded and stepped forward to grasp his friend's outreached hands but was instantly taken aback at the feel of the knotted fists that were extended to him. He had not realized that several of the man's fingers had been methodically broken, but the proof lay in his own hands. Yet, even now, they were unbandaged.

"I have been waiting for you." The spark of life that so invigorated Imanuel in the past was glowing once again despite what he had suffered.

"I wanted to come sooner, but I was afraid you were not up to visitors," Rick stammered. "You gave us all quite a scare."

"Me, too." The old man wheezed, and it took Rick a few seconds to realize he was laughing. "It is good to laugh again. I was afraid for a while I might never be able to again."

Rick nodded, not sure of what more to say.

"I am glad now that you and Mariana were not here for Christmas. I was not so happy when you left, you know. It was selfish, really. I wanted you to be here, for our Christmas *misa*. And then, in the end, none of us were. *Gracias a Díos* for Paz and Gilberto. Emelina tells me they took care of everything."

He took a deep, ragged breath. *"Por el amor de Díos*, it was awful. One minute I was praying for my life, and the next I was praying, Lord, take it, please. I was glad you two were not here because then it might have been you and Mariana as well. I know now what they can do to a man. I could not bear the thought of what they might do to a woman." He gasped and coughed, long and hard, before leaning over the edge of the bed and spitting into a small pail that Rick had not noticed before.

"It is okay. Maybe you shouldn't talk anymore right now. We can just sit here."

"No, I have to tell someone." He pulled at Rick's arm in an urgent appeal, and the coarse whisper hurt Rick's ears so, he hated to think what it was doing to the old man's throat.

"Okay, but rest a little first. Something to drink?"

Imanuel accepted a glass of water from the pitcher on the small table next to his bed. After a few more hard-won breaths, he tried again.

"They were very funny in some ways. One told me, we know you are not a *comunista*, yet you organize the people, and we cannot have that. So, we will continue to call you and all like you, *comunista*.

"The church and the people of the church. It is just like Monsignor Romero says. These are the men with no conscience, men who fear only one thing, the church. They fear the people's allegiance to something they themselves cannot understand."

"Then, do you know who took you? A boy by the *estero* saw that you were led away, but someone else said it was soldiers, and we were never certain."

"And they will be led by a little child? Is that not what is written?"

Rick smiled at the connections his friend could make, even at a time like this. "That is what is written by the prophets."

"It was soldiers, but I do not know which ones. Maybe none from around here. The one who did most of the talking, you could hear it in his voice, that he often gives orders."

"Was it Hernandez?"

"No, it was not Hector. I have known him since he was a little boy, and I am sure I would know his voice. I do not know this man, but I will never forget that voice. Of that I am certain. I had that black sack over my head, so I never saw him, but I could hear. He was the one who talked about being a *comunista*. He asked me some questions, mostly about other people. Some I knew, others I did not. I would not answer any of the questions, and that, of course, made him angry. How could I say something that might land someone else in the same kind of trouble?"

He took another swallow of water before continuing. "I was tied to a tree, outside in the dark, the way you say they did Augustín Rivas. When they left, I thought it was over, but the worst had just begun.

"After a while, some others came. I do not know who they were because they did not talk. They beat me, with poles and sticks. They opened the hood at the bottom, and I thought I would be able to see, but they only threw something in and tied it tighter. *Cal*, I think, because then it hurt so to breathe." He began to tremble.

Rick took the glass from his hands. "*Cal*?" Rick asked, confused. "Like they use in cooking the corn for the tortillas?" Good God, that can't be right. Rick hoped his friend was mistaken. Lime tossed into a hood, tied over a man's head, and then he would be forced to breathe it in. His skin turned to goose flesh at the thought.

Imanuel nodded. "One went behind me and untied my hands but only to throw me on the ground, spread my fingers out, and stomp on them with their boots. Soon it was hard to know what, where hurt the worst. They pulled off my clothes and beat me more. I knew I was naked but could do nothing. Only that hood, that damnable hood. They did not take it off, just filled it again with the lime. After a while, it did not matter anymore. I wondered if there would be enough of me left to bury or if anyone would ever even find me. I prayed it would not be Paz or Mariana or you. Let it be someone who did not know me or care."

He was crying now, and Rick moved onto the edge of the bed to wrap his arm around the gaunt quaking shoulders.

"*Ya estuvo*. It is over now," Rick repeated several times. He had wanted to stop him sooner, but the need was too great to tell what needed to be told.

"*Gracias a Díos. Ya estuvo. Es cierto*." Imanuel sobbed freely before he began to pull himself together. He wiped his face on the sheet in front of him. "I do not remember much at the end. I was dreaming about being on the water, and then I saw your face, and you were lifting me up. No one has told me how you found me. These women mean well." He peeked at the doorway as if he might be overheard. "But they do not tell me anything at all."

Rick smiled at that. "You weren't dreaming. They sent you back the same way they took you away, in a *cayuco*. Someone saw men push it off from the far side by itself, and when they realized who was inside, a boy called for Paz, and we all came running. I did lift you out of the *cayuco* because, like you said, you were naked, wrapped in a sheet. I don't know where it came from. I brought you in here, and that's all I know. Mariana and I came back that same day, Christmas Day, the 25th, as soon as we received the telegram from Paz, saying you were missing. Carlos drove us. He was here, too, for a couple of days."

"I remember. He came in and talked to me, but he said he had to leave. His life is like that," Imanuel nodded as if deep in thought.

The two visited a while longer about fishing conditions and what others in the village were doing.

"How are Niña Ana and the others?" Imanuel asked about each of the families in the church's assistance program.

"I think they are all doing fine." Rick was afraid to say anything else. "I talked to Mariana, you know," Rick spoke more slowly, uncertain how to broach the difficult subject. "About whether you should go away for a little while. Until it is safer for you here."

"Until it is safer." Imanuel seemed willing to consider the idea. "Safer, for what? Safer for who? For me? And when do you think that will be? There is no safe time, no safe place for those who follow what they know is right. The work for God, following the mandate He left for us. I will need to be more careful. I can see that. Maybe I can find other ways of doing what it is that needs to be done, but I cannot just leave the work behind. There is still too much to be done."

"But don Imanuel—"

"Understand one thing, my young friend," Imanuel wheezed loudly, and Rick regretted having upset him. "I have had a lot of time to lay here in this bed and think about nothing else. I will be more careful, but I will not stop. Never will I stop."

"But—" Rick tried again but to no avail.

"Think about your own home, where you live, Ricardo. If a civil war was to come there, would you simply pick up and leave and let others drive you out of your home, your town, your life? I think I know you well enough to know you would not go. Christians are not afraid of combat. We know how to fight, but we prefer the language of peace. The language of love."

"However, when a dictatorship seriously violates human rights and attacks the common good of the nation, when it becomes unbearable and closes all channels of dialogue, when this happens, the Church speaks of the legitimate right of insurrectional violence." Rick whirled at the sound of the familiar taunting voice coming from behind him. He found Franco standing in the doorway.

"I listen to the radio, too, *Tío*. You quote Monsignor Romero well. So can I. The man made both statements."

"You are listening to Monsignor Romero now?"

Franco acted as if he had been grievously wounded. "I am willing to listen to everyone's opinion."

Imanuel lay back on the pillows, his energy spent, yet a wide grin crept across his tired face. "If you are seriously considering Monsignor's words, Franco, there is hope, hope for all of us."

"I am sorry." An anxious Mariana came in behind Franco. "I did not know until just this minute that he was here."

"It is all right." Imanuel lifted a hand toward her. "I have been expecting him. Franco always seems to know just what is going on in this town even without living here."

His nephew grinned at the backhanded compliment. "I would have been here sooner, but—" He shrugged.

"I should go." Rick stood up. "And you should rest."

"I will, soon," Imanuel promised as Franco sat down.

Mariana followed closely behind him. "I heard it all," she told him resignedly as they walked into the living room behind the empty store. "He is a stubborn man. I do not think we will change that." She shook her head, but a small smile remained on her lips. She wrapped her arms around his neck and pulled him close. Their lips met, and a wave of the ecstasy of the night before swept over him. "Wait, wait," she broke away, laughing. "That was just to say 'I'm glad' about last night. We cannot pick up where we were then."

"And why not?" He stepped toward her, playfully, reaching for her once more.

"Because I am the one watching the store just now."

"Can't pay attention to two things at once?"

"Hmm. More like, I am not ready to make a public announcement to this town as to where we were last night. Are you?"

"No, that probably would not be wise," he agreed with a sigh and settled for one last long kiss and embrace before letting her go.

"*Que tal, gringo?*" Franco stepped jauntily from the connecting door behind them, and Rick released her more quickly than he had intended. Franco frowned and then smiled as if he were the one caught in the act.

"My uncle was more tired than he thought. He fell asleep while we were visiting. I will see him later this evening. And you? Are you ready to visit a real rebel camp?"

CHAPTER 12

January 23, 1980. San Salvador. The largest demonstration in this nation's history took place yesterday, as nearly 200,000 men, women and children gathered to protest against the current government. The gathering was originally planned to mark the anniversary of the peasant uprising of 1932, in which 30,000 people are believed to have died. Beginning at Cuscatlan Park, not far from the National University, the demonstration turned into a blood bath when shots rang out as the crowd passed the National Palace. At least 21 demonstrators are known dead, and an estimated 120 others were injured.

The government has seized all local radio stations and continues to broadcast only their version of the shooting, which states that the demonstrators fired first.

Archbishop Oscar A. Romero stated that the National Guard fired first from within the National Palace. In a statement released today, he condemned the "irrational massacre."

"There certainly are times in your life when you stop and wonder how you came to be in a certain place at a certain time," Rick spoke aloud, more to himself than to anyone else. Mariana slipped up beside him, and he slid an arm around her waist as they stood together at the edge of the precipice, surveying the peninsula, the nesting place of *Las Palomitas*, far below.

Clothed in the mists of distance and sea spray, the tawny green arm of land stretched courageously against the powerful buffeting waters, fighting daily to justify its very existence. Delicately edged in the white lace of breakers on the far side, verdantly outlined against the creamed coffee-colored waters of the estuary on the other, he marveled at the deceptively peaceful scene.

"What did you say?" She asked as she followed his gaze.

"Nothing important."

"It is beautiful here."

"Yes, it is," he replied in a dreamy voice of sumptuous satisfaction as he watched the breeze make an ebony halo of her hair, further gracing her lovely face.

"And to see it from here, you would never know anyone there had any worries at all, yes?"

"It's a wonder that some hotel chain or real estate developer hasn't snapped it up." Rick was irritated by his own train of thought. God, I must be more closely related to my father than I think.

"Oh, somebody already thought of that. You did not see the pictures in don Raúl's house the day you were there?"

"Pictures? I wasn't there to check on his interior decorating if you remember. Scared out of my mind and terrified for you comes closer to describing it."

"I'm sorry." Her sweet laughter added to his delight as she leaned against him. "I thought maybe you saw them because they were there in the hallway where you were waiting. *Condiminios Las Palomitas*. They are paintings, I think, artistic works of—"

"I did see those. Across from the kitchen where the maid came out. I didn't pay much attention at the time. They're named after the village?"

"Not exactly. They were supposed to be built here. I mean, there." She pointed off in the distance. "Don Raúl's brother-in-law was the one who wanted to build them. He owned the land where the fishermen's cooperative is now, close to the beach. He was involved with many things like that, what do you call them, investeds?"

"Investments."

"That. He had all these plans, but then he got caught in other deals in San Salvador, making out with government money."

"Making off with government money is the phrase you want," he interrupted with a smile in his voice.

"All right. Making out. Making off. What is the difference?"

He laughed. "I'll show you later" and hugged her closer.

A slight frown of confusion creased her brow as she continued. "Anyway, it must have been really bad because even don Raúl could not protect him.

The man lost his money, and the government took away much of his property, including the land the fishermen now own."

Rick shook his head, only half-listening to her story. "Well, I'm glad they didn't build them. They don't need any high rises on this stretch of beach."

She nodded. "Don Raúl always swore he would build them himself, but maybe he is afraid he might end up badly, too. There are spirits at work, in the natural places of this country, you know. Spirits in the mountains and in the waters that take offense at what some men do."

"What?" She had his full attention now. "What are you talking about?"

"You think I am foolish, yes? Superstitions, you call them, but there are those, like don Emil, Raúl's brother-in-law who found out too late."

"Hey, are you two going to stand out there all day?" The shout from behind pulled them back to their current situation.

"I forgot. I came out here to tell you to come to breakfast. Franco's getting impatient." Mariana turned to go, and Rick followed her lead.

They had been at the camp for three days already. It was reflections on his life in Texas—and the thought then, of ending up in a Latin American revolutionary camp, less than six months later—that had him talking to himself earlier. For some reason, Ana Luisa and their childhood runaway trip to *los barrios de San Antonio* had come to mind. Is this what it had led to? He could not be sure.

He wondered if David might already be back in *Las Palomitas* while he was up here on the mountain with Franco, and he hoped if he was, he was not blowing too many holes in the story Mariana had told Paz and Imanuel before they left.

Franco's appearance that day at the house was nothing if not unexpected. He said he had all the arrangements made for Rick's visit, but it was Mariana who surprised them both.

"*A la gran puta!*" Franco had cursed her interference. "You think I want to drag you along, too?"

"I really do not care what you think." Mariana's cool reserve slid easily into place. Rick almost felt sorry for Franco.

"If he goes, I go. *Ya estuvo.*"

"And have you forgotten a few minor details? What about *mi tío*? What about your brother? *Por el amor de Díos*, what about Carlos, your dear and devoted husband?"

"You can leave my relatives to me, thank you very much." Her voice was low, almost threatening. "Carlos is certainly none of your concern. He is not here and is not expected back for some time. I can tell Paz and Imanuel that he called for me to come back to San Salvador for a few days, and Rick is going along to escort me. Good enough for you?"

He sidestepped the direct challenge. "How is *mi tío*, really? I meant what I said before. I wanted to come sooner, but I was afraid to... for his sake."

Her voice softened at the genuine concern. "He is healing. It is slow, but there is true progress, I think."

She looked at Rick, who nodded. "You were right not to come right away. It would not have helped. Emelina is doing a good job caring for him, and if he thinks I am only gone to San Salvador, there is no harm done. Carlos seems to think he is safe enough for the time being."

"What does that mean?"

"That unless or until he returns to his usual activities, he probably will not be bothered anymore. His idea is that he was kidnapped because of his work with the church and *la comunidad*, and not because of me."

"That sounds reasonable." Franco pursed his lips and ran a hand across the stubble on his chin. "He is not the only one to be blamed for some of what goes on in the church, *la clinica*, all of it together."

"I do not understand."

"Never mind. For once, I agree with Carlos, at least about Imanuel. And I think Carlos would agree with me. I do not think he would stand for the idea of you going off with us if he was here."

"But he is not. And even when he is, he does not tell me what to do."

Franco continued to spar verbally with her but to no avail. In the end, he visited that evening with Imanuel. Mariana made a short trip to the telephone office that same afternoon and then announced her need to return to San Salvador in two days and asked Rick if he would accompany her. He hated the play-acting in front of people he trusted, and he seriously considered not going at all. One look at Imanuel was enough to convince him the danger was all too real.

"Losing your nerve, *gringo*?" Franco asked when it was just the three of them, late that evening, after Paz had gone to play cards with his father.

"Excuse me?" Rick countered.

"You have the look. The look I see in the young recruits sometimes, who cannot decide if they want to go and fight or stay home with *mamá*."

"Franco, you really are—" Mariana began, but Rick cut her off.

"Maybe now is as good a time as any for us to get a few things straight. I'm not going to fight anybody. You made a point the last time you were here, saying I didn't know enough about the other side to condemn it. Maybe you're right. The only reason I've agreed to this at all is to see a few things for myself. What I hate is the lying to people, especially to people who have been good to me, like Imanuel and Paz."

"Do not worry. You get used to it."

"I don't think so."

"*Vaya, vaya*." Franco threw up his hands in mock surrender. "I was just checking. The truth is you should be less concerned about the ones who are staying behind and more concerned about this *loca* who is insisting on taking over where her father left off."

"What are you talking about?"

"It is nothing, really." Mariana wore the demure expression that Rick had seen the night they had spent helping Fabiano. "He is just bothered because I told him we cannot go until after tomorrow."

"And what's tomorrow?"

"The visiting nurse is coming," she chattered on quickly before he could ask any questions she would not want to answer. "She was supposed to come a couple of weeks ago, but then Imanuel was gone and then hurt too badly to be of help. He does not want it postponed again, and there is no reason I cannot take care of this."

His eyes rolled, and she knew he, too, was thinking of the last time they had talked of the clinic and the long night they spent there.

"See, then it is settled," Franco interrupted. "You cannot go, so the *gringo* here can go alone. He is a big boy, Mariana—honest." His gaze ran over Rick from head to toe. "You should tell her to stay here," he finished lamely.

Rick laughed out loud. "You are as far wrong as you could possibly be. You've already told her, and she didn't listen to you. I don't think my luck would be any better. Besides, if she comes, maybe you'll be more careful about what you get me involved in. Am I right?"

Franco gave him a sharp sideways glance before a quiet little smile crept across his face. "You are not wrong."

* * * * *

As he walked into town the next day, Rick could see the line long before he could see the clinic. Mothers, grandmothers, older sisters lined up one behind the other, with what looked to be hundreds of children, most of them quite small. Glancing at the sun just breaking free from the tree line, he realized most of them must have arrived without breakfast. From the length of the line, it was clear many of them would be there past midday.

"Where did they all come from?" he asked when he finally found Mariana holding one child on her hip and giving directions to the next and his mother to wait their turn.

"I am glad you came," she said breathily. "Take him!" She abruptly handed over the toddler she had been carrying. With both hands free, she shuffled furiously through a stack of paper slips lying on a makeshift desk near the door. A nurse in a starched white uniform, amazingly clean considering where she was, Rick thought, stood in the far corner. With impressive rapidity and efficiency, she checked the paper each mother held and administered a syringe full of vaccine to each child brought to her. Rick and the boy in his arms peered at one another. Judging from the dusty tear stains streaking his face, this one had already had his turn with the health nurse.

"Thanks." Mariana just as quickly whisked him off and handed him over to a little old woman, who kept repeating. "*Gracias, gracias.*"

"Sorry," she shrugged sheepishly. "His grandmother needed to leave him here for a minute while he got his shot, and then I got busy."

"Like I said, where did they all come from? They are not all from here in *Las Palomitas*."

"Oh, no. They come from all the neighboring towns and villages, some as far as 50 kilometers. It did not used to be this way. I can remember when they first started these programs, the mothers were afraid. They would not bring their children because it made them cry." Her hands never stopped the entire time she was talking. Once the papers were in order, she turned to organize the waiting line better, gently pushing and pulling the women and children into place.

"What changed?"

"*Mandé?*"

"What changed? Why do so many come now when they didn't before?"

Her smile was bittersweet when she glanced at him. "She is giving DPT vaccines. You know what those are for? Diphtheria and tetanus and some kind of cough but the first two, those are the worst ones here. They started to bring their children when their babies did not die after getting the shots. Going to the funeral of your child or the child of your relative or your neighbor—that can move you to do things you would not normally do." She turned back to organizing the mass of humanity before her.

"What can I do to help here?"

"Are you serious?"

"Yes." He laughed. "You don't think I can do this?" He waved a hand over the chaos before them.

"*Vaya pues*." She shoved a pencil and stack of blank forms at him. "I need the child's name and age and the mother's name on the paper. Wait—" She stopped and looked at him. "That will not work so well, will it?"

He laughed again. "Probably not."

"Come, do this." She took him by the hand and showed him how to get them all back into line and who needed to stand where. Then she handed him a bottle of alcohol and a bag of cotton balls and showed him how to wipe off each child's upper arm. She picked up the pencil and papers and headed further up the line.

Awkward at first, he soon developed a rhythm to the work. Whether it was his size, the fact that he was a foreigner, or simply the only man in the place, he had no idea, but it was not difficult for him to get anyone to move where he wanted them to go. A single word or two was all it took.

The sharp odor of the alcohol brought back the surreal images of the last time he had been in this clinic, in the middle of the night, with a lovely lady and a wounded boy. Looking around in the clear daylight, it was hard to remember how frighteningly real that night had been.

The hours flew by as he remained preoccupied with the task at hand. At one point, he was far enough ahead to walk to the door and look down the line. He spied Mariana, papers still in hand, sitting outside the door, talking with a young mother, whose child stood close by. The little girl, no more than five years old, held one bloody bandaged hand, cradled in her other.

"But you can make it right, Niña Mariana." The woman was pleading.

"Listen to me carefully." Mariana's tone was deadly serious. "You must take her to the doctor in the next city. I know it is a long ride, and you will miss the rest of your work today, but if you do not, she will die. A doctor there may be able to sew her thumb back on, maybe not. I am not certain, but she cannot go on like this. I know she is frightened, as you are, but you cannot take the chance. Please, believe me."

"You are certain? She is afraid. I think the other children have told her lies, that the doctor will cut off her thumb."

"It does not matter what they say or what that witch doctor of a sister-in-law of yours has said either, do you hear me? I am the one telling you the truth. Your child will be dead within days if you do not take her."

"*Vaya pues.*" The young woman did not argue further. "I will take her. Thank you, Niña Mariana. Thank you very much."

He turned away without her notice.

Early in the afternoon, Mariana came back in to check on him and to toss down the few papers she had left.

"*Ya estuvo.*"

"What?" He asked without ever breaking his stride as he swabbed a patch antiseptically clean on yet another small brown arm before looking up. His eyes fell on the message printed in Spanish in large letters on the back of the paper slips. He had not noticed it before.

THERE ARE THREE (3) VACCINES NEEDED TO KEEP YOUR CHILD SAFE. IF THIS IS THE FIRST, TWO MORE ARE NEEDED. THEY CAN BE OBTAINED AT THE FOLLOWING DATES AND PLACES.

"The last slip given out for the day. We cannot do any more than that. It is all the vaccine we have anyway."

"How many is that? Or should I ask?"

"Three hundred. Not bad for one day, yes?"

"Incredible." He shook his head and felt a real sense of elation and accomplishment.

"Yes, you are," she countered. "I cannot get Paz to come in here and do a thing for me, on a day like this. He says too many dirty kids, too many wet noses."

Rick smiled, silently giving thanks for the fact that she spoke in English.

"I will be back." She disappeared out the door but soon returned with cold drinks for the three of them.

She sat contentedly watching as he and the nurse, Niña Dorita, finished. "So, how is Imanuel today?" Rick asked.

"A little better, I think. He is starting to give Emelina all kinds of trouble, so that is surely a sign that he is feeling better."

He nodded in agreement. "And yesterday's visitor? I take it he left with no problem?"

"No problem." She repeated in English, her eyes locked on his.

"What happened to that little girl I saw out there earlier, the one with the injured hand?"

"Carmen." She nodded. "She is a sweet little thing, but both of her parents work in the fields, and she is left with her older cousins. She slipped with a machete, trying to open a *coco*, and her thumb is all but cut off. Her aunt, who thinks she is something of a curing person, like Niña Ana wrapped it up and said it would get well, with a little *tela de araña*.

"What's that?"

"Spider web. Some of the old ones here still think it has magical powers, and they put it on open wounds to cure them. *A la gran puchica*, it is pure dust and dirt and has caused a lot of children's deaths through tetanus."

"So you weren't lying when you told her if she didn't take her to the doctor, she would die."

"Did you think I would make it up?" She sounded insulted. "Some of our people have learned a great deal over the last few years, and others, they live as they did five hundred years ago. She and the child were so worried about losing her thumb, and the truth is Carmen might lose her life. Who can understand it?"

"I hope she'll be okay," he answered lamely. He stood up straight, stretching his back, more than a little relieved as the last child to be vaccinated stood before him. Niña Dorita still looked as primly starched as when she began the day.

She approached them after gathering up her supplies. "We gave vaccines to 302 children today, which is good because I only had enough for 305. The driver from the Ministry of Health will be waiting outside for me by now. I will see you in three months to do this all again." She went out the door, laughing at Rick's startled expression.

"You really do it every three months?"

"And why not? Think how many more babies there will be by then, plus so many of the children will need a second or third injection at that time, too. This is one of Imanuel's dreams-come-true. Health care and the church—things he has been working toward ever since I can remember." She let out a sigh from her lower lip that blew the hair on her forehead.

"That reminds me. I've got to go check on Niña Ana. Your father asked about her the other day, and the truth is—"

"The truth is she is gone." Her voice was completely flat.

"What?"

"I do not know any more than that," she sighed again. "Only that I went to see her early this morning, and there was no one there and nothing left. Her house is empty, abandoned. Maybe she went to live with her sister on the other side of the *estero*. I really do not know."

"Now what will I tell your father?"

"It is like Franco said the other day at the house. Maybe we have to get used to lying, at least for a little while. It serves no purpose to tell him the truth right now."

"Maybe you're right." But it did not lessen the uneasiness he felt deep within.

"How is your stomach?" she changed the subject.

"Fine, why? How's yours?"

"Empty. Shall we go see what Emelina has left for us?"

"I thought you would never ask," he answered, offering her his arm.

* * * * *

According to plan, Rick and Mariana left the next morning, crossing the *estero por cayuco*, having told Paz they would walk the kilometer or so to the highway where they could catch the bus to San Miguel. Halfway to the highway, they found a pickup truck with two men in the cab, waiting along the roadside. They climbed aboard to share space with a few melons, some dried corn, a large sack of dried beans, and other foodstuffs.

It began like a ride to a Sunday picnic. The truck whizzed along the main highway for several miles, and Rick enjoyed watching her hair blowing free in the wind. A few miles later, they turned onto a rough track that cut through the thick woods and underbrush like a tunnel through a mountainside. Halfway up, though, the truck came to an abrupt stop, and the two men climbed out and began walking back down the way they had come.

"Hey!" Rick called after them. "Now what?"

There was no response.

"We wait," Mariana advised quietly. "It might be better if we get out, too. You never know who might be coming or watching." They scrambled over the back end of the truck and made their way through the wall of trees that nearly enclosed the road. They stopped beneath a large *ceiba* tree, Central America's answer to the mighty oak, where they still had a clear view of the truck. Their wait was not a long one.

A teenage boy darted from beneath the trees on the opposite side and was into the back of the pickup in a single fluid movement. With an efficient style, he tossed the contents of the truck bed out to three waiting companions.

Only the extra heavy sack of beans gave him a problem. When he attempted to lift it, he fell back, clutching his shoulder.

"Fabiano," Mariana called out, just loud enough for him to hear as she stepped into the open. Suspended animation struck the four at once, Rick thought, and then, the change came, and the three on the ground melted instantly back into the woods from whence they had come. Only the boy in the truck stood up straight, to wave.

"Niña Mariana. He told us we would find a surprise when we came today, but I had no idea—"

Rick also stepped clear, and as he did, the others, fearing no danger, re-appeared. They were all teens, three boys and a girl. Fabiano looked to be the youngest.

His eyes rolled wide at the sight of him. "You brought your American friend, too." He jumped from the back of the pickup. "I am glad." He held out his hand in a polite, formal greeting. "I never had the chance to tell you thank you, don Ricardo. For saving me."

Rick shook the diminutive hand and looked at Mariana, unsure of what to say next.

"This is the one, *verdad*?" The girl stepped up beside Fabiano as their two companions wrangled the sack of beans from the truck behind them. "The *gringo* who stayed in the closet with you to protect you from the *guardia*?"

Fabiano nodded.

The look on her face was a combination of amusement and disbelief, with a bit of newfound respect mixed in as well. Rick had seen that expression before on the faces of new arrivals at the Boys Club—Tex-Mex youth who were unsure what to make of a college-bound *Anglo* who chose to spend time working at their community center.

"I always wondered if you made up part of that story," she teased. "I mean, it sounded pretty wild, an American you do not even know risks his life to save yours. But I guess now I will have to believe you." She gave Rick another once over with her eyes. "You did not tell me he was so good-looking, Fabiano." She gave her friend a playful shove and turned to help the others with the items they now had loaded on their shoulders.

"That is Blanca," Fabiano made hurried introductions with a chagrined smile. "That one is Luis, and that is Ramón."

The boys ducked their heads in shy acknowledgment as they hurried to catch up to Blanca, who was already several paces ahead.

Mariana and Rick followed the teens, who scampered over the rough terrain at a surprising rate, despite their burdens. The party wended their way up the mountainside, following trails that Rick thought must be older than time itself. They passed an occasional thatch hut, nestled under the trees or set against the hillside but never too close to the trail, the only thoroughfare in this part of the country.

As they neared what surely seemed to Rick to be the mountain's crest, they broke into a large clearing of long yellow grass, eclipsed at the far end by a small log house, sitting on a stone foundation.

"Do you know where we are? Whose house this is?" Rick asked Mariana.

She looked pale and slightly fevered from the long climb, reminding Rick of the day she fainted in the cemetery. "What's wrong?" he asked as he reached out a hand to steady her.

"I just need to find my breath," was all she said in a thin, forced voice. "I will be fine in a few minutes."

He stopped and called out to Fabiano to do the same.

"It is good," he said, dropping his load. "We are ready, too. I do not know how to say—" The boy looked at the ground in embarrassment as he pulled two black swatches of material from his back pocket.

"Franco told me you must wear these the rest of the way from here. I am sorry, don Ricardo, Niña Mariana. You have been so good to me—"

"It does not mean we do not trust you." Blanca did not hesitate to explain as she helped Mariana tie her blindfold in place. "But no one knows what will happen here or anywhere in our country, day to day. This way, you cannot tell anyone where you have been, no matter what the situation. It is safer for everyone this way."

Rick decided he would rather not dwell on the implications of her explanation. Blanca took Mariana by the hand. Rick felt a little less uncomfortable, covering his eyes as Fabiano moved in closer to become his personal guide. His hand securely resting on the boy's uninjured shoulder, they began moving downhill in the opposite direction from where they had come. He could hear Mariana's voice clearly, close in front of him.

"You asked about the house. It belonged to a young couple from San Salvador years ago, Pablo and Marta Gloria. I was here once a long time ago, but we came by horseback, something arranged by one of the American priests from Chirilagua, as I remember. There were several people from area churches, and Pablo was one of their leaders, the lay teachers. We were here for a couple of days, like a long weekend, and there were classes. They were such kind people."

The sweet taste of the nearly forgotten memory could be heard in her voice. "I remember how proud Pablo was of his house. He said the only things he brought up the mountain were nails and cement mix. Everything else—the logs and the stone came from the mountain. He was the son of a rich man in the city, but he had come here to build himself a house on the mountainside and to break with many of the traditions of his father. I think that is why he was working with the church people so much because I remember when my father first heard his name and met him, he was surprised."

"What was his name?" Rick asked.

"I do not remember," she sighed. "Do you know the people who owned that house?" she asked the others.

"Pablo Villanueva," Ramón spoke up. "He is the man who built it."

"That is right," Mariana continued. "I never met a man so proud of a house before. I suppose he cannot live there now, but I would never have thought he would leave it."

"He did not leave," Ramón spoke so softly, Rick had to strain to catch the next words. "The army blew up his truck, with him inside, at the bottom of the road. His wife and children left after that." They went a few paces more before he added. "Marta Gloria is my sister."

"I am so sorry," Mariana replied immediately. "I did not know."

"I know," the soft voice came again. "It was nice to hear the things you had to say about Pablo and

Marta Gloria. It is true. He was a very good man, and nothing like his father. *Ya.*" The column stopped, and Rick heard some scrambled sounds he could not identify, like rustling branches and something heavy, dragging, scraping along the ground. Fabiano seemed to drop below him. Rick's hand was taken from his shoulder and placed high beside his head, on a stony crumbling ledge for support, as they made their way down a set of homemade steps. Rick's long feet just barely fit on the narrow stairs as he slid each foot forward, searching for the edge, before taking another step. After a half dozen or more, he found himself on solid gravel-covered ground.

"Hey, *gringo!*" He recognized the shout and reached up to take off the blindfold. "Wait!" Franco's voice commanded, and Rick's hands froze. "I think maybe I like both of you better this way."

"Franco! *Bayunco!*" Mariana chided. "You never change."

Rick felt her hands pulling at the knot behind his head. He opened his eyes to the shadowy shelter of a wide-mouthed cavern that opened up like a long, low-ceilinged lean-to. At the front edge, a string of large trees provided an extra measure of shade and shelter, like the homey security of a front porch designed by nature.

At the front edge of the cave, two cook fires burned. Tortillas were the order of the day at one, as a few women gathered around the large *comal* perched close above the glowing coals, balanced on a handful of large rocks. They patted out tortillas on their flat palms while they chatted with the lady at the other fire who was stirring a large pot of beans. Rick thought the old woman looked familiar as she turned away, but he could not be sure.

Other members of the group were sitting or standing in small groups while they cleaned weapons, worked on other gear, read, or dozed. A small group of youth not far from where they stood were seated listening to a teacher dressed in green camouflage pants and a t-shirt. Against the far wall, bedrolls and a few blankets hung to provide a sort of make-shift communal bedroom with separated areas for some. Directly behind where they stood, a set of stone steps cut into the hillside led up to a solid wall of rock. While Rick was busy trying to take in everything at once, Franco introduced them to the others.

Rick recognized a few faces from previous encounters, two in particular. He shook hands with Elio, a former student of the National University, and was loudly welcomed by a very large man who sat alone, cleaning a new M-16.

"*Qué tal, gringo*?" Lito grinned at him. "Been on any bus rides lately?"

"Lito." Mariana put her hands on her hips. "A better question is, have you been raiding any buses lately?"

Lito turned toward Mariana. "It was you on the bus that day! Franco did not believe me when I first told him. What are you doing here now?"

"We just came to see," came the cheerful, almost saucy reply. "To see what you are up to, besides making trouble."

She must be feeling better, Rick thought as he began to relax a bit.

"Oh, Niña Mariana," a whine crept into Lito's voice. "We only make trouble for the *guardia*, nobody else. And no more buses, either. Your cousin says it is not a good idea."

"Some people do listen to me." Franco directed his comment toward Mariana.

"That is nice," she answered.

"So, *gringo*, what do you think? It does not exactly look like the Army of the People that is going to overthrow the government one day, yes?"

Rick shrugged. "I suppose you would know better than I."

"Maybe we can show you something about that while you are here. Come."

Franco spent the next half hour showing him around, explaining with more than a touch of pride how they took care of their own, repaired older weapons, and even manufactured their own contact bombs. Rick's first impression of the long, low cave proved to be more than accurate, as Franco explained that they had built walls from stones, subdividing the original cavern into separate sections, which included a schoolroom that also served as a hospital and an arms storeroom. He continued that those studying in the great room today were doing so because the other room was serving as a hospital at the moment. Two of their members had been wounded in a recent foray with the army, and a woman who had a baby three days before was also resting there.

"She really does not need to be there now, though. She is proof of how strong this revolution is in the people's hearts," Franco continued.

Rick raised an eyebrow in his direction but said nothing.

Franco's voice turned to a monotone. "There was another massacre, up north, last week."

"*Por el amor de Díos, no*," Mariana gasped. "Where?"

"One of the smaller villages, *El Rosario*. The woman with the new baby, she and a dozen others came from there. They were able to slip out before the shooting started, sneaking past the army patrols. Someone they knew in their village told them that the army was coming, but most of the people did not believe it and refused to leave. By the time she and her group did, it was nearly too late. They walked for two nights, hiding during the day, but she gave birth on the second day."

"And then what?"

"And then she got up and walked two more nights. That is how badly she wants a new life and a new life for her daughter. She knows as we all do that the army makes no distinction between killing men who fight and children and babies who cannot. That is why we will win in the end, you see. The army does not fight at night. They are too lazy and too scared to get out of their beds to walk patrols. They have commanders who sneak back to the big city whenever they get the chance." He snorted with contempt. "We will win in the end because we have to. Because there is nothing for us to go back to if we do not. Nothing. And nothing that another army can bring to this war can defeat a woman or a man with that kind of strength."

"And once you win. Then what?" Rick asked the question in a guarded tone, not wishing to make light of that which Franco spoke.

"Then we will establish a government based on what the people want and what the people need, not what the man with all the money wants," Elio interjected as he came up behind them.

"And is it really that simple?"

"No one ever said it was simple. Only that it has to be done."

"And what about the leadership, the people behind all of this? What we are told in my country is that it is revolution, imported from other places."

"What other places?" The exasperation in Elio's voice was no longer concealed. "Cuba? Nicaragua? How long have you been in El Salvador?"

"Since September. About four months, I guess."

"And in this time, what have you seen? If you lived in a shack, would you join the revolution, or would you continue to wait for the *guardia* to arrive at your door one night? Or maybe you do not believe the army here treats the people all that poorly?"

"I know something about the soldiers and the way they abuse their authority."

Elio studied him carefully for a moment. "Somehow, I think you do. If that is the case, then you know the truth. Yes, there are others, a political arm of the revolution, if you will, and we must work together with them. But what they believe does not diminish what we believe, what we know. At this time in our country's history, our only hope of attaining any political goals, any significant changes of any kind, lies in armed insurrection. It is not what any of us wants. Everyone here has tried other ways first. Many of these men were in the army but left when it became clear to them that what they were expected to do was completely without reason; killing women, children, torturing those who chose a different way of life. We are here because we have been forced into it. Now that we are, however, we will do whatever we have to, to make the necessary changes." He stopped. "Excuse me, I have to check on something on the other side."

Rick decided not to ask any more questions for the moment. They looked in on the patients. Franco spoke to the injured men from the doorway, but Mariana slipped inside to greet the woman resting in the third bed. Rick watched with a full heart as her face lit up when the new mother shared her greatest treasure. Mariana cradled the tiny life in her arms, cooing softly, the radiance in her face a reflection of the tiny new life she hugged to her breast.

"What is her name?"

"Victoria," came the shy answer.

The woman nursing the injured men had her back to them, but she turned from the wounded man she was tending at the sound of Mariana's voice.

"Marielos!" Mariana's surprise was genuine. "We were worried about you."

"We are all right here now." Marielos reached out to give her friend the traditional exchange of half an embrace and a kiss on the cheek. "After what happened to my brother and your father, I knew we could not stay in town any longer. We are all here— my grandmother, my daughters, Fabiano, and of course, Orlando. I needed to be with him again. We may be here in the mountains, but now we are a real family, together again."

"I am so happy for you." Mariana returned the baby to her mother and gave her old friend another hug.

Franco and Rick left the women to their reunion. "They have a lot to talk about, I imagine," Franco said. "It is good to see them together again. Maybe it is not such a bad thing that she came after all. Come. I can show you something that would not interest her much anyway."

As they stepped back into the other room, Rick nearly tripped over a collection of small potted plants. "Just like home," he joked with Franco as he pointed to them.

"Those were nearly the death of that old woman, Ana, dragging them along. Marielos said she would not leave the village without her 'cures,' but I could not believe it when she came hauling them up the mountainside."

"Well, I've seen them work pretty well a time or two. There's a guy back in *Las Palomitas*, Andres Parada, who was poisoned while working in the cotton fields, and what she gave him sure seemed to help. I got a taste of some of her medicine one day, too. Tastes pretty bad, but sure did put me back on my feet pretty quick."

Franco looked at him anew. "You really are becoming one of—" He stopped speaking and leaned back to take another look at the American.

"One of what?" Rick asked.

"Nothing." Franco turned away, shaking his head with a wry smile. "Nothing at all." They walked past the women at the cook fires when the woman stirring the beans looked directly at him.

"Don Ricardo," Niña Ana opened her arms wide and gave him an unexpected hug. "I am so glad to see you."

"I wondered if that was you," he returned her greeting. "How are you? It is good to see you again."

"It is good to be here, for our family, to be together again. I never got to thank you for what you did for Fabiano. Before I could say anything, he and Marielos had whisked us away."

"Then, you are doing all right here?"

"Ay, don Ricardo. We are a troubled country, but the Lord takes care of His own."

"Excuse me?" He was not following her words well.

"My mother used to say, whenever you think the worst has come and your life is over, wait three days."

Rick shook his head with a smile.

"You do not understand? When the soldiers shot and came looking for poor Fabiano, I thought everything was lost, but you and don Imanuel and

Niña Mariana saved him. Three days later, he was safe here in the mountains with Franco and the others, and we arrived right after that. The worst day the world has ever known is coming. We call it Holy Friday, no? The day our Lord was hung on the cross. And the faithful thought that all was lost. They went into a locked room for three days, and they prayed. And then came *la resurrección*, and their faith was rewarded with the best day the world will ever know. Whenever you lose hope, my friend, wait and pray for three days, and your faith will be rewarded."

Rick smiled and shook her hand before following the impatient Franco. "I'll try to remember that," he told her. "Thank you."

Franco stopped outside the far doorway, on the opposite side of the cave from where they had left Mariana and Marielos.

"This is what I wanted to show you," he said as they stepped inside.

To call the makeshift room a bomb factory might be stretching things, Rick thought later, but he could think of no other name that fit. Contact bombs—created from small amounts of chemicals, common plastic sandwich bags, masking tape, newspaper, and broken pieces of metal—he soon learned were an essential and lethal part of the guerrilla war effort.

One of the older boys was using a heavy hammer on the last vestiges of a refrigerator motor as Elio supervised. "The pieces make the shrapnel," Franco explained. "We survive by using everything we have for some purpose. We got this last week in a raid on a nearby town. It did not work anyway, the man told us, so we found a way to make it work for us.

"There is a problem with you coming now," he further explained to Rick, "but maybe Marielos just solved it for us. We have to go up north of here. We will not be long, a couple of days, no more, but it would give you a chance to see what we are really made of, why we do what we do and how. If you are interested, my friend. This might be your chance to learn a great deal. What do you think, Elio?"

"He should think about why he is here and why he would want to go." Elio left the bomb-making to re-join them. Rick did not like being spoken about as if he were not present. He waited politely, but Elio did not add anything more.

"What's the catch, Franco? I hear something more."

"Nothing, except, of course, we will be walking a great deal, mostly at night, and I do not think Mariana can make the trip. She does not seem so strong right now. It worries me. Have you noticed?"

"Sure." Rick could not tell if he was deliberately swinging the conversation in another direction, but he was glad to know he was the only one who was concerned about her health. "I've asked her about it a couple of times, but she always tells me it's nothing. I'm not convinced but—"

"But you do not want to argue with her. I know that feeling."

"One thing I have seen is that she's better now than she was when she first came back. I don't know what it is, but she's not as weak. Just now, coming here, she climbed that mountain. It was still a struggle, but she did it. I'm not sure she could have done that a couple of months ago." Rick shoved a hand roughly through his hair. "But I can't get any straight answers out of her about anything more."

Franco grinned. "If she does not want you to know something, I can tell you right now, she will never tell. She was always like that even when we were little. Nobody can keep a secret like Mariana." A puzzled frown crossed his brow.

"What is it?"

"Even when we were little," he repeated. "I hope she is not getting sick again."

"What do you mean?"

"She had some sort of fever when we were younger. I remember it because Imanuel took her to a doctor, which was a pretty unusual thing. No one then could afford to take a child to a clinic. It was not too long after my Aunt 'Lupe died, so maybe that is why he did it because he was afraid he would lose her, too. Anyway, the doctor said she had to stay in bed for months, and Imanuel saw to it that she did, too. He would yell at her every time she got up, so we all learned to play and work with her in the bed or in the hammock. I remember I was mad because it meant I had to look after Paz much of the time. He was just a baby, and I was not a very good babysitter." The memory of gentler times brought a softness to Franco's usually taut serious face.

"What did she have? Did they ever tell you?"

"Some kind of fever is all I remember. They told us she had to rest, or it would damage her heart. I hope it is not something recurring, like malaria. People here get that quite often, and then it comes back, time after time."

He shook off the childhood memories. "At any rate, I do not think she could make the run with us. There will be others who stay here, including Marielos and Niña Ana, people she knows. She would not be alone. You want to think about it."

And think about it, he did. He spent the next two days watching Franco, Elio, Lito, and the other men at drill practice in the field behind the house. He was allowed access to any part of the cave and to talk freely with anyone there. The only thing that remained hidden to him was the entrance to the cave. The blindfold was replaced each time they left or entered.

It was at night, however, sitting around the fire, listening to the men and women, boys and girls, tell their stories that he learned the most about what was truly happening in this country he had come to love, this country that had become a war zone.

Ramón told the story of his sister, Marta Gloria, and her husband, Pablo, who once owned the very land where they now camped, although even they did not know about the existence of the cave. Completely obscured from the land below by the wide band of trees at its mouth, it was the perfect hiding place because it could not be seen from below or even from above by a helicopter. There had been no hiding place good enough for Marta Gloria, though, after her husband's murder. She received telephone threats once she moved to the capital, and a man she did not know gave one of her daughters a note after school one day. All it said was 'next time.' She did not wait.

"She is living in Miami now," he concluded. "She works as a maid for someone else. She was a teacher here but not there. Still, it is better than ending up like her husband or losing one of her daughters."

"Even after she left," he sighed, "I was not ready to leave who and what I was behind. It was not until the day the soldiers closed the National University, and I saw them shoot three other students from one of my classes. One of them was a leader of a group advocating change, and he was handing out fliers. We were all talking and laughing together, and I had just walked away from them. I turned at the noise and saw them all fall dead. That was when I knew, and I just left. Living here is hard, but fighting for something is better than being shot down because you are talking to someone who wants to change life for the better."

"For me," sixteen-year-old Sara spoke up next. "It was different. You all know that." She cocked her head to one side and smiled nervously as she told her story. "My mother and father were both members of the church. They went to Mass faithfully, and when the priests began to say they were one with us, the poor, and that they would teach us better ways to feed ourselves, to build up our towns, they believed.

My father was with the priest in our town when he was murdered.

"They killed them both together in the church. My mother took my two little sisters and went to the refugee camp in Honduras. She told me I should choose—to go with her or to stay and fight. I told her I could not help anyone sitting in a camp and that I would fight for her and my sisters and for the memory of my father." She choked on the last words. "I still miss them so," she whispered with tears in her eyes.

"Of course, you do." Rick was startled by the compassion in the voice that followed. "We all miss our mothers, our sisters, our brothers, our fathers, all who have died in the struggle or now have to flee for their own safety. But their strength lives in us now. Never forget that." Rick was not accustomed to empathy from Franco.

"My parents were teachers." Blanca picked up the narrative. "Maybe somewhere they still are. I hope so. They wanted me to go with them when they escaped to the United States, but I told them no. I would not go to the country that sends weapons to mine to kill people who never did any harm to anyone. I hope to see them again one day, but in the meantime, I will fight here."

A silence fell over them for several minutes, and after a time, he felt compelled to give them some explanation for his presence. "I was invited here by a friend of yours. He told me I did not know enough about this struggle, and after listening to him and to you, I think he is probably right. I came to learn and to try to understand. I know part of what you study about the United States says that everyone there gets to make their own decisions and that the government there is controlled by the people. One thing you should know is that the people there do not know, do not understand what is happening here. They are not supplying aid to your government because they hate you or want to hurt you. I want you to know that when I go back, I will do my best to make them understand. You have to remember, though, that I am only one small voice—" He quit speaking, searching for the words to continue.

"One small voice crying out in the wilderness. That is where Monsignor Romero says you have to be to hear the voice of God, in the wilderness." Fabiano stood up. "If you cry out in the United States, don Ricardo, there are Christians there, too, and they will hear you."

"I hope so, Fabiano. I hope so."

The days passed swiftly, and Mariana looked more radiant than ever. She probably gets more rest here than at home, Rick realized, as he watched her at breakfast that morning.

"Come here," he told her when they finished eating. Arms around each other, they walked back to the edge of the cliff where they could survey all of *Las Palomitas* from above.

"Franco wants me to go with them tonight. I am not even sure where they are going, but—" He shrugged his shoulders, leaving the thought unfinished. "After I get back, we can go 'home' back down there, but I wanted to ask you about tonight."

"Do you want to go?" she asked, almost nonchalantly.

"Yeah, I do. Now, if you ask me why, I'm not sure I have an answer for that, but the basic answer is yes, I want to go."

"I know why." She continued, looking past him to the sea and the village below. "The why is because you are a man and men like to know why and they like to fight, no matter what they say. And it is also because that is the way Franco is. He can make you feel like you should go with him, whether you really should or not." There was no accusation despite her words, just a statement of fact with a resigned sense that the decision had already been made.

"You are not angry? I'll not go if it upsets you. Tell me the truth."

Her dark eyes pierced his heart as she looked through him. She wrapped her arms around his neck. "The truth?" She spoke softly, standing on tiptoe to bring her face close to his. Her sweet scent was even more intoxicating here in the mountains, was all he could think.

"The truth is that it scares me to death. But if you do not go, you will always be sorry you missed this one chance. You must go. Do not even think about it anymore. But be careful and come back here safe to me. I do not want to be taking bullets out of you like Fabiano or even worse. Do you understand?"

"Yes, ma'am," he muttered dutifully in her ear as he kissed her neck. "That is exactly what I intend to do."

They sat around the fire again that evening, but it seemed a completely different group than the one from the night before. Orlando had a guitar, and they sang of the revolution and the life that they hoped to attain one day.

"Tell us a story, Niña Mariana," Fabiano asked after a while, and the others chimed in. "She tells the most wonderful stories, did you know?" He asked Rick. "I remember from long ago—" He stopped suddenly as if he had said something improper.

"It is all right, Fabiano," she said. "It was a long time ago."

"Tell us about the spirit of the mountain at *Izalco*."

Delight spread over her face at being included in their inner circle. She leaned forward and began her tale in earnest. Rick could not catch all of it as she talked about the Indian spirits of the *Náhuatl* and specifically about the spirit that lived in a mountain called *Izalco*.

"*Izalco. Izalco.*" She repeated the name like she was mulling it over, having heard it for the first time. Rick realized it was the storyteller coming out in her as the adoration in her voice soon captured the attention of all who listened. "You all know that name, yes?"

They nodded.

"*Izalco* has long been famous for its spirits. The very name means the place of the witches, for that was their gathering place long before any of our grandfathers were born. It is no surprise then that a few of those spirits remain there. This is the story of one of those spirits who lives even today, the story of the volcano at *Izalco*, the most famous in all of El Salvador.

"The sailors from all the countries who sailed the Pacific used it as their guiding light. They called it the Lighthouse of the Pacific. It was not like the volcanoes we know today, which churn out tons of black rock and ruin everything in their path. *Izalco* was a thing of beauty, a fiery reminder of the strength of Mother Earth and one who chose to be a friend to the local farmers by not destroying their crops and homes."

Franco handed her a cup of coffee. She took a sip and then continued. "One day, men from the city came, and they decided everyone should have the chance to see *Izalco* for themselves. They went up on the nearby *Cerro Verde*, which is actually a little taller than *Izalco*. The men decided to build a big fancy hotel on the side of the *Cerro Verde* so visitors could look right down inside *Izalco* and look in on the spirit who lived there as he spewed his fire each day.

"Now you must understand, there had always been something of a rivalry between the two mountains. *Cerro Verde* was always a little too prideful about his height because he was just what his name says, a big green hill, and nothing more. He was jealous of his neighbor, the mighty volcano, *Izalco*.

"Now *Cerro Verde* was even more prideful, bragging to *Izalco* that the men from the city favored him since they had decided to build their hotel there. And so it continued, as the men came with their machines, tore up the land, and built their grand hotel. But when it was all done, *Izalco* had the last word, and that was no word at all. After so many years of being the Lighthouse of the Pacific as the sailors called *Izalco*, and after the men had finished building their hotel, *Izalco* fell silent and stopped speaking altogether.

"He closed up his mighty mouth and refused to make another fiery sound or share any more of his beautiful light in the night or day. Now the sailors of the sea have to depend on other ways to see the coast. The farmers worry that someday *Izalco* may explode like the other volcanoes that sit quietly for years and then suddenly erupt and do much damage. The spirit of the mountain sits patiently waiting down deep inside the volcano, and the men who built their hotel have a big building but now no reason for anyone to come there. There is nothing to see. The people say the spirit of *Izalco* was so incensed by the audacity of men to try to look down on him from above that he will not speak again, until that hotel is torn down."

She concluded. "The *Cerro Verde* is still a bit taller than *Izalco*, but he is the one who looks foolish now as he holds a big empty hotel. Bigger is not always better, and bragging is never the way. Even the smallest among us holds more power than we know."

The story was well-received. "Tell us another," the cry echoed around the fire. "Tell us about the Siguanaba and the Cipitio," someone else implored.

"Not tonight," Franco interrupted. "There is still work to be done before we leave, so let's get going. One last song is all we have time for, if Orlando is willing."

Marielos sat close to her husband's side as he began another song, this one about the victorious people who would not be dissuaded from their righteous struggle.

"Is that what you were talking about earlier this morning?" Rick whispered to Mariana. "When you mentioned something about the spirits of the land?"

She nodded. "It is a true story, the one I just told."

"About the spirit of the mountain?" Rick squinted in disbelief.

"Believe whatever you like," she shrugged. "The facts are that *Izalco* was as regular as what do they call the famous fountain in the park in Wyoming—Old Faithful? *Izalco* was the Old Faithful of El Salvador until they built that hotel a few years ago on *Cerro Verde* and now, nothing. Men have even climbed down inside. It is completely closed up. Now, I am sure the scientists have some explanation, but here, this is the one that makes sense to us. Until that hotel comes down, *Izalco* will not speak again."

Rick pulled her close in the chilled darkness. "Then it works for me," was all he said.

He was asleep, dreaming of her as he held Mariana close under the thin blanket they shared when he was roused by a sharp prodding on his shoulder.

"It is time." Franco's harsh whisper somewhere in the dark jerked him from slumber faster than any alarm clock. He had not intended to fall asleep, only to hold Mariana for a few minutes until she slept.

On his feet, blindfold in place, Rick followed the others as they trooped out of the cave. A few hundred feet later, Franco pulled the covering from his eyes. They were in the field behind the house. It was a night of constant movement. Rick could not be sure how many miles they covered, but at the steady pace, he was certain it was no small distance. He carried a pack of supplies Franco had given him, assuring him there were no weapons, bombs, or the like inside.

"Only non-lethal assistance," Franco promised him with an ironic little smile. He also handed him a plastic bottle with a handle that had a small piece of rope attached. It reminded Rick of a small bleach bottle from his mother's laundry room. "Here. You'll need it," was all Franco added. It took a moment for Rick to understand he had just been given his own water supply.

Halfway to wherever it was they were going, they found a wizened old woman by the trail, who served them hot rice and beans, rolled up in plate-sized tortillas. "*Que te vaya bien*," she told each one as she handed them what Rick thought of as Salvadoran fast food. "May all go well with you." It was a phrase he had heard often since coming to El Salvador, but never more needed than tonight, he reflected, as he scrambled after the others. They ate while still on the move.

Dawn's early light found them laying along the crest of a hillside. A small village lay further down the valley, but directly below them was a low bunker of a building, white stucco with a traditional red tile roof. Franco reached into the pack he had given Rick and pulled out a child's school notebook and scribbled a note on the first page. Tearing it out, he handed it to one of the youngest boys who ran just below the ridge, toward the far side of the hollow.

"What do you think?" Elio slid up alongside Franco and Rick.

"I think they will be there," Franco answered. 'If so, we will have some real action for you in a few minutes, my friend."

Rick could not remember when his name had been converted by Franco from *Gringo* to Friend, but he was grateful for the change, particularly at a moment like this.

They laid in the sparse dry grass, quietly waiting, for what Rick was not quite sure until he saw the messenger stand high on the far ridge and wave, hand high above his head. The next sound was the crack of a rifle echoing down the valley, and after that, it all became a blur, a kaleidoscope of bits and pieces, falling haphazardly together, to create an image the like of which he hoped never to experience again.

The men fired en masse at the building and began heaving the contact bombs he had seen them making at the camp. The air was filled with shouts from within the building as the sleeping soldiers tried to make sense of the deadly reveille that resounded from the hills around them. Men scampered over the far ridge from the direction in which the messenger had last been seen, and at last, Rick understood the group he was with was one of two involved in the attack. A handful of soldiers came running from the village—those on guard or patrol, Rick thought, but they were intercepted by gunfire, courtesy of some of Franco's men, strategically located high up in the rocks between the town and the garrison. They were neatly pinned down and cut off from those hoping to rejoin their fellow soldiers, making both retreat and advance impossible. The rebels crept down the hills, getting ever closer to the building and yet seemed to be having little impact on those locked tightly inside. Their contact bombs, while impressively explosive, had little effect on the garrison's thick adobe walls. The same could be said for their bullets. The air was soon a pale blue-gray, painted with the thin smoke of discharged gunpowder.

While the others continued firing and slipping closer, Rick lingered in his original hiding place along the ridge, observing all, yet feeling ridiculously helpless. He was not a part of the conflict, yet he could hardly be considered an impartial observer, he thought in disgust as another piece of rock splintered beside him in response to a bullet fired from the bunker.

Lito lumbered over the edge, at last, tossing his rifle over his shoulder as he went, where it hung from a homemade twine strap. Halfway down the hillside, he lifted a small boulder onto his shoulder and heaved it, Goliath style, onto the roof of the bunker below.

Great, Rick thought. When they can't get the job done with guns, they go back to the old tried and true methods of throwing rocks.

To his surprise, the huge rock crashed through the red tile roof, leaving a mammoth hole in its wake. Contact bombs were then expertly lobbed through the opening, and in short order, the front door swung open and men, some still only half-dressed, began pouring out, their hands in the air.

As quickly as it began, it was over. The remaining rebels from both sides of the valley scooted down the hillsides and, once united, began to take stock—of the prisoners, the captured arms, and other plunder, as well as the dead and wounded on both sides.

"Come on." Franco motioned to Rick, who joined the others and surrendered his pack upon command. Rick discovered what he was carrying were first aid supplies. One of the women, sometimes hard to distinguish from the men in their makeshift uniforms, began to work over the six wounded guerrillas. She quickly passed over those with lesser injuries and handed over some of her supplies to another rebel who in turn tried to staunch the bleeding of a wounded National Guard's soldier's shoulder.

"What happens to them now?" Rick was almost afraid to ask as he surveyed the group of soldiers. Like their revolutionary counterparts, they were mostly young, and at the moment, more than a little afraid, Rick guessed from the faces that he saw.

"*Rebelde gringo*," the quiet epithet that slipped from one young soldier's lips seemed to surprise him almost as much as it did everyone else. Lito raised his rifle butt, threatening to silence him once and forever. Franco whirled as the soldier dropped his eyes but not before Rick realized as his heart plummeted to his feet, that he, too, recognized the man.

"Alfredo," Franco said quietly as he held up a hand to stop Lito. "Alfredo Chicas. Come, Alfredo, let's go for a little walk. You should be more careful, little soldier. I know you. I know all of your family, yes?" He motioned for Rick to follow along behind as they walked away from the others. "Is that not what you tell our women and children who are home in the villages when you discover they have a relative amongst *los muchachos*? Well, now things are a bit different, yes? I do know your sister, Ofelia and your cousins, twins, yes? Alberto and Gilberto. You know Gilberto, yes?"

Rick nodded, cringing himself at Franco's mincing tone.

"*Por favor*, don Franco. I did not mean anything. I just remembered, that's all." The man began to snivel.

"That is enough sometimes, to get you into a great deal of trouble. Surely, you know that?" Franco sounded more like a threatening older brother than someone who literally held this man's life in his hands.

"*Sí*." With his head down and his shoulders beginning to shake, the answer was barely audible. He didn't look to be much older than the teens they had listened to the other night around the campfire. God, what this war is doing to both sides is unconscionable, Rick's soul cried out in silence.

"Where do you know this man from?" Franco's manner was now crisp, strictly military, with no more preambles.

"From the beach. The first day I was assigned there. He rode in the Jeep driven by the other *gringo*."

Franco looked sharply at Rick for corroboration, and Rick nodded while remaining silent.

"So you serve under Lt. Hernandez?"

"I did but not now. I was transferred a month ago."

"Why? Why were you transferred?"

"Because I asked for the change."

"You did not want to be near your family?" Franco did not bother to hide his surprise.

"I did not want to stay under the command of Lt. Hernandez."

"And why not?"

Alfredo lifted his eyes momentarily before answering. "Because as you say, my family lives close by. Lt. Hernandez is not so particular about who he singles out for punishment if he thinks they are against him or those he works for. I did not want to stay and have to be after my own family and friends. My sister Ofelia and her husband and his brothers and their children all live there."

"Why did you join the armed forces of El Salvador?" The next question was a surprise to Rick as well as to Alfredo, who hesitated again before answering.

"Because." His shoulders drooped as a sigh escaped him that seemed to come from his boots all the way to his quivering lips. "Because there was no work and I could eat and wear uniforms and give a little money to my sister. I just wanted to be somebody."

"To be somebody. Is that what you are doing now? Is that what you were doing in *Las Palomitas*? You were being somebody? So much so that you had to leave town because you might be ordered to hurt one of your own one day?"

The young man hung his head and cried unabashedly, his tears slipping between his fingers as he covered his face.

"And do you know what happens now?"

He nodded, without speaking, his face still covered.

"What?"

"You will kill me."

"You are wrong again, my young friend. Just as wrong as the day you joined *la guardia*."

Alfredo stopped crying for the moment and looked up, not believing what he had just heard.

"You are leaving this place, and maybe if you are lucky, you are leaving *la guardia*, too. Do you see that man over there?" Franco put one hand on the boy's shoulder while he directed his attention to the commander of the rebels who had come from the other side of the valley. Already, most of the other soldiers had been organized and were preparing to march off to God knows where, Rick thought.

"You are going with him. He and his men will be taking all of you prisoner, it is true, and you will go off to live in the hills with them for a time. No one will shoot you unless you do something really stupid, like try to run away or fight back. Do as you are told, and you will be fine. After a few weeks, you will be allowed to make your own choice—to go back to being a soldier or join the revolution. If you wish to return, you will be permitted to do that but only on one condition. See this man?" He pointed to Rick. "You must forget you ever saw him here. He has no gun. He did not fight today. You saw for yourself, the only thing he carried was bandages, and they were used for some of your fellow soldiers as well as on our fighters. Do you understand?"

Alfredo eagerly began drying his tears and wiping his runny nose on his sleeve. "*Sí, entiendo bien*, don Franco," he answered obediently.

"Forget that name, too, Alfredo. It could only get you into trouble at this point. *Me entiendes*?"

A little smile appeared on Alfredo's tear-stained face. "*Sí, es cierto*. I understand. I will do as you say."

"Go now. It may be the only chance you ever get in this country for a new life."

Alfredo took a few steps toward his new captors before turning back. "*Adíos, señores. Muchas gracias*. I will never forget this day, this chance. I swear it." He walked toward his waiting comrades. With each step, his back straightened and his steps quickened as he joined the prisoner line up.

"Not what you expected, *verdad*?" Franco glanced at Rick. "No firing squads here. We take our prisoners to the hills and keep them a while. Alfredo will be busy for at least a month, and then, unless I misjudge him greatly, he will not be wearing an army uniform again. He was not exactly a contented soldier in the first place. Most of them are not. Many are little more than *putas*."

"Prostitutes?"

"Certainly. What is a prostitute? Someone who sells herself for the money. With what she earns, she eats, feeds her family, buys nice clothes and shoes, and earns a sick sort of respect because she can manage to do that. But at the same time, everyone spits on her, at least behind her back, because of what she does for a living."

"Yeah, but soldiers—"

"The average foot soldier in the military here is in it because he was in the kidnap draft or because, like Alfredo, he wants to eat regularly, wear a uniform and boots, and earn a sort of sick respect—to be somebody as he called it. You get to be somebody when they give you a gun and let you use it to make people afraid. And at the same time, behind his back, everyone spits on him because of what he does. So tell me, what is the difference?"

"I'm not sure," Rick stuttered, trying to follow the peculiar train of thought. "What is the kidnap draft?"

"Just what it sounds like. You go along, walking down the street, drinking in a bar, minding your own business, and then you are kidnapped into the army. If you refuse, they assume you are sympathetic to us, the other side. You lose either way. They take the poor and the middle class, even university students. The only ones they do not take are the ones who have rich relatives and friends."

"What about the ones who attend the military school?" Rick countered. "There is military training for—"

"*Ay, sí, la Escuela Militar General Gerardo Barrios.* The school of how to cheat everybody you have ever known and will ever know. The school of how to make big money while you are in the military by blackmailing half the people you know and threatening or working illegally for the other half. Many of the presidents of my country graduate from there. You remember, the ones we talked about before—the puppets. Also nice people like Roberto D'Aubuisson, a man so brutal he was actually thrown out of the National Guard. It is a school for teaching men how to get the most out of their country and how to put it into their own pockets. A very nice school indeed."

"Then there is nothing good about the military here?"

"Sure, they are good at getting what they want, and they will do anything they have to, to get it. Officers make lots of money, bleeding it out of the country around them. The ones of low rank, like Alfredo, can work up to that, or they can just threaten poor people to get what they want at the moment. The only good thing about the military in a country like ours is a solution like Costa Rica."

"And what's that?"

"No real military at all. Come on."

Rick followed him as they rejoined the others. The group from the north appeared ready to go back that direction. A cache of captured weapons, all army issue, mostly US-made, Rick noted, was being handed out. The northern group took their share before leaving.

"This is the way you get your weapons?" Rick's surprise was written across his face.

"Many of them," Franco replied nonchalantly. "Others we buy."

"From whom and with what?" Rick's questions were popping out of his mouth as fast as they came into his head.

Franco's laughter had a hollow ring to it. "You ask a great many questions."

"I know," Rick frowned. "I just couldn't imagine you walking in somewhere and—" He stopped speaking and looked down at his tennis shoes.

An exasperated sigh escaped Franco. "We buy guns from the only ones who have guns. The army, *por supuesto.*"

"Now, wait a minute." Rick's confusion deepened. "How can you buy—"

"How does my cousin stand it?" Franco stood back and looked at him with total disgust. "The *chafa*," he began with exaggerated patience, invoking his favorite profane term for the military, "is full of men who would rather fill their own pockets than win against any enemy. For a price, they would sell their own grandmothers or anything else, and that includes weapons and ammunition."

The *revolucionario* cocked his head to one side in a sly fashion as he continued. "The tricky part is getting the money, but there are those who kidnap the wealthy and the powerful and make a tidy sum at it. Did you think I was just making a joke when I spoke of kidnapping one of your hunting *compañeros* that day below Conchagua? There are others who do so, and that, along with this, keeps us in military hardware."

Franco turned and started down toward the village, followed by several others.

"Now what?" Rick asked, catching up.

"Now we do a little shopping for necessities, and then we got out of town quick before the helicopters come."

"Helicopters?" They could just as easily have been discussing the daily appearance of the mailman, Rick thought nervously.

"Yes, they will be here soon." Elio squinted at the sky as if expecting their imminent arrival. "But never before mid-morning. If we are quick, we will be gone before they come."

"How do you know these things?" Rick, bewildered, searched the sky like Elio, but saw nothing. "What makes you so sure?"

"You learn a lot of things about your adversaries in this line of work," Franco quipped. "Helicopter pilots do not fly before certain hours. I do not know why it is. I just know it is, and we use that to our advantage."

In the two stores in the village, the group stocked up on basic personal supplies, items ranging from toothbrushes to playing cards to packets of cheap drink mix. The owner of the store that Rick entered appeared slightly nervous in serving these particular customers but also refused to take any of the money they offered for payment.

Rick walked out with the others but made a quick excuse while strolling up the street and returned to the store. "Here." He told the man behind the counter. "I came back to pay for what they took. It's all right now, truly," he explained. "They are gone."

"It is all right, truly." The store owner echoed his words back in Spanish. "I do not want their money or yours either. After all, you are fighting for all of us. Is that not true? What they took is nothing compared to what the army takes from us, any time they want to. This is the one small way I can help. *Que le vaya bien, amigo.*"

Genuinely surprised, Rick returned the man's friendly wave and ducked out the door. With his long stride, he caught up to the others with little effort. The menacing echoes of helicopter blades, like fleece-wrapped sledgehammers pounding on distant anvils at breakneck speed, shattered the quiet mountain morning as two helicopters appeared over the treetops.

"*Vamanos!*" Elio's shout was barely heard, lost in the deafening approach. The group scrambled over the top of the ridge above the now-empty garrison and scattered into the meager cover offered by the thin line of trees, as one of the helicopters followed after them.

This isn't happening to me was all Rick could think as he sprinted after Elio and Blanca. A strange sensation of watching the action transpire yet feeling no pain, no immediate danger, engulfed him despite his fast-moving feet, pounding heart, and gasping breath.

I should be terrified, Rick kept telling himself, not unlike that day on the bus with Lito pointing a gun in his face, but the only thing here was an ineffable sense of exhilaration. It was something akin to his days on the track team when, having found his pace, he felt like he could run forever, yet this was so much more intense. Today, he knew he could run all the way back to *Las Palomitas* or the mountain hideaway where Mariana was waiting. Nothing could stop him. Not even the man firing a machine gun from the door of that helicopter overhead.

Despite the amount of ammunition being hurled at them, the gunman above seemed incapable of hitting anything except the ground and an occasional tree limb. Chunks of dirt and rock spit in all directions, sending up clouds of dust in the wake of their passing, as the bullets tore up the earth in what was more like a temper fit of frustration than a true attempt to hit anyone. The rebel soldiers, constantly on the move, appeared to be in little real danger. A large tree branch directly above them crashed to the ground, and Elio tapped Rick roughly on the shoulder as they took off again, running after the moment's hesitation, taking shelter under one of the larger trees.

As the trees thickened, the advance of the lone helicopter lost not only its intensity but direction as well. The rebels now strewn across a kilometer presented no distinct target. As the second chopper rejoined the first, it occurred to Rick that it must have first gone in search of the band that had previously headed north. The pair wobbled in the air barely above the treetops, as if unsure of what their next move should be. At times, they appeared to be dangling from invisible strings that allowed them to swing dangerously close to one another. A closer look revealed that the gunmen on the two airships were trying to communicate with hand signals. At least one of them cannot read sign language, Rick thought, as the double sets of rotor blades whirled in alarming proximity, while those on board made wildly animated gestures. A shower of sparks resulted as the blades from the lead chopper barely nicked those of the other. The two helicopters blew away from each other like magnets with like poles. The gestures of the men on board were wilder than ever, but even Rick crouched behind another tree far below on the ground could read those, as both crews blamed the other for the error. The lead helicopter slowly lifted and turned toward its home base, and the other, after hurling a last few sporadic shots in their general direction, did the same.

"*Vaya pues, muchacho!*" Elio pounded Rick on the back in obvious relief that the final attack was over. The rebel stood up straight and stepped clear as he began looking around for the others. Gradually, they re-grouped and continued to head in a southwest direction. Franco joined them as did the others. No one had been hit directly by the helo fire, although a few had sustained superficial cuts from the flying bits of rock.

Franco took time out, once most of them had reunited, to tend to their cuts, minor though they were. It also gave everyone the chance to rest and eat a few tortillas they'd bought earlier in the village.

"What a day," Rick told Franco as they sat beneath the sheltering limbs of a *ceiba* tree. "This is the kind of adventure David was always looking for, not me. I would never have thought—" He hesitated, as a wave of guilt swept over him for the heady exhilaration that had overtaken him, although he had no real idea as to why.

"This is not the kind of thing American university students do regularly?" Franco feigned surprise.

"I didn't mean to make it sound so...so casual."

"It has been a fine day." Franco seemed to take no offense. "I feel pretty good about it, too, only three wounded, no dead. It is an especially good day when we do not have to conduct any funerals." He stopped speaking, his gaze drifting off into the distance. When he spoke again, there was a darkness in his voice that sent a shiver down Rick's spine.

"There are other days that are not so good." He took out a full pack of cigarettes, something that Rick had not seen many of since his arrival in *Las Palomitas*. Most men smoked only from the tiny bundles of four cigarettes, tied up by local shopkeepers, like Mariana and Imanuel, who broke up the packs so locals could afford them. Franco passed the slightly mashed cellophane package around to the others. It came back to him with only one *cigarillo* still inside. He stuffed it into his shirt pocket and lit the cigarette that dangled from his lips.

"There is a canyon a short distance from here, where we will spend the rest of the afternoon. We have friends near there who will feed us, and then tonight, we will move on. Tomorrow we go back to the cave after we make a short detour." Franco climbed to his feet.

"Detour?" Fatigue had slipped up on Rick in the short time they had rested, like a silent thief stealing his newfound energy. His first attempt to stand was not entirely successful.

Franco shook his head. The others struggled to their feet, and looking around, Rick could see he was not the only one who was dog tired. Too much exercise, too much adrenaline, along with too little food, water, and rest had taken its toll. It was a devastating combination, even for the few hours he had been exposed to it. He marveled at how these young men and women survived on this kind of starvation fare and still had the energy to continue their fight.

"What kind of detour?" Rick asked more specifically as he rose, carefully gauging his balance this time.

Franco's earlier effusive mood was gone. "Tomorrow, you will see what it means to have a bad day," was all he said before he led them on a long downhill march to the aforementioned canyon.

The three-sided gorge that plowed deep and narrow between short hills could be an excellent hideout or a hideous trap, Rick considered as he surveyed their current location. They lounged on the sparse grass under the thick grove of trees that neatly obscured the entire chasm until one practically fell into it.

Rick lay on his back, watching white drifts of puffy clouds slip past the one tiny patch of blue he could see between the heavy green branches above him. Franco's friends had proved generous, filling them up with hefty portions of rice and beans that even had pieces of roasted pork mixed in. Ladled once again and rolled up in large thick tortillas, they were quickly and gratefully devoured. Some of the younger ones sat talking to those who brought the food, telling them of the day's events. He heard himself mentioned, *el gringo*, and assumed they were explaining his presence among them.

After the morning's activities, weary and with a full stomach, Rick was ready to sleep and did so for several hours. The nearly full moon was already on the rise when Franco woke him with a rough shake of the shoulder.

"*Vamanos*," came the harsh whisper from the shadows.

Rick started, rose quickly, and regretted it immediately. Sleeping on the hard ground had left him chilled in the mountain cool after the wild, frenzied run. Every muscle ached, and he stopped to stretch, another lamentable move. Franco hit him low and hard, like a football tackle, a game Rick was fairly certain the rebel fighter had never played.

"What the hell—?"

"*Calláte!*" Franco hissed, his mouth close to Rick's ear, his hand roughly across his mouth. It was then that Rick heard them. Marching feet, dozens of them, and close, touching close, he feared.

He searched the contours of Franco's face in the silvered moonlight. Convinced that Rick understood the real and present danger, Franco removed his hand.

"Who?" Rick formed only the word with his lips, no sound escaping him.

"*Chafa.*" Franco answered in a like manner.

He pointed above their heads to the top of the gorge. They lay, motionless on the rocky ground while the column marched on. Franco's own shallow breathing did little to calm Rick's thundering heart. Watching, waiting, listening to the men's shuffling boots as they passed, paying no heed to their surroundings, the scene became clear to Rick.

The soldiers had come perilously close to falling into their hiding place, unaware how close their adversaries were to them at this very moment.

What a disaster that would have been! Rick considered the near-miss with a shiver. As the tramping of boots faded in the distance, he dared to roll over.

"*Puta!*" Franco cursed under his breath. "The army hates to move at night, and they usually do not. When they do—" He did not finish the thought.

"Fabiano! Ramón! Luís!" He cried out softly with such urgency, it made Rick jump. He took them aside and, with some curt instructions, sent them tearing down the hillside after the retreating soldiers.

"Now what?" Rick knew he should not ask, but he had to know.

"They have gone to sound a warning."

"And the rest of us? We aren't going to follow?"

An amused little smile played at the corners of Franco's mouth. "The rest of us, heh? And when did you become one of us?"

Rick stopped to think about what he had said. "I don't know. Maybe about the same time you stopped calling me *gringo* in such an insulting manner."

"*Vaya pues*," Franco chuckled in spite of himself. A worried frown crept around his eyes. He pulled off his hat and ran his hand through his thinning hair. It occurred to Rick he was far too young to be losing his hair already. Dust from his hair sifted onto his shoulders. He replaced his khaki military-style hat, tugging on the bill to pull it low over his eyes.

"I sent those three to warn our friends in neighboring villages. It is possible, like us, the soldiers will pass them right by. If they are warned, however, they will still have a chance if they are on somebody's list. Those boys are young, strong, and can move more quickly than the rest of us. Just the three of them, if they are lucky—they might save lives yet tonight.

"The rest of us," he repeated the phrase, savoring it once again. "We are headed in the other direction." With a few sharp orders, the group pulled itself together and was once again trekking across the countryside under the pale moonlight.

Rick was both thankful and distressed by the radiant clear night as it made their path easier to follow yet simultaneously made them more easily seen by others. He found himself clenching his teeth, shivering nervously and waiting for the first shot, the shattering moment of discovery. All around him—the greens of the grasses, the red clay earth, and the yellow hued-rocks—had been drained of their daylight colors by the pale blue frost of the moon. He wanted to relax and enjoy the eerie contrast between the day and night, but the dread of what might happen next kept him from such pleasure.

Well into the wee morning hours, they walked, until Franco determined they had reached their destination. They lay down, spread out along a grass-covered hillside, not unlike the one where they had begun the day, so many hours ago.

Rick was so tired, he could only wonder if it was some sort of cruel joke, where they had marched around in circles half the night and were now right back where they had started. At daybreak, Franco rousted them all, and after a short walk, he brought them to an abrupt stop. He sent a scout up ahead, and when he returned a few moments later with an apparent 'all clear' report, they proceeded around a short bluff. The others ran ahead, gleefully, jerking their water bottles free from their belts. A narrow waterfall flowed from the rocks overhead and filled a shallow pool below. It overflowed from there, and a portion of it was channeled to one side into a rough concrete animal trough. A watering station for both humans and their herds and flocks, Rick thought as his companions immersed their water jugs and splashed each other as they frolicked in the shallows. He noticed Franco posted sentries who kept a close eye on surrounding rock cliffs and that they spent little time loitering there, despite the others' willingness to enjoy the cool refreshment.

On the move again, they soon encountered a strangely sweet, yet sickly smell hung heavy in the air, like that of some sort of exotic flower that was rotting as it grew. Rick had no idea what it was, but he was certain he did not care for it and hoped they did not stay in the area long.

In the early morning mists, he saw for the first time the source of the stench. It sickened him to his core. Never again would he need to ask Franco, Elio or any of them, why they made the choices they did, why they chose to fight.

Twenty-four hours before, they had peeked over a similar ridge to discover a soldiers' camp and a living breathing village in the valley below. This ridge and this valley held only ghosts and memories, horror and death. The village that had once been here was no more. Only charred ruins of the buildings remained, surrounded by a few remaining corpses of those who had once called this place home.

"This was the village of *Santa Maria de la Aguas*," Franco explained. "Like *El Rosario*, it was wiped out by the army along with everyone who lived here, men, women, and children. Come. Take a closer look."

"I don't need to see any more." Rick's voice was barely above a whisper.

"You do not have to be quiet here anymore. There is no one here who will be bothered by anything you have to say. And the army has long since moved on." Franco's voice was too normal, as if he regularly discussed proper etiquette at village massacre sites. "And you did say you wanted to see it all. Well, this is part of it, too."

Slowly, Rick climbed to his feet and followed in obedience. Only he and Franco descended into the village. It was worse than anything he could have imagined. To see them, the remains were more bones than anything else, but the cruelty was exacerbated by the fact that several bodies were so much smaller, obviously women and children. So many children. His heart broke for those he had never seen, those he would never see.

All around them, pieces of shattered lives— chunks of wood that had once been furniture, broken dishes, and water jugs, a smashed crucifix, the remains of a few cherished photographs cradled in pockets of broken glass that had once been frames—lay strewn throughout the deserted dirt lanes of the town. A passing attempt had been made to burn much of what was left, but apparently like the original attack, it has been haphazard, and the result had left some shacks and huts burned to the ground while others had sputtered out before being completely consumed by the flames.

Heavy footprints, many clearly those of combat boots, imprinted in the thick mud apparently at the end of the rainy season, were now starkly preserved as the mud hardened and dried in the long days of the past months of the dry season. All about, in the longish grass and on the dusty bare spots, the spent brass cartridge cases of M-16s glinted in the early morning sunlight.

Rick bent down to more closely inspect a bright red item that caught his eye at the bottom of a heel print. 'Made in the USA,' the small print was still visible along the bottom of the little metal and wood harmonica, despite its soil encrusted condition. He glanced at the shack closest to his right and saw the collection of bones in the doorway. Upon closer inspection, he realized he was looking at a child's skeleton, covered by a larger one, undoubtedly the child's mother.

"The vultures have been busy here." Rick jumped at the sound of Franco's voice. "The last time we were here, it was not possible to walk through here. The smell. The birds. It is still not good to come here in the heat of the day—"

"For God's sake, Franco! Why did you bring me here? What the hell do you want? I swear if you go on chattering nonsense in the face of all this, I'll kill you myself and leave you here with them!" Rick pointed to the skeletons behind him.

"It was never me who chattered nonsense," Franco's voice was low and intense. "Even now, Sara, remember her? She waits with the rest on the other side of the hill. She cannot come here. This was her village. These were her people. Right over there is the church she spoke of the other night at the fire. Remember? There must have been a trace of religion left in some of those soldiers because it was one of the few buildings they did not try to burn. They just murdered the priest and the catechist, her father, right over the top of her head. She was hiding down below, in the space under the floor where her father had put her for safety. We found her in that tiny space under the church. The blood of the two men upstairs had leaked through the wooden floor and dripped all over her. She was nearly deaf when we found her a day later. The roar of so many guns at such a close range echoing through these hills damaged her ears. Even now, she tilts her head to one side to listen. Did you notice that?" He stopped to catch his breath and allow some of what he had said to sink in.

When he spoke again, his voice had softened. "I asked her permission to bring you here, but even so, she will be an emotional wreck for the next couple of days, I imagine. Who could blame her? She just barely got out of here alive. All of her life lies there, scattered at your feet."

"What about her mother and her sisters? She spoke of them the other night, too." Rick could barely force the words out.

"They were lucky. They were visiting an aunt in a nearby village when this happened. They had no idea what had happened until we found Sara. She said I could bring you here today because it would be worth it if you could see and believe and tell the rest of the world. Tell them what they are trying to do to us—what THEY WILL do to all of us if they get the chance! If we cannot convince the United States and the rest of the world, that we have serious problems here and not the kind manufactured in another country, we are all as good as the ones you see here. If you understand that, if there is no longer any doubt in your mind, then you have seen all you need to see here."

Rick nodded. He dared not look up. There were no words left in him to describe what he had seen, what he felt at this moment. He thought about the many times he had observed some horrific scene on the nightly news and felt little or nothing, other than a mild twinge of pity. Seeing and hearing something on televised news does not make something real, he realized. You can't smell it. You can't touch it, and perhaps, most significant of all, it can't touch you.

They went back the way they had come, climbing the ridge to find the others, but not before Rick took one last look over his shoulder at the barbarous evidence spread below. He made the long trek back with the others, as a changed man, someone different from who he was when he awoke that morning, a man with a child's tiny harmonica in his pocket.

CHAPTER 13

*F*ebruary 18, 1980. San Salvador. Archbishop Oscar A. Romero has written a letter to the American President, pleading with him, one Christian to another, not to send $5.7 million in military assistance already promised to the Salvadoran government. The Archbishop read much of the letter during his Sunday homily yesterday. Charges listed in it include the fact "that neither the junta nor the Christian Democrats govern the country. Political power is in the hands of the armed forces... and they use their power unscrupulously." The country's controversial archbishop further stated that [the armed forces] know only how to oppress the people and defend the interests of the Salvadoran oligarchy."

Monsignor Romero also made mention of the $200,000 in non-lethal military assistance and the six military advisors now in the country, sent here by the US in November of last year.

The proposed $5.7 million in military aid represents an amount greater than ten times the amount of such assistance sent to El Salvador for the past thirty-plus years, according to the US government's own figures.

In a related story, the Salvadoran Commission on Human Rights reported at the end of last week *that during the last ten days of January, more than 160 persons had been killed and another 42 taken prisoner or 'disappeared' by the armed forces.*

Coming home. That's what he had called it, talking to Mariana that day on the mountain, *Conchagua,* before he had marched off with Franco, Elio, and the others. He watched the waves once again from beneath his favorite palm tree. That's what it felt like, coming home. Back beside the waves, the ever faithful presence of the sea was more comforting to him than he could begin to understand or ever try to explain.

They had returned to *Las Palomitas* the day after their reappearance at the cave. Fabiano, Luís, and Ramón were waiting for them when they arrived, and their young faces shone with good news. They had arrived in time to warn those who were in danger, but even more fortunate was the fact that the marching soldiers had passed the villages by without incident. In all the exuberance, Rick found himself standing outside the entrance to the cave, like all the others, only this time with no blindfold.

He cast a startled, half-apologetic glance at Franco, who only shrugged. "You said it yourself. You are one of us now. I guess we cannot worry about some details."

It was an impressive detail, and one Rick now understood all the better for having seen it. The entrance to the cave, originally little more than a large hole in the side of the rock, was obscured by a heavy door, expertly crafted of hewn wood, laid on the bias and framed together. Lying out here, by itself, it practically screamed to be noticed, the handcrafted work of a master, lying alone on an otherwise untouched hillside.

"It came from Pablo's house up there," Ramón explained. "It was his back door. We thought it a proper tribute to the man who was with us in his heart, even though he is gone now."

The genius for its use lay in the camouflage that disguised it. Their own version of a screen door, one constructed of small trees bent and attached to a frame that was pulled open from the outside, yet fit flawlessly over the other, obscuring the heavier door. To the roving eye, the entrance was invisible. A stand of thin trees, growing close together, bent at their base, as their roots struggled for a hold on the hardscrabble ground, was all there was to see.

Standing next to it, once it was closed, Rick noted there was nothing that even hinted it was anything more than it appeared to be. Even the ground up bits of rock from the interior of the cave all around the outside of the door gave no clue that it wasn't all native cover. The natural gravel was endemic to the area and could be seen throughout the mountains, wherever the scant patches of grass could not get a permanent hold in the thin topsoil. Scattered here, the same natural gravel was the perfect material for obscuring all traces of the heavy foot traffic.

Franco had called it a detail, one that Rick knew he could never forget. Franco had now entrusted him with the knowledge that could threaten the safety of them all. It should have made him feel better, but for some reason he could not fathom, it did not.

The sight of Mariana, waiting just inside that doorway, was a tonic to his tired body and soul. He wrapped her up in his arms and hugged her so tight, he feared he might hurt her and yet it still was not tight enough. He wanted to hold her even closer, to curl up inside her, to feel safe and protected in the sanctuary of her love. He wanted to be like he was before that morning's walk through a decimated village, and yet he feared he had lost something there in the morning twilight that he might never be able to regain.

She said little but rather led him back outside to sit quietly, just the two of them, concealed under some nearby foliage.

"What did he do?" she asked when they were alone. "He promised me he would not put you in any real danger."

A mirthless little laugh escaped him. "Oh, he didn't lead me into anything any more dangerous than anyone else." He sat quietly for a few moments. "He showed me the truth. That's what he did. And I don't know if I'll ever be able to forgive him for that."

Back along the beach, the warm days, the balmy nights, the welcoming faces of Paz, Emelina, and an ever-improving Imanuel all helped to heal his wounded spirit.

They returned the way they had gone, paying twenty *centavos* a piece to be ferried across the *estero* in a *cayuco*. When they arrived late in the afternoon, Paz was on the fishermen's beach, working beside Miguel.

"So how was San Salvador?" he asked with a bright smile.

Rick winced at the thought of more lies to be spread to cover their absence.

"It is the same as ever." Mariana threw an arm around her brother's shoulders and guided him gently away from her companion. "We will tell you all about it later, I promise. First, tell me, how is Imanuel?"

"See for yourself," he answered amicably as he pointed toward the back door of the store.

Imanuel sat on a wooden chair on the elevated back porch and waved with a club of a fist, a welcome home smile creasing his face. Mariana ran up the steps and gave him a hug. Rick waved and started up the beach toward his own house when a familiar figure drew up beside him in a battered Jeep.

"I was worried I wasn't going to get to see you before I left." David was talking almost before the vehicle came to a complete stop. "Come on. I'll give you a lift."

"We tried," David began, talking so fast, Rick could hardly take in his words. "We tried for all we're worth and every way we knew how to explain it to 'em, but the big brass decided. We're the ones that got hung out to dry."

"What are you talking about? You've been in the city for a couple of weeks now, and you're going... where?"

A mischievous grin spread across David's face as he enjoyed the moment. "It's kinda nice to know you missed me. I got back yesterday, and they told me you were gone for a few days, too."

Rick just shook his head.

"Okay, well, it doesn't really matter. You need to pack it up. I'm outta here, homeward bound, as they say. Back to the good ol' USA."

"When?" Rick sat up straight in the passenger seat. "Now?"

"Tomorrow. That's what I meant when I said I was worried I wasn't going to see you. As of the day after tomorrow, this boy no longer has a legal right to be in this country. They're shipping us all out at once, buying us our plane tickets, and yanking our visas. They mean business." David had passed Rick's hut on the beach and pulled the Jeep to a sharp stop in front of his own house.

"Who?" was all Rick could think to ask.

"Come on. I'll treat you to a cold one." David motioned Rick out of the Jeep as he continued to explain. The gravity of the situation struck Rick as he walked past David's personal belongings, more packed than not, stacked near the door.

"Who? Well, that's an interesting question. Officially, the US government. Unofficially, who knows? They claim it's 'cause one of the girls got kidnapped in the marketplace in the city, but I don't know if I buy that one or not."

"Kidnapped? Is she all right?"

"Oh, yeah." David took the time to enjoy the beer in his hand. "She was in there doing some sort of nutrition classes, I think, and a bunch of the guerrillas took over the market and held onto it for several hours. They wouldn't let anybody leave, her included. I talked to her afterward, and she wasn't upset. She said they came 'round and talked to her and were really pretty nice. They even told her our program was one of the best things the US has ever done here. But they also said they couldn't extend any special favors to her, so they held onto her along with everybody else in the place. Like I said, I don't know if it's that big a deal, but Washington is going to make it one whether we like it or not." He sighed and leaned back in his hammock. "So, the basics are, they're putting us out. Are you ready to go?"

The shift in the conversation startled Rick, but time spent with Franco was making him something of an expert at covering his initial reactions.

Deliberately, he pulled up a wooden chair and straddled it, facing his cousin. "In a word," he answered politely, "no."

"So how long do you figure? I can hang around one more day if you need it." He stopped speaking as he took a closer look at Rick's face. "You aren't going at all, are you?"

"Not now." Rick shook his head.

They sat for a moment in a confused silence, drinking and contemplating the other. "Do I want to know why?" David broke the silence as he finished his beer.

"Probably not," Rick answered, matching David's equanimity.

"Does this have anything to do with where you've been for the last week? I mean, I saw Paz, and he told me you'd gone to the capital, but I didn't believe it although he seemed sincere enough."

"You didn't tell him that, did you?" A note of concern crept into Rick's voice despite his best effort.

"No, I didn't tell him anything. He's a kid, for chrissakes. Why would I wanna get him involved in anything he doesn't need to be in?" David's patience was wearing thin.

"That's just one of the things you wouldn't understand, I suppose. Look, if you're leaving tomorrow, I really don't see the point of getting into it now, over things we'll never agree on anyway."

"Okay, okay." David gave up the battle. "Just tell me. Is it the woman?"

"She's part of it."

David gave him a strange look.

"Okay, she's a big part of it, but maybe not all of it."

David started to speak, stopped, and then tried again. The note of distress in his voice was genuine. "Do you know what you're risking? By staying, I mean? And by staying with her?"

"I think so." Rick took a deep breath, weighing each word with care. "I have never felt so at home, so much like I belonged anywhere in my life, than since I came to be here. I know that doesn't make any sense in some ways because you can take one look at me next to anyone in this place, and it's obvious I don't fit in, but in a very real sense, I do. More importantly, they treat me as if I do. I know

I can't stay forever. I know Mariana can't ever really be mine, but I'm going to take any of it, all of it, that I can get and hold on to it, and that includes her, for as long as I can. After that, it doesn't matter that much what else happens, in one way because I'll always have this, this one time in my life, to look back on, to live through again and again. A time that belonged just to me, to just what I wanted, which in this case, happens to be helping out some other people, much of the time. Now maybe that doesn't make sense to you, but it does to me, and for that reason alone, I'm going to do it, and that means staying just a little while longer."

David looked more than a little amused. "Damn, and I always thought of you as my little lost cousin. Remember that time in San Antonio with Ana Luisa? You got lost, and we had a heck of a time finding you. I thought SHE was gonna have a heart attack, she was in such a panic. I've thought of you as a lost little kid, hiding under a bakery cart ever since, I guess. Not anymore, heh?"

"Not anymore," Rick shared with half a smile. "I'm the one who always moved around as a kid. I've known more new schools and more new towns than you can probably imagine, and none of them has ever felt as right as this does."

David got himself another beer and settled back in his hammock once again. "And I always thought of this as just another village of illiterate fishermen."

"I told you we'd never agree on most of it." He stood up as if to leave.

"I'm sorry." David raised his beer in salute. "You're being honest, and I didn't really mean to be a jerk. Just tell me this. You aren't taking up a gun, are you?"

Rick laughed out loud, breaking the tension between them. "No, no guns. You're right to suspect where I've been but no guns, I swear. Even up there." He stuck out his chin, Salvadoran-style toward the mountain of *Conchagua*. "I only carried a bag of bandages."

"Thank the Almighty for that." David breathed a sigh of relief. "Hey, what are you going to do now?" He twisted around as Rick stepped away from his chair and headed for the back door.

"I'm going to borrow a towel and your soap." Rick stretched his full frame, brushing the underside of the roofing tiles with his fingertips. "And then I'm going out to that well and take a bath. Not a lot of chance to do much of that where I've been. Then I'm going to my house. Why?"

"Oh, just wondering if you wanted to go tie one on, just for old time's sake before I go, but I guess not." It was a sad little smile that played at the corners of his mouth.

"I guess not. I'm pretty tired," Rick answered honestly.

"Maybe you ought to think about moving in here after I go. You got more space, and there's electric and water, of sorts, anyway."

"Thanks, but I'm pretty comfortable where I am. The electric might be nice, but from what I've seen, it goes out almost as often as it's on."

"That's true," David agreed with a chuckle. "I just thought—"

"What?"

"That it might be better for you, away from the main road."

"Oh, that's never bothered me. Besides, I'd miss the beach. That's the best thing about where I live now. Why don't you come over tonight whenever you're done here?" He jerked a towel off the outside clothesline as he went out the back door.

Showered and refreshed, Rick puttered around his own little kitchen, ravenously devouring a couple of scrambled eggs. He would need to light the kerosene lantern tonight, he reminded himself as the lengthening shadows fell across the floor and the table. He laid the matches next to the lamp so they would be easier to find in the growing darkness. A knock at the door surprised him since David never announced his arrival in such a formal fashion. He turned to discover Paz and Mariana in the open doorway.

"*Pase adelante.*" Rick found himself making a conscious effort to curb his delight, lest Paz might perceive more than he or Mariana would find convenient to explain.

"Paz brought you a surprise," Mariana announced as the three stood awkwardly in the small room. "Come outside, and he can show you."

"Sit here," the youth instructed as he patted two places in the sand in front of Rick's hut. He then busied himself, building what looked to be a small campfire.

"Not another bug fire tonight," Rick teased. "There's a nice breeze. I don't think we need to burn any more cow chips."

"No," Paz giggled, remembering Rick's aversion to the whole thing. "It's much better than that. That did work, though, yes?"

"Yeah, it worked," Rick agreed with a grudging smile. "No self-respecting mosquito came near the place. Of course, as I remember, neither did anybody else."

"No, it did not even smell bad. You just think it did. It is the idea of it."

"That must be it," Rick agreed as he settled into the place Paz indicated. Mariana came to sit beside him. "So, what are we doing here?"

The fire, fueled by dry grass and twigs, flared hot immediately. Paz settled a large flat beat-up metal plate on top of the flames. It had almost certainly been a large lid in another life, Rick thought. Paz next emptied a small string bag of odd-looking gray-green hulled fruits over the metal plate.

"Are these what I think they are?" Rick asked, poking at one of them.

"Seeds of the *mariñon*," Paz announced proudly. "I collected them for you. Mariana likes them, too, so I told her I would roast them for you tonight."

"What do you call them in English?" Mariana asked. "I forget."

"Cashews. In my country, they call them nuts," he explained to Paz.

"But they are not nuts at all. They are fruit seeds and hard to get since there is only one for each fruit."

Growing at the bottom of the soft and pithy *mariñon* fruit, Rick had encountered cashews in their natural state here before. The local children used them like an ice cream treat handle, to hold unto the fruit while they ate the soft upper part. The seed in its heavy husk was useless until it was roasted. Rick had attempted to crack one open with his teeth, shortly after his arrival, but had been seriously scolded by Paz for doing so.

"The oil inside will burn you," he warned. "Only after it is cooked is it safe." Presented with something even Paz would not eat, Rick was certain he wanted no part of it.

Mariana leaned closer to Rick in the balmy twilight, her face enchantingly lit by the flickering firelight. He discreetly slipped his arm around her waist while keeping a close eye on Paz. He, however, was totally absorbed in the task before him, using a stick to stir the frying husks. As they split from the heat, their caustic oil leached onto the hot metal.

"Are you ready?"

Rick wondered what came next as Paz reached under the homemade griddle and pulled out a burning twig, which he dropped onto the sizzling seeds.

"Cashews flambé!" Rick exclaimed as the contents of the grill went up in a sudden whoosh of flame and smoke.

"Perfect!" Paz squealed with delight, stirring down the flames with a large stick. He kept the burning mixture moving, being careful not to stir out the flames entirely. After a few more minutes, he slid his stick under the edge of the makeshift griddle and flipped the entire thing upside down. Fifty tiny fires, each individual seed, lay sputtering in the sand as Paz moved swiftly to put them out, then flip them back onto the griddle.

"Now we wait a few minutes until they are cool, and then we eat," Paz chortled. Paz jumped as he looked over at Rick and Mariana, and Rick was afraid he suspected the truth.

"Sorry. I didn't mean to interrupt." David's voice drawled from out of the shadows.

"Hey, you're just in time for some freshly roasted cashews." Rick jumped up to welcome him into their circle, but David hung back.

"No, I just came by to say, so-long and to talk to you for a minute," David began as he moved back from the fire and the light. Rick excused himself and followed a few steps away from the other two.

"To be honest, I don't know what I came to say," he stammered, following Rick's gaze as it rested on the pair still by the fire. "I started over here to tell you not to be a damn fool, that you can't stay, not without me. But I have been standing here a minute or so, watching. You've gone and found your own little family, haven't you?" David did not wait for Rick to respond. "And the truth is, it looks good on you, Cuz. It really does." Rick thought he heard a trace of envy in his voice.

"I ain't never heard you sound so sure of yourself as you did this afternoon. I'm still not certain about leaving you here. I figure I'll have to sneak into Texas

and stay as far away from your old man as possible."
He gave a little laugh. "But, if I was you, right now—"
He glanced back at the beach one more time, as
Mariana strolled over toward them. "I'm not sure I'd
be doing any different." He finished quickly as she
came to stand close to Rick.

David stuck out his hand. Rick shook it heartily
and then reached out, and the two men embraced.
Rick took a step back, pulling Mariana close to his
side as he did so.

"Promise me one thing," David said as he turned to
go. "Don't stay here too long. Overall, I think things
are still pretty safe for foreigners at the moment, but
who really knows how long that will last? If things
start to get too hot, you get the hell out, you hear?
You promise, too." He looked directly at Mariana.
"You know how it works here better than either of
us. You send him packing if—"

She did not let him finish. "I will. I promise." Her
tone was deadly serious.

"Hey, Paz, *adiós, amigo*," David called out with an
exaggerated wave.

Paz scampered over to say a proper goodbye. "Take
care, don David. *Que le vaya bien*."

"You take care of you, buddy," David called over
his shoulder. "And your big blond friend there, too."

They returned to their cashews, cracking and peeling
them in silence at first. They collected the meats in a
moro shell and discarded the charred husks.

"It takes a long time to get anywhere with these
things," Rick said after several minutes.

"So, don David is leaving, and you are not going with him?" Paz could contain himself no longer. "I am very glad you are not going, but I do not understand. He is your family. How can he leave without you?"

"You have to remember he came without me." Rick attempted an explanation after exchanging glances with Mariana. "He came here with a specific job to do. Now his bosses in the capital say that job is finished, and they are sending him home. I don't think he's ready to leave either, but he has no choice. I do."

"And you choose to stay?"

"Yeah. Does that surprise you so much?"

"In one way, yes. In another way, no." Paz squealed and dropped the cashew in his hand, having inadvertently broken open a still smoldering one. He stuck his burned fingers in his mouth briefly and then examined them by the firelight before continuing. "I think there is more to all of this than you are telling me."

A furtive look in Mariana's direction was no help as she bent over the hot seed in her hand. Rick had the distinct impression she was struggling to cover a sudden case of the giggles.

"What makes you think that?" Rick stalled for time.

Paz shrugged. "Just a feeling, I think." He reached for one of the last cashews and looked Rick straight in the eye. "Is it true?"

Rick looked down, unable to answer.

"Did Imanuel tell you where we were this past week?" Mariana interrupted in a soft voice.

"No, you did. You said you were going to San Salvador when you left. That reminds me, you told me earlier today, you would tell me all about your trip later. Well, now it is later."

"Yes, it is," Mariana sat up straight and laid her hands to rest in her lap. "We did not go to the city. We were with Franco."

"You went with my cousin, and you did not tell me?" Paz was incensed. "How could you—"

"Lower your voice this instant, or I swear I will not tell you another word." Mariana could do a fair imitation of Imanuel's 'general' voice, Rick mused as he sat, watching and listening to the two of them.

"I am sorry." Paz was instantly contrite. "I want to hear the rest. It is just that you know how much I want to go."

"I know. I know." She patted him on the arm. "But it is not a game, you know, and not a very good place for younger people."

"But I have heard that there are some there as young as me. Is that not true?"

"It is true," she sighed. "There are a few, but Paz, their life is not easy. They are not there so much because they want to be but more because they have no place else to go. They are the ones like Fabiano or others whose families have been threatened or murdered and—"

"And it has not nearly happened to us? *Mi papí?*"

"I know. It is true. We have been luckier than most. Look. I do not want to argue. Do you want to hear about this or not?"

"I want to hear it. All of it. I will be still. I promise."

She relayed all that she could remember, all that was safe for him to know, about the camp, the people there and how they spent their days.

"And many of the evenings, they sit around a fire, just like this. Except they do not have anyone nice enough to collect *semillas de mariñones* for them. Look, they are nearly all done now."

Rick stood up, turning toward his cabin as he did so. "Who's there?" He cried out to the darkness, at the unexpected movement of a nearby shadow. "David. Is that you?"

"What is it? Who is there?" Mariana jumped to his side.

"I don't know." He answered as he peered into the nearby wild growth. "I thought maybe David came back for something, but I do not think so. Whoever it was, moved away quickly when I called out."

He went inside and brought out a small bag of sea salt, the most common salt available in the country.

"You bought this at our store, yes? What is it for now?" Paz asked. "Intruders?"

"No," Rick laughed out loud, breaking the tension. "It's just salt. For the cashews."

Paz gave them both a puzzled look, and Mariana was amused.

"They put salt on them in some places," Mariana explained.

Paz wrinkled up his nose. "Really?"

"Sure. Don't you?" Rick replied.

"No, never." Paz smiled as he nibbled on the burnt brown bits in his hand.

"What do you think?"

"I do not know." Mariana's brown eyes caught his in a serious exchange that had nothing to do with toasted nuts. "Maybe a dog, a drunk? I do think we best talk about something else, just in case."

"That is what you need, don Ricardo." Paz seemed to take no notice of the more serious undercurrent. "A dog, a good dog."

"What does Rishard need with an *aguacatero*?"

"A what?" Rick looked up, puzzled.

"An *aguacatero*, a mutt dog, I think you call them," Mariana explained, but the question on her face remained focused on Paz.

"He needs a dog here to watch out for him, to guard his house," Paz explained in earnest.

"You want a dog, Paz. I have heard this conversation before, and Imanuel will not permit it. That is why you want Rick to have a dog so that you can have a dog," Mariana said.

"A dog would be a good thing for protection. To sound an alarm."

"Rishard is not home enough to take care of himself. How could he take care of a dog?"

"So this is an avocado-eating dog? A green dog?" Rick was still focused on the strange name.

"*A la gran puchica!*" Mariana lost patience with both of them. "You two are crazy. It is not a green dog.

It is a poor dog, a dog so skinny and hungry, it will eat almost anything. I do not know where the name comes from, really. I always think of them as ditch dogs—they are born in the ditch, live in the ditch, and die in the ditch."

"Third world dogs. Got it." Rick nodded. "It is not like there is a shortage of them here."

"See? He thinks it is a good idea, too," Paz chimed in.

"Is that what I said?" Rick's eyebrows shot up.

"He just wants a dog. Most boys do, yes?" Mariana smiled wearily. "Imanuel says we do not need a dog since we live in town. He says in town, the dogs are barking all the time at every little noise the neighbors make, and it is true. Also, he does not need something else to look after. I think he feels Pazito would not always remember to feed it and clean up the mess, yes?"

Rick nodded.

"But you live outside the village, so you need a dog, yes?" Paz tried once more.

Rick laughed at the boy's indomitable spirit. "Well, let me think about it."

A comfortable silence fell over the three of them momentarily as they watched the fire melt down to glowing coals.

"Padre Dionisio and Madre Elenita came to visit us while you were gone," Paz spoke up after another minute or two. "They came because they heard about how badly *mi papá* had been hurt and to help him make plans for the church."

"Who are they?" Rick asked.

"They are Americans who work with the church in *Chirilagua*. They are such good people," Mariana answered. "They are from—Pazito, do you remember?"

"Ohio," Paz pronounced it slowly. "Cleveland."

"That is right. They have lived in this area for years. They have a large mission and do different types of educational work in all the little towns. They have helped Imanuel many times over the years."

"I'm sorry I didn't get to meet them," Rick said.

"We told them you were in San Salvador," Paz laughed. "But they will be back. They love to come here and visit, for the church and also because Padre Dionisio loves the seafood, especially lobsters."

"Well, I hope they come back soon."

"Hey, these are good."

"But of course. I am a master at roasting these seeds."

Mariana laughed. "I hate to admit it, but it is true. Ever since he was little, Paz could make the best ones. I really think he is a firebug at heart and just likes the excuse of playing in the fire."

"Not me," Paz countered. "My cousin—he is the worst firebug of all. *Mi papá* and *mi tío* could never get him to stop playing with the fire."

"I forgot about that. I can remember Miguel beating him half to death as a kid because he set a trash pile on fire so close to their house, it caught the thatch on the roof. I do not know who was fastest. Miguel carrying water or Franco once Miguel started after him." She laughed in delight at the memory. "He did not mess with fires for a while after that. He is the one who taught you how to toast these, yes?"

"Yes, but mine are never as even as his. I always burn a few and have a few that are not quite done. His were always browned just right."

"Hey, I think these are good just the way they are," Rick added. "You wouldn't believe what these cost you in my country."

"They are expensive there, yes?" Mariana remembered.

"Of course, I never knew where they came from and what you had to do to make them this good. I didn't understand why they were so much more than peanuts, for instance. Now I understand a little better."

Rick looked back at the fire and changed the subject, after downing another handful of the roasted treats. "There is something I've been wanting to ask you. Up there on the mountain, someone asked you about a couple of characters, story figures, I think, *El Cipitio* and...what was the other name?"

"You were telling stories?" The elation in Paz's voice was unabashed. "You have not told stories for such a long time. And did you tell them about the *Siguanaba* and the *Cipitio*?"

"No, I did not. There was no time."

"Who are these people, anyway?" Rick asked again.

"They are not people," Mariana laughed. "They are spirits, a little like your fairy tales, except many people here, believe they are real."

"And everyone here knows who they are?"

"And does everyone in your country know who Cinderella is and the Sleeping Beauty and who else? Maybe Howdee Doodee?"

He answered, laughing. "Well, I think you have that last one a little mixed up, but yeah, I guess they do."

"See?" She turned her face toward his. "It is the same thing."

"So, what's so special about these two?"

Mariana settled back. "The *Siguanaba*," she began her explanation, "was originally a beautiful woman, a princess. She was the daughter of the Indian god, Tlaloc, the god of the water and the wind. Because she was the daughter of a god, she was supposed to be a chaste and virtuous young woman and marry only another of her station. But she disobeyed her father and took a mortal man as her lover instead. When her father found out, he was furious. He cast a cruel punishment on her, one that condemns her to spend the rest of her days living always near the banks of the rivers and streams, or even around deep wells. Any place where men go for water.

"When they first see and hear her call out to them, she is her original lovely self, the beautiful princess the whole world loves. But when they approach her, she becomes a horrible witch, shrieking and cackling and beating her breasts on the rocks. She nearly always attacks them with her long fingernails, leaving the poor man scratched and beaten, when the whole time he thought he was approaching a beautiful maiden."

She cast a glance at Rick before continuing. "They say she always goes after men who walk alone at night and that a *cuma* or machete is useless against her. Some men believe that if they smoke a cigar as they walk, that will ward off her advances because she does not like the smell of cigars."

"And people believe this?" Rick was more than a little skeptical.

"Some, yes, some, no." Mariana gave him a level gaze. "It makes a better story when a man arrives home with scratches on his face than to tell his woman he has been with a *puta*, yes? Or even admit he was drunk, fell down in the dark, or got lost. A visit from the *Siguanaba* sounds much more exciting." Her laughter in the darkness drove all the evil spirits away from Rick's heart.

"There is even an opera written about her. Some call her *Sihuelut* or the *Sihuehet*. It is all the same. Her punishment is supposed to be a lesson to all—what happens if you do not do as you should."

"And the other one?"

"The *Cipitin* or the *Cipitio*. He is her son, a ten-year-old boy who is half-god and half-human. That means he lives forever but always as a child. He sleeps in flower beds, especially among the lilies. They are his favorite, and he too can be found along the waters of the countryside, like the rivers and the streams. Like all little boys his age, he is mischievous and always causing trouble. The worst thing is that he steals the spirits of children who fall asleep near the river. The belief is that women who go to the river to wash clothes should not let their babies sleep there or they should wake them up often while they are beside the river, to make sure the *Cipitio* does not get their souls."

She smiled. "You can tell if the *Cipitio* is around if the ashes disappear from the cooking area at night."

"What?"

"The *Cipitío* eats ashes, so if the ashes are gone from your cookfire table in the morning, you must be extra careful that day because it means the *Cipitio* has been nearby."

Rick laughed out loud at this last. "I've never heard of characters like this before," he admitted. "I remember Andres Parada saying he wouldn't drink Niña Ana's tea because it was made with charcoal and he wasn't the *Cipitio*. At the time, I had no idea what he was talking about, but now I understand."

"They are part of the local mythology," Mariana finished. "I guess you could say part of who we are."

The cashews were gone, the fire burned down to gray hooded embers, but at least two were not ready for the evening to end, as they leaned against one another, seated in the soft sand.

"I think this fire is nearly gone," Paz spoke up. "I do not think it will do any damage, like one of Franco's," he finished in a hoarse whisper. "I am going down to check on my aunt. She was not feeling so good today. Remember?" His eyes traveled to Mariana's face, still aglow despite the waning coals. "I can wait for you there."

As fast as he finished speaking, he was up and gone.

"Paz, everything all right?"

"Fine, don Ricardo. *Hasta mañana. Buenas noches.*" He called back from the darkened beach.

"Is he okay?" Rick asked Mariana a few moments later.

"Oh, he is fine, I think," she answered dreamily, her head resting on Rick's shoulder. "He is a very perceptive young man, you know?"

"Yes, I think so, too but—"

"But he will never say a word to anyone. Believe me."

They sat quietly, curled up together, each lost in their own private thoughts as they listened to the gentle waves on the beach.

"I think Paz is right about one thing," Mariana spoke again. "There is more to it, the reason why you came here, and the reason why you stay. I told him where we went, and that satisfied him, but it does not explain it to me."

"And what is it you want to know?" Rick's voice was low, barely audible.

"Why you came, why you stay, only that. Paz said it was something about a fight with your father and working with him, but..."

"But what?" His answer was sharper than he intended.

"There is something more, yes?"

He sighed deeply and pulled her closer. He savored the echo of his own heartbeat against her momentarily before attempting an explanation.

"All that I told Paz was true. About working in my father's bank this summer but I did not tell him about a friend there, an older man. His name was Stanley, and we shared an office. We visited sometimes while we worked, and I came to understand that he didn't like the work we were doing any better than I did. He loved the outdoors and fishing, but he was set to retire in another couple of years. Then he would have all the time he wanted to fish and be outside. He had this plan to buy himself a little fishing cabin somewhere off in the woods beside this lake he knew. He was always talking about how he was going to be there once he got the chance." He stopped talking.

"And what happened?" She prompted.

"Stanley had a heart attack and died a week before my summer ended there. He died on the floor of that office, his face on that gray carpet."

"How awful," Mariana breathed the words. "Were you there when it happened?"

"No. I was out to lunch. I even tried to get him to go with me that day, but he said he had too much work to do. He was not terribly good at what he did, and he was always behind. I think that put extra pressure on him as well. When I got there, people were trying to revive him, but it didn't work. The paramedics came and took him away, but they never could get his heart going again."

"That must have been so sad for you. Is that what made you leave?"

"I already knew. I knew it was over, that I could never do that kind of work for the rest of my days and that if I did, I'd end up just like Stanley. Dreaming of one life while living another that I hated. I knew before he died, but he was definitely the last straw, the last little push that made me do something about it. I went back to school, still in shock, I think, but once there, I knew I had to find a way out."

"And that brought you here?"

"Pretty much. It must sound ridiculous, like some rich kid, whining about his troubles, compared to what most people struggle with here. It's not the same, and it's not like I've ever been poor or gone hungry, but it's still important to me to do something, to be something I can be proud of. I can't explain it any better than that."

"You do not have to. This is not Franco you are explaining these things to. I did not say it was not important, did I?"

"No, you did not." He gave her a little hug. "Thank you for that."

"And the reason that you stay now?"

"Hey, I have a limit. One difficult question per night."

She laughed. "That is fair."

Far beyond the mountain islands out to sea, a golden sliver of moon began to emerge over the highest peak.

"How many nights I've sat right here and watched that moon rise, all alone," his thoughts seemed to slip from him, unbidden, his arms wrapped securely around her.

"How many nights I have sat and watched that moon set, in the early hours of the morning, all alone." She echoed his thoughts, if not his exact words.

"You stay up all night to watch it?"

"No." Her voice was quiet and serious. "There have been, I think, more nights in my life that I did not sleep well than nights when I did. Sometimes when I cannot sleep, I watch the moon. It is as if we are up together, the only two, while all the rest of the world sleeps. At least, I can say I am not afraid of the night like many people are."

"Not like the ones who worry about the *Siguanaba*?"

A tiny laugh escaped her. "No. I do not worry about spirits like that."

"Then what? I know so little about your life, and yet, it seems, from what I do know, it has not been a very happy one."

"Hmm." She nestled deeper into his arms. "Maybe, finally, it is changing, at least for a little while."

"Do you want to go inside?"

"No. I cannot. You heard Pazito. He will wait for me at Emelina's just down the beach." She turned her face toward the incoming waves. The rising moon cast its light full upon her face. It was all Rick could do not to steal her away into the night.

"I will not have to explain to him," she added with a sigh, "but Emelina, if she is up waiting with him, that could be a much different story."

"Tell me. I'm confused. Paz went toward the village to Emelina's house. I thought she lived with

Candelario. Doesn't he have a house at the back of Carlos' estate, further up the beach, in the opposite direction?"

"Yes, both are true. They have two houses, little ones, just one room each, like yours. Emelina was for many years, by herself, not married. Now she is with Candelario, but they move back and forth, stay here, stay there. She had her house first, and he must stay at the one at Carlos', much of the time as the *cuidandero*, the one who watches over the big house. She says she does not want to give up her house on the beach, so that is the way it is."

"Are they married?"

"No, not really, no more than anybody else here. Most of the people here are not married, not in the way that you think of, by the government or the church. Imanuel and Guadalupe, yes, but they were one of the few couples here in the country who were ever married in the church. I think Imanuel must have saved his money for a very long time to be able to marry her. It was very important to both of them."

"I'm not following you."

She twisted around, still in his arms, but now she could see his face. "The government has a law here that says before you can be married by a priest, you must have a civil marriage. They do it that way in England and much of Europe, too, I think. The reason here is to make one more way to take power away from the church. They also put a big tax on it. It costs maybe $200 in taxes now, to get married by

the government judge and then put the ads in the
paper before you can be married by the priest."

"What ads?"

"You have to publish for so many weeks before, for
instance that Fulano de Tal is going to marry Maria
Perez, three weeks from this date. Then, if anybody
has a reason why they should not get married, they
have a chance to say so before the wedding."

"What kind of reason? I don't understand."

"The main one is that Fulano is already married
and has run off and left his wife and children in
another town, or maybe that Maria has a child
somewhere, that she has kept as a secret."

"Sounds pretty complicated to me. In the US, if
two people want to get married, they get married.
Sometimes, they might have to wait a day or two for
licenses or the like, but basically, they don't have to
ask anybody else's permission if they are both old
enough. They put it in the ceremony sometimes—
does anybody have any reason to object—but
you can tell the priest, pastor, or judge to leave
that part out if you want, and a lot of people do
just that."

"Hmm. Well, here once they have satisfied the
government, then they can get married in the church,
and that is usually the only thing anyone wants
anyway. To be married by the priest. But most poor
people cannot afford the first wedding, so they do
not get married. They just live together. If you ask,
the man, he will often still say he is single because
legally, he is, even if he has lived with the same

woman for twenty or thirty years. Still, they are like the doves."

"What do you mean?"

"Like the doves. They mate for life, staying with the same partner until one dies."

A momentary silence followed as he contemplated this last. "And what if they find a priest who will marry them without the civil marriage first?"

"Oh, that is dangerous for the priest. I have heard stories of priests who were put in jail and foreign priests who were thrown out of the country for simply marrying a couple without the civil ceremony first. Like I said, the reason is to take power away from the church.

"The government here always seems to think if they can take just enough power away from the church, then somehow that will make the people more loyal to them. They have never understood what the church really is to the people, the church holds the people's hearts. The government, with all their history, all their power, can never do that here."

They sat quietly for a time before he finally asked the question that was holding his heart hostage. "So tell me, you and Carlos, are you married by the government and the church?"

"Did I tell you he called earlier today?"

Rick stiffened, forgetting his question for the moment. "When is he coming?"

"Oh, he is not, at least, not for quite a while. He called to ask about Imanuel and to apologize. The time was good, no? If he had called yesterday, that would have left all of them wondering where we were. Of course, when we went off with my cousin, I did not really know we would be there for so many days. Anyway, Carlos said he was sorry, but he was going to have to leave for Europe sooner than he thought. He called to make certain everything was still calm here and that Imanuel was doing well. When I told him, he said he was not coming until after he returns from Europe."

"And you? What about you? You said before you didn't plan to go with him. You don't mind that he'll be gone so long?"

"Carlos is a very good man. You must understand that. I would never do anything to purposely hurt him, but I have to live, too, even if it is just for a little while. That is all I am doing. He will not ask me anything, and I will not tell him anything. That is all. I must go." She stood up and began to brush the sand from her skirt.

Bathed in the pale moonlight, her thick black hair sparkled as it fell across her shoulders. Her long earrings, made with tiny seashells, dangled and mixed in her curls. Her skin shone like mahogany. Watching her, the raging swell within him would not allow her to simply walk away.

He took her back into his arms, scooping her up and lifting her lightly off her feet as he kissed her, his lips drinking hers in. Her sweet mouth responded eloquently, returning his affection fully, as they stood wrapped in each other beneath the palm trees on the moon swept beach.

"Rishard, oh Rishard," she repeated his name softly in his ear. "I must go home tonight."

"I know," came his whispered reply. "But that doesn't mean I have to like it."

"Another night. I will be back another night soon, to stay with you, I promise."

"Tomorrow night?"

"Hmm, not tomorrow." She threw her arms around his neck once more. "Tomorrow is *miércoles de ceniza*. How do you say, Wednesday of Ashes?"

"Ash Wednesday?"

"There will be a special *misa*, tomorrow night. Will you come?"

"That's not an easy question. Imanuel and Paz have invited me before but—"

"But you never come." She hesitated. "This time, I am inviting you."

He refused to let his eyes meet hers. "I'll walk you to Emelina's house."

"No," she answered, letting the other matter drop. "That is not a good idea. It is not far. You can practically watch me all the way from here, in this light, if you are worried about me."

Reluctantly, he released her, kissing each of her hands as he held them gently in his. "*Que te vaya bien*, Mariana," he called softly after her as she walked across the lighted sand. He kept a vigil from beneath the tallest palm until he saw her turn toward the safety of her aunt's little house.

* * * * *

The heat of the sun woke him the next day, halfway through the morning. Sun stripes filtered through the windows and walls, crisscrossing the floor with their warmth as he awoke in a sweat. The trip to the mountains had taken more out of him than he cared to admit.

There was nowhere to shower other than the well behind David's house, even though something inside warned him not to go. As he walked through the abandoned house, now stripped of his cousin's belongings, he, too, felt an emptiness inside.

In the kitchen, only the small refrigerator remained, and he was surprised to still see it connected to the power and running. He found a note inside along with one last cold bottle of beer.

'Have one on me, Cuz. I promised the fridge to Julio. His daughters are the ones who kept me from starvation these last couple of years. See that he gets it, okay? Thanks, David.'

The beer made a refreshing compliment after the bath. He spent much of the day helping Julio and his son-in-law Simón move the refrigerator. David would love this, Rick found himself thinking. The old clashing with the new, Rick mused as he and Simón attempted to hold the appliance upright once they had it loaded onto an ox cart with solid wooden wheels. Holding it steady as it jounced along the rutted dirt road was no simple task.

"Be careful. Do not let it fall," Julio implored. Rick's suggestion that they lay the thing down had been immediately rejected. Julio explained he had been warned against that as it did something to the cooling gas inside and disturbed the operation of the entire appliance. The refrigerator, Rick discovered as he listened, was more than a mere addition to their belongings. Juana, Julio's daughter, planned to open a small store, a business move that was affected in this country in a similar fashion to opening one of the small *comedores*, little diners which dotted this part of the world.

In the case of a store, David had once told him, they simply stocked a dozen different items in the living room and filled a refrigerator with a few cold drinks and then called their new business, a *tienda*, a store. A great deal more than a simple kitchen appliance was riding in that wagon, Rick thought as they struggled to move it into the front room of Julio's little three-room house.

He had not seen Mariana all day, and perhaps that, as much as anything else, drew him down the beach at sunset. He told himself more than once he had no intention of going to church. Maybe he would just listen from the safety of the beach.

The church was full to overflowing, and many others stood in the street outside, as Rick approached the gray stucco building. Despite their numbers, there was a respectful hush over the crowd, and Imanuel's voice could be heard clearly as he began with a prayer.

"Lord, protect us in our struggle against evil as we begin the season of Lent. Grant this through our Lord, Jesus Christ, your son, who lives... and the Holy Spirit..." Rick found he could not grasp all the words, but he understood nonetheless as

Imanuel further expounded upon God's presence in their daily lives.

"Those of you who listened on Sunday to Monsignor Romero, heard him speak of many things, including the fact that today is *miércoles de ceniza*, Wednesday of Ashes, the beginning of Lent, a time of preparation. You heard him speak of great hopes for our country—the poor and the young. That is what many of us are here; some of us are only one, poor and others, are both. It is by your faith that you will be saved. It is by your faith and your works that our whole country will be saved.

"Those who listened know that at this moment, he is celebrating *misa* in the capital as we do here. The ashes we have were blessed by the priests in La Union. They apologize to us for not coming, but as we all know, it is far too dangerous for them to travel at night. There are many communities like ours, with faithful believers and a church but with no priest. But we have each other, and tonight we will celebrate together, believers helping one another."

Rick drew closer, slipping past those along the outer edges of the crowd until he could peek inside. The tiny flickering flames from dozens of candles illuminated the interior in a smoky haze. Imanuel stood before the crowd, a small table to his left.

He read from the Bible and then prayed. "Lord, bless these ashes, which are to remind us all that we are dust. Pardon our sins and keep us faithful. Lead us in this special season down this long road of our lives, a journey that will bring us to hope, *la resurrección*, and a new life." The entire room began to recite, and after a few lines, Rick recognized the Lord's Prayer in Spanish.

Imanuel dipped a crooked finger in the small bowl of ashes that he cradled in the crook of his elbow and made the traditional cross on the forehead of the first person, standing in a front row. Upon receiving the ashes, Paz stepped away to his father's right side and began to play a small homemade flute. The next person stepped away to the left side, and Rick recognized Mariana. She began to sing a loving yet mournful song as Paz played and Imanuel administered the ashes. He could understand none of the words, but the look of serenity and joy that lit her face while her melodious voice rose and fell, was unmistakable.

As Imanuel approached him, ashes in hand, Rick thought he should turn away, but it was as if his feet were rooted to the spot, and he could not do so. His heart yearned only to hear more of Imanuel's prayers and her haunting song.

Imanuel reached up to make the cross on one more forehead, a tall blond one. "Remember, you are dust and to dust you will return," the catechist whispered as an unexpected radiance lit his face before he moved on to the next person.

"Peace be with you," Imanuel called out to them as he walked back to the front of the church.

"And also with you," they echoed his greeting.

"Then share that peace with your neighbor," he instructed, and suddenly, the service was over. They shook hands with one another as they greeted their neighbors in the name of Jesus Christ, each wearing the small symbol of their own mortality.

"I am glad you came." The soft voice he knew so well was at his side. "Surprised but glad."

"So am I," he replied. "On both counts."

"What?" She frowned.

"I'm glad I came, but I am also surprised. I can't say I really planned on it."

"Sometimes, God has plans that go beyond ours." She laughed easily as they walked out into the street.

"The song was beautiful. I didn't know that you sang."

"And who says that I do?"

"Probably everyone who was in that church just now. It does something to your face, you know, when you sing like that."

"What?" She clapped her hands against her cheeks as if she might be able to contain what he was speaking about.

"You had a glow about you as if you were all lit up from the inside out."

She smiled in a shy, little girl fashion at the unexpected compliment. "I should go and help Paz and Imanuel clean up." He followed her back into the church, but Imanuel shooed her out.

"You have already done your part here tonight," Rick overheard him say. "Paz can help with the little bit that needs to be done."

Together, they strolled out onto the beach behind the fishermen's cooperative. He leaned against the darkened building, and she joined him there. It was too early for the moon, and the sky was ablaze with thousands of fiery stars, so close in the still clear night air. Rick felt like he could reach out and pluck a few from the heavens.

"There's Orion." He pointed at the renowned three-in-a-row formation.

"Do you know the stars?" The enthusiasm in her voice caught him by surprise.

"Not really. Just a few constellations," he admitted and regretted not having paid more attention in classes where they had been discussed. "I can often find Orion at this time of year, and from there, there's the Seven Sisters, and over there is Taurus and Gemini, the twins and away to the north is a part of Virgo—"

"Wait," she stopped him with her laughter. "I thought you said you do not know the stars."

"I don't, really. It's just a handful of constellations that I can identify, not very much at all."

"It is still more than I know. I always wanted to learn them, but there was never a good time."

"Maybe, there will be soon," he sighed as he reached for her.

"Mariana," Paz appeared out of the shadows. "Where are you?"

"Right here." She stepped out of the shadow of the building. "What are you doing?"

"Looking for you. *Mi papá* said to find you and escort you home. I am sorry if this is not a good time," he finished lamely.

"It is all right. It is not your fault." She leaned back into the darkness for a quick good night kiss and spoke to Rick. "I will see you soon, unless, of course, you want to come home with us and play cards or something."

"Not tonight. I'm afraid it would be too clear how I feel about you. Another time, soon."

"*Pasa buenas noches*." She walked away with Paz.

"*Buenas noches*," he told them both as he went back to stargazing.

CHAPTER 14

*M*arch 17, 1980. San Salvador. As a part of his Sunday homily yesterday, Archbishop Oscar A. Romero read from a letter written to him by US Secretary of State Cyrus Vance, in reply to the letter the archbishop sent earlier last month. At one point, he read, "The United States will not interfere in the internal affairs of El Salvador." Monsignor Romero told those attending the Mass, "We hope that the events will speak better than the words."

Much hope and attention will be focused in coming weeks on the new US Ambassador to El Salvador, Robert White, whose recent arrival is being interpreted as a sign that the US is finally getting serious about the human rights situation in this country, which continues to take civilian lives on a daily basis.

The dead and tortured bodies of labor leaders, opposition politicians, lay and clerical leaders in the churches, as well as those of rural peasants are regularly discovered on the streets and rural roads throughout the country. Amongst those killed in past weeks was El Salvador's attorney general Mario Zamoro and his wife, who were murdered in their home. Zamoro's brother, Rubén, long active in this country's political opposition, has reportedly gone into exile.

"I cannot believe *Semana Santa* will be here in just two more weeks." Paz leaned against the bow of the *cayuco*, facing Rick after they had finished dropping the net, early on a glorious sun-drenched morning. "It is the best time of the whole year." The canoe rocked gently with the undulations of the passing waves.

Rick did not answer right away as he sat, staring absent-mindedly at the far island's shore.

Paz sat up. "You will be here, yes?"

"Yeah." The answer came slowly. "Yeah, I'll stay here through *Semana Santa*, but I don't know how much longer after that. One of these days..." His voice trailed off. "One of these days, I'll have to go back." There, he had said it aloud for the second time, and still, the words sounded hollow.

It was a week after David's departure, and she had managed to slip away and spend a night at his cabin as she had promised, but it was difficult for her. Concern for her safety, her family's opinion, and placing her in a compromising position took much of the joy away from the evening.

"I have a better idea," she told him that night. "Tomorrow, when you come back from fishing with Paz, fill both the gas tanks, and I will meet you at the station after Paz has taken the fish to the cooperative. I know a place where we can spend the whole day, and no one will bother us."

Her light steps echoed on the wooden walkway built out over the floating dock where the boats tied up underneath the gas pumps, as Rick finished pumping the last tank full. She carried a square wicker basket in one hand, its contents covered with a dishtowel tucked neatly around the edges, and a large container of fresh water in the other, like the ones the workers carried to the fields. Two soldiers leaned on the bridge rails as they lazily watched the comings and goings of the estuary traffic that morning.

"*Buenos días*, Niña Mariana," Juan, the station keeper greeted her, as he pulled the gas hose back up to the bridge level from where Rick had released it. "You have a heavy load today."

Her tone was cool, but her smile friendly as she returned his greeting. "Don Ricardo has been kind enough to offer me a ride. This food goes to some friends on the other side of the *estero*, around the point." She waved a hand in the general direction they were heading.

"And what are your friends' names over there?" One of the soldiers spoke up as he strolled over for a closer inspection of the boat. A cold chill passed over Rick as he recognized Sgt. Fidel Fuentes. He wondered about Alfredo and if he was still in the mountains.

Mariana's friendly manner with the station keeper shifted as she contemplated the interfering soldier. "I only know their first names."

"I thought you said they were friends of yours."

"They are friends through the church. That makes them friends of mine. Their names are..." she hesitated as she caught Rick's fleeting glimpse of concern. "Their names are Pablo and Marta Gloria. They have two children as well."

"I see. And you, *gringo*? I suppose you have your papers in order?" He turned his attention to Rick.

"Papers? Out here?"

"This is don Ricardo," Juan intervened. "He lives here. Everyone knows him." He hesitated and then added. "No one who goes to sea carries important papers with them, like *cédulas* or passports. They could be too easily lost. He lives right over there on the beach." Juan pointed toward Rick's hut. "I am sure he would have his passport ready for you to see anytime."

"Yes," Rick nodded, slowly, watching the station keeper closely for any needed cues. "Any other time."

"Very well." The soldier suddenly lost interest. "Another time. I will stop by to see you one day." He touched his hat in Mariana's direction and walked away briskly. He snapped his fingers, and the other soldier fell quickly in step beside him. They headed toward the road on the other side of the station, where fuel was also sold to drivers on land.

Rick let his expression, rather than words, express his gratitude to Juan as they pushed off and headed downriver to the ocean.

Rick motioned her back toward the center of the boat once they were near the point. "What was that all about?" he dared to ask in English. The water often carried conversations farther than the speaker intended, and he was grateful for the engine noise that helped to cover their voices.

"I am not sure," Mariana frowned. "I only told the lie about friends on the other side because I wanted to give Juan and the other gossips a little less to chew on. I did not think one of Hector's men would want to start a full investigation. *Por el amor de los cielos!* A little power, and they just go crazy. What does he care about the names of our friends? I thought you were going to have to go find your passport for him!"

"I was more worried he was going to ask you more about your friends, Pablo and Marta Gloria. Was that a wise choice?"

She sighed with a little giggle. "Probably not, but I really did not do it on purpose. The only other names I could think of were Marielos and her family, and I certainly didn't want to mention them right now. He is an idiot. He was in the store the other day. The problem would have been if he had asked to look in the basket." She flipped back the towel to reveal a complete picnic lunch of fried chicken, white cheese, tortillas, *quesadilla*, and two bottles of beer. She leaned back against his knees.

"I do have one question." He mentioned as they rounded the point. "Where are we going?"

Mariana pointed straight out to sea, and he directed the boat accordingly. At nearly high tide, it was easy to guide the small craft over the sand bars since most were inundated, and the shallow keeled *cayuco* glided through mere inches of water without a problem. The light, smooth seas were ideal for speed this morning, and they flew across the water's surface. He loved the feel of the feathery spray in his face and the illusive ecstasy of the freedom that surrounded him this morning. More to the point, he loved the woman who sat perched before him, more than any other he had ever known, more than any he would ever know, he was quite certain. Less than an hour later, they faced the island and its strong pounding surf as it plunged against the sandy beach. It was the farthest out to sea Rick had ever ventured from the Salvadoran coast, and the beach before them looked hazardous.

"Do not worry so," Mariana told him, as she glanced up at his tense frown. "There is a better place to land, over there by the *muro*."

At the far end of the beach, a high rock dike thrust out into the incoming waves, providing a breaking point and a safe harbor for small craft like theirs. Rick guided the *cayuco* alongside and discovered two heavy iron rings and a thick sisal rope, waiting there for any who cared to make use of them.

"Whose place is this?" Rick asked warily as he tied the bow securely to one of the rings. "Are we going to be in trouble for trespassing?" He jumped out onto the rock wall.

"No, not today." Mariana took his hand and stepped gingerly out of the *cayuco*. "Today is a day of no worries." She reached for the things she had brought along, but Rick quickly scooped them up. "There is a house further inland from here. It belongs to a friend. The wife of the *cuidandero*, the caretaker, the man who works like Candelario does for Carlos, is a relative of Marielos. It will not be a problem, wait and see."

She had barely finished speaking when two small children came running toward them. Halfway there, they stopped, turned around, and ran back. "The welcoming committee," Mariana laughed as they walked to the end of the dike and made their way down to the sand.

"Niña Mariana, is that you? It has been such a long time." Rick could hear the friendly voice but saw no one.

"Sí, Niña Sofía. It has been a long time. I was not certain you would remember me."

"I could never forget." A small woman, dressed like many of the country women in the area, in a faded cotton dress and white apron, slipped from behind a tree. She reached for Mariana and gave her half an embrace in welcome.

"You look thin," she chastised gently. "And pale. Do you not eat? Come in, come in." She ushered them along a sand path that led from the beach inland. "Tell me about my niece Marielos and my good-for-nothing nephew, Fabiano. What do you hear from them? And Ana? How is she?"

The woman living alone on this side of the island with her fisherman husband and their two small children was starved for information and company. Mariana introduced Rick as the woman dragged three chairs out of her tiny thatch hut and bid them sit down. Mariana told her friend's aunt a few of the details of their recent trip up the mountain.

"So that is where they all are now? God bless them and keep them." She crossed herself. "Rodrigo, my oldest son, we could not keep him on the island, no matter what we tried. His father told him to just fish with him, and he would be safe, but he would not listen. He spent too much time in La Union, especially in the bars there. One day the soldiers who recruit people into the army came and they took him. He was not one of the lucky ones, though." Her hands drew her apron corner up to her face to wipe her wet eyes.

"His friends brought him out here to us one night, and we buried him up there." She pointed to the hillside above the house. "We do not know who shot him, the soldiers? A *guerrillero*? Who knows? His father still wants to know, but I say, what difference does it make? The only comfort we have is that we did get him back. He is not one of the dreadful ones we hear about so often now, another body left along the roadside. When will it all end, Niña Mariana? Where will it all end? Will it be that every mother in El Salvador has to bury at least one child before things can get better?" Her eyes filled with more tears.

"I do not know, Nina Sofía," Mariana answered as she patted the other woman's hand. "None of us have any answers." Mariana slipped her hand into the bottom of her basket and pulled out two small bags of penny candy. "I brought these. I hope that is all right."

"But of course. You give it to them. They should know they come from you." She looked hard at Mariana. "It is hard to believe you are all grown up now, you and Marielos. I can still remember when your father first came to *Las Palomitas*. You were just a baby then, yes?" She shook her head in reminiscence.

"Well, you did not come all this way to spend your day with an old woman, listening to her sorrows and her memories. I imagine there is a fine lunch in that basket if you and Emelina had a hand in it. Does she still run the restaurant? I need to go to the mainland more often. Maybe I will go and see her one day myself."

Mariana laughed. "She would like that, I am certain. We only came to use the beach for a little while today, if that is acceptable?"

"You know that it is. And that," she pointed to the bags, "should be enough to convince those little ones to leave you in peace as well." She looked at Rick, who had not said a word. She winked at Mariana. "He is a fine-looking one, Mariana. Fine looking." She giggled when Rick blushed and dropped his gaze to his feet.

"We should go now, Niña Sofía." Mariana gave her a quick embrace. She handed out the bags of candy to the two who were peering around the corner of the little house, hiding in their shyness of the strangers.

"Even here..." Rick hesitated, wondering how to finish the thought as they walked back to the beach.

"Yes, even here," Mariana answered.

They spent the afternoon on the beach, teasing the waves, which were much stronger here than the ones on the mainland. No sheltering bay here. The island beach faced the open ocean, and the waves that attacked were fierce ones with a surprisingly strong undertow. The sand, too, was heavier, almost like small pieces of gravel that swirled in the churching waters.

Like Paz, Mariana did not swim, and chose the safety of the shallower breakers as they rolled in over the sand. Rick, however, could not resist the temptation to try a little body surfing, in the heavier curls. He tumbled onto the sand after his first couple of attempts, but with Mariana's encouragement, he tried again. This time, he caught his wave, at the perfect moment, and sailed along for a couple hundred feet before slowing. He turned and swam back out and caught another. He rode this one, even guiding his direction and coasted in to catch Mariana and take her with him, tumbling to the sand. He held her there beneath him as the water drained away from them.

"I didn't come out here to swim or to surf. This," he emphasized the word, "is much more exciting than that."

She wrapped her arms around his neck and reached up to kiss him. He rolled her over in the embrace as they lost themselves in each other. The tantalizing opportunity, their own passion for one another, caused them to forget the incoming waters, which suddenly engulfed them both. She panicked as she broke free.

"It's okay. You are all right," he told her. "I've got you," but it was too late. Something else had taken hold of her as she gasped for breath and clutched her chest, struggling to breathe.

"What is it?" Rick quickly pulled her to a half-sitting position.

She reached out, grabbing hold of his hand and squeezed it hard, as if that would somehow ease her pain. She relaxed, and the crisis passed, but Rick's determination to discover the source of the problem was not so easily assuaged.

He helped her to higher ground, close to the rock wall where they had left the picnic basket in the shade. He poured her a drink from the water jug.

"All right, young lady." He did his best to imitate her own father's tone of voice. "I'd like some straight answers. What is wrong with you?"

Her wide-eyed innocence gave nothing away. "That is a nice thing to say to a person who nearly drowns in her lover's arms. What is wrong with you? Nothing. I am like most people who swallow water when they are not expecting it. I choked."

"There's more to it than that, Mariana." He tried to maintain his gruff approach as he stretched out beside her. "You've had these kinds of attacks before. It's like you can't catch your breath, like there is some great pain in your chest. I've seen you faint twice. All the women I've known in my life, and I don't believe I've ever seen one of them pass out before. And now you—" He left the thought hanging in the air.

She sat quietly, watching him, before she looked out to sea. "When I was a little girl, I was very sick for a while. I had to stay in bed a long time, for months."

"Franco told me about that."

"He did? When?"

"When we were in the mountains. When I was off with him by myself."

"If you know, then why do you ask me?" She sounded insulted.

"Because that was when you were a child. What does it have to do with now?"

She shrugged. "Sometimes, it causes trouble with your heart, later on. It is not serious." She forced a laugh. "The only reason I had trouble over there," she pointed to the waterline, "was because I was lying flat on my back. I cannot do that. I never sleep like that. It makes a terrible pain in my chest when I do that, but it is not like I am having a heart attack or anything. You saw how quickly it passed when I sat up."

"What I saw," Rick kept his voice deliberately calm. "I saw that you couldn't even sit up by yourself. Heart trouble is always serious. I think whatever it is that's bothering you, is more than you let on."

"Do not be ridiculous." Mariana pulled the picnic basket closer and began to lay out a meal for them. "I am fine now. And just ask yourself if I am not better than I was before. You said I have fainted twice. When? One time when I thought my brother was drowned and the other, when my father—that could happen to anyone, yes?"

He had no answer for her and felt forced to let the matter drop for the time being.

"Are you hungry?"

"Yes!" He hated to admit that he was famished. "Swimming always does that to me." He frowned.

"Tell me something. Up there," he motioned toward Sofia's house. "She said something about remembering when Imanuel first came to *Las Palomitas*. I thought he always lived there."

Mariana looked surprised. "You did not know? My father and Miguel were mountain people first. They came to *Las Palomitas* years ago, but they are not from there. Miguel always loved the sea, and he left the mountains first. He learned to be a fisherman, and I guess he was the one who convinced Imanuel to join him. I have been back once to the little village up in the hills, and it is beautiful but no more than the beach. Only it is cooler there. It is funny, even there, the rich have their vacation homes, just like here. The people who live there are just like the ones here, poor *campesinos*. There, they are farmers, and here, fishermen. When my father came, then my mother and then even Emelina, my mother's sister, followed. Paz is the only one amongst us who was born to the life that he knows here on the beach."

They lingered over the food, which helped to fill the void in Rick for the moment. Even the warm beer, which Rick had learned to drink after months of being served a semi-cool beer at the best of times, tasted good.

"How is it no one ever gets the beer cold here?" he asked playfully.

"Many places only have ice to keep it cold, and if they do not have very much—" She shrugged. "Everyone knows Americans only want it if it is cold, so sometimes, they roll the bottle in cold water, if they do not have time or enough ice to make it cold. It makes it feel cool when you touch it, but it does not help what is inside, yes?" Her explanation was trimmed in laughter.

"You've done that yourself, haven't you?" He tickled her ribs. "I can tell by the way you are laughing."

She confessed. "It is true. Marielos and I used to, in her mother's seafood café. There was no refrigeration in all of *Las Palomitas*, then and her mother could not afford very much ice, so we would put the bottles in cold water."

"Marielos' mother had the café before she did?"

"Yes, she did. That was a long time ago."

"And what happened to her?"

"She left."

"Where did she go?"

"North, like so many others. She went to the United States illegally to get a better job."

"And she never came back?" Rick was shocked.

"It happens sometimes. She wrote a few times and then they never heard from her again. It was like she just disappeared. Of course, once I lived in the US for a while and could read the newspaper, I understood better. Illegals have no rights, and they often work in the worst places. Anything can happen. She may have died in any of a hundred ways, working in an illegal factory that catches fire, working as a prostitute, even just sick at home in her own bed or on the street. Who would know? Who would they tell?"

He did not say anything but simply laid there, looking at her.

"What is wrong?" His stare made her uncomfortable.

"You make death sound like it is such an ordinary part of life."

"Well, here it is. People die every day, the children of disease and malnutrition, the rest from bullets and fights of every kind, as well as from disease. Death is a part of life. Only in the United States have I seen people work so hard to make it different than that." She picked up a stick and began to draw in the sand.

"It is different there than here, that's for certain." Rick rolled back and looked at the sky, away from the blinding sunlight, before his eyes dropped to the rolling surf. Something large was turning over and over in the waves.

"What is that?" He sat up straight for a better look. He trotted down to the water's edge and tried to grab it, but getting a hold of a forty-pound sea turtle is not easy under the best of conditions.

"Take it by the hand," Mariana called out as she ran up alongside him. It washed back close, upside down, and she showed him how to grab one of the furiously beating front flippers, while the animal was still on its back.

"Like this, it will not hurt you," she told him as they dragged it to the line between the wet and dry sand. "Turn him over."

Rick did as he was told and was pleasantly surprised to discover the animal seemed more alive than dead as he had first feared.

"What's wrong with him?"

"He was probably in a net. The shrimp boats catch them sometimes, and since they pull them for long distances, the turtles drown before they can get out. Sometimes, they get free but are like this one, *mariada*." She twirled a finger in the air, in a universal sign for dizziness. Rick remembered the word as the one used for seasick as well and thought, how appropriate.

"Will he be all right?"

"Probably, after a chance to rest a little," Mariana answered. "At least he is still breathing, so if there are no cuts anywhere, he might swim away. Do you see anything?"

"I'm not sure how close I want to get," Rick admitted, remembering the big river snapping turtles of his youth. The animal before him dwarfed those fierce creatures, but not the memories of the tales people told about their ability to sever a man's finger if the beast was so inclined.

"Have you never seen a sea turtle before?" Mariana asked in surprise.

"Only in a zoo."

"They were once common here, but now too many people like to eat turtle eggs, and others hunt them. Then they are caught in the fishing nets, too. They say there are not so many left. It is very sad." She patted the head of the huge reptile, which seemed to take no heed. The turtle's large eye blinked, the only sign of life Rick could see, beyond the flapping flippers.

"We can just let him rest here for a while. If he feels better, he will make his own way back into the water. If he starts to get too hot, we can put some water on him."

They walked back to their picnic site. Rick looked down at the letters she had traced in the sand. His initials and hers, side by side.

They were quiet for a time. "One of these days, I will have to go back."

"Where?" Her mind was still on the turtle.

"The US. I can't stay here forever, much as I'd like to."

"Why not?"

"Oh, little things, like your government and mine. Entry visas, little details like that. Mine will be expiring soon. Then I'll have to go."

"Soon?" She said only the one word, but the way her nose wrinkled up, it was as if the whole idea was painful to her.

"Why don't you come with me?" He dared to utter the words that had lain heavy on his mind and heart for days now.

"It is a nice idea," she smiled faintly.

"We can make it more than that."

"No, we cannot. I cannot. Rishard, I care for you, more than I should, more than I dare to say, but please, you have never asked for a part of my future, and I have not asked for any of yours. That is not possible. Please, let's just enjoy the time we have. That is all either one of has a right to ask."

She stood up and walked back toward the water as the next wave ran up to her.

"Okay, okay, I'm sorry. Don't be angry with me. I had to ask." He ran after her, taking hold of her shoulder to turn her back to him as he took her in his arms. "I love you. There is no doubt in my mind what I feel for you. It doesn't matter if you can't go. I'll just have to find a way to stay longer, that's all."

They spent the rest of the afternoon further up the beach, in the shade under the trees, expressing their love. Enjoy the time we have now, Rick told himself as he delighted in her laughter and her touch. There were a thousand things about her he wanted to make an indelible part of his memory. The way she tilted her head when she did not understand every word he said; the light that shone in her eyes when he reached for her or caressed her face; the smoothness of her skin, and the silkiness of her luxurious thick black hair; her melodious laughter, her essence when they lay side by side, everything there was to see, hear, feel, and sense about her. The afternoon ended far too soon.

"It is time to go," she said as she rolled away from him and sat up. "Look." She pointed to the trail in the sand where something heavy had been dragged. It began where they had left the turtle and ended at the water's edge. "He must have dried out enough to go home."

Rick grinned at the little girl way she said it. "Maybe we embarrassed him," he added.

"More likely, he looked up and remembered his own girl somewhere out there. Now look at that." She pointed toward the horizon. "The pelicans are diving."

Flying low across the water's surface, the large birds cruised along, wings arched in search of their quarry. Once they spotted what they were after, they soared gracefully up into the air, to fall almost clumsily from the sky, onto the unsuspecting school of fish.

"They look so funny," Rick laughed, as another one made a headfirst dive.

"They may look silly," Mariana agreed as she reached for her sandals. "But they get what they are after. Look." The bird that had Rick laughing emerged from the water with a heavy bill full of fish. "It is a good omen."

"What is?"

"The birds, catching lots of fish and the turtle, returning to the sea. It is getting late." She pointed toward the sun, settling low in the sky. "We have a long trip yet."

They tossed their few belongings into the boat and were ready to go, but Rick took Mariana's hand before helping her step in. He dropped his arms lightly around her waist as he faced her. "I want you to know I have never spent such a beautiful day as this one." He kissed her lightly, and she returned his kiss.

"I am glad," was all she said.

* * * * *

"I am glad." Paz's words brought him back to the present. "I am glad you will be here with us. Do you celebrate *Semana Santa* in the United States?"

"Most people observe Easter one way or another," Rick answered, struggling back from his daydreams of Mariana, "but I doubt if it is much like here. I spent *Semana Santa* in San Antonio with a Salvadoran family once." He smiled at the memory.

"And how was it?"

"Oh, it was great. David and I went together. We were just little kids, but we had quite a time. We spent the days eating, playing with the other kids in this big family, and we made a huge *alfombra* down one of the streets there."

"You made an *alfombra*?" Paz was duly impressed. "I did not know. We do not have any streets to decorate with colored dust here. The people of the western side of El Salvador do that and, of course, the *guatemaltecos*," he laughed. "We have our own style here. It is the biggest party of the year. The carnival comes to town—all the rides with bright lights. There are *ramadas* all along the beach—"

"What is a *ramada*?"

"The little rooms, made from wood frames with palm walls and roofs. There are many tourists who come, and we have no hotel, and they need a place to stay. They are big enough to hang a couple of hammocks, and that is all the people need—a place to sleep, change their clothes, and of course, someone to stand guard over their things. Gilberto and I can usually make some money, as *cuidanderos*, during that week. Then there are the *músicos*. Wandering musicians who come and play guitars all week for the people and finally, the *misa* as the sun rises on Sunday. A big party with people coming from everywhere! It is wonderful! You will like it, too!"

They made a generous catch that morning, and it certainly seemed like a good start to the day. As they pulled into the fishermen's beach, however, Emelina surprised them.

"Please, don Ricardo," she began. "You are the only one who can talk to him. He will not listen to Mariana or any of us. Please. Come now."

"What's going on? You need me to do what? Emelina, we have all these fish—" He waved a hand over the contents of the *cayuco*. Miguel was close behind her.

"Go with her," the older fisherman spoke up. Rick did not care for the serious note in the usually jovial man's voice. "I can help Paz. My brother needs your help."

Rick scrambled to catch up with her fleeing figure as she hurried toward the store. Julio was inside, hoping to be waited on, Rick assumed as he glanced around the empty store. He looked haggard and wan as if we were ill. Emelina pointed toward the curtain without saying another word. Rick found Mariana on the other side, arguing with Imanuel.

"I know you mean well, but you have barely gotten your strength back. You cannot do this. You know what it will mean."

"I know what it will mean if I do not go when I am needed. That I know very well." There was more than a touch of anger in his words.

"And you think we do not need you here?" Her voice rose to a high pitch.

He reached out and patted her cheek in a loving fashion. "Of course. Just like I have always needed you. And in the same way, we will always have each other. Please do not worry so. There are always threats, but they rarely mean anything."

She took his hand in both of hers and stroked his curled fingers, now healed but forever crooked into unnatural hooks after the beating. "Do not tell me what I want to hear, old man. We both know better."

Rick cleared his throat, unsure of how long he should remain without making his presence known.

"Ricardo." Imanuel gave him his full attention. "I am glad you are here. You can drive, yes?"

"Drive? Drive what?" Rick was confused.

"A car, a truck," Imanuel replied. "Don Julio is outside, waiting for me, and I have managed to find a vehicle, but I do not drive. This is a very special mission. I cannot ask just anyone."

Mariana turned away but not before Rick saw the tears in her eyes.

"What's going on?" Rick was not able to make sense of anything he had heard so far.

"Julio's son-in-law is dead." Imanuel began to explain, although the way he kept stealing sideways glances at Mariana, it was apparent he would have preferred to do so elsewhere. "He is laying up the road a couple of kilometers from here. From what Julio says, it is pretty gruesome. He has already been up there but has no way to carry the body home. There are also signs, so he is frightened."

"Signs?"

"I can tell you on the way. Shall we go?" The older man gently pushed him toward the curtains. "You do not mind giving me a ride?"

"Tell him. Tell him the truth about all of it. You cannot involve him if you do not tell him all of it first." Mariana turned back on them. "Tell him what they say."

Imanuel sighed and looked down at his feet for a moment before speaking again. "There is a sign by the body which threatens any who attempt to bury him. They are the work of terrorists, but they mean nothing."

"Terrorists? Leftists?" Rick frowned in confusion.

"Leftists." Mariana sniffed. "Franco is a leftist by the standards of this country, but the true terrorists are the *derechistas*, the right hand, the ones who kidnap people, beat them, suffocate them, electrocute them, cut them and then finally, kill them while they terrify everyone else.

"I am going with you," she announced as she reached for a headscarf hanging near the curtain going to the store.

"No, you are not." Imanuel was emphatic.

"Why? It is safe enough for you but not for me." It was the first time Rick had heard her openly challenge him.

"Because it is not necessary. We can take care of what needs to be done."

"Fine. Then you can leave me at Julio's house. I can sit with Juana, the man's wife, while you do what it is you feel you have to do."

"Juana? It is Simón who is dead?" Rick was finally beginning to fit some of the puzzle pieces together.

"You know him? Oh, I am sorry. I forgot he lives across the road from you," Imanuel stopped. "I thought since he worked in the fields—I am sorry. I should have told you differently." He sighed. "I think I am getting too old."

"It's all right," Rick added quickly, hoping to make his friend feel better. "I knew him a little, but I am just so surprised. I guess I don't understand. Just tell me what you need me to do to help."

"Come." Imanuel protested Mariana's plans no further, only picked up a sheet that lay folded on the couch. They walked through the store in silence, and Julio fell into line behind them. Emelina made the sign of the cross as they filed out.

Imanuel led them to a small blue pickup truck with the keys in it that was parked in front of the cooperative. Rick climbed into the driver's seat as Julio scrambled into the empty truck bed. The older man and his daughter slid in beside Rick.

"Whose truck is this?" Rick asked as the engine coughed to life, and he backed it into the road.

"It belongs to a man who comes here regularly to buy fish. Miguel knows him better than I. He told Miguel he needed some time to rest and enjoy a little beer before returning to the city this afternoon. He promised not to notice if his truck was gone for a little while."

"Are we driving a stolen vehicle?"

"No, no," Imanuel assured him. "The man does not wish to become involved, so he told Miguel to use the truck and not tell him what for. That's all."

"I see." Rick pulled up in front of Julio's house, a three-room shack across the road from his own. Already black dead palm branches had been hung over the door as a sign of a household in mourning.

Mariana stepped out of the truck and put the scarf over her head as if she were walking into Mass. Julio's wife, Yolanda came out to meet her at the door, and the men continued up the road.

Julio guided them to a curve, half a kilometer past the cemetery where his son-in-law's body lay. The man was naked, a ghastly sight as what remained told the horrifying story of what had been done to him in the past hours and days. His eyes had been gouged out, and his fingers broken, not unlike Imanuel's. He had been beaten all over, and one arm was obviously broken due to the cock-eyed angle it lay above his head, but the most hideous of all was that his genitals had been hacked off and shoved in his mouth. Across his chest, a sign made from a cardboard box warned: DEATH TO ALL COMMUNISTS AND TO THOSE WHO BURY THEM.

With a tremendous effort, Rick willed himself not to be sick. Just a few days before, he and Simón had stood together on the back of an ox cart, cracking jokes. The man had a quick wit, and from the things that he said, Rick had taken him to be a devoted family man. He was most excited about the impending birth of their second child. Rick had noticed that many men here did not talk much about such things, leaving the domestic issues to their wives and mothers, but Simón was different. He had proudly told Rick that, like the Americans, he and his wife only wanted two children, no more. They wanted to raise those two well and provide the best for them, instead of starving while trying to raise half a dozen or more.

No wonder Julio looked so gray and sick in the store this morning, Rick thought. Imanuel used the sheet he had brought along as a shroud to cover the dead man. Then he knelt and prayed. Rick looked over his shoulder at the deep blue ocean behind them and sea spray flying as it hit the large rocks near the shore. He tried not to think of the dire warning scrawled on the cardboard sign but still couldn't help but worry about who might be watching or even waiting.

He had come here to dive and wander amongst the tide pools on more than one occasion. It was nearly impossible to imagine the horrific circumstances

that had led to this, the mutilated body of a neighbor
lying so close to this idyllic scene, and yet the tragic
proof was right there before him.

The three men lifted the corpse into the truck bed.
Rick took his ankles while the other two each slid
their hands under his shoulders. Julio climbed into
the back again, his hand resting on the sheet as he
sat beside his dead son-in-law.

"Julio has no sons," Imanuel told Rick, once they
were back in the cab of the truck. "He has three
daughters, all with *maridos*, husbands, and all of
them are good boys. To him, they have been the sons
he never had, and this one especially, Simón, was
his favorite."

"Does he know what happened? Did he say
anything?"

"He belonged to a farmworkers' union. Like
Andres, Sonia's husband, he worked mostly in the
fields out along the highway, but Simón joined the
union. He believed working together, they could
fight for better working conditions and better pay,
but this is what he got instead." Imanuel stared
straight ahead.

"He talked to you about it then?"

"I am the one who told him, working together,
we could make a difference." He hung his head and
covered his eyes. "How could I not come today to take
care of him when I am the one who may have sent
him to this kind of death? I am afraid to walk into
his house, even now. What do I say to his wife, and
how do I look at his son who will grow up without

a father? Am I the one who left his woman a widow and his children orphans?"

"Hey, hold on." Rick grasped his friend's shoulder but immediately had to put his hand back on the steering wheel to keep the truck on the road. "He was not a child. I talked to him a little. Simón was old enough to make up his own mind, and the tragedy here is that he was the one who knew how to use the bright mind that he had. This world needs more, not less, men like him. He made his own decisions, so it is not your fault. If he was killed because of his work in the unions, then you have to remember he died for something he believed in." Rick wondered where the words were coming from.

"I hope that is true." Imanuel lifted his head from his hand, but his eyes were still wet. "I pray to God that he did what he did because he wanted it and not because of anything I said. Who am I to send lambs out to be slaughtered before lions? Poor Simón. He did not deserve to die like this."

"Nobody deserves to die like this," Rick added.

"Did I not tell you that this was the sort of vanity I thought of myself when I was taken? Who will find me? Will it be those who care for me? Better to be buried by strangers, I told myself, and yet when Julio arrived at the store this morning, I knew I had to come. How is it that a man can believe two ways at once?"

"I don't have an answer for that one." Rick shook his head as he pulled to a stop in front of Julio's house.

Inside, they found Juana and her mother Yolanda and the other two daughters, as well as another son-in-law and Mariana. The bracing aroma of fresh cut pine filled the air, and a virgin wood coffin sat empty in the middle of the main room, resting on two chairs. The carpenter who had just delivered it was leaving. He greeted all three men and then expressed his condolences to Julio. He stopped to speak to Imanuel.

"Is it as bad as they say?" the man asked.

Imanuel nodded without speaking.

"Making these boxes is part of my business, but nobody wants work when it comes like this." He wagged his head from side to side as he went out.

Julio and his younger son-in-law brought Simón inside. They placed him, shroud and all in the freshly hewn casket. A heated discussion erupted as Juana started to draw back the sheet for one last look at her husband. Rick's head began to spin, and he headed outside. He was not unhappy to discover Mariana at his side, as anguished voices flared behind them.

"Come on," he said. "Imanuel would like for me to return the man's truck as quick as I can. Would you like a ride back to town?"

"I was planning on staying with Juana a little longer. They are making plans for tonight."

"What is tonight?"

"The vigil, when everyone comes. Sort of like the visitation they have in your country, but this is, of course, at home. Tomorrow they bury him."

"She has her family with her right now, doesn't she? Believe me, you don't want to be in there if she does manage to get a look at him. It's like something out of a nightmare—"

The wretched scream that cut him off explained more than any words of his could.

"There's nothing you can do for her right now." Rick eased her toward the truck. "Give her a little time. We can come back tonight."

She did not resist.

He parked the truck where he had found it, and just as Imanuel said, no one seemed to notice. Paz's name was listed on the chalkboard on the outside wall of the cooperative, along with the amount of fish he had sold that day. Rick was relieved to know he and Miguel had already turned in the catch.

He walked with Mariana, past Marielos' empty café, toward the restaurant and store. They could see Emelina in the kitchen and Paz, bent over his schoolbooks, spread out over the store countertop, as they passed by both doorways.

"Where are you going?" What are you planning?" Mariana was uncharacteristically curious.

"I don't really know," he replied. "I just know I can't go back to business as usual right now. I'd like to go for a nice long walk and try to think things through, but I don't want to go back to the beach with the big rocks right now. That's practically where we found Simón's body. Maybe I'll just take the boat and go."

"Go where?"

"I don't know. Up the *estero*, maybe. The tide is nice and full, and it is a beautiful quiet place."

"That is crazy."

"Is it?"

"It is a dangerous place. I told you that before."

"I'm beginning to think every place here is dangerous, one way or another. It seems to depend on when you are there and who you are with." He flexed his shoulders. "I just need a little quiet at the moment. Going home, across the road from Julio's house, doesn't sound so good right now."

His meanderings brought him to the *cayuco*, tied to a heavy barrel, outside Miguel's house, still afloat as the high tide waters lapped at the edge of the dry sand.

"Tell Miguel, I took the boat for a little while, will you?" He untied the halyard.

"No." Her answer was a surprise as she came to stand near him. "If I go and tell him about the boat, there will be too many questions to answer. I will go with you if you do not mind."

"But—"

"Watch." She reached down and tied a funny-looking cross between a square knot and a bowknot, leaving only one loop, sticking straight up. "Now Miguel will know who took his boat and there will be no problem. That was our signal to one another for years. Chances are he will never even notice we are gone."

Rick guided the boat slowly in the same direction he and Paz had gone that afternoon weeks before.

"I didn't invite you along," Rick broke the silence between them after several minutes. "I didn't think you would want to come."

She rose up from her position in the middle of the boat, once they had pulled away from the fishermen's beach and crept to the back of the *cayuco*, turning to sit down close to him, nestled in the safety of his arms.

"I do not know, even now, why I told you that I would." The look on her face was a mixture of trepidation and confusion at her own bravado.

He chuckled slightly as the sound of the engine echoed off the water and mangrove forests around them. "Maybe because you know it's foolish to be afraid of something if you can change it. Maybe because you thought I'd be your protector." He reached out and hugged her closer to him.

"Protect me from what?" She pushed at him playfully yet jumped when a rush of wind and feathers raced close by overhead.

"It's a kingfisher," he laughed again. "Highly un-dangerous."

"Please do not laugh at me." The earnest ring to her voice brought him up short.

"I would never do that." He leaned forward, half-whispering the words in her ear. "I'm sorry. It must be frightening for you, coming back here. It takes a lot of courage to face your fears. I know that." He rubbed the back of her neck and noticed the line of goosebumps that ran along her arm. "Now, are those from being scared or from something else?"

She smiled her answer to him and took his hand in both of hers, the way he had seen her do with Imanuel earlier in the day. She laid her face beside his hand. "I am so glad you have come into my life. Even if it is only for a short while."

He reveled in her affection and squeezed her two hands in his one. "Look," he pointed ahead to a huge white crane, standing knee-deep at the water's edge, a short distance in front of them. Rick trained the motor as low as it would go without cutting it out completely as they continued their approach. A few feet more and the huge bird spread its mighty wings, lifting gracefully out of the stream and into the air, in a magnificent display, seemingly arranged just for them.

"That was lovely," she said in a rush, as if she had not dared to breathe upon seeing the elegant creature.

"I told you there were beautiful things to be seen here."

Tiny birds dove overhead, skimming close to the water as they flitted past. The long finger-like roots of the mangrove made the trees look as if they were standing on tiptoe. He wondered what they must look like at low tide, with so much more of the roots exposed. The canoe continued to meander slowly upriver, winding its way further inland.

"Imanuel says this river will take you all the way to the village of San Marcos, out by the highway," Mariana spoke softly as if she were fearful of being overheard.

"That'd be one long trip. I don't think we'll go that far if it's all the same to you."

"I do not need to go that f—Oh, Rishard, look!" A doe and her fawn stood statuesque and motionless on the bank. Rick cut the engine at the unusual sight of deer in this part of the world, especially this pair, a donnish gray mother and her lighter, buckskin offspring. They glided by in a moment of silence before the two turned and walked back into the dense underbrush, disappearing after only a few steps.

Mariana was nearly beside herself. "Can you believe what we have just seen? I did not think there were any deer left in this country. Not since I was a very little girl have I heard of any deer or monkeys here. They have all been hunted away. They were so beautiful." She stopped to catch her breath.

"Yes, they were." He so enjoyed watching her, these rare times when childlike delight took her over.

"Why were they here?" She was consumed and mystified by the pair.

"What do you mean?"

"Why did they come to the *estero* like that?"

"I don't know, to drink, I guess." Rick could not answer the question, but he restarted the engine and guided it in closer to the spot where they had disappeared.

"They cannot drink this water," she corrected him. "Nothing drinks this, only shrimp. Too much salt."

"I hadn't thought of that," he admitted, realizing his own upbringing far from any ocean was showing again. He peered into the forest beyond the mangroves that lined the river's edge and could see the bank blended into a steep incline. A few feet above, a string of colorful wildflowers traced its way down the hillside. In the hush of the forest depths, the telltale murmur of water falling, just a trickle, was the only sound that breached the silence.

"Like I said," he pointed inland and turned back toward her. "They must have come for water."

"*Díos mío*. This is the place." She closed her eyes as if she were praying while all the color drained from her face.

"What?" He struggled to follow what she was saying. "What place? We just saw the deer here, that's all. What's wrong?"

"This is where—" The words caught in her throat, and she tried again. "This is where they left me, where I spent the night. Oh, Rishard." Her hands covered her face.

"It's okay. Don't panic." He started to swing the boat wide. "We'll get out of here. It was a long time ago. You don't need to think about it anymore."

"No, no. Wait." She swallowed hard as she tried to regain control. "I want to see it. I need to see it."

"See what, for crying out loud?" He cut the motor midstream, and they drifted along in silence.

"I need to see it again. Please, take me back."

"I'm not so sure this is a good idea—"

"I will be all right. I promise." She wiped the tears from her eyes and gave him a brave yet trembling smile.

He watched her out of the corner of his eye as he turned the boat back in the direction that had come and ran it up close to the *mangle* roots. "Do you want to get out?" He was not certain he wanted to hear the answer.

"Yes."

On the bank side of the *cayuco*, just beyond *mangle* roots, the sloping ground was covered with thick moss. Deep hoof prints covered the muddy ground in front of the spring-fed watering hole. Rick climbed out first, tying the boat firmly to the closest mangrove tree, before helping her out.

"I found the water." She began to talk as she approached the flower-frilled pool. Trickling water from the rocky ground above had made a natural open-top well, a godsend to the animals that lived in the *mangle*, judging from the surrounding tracks, which included deep-set deer hoof prints.

"I found the water that night," she repeated and dipped her hand in the cool refreshing liquid. "And I tried to wash." She choked and coughed before going on. "I tried to wash it all away. I sat down after a while and leaned against a tree...there, maybe."

A huge twisted tropical trunk to the right and behind the spring hole provided a half-dozen recesses, inviting places to hide and weather out a storm. "I was so tired. More than tired, the kind of tiredness that old people must feel, I think. I just wanted to rest for a bit before trying to go home." She stopped speaking and took a deep breath.

"You don't have to do this." Rick tried to spare her.

"I need to tell you so that I can understand it, too."

He nodded, saying nothing more. The enveloping forest protected them from the sun's hot rays. Standing in the afternoon shade, Rick noticed the air was so still it was as if every tree, every living thing was leaning in close, listening to the horrific account they had witnessed years before.

"I had come to collect wood, lots of people did that back then. And when I first saw them, I did not think too much about it, but when they stopped their big fancy boat, I could see they were drunk. *Campesino* girls may not know much about some things, but we always knew that a rich man's son could be a dangerous thing, and a drunk one is even worse.

"I moved away from them, deeper into the *mangle*, but I never thought they would follow. When they did, I was filled with panic, and I ran. I never knew how much faster a man could run then, especially one that is after only one thing. There were two of them, and they were so strong. I fought them, but they did not even seem to notice. Roberto hit me in the face once or twice and pulled a gun from his belt. He pushed it in my face, and after that, I had no strength left. I think they would have killed me. Maybe that was their plan except that after they had both had their turns with me, they started to fight with each other. By then, I was hurting too much to know over what—fighting over me, what to do next, I don't know." Her shoulders sagged.

Seemingly unaware, she had moved to the safety of one of the hollows in the large tree trunk. She sat with her ankles crossed, holding onto them as she rocked slightly, her arms tightly pressed between her legs, her full skirt falling around her hands.

"Roberto's friend, Tomas Escobar, was on top of me, leaning over me. I am not sure, and Roberto hit him. I remember because it was the first time since they took me that one of them was not holding onto me. They kept fighting, the way drunk men do sometimes, much yelling, falling down. I started slow, just doing like a baby, crawling until I was a little distance from them. Then I got up and tried to run. It hurt so bad. Then I heard Roberto's gun. I thought he was trying to kill me, so then I really ran. I did not stop until I could not hear anything more. When I did stop, all I could do was cry and think about how I could not go home because I would not be able to say anything to anyone, especially Imanuel. A young girl cannot tell a man, any man, that another man did things like that to her. I was also afraid he might not believe me."

"Imanuel? He adores you. How could he not?" Rick had not meant to interrupt, and he bit his lip.

A sad little smile swept across her face. "Remember, rich men hold the power here. What good would it do? Even if Imanuel believed me, what could he do? Get himself killed if he complained too loudly about it? It was already a nightmare, and it had just begun."

"What do you mean?"

She continued. "I found this place, a place to rest, even if for just a short while. After the water, I sat down here." She spread her hands in front of her.

"And I suppose it sounds strange now, but I fell asleep. When I woke up, it was so dark. It took me a few minutes to remember where I was."

She took a deep breath. "Then I heard them. I did not think about this being their place to come for water. All I knew is that I could hear things, like footsteps and the sound a branch makes when it moves. I thought it was Roberto and Tomas coming for me. I thought this time, they will kill me." Her eyes brimmed with tears.

"It took a long time to know it was the animals coming for the water, but then that was almost as frightening. Everyone knows there are snakes up here, big ones as well as iguanas and *garobos*. Back then, people still talked about wild cats and deer, lots of forest animals. I was sure I would die that night, one way or another."

She brushed at the tears on her cheeks. "Until we saw the deer today, I thought most of the animals were gone now. I have heard that they were all hunted away, but who knows?"

She let out a little sigh and went on with her story. "Imanuel, Miguel, and Franco came, sometime the next day, they told me, but by then, I could not remember anything. I do not know where I was, if they found me here or somewhere else. I was so scared, I could not talk about any of it, what had happened. I was afraid if I told them anything, I would not stop until I told it all. And that would get all of us in trouble, so I did not tell them anything at all."

"So, it was Roberto who killed his friend?"

"Maybe that was the shot I heard when I was running away. I know it was not me. I could not fire a gun at anyone, not then, probably not even now." She sat quiet and calm despite all she had said. The tears rolled down her cheeks, a moment more before she held out her hand to him. He helped her to her feet and wrapped his arms securely around her. The sobs came almost immediately, and he held her tight. He made no attempt to staunch the flow of her grief. She had held it inside far too long, and he listened as her weeping echoed softly off the forest around them.

After a time, she pulled away, drawing a small handkerchief from her skirt pocket and dipped it in the cool water before wiping her face.

"She said I could face it all now. I would not have thought it was true." Mariana gazed down into the pool.

"Who said?"

She gave him a small, tremulous smile. "The psychologist who helped me to put my life back together, a couple of years after I left here."

"I had no idea." He stood watching her, shaking his head. "Can I ask one question?"

"*Por supuesto*," she replied. "Only one?"

"If Roberto killed Tomas, who killed Roberto?"

She regarded him in silence before replying. "You do know the whole story, no?" There was an undercurrent of accusation in her voice.

"The truth? I wanted to know everything there was to know about you after that first meeting on the bus. I knew I shouldn't, but I asked a little and listened a lot. I don't claim to know what is true and what is not. Whatever you tell me, that is the only truth I care to know. I would have asked sooner, but..."

She eyed him curiously before slipping back into his arms. "Then I will tell you. I spent a great deal of time with doctors after I left here."

"With Carlos?"

"Yes, with Carlos. He saved my life."

"I don't understand."

"When I left here, Raúl Gomez was after me because he said I killed his beloved Roberto, but there was more." She squeezed him tight as if hanging on for her life. Suddenly, she threw her head back and looked Rick full in the face.

"When I left here, I was also pregnant. I did not know who the father was, Roberto or Tomas. If Raúl Gomez had known... with all the rest, I do not know that I would have survived here. A month after I left, I had a miscarriage."

"My God." Rick barely uttered the words as he hugged her to his breast again.

"The day Roberto Gomez died, I was nowhere near him. I took Miguel his lunch that day, and I walked by looking at the other side of the road. I did not want to see that house. I certainly did not want anything to do with any of them."

Her smile was small, but he thought it was more beautiful than ever. "Just like here in the *mangle*, I never fired any gun. I have no idea who killed him, but whoever it was, I think they deserve a prize."

"Then tell me this. Why did you offer yourself to don Raúl that day in his house?" Rick hated himself for asking, but he could not stop.

"Don Raúl had the man who raised and loved me all of my life, or if he did not have him, he knew who did. If someone loves you like that and is in terrible danger, you do anything to free them, no? I was willing to make a trade with don Raúl if he wanted me that bad. The important thing was to get Imanuel home alive. That is the only thing that mattered to me. If admitting to a murder I did not make is what it took, then I admit to murder. But I did not kill anybody. Do you understand?" She released him and moved toward the boat.

"I'm not sure," Rick answered as he contemplated the kind of devotion she was describing. "I'm not sure I ever loved anyone like that... before now."

She looked back at him over her shoulder and threw him a fetching smile. "Besides, you said one question. That was two. Shall we go?"

"*Vaya pues*," he answered, still pondering all he had heard. "*Vaya pues.*"

* * * * *

An overwhelming sense of dread swept over Rick as he approached his own hut and saw the number of people already gathered across the road. Against his better judgment, he changed his clothes and walked across to join his neighbors. He was surprised at the almost jovial atmosphere he found as two different groups of men gathered around folding tables to play cards in Julio's front yard.

The women sat on the opposite side of the yard, talking softly, sharing stories, and trading benign bits of gossip. Inside the house, Simón's still open pine casket was full to overflowing with fresh-cut wildflowers. The sheet that Imanuel had wrapped around him earlier had been rearranged. He wore a shirt now and the lower portion of his face—his nose, mouth, and chin had been cleaned and peeked from beneath the mound of flowers. Despite the fact that Julio's was one of the few houses outside the village with electricity, only candles lit the interior of the house.

Rick greeted Yolanda and Juana and shook their small hands in consolation as he might have had they been in his country. He was soon invited into a game of poker. When Mariana arrived, along with Imanuel and Paz, she joined the women on the other side of the house. From time to time, Rick could catch a glimpse of her watching him, but no words were exchanged between them. After a time, he excused himself from the game and sought out Paz and Imanuel, inside the house. He was moving in their direction when a terrible screech outside caught everyone by surprise.

It was like an animal's scream of pain, Rick thought at first, like a dog pinned under a car. Those in the house rushed outside, but being taller than the rest, Rick looked over those gathered. A small knot of men were pulling a clench-fisted Juana away from

Lt. Hernandez's Jeep, which had apparently just stopped on the road in front of the vigil.

She continued to hurl sobbing insults and accusations as she was led away. The startled lieutenant attempted to recover his dignity as he addressed Julio. Much to Rick's surprise, the soldier looked more shocked than angry.

"Don Julio," he began, "in all sincerity, I came to offer my sympathies to your family."

"I understand, *Teniente*," Julio answered humbly, his hat in his hand, coming from one of the card tables. "We appreciate that."

Juana's cries could still be heard, coming from the house.

"I had no idea this woman somehow blamed—" he frowned, uncertain of how to continue.

"Please, *Teniente*, my daughter is not responsible for what she says right now. She is out of her mind with grief. I trust you understand and will accept my apology."

"You are the one who should apologize, Hector." Mariana came forward from where she had been with the other women. "There is no place for you here."

"Every place in this country is open to the military, woman," Sgt. Fuentes spoke up from the back of the Jeep. "This gathering could quickly be declared illegal if it is determined that it is adding to the unrest in this area."

Lt. Hernandez held up his hand and cut him off. "Mariana, do not be harsh. I grew up with these people, too. It is not only you." There was almost a pleading note in his voice.

"You made your choice, Hector," she continued but in a lower voice this time. "We all have."

"Don't do this, Mariana. Don't put me or yourself in a position we might later come to regret."

"You have said what you came to say, yes?" She seemed to take no notice of his words.

Imanuel came to her side and laid a hand on her arm. "It is all right. Everyone has the right to express their sorrow here tonight."

The soldier was once again, all business. "Don Imanuel, you are a man of the church and as close as anyone is to being in charge of this gathering tonight. I urge you to keep it under control. Crowds of all kinds are of particular concern to the government at this time in our country. That includes all of those in attendance." His scrutiny fell upon Mariana and Rick, who had just come to stand by her side. He signaled the soldier at his side to drive on.

"*Buenas noches.*" Even his farewell echoed with the sharp ring of an order.

If Hector Hernandez's purpose was to disperse the mourners that evening, he did a good job of it, Rick thought as people began to leave almost before the dust behind the departing vehicle had settled. He, too, went home after bidding Imanuel and his family good night.

"Will you be all right walking home in the dark?" Rick inquired.

"You do it all the time," Mariana answered, only half-teasingly.

"We will be fine," Imanuel stated. "I have apologized to Julio and his family. It is probably best that we all go now while so many others are also walking back to town. We will be back first thing in the morning."

Rick did not sleep well. The strong winds of a month ago were back, and although he knew it was not cold by the standards he was accustomed to, he still felt a chill in the air, nonetheless.

The gathering of mourners the next morning was quite small, compared to the number that had come the night before. Maybe it had to do with the sign they had found on Simón's body, Rick thought, making people afraid to join the funeral procession in the light of day. Maybe it was as simple a matter as people felt they had to fish or attend to other types of work that day, or maybe it was a result of the military's visit the night before.

Rick watched from his own house as Imanuel arrived, alone and organized the proceedings. After a couple of false starts, the sad little group clumped around Simón's ox cart that now carried the owner's coffin and plodded up the road to the strains of the women's wailing song. Rick turned the other way and walked out to the beach to lean against a palm tree, watch the glittering waves, and contemplate final solutions.

CHAPTER 15

*M*arch 24, 1980. San Salvador. Archbishop Oscar A. Romero continues his fight from the pulpit against the government forces here, who are believed to be responsible for the death of nearly 900 civilians since the first of the year, according to a report released last week by Amnesty International.

In his four-hour homily yesterday, Monsignor Romero made an unprecedented personal appeal to the members of the National Guard. He stated, "Brothers, you are part of our people. You kill your own peasant brothers and sisters. Before an order to kill... the law of God must prevail that says, thou shalt not kill! No soldier is obliged to obey an order against the law of God... In the name of God, and in the name of this suffering people whose laments rise to heaven each day more tumultuous, I beg you, I ask you, I order you in the name of God: Stop the repression!"

Grave concerns have been expressed by officials in Washington D.C. as well as by friends of the archbishop in San Salvador for Monsignor Romero's safety.

"I am your friendly letter carrier." The breathy whisper close to his ear startled him from his dreams. He awoke to find his dream come to life, bending over his cot, brandishing a postcard. She let out a shriek of delight as he grabbed her and rolled her over him onto the far side of the bed.

"And I am your friendly big bad wolf," he growled, leaning over her, "who is going to eat you up." He ferociously attacked the soft tresses of dark hair that curled along her neck.

She squealed again, laughing and throwing her arms around his neck. "Now I am not surprised the postman will not come to your house, if this is what you do to letter carriers," she giggled.

"I beg your pardon." He sat up in mock indignation. "I am very particular about who I do and do not attack."

"Oh, I see. Well, here is your postcard from David, just the same. What does he say?" She stretched out beside him, her head resting on his ribs.

"Oh, as if you haven't read it already. Don't give me that."

"You do not believe in the postman's code of honor?"

"Not in this country."

"Well, it is a very simple code," she laughed. "Read all you can and take much of the rest."

He studied David's scrawl. "He made it home and still hasn't found a job. Says he's avoided my father so far, which is good because he's still mad. Also says US news is not too good. I imagine he's referring to the politics here." Rick glanced at the picture of the jack-a-lope on the other side, a jokester's depiction of the animal that would result from the crossing of a jackrabbit and an antelope.

"Just his style," Rick muttered.

"Do you want some breakfast?" Mariana swung her legs over the side of the cot and stood up.

"What? Where? Here?"

"Oh, I do not think so." She dismissed the meager contents of his kitchen with one glance. "There is nothing to eat here, is there?"

"Not much," he admitted.

"Then let's go to Emelina's. I will even cook for you. What would you like?"

"Oh, let's see..." He pulled on a T-shirt and reached for a comb. "We could start with bacon and a big stack of flapjacks and a large cup of hot chocolate, with some toast on the side."

"Oh, you are so funny." She shot back as she waited for him by the door. "You know I cannot make toast here, there is no bread, only tortillas. I could fry some *chicharrón* instead of bacon but flapjacks?"

"Fatback? No, it's just not the same for breakfast."

"Oh, come on then. I will make you some fried *platanos*, scrambled eggs, and some white cheese on the side and tortillas. I will even make some *leche con café* instead of hot chocolate if you are tired of coffee. It will all be good, yes?"

"If you are there, yes, it will all be good. *Leche con café?* You make that? I had that once when I was little, sort of like hot chocolate only with coffee, right? It was great, as I remember."

"Where did you have that?"

"I'll tell you about it on the way."

At the far end of the beach, they found Paz watching a group of men unloading three large trucks, as true to his prediction, the carnival had come to town.

"*Buenos días*," he called when he saw them. "Look at this." The men tromping about in the sand, in the midst of the newly-slapped together *ramadas*, were busy assembling the mechanical workings for half a dozen rides. Rick recognized old familiar favorites, including a small Ferris wheel, a canopy-topped merry-go-round that carried swings, a more traditional carousel with shiny plastic animals, and a down-sized version of something he and his friends had always called the wild mouse. They joined Paz, watching with interest and yet staying back out of the way.

One man began pounding long spikes into the sand. "What are they doing?"

"Making *anclas*, anchors," Mariana responded. "That is how they tie them down."

"That's it?" Rick was flabbergasted.

"It is enough," Paz sounded defensive. "Besides, that is not the important part. Getting in line soon enough. That is the tough part."

"Remind me not to get on any of that stuff, will you?" Rick laughed as he and Mariana continued on their way. "Stakes in the sand." He shook his head.

They found the kitchen empty and true to her promise, Mariana went to work cooking breakfast while Rick stood in the doorway, kibitzing.

"Would you like some *frijoles*, too?" She lifted the lid on a pot at the back of Emelina's large cooking table. "These look ready."

"Ready for what?"

"To make into refried beans. How do you think they get that way, anyway?"

"I dunno." He shrugged. "You mash them up and then fry them, I guess."

"Americans," Mariana laughed. "You think people fry beans for no reason? The beans are fried because they have been cooked so long in the pot, that they are like—" she stopped looking for the right word. "Like *masa*."

"Like dough?" He wrinkled up his nose and walked closer to take a look as she tossed a handful of chopped onion into a hot oiled skillet.

"The beans were made at the end of last week and cooked every day, and now they are not really beans anymore, you see?"

Rick peered at the cold brown porridge-like contents. "If she cooked them last week, where have they been since then?" His apprehension was beginning to show.

"Right here. She puts them back on the fire each day, whether she serves them or not. As long as they come to a boil every day, they stay good. Nothing can grow in there. What is the harm?"

Rick made a face.

She threw an impatient hand to her hip. "I suppose you think they have to spend every night in the refrigerator to make them good?"

"Well, it seems like the thing to do."

"People here learned how to do things they need to do, long before anybody brought a refrigerator to this village. They cook them this way, all at once, because it takes less firewood. Each day when the fire is already going, it costs nothing to heat them again. Besides, there is no room in that refrigerator. Do you think Imanuel is going to let us put food in that thing when he has it full of things to sell in the store?" Mariana snorted. "Do you know Tila Rodriguez down closer to the point?"

"No, I don't think so."

"Well, she has a store, too, and a refrigerator, and she puts her beans in there day after day. I can tell you in four days, they smell and taste terrible. Emelina's beans last all week, and they still taste... well, you tell me. You have been eating them for months now. Is the food good?"

"Well, yes, they are good."

"So do you trust me?"

"Uh, yes, I do, but..."

"Do you want beans with your breakfast or not?" She stood perched with the pot balanced over the aromatic skillet of simmering onion, *chiles*, and tomatoes.

"Yes, I want the beans with breakfast. I am sorry I asked." He grinned at her agitated state and went back to the post beside the door, taking in her every move.

Miguel came in through the back just as Paz did the same from the front.

"Finally, I have the two of you together," Miguel announced, as Rick's heart took a guilty leap at his phrasing.

"Were you looking for me, *Tío*?" Paz's face was pure innocence.

"Which one of you *burros* has my big net shuttle? I am out here in the hot sun," he wiped his brow melodramatically, "trying to repair the nets and keep you two in fishing equipment, and I have only the little shuttles to use."

"You have it." Paz pointed a quick finger at Rick.

"Now wait a minute," Rick countered. "It's at my house, but who left it there?"

"Just what I thought." Miguel was self-righteous. "I knew better than to ask one without the other beside him. I have to find the two of you together to get any answers."

"I'll go get it for you," Rick volunteered.

"*Vaya, Tío*," Mariana intervened. "Let the man eat his breakfast first, then he can go after whatever it is you need."

"*Vaya pues*. That will be fine." Miguel went back to his play-acting. "I will just suffer out here with the little ones. Of course, there are two of the little ones. One would just fit, let's see—" He made a grab for Paz's hand. "Yes, I think it would fit this hand perfectly right here."

"I have to go with don Ricardo to help him find the other one. I mean, I left it at his house, but he does not know exactly where, right?" He threw an imploring look Rick's way.

"*Vaya*, and it is such a big house to search." Miguel acquiesced with a touch of sarcasm. "But after that, you come help for a while. There might even be some extra coins in it for you. They are not going to let you ride on all that fancy machinery over there for nothing, you know." Miguel stuck his chin out toward the beach.

"I will be there soon, *Tío*. I promise."

She laid a small breakfast banquet before him. The last thing she brought to the table was a steaming cup of *leche con café*. Mariana started to sit down beside him until she looked up at Paz. "I suppose you need to be fed again, too?"

"No, I already ate."

"I know that," she answered as she reached out and tousled his curls back from his face a little. "But that was three hours ago, and at your age, you are no doubt hungry again."

He laughed and dodged her attempts to make him look a little less bedraggled. "I will just steal some of his tortillas." He helped himself to one of the hot ones wrapped in the thin towel. "He never eats them all anyway."

"So no fishing today?" Mariana sat down beside Paz, across from Rick.

"Still pretty windy out there." Rick tried to cover his mouth that was full. "You could really hear it at my house last night. That usually means there's no point in getting up early. Maybe this afternoon."

"Yes, this afternoon," Paz echoed.

"This afternoon, that would just be me, all by myself." Rick did not want to leave any false impressions. "You have school."

"Oh, I did not tell you. School is out now for *Semana Santa*."

"Already?"

"That is next week." Mariana popped him on the top of the head.

"Well, it can just start a little early for me." He grinned, caught in the lie.

"I don't think so." Rick finished his meal and leaned back. "Now that was a breakfast," he commented and patted his stomach. "I have to walk home just to work some of it off. Thank you." His eyes said more than his words as they settled momentarily on hers.

"You are very welcome." She returned.

On the road, Rick noticed Paz watching one of the local girls with more interest than just a few months ago as she passed by, the water jug on her head, accenting her perfect posture. She smiled at Paz but said nothing.

"Pretty cute, huh?" Rick commented.

"Who? Her? No, I never noticed." His face colored as a goofy grin spread across it.

"Sure, sure." Rick smirked as they neared his cabin. "Hey, I didn't leave the door standing open." He took a few more quick steps and found there were a great many other things not as he left them just a short time ago.

The entire insides of the cabin had been tossed about as if a small tornado had come and gone within the four walls.

"Don Ricardo, *qué pasó aquí?*" Paz stumbled in behind him.

"That's what I'd like to know, too," Rick repeated in shock. "What happened here?"

The kitchen table lay on its side. and all of the jars it once held were smashed on the floor, their contents now mixed with shards of glass. The cot had been sliced down the center, and the crate, small table, and bookshelf had all been upended. Books, some with their pages torn out, were scattered throughout the room. His duffel bag had been emptied, the clothes in it tossed about the place. Only the hammock appeared untouched, still hanging where it was when Rick left that morning.

Paz started to follow Rick inside, but Rick stopped him. "Bare feet and glass," he warned. "Not a good mix."

"Did you make somebody mad?" Paz was still trying to fathom the reason behind the disaster before his eyes.

"I don't know. I sure don't know what to tell Miguel about his net shuttle now."

While Paz went to deliver that message, Rick began to sift through the bits and pieces that were left as his mind sifted through the possible motives behind such an intrusion. Back outside, he noticed the several sets of footprints that led toward the beach, away from the road. Rick's mind leap-frogged ahead. He could come up with only one very chilling answer as he stared at the boot prints at his feet. The fact that they went only a short distance, ending at a set of tire tracks, lent confirmation to his worst fears. Only one kind of vehicle was ever driven across the beach sand.

Back inside his cabin, he started in the center by picking up the now worthless cot. *Tijeras*, the locals called them, because of the way they folded up like a pair of scissors. He set the frame outside. He shoveled a clear place in the corner with his foot and righted the bookcase. He began collecting its contents from around the room. Suddenly, he knew what would be missing. He could spend the rest of the day looking, but he knew they were gone— his return ticket to the US, five twenty-dollar bills that he had set aside for traveling money, and his American passport.

When Paz returned, Mariana was with him. "Oh, Rishard." Her voice startled him, and he whirled to find her standing in the open doorway, surveying the damage. "Paz told me, but I had no idea."

"Quite a mess, huh? Somebody really did a job on this place."

"We will help you to fix it back." She stepped inside with a push-up-the-sleeves air of getting down to business. "Come on, Paz." She picked up the packing crate and began to collect the bigger pieces of broken glass.

"You don't have to do that," Rick protested. "Be careful. You'll cut yourself."

"I will be just fine. Pazito, go over to Julio's house and ask to borrow a broom."

"I have a little homemade one over there in the corner," Rick pointed, but of course, it too, was not where it had once been. "Oh... well..."

"It does not matter," she said. "For this big mess, I think we need a real one, anyway."

She began picking up his clothes, folding each piece and making a tidy stack near the door.

With Paz gone, her tone was less cheerful. "Do you know who did this?"

He sighed. "I have an idea."

"But you are not going to tell me?"

"I don't want to say if I'm not sure," he stalled. "It would be unfair to make accusations right now. After all, there are many strangers coming into town right now and from what Paz says there will be more, with the coming of *Semana Santa* and—"

"What kind of a fool do you think I am?" She stopped cleaning and tried to look him in the eye, but he turned away. "You are trying to tell me you think someone did this as a trick, or it is just common thieves? I do not believe it. There is something more. It is something you cannot tell me? What?" She reached for his arm and pulled him around to face her.

"I don't want to scare you. That's all. I've got my suspicions—"

Paz burst back through the door, borrowed broom in hand. "Don Ricardo, I know who was here! Niña Juana says the soldiers came, and one stood outside, while others came in..."

His words were cut short at the sight of their faces.

"Is that it?" Mariana demanded. "Is that what you suspected?"

Rick looked at the floor. "There are tracks outside that led away to the beach, and they stop where a set of Jeep tracks begin."

"*Madre de Díos*, Rishard. You cannot stay here. You know that now."

"I don't know what to think," he countered, the anger mounting in his voice. "I know I sure as hell can't leave just now either. I don't know what else is missing, but they took all the money I had plus my passport. Traveling back to San Salvador on the bus could be a tricky business without that."

"*A la gran puchica.*" Paz let out a long breath.

Mariana watched Rick closely. "I did not mean, leave *Las Palomitas*. I just meant you should not stay here, in this house, alone. You can come down and stay with us. We will figure this out. Maybe Imanuel will have an idea of what we should do next."

A crooked smile warmed his face, despite his mood. "He probably will. I'm sorry. I hope this doesn't get all of us into more trouble."

"Niña Juana said she was scared when she saw them here. She was afraid you were home—" He left the thought unspoken but brightened as he finished. "She said when she saw the soldiers come out quickly, as if they were looking for you, at least she knew you were not here."

"I can't imagine what they're after or why. I've been here for months. Why should they suddenly take an interest in me?"

"That is what we need to find out," Mariana nodded.

They spent much of the day, attempting to right the cabin, salvaging what was left. Late in the afternoon, Rick packed a small bag and walked down the beach, hoping not to attract any notice. Mariana was behind the counter in the store when he walked in. Imanuel was high up on a ladder in the far corner, attempting to retrieve some boxes from the highest shelf.

"Be careful up there," Rick teased, as he tossed his bag behind the heavy curtain. "What are you after, anyway?" He wandered over near the ladder.

"Oh, one of the ladies from down near the point asked if we had any white lace, and I thought I had some stored up here in one of these boxes. She said she is making a gown for her baby granddaughter's baptism and wanted to—"

"*Buenas tardes.*" The deep voice at the door startled Rick as Sgt. Fidel Fuentes stepped inside.

"*Buenas tardes,*" Mariana answered with cool politeness.

"*Cigarillos.*" He pointed to the shelf behind her. "And a box of matches."

Rick was watching the man while trying to appear not to do so when the bundle of white lace came unraveling down across his shoulders. He looked up to discover Imanuel barely clinging to the ladder. Rick climbed up behind his friend after a quick glance over his shoulder, assured him the soldier was still occupied at the counter.

Imanuel's trembling hands gripped the ladder, but his labored breathing and sweat-covered brow had Rick wondering if his friend was suffering a stroke or some other health crisis.

"What's wrong?" Rick whispered, leaning in close to protect his friend from whatever was troubling him.

"That is the voice." Imanuel barely breathed the words aloud.

The now-empty box above their heads lost its delicate balance and clattered to the floor as the sergeant turned to go. He looked up at the two of them as he stopped in the doorway to light a cigarette.

"*Buenas tardes*, don Imanuel," he called out. "*Buenas tardes, gringo*," he finished with a laugh and disappeared out the door.

"What is going on up there?" Mariana flew to the bottom of the ladder.

Rick shrugged in confusion in answer to her question. Gradually, he was able to help Imanuel ease his way down the ladder. He was pale and shaking, and Rick half-carried him to the couch behind the curtain while Mariana went to fetch a cool drink from the refrigerator in the store.

"Quick, before she comes back. I must tell you. That is the voice." Imanuel clutched at the front of Rick's shirt. "The one who directed the others when I was taken."

"Fuentes?" Rick thought his friend might be confused. "But you've heard him before, haven't you? You must be mistaken."

"No, I have seen him, sometimes, walking or riding with Hector, but I never heard him speak until today. He is not the sergeant who first came when Hector arrived here. Remember? Fuentes came later, after *el día de San Rafael*. Only once before have I heard that voice, when I could not see his face. I will never forget, not if I live to be 100 years old."

Mariana arrived with a cold bottle of Coke. "What happened?"

Rick's gaze dropped to the floor, but Imanuel spoke up.

"I think it was just too hot up there close to the ceiling. I should have waited until later in the day to look for Niña Marta's lace, but I was afraid I would forget."

"You have been working too hard lately." Mariana chided as she wiped his forehead with her handkerchief. "When will you learn? Now her white lace is all over the floor. I have to go pick it up before Paz or someone else comes along and walks on it. You stay here and rest. Promise?"

He nodded, taking a long drink. Mariana signaled for Rick to follow her.

"That was a very nice little story." Her tone was acidic. "Now, you want to tell me what is really going on?" She began to wind the lace back onto its cardboard reel.

"Hey, I was glad to find out it was only the heat. Did you see him up there? I thought he was having a heart attack or a stroke or something. He's not a young man, you know."

"You really think that's it?"

Rick breathed a tiny sigh of relief at the thought she might actually accept his explanation. "What else could it be?"

"I am not certain. I thought it might have something to do with Fuentes, the soldier who was in the store."

"I can't imagine what that would be." Rick was appalled at how easily the lie fell from his lips.

"I do not know." She sounded lost in her own thoughts as she looked back at the curtain. "It is just a feeling I had."

* * * * *

After a long nap, Imanuel came back into the store that evening and insisted on stepping behind the counter. He refused to discuss the earlier incident with Rick and silenced Mariana's protests. He insisted that she and Rick join Paz in enjoying the festivities across the way. The carnival rides lit up the beach with their bright, whirling array of lights, spinning in half a dozen directions. Paz wore the carefree expression of a child who had just been given the keys to the proverbial candy store.

"It is wonderful, yes?" he asked as Rick and Mariana left the store with reluctance. "This is the most exciting thing that happens each year here."

"This?" Rick was not convinced. "What about the National Marimba here a few months ago for the *fiesta de San Rafael*?"

"I told you then. That is old people's music. It is all right to listen to if there is nothing better."

"This is better than Christmas?"

"Well, if you remember, Christmas was not a very happy time for us this year—"

"Okay, okay, that's true for this year but—"

"But why argue with him, anymore," Mariana interrupted. "What does it matter? For all of the children, this is the best, no? This is games and fun and no responsibilities, something all of our children need from time to time. What have you done so far?" she asked him.

"Just the swings, they are always the best, I think. Gilberto promised to join me here soon, but I have not seen him yet. I was going to take a look on the other side, and then I will come back."

"Go on with you then. You can find us here." She turned back to Rick, who was leaning on the wooden split rail fence that separated the buildings from the beach.

"I'm sorry."

"About what?"

"Snapping at you that way when you were talking to Paz. I am glad at least he can have some fun right now. It just feels like..."

"Like what?"

"I do not know. I am worried about Imanuel. You said his health is not so good, and yet he chases us out of the store like a mother hen, taking over. It makes me nervous."

"Do you want to go back over to the store? We can, you know."

She shook her head. "It would not do any good. He would run us off again. There probably will not be much business tonight. Look around you. Anyone out tonight is here. He just seems to think he has to do everything himself lately, and he will not let anyone else help. That is not like him."

"What do you think it is?"

"I truly do not know. I suppose that is much of what bothers me. Not knowing."

He nodded in understanding without saying anything more.

A popcorn vendor loudly hawking his wares passed by, and Rick motioned him over. He bought a paper cone full of the light confection.

"What did he call this?" Rick asked Mariana in English as the man walked on, singing out what he had to sell.

"*Palomitas de maiz*," she answered. "Little doves of corn."

"What a sweet name," he mused, half a smile on his face.

Paz returned with Gilberto, who was also obviously enjoying the carnival atmosphere. "Here," Mariana reached into her pocket and handed Paz a few *colones*. "Ride one for me. Have a good time."

"There was a time you would have been on every one of these yourself," Paz teased. "Some of them twice in one night."

Her smile had a tranquil weariness to it. "Not tonight, Pazito. The carnival will be here for more than a week. Another night, perhaps."

He shrugged and slipped the bills into his pocket. "*Muchas gracias*." He tapped Gilberto on the shoulder, and the two scooted off together. On the far side of the merry-go-round, Paz stopped in front of a wandering group of boys his own age. They wore white *guayaberas* and blue slacks as if they had just slipped away from a school celebration of some sort. They carried various sized guitars, some professionally made and some apparently home-fashioned. He gave them one of the bills Mariana had just shared with him and some brief instructions before continuing on his way with his friend.

"So, you were also a big fan of the carnival?" Rick asked after Paz and Gilberto had gone on their way.

"All village kids are." The sweet light of reminiscence graced her face. "Paz is right. It is the most exciting time of the year for them."

"For them?"

"Yes, for them, the children. I am not a village child anymore. Once I was, but not anymore."

"But you are back here. Back where you started."

"Back where I started." She said it slowly as if trying to take in the meaning of the exact words. "I like that."

"I don't understand."

"You do not have to. It does not matter. They are just silly little meaningless thoughts."

"Don't do that. Whenever I get too close to something, I'm not sure what, you turn away and tell me, it's not important and yet it must be, or you wouldn't turn away from it." His attention was diverted by the group of schoolboys who arranged themselves in front of the two of them, guitars in hand.

"It is all right. *Gracias, pero no*. Not tonight." She tried to tell them. "Another time."

"But we have already been paid." The leader spoke up. "You will like the music."

The leader counted softly, nodding his head to the others, and they strummed their instruments together. It was refreshing and quaint, yet surprisingly melodic and soothing, Rick thought, as they began to sing.

"*Una promesa, como una sonrisa en la mañana—*" He could not catch all the words, but the young man was right. He liked the music, as the words he did hear described Mariana, "a promise, a smile, like the dawn of a beautiful morning."

"*Mi esperanza—*" they continued, "my hope for the future, the light of a new life I've found." She was all of those things and more, he thought, listening while watching her, swaying gently to the rhythm in the flickering lights of the fair rides. The boys' song rose to a final high note, and Rick applauded as did several others who had stopped to listen. Mariana's face colored as she looked down.

"It is terribly warm this evening, yes?" She made nervous fanning motions around her face with her hands.

"It is the warmest it has been in days." Rick returned the nonchalant banter as a few others drifted over closer.

"Play another." Someone held out another crumpled bill to the boys. They struck up a lively tune this time, still in a minor key.

"What is that one?"

"The song of *Las Palomitas*, this place, this town. Almost every town in El Salvador has its own song."

"Really?"

"Certainly. Some of them are quite famous and all the *conjuntos*, the local bands play them, like the one for San Vicente."

They listened for several moments as the troubadours sang of smooth glistening beaches, riding in *cayucos*, and enjoying the holidays, swimming in the sea at *Las Palomitas*.

"Do you not remember when the *Marimba Nacional* played this song?"

"There is a lot about that night I don't remember clearly," Rick admitted sheepishly. "Like most of the music, but one part of it I'll never forget."

"Hmm?"

"Dancing with you, that's the one thing I want to remember. I'd do it again right now, if—"

"Oh, you would start a scandal!" Her nervous laughter said she almost feared he might try.

"I don't care about a scandal or anything else. Don't you know that by now? Only about you." Even though he spoke in English, he leaned in close so as to not be overheard by the others. "A decision is being forced upon me, whether I want it or not. After this afternoon, I'm going to have to—"

She cut him off. "A decision is being forced on you, so now you are going to force one on me. Is that it?"

"No." He shook his head emphatically. "That's not what I mean. It's just..." He heaved an exasperated sigh as he met her eyes. "I could have left here any time if I had never met you."

She dropped her eyes. "I know, and for that, I am sorry."

"Don't be." He touched her arm. "It's made my life much more complicated, but I don't regret any of it. Only the timing."

"Did you like the music?" Paz's enthusiasm matched his bouncing steps.

"It was beautiful, Pazito. Thank you. I am glad you came back. I wanted to say good night."

"You are going so early?"

"I am very tired. It has been a long day. I will see you tomorrow."

"*Vaya pues. Buenas noches*. You better rest up. There will be other nights yet of this celebration. You will need your rest."

She smiled and waved as he scampered back to the festivities and his waiting friend, Gilberto.

"You do not have to come," she told Rick as he started to follow her.

"And what am I going to do here? I have no intention of climbing on any of those things. If languishing in a hammock in your living room all night, while you sleep safely in your own bed is to be my fate, it might as well begin now as later."

She eyed him sideways as they crossed the street. "And what is that supposed to mean? You expect me to invite you into my bedroom with Imanuel sleeping next door?" The words came out in a hoarse whisper as she tried to suppress her laughter. "Are you completely crazy?"

"No, not completely." He grabbed her arm, once they were in the shadows of the buildings on the far side of the street and whisked her toward the fishermen's beach, beyond her own front door. They held hands and ran like school children up the beach away from the village.

"Look." He stopped and pointed off toward the trees. "There's David's house. There's no one around." He wrapped his arms around her, and kissed her and then began to disrobe.

"You have lost your mind." She began to giggle. "What are you doing?"

"Going swimming. You said yourself it was a hot night. It's dark enough up here. No one will see. No moon yet tonight."

"Yes, but Rishard, this is not the United States. You cannot drop your shorts wherever you choose and just—"

"Too late," he teased as the last of his clothing hit the sand. "Come on." He grabbed her hand, but she pulled back.

"You must be crazy." She looked at him an instant longer before she began unbuttoning her dress. "And I must have caught it from you." It slid down over her shoulders and dropped to gather around her feet. Her bra and panties followed.

How he longed for the return of the full moon to bathe her lovely curves in silvery light, but he gladly settled for her dark silhouette against the village's meager lights. She took his hand again, and he forced himself to leave his baser thoughts on land as the look of total trust that came his way, blessed him unexpectedly.

The warm sultry waters of the *estero*, caught between tides, produced a body of water that was almost static, like a wide, serene lake.

"Oh, look at that! What is that?" She squealed as her body broke the smooth surface, producing a wave of iridescent sparks skittering in front of her with every move she made.

"David and I swam out here a couple of times. He said they were some kind of microscopic creatures that live in the water. They won't hurt you, and you can only see them on nights when there is no moon."

"They are wonderful!" She exclaimed in pure delight. "They make me feel like Cinderella. They look like the magic dust in a fairy tale." She moved her arm in a wide arc just below the surface of the water and marveled at the lighted sparkling waves before her.

"All the years I lived here, I never knew there was magic in the *estero*."

"Maybe you just never went swimming at night with the right guy."

She giggled. "More like I never went swimming in the night at all. Who does such crazy things?"

"Lots of people." He ducked under the water, and she giggled when he came back up, right in front of her.

"*A la puchica*," she exclaimed. "They are on you, too. The little glowing things. There, they fell off."

He reached out and pulled her close and kissed her. Her arms encircled his neck, and she held on tight as he walked her out into deeper water. "Please, you make me nervous. You know I do not swim."

"I know." He whispered in her ear. "I will be careful. I promise. I needed to be where I can stand up. There. That's better." She leaned away from him slightly, her legs still locked securely around his waist. "I've got you," he further assured her. "You're safe."

"And why is that?"

"Excuse me?"

"Safe. You said I am safe. And it is true. I always feel perfectly safe when I am with you." She kissed him back this time. "Ever since that first day on the bus." Their arms tightened around one another as they both grasped, looking for something they could not quite attain. As their passion intensified, he slowly began to make their way toward shore.

She whispered in his ear. "Now what?"

He left her in the shallows while he spread his T-shirt wide on the dry sand. Lifting her out of the water, he set her down on the makeshift towel before dropping over her.

Passion on the sands of the fishermen's beach. In all the times he had been here, never had he thought of it a place of romance. It was a long way from their first lovemaking in his cabin on the ocean side beach, and yet they too had come a long way since that first time together.

This was the woman he could—he would—go on loving for a very long time. No matter how often, or how rarely they could find the opportunity to make love, whether like this, in moments stolen from both their lives, hidden from prying eyes, or side by side, sleeping together each and every night. He had no idea how he would do it, but he knew he had to find a way to meld his life with hers, and make their separateness, one, as they were one, now and always, in his heart.

She rolled, and he lay down beside her, their ardor spent for the moment. She ran her fingers through his hair as he caressed her ear. "Rishard, what are we going to do?" She asked in a breathless, almost hopeless voice.

"I think we have already done it."

"You know what I mean."

He reached out and kissed her lightly one more time. "I know exactly what you mean, but I haven't got any answers for you. Not yet, but I'm working on it." He slipped from her arms and walked back into the water. She joined him there.

"We must go home soon. What if Paz arrives before us?"

Rick stood on tiptoe briefly, looking down the beach in the direction of her house. "I don't think he is there yet."

"*Chiflado*, as if you could see him or the house from here."

"I can see the lights of the Ferris wheel, and it's still turning."

"So?"

"So, what are the chances that your brother has gone home if anything on the beach is still operating?"

"Okay, you win," she chuckled.

They walked back the way they had come, hand in hand in the dark. When they neared the occupied buildings, they separated and climbed the stairs to the back of her house in silence.

"Watch out!" Mariana let out a loud whisper. "Not this one." She indicated the second step from the top. "It squeaks." They both dissolved into muffled giggles as they snuck into the silent house.

"This is the most difficult thing I have done since I've been here," he muttered close to her ear, standing in the darkened living room next to the hammock. "Sending you to bed in one room while I stay in here. Sleep well, love." He kissed her on the forehead. "I know I won't."

The tantalizing music of her laughter echoed back to him as she slipped away into the darkness. "*Buenas noches*," she whispered back.

* * * * *

He surprised himself by sleeping more soundly than he had in days and awoke, guilt-ridden, knowing despite the lack of a watch or clock that he had slept well into the morning. All was quiet throughout the house. It was not until he made his way into the store, still struggling to come fully awake, that he realized he was not alone in the place as he first feared.

Mariana greeted him from behind the counter, where she sat perched on a stool, filling out lines in a large ledger. "I thought maybe you were going to sleep all day."

"I feel like I already have," he admitted, rubbing his unshaven jaw.

"Well, you look like it, too," she teased, running her fingers over his face, tracing something there. "You put your face against the hammock, yes? Because it is there."

"Oh, fine," he grimaced. "Maybe I'd better wash up before anyone comes in."

She showed him to the back of the house and a metal washbasin with a large pitcher of water, like the ceramic versions he had seen in many a Midwestern antique store. Funny what one place considers an antique, another still finds to be an item of daily necessity. Their water here, he knew, came from a well like he had not seen anywhere else in town—an indoor well, located in the concrete floor, between the restaurant and the store.

She chatted with him momentarily while he washed and fumbled with the razor from his bag.

"So how late is it anyway? Where is Imanuel this morning? And Paz?"

"It is nearly nine. Paz is helping Miguel make *arañas* this morning, you know, anchors for the nets. He has not said anymore about his net shuttle. I guess after what he heard about your little house, he didn't want to fuss about that anymore. I'm not sure where Imanuel is. He was gone when I got up, but I imagine Emelina knows. She is cooking. If you hurry, she might even make you some breakfast."

"And I'll hear about sleeping all day, too that way."

"She is up every morning by five or better. She does not understand people who are not, but then she is in bed by eight, too. She has no electricity in her little house on the beach, and she's—" She touched her elbow with her hand, the local sign for thrifty or cheap, depending on the point of view. "So much so that she only spends a little money on candles or kerosene, certainly not on electricity. She has always been that way." She grinned as she handed him a towel. "I am not sure she even knows there are people like you, who are still up at the outrageous hour of ten or eleven o'clock at night!"

A noise in the front pulled her back toward the store. Rick finished and made his way to the restaurant. He found Emelina, still in the kitchen, but her apron was pulled up around her wringing hands once more, and her tears fell freely.

"Niña Emelina." Rick was uncertain as to how to approach her. "Why the tears? What has happened?"

"Oh, I beg your pardon, don Ricardo." She dried her face at once and began to tend to the simmering rice and beans, bubbling over the fire. "I bring you your lunch at once."

"Calm down. There is no rush," he assured her. "I'm not that hungry right now. I can get something from the store later if you are not feeling well."

"There is nothing wrong with me," she sniveled. "You are simply looking at a foolish old woman, crying about things she can do nothing about."

"Everybody does that sooner or later." He tried to console her.

She gave him a little smile, although it did not reach her tear-swollen eyes as she prepared a plate for him. Mariana joined him.

"Paz came in and agreed to take care of the store for a few minutes," she explained as she sat down. "Of course, it will cost me a bit tonight when the carnival opens up again." The smile on her face said she really did not mind.

"Emelina," Mariana called out half-distractedly. "Where is Imanuel this morning?"

Silence was the only response.

"Emelina," she called again. "*Tía*, where are you?"

"I don't think she's feeling too well this morning."

"Why? What is the problem?"

The older woman came around the door, but she hung back, like a small child afraid of punishment, and the tears began again.

"Mariana." Her sobs punctuated her words. "He has gone for another body."

"*Santísima Madre de Díos*," Mariana crossed herself. "Where? Who?"

"The man's sister was here this morning at dawn, waiting for him when I arrived. From what she described, this one is the worst. They tortured the poor man with cigarettes. She said there were little burns all over him, and then she told about all the other things they had done to him. It was just like poor Simón." She heaved a ragged sigh.

"Ofelia said they were taking him back to her house, but she needed Imanuel to come to help with the burial preparations, as one representing the church. Her whole family is very Catholic, but they live so far up the road, they usually go to the church at San Marcos, rather than the one here."

"Ofelia? But isn't her brother—" Mariana hesitated.

Rick choked on the food in his mouth as something turned over sharply inside of him at that name. Up until this point, he had listened quietly, anxious for his friends and concerned especially for Imanuel, wondering why he did not ask him to go along this time.

"Are you all right?" Mariana frowned at him, as she continued to question her aunt. "Is her brother a soldier? Did she say? Who would do this to him? This is not the kind of thing the *muchachos* do. I do not understand."

"Who understands any of it?" Emelina snapped. "And who knows who does any of it? How can a person, any person, do these terrible things to another human being? They are not Christians. They are animals, every one of them."

"What is his name? I think I remember seeing him with Hector." Mariana continued to think aloud.

"His name is Alfredo." Rick's voice was so flat, both women turned to stare at him.

"You know him?" Mariana's surprise could be seen on her face.

He shook his head. "I came across him in the mountains with your cousin. And up there, I found out he has a sister named Ofelia." He pushed the food away. "Why did Imanuel go alone this morning?

Do you know?" He turned back to Emelina, his tone almost accusatory.

"I do not know. She was here so early and in a great hurry. Maybe he did not think about it. She was with a friend in a truck, and he went with them. Why? Does that mean something?"

"Maybe nothing. I'm not sure. I just don't like it." He stood up and walked out the back door toward the fishermen's beach. Mariana followed.

Once outside, she caught his arm. "What is it? You know something more. You can push Emelina aside like that, but not me. Now tell me."

He cast his eyes up to the brilliant sky and then back down to his feet, holding his head as if it might burst. "God, I don't like the way this is all coming together. They tore up my house yesterday, and we weren't sure why. But now maybe I know. How long would they have had Alfredo, do you suppose? A day or two, maybe more, to do all that they did."

"What are you talking about? Who is he?" Her voice rose in frustration.

"Alfredo was a soldier. The operative word is 'was.' He was one of the soldiers at the garrison that Franco and Elio took when I was with them in the mountains."

"And this Alfredo, he saw you?"

"Saw me? Franco had an entire conversation with him about me because he opened his mouth about the *gringo* rebel. That's how I knew his sister's name was Ofelia. Franco mentioned it. By the time Franco was finished with him, it sounded like his career in the army wasn't of his own choosing anyway. It sounded like he might decide to stay in the mountains. I don't know. I just had the idea from the things that were said that he would never say anything to anyone. It never occurred to me that the army or right-wing would get their information from him like this. Whoever it is that tortured him, he surely told them everything he knew, and what he thought he knew was that I was in the mountains fighting with Franco and his men."

"*Por Díos*. Imanuel. What has he walked into?" Her eyes filled with tears.

"Exactly." The last word escaped under his breath as he reached for her.

They collapsed in each other's arms, fearing the worst, afraid to say more.

"I'll go up there, wherever it is he went," he began, his mind racing, trying to determine the best course of action. "Maybe I can find him and get him out of there before it is too late."

"And what will that do?" She choked on her own words. "Then you will both be missing. I do not think it will help for you to go anywhere. You do not know who is there or what they really know. I could not bear to lose you both in the same day." She closed her eyes tight, trying to bring her own emotions under control.

"Do you know where he went?" Rick posed the question despite her objections.

"I know where Ofelia and her family used to live, but it has been a long time. Please, Rishard, we need to find another way."

"Do you have any ideas?"

"No," she sniffed. "But I do not like this one."

In front of the restaurant, Rick allowed Mariana to explain what little she felt was necessary to Emelina. Imanuel's sister-in-law confirmed the location of the family's house while Mariana made a case for the two of them simply going there to make certain Imanuel did not need any help. Meanwhile, Rick found the fishermen's cooperative truck was about to make a run for supplies to San Miguel. The driver was willing to give them a lift up the road.

The young driver, Chevez, was a cheerful sort and asked Rick a steady stream of questions about life in the United States on their drive. He related how he had made the trip once to California, entering the country as an illegal, in an attempt to work there. Chevez's adventure was short-lived, however, courtesy of an encounter with US Immigration officials. Despite the fact that he was deported back to El Salvador within weeks of his arrival, his opinion of the US remained jubilant.

"Even in jail, they fed us, and we had a bathroom, even a shower. The most amazing thing is that they gave me back my money that they took from me when I was arrested. No police officer here ever took your money and then gave it back." He laughed heartily. "Yours is a wonderful, exciting country."

Rick smiled in spite of his grim mood. At any other time, he would have had a number of friendly questions for the loquacious driver, but not today.

They thanked the driver for the ride as he dropped them off, just a kilometer or so from the village of San

Marcos located near the main highway. He refused to take any payment at Rick's offer. "My pleasure," he waved as he drove off. "*Que les vaya bien.*"

"The house was along this road," Mariana started off, down a dirt track, and Rick hurried after her. "There it is," she cried out as they topped the hill that blocked the view of the house from the road. "*Madre de Díos.*"

At first sight, only the roof was visible, but as they drew near, they could see the small house, which was not much bigger than Rick's own cabin, with a kitchen-porch attached at the back, had long been abandoned. Despite the obvious, they pushed open the creaking gate. Long grass surrounded the house on all sides. The front door stood wide open, and what remained of the shutters on the window hung in tatters at odd, useless angles. A thick layer of dust and sand lay undisturbed on the wooden slat floor.

"No one has been here for months." Mariana gave voice to what they both knew to be true. "There is nothing left for us to do here." They walked dejectedly back to the main road and were fortunate to catch the bus that was headed to *Las Palomitas*.

They saw Candelario standing at the back of the bus as they got on, but Mariana seemed in no great hurry to speak to him. Rick followed her lead, and after lifting his hand in greeting, they stood at the front of the bus while he remained at the back for the rest of the trip. Mariana told Rick she would think of something to share with Paz and Emelina but that she wanted to tell them as little as possible for the time being, and Rick agreed. Imanuel had beaten the odds once before.

"I know it is too much to hope for again," she acknowledged. "But a little hope and a great deal of prayer are all I have left."

It was a long hot afternoon followed by a sultry evening. Paz was eager to be off to the carnival again. Mariana encouraged him to go, despite his questions about Imanuel's whereabouts.

"There is another vigil up the road tonight," she told him as she handed him some extra spending money. "You know how faithful he is about that sort of thing. I am sure he will be home soon."

Emelina was not so easily persuaded. "You have not told me what you found at Ofelia's house," she told Mariana after Paz left and the kitchen was shut down for the night.

"Nothing," was Mariana's one-word answer.

"What do you mean? Nothing? What did the woman say?"

"I mean, nothing." Mariana did a poor job of fighting the rising panic in her voice. "There was no one there, and no one had been there for a very long time. I do not know where she lives now, but it is not the place we know."

"What do we do now?" Emelina whispered fearfully. "How can you sit here so calmly?"

"I am anything but calm, *Tía*," Mariana replied with strained kindness. "I do not have any answers for you. There is only one chance for him now." She came away from the doorway where she had watched Paz scamper off toward the bright lights. Inside, she swung the heavy door shut and threw the bolt across. High above on the hook to the right of the doorway, she retrieved a large key on a short leather strap.

She pulled a rosary of shiny black beads from her pocket. "It belonged to *mi mamá*," she said as much to herself as to anyone else.

Rick watched the two women walk toward the church.

He walked back through the restaurant and store, closing the connecting door between the two, before slipping back behind the curtain. He stopped at the little closet door. Up on the roof, alone, he surveyed the entire town, one last time in the fading twilight.

This was once mine, he thought, but no more. When the end would come, he was not sure, only that it would come and soon. He could barely see to the point in the hazy evening gloom, and the road disappeared to the left, lost in the shadow of the enveloping trees. Life as he had known it here would be no more. He could feel it. Even now, he could look across at the skittering lights of the carnival, and it was as if the world of the outside had invaded his private haven here. Maybe it was his own fault. He had listened little to David once he had arrived. His last words had held a powerful warning—don't stay too long. Now it was too late. How could he leave? He was without a passport, but more importantly, Mariana was without her father. He could not bring himself to abandon her at this moment, no matter what it cost.

"Fall down and worship me, and all of this shall be yours." The words came back to him from some faded Sunday school lesson. Is that what he had done? Concentrated on his own pride and his own needs alone. He thought of the two women in the church down the street and what he had received as a result of his time in this place. No, his was not the mortal sin of pride. He descended the narrow stairs and wandered down the street, entering the back of the church with caution, so as not to disturb their prayers.

Shadows danced on the walls in the weak flickering lights that came from the table on the sidewall, ablaze with multiple candles. They blended into a mass of melted wax as the flames carried their votive prayers a bit closer to heaven. Mariana knelt, alone on the hard tile floor at the front, her head covered and bowed. Rick sat down on the last pew and dropped his head to offer his own private petition.

After a time, he raised his face to watch the solitary figure before him. Her silhouette appeared to quiver in the weak illumination provided by the sputtering candles, but he was equally certain she was solid and unmoving in her station of solitude. He crept forward, tempted to listen to the whisperings of her lips that he could hear, but not quite understand.

"Bring him back. He is your servant. Bring him back." She repeated again and again, the rosary beads still wound tightly around her cupped hands.

Closer now, he could see that the candles had not deceived him. She was swaying, rhythmically as if in a trance, moving in time to her own words. "Bring him back. He is your servant."

Startled, he reached out and touched her. She leaped as if he had dripped hot wax on her shoulder, before sagging into an exhausted heap. "Rishard, *por el amor de Díos*. I did not know anyone else was in here!"

"I'm so sorry," he began at once. "I was worried about you. I didn't mean to scare you."

"It is all right," she said as she climbed to her feet. He put out a steadying hand to her. "I should have left earlier. Emelina decided to go home. She said she would say her prayers there."

They walked out, and she locked the heavy door behind them.

It was both too early and too late, Rick thought. Too early to go home to bed and try to blot out the reality of this day with sleep and dreams. Too late to do anything that might have any effect on Imanuel's fate.

The two of them sat in the darkened restaurant, silently watching the carnival celebration in the distance. A light breeze brought the scent of cold ashes from the kitchen.

"A penny for your thoughts, you once told me when we sat across the way at Marielos' café." Rick finally broke the silence.

She looked down at the floor. "And you told me that day that they were not worth even that much."

She continued in a wistful manner. "I was just thinking of Imanuel, praying even now for him wherever he might be. He is like Paz, you know. He loves the carnival. He may be an old man, but he is still child enough that he always rides, too."

"Really? I'd like to see that."

"Maybe if we are extraordinarily fortunate, you will."

He slipped an arm around her and the dam that had held all day in the face of others, broke as she sobbed softly on his shoulder.

A shadow slipped into the restaurant from the side, a movement Rick only half saw before the voice calmed his alarm.

"He is not at a vigil, is he?" was all he said.

"Oh, Pazito. I am so sorry," she spoke through her tears. "I did not want you to know, to worry any more—"

"I know." He let out a heavy sigh as he seated himself on the table, his feet resting on the bench where she sat. "No one ever wants the children to know anything bad."

She patted his leg. "I should have known better. That you are not a little boy anymore."

He leaned over and kissed her lightly on the forehead. The three stayed there, in the darkness, silently leaning on one another, for quite some time. As the carnival lights shut down, Paz announced he was going to bed.

"Come on." Rick urged Mariana in the same direction.

They curled up together in the hammock, neither expecting to get any sleep, but knowing, too, they would not sleep separately either. He pulled a thin bedspread over the two of them. Somewhere before dawn, they both drifted into a fitful doze.

CHAPTER 16

*M*arch 24, 1980. San Salvador. El Salvador's Archbishop Oscar A. Romero was assassinated by a lone gunman while he celebrated Mass in a cancer hospital in the capital tonight. The martyred archbishop, a former Nobel Peace Prize nominee, was the leader of the church in this country that is 80% Catholic. Since becoming archbishop, he has been viewed as a controversial figure by both the Salvadoran and US governments, as he led the church in demanding greater emphasis on human rights issues. Earlier this year, he wrote a letter to the American administration asking them to halt a shipment of US military aid to the Salvadoran government armed forces which the archbishop and others have accused of assaulting and murdering their own people.

A woman's excruciating scream roused them in the first gray light of dawn. Rick slipped from Mariana's grasp as she began to rouse and headed quickly out the door.

"*Qué pasa?*" she called after him but he did not take the time to answer.

Others were scurrying as he stumbled into the street and followed the dreadful sound, coming from around the corner.

He hung on the church door, crucified there, in an old-fashioned monk's robe, which hid his face. The pool of blood gathered beneath him from where it had run down and dripped off of his bare, lifeless feet, said that the poor man no longer felt the pain of what had been done to him.

Two women were trying to comfort the now sobbing woman who had apparently made the grisly discovery. The others stood in various stages of shock, staring, yet not believing. Rick gingerly pulled the hood back far enough to reveal his friend's face, a map of agony and torment to the last. A small cardboard placard around his neck read DEATH TO ALL PRIESTS.

He dropped the covering back into place and turned back, hoping to be in time, yet knowing he could not stop her. Mariana reeled around the corner as he caught her up in his arms.

"No!" he shouted, but her scream too was already in the air. He gathered her up as she broke down, abandoning her last reserve of hope. A sleepy-eyed teenager met them as he carried her in the front door.

"What's going on?"

"Don't go out there!" Rick commanded.

Paz jumped back without question.

"I'm sorry." Rick laid the comatose woman on the sofa. "Get me a pillow, please. And a little water."

Paz did as he was told. "Is she hurt badly?"

"It's your father." Rick's own words welled up in his throat. "They killed him, Paz. He's outside, his body. You don't want to see."

There was no keeping him now. Rick let him go, and the rest of the day seemed to pass by his eyes in similar chaotic fashion, bits and pieces falling together and then apart.

Emelina's arrival, after she, too, had followed the crowd to the tragic site at the door of the church. The borrowed hammer he used to pull the nails from his crucified friend. The wretched touch of the broken bones as he held the fractured body in his arms before laying him in the fresh pine coffin, now in the restaurant. The cascade of fresh flowers, the perfume of the flowers and pine branches, collected by Paz and Emelina. Miguel's clumsy movements as he tried not to show how deeply he hurt and how much he already missed his younger brother. And worst of all, the hollow-eyed leaden movements of the beautiful woman who was once again reduced to silence by ineffable grief.

"Maybe we should call don Carlos," Emelina finally voiced an opinion as she watched Mariana touch each of the flowers encircling Imanuel's shrouded form as she stood before the casket.

"Do you know where he is?" Rick was surprised that he did not find the thought particularly alarming. Any kind of help for her would be agreeable to him at this point.

"No. I thought maybe you did." Emelina turned to Rick.

"I only knew he was going to Europe on business. He told Imanuel and Mariana, I think. I thought you knew, too."

"Europe," she sighed. "That is all I know. There is an office in the capital where we sometimes call to leave a message. I called Chirilagua, and they are sending someone tomorrow. I did not want him to be buried without a priest."

Rick smiled sadly at the thought.

As the villagers began to stop by that evening, it was clear that the people had lost their earlier reticence that had kept them away from Simón's funeral. Most of the town filed through, filling the restaurant with those who had once been helped by this simple church catechist. With the outpouring of affection and concern, from her childhood friends and neighbors, Mariana seemed to return to the world before her, responding to the greetings and embraces showered upon her.

Sonia and her husband Andres came, as did so many whose children had been vaccinated. Members of the fishermen's cooperative entered the house as a delegation while others gathered closely around Miguel, their brother fisherman. There were dozens of people Rick had never seen before as well as familiar faces, like five-year-old Carmen, who now sported a singularly stiff but still very present thumb, along with her mother. Gilberto and Silvia and different ones Rick recognized from the day of the parade as well as many recipients of the clothes and food he had helped Imanuel distribute—they all came to tell Mariana and Paz of their appreciation of their father. Rick wondered how many others, like Fabiano, Ana, and Franco would also have come if they did not fear a similar fate. Into the late hours of the night, the vigil continued.

Even into the next morning, Rick discovered a number of people standing outside the restaurant, waiting to make the long walk with them to the cemetery.

By mid-morning as the appointed hour approached, the large crowd blocked the street. The bus was obliged to unload a block from its usual stop beneath the large tree. A small sedan pulled up behind the bus, and Rick was surprised to see three Americans climb out and come toward the restaurant.

"Great," he thought at first glance. "Someone else to tell, sorry, no food today." As he watched them make their way through the crowd, he realized he was mistaken.

The tall thin man dressed in black slacks and a black shirt and the women dressed in white blouses and dark skirts were not dressed for the beach. Mariana came out of the back in a black dress of mourning, a black lace scarf falling across her shoulders as they came in the front door.

"*Padre*." She welcomed the tall Irish-American priest who greeted her with an embrace. "Sister Dorothea, Niña Elenita. We so appreciate you coming today."

"We are the ones who come to express our appreciation at your father's incredible sacrifice, Mariana. Appreciation and sorrow that it would all end this way."

The crucifixes that all three wore sparkled as Rick was introduced to Father Dennis, Sister Dorothy, and Elena, a Catholic volunteer, all of them originally from Cleveland but now of the mission in Chirilugua, just up the Salvadoran coast.

"How long have you been here? Where are you from? So you are the one Imanuel spoke of who was helping him." Their questions were friendly, far from intrusive, and yet suddenly overwhelming to Rick as he thought about the many simple questions he would face once he returned to the United States. It was the answers that would break his heart, he thought.

Emelina handed out cold drinks, and after a sip, Dennis's attention turned to the restive crowd outside. "They are still coming. I suppose we'd best get started."

The fishermen's cooperative truck, parked since early morning in the alley alongside the store, was now brought to the front where Miguel and a few of his fellow fishermen loaded the casket into the back.

Padre Dionisio donned his priestly vestments, and the ladies flanked Mariana, one on each side as they began the long walk, following the truck. Paz, Rick, Emelina, and Miguel, as well as much of the village of *Las Palomitas*, trailed after them.

He had walked this road dozens of times now, but never before had Rick noticed how many dwellings were nestled back in the trees as well as the number that were built up close along the sandy drive. He would not have seen them today except that in front of so many otherwise invisible grass and stick shacks, someone came outside to stand watch, bow their head, and acknowledge their passing.

Women with small children, old people who were not strong enough to make the trek with them, individuals who, for whatever reason, did not join the mourners, still came out to add a prayer to the procession.

The heat of the late morning had intensified by the time they neared their destination. Rick kept a close eye on Mariana, who seemed surprisingly calm this morning. He was grateful for the gentle sea breeze that provided a cooling touch as they rounded the last curve before ascending to the tiny cemetery.

The grave had already been dug, much to Rick's surprise, until he looked at Paz, who turned up palms that included a new blister.

"I always knew it would be my place to do this for my father one day," he whispered to Rick alone. "I just never thought it would be so soon."

The pine box was lifted from the truck by many hands and gentled settled beside the grave. Father Dennis spoke in Spanish, delivering a heart-wrenching eulogy. As he listened, Rick learned that Imanuel had been one of the first catechists that the American priest had trained years before upon his arrival in El Salvador. He spoke of Imanuel's faith and incredible devotion to do what he knew to be right, even when the personal risk involved was so great.

"Most of you who stand here today have been helped over the years by what this man did. You knew as we all know now that it was not safe or easy for him to do the things he did, but he never stopped to consider that. His only thought was that a need existed and that a person with that need waited for him.

"Our hearts are heavy as we come here today, trying to understand that which cannot be understood. Our Lord told us that to follow him would not be easy and that it would mean hardship and even death for some here on earth. Imanuel Flores knew that, but it did not stop him. If we each leave here today with that same spirit in our hearts, the one that empowered him, I think he would consider it the finest compliment—to live as he did, to care as he did for each and every one, neighbor or stranger, old friend or newcomer..."

Rick did not hear much of the rest as he dropped his eyes and tried to control the burgeoning sorrow welling up inside. Mariana's head was also bowed, but she seemed to be holding up well from what he could tell.

The priest finished, and the lid was fastened into place. The casket was lowered by ropes into the waiting earth. Mariana took a fistful of soil and dropped it in afterward along with one of the flowers. The dirt made a hollow thud as it hit the top of the wooden coffin. Paz did the same as did Emelina and Miguel and even Rick. Soon all those who had come made a long line, each adding their small contribution.

The Americans stood outside the gate and makeshift fence and spoke to many of those in the crowd as they filed past. "*Gracias, muchas gracias*" was repeated again and again. Only one older woman stopped to ask Father Dionisio, "who will care for us now, *Padre*? Who will care for our church?"

"I don't know," the cleric answered honestly. "We will see in time. God will let us know in the days to come."

She nodded. "Yes, He will. We must have faith." She went on her way with her head bowed like all the rest.

"Mariana wanted us to talk to you." The priest looked directly at Rick, speaking in English for the first time. "She says your passport was stolen, and you need to get back to the American Embassy in San Salvador."

Rick was mildly surprised but couldn't deny the truth in the statement. "Yes, that's true, I suppose."

"When we leave here, we're on our way there," Elena explained. "We'd be glad to take you along. It would certainly make a much safer trip for you than trying to go across the country any other way, with no passport or other identification."

"Yeah, I'm sure that's true but..." He turned back to look at Mariana. She was sitting on the remains of the pile of dirt beside the grave. All the others had made their additions and were on their way out, many already walking back toward *Las Palomitas*. She picked up another handful and let it trickle between her fingers.

"It does not matter now, *Papí*." Her words were soft and hard to understand, almost as if she were in prayer. "I'll be with you soon—"

Emelina's shriek spun him around. "You witch! I could kill you with my own hands! How dare you show your face here after what you did!" Emelina was a formidable sight as she lumbered down the hill, directing her fury at a woman close to Mariana's age who had come from the direction of the highway.

"Emelina!" The reproof came from above as Mariana stood up and made her way, like a princess from on high, toward the two of them.

"Ofelia," Mariana spoke first.

"Niña Mariana. I came only to beg your forgiveness and to tell you the truth. I did not know when I came for your father's help. I swear I had no idea what they would do."

"What who would do?"

"One of the soldiers told me to go for don Imanuel. He said that they had my brother, Alfredo with them and that he was badly hurt. He said he needed a priest for last rites and that we should bring the catechist since there was no priest closer. We had not heard from him in so long. We did not even know where he was, if he was alive or dead." She began to cry as she continued. "He told me to go and ask for the catechist at *Las Palomitas.* I told him we go to the church at San Marcos, but he said they had already been there and that no one was at that church. I did not know. I had no reason not to believe him. He said Alfredo was in trouble and that he was a traitor. He scared me so, and I believed him. I just wanted to help my brother."

"And you believed him?" Mariana echoed her words.

"I wanted to believe there was a chance for my brother. I had no idea what he was really talking about. The last time I had seen Alfredo, he was in a soldier's uniform, but when I returned with don Imanuel, we found Alfredo dead, and they grabbed don Imanuel and took him away." The weeping took her over. "I swear I did not even know about don Imanuel's death until this morning."

"Liar," Emelina hissed. "You are worse than Judas. At least he did not lie about what he did."

"No," Mariana reached out to her. "We are all doing whatever we have to right now, to save the ones we love. I am sorry for your loss, too, Niña. From what I was told, Alfredo made his choice to try to be a good man, but it is dangerous now for all of our young men. Tell me just one thing. Do you know the name of the soldier who told you this?"

She shook her head. "No. I was too afraid to ask anything. I do not know any names, only that he is one of those who commands the others."

"One who commands," Mariana repeated the words, more to herself than to anyone else.

She hugged the struggling woman. "Can you make it home?" she asked. "Where do you live now?"

"Not far from here," was her reply. "I am so sorry about your father."

"And I, for your brother." Mariana turned back toward Rick and the other Americans.

Paz was finishing the job he had begun, with the shovel in his hand.

"Wait, Paz," Rick headed in his direction. "I will help you."

"No." The youth smiled at the offer through his tears in a way that made him look so much older than his years. "I need to finish this myself. You do not need to wait for me, please. It will be good to be alone for a little while now."

"Of course." Rick moved back toward the others.

"The fishermen want to know if you want to ride back in the truck," Miguel asked.

"No," Mariana shook her head. "We have plans to make as we walk. You are going with them, yes?" She looked at Rick as if she were discussing the weather or something equally unimportant.

"Now wait a minute," he began to protest in English. "I do need to get back to San Salvador, but not today. Now is not the time—"

"Now you have a ride, a safe ride to get you where you need to go. It is the perfect time, really. Heaven only knows when you might get another chance like this." She set a brisk pace for all of them, walking back toward the village.

"Things are getting worse, more dangerous, even for Americans," Sister Dorothy added in a gentle manner. "I worked in La Union until recently, but now we've been transferred to Zaragoza, a city closer to the capital, outside La Libertad. If you are without identification, it really would be better for you to come with us."

As he glanced at the perky blond nun, Rick thought how she could easily have been a former cheerleader, lifeguard, or girls' camp counselor. How did she end up a missionary in the Third World, he wondered vaguely.

"I appreciate the offer, I really do." He tried to explain. "Please don't misunderstand." He was trying to recall something he had seen or heard but not quite understood, something that didn't quite make sense yet. "It just really isn't practical right now."

"Of course, it is. We are even walking past your house." Mariana's sudden efficiency was maddening.

"What are you doing?" he muttered under his breath as he dropped in to walk beside her. "Are you suddenly that anxious to see me go?"

A sober gaze, all but devoid of emotion, was her only immediate response. "Please, Rishard, don't fight this anymore. It is the only way. Even you said you cannot stay here forever, and you are right. Today is as good a day as any to go back to your life. You have a safe way back now. Please take it."

She stopped at the pine grove where the road came closest to the beach, just outside his cabin door. "If you pack your things, I am sure they will wait for you. Emelina and I will make all of you something to eat before you go," she announced to the others.

"Please, Mariana, not on such a day would we expect you to do that." The priest shook his head. "Our time is short. It is still a long drive to the capital. We can take some of Emelina's wonderful tortillas with us, a little cheese and some cold drinks. We don't need anything else."

"I understand," she answered with a small nod. "God bless you, *Padre*." The group continued on, leaving a bewildered, tall blond man standing alone in front of his cabin door.

Despite their best efforts, the interior was still little more than a tattered remnant of what it had once been. Unwilling to spend any more time and emotion on things he could not change, Rick angrily stuffed a few possessions and the last of his clothes into his duffel bag and threw it in a corner.

He allowed himself a last look at the ocean from beneath the palm tree and *caserinos* outside, before marching down the beach toward the elephantine steel structures of the carnival, asleep in the midday sun.

At the restaurant, he found the Americans waiting patiently. To see them from the street, they looked like nothing more than friends who had come for a visit. Mariana's cool mask slid into place upon his arrival. "Nobody can keep a secret like Mariana." Franco's words echoed in the back of his mind as his heart sank at the sight of her.

"Ready?" the priest asked cheerily. "No luggage?"

"I left it at the cabin," Rick mumbled. "I thought it would be easier to just pick it up along the way."

"That'll be fine. Ladies?" He turned and waved to Emelina, who was once more at her station in the kitchen, patting out tortillas.

"With all my heart, I wish we had come for some other reason." Father Dionisio sandwiched Mariana's one hand, between his two. "You know I have not been here for some time now, as I have been assigned elsewhere. I am here only on a visit, but when Emelina called, I knew we must come. If you need anything at all, you know you can call the mission. There are still some old friends there, like Elena here, and there are others, too. They are all always willing to help. Promise me, you will call if any of us can be of any help to you."

"Thank you," Mariana answered in English. "For all that you did for my father over the years and for today. We will manage. Your training, his work in the church, it gave him a life he cherished, *Padre*. Thank you for that, too."

She took a deep breath. "We must find the strength to go on. God will give us that. He always gave it to Imanuel. Come and see us when you can, *Padre*. Niña Elena, Madre Dorotea, you, too. I know you love the beach. We miss you. Come back to us soon."

They each hugged her in turn.

"I want to talk to you," Rick said, none-too-politely as he took hold of her arm.

The priest took in the scene and cocked a curious eye in Rick's direction. "We'll wait for you at the car."

"What the hell is really going on here?" he demanded once they were behind the curtain. "What are you doing to us?"

"Us?" she snorted. "You Americans are always so *dramático*. What 'us?' There is nothing. We are nothing. You have a life in the United States. Go back to it. I have a life here. I have a brother and an aunt to take care of now, and Carlos will be back from Europe soon. There is no place left for you here."

He struggled for the words that would not come. "We buried your father a short time ago, and now you expect me to just walk away? I love you. You must know that by now, and I'm pretty damn sure you love me. I can't just walk away, Mariana."

"Fine, have it your way. Then I will." She tried to push past him on her way back to the store, but she was not quick enough. He had never held a woman against her will, not even for a moment, but she responded to his kiss and his passion as she held him as tightly as he held her. Thank God, he almost breathed a sigh of relief as he loosened his hold on her.

She tilted her face up toward him with a small tight smile. "Go home, *gringo*. You have a few memories now to take with you. *Que te vaya bien*." She turned toward Imanuel's bedroom door and slammed the door behind her. He heard the bolt lock into place.

He picked up his bag and slipped into the back seat of the waiting car. "I'm sorry to have kept you waiting," was all he said.

"It's no problem," the priest assured him, looking at him by way of the rearview mirror as he started the engine. At the cabin, Rick grabbed the duffel bag and threw it into the open trunk.

"You sure had a beautiful view here. I would imagine you'll miss this place a great deal, won't you?"

"Yeah," Rick slumped into the back seat once again beside Elena. "More than you can imagine."

The car lurched back onto the main road, and Rick nearly missed Paz as he walked by, carrying the shovel. "Wait!" he spoke more sharply than he intended as the youth caught sight of him. The priest brought the car to a quick stop, and Rick stepped out, but Paz did not stop. He waved but began to trot in the other direction, away from them.

Dumbfounded, Rick climbed back inside.

"Don't take it too hard." Dennis's words of comfort floated to him through the fog of hurt and confusion that enveloped him. "He is a special friend to you, isn't he? No boy that age wants to be caught crying."

"I didn't even think of that," Rick stammered.

"Didn't you?" The man's voice was barely audible. "I'd say you feel about the same way right now."

Rick stared out the window as the beach slipped further away. He dared not look at any of them, and his chest ached, and his head throbbed as they passed the curve of the cemetery once more. A colorful clutter of flowers covered the newest grave. A farewell caress, the soft breeze from the beach touched his cheek as he glimpsed the blue water and tawny sand at the last turn.

He leaned his head back and closed his eyes. What was it she said, there at the last? The memory from earlier in the day that he could not let go, even now.

She had said so many things to him over the past few months, yet her behavior today seemed to say none of them mattered. Why was it he could not make himself believe she really wanted him to go?

He had watched her these last weeks and months, dealing with Raúl's fury at the dance and at his house, "There is nothing you can do," she told him bravely withstanding his scrutiny in front of the whole town. And she had repeated that same thing later that evening when Rick asked her about it. "They cannot hurt me anymore," she said. "Whatever you do, it changes nothing for me," she told him when she demanded Imanuel's release. Then there were the fainting spells, the times when she couldn't breathe, but it was more than that. There were Franco's words echoing in his head again. 'Nobody can keep a secret like Mariana.' And now this morning, her words as she sat at Imanuel's gravesite, "I'll be joining you soon."

"Stop! Stop, please." Rick lurched forward and grabbed the driver's shoulder, startling the man into an immediate halt.

"What? What is it? Did you forget something? You scared the heck out of me, son!" The priest spun around to look at Rick, but he was already out of the car.

Father Dennis followed as Rick danced with impatience beside the trunk of the car.

"I'm sorry to have been such a pain in the neck," Rick apologized. "I did forget something, and I've got to go back and take care of it. There isn't time to explain, and for that, I apologize." He heaved his duffel back onto his shoulder and shook the startled priest's hand. "Thanks again for all your trouble."

"Do you want us to take you back?"

"No, I'll catch a ride. Somebody will come along. Thanks again," he called over his shoulder as he started off at a brisk pace.

The two women were also out of the car. "Dennis, are you really going to let him go?" Elena asked her in her best imitation of a mother hen. "He does need to get to San Salvador in the worst way."

"I don't see what else I can do about it." The priest shrugged as he returned to the driver's seat. "He's obviously made up his mind. He's young, and if I don't miss my guess, in love, one way or another. All we can do now is pray he'll be all right."

"May God bless him," Sister Dorothy spoke softly, watching him go.

The sedan went on its way, moving to the far side of the road to allow a passing flatbed truck the space needed to get by.

"Hey, *gringo*, you need a ride?" The leering face of Sgt. Fuentes appeared in the passenger window as the truck pulled to a stop alongside Rick.

His blood chilled at the sight of the man who had undoubtedly had a hand in the murder of his friend. It has not occurred to him until this moment that he might have been the one that Ofelia had spoken of, one who commands? Or was it Hernandez? He debated silently whether refusing the lift might make the officer even more suspicious.

"Where is your Jeep today?" Rick forced himself to be friendly despite his suddenly parched throat.

"The lieutenant had other business," Fuentes smiled with no warmth. "And the vehicle goes with him. Are you coming? There is no room up here, of course."

"*No problema*. I prefer the fresh air." Rick tossed his bag onto the flatbed and clamored in on shaking knees.

Standing over the cab with the sea breeze in his face, he gained a new appreciation for why so many in the country, rode in open trucks and the *cobradores* who rode the buses on the outside of the big vehicles. The rushing wind in his face afforded a sense of freedom, denied to the common people here in so many other aspects of daily life. Although he could not explain it, he felt better now than he had in days. How could he have not seen it sooner? All the signs were there in front of him, and yet he had not put it all together until now.

The truck slowed for a small herd of cattle. Rick took comfort in the charming antics of the newborn velvet-skinned calves, running full tilt with their tails in the air like miniature flags, warning all of the imminent danger.

Fuentes left the truck a short distance from where Rick was picked up.

"*Adíos, gringo*," he called back as he sauntered away down a side road. "Hey." He turned back sharply. "I never did see your papers."

Rick shrugged as if he could not hear over the noise of the shifting gears and threw his hands high in exasperation. The soldier laughed, waved, and continued on his way. "At your house one day soon," he called over the noise of the departing truck.

The soldier continued walking away and a shiver passed over Rick as he considered how he might best avoid the inquisitive Sgt. Fuentes in the future.

Back at *Las Palomitas*, Rick threw his bag in a corner of the living room behind the store, past the separating curtain. The store remained closed. The sound of muffled weeping guided him to her small room, a place he had never seen, tucked behind Imanuel's room.

He stood for a moment in the doorway, watching her, his heart breaking as she sat on the bed, her face in her hands.

"I know the truth now, Mariana, and I won't be leaving again." His words were gentle, but the resolution in his voice was ironclad.

She nearly fell in her surprise as she jumped up. "What are you doing here?" She flew at him with fists pounding on his shoulders. "You are supposed to be gone, to get out and never come back! What have you done? Why?"

He grabbed her flailing hands. "Because now I know. I know the truth."

"What are you talking about? You do not know anything."

"I know you lied to me that day on the island when you said there is nothing seriously wrong with you. Is that why you came back? Why you would never answer my questions before? I know your heart is weak, so weak that..." He didn't finish.

Her eyes widened in horror. She stopped fighting, but her words were no less angry. "How did you find out? No one knew except Carlos and Imanuel, and they swore they would never tell."

"You told me." His words were loving now, and he reached out to hug her close. "You told me in a dozen little ways. I just never realized it until today."

They sat down together on the bed, and he held her while she cried anew at the revelation of her secret. "Now you know why I cannot leave with you, no matter how many times you ask."

He did not speak at first. He just held her, while leaning against the iron bedstead, stroking her hair in comfort like he would a child.

"Tell me, what is really wrong with your heart?" He asked after a time. "Was it rheumatic fever?"

She nodded. "Nobody knew for a long time. It comes years later sometimes, the doctors said. I saw specialists in Houston and in New York. Carlos took me, and he wanted to take me to another doctor in Europe, but I said no. They all said the same. The valves in the heart are damaged, and they cannot be fixed. They cannot replace them, even as they replace a whole heart sometimes now. Someday, they say, maybe but not now. I told Carlos I was tired. It was time for this little village girl to just come home. We argued about it more than once, and that is why I came home on the bus the first time. I left him a note and just came by myself. Once I was here, he finally agreed."

She sighed. "I knew coming home would not be easy, but I never thought it would cost Imanuel his life. I never thought I would come back here and meet someone..." She began to cry again.

"I know." He hugged her closer, but he did not try to stop her tears. "I know."

She cried herself to sleep in his arms, and he too dozed in the afternoon heat. A noise in one of the other rooms startled him awake, and he slipped from beneath her to go investigate.

"*Puchica!* I thought you left!" Rick's appearance made Paz jump. He put down the cold beers he was carrying and threw his arms around his friend in a sudden display of emotion. "I am glad you did not go. It probably would have been better for you, but it was too much, especially today." He picked up the chilled brown bottles again.

"What are you doing with these?"

"My Uncle Miguel and some of his friends are next door. They are resting and remembering, telling stories about my father and Miguel and their older brother when they were younger."

"Older brother? There is another? I never heard about him."

"He is older than Miguel even. Ricardo was his name, too, just like you. He left them when they were still in the mountains. It has been years since they saw him, but Miguel is a little—" He made a tipsy motion with his head since his hands were full. "Today is the kind of day when you do things you do not usually do, yes?"

Rick nodded with a grin and rubbed the back of his neck.

"Do you want to come and sit with them?"

"No, maybe later. I want to stay close to her right now." He tipped his head back toward the bedroom. "She's sleeping now, but I don't want her to wake up and be alone."

"That is good," Paz agreed. "She is not doing nearly so well as she likes to make people think. Emelina is worried about her, too."

"Where is she anyway?"

Paz made a face. "Candelario came by and took her to his house. He said she needed to rest. He was trying to be nice to her, I think, but he does not know her so well. She is better if she is busy. She did not want to go. Up there, there is no one to cook for, no one to fuss over."

Rick laughed in spite of the situation. "You don't think she would just like to be alone and rest for a time by herself?"

"Not *mi tía*, no. That is not her way." Paz was emphatic.

"And you, Paz. How are you doing?" Rick could not help but ask.

"I will be all right, I think. I have to be, yes? My father talked to me more than once, warning me that something like this might happen. I have known for a long time it might end this way. It does not mean I will not miss him terribly." His eyes dropped to the floor. "I have to get these to them. Come out later if you like."

"Thanks, maybe I will." Rick slipped back into the bedroom and was soon fast asleep beside her once again.

He awoke later, disoriented, unsure of where he was, at first. It was the first time he had slept in a bed with a regular mattress in months, and he slept much more soundly than he had expected. Outside, on the back porch, he discovered the last rays of the setting sun could still be seen, reflecting off the water. Mariana slipped up behind him, still rubbing the sleep from her eyes.

They stood together on the porch, their arms wrapped securely around one another as they looked over the waters of the *estero*. "Is it possible that only a few days ago, we played in this water as if we had not a single worry in the world?" she whispered.

"Yes, it wasn't so very long ago."

"Are you hungry? Maybe Emelina left us something in the kitchen," she continued. "Did you know she went to Candelario's house?"

"Paz said he came by to get her." They walked through the silent house together. The harsh reality of the situation stung him once again at the sight of Imanuel's desk in the corner, with its dog-eared Bible, lying in the midst of the business paperwork.

"It was strange," Mariana continued. "She told me *en secreto*, she would be back at her own house tonight and that I should come by and see her later, but he kept insisting that she should plan to spend the night up there with him. He said she works too hard here and that she should rest."

"Paz didn't seem to think much of the idea either. He said that wasn't the kind of thing Emelina would like."

Mariana snorted. "That is the truth. Emelina is not a sitting still person. She does work hard, but that is the way she is. Everybody works harder than Candelario. Maybe that is the part he cannot understand."

He laughed. "You and Paz don't think much of him, do you?"

"Oh, he is all right, I suppose. He does not bother me, so why should I care as long as he makes her happy? Look here. She left us a pot of fish head soup and tortillas."

"Sounds great." His enthusiasm did not match his words.

"Oh, it is fine. I swear Americans get such funny ideas. The fish is just what is left when fillets are cut from a big *corbina* or red snapper. That is a lot of fish. There are no bones or eyes or anything else left in the soup, just fish."

"Well, if you said fish head, that is what it sounds like is in there." He tried to justify his reticence.

"It has fish and vegetables and potatoes. You will like it. With *Semana Santa*, you are not going to find Emelina cooking meat right now. Be glad she did not make us salt fish."

"I suppose that is true." Rick thought of the dried fish he had seen around the fishermen's cooperative and different people's huts. For months, the fish had been salted and hung on lines like laundry to dry. Once dried, it could be stored anywhere and then cooked in boiling water to wash out the salt, when it was time for a meal.

"Emelina loves to make that. She says it shows proper respect, *sacrificio*." Mariana sat two bowls of the steaming soup on the table, along with a stack of cold tortillas, which they tore into pieces and dropped into the soup. They ate alone in the darkened restaurant.

"I hope you do not mind if I do not put on the lights."

"It's fine with me."

"If I put on the lights, people will come, and I am not ready for that."

"I understand." He took a sip of the broth and was pleasantly surprised at the smoky flavor.

"Even the people of the carnival said they will run their machines tonight but with many fewer lights, out of respect for Imanuel," Mariana told him. "I thought that was especially kind."

"It is," he agreed. "Oh, did you see this?" She pulled a slip of paper from her pocket, a note from Paz. "He says he has gone to your cabin tonight for a little while, to be alone. He is a funny boy, sometimes." There was half a question in her voice at the look on Rick's face.

"No, it's fine. I just worry. After what happened there and..."

"What? What is it?"

He heaved a sigh, irritated with himself for having even mentioned it. "I saw Sgt. Fuentes today. He was in the truck that gave me a ride back to town, and as he left, he asked me about my papers again."

"He what? When he is probably the one who stole them in the first place. *Hijo de*—"

"Mariana," Rick was mildly surprised. He had not heard her talk that way before.

"Well, he is. He and Hector both. I cannot believe still that it might have been Hector who took Imanuel away. He must have handed him over to someone, some group. I don't know—"

"Don't. Don't think about it now. Please." Rick reached a hand across the table. "Come on. You were the one who was hungry, remember? Go ahead and eat up, and don't think about the other."

She nodded and swiped at her nose with a handkerchief. "Maybe we should go find Paz if you think it is not safe."

"I don't know for certain, but I'd feel better if he was here. He was with Miguel at his house this afternoon and some of the other fishermen. I guess they had a sort of fishermen's wake for Imanuel there."

She smiled. "They do that sometimes. It is the only time Miguel drinks." She took a deep breath. "I can walk to Emelina's little house while we go. That way, I will not need to stay too long, and you and Paz can stop for me on your way back, yes?"

"Sure." He was pleased to see she was making plans, even little ones like this. A few hours ago, she had all but thrown him out. "I'm coming back here."

"And tomorrow? What will you do then?"

"Tomorrow," he sighed. "I'll call the American Embassy and try to figure out how to straighten out at least a part of this from here. After that, I don't know. I can only take things one step at a time. That's what I've done ever since I came here, you know." He looked at her with a hint of laughter in his eyes.

"Be careful, Rishard." This time it was her hand that came across the table to grasp his. "I wanted you to go because I know it would be safer for you. Only God knows what will happen in this place tomorrow."

"Safer is not always better." He smiled back at her. "We'll worry about this later. Let's go get Paz for now."

They left the dishes on the table as they went out the door. After a couple nights of bright carnival lights, the street was noticeably darker tonight, Rick thought as they strolled along. The stars, clinging to the treetops in the black velvet sky, were clear and bright enough to provide their own weak light. Once in the shadows, he found himself wishing they had walked up the beach instead. As she slipped her warm hand into his, he knew he was not the only one made uncomfortable by the imposing gloom.

"Are you sure Emelina will be there?" Rick asked as they neared her house.

"Yes, I am sure that is what she said." Mariana nodded as she released his hand. "Go tell Paz it is time to come home, and by the time you get back here, I will be ready to go home." She slipped off into the darkness and was instantly out of his sight.

He picked up his pace, trying to shake the nervousness that had descended upon him ever since they left the lights of the village behind. In the dark, he could hear, or rather sense, the passing of another person, since feet made little or no sound on the soft dusty sand of the road.

"*Buenas noches*," Rick finally spoke.

"*Buenas noches*." The voice at his side was heart-stoppingly close when the man did speak. The lit end of a cigarette glowed as the man brought it up near his face. It made Rick think of Mariana's story of the *Siguanaba*. He walked on, without further incident, but Rick was more than happy to see the lantern burning in his own cabin as he approached.

"Paz," he called out, and he heard a sudden scramble as he pushed the door open. "Oh Paz..."

The youth sat on the floor before him, a large wooden cross in front of him. Paz held Imanuel's carving tools in his hands, where he was fashioning a cross with Imanuel's name on it.

* * * * *

As Mariana walked toward her aunt's small house, she regretted not having asked Rick to accompany her. Maybe it was the oppressive darkness, made worse tonight by the moonless sky over *Las Palomitas*. Maybe it was the guilt, worrying what her aunt might say, knowing she would say nothing if Rick was at her side.

The light coming from inside the cabin was so bright that it burned through the cracks in the clapboard walls, a circumstance that struck a strange irony with her since she knew Emelina rarely used more than one or two candles at a time. The windows were tightly shuttered, but she stepped cautiously around to the back of the house, where she knew two of the boards did not fit together well. It was a secret she and Paz had shared for years, a place where they had spied on her when they were little. For whatever reason, tonight, it came to her, and she sought out the narrow crack before going to the door.

Her knees nearly gave way as she saw, not her aunt inside, but instead Candelario, Sgt. Fuentes, and Jorge, don Raúl's bodyguard as well as an unknown soldier.

"I tell you, he is not dangerous," Fuentes told the others while leaning back in his chair next to the table. "Did I not look through everything the man owns already? Killing Americans is a messy business, and rarely worth the trouble it brings down on everyone."

"This one is different," Candelario insisted from where he was seated at the table. "We know he has been off in the mountains, fighting with *los muchachos*. How do we know he is not a spy for who knows which group? Even as we speak, they could be making plans to ship weapons to them." He pounded the table with his fist, causing the Uzi and the empty liquor bottle next to it to jump.

"The only thing you know is what that little shit Alfredo said, and by the time you boys were done with him, he would have said anything to anybody," Fuentes continued.

The soldier in the far corner where he leaned against the wall, grinned in satisfaction. "We did the job that was needed." He dropped his cigarette and crushed it out with the butt of his M-16.

Fuentes shuddered. "I had him in my command before *los muchachos* got hold of him. He would do anything he was told. There was no need, I tell you. I could have scared the amount of information out of him that it took you idiots two days to squeeze from him."

"But that is the point," Jorge spoke up. "After the guerrillas have them for a while, they are not nearly so cooperative."

Fuentes snorted with contempt. "It does not change things with the American, I tell you. He was not the problem. That was Flores. He has been taken care of. The *gringo* is of no real importance, and he is not going anywhere. Believe me." He pulled the Colt .45 out of the holster on his hip and laid it on the table. With a dramatic swoop, he dropped a dark blue passport drawn from inside his shirt pocket on the table beside the pistol.

"That belongs to him?" Candelario raised an eyebrow. He folded his arms across his chest. "What about the girl?"

Jorge stood up to speak. "The woman will have to be dealt with. My employer cautions that if these religious types get together with the union workers in the fields, we will have more trouble than any of us wants to deal with. My employer is opposed to any more violence than necessary, however, he says that at all costs, we must stop this rabble from going any further. My employer—"

"*A la gran puta*, Jorge," Fuentes cut him off. "Stop making speeches. We all know who your employer is, so you do not have to make it sound as if it is some big secret. Candelario, you want to kill the American. I tell you it is a mistake. If you do it, I want no part of it. Searching and stealing his things is one thing. Killing him is something else. Now when you get around to the girl, let me know." He raised his eyebrows with a malicious grin.

"It cannot be a question of 'if.'" Jorge dropped the beseeching mannerism. "After all, she is Flores' daughter. The puppies of the *aguacateros* may be cute when they are young, but they grow up to be the same kind of ditch dog cur in the end."

She was shaking so hard she could hardly make her leaden feet move. Her head was spinning. She had to warn him and to tell Emelina and—she stumbled in the dark, kicking a metal wash basin leaning against the outside wall. An involuntary cry escaped her lips as it jangled against the back of the house. A scraping of chairs on the wooden floor and raised voices told her those inside had heard it, too.

She kicked off her shoes with her first steps, snatched up her skirt, and ran blindly toward the beach, the clearest way to Rick's cabin. The lights in the hut went out as ominous shadows scattered across the beach behind her.

Free of the trees, running on the beach, she could see better, but it meant they could see her as well. After only a few feet, her heart began to crash against the walls of her chest like a caged tiger. She could hear them behind her. She had been a fast runner as a child. How was it now her legs moved so slowly, as if she was running in water?

All the parts of her body were betraying her at once, adding to her panic. Her feet dug deep into the sand, slowing her pace. Her legs ached as her mind reeled, and her lungs were threatening to explode. It was her heart, however, her thundering heart that was refusing to do the impossible.

"Rishard!" The scream caught in the air as it echoed down the beach, reverberating off the trees. "Rishard!" she tried once again as the men behind her stopped to take their positions.

Still standing in his own doorway, surveying Paz's handiwork, Rick sprinted onto the beach at her first cry. For an instant, he saw only her, coming at a pace he knew must be killing her while a second throat-splitting scream split the night. It was then he caught sight of the dark shadows skittering across the sand behind her.

She fell into his arms, spinning them both around, as the first shots whistled past. He could hear the crackling of the nine-millimeter gunfire as the Uzi rounds strafed the sand around them, but a louder clap followed, and something struck him on the right hip. As he spun to the ground, she flew from his arms. The echo of gunfire reverberated down the beach, resounding in his ears as he lay, stunned, the side of his face on the wet sand. Suddenly, the beach was bathed in light, and he could hear voices and the trampling of feet coming toward them. None of it mattered. He blocked it all from his mind as his eyes fastened on her still form, lying just ahead of him.

He tried to stand, but the searing pain in his side made that impossible. If he was to die on this beach, in this way, it would not matter as long as he held her in his arms when the final blow came. He dragged himself forward on his elbows, reaching her, despite the blinding light, the torment in his side, and the impending chaos coming toward him. Struggling to his knees, he rolled her into his lap and hugged her to his chest.

"Oh, God." The words fell from his lips. There was only a small amount of blood on her dress, down low. She had to be alive, he told himself. It was then that he noticed the blood running down her hairline, dripping onto his arm.

She opened her eyes and whispered his name.

"I'm here," he told her, smoothing her hair back from her face. "I'm here."

"You have to run...they are coming..."

"Shh," he hugged her gently again. "Don't worry. It will all be done soon."

He glanced up at those who were gathered around. Surely the gunmen had heard, but only confusion ensued as he caught sight of Paz and Carlos, huffing up to them.

"*Por Díos*, don Ricardo." The tears ran freely down the young man's face as he threw his arms around his friend's neck.

"Carlos." Mariana reached a hand toward the man who was still breathing hard from his run from his vehicle. "Take care—take care of them," was all she said. A weak cough escaped her, and she stiffened in Rick's arms at some unseen pain. "I love you. Never forget that." She twitched and then caught her breath before she slumped, unmoving, against Rick.

"Mariana!" Rick's desperate cry echoed down the empty beach as he hugged her lifeless form one last time.

* * * * *

Nightmare is the only word that came close to describing Rick's last few hours in *Las Palomitas*. After a time, Carlos lifted Mariana from his arms, and he had no choice but to let her go. His strength was gone. He vaguely remembered Paz, helping him to Carlos' Land Rover, parked near the cabin, the source of the blinding light on the beach. He continued to worry about the gunmen, but Paz, who stayed by his side throughout the night, kept reassuring him that they were gone. Paz tried to tend to the bullet wound on his hip, taping new bandages over it every hour or so it seemed.

"Let it go," Rick told him, as he lay in the hammock behind the store. "Mariana?" he asked through the buzzing cloud that filled his head, but Paz only shook his head as his eyes filled with tears.

"Don Carlos said he would put her somewhere safe so that they cannot come back for her. He did not tell me where. It does not matter now."

Rick dozed in the hammock, oblivious to what might come next. After a time, Carlos appeared in the doorway, sucking his pipe that was clenched in his teeth. The memory of Imanuel, lying in a bed, with only Emelina and Mariana to care for him, serpentined through Rick's muddled head. Carlos had said then that was the best possible care for him, that no doctor would touch him. What was his remedy for bullet wounds? He wondered in a painful fog, his thoughts strangely detached from the reality of the situation.

"Should we wake *mi tío*?" Paz asked.

"No, let Miguel sleep," Carlos answered. "You said he was drunk. Let him rest. He does not need to hear about any of this any sooner than necessary. It is time to go." Carlos looked at Paz, who again helped Rick to his feet and into the front seat of the Land Rover.

It was as if he did not exist anymore, Rick thought. Carlos was not speaking to him, only seeing to it that he was shuttled like so much baggage. Did he blame him? If I were him, there would be murder in my heart was the confused message floating around inside of Rick's head. He did not even ask where they were going. It did not seem important anymore.

Carlos climbed into the driver's seat and started the engine. Crossing the road, Paz trotted in front of the vehicle. Carlos followed, positioning the car at the top of the ridge, overlooking the wet sand of the open beach at low tide.

The first pale shades of an orange dawn painted the eastern sky. How many times I have watched this from under that big palm tree Rick thought. Never did I expect to see it like this. He hung his head in agony.

"Go watch for it." Carlos told Paz, who went to rest against the hood of the car.

"After today, forget this place." Carlos was now giving him definitive orders. "Forget what you have done here. Forget who you have known here. Do you understand?"

Rick's head snapped up, and he coughed painfully, realizing one of the bullets may have lodged in his back. "No, I don't. What are you talking about?"

A new droning sound could be heard, another aching inside his own head, Rick first thought. It grew louder as Paz pointed at something in the sky.

"What I mean is you have a way out of here now, but if you try to contact Paz or Miguel or anyone else here, you could put their lives in danger. Forget them. Leave them what little peace they have left."

He sat up straight and squinted past the steering wheel. "It is time."

"Time for what?" Rick asked before he caught sight of the small plane.

"To send you home." Carlos climbed out and made his way around the front of the Land Rover. The plane came down low, dipping its wing as Paz waved. It circled once more, making a perfect landing on the wet sand, left bare by the outgoing tide. Back at his side, Paz helped Rick to move toward the now stationary plane. Rick looked back for Carlos but caught sight of him on the other side of the plane, speaking with the pilot.

"Take care of yourself." Rick gave Paz's shoulders a firm squeeze as he slowly eased himself into the two-seater. "Stay in school and study hard, okay?"

Paz nodded obligingly. "I will, don Ricardo. I promise. For you and my father." The words caught in his throat. "Goodbye, my friend," he stammered in English, as he stepped back from the plane, waving furiously. "I will miss you."

Rick's body sagged at the effort it had taken to climb into the plane. He waved in return and keenly felt even that small movement. The small plane taxied down the long stretch of beach in the glow of the rising sun. He wondered about the unlikely runway, but despite his initial doubts, it proved to be the smoothest takeoff he had ever known as the plane raced over the cushioned sandy surface.

They banked sharply, coming around, giving Rick one last look at the peninsula, the village, the beach, and still, there was no peace in *Las Palomitas*. Where his cabin should have been, a fire raged, the entire roof ablaze. He could see Paz running down the beach and the Land Rover speeding up the road in the same direction.

Even as I leave.... His thoughts tumbled one over another. He collapsed against the door of the plane. He could see no more. He did not see the youth who stopped to watch the plane as it grew smaller in the distance. He could not see that particular morning's glorious sunrise as it climbed into the azure sky, pouring its light and warmth over the volcanic sand, the green palms and verdant *caserinos*. Paz watched a moment longer before resuming his run up the beach toward the flaming remains of his friend's cabin.

March 25, 1980. Washington D.C. A US House subcommittee will begin hearings on $5.7 million in military assistance to the government of El Salvador later today. While some mild opposition is expected, state department personnel seem confident that this aid will help the Salvadoran government in its effort to stem the tide of violence that has taken the lives of 1,000 people already this year.

March 26, 1980, Palm Sunday. San Salvador. Violence marred the funeral of martyred Archbishop Oscar A. Romero today as forty or more persons were killed, many of them crushed, when the thousands in attendance panicked after a bomb was thrown into their midst. Gathered in and around the city's municipal cathedral, the mourners included foreign journalists and visiting bishops from Brazil, Britain, Ecuador, France, and Panama, several of whom stated that they saw gunfire coming from the second floor of the National Palace. Others have reported that the bomb which started the hysteria was also thrown from a window in the National Palace.

American clergy inside the cathedral stated that despite the crush of people inside the church, those present remained calm and assisted one another until the crisis was brought under control.

December 1980. Zaragoza, El Salvador. The bodies of Jean Donovan, age 27, a Catholic lay worker, Sister Dorothy Kazel, age 40, an Ursuline nun, both of Cleveland, Ohio and Maryknoll sisters, Ita Ford age 40 and Maura Clark, age 49, both from New York, were discovered in a single grave on a deserted stretch of road between the airport and San Salvador. All four had been raped and executed at close range. Dorothy Kazel and Jean Donovan were last seen having picked up Sisters Ford and Clark at El Salvador's airport outside the capital.

The women, who worked closely with the Salvadoran poor, had been threatened in their work and accused of subversive activities, as they distributed food and medical supplies to those in need, and often buried the dead found more and more frequently along the roadsides of this war-torn country. Salvadoran security forces are suspected in the murders. The US government has asked for an investigation, and Salvadoran officials have promised to look into the matter.

January 1981. San Salvador. The director of El Salvador's land reform agency, José Rodolfo Viera, age 43, and Americans, Michael Hammer age 42 and Mark Pearlman age 36, both of the American Institute for Free Labor Development (AIFLD), an extension of the AFL-CIO, were murdered in a hail of gunfire as they met for dinner at San Salvador's Sheraton Hotel. The US government has demanded an investigation, as once again, the Salvadoran military, one of the primary forces set against land reform in this country, is suspected of complicity in these murders.

April 1982. San Salvador. In last month's most widely published election in this nation's history, the right-wing party, ARENA, headed by Roberto D'Aubuisson, is claiming victory, as they came in a close second behind Duarte's Christian Democrats party. Despite the assurances of a wide range of international observers, the local Catholic University has stated publicly that there was 'massive fraud in the number of votes', stating there were no more than 600,000–800,000 votes cast nationwide, as opposed to the more than 1.5 million claimed by government figures.

Neither Duarte nor D'Aubuisson has emerged as president of the country, despite the vote. Alvaro Alfredo Magaña has been named as president, and Roberto D'Aubuisson, long associated with death squads and the murder of Archbishop Romero and the US labor leaders, has been named leader of the General Assembly.

April 1983. Washington D.C. President Ronald Reagan made history this month when he became only the seventh US president to speak to a joint session of Congress on a foreign policy concern, as he took his fight to continue support for the government of El Salvador to new levels. He praised the Salvadoran government for 'making every effort to guarantee democracy, free labor, freedom of religion and a free press.'

July 1983. San Salvador. According to the Catholic Church's legal aid office, during the past fourteen months, the guerrillas, known politically as the FMLN (Farbundo Martí National Liberation Front), have been responsible for the death of 63 civilians. The government armed forces were responsible for killing 4,867 civilians during the same period.

EPILOGUE

*M*arch 1984. San Salvador. According to figures released last month by the legal aid office of the Catholic Church here, 40,000 innocent civilians were murdered in El Salvador between October 1979 and January of this year. Most were peasants, children, and the elderly. More than 90 percent were killed by the death squads, which are now widely recognized, even by the American Embassy staff, including the new ambassador, Thomas Pickering, to be members of the Salvadoran military and police forces.

During this same period, it should be noted that the US government, primarily under the administration of Ronald Reagan, has sent almost $300 million in military aid to the Salvadoran government and brought 500 Salvadoran officer trainees and over 1500 troops to the US for training at US military bases.

March 1984. San Salvador. As the country prepares for a new round of elections the end of the month, allegations made by a former high ranking Salvadoran government official in Washington D.C. have linked presidential candidate and former president of the Constituent Assembly, Roberto D'Aubuisson, with various death squads, including those responsible for the murder of Archbishop Romero, Mario Zamora,

El Salvador's attorney, and land reform workers, José Rodolfo Viera, and American labor advisors, Michael Hammer, and Mark Pearlman. In addition, the official, who requested anonymity for fear of reprisals, implicated several high-ranking Salvadoran officials, claiming that former Minister of Defense José Guillermo Garcia, as well as the current Minister of Defense, Eugenio Vides Casanova, were aware of many who were involved in the death squad activity. One of those accused in the murder of the American churchwomen, Colonel Oscar Edgardo Casanova is the cousin of the current Minister of Defense.

*The official also maintained that although Roberto D'Aubuisson was ousted from the army, he continued to receive a substantial army salary secretly while he was organizing death squad activities in 1979. The unnamed official is meeting with various members of Congress as well as with reporters from the **New York Times**.*

Walking down the beach, with Mariana beside him, he had never felt happier. She was more beautiful than ever. As they strolled along, he slipped his arm around her waist. The sunshine and a soft breeze made a halo of her hair around her face. She smiled at him, and then she laughed, that wonderful musical sound that always had the power to lift his heart. Everything was as it should be.

Suddenly, the sun's glow turned white, and a chill swept over him. The sun had become the moon, and under its silver light, everything began to shift as he watched in horror, helpless to stop what was to come. The breeze became a wind, and the waves that had lapped gently at the shore a few moments before were now pounding the sand with a roar.

Mariana was no longer laughing. She was screaming. He turned with agonizing slowness. He reached out to wrap his arms around her to stop her screams, but when he drew his hands back, they were wet and sticky with her blood. As he stared at them, the screaming stopped. When he looked up again, she was gone.

Frantic, he began to search in the darkness. This time when he saw her, she was silent, motionless, lying in a heap on the sand. When he reached for her, a hot burning in his hip threw him to the ground. He touched his side and found more blood. He opened his mouth to cry for help, but no sound came out. And then he was simply falling.

Rick jumped so violently the antique wooden bed frame creaked in protest. He lay motionless, taking stock. He was warm and comfortable, nestled deep in the cotton bedclothes and feather pillows. Damp with perspiration, the pain in his hip was still there but not so sharp, just a dull ache at this point, the way it always plagued him when a change in the weather was coming.

He had survived the dream again. It was always the same. How many times in the last four years had he lived through it all, warped as it was by the surreal shadows, the collision of memory, imagination, and subconscious? As he lay staring out the window at the cold gray Texas sky, he wondered how many more times he would have to live through it again before he died.

The bedroom was the one he had called his own in his father's house since he was a teen. It was a place that should have wrapped him in nostalgic comfort like a family quilt, but instead, he felt uneasy, almost as if he had snuck uninvited into a stranger's home. He threw back the bedcovers and dressed as usual in blue jeans, a T-shirt, and worn leather loafers.

His mood matched the oppressive sky. In the large exquisitely designed kitchen downstairs, he fumbled with an electronically-controlled coffee maker. He cursed it silently as it failed to produce the hot liquid he craved. Still muddled by the nightmare, he gave up in frustration and slapped a mugful of water into the microwave. While he searched for a jar of instant coffee, his sister, Amy breezed in, on her way out the door.

"Well, it's about time," she began cheerily as she slipped a raincoat over her tailored suit. "I thought maybe you were going to sleep all day."

He heard only the implied criticism. "I didn't sleep much last night, okay?" he began in his own defense.

"I heard you and Father arguing until all hours. Honestly, Rick, he's barely out of the hospital. Why do you fight with him so? Can't you see he's still so weak?"

"Weak?" He choked on the word and slammed the microwave door, spilling scalding water on his hand. "If he's weak, the rest of us are dead! Take a look at the calendar, Sis. It's been two weeks, and he's a lot better than either one of us knows. He may have had a stroke, but weak, he's not. I came here like you asked to try and help, but there's nothing more I can do. I've had enough. I'm going home." He floated a spoonful of brown powder on the surface of the hot water in the cup.

"Home? What do you mean 'home'? You are home, Richard Mercy." Her voice took on that imperial tone he had heard so often in arguments with his father. "What you mean is, you're going back to the Rio Grande Valley and that squalid little camp of refugees. How can you?" Her voice droned on, but he no longer heard anything she said. He had taken his own advice and glanced at the ornate calendar on the far wall, a move he now regretted. No wonder he felt so miserable. Day after tomorrow, it would be four years exactly that he and Mariana were gunned down on the beach, the anniversary of her death. Sunday would be the anniversary of her death and the funeral he never saw.

He had no memory of it, of course, but he had imagined it, time and again. The simple wooden coffin, just like her father's, lined with a sheet or maybe even a woven blanket, flowers and *caserino* branches, tucked in around, surrounding her in a fragrant wreath. Most of the town would have walked the road, the same way they had for Imanuel. Paz, Emelina, and Miguel would have been there, and Paz would have another marker to carve, a simple wooden one to mark her resting place, the only symbol of one more murdered Salvadoran peasant.

Rick closed his eyes, but that failed to shut out the painful memories.

"Have you heard a word I've said?" Amy's whining intruded on his private thoughts. "We need you here. Father and Charles need your help at the bank, and I need you."

"Need?" His voice was sharp-edged as he brought himself back to the jarring present. "You've never known the meaning of the word. No one here needs anything from me. He has his full-time nurse and his visiting physical therapist. He's getting better, and he'll soon be in top form again, you'll see. He was more than strong enough last night to go through the whole of my life again."

He took a deep breath before he continued. "You've got all the help you need around here, although heaven knows some of them probably need a degree in engineering to run this kitchen." He pushed the mug across the table, sloshing the contents onto the fine-grain wood. "Is it too much to ask for a decent cup of coffee? Is there a reason this place needs to look more like a science lab than a simple kitchen?"

Amy said nothing. She picked up his cup of coffee, dumped its contents into the sink, and refilled it from the machine that had earlier refused to perform for him.

"It's the cook's day off, and Carmelita is downstairs, tending to the laundry," she told him as she handed him his coffee.

"As for that 'squalid little camp,'" his anger was fading despite his words, "I do more good and get more accomplished there in a day than I have here in two weeks. I help people there, really help, not just hold their hands."

Amy sat down across the table from him.

"And you have Charlie to run the bank. You sure don't need me for that." He took a gulp of the steaming coffee.

"He hates it when you call him that. His name is Charles."

A sideways smile escaped him. "Yeah, well, don't tell him. Whatever you call him, your husband fits into this family better than I ever did." He finished with a sigh.

"Don't say that." She gave him an apologetic look. "I thought you coming back here would make things better somehow. Nothing has been the same ever since you left the first time." Her lips dropped into a pout.

"Don't try to lay that on me, too. I'm not the magic here, and I never was." He hesitated and then plowed on. "He wasn't an easy man, to begin with, but now he's truly impossible. I can't fix that. I'm not sure anybody can."

His thoughts slipped back to the day last summer when his father had arrived at the gate of the *Casa Oscar Romero* in the Rio Grande Valley. Rick's step had quickened, thinking that his father had finally come out of interest and concern for his only son. His hopes were soon dashed when Rick discovered the truth. He cut off the ugly train of thought. It was still early, and already his mind was filled with the only two women in his life whom he had ever really loved and who cared to understand him—his lover and his mother. And they were both gone.

"But what if we lose Father, too? Rick, I just can't—"

"Amy, it will happen one day," Rick continued, choosing his words carefully. "You know it will. He is an old man, and I can't imagine the way he lives, so stubborn, unwilling to bend even a little, is going to increase his life expectancy. Even his doctors say that. But having me here isn't going to help either." Rick chuckled. "I'm not what you need." He made a move to stand up while still speaking. "And despite what you say about my work—" He fell back heavily into the chair.

"Rain days are cane days," he muttered.

"Ricky, are you all right?" She had not used that form of his name in years, and especially under the circumstances, he found it touching. "I thought you were finally all well."

"Things are healed as well as they probably ever will be." He shrugged as if it was unimportant. "The doctors say I was lucky. They said a nerve center is damaged and that it could have been a lot worse. The worst is days like this, rainy days. The vets at the rehab center say the same thing."

"I try not to think of you in that place," she answered with a frown.

"A little too real for you, Sis?" He raised an eyebrow in her direction.

"It was awful, Rick. Maybe you don't remember it as well. You were so sick by the time they called us.

First, it was the hospital and then that recuperation center."

"Rehabilitation center."

"Whatever it was, it was full of people in terrible condition. I just couldn't stand it. It wasn't that I didn't care, but how can you look at those people, day after day, knowing—" She bit her lip. "It just hurt too much to see you there with them."

"Maybe that's your problem." Rick didn't try to keep the accusation from his voice. "You see them as a breed apart. They're people, Amy, like me, who were in the wrong place at the wrong time. That's all. You have to look at them when you live there like I did. You talk to 'em and find out they have parents, wives, kids, girlfriends, whole lives that have nothing to do with what happened to them and what they have left."

A scowl settled on his brow. "When I was there, all I could think about was what I'd lost, but in another sense, while I was there, I guess I also learned how lucky I really was."

"Lucky?"

"Yeah, lucky. Maybe blessed is an even better word. I'm walking around, able to do what I want to do. Not everybody gets off that easy."

She shook her head, and when she spoke again, he knew she was no longer talking about hospitalization. "I still can't believe you were there and got yourself in the middle of that whole thing. We tried to ask David, but he wouldn't tell us anything. Sometimes, I swear, I hate to admit that we are related to someone like him." She gave an exaggerated little shudder. "He's such a hillbilly, if you know what I mean. He said it was all over some woman, but I never did believe you'd be so foolish. Still, you never did explain—" She quit speaking as she caught the expression on his face.

"Leave it alone, Amy." The warning in his voice was clear. "It isn't something you'd understand even if I did try to explain."

"Oh, Rick, really—I didn't mean anything by it. I just hate it when you talk of going away again. Can't you find a way to stay here? Do you have to go back to them?"

"You haven't heard a word I've said, have you? Them again?" Abandoning any attempt to cover his anger, he went on. "I help them! They are Salvadorans and Guatemalans and Hondurans, but first and most importantly, they are people. Most of them are in this trouble through no fault of their own. Did you know, in their countries, it can be seen as a crime to help poor people and that alone, can get you killed?" The memory of Franco standing in Imanuel's tiny living room, telling him that same thing a few years ago, flashed through the mists of memory.

"Rick, don't talk about it. All that going on down on the border, it's so tedious."

"Tedious? Well, I could say the same about garden club or bridge club and so many things that keep you busy, Sister Dear. Maybe that's the difference between us. I don't know. All I know is if it's important to you, then I can extend some value to it, simply on your say so. Too bad you can't do the same for me." He started out of the room and then turned back to add one last challenge. "Maybe you ought to come see for yourself sometime."

"Oh, Rick, honestly. You can't be serious. I just wish you could be more like—"

"More like Charles?" He finished the thought for her. "I can't be who you want me to be, Amy. I walked away from the life you are talking about a long time ago. Nothing that's happened since has made me sorry I did."

She stood up, shrugging the raincoat into place. "When are you leaving?"

"Later today or tomorrow at the latest. I'll call the center and see if they need anything first, and then I'll go."

"Keep me posted on where you'll be. I've really got to run now."

"You know where I'll be."

Amy hesitated. "I just mean when you get done there. I mean, how much longer can it continue?"

"Ask your friends in Washington, not me."

"I don't want to talk about it anymore." She gave him a peck on the cheek. "I have a great deal of shopping to do, and I'm meeting some friends for lunch, so if you're not here when I get back this afternoon, I'll know."

"Bye, Amy," was all he said and turned to go back upstairs.

*   *   *   *   *

After threatening for hours, the rain finally came while Rick was standing in line at the teller window at the bank. The water made tiny rivulets down the great slabs of grey-green glass as he watched. He had called the center before he left the house, and everything was fine, Elena said. She had been such a comfort to him, the same woman he had met so briefly that last day in *Las Palomitas*. She worked for the diocese and was now at *Casa Oscar Romero*, the Salvadoran refugee center. It was such a surprise to find her there and such a relief. She was one of the few he had found since coming back to the US who could truly understand what he had been through, the things with which he still struggled.

A little money, he tried to concentrate on the task at hand, as he leaned on his cane. He hated coming here in one sense, but once he had a little cash in his pocket, he could be on his way. His father's name crested the top of the huge plaque that hung in the vestibule. President of the Board of the Directors when the building was erected, and he still was all these years later. He would not have come at all, but his mother had left him an account here after she died last summer, so he tried to slip in unnoticed and wait in line, like everyone else. Sometimes it worked, sometimes not.

"Ricky, what are you doing standing here?" Claire Bingham, the head teller, caught sight of him, as she came through the polished wood and granite barrier that separated those who came for their funds from those who had charge of them.

"I do declare, child, you know better. Come right over here to Deacon's desk and sit down so we can take care of you proper. You need to cash a check, honey?" She looked up at him from over the top of her over-sized half-glasses, perched on the end of her tiny, pinched nose. "Why do you do that? Stand in line there with the rest of the world. Why if your daddy saw that, he'd simply have a str—" She bit her lip and blushed almost as deep a shade as the red lipstick she was wearing. "Oh, my stars. I am sorry. George always says I talk too much. I suppose there are times when he's right."

Rick handed her his signed withdrawal slip and fidgeted nervously, but he did not sit. "How is George?"

"Oh, he's all right, grouchy, is all. He manages fine, but of course, he is no William Joseph Mercy. How's your daddy doing? Any idea when he'll be getting back to us?"

"He's much better. I wouldn't think it will be too much longer, but I don't know for sure. It's all up to the doctors and Amy, of course."

"Amy, yes, well. I'm sure she'll be happy to have the pressure off of Charles, too. I'll run get your money." She finished filling out the form in her hand. "Have a seat. I'll be right back."

Her frosted, fluffy hair bobbed out of sight in the crowded lobby. Glancing around, something inside began to scream deep down inside him. Too many bitter memories reaching out as if they might snatch and hold him against his will if he did not escape soon.

"Here you are." She was back, handing him one of the bank's gray printed cash envelopes. "You're taking off soon, are you? Back to—where is it you live now? Brownsville?"

"Yes, ma'am."

"You don't ever think about moving back here, back home?"

"Not now. I'm busy there with a job I like so—" He edged toward the door.

"You take care, hon. Come back and see us real soon now. And next time, don't be standing in those lines over there, you hear?"

"Yes, ma'am." He nodded and made a straight shot for the door. The downpour outside would be a welcome respite from what he was feeling at the moment.

With eyes downcast, he pushed open the heavy inner glass door to the vestibule. He glanced up at the young man who had entered from the other side, shrugging out of his dripping dark blue jacket, emblazoned with the symbol of one of Houston's finest private schools. He came to an instant standstill as the younger man looked him full in the face.

The wide grin in front of him was as familiar as it was heart-breaking. "I knew I would find you one day, don Ricardo" was all he said.

"Paz?" Rick was afraid to hope, certain he was mistaken. "Is it really you?"

"*Por supuesto.* Of course." He stepped forward and embraced his friend with a bear hug.

Overcome, Rick enfolded him in his arms, embracing and embarrassing his friend only slightly less than he might have on the beach years before.

Paz stepped back, chattering so fast, Rick could hardly keep up. "I knew I would find you, and I always thought it might be here. Did you know when I first came, I sat in the lobby here to wait for you to walk in?"

"What?" A frown of confusion creased Rick's brow.

"I knew I would find you here, but you do not look much like a banker, no?"

"No, I'm not a banker. Paz. What are you talking about?" He stared at the youth who was considerably taller than the last time he had seen him. "Here, come in here." He pulled him inside, and they made their way over to an upholstered bench inside the bank.

"There is your father's name, yes?" Paz pointed to the top of the full-length bronze plaque across the room, even as others filed past, intent on their own errands. "I remember from one day when you told me in your cabin in *Las Palomitas*. And then, when you sent for me and put money here for me, I knew it was you."

"Paz..." Confusion threatened to overwhelm him. "Look. We've got to get out of here." A large man nearly tumbled over them in his rush to get to an open teller window. "Do you have business here?"

"It can wait."

"Then, let's go someplace where we can talk."

"There is a place close by. Come." Paz pulled his wet blazer back on and led the way out into the rain. Paz ran to the next block with Rick in close pursuit, despite his double-hop gait as he favored his right leg, using his cane. He thought of the day he had followed Paz, running through the rain from Hurricane Ella, years before in *Las Palomitas*.

"Here." Paz stopped abruptly and jerked open the door of a small coffee shop. They were dripping, but no one seemed to notice as they tumbled into one of the roomy dark wood booths along the dimly lit back wall.

"Some of the food is very strange," Paz explained. "But it is quiet, and they never mind how long you stay. I will get us some drinks."

Rick took a moment to scan the menu, hanging on the wall behind the counter. Pastrami on rye, corned beef, pumpernickel, bagels, knishes made with beef and wild rice. No doubt a boy from El Salvador would find the cuisine of a New York-style delicatessen to be more than a little strange.

"I just want to look at you," Rick began when Paz returned, a soft drink in each hand. "You are all grown up." The once-skinny village child was now a lean young man who stood taller than Rick would have expected. His shoulders were broad, his arms and legs long, with a solid muscularity that was apparent even in his school uniform.

"You sound like someone's *abuela*," Paz laughed as he sat down.

"Somebody's grandmother, heh? Well, sometimes, I feel about that old." He leaned back against the back of the booth, pulling his right leg up onto the bench seat.

"That is still from the last night on the beach, yes?" It was a statement of fact, not an actual question. Rick studied the young face across from his. The plump contours of early adolescence had given way to a strong jawline and a lengthening of his countenance. The quick, bright smile that was nearly always at the ready remained unchanged, however, despite all he had been through.

"What are you looking at?"

"You. Just you. I can't believe you are here. You speak English now. And look at this jacket. You go to St. Francis? I'm impressed. How long have you been here? Why didn't you call me?"

Paz's smile faded to one of bewilderment. "You know where I go to school, and you know how long. How could you not know? The part I do not understand is why you never wanted to see me. You act so surprised, now, but all the time I have been here, you never came or called."

"Paz—" Rick hesitated, suddenly fearful of disillusioning his young friend with the truth.

"Don Ricardo," Paz continued. "You put money in the bank for me. The solicitor, he told me all of this. It is in your father's bank so I know it must be from you. I thought you worked there, too, but I never saw you. When I asked, they say you are not there now but nothing more. I was afraid to ask too much. I think if you do not want to see me, there must be a good reason. Maybe you are not well. I remember how you looked when you left *Las Palomitas*. I was afraid you would die before you ever reached the United States. And I thought maybe it was all too sad, with all of us losing Mariana that way..." His voice quavered, and he stopped speaking, noting the effect his words were having on the man across the table.

"I don't know what to say," Rick stammered. "Except that I didn't know you were here, and I didn't do any of it." He gulped. "I wish I had, though."

"But don Ricardo." A frightened expression crossed his face, and his voice took on a strident tone. "You must be *mi patrón*. You must. If it is not you, then who?"

"Paz, calm down. I don't know, but it is definitely not me. It's a great idea, but I'm no banker. I never went back to the bank after I left *Las Palomitas*. And I didn't ever try to get in touch with you again there because I was warned it might be dangerous."

"Here? Dangerous? You think the ones who shot you there would come after you here?" Disbelief colored his face and his words.

"No, not for me. For you."

"Who told you this?"

"A couple different ones," Rick lied and wondered why he did so even as he spoke the words. "I've talked to a lot of Salvadoran refugees as well as political scientist types over the last few years. I was afraid to write to you, for fear someone there might go after you."

Paz nodded solemnly. "That makes sense. For certain, things did not get any better after you left."

"I know."

"How do you know? What do you know?"

Rick took a deep breath. "Juana, Julio's oldest daughter, Simón's widow. Remember her?"

Paz nodded. "Of course."

"She came through the center where I work, about a year ago and she told me a number of things. I didn't know if it was all true or not, but..."

"What did she tell you?"

Rick picked at the wax-coated cup in his hand as he began his story. "She said that after I left, everything got worse. I asked about you, about Emelina and Miguel, everyone I could think of. She was only with us a couple of days, and there is always so much to do so we did not get as much time to talk as I would have liked, but—"

He took a sip of his drink before he continued. "She said there were several stories about you. Some said you went to school in San Miguel or San Salvador, but others said you'd gone off to the mountains with your cousin. She said she thought you had gone off with Franco, and frankly, that seemed the most likely to me, too. It made me feel so sad and helpless, like I had failed you somehow, but I certainly couldn't blame you either. She didn't seem to know what happened to Miguel, only that he didn't live in *Las Palomitas* anymore. After all that had happened to his whole family, that was no surprise. The saddest story she told me was about Emelina and Candelario."

"Did you know he was one of the ones who shot you?"

"I figured as much," Rick admitted. "Mariana said his name that night, didn't she? Fuentes and Candelario is what she said. It was a long time before I could make any sense out of it, though."

"After you left, I did not see *mi tía* for a couple of days. Miguel and I just stayed at his house or went fishing. There was no one in the store or the restaurant. We just left them closed." Paz stared at his hands spread out before him on the table. "Miguel drank a lot those first few weeks. First, it was only beer, but then he turned to *chicha*. You remember?"

Rick nodded. "*Chicha*. Mother's milk." He had always thought it an ironic twist that the same name was used for both mother's milk and homemade liquor. "White lightning is what they call it here. Homemade liquor."

"It made me afraid. I was worried about Emelina, but Miguel would not let me go anywhere where he could not see me. When she did come, she was completely crazy. She whispered to everyone, and when we talked to her, it was as if she did not even hear. She wandered around town, looking for Mariana and *mi papí,* and even for Candelario. If you tried to keep her inside when she wanted to go out, she would scream in a strange way." Paz grimaced at the memory. "*Salvaje* is what Miguel called it. I do not know how to describe it."

"Savage." Rick nodded.

"I worried about her walking around in the day and the night, but Miguel said we just had to let her go. He said the people with that kind of sickness in the head from too much grief do not usually hurt anyone. It was true. She never did. She slept at her own house, but even there, it was like the little house went crazy, too. She never cleaned anything anymore. I only went in there once after that. It looked like a wild animal lived there, and it smelled terrible. When I left, she was still there. But it was as if *mi tía* was already gone, and there was just some crazy woman, who wore rags and never combed her hair had come to take her place."

"When did you leave, Paz?"

"It has been more than three years now. It is a long time to live away from home." There was a heaviness to his voice that his best effort and a smile could not disguise. "And Juana? She told you other things? I have a couple of letters from Miguel, no more than one or two a year."

Paz grinned as if at a private joke. "Someone else must write them for him, so I do not imagine he enjoys that part. *Mi papí* knew how to read and write well, but not my *Tío* Miguel. He could just barely read and write. He would be surprised to see me now." He shook his head in amusement. "His letters come from San Salvador, and he says he is working and doing well. He said that Emelina had drowned in the *estero* one night, but I do not know much more than that."

Rick sighed, burdened with information he did not relish, sharing. "Juana told me, but I'm not sure you'll want to hear it."

"You have something worse to tell me than all the rest? Don Ricardo, my family is gone, all gone. What could be worse?"

Rick traced a long scratch in the table with his thumb. "You said Candelario was one of the men who shot us that night on the beach. What happened to him after that?"

Paz shrugged as he sucked in a mouthful of ice from his nearly empty cup. "We do not know. I never saw him again. Miguel said, once people knew he was responsible, that he was a member of *ORDEN* and had been spying on the whole town for who knows how long, he would be dead if he came back. Miguel said people like Juana or even Miguel himself would kill him since he had a hand in killing their family members. It made sense.

"Miguel told me this one day while we were working on the fishing *equipo*. I remember because when *mi tío* talked about Candelario, he twisted one of the thin steel pieces we used for the *anclas* for the nets, right in half." The young man illustrated his point with a quick snapping action between his hands.

Rick added without looking up. "Like you, Juana said Emelina drowned one night in a storm in the *estero*. After they went to her house and it was so bad, they decided to just tear it down, and that is when they found Candelario."

"What? Where?"

"Under the floor of the house. Juana said they figured that when Emelina found out Candelario, the man she lived with, had a hand in killing her brother-in-law and her beloved niece, she killed him herself. Then she must have stuffed his body under the floorboards of her house. I guess all that would be enough to make a person lose their mind."

Despite the flatness in Rick's voice, Paz began to make a strange sniffling sound. He covered his mouth, but despite his best attempt, he could not stifle his amusement. "*Por Díos*, don Ricardo." Paz made an abbreviated sign of the cross. "God forgive me. I know it is not funny. There is nothing funny about what goes on in my country right now, but I cannot help it. That news about Candelario makes me laugh."

"You are a sick young man." Rick's smile slid sideways.

"That man was one who ended my life, our life, the life we all knew in *Las Palomitas*." Paz swiped at the corner of his eye. The humor that had been in his voice a moment before was gone.

"He killed my father, or helped the ones who did, and my sister, and in a way, my aunt, too. For a time, I thought he had killed you, too. I know the priests teach us at school to forgive, and I suppose I can do that, but I can feel no pity for him. If Emelina took his life, well, she had the right. The truth is she was the one who got to him first." He sat quietly, staring out of the tiny windows across the room.

So many questions burned in Rick's brain, but he was afraid to give voice to any of them at the moment. Instead, he tried a different tack.

"Paz, what happened to Carlos? I remember it was the two of you that put me on that plane. It taxied down the beach and then, and then—" A long-forgotten heartbreak returned. "And then, my cabin was on fire." The words seemed to surprise even him.

Paz made another furtive swipe at his cheek. "Yes, it was. Do you want something more? Something to eat? The food here is *raro*, strange, you know, it's true, but it always tastes good. The ones at my school all like it, and we spend a lot of time studying here."

"Sure, sure. A bagel with cheese, something simple. And you?"

Paz was already back at the front counter, and Rick waited patiently for his return. He carried a tray this time, with bagels and two more drinks.

Paz sat back down. "You asked about Carlos. There is not much to tell. He left the next day after you did, and we never saw him again. With Mariana and *mi papá* both gone, I suppose he had no reason to come back. It was not a surprise." He shrugged. "It has quit raining."

Rick glanced at the windows. "What about the fire at the cabin?"

Paz shifted in his discomfort but did not answer.

"Oh, hell. I don't care about that. What I really want to know is about Mariana's funeral. I have imagined it so many times, what she must have looked like. All of you there, Miguel, Emelina—"

"There was no funeral, don Ricardo." Paz practically whispered his answer.

As Rick leaned across the table, a loud crack, like a pistol shot, rang out, focusing the entire room's attention on the two of them.

"Sorry," Rick muttered as he picked up his cane from the floor where it had dropped from the end of the booth.

"What do you mean there was no funeral? You didn't—"

"*Por el amor de Díos*, I wish there was someone else who could tell you this," Paz moaned. "You saw the cabin burning. Do you remember that night I told you, Carlos put Mariana somewhere safe because he feared the ones who shot you might come back to steal her? He knew, as I did and you, that she was dead, but he was still afraid of what they might do."

He took a deep breath and continued. "Carlos put her in your cabin. They knew we had you, so he thought she would be safe there. After the plane was in the air, I saw the smoke. I ran, and Carlos drove, but when we got there, there was nothing we could do. The fire was over everything. It was the hottest fire I ever saw, and it was a whole day more before we could touch anything. And then there was nothing left. There was no processional, no funeral. *Nada*. I am so sorry to tell you this."

Rick sat with his eyes closed, his head leaning back against the wall behind him. All these years he had imagined every detail of her funeral, perhaps in a grim way to ease his own guilt and retain a grip on his sanity, when heartbreak and despair had threatened to overwhelm him. Only it never happened, and now on the anniversary of her death, he was learning the truth.

He wondered if he should laugh or cry, but the truth is, he felt numb. The deadening sense of sorrow came creeping back to eclipse all hope, to overshadow every fiber of his being, the way it had for months after his return.

"Don Ricardo, are you all right?" Paz interrupted his reverie, reaching across the table to touch his arm.

Rick jumped. "Yeah, I guess. I'm sorry, Paz. Hey—" He tried to laugh, but it did not come out well. "We are in America now. Don't call me don, just Ricardo or Rick is fine."

Paz grinned, remembering how the American had been uncomfortable, his first days in *Las Palomitas* with the common title of respect there, too. He asked Paz then, not to use it, and the boy had explained why that was not possible.

"People would say I have no respect, and they would blame my father, saying his son is *mal criado*, poorly raised."

Rick had laughed at that and let the matter drop, but it amused Paz that it was still a source of concern, even now.

"*Vaya pues*," Paz answered. "In America, I can call you Ricardo."

"Paz, I had no idea that things happened the way they did after I left. Until just now, I had forgotten about seeing the house on fire as the plane took off. I just remember waiting there with you, and then

Carlos came. He was so quiet, it was scary. I never expected him to do anything to save me. If I'd been him, I'm not sure I'd have done the same."

A contemptuous snort escaped Paz. "Carlos left while the ashes of your cabin were still smoking. He told me that morning after the plane left, he did what she asked, by taking care of you. The next day, he was gone and *ya estuvo*. I cannot say I have missed him."

"He took care of me," Rick repeated the words, lost deep in thought.

"So where did the plane take you? What did you do?" The worst seemingly behind him, Paz babbled like a sinner who had just received absolution.

"The plane?" Rick came back to the present. "We landed in Guatemala, but I don't have any idea where. There was a large hacienda and Rutilio, Carlos' driver, the one who couldn't speak, was there. He helped me from the plane and put me to bed. There was a doctor who said I needed surgery and that he couldn't do anything about that. He gave me something to kill the pain, and after that, I could barely stay awake. First, he explained that since I had no papers, they would have to smuggle me back into the US, that there would be fewer questions for everyone that way. I was hardly in a position to argue.

"After another day, they flew me on to Texas in a different plane, with another pilot. This guy looked pretty rough, and we landed way out in the west Texas desert somewhere. I had the feeling he was used to flying illegal cargo but probably not the living, breathing kind. At any rate, my father was there with his Lincoln Continental. Pretty classy ambulance. It was funny because it was the first time I'd ever seen him look really worried about me or anything I was involved in. Someone had called him and told him to meet us there. I thought he was going to have a fit when he got a look at the pilot. I realized later he probably thought everybody I had been with in El Salvador was like him."

Rick shook his head as he concluded his story. "Anyway, he had blankets, pillows, drinks, and everything all fixed up in the back of this car since he was all by himself. We drove straight through to Houston, and I can tell you that's one long drive. He took me to a small private hospital there, and after that, things got pretty blurry. I know there were some questions about me having gunshot wounds, but he managed to get those taken care of, one way or another. That's pretty much all I know."

"How long were you there?"

"Which place?" Rick answered one question with another and half a smile. "I was in the hospital, and then a rehabilitation center, and I guess they talked pretty seriously about a psychiatric hospital commitment but—" he shrugged. "They gave up on that after a little while. It was a couple of months altogether."

"Don Ricardo. I mean Ricardo," Paz caught himself. "I am so sorry. I did not know. All of this because... because of us?" Paz could not seem to make it all fit, as he eyed his friend with a still broken heart.

"All of this, Paz, because after looking for something I needed for most of my life, I found it in *Las Palomitas*, and just as quickly, I lost it. If you want to say it was because of you, then it was because of all the good you and Imanuel did for me. And then I fell in love with your sister. I know that was crazy, but it was like I couldn't help it. All that you shared with me and you didn't take it away. That was somebody else's doing."

Paz nodded. They sat without speaking as the restaurant around them began to fill up with those in search of a midday meal.

"*Y don David*?" Paz finally broke the silence. "What has happened to him?"

"Well, you know David," Rick chuckled. "He is still pretty much the same. I have not seen him much. He came to see me at the rehab center, but it made him pretty nervous." Guilty thoughts of Amy came to mind, unbidden. That David could not tolerate 'sick people' as he called them, did not surprise him. Why did he find the same so intolerable in his own sister?

"He has a new wife and baby," Rick continued. "That means, of course, he's had to settle down some and take a regular job. The last I knew, he was working at a marina at one of the big lakes."

"David, the father. It is hard to imagine, yes?"

"Well, I didn't get the impression that any of this was too well planned. You know, David. I think it just sort of happened."

"Hmm. You said you work at a center, and that is where you saw Juana? What kind of a place is it?"

Rick smiled in relief. "It's a refugee center near the border. That's where I've been for nearly two years now, and it's good work. Frustrating, fighting to get people what they need, but it's been good for me. Juana fled with her children. After Simón died, she tried to open a store at her parents' house, but it didn't do well. The field workers were threatened and told not to go there, so she went to the fields to try to get work instead. Because of her name, people thought she would help with the union organization, too. She said she told the ones who asked her 'no,' but it was as if no one heard her, and then the threats began. She left after a note was nailed to her door, threatening her and her kids. She told me it looked like it was written in blood.

"Her parents and sisters moved to another village, but she couldn't stand it anymore. She was afraid whatever happened next might cost her one of her children, and after losing Simón, she couldn't bear the thought. Who could blame her? Julio has a brother who lives near Seattle, and we helped her to get there. That's the kind of work I do now."

He swallowed the last bit of bagel. "Do you remember Niña Elena from Chirilagua? She came with the priest and the nun, the day of your father's funeral. She works there, too. She has been a big help to me, and every now and then, she finds someone from the villages where she used to work."

"It is good to know she made it out alive. You know what happened to the other one, the nun, Madre Dorotea, who was with her that day?"

"Dorothy? Yes, she was one of the four churchwomen murdered in El Salvador in 1980. I couldn't believe it when I heard. It is still so hard for Elena. One of the reasons she left is because she was also threatened for helping the people. After what happened to her friend, she didn't wait. She works hard at the center. She is in her fifties or sixties now, I can't tell. We have sat up, talking a number of nights. You should see how well she gets things organized."

"You like that, yes? You were always good at this kind of work. I remember you at the clinic on vaccination day."

A nostalgic smile spread across Rick's face. "How would you know? You never showed up to help that day," he teased.

"I was there. You did not see me, but I came. I was outside for a little while with my sister, but she said you were helping and doing such a good job, she did not need me to stay." A knowing wink punctuated his explanation.

"She did know what she was about, didn't she?" Rick leaned back, content for the moment, with his memories.

"And you?" Paz hesitated over the next question. "You are still *soltero?* You have never found someone else?"

There was an apologetic air to his answer. "Still single. You can't move on when you haven't settled with what came before. I'm not sure I could care for someone else after Mariana. I've thought about it, but I just can't wrap my mind around it."

"You still love her." It was a simple statement of fact.

Rick nodded. "I still love her. I can't imagine ever not loving her."

"But, Ricardo, she is... she is dead. You did not die with her."

"Oh, don't be so sure. Part of me did. Believe me, I've been on this merry-go-round with the shrinks. Don't start. Life just has to take its own course. I'm at the *Casa Oscar Romero* now, and that's a big help and a big part of my life. There's not much room for anything else, and that's fine with me. I may have fallen in love with the right girl in the wrong place and time, an impossible situation, but I'm all right, really."

He sat up straight in the booth, pulling his right leg off the bench to look Paz full in the face. "Tell me about you. When did you come?"

"Oh, not so long after you left. At the end of May, I think. I went to a summer school, as it is called here, with other boys who did not know so much either. Most of them were from America, though. There were just a couple of them from other countries, like me. We were taught many things— the wearing of a uniform, how to eat the proper way, personal care, how to be polite to adults and other students—cultural lessons, they were called. They taught us English, too. There were a few boys from the Middle East who also needed to learn the language better and some black ones from here in America who come on scholarships. The same for the other Latinos, Chicanos. Some speak English, but some of it was not good enough, and they had to study like a foreigner.

"Then the next term, in the fall, I started to regular classes. I live at the school and work there some, too, but I thought you knew all of this."

Rick shook his head. "But how did it all come about?" Rick could not yet grasp the source of Paz's transformation.

"A letter came from a solicitor, a lawyer, yes? From here in Houston. Señor Roberto Morales. It explained everything. It said I should take the bus to San Salvador, and there, another lawyer would find me a passport, a visa, and an airplane ticket, all the business to get me to Houston for the purpose of going to school. The letter said *mi patron*, my sponsor, wished to remain anonymous, but when I read it to Miguel, like me, he thought it must be you. We did not understand why you wanted to do it this way, but all Miguel heard was the word 'school.' With that, he was packing my bag for me." He laughed softly.

He looked Rick square in the face. "I was so sure it was you that I did not even mind the idea of more school. The priests at St. Francis. You know them?"

"I know of them." Rick nodded.

"They told me they did not know who *mi patron* was either. The money comes to the school from the same lawyer. He is the only one who knows, Señor Morales and although he is very polite, he is very much the businessman. He has never told me anything, even when I asked."

"You asked him?"

"Well, mostly, I asked him how to find you. Maybe I should have believed him when he said he did not know you. I thought he was lying."

"I know it's not what you want to hear, but he was telling you the truth."

Paz rolled his shoulders forward. "Are you done here? Do you want to walk? I mean, is that all right?" He cast a dubious look in the direction of Rick's cane.

"Me? Yeah, I can walk, and most days, I don't need the cane. I kept up with you in the rain, didn't I?" Rick was already on his feet.

Paz grinned. "Yes, you did."

Outside, they found the morning gloom had been replaced with mild spring sunshine, leaving only the wet shining streets as a reminder of the earlier downpour.

"Do you want to see my school?" Paz asked with more than a touch of pride in his voice.

"Well, I was just wondering about that. Were you supposed to be in classes right now?" He let his words trail away as he caught sight of the sheepish expression on Paz's face. "I thought as much."

"It is not that bad," he began to explain. "I had an hour off for lunch, so I am only a little late, and when I explain to Father Emil why I am so late, I do not think I will be in too much trouble. This is a very special day. That is for certain."

"Who is Father Emil?"

"He is one of those who runs the school. He is older and the one who—" He took a deep breath. "The one who reminds me most of my father. He is French and has always been very kind to me. He speaks Spanish and English and French, and also Latin and Greek. He is the most help when I get too homesick, as they call it here. In the beginning, it was really bad sometimes, but he always understands. He says it is because he, too, knows what it is to be a stranger in a strange land."

A melancholy expression slipped across Rick's face. "He sounds like a good man, especially if he is anything like Imanuel."

"He has been asking me to think about staying in school after graduation here in two months. He says I should think about the seminary, about becoming a priest someday."

A sudden intake of breath gave away Rick's feelings on the subject.

"You do not think it is a good idea?"

"No, that's not it at all. I was just thinking of your father, of how proud he would be right now to know you are even considering the idea."

A crooked little smile lit Paz's eyes. "I suppose that is true. I have thought about what Father Emil says, but I also think about going home."

"And you don't think you can do both?"

"Not right now. I do not want to wait any longer to go back. It has already been so long." A deep sigh racked his whole body.

"Paz, it's not exactly the best time. We have more people than ever coming out of there. It's not safe."

"I know. I have thought of that, and I was willing to wait because I thought it was you who was paying my way. I was willing to wait before, but now I'm not so sure."

They had reached the manicured grounds of St Francis School for Boys. Beyond the brick pillars and black cast iron fencing lay a campus of green grass and hundred-year old buildings still in surprisingly good condition despite the hundreds of boys who had passed over their lawns and through their doors and halls over the decades.

"Paz," Rick stopped at the front gate. "I was thinking. It might be better if I come back later, if that's all right. It is beautiful, and I want to see it. I know where you are now, and believe me, I will be back," he added as he noted Paz's startled expression.

He cast an appreciative eye over the red tile roofs, perched above deep-gold colored brick walls.

He pulled a card from his wallet and scribbled a number on the back. "Here's the phone number to my father's house as well as mine at the center."

Paz studied both sides of the card. "Director. You did not tell me you were the director there."

"It sounds more impressive than it really is," Rick assured him with a self-deprecating smile. "I've got to check out a couple of things, and I'll be back in touch soon. I promise."

"*Vaya pues*, Ricardo." A cloud of uncertainly hovered over the youth. "You will not forget?"

"Forget what? That you're here? Not a chance." Rick was emphatic. "This is the best day I've had in a very long time. You have no idea. I'll get back to you very soon." He slipped an arm around his friend's shoulders. "Get back to your studies for now, okay? Gee, that sounds strangely familiar, doesn't it?"

He was rewarded with Paz's wide familiar smile. "Yes, it sounds like my father and my sister. I will wait to hear from you. Just do not make me wait too long."

"No problem. We have both already done enough of that."

He made his way back to the fatigued pickup truck he had parked near the bank, hours before. Even the parking ticket jammed at an awkward angle under the windshield wiper could do nothing to damper his spirits. He ignored it and stepped inside the public telephone booth on the nearby corner. He flipped through the heavy telephone directory there.

"Roberto Morales," he muttered to himself as he scribbled down the address and number he sought.

* * * * *

The thick plush carpet beneath his feet was the kind that always made him feel just a little off-balance, Rick noted with a grimace as he opened the solid core door to the lawyer's office. He had to step around the dividing wall that blocked his view before he caught sight of the receptionist, a severe-looking woman, who tried to hide what nature had taken from her with an extra layer of rouge and lipstick. Having already spoken to her on the phone, Rick was not surprised to discover her harsh appearance matched her less than-friendly-voice.

"Mr. Mercy," was all she said as she notified her employer of his arrival. He had barely managed to convince her that his business with Mr. Morales was of a legitimate nature. It was not until he mentioned the name José de la Paz Flores that she deemed the conversation to be worthy of a few minutes of the attorney's time.

Roberto Morales, a slightly built man with dark hair, sallow skin, and dark green eyes, peered at Rick through heavy-lensed glasses as he shook his hand briskly. He was the antitheses of his receptionist, seemingly open and friendly.

"It is a pleasure to meet you." He waved Rick to a richly upholstered chair in his inner office. "It is always a pleasure to meet a friend of a friend, no?"

"A friend of a friend?"

"You are a friend of José de la Paz Flores. Is that not correct?" he continued as he seated himself behind a huge, dark cherrywood desk, the surface of which was empty except for a single desk set, containing two ridiculously long fountain pens. Rick tried to imagine it covered with papers, contracts, or other manner of paperwork that would indicate that something of import was accomplished here but could not make the image take hold.

"Yes, Paz is a friend of mine. A friend I didn't even know was in Texas, right here in Houston, until today. He explained a little to me about the arrangement that you oversee that brought him to school. Apparently, he was under the impression that I was the one behind it all. It upset him a great deal to find out otherwise."

"I see." Morales balanced his fingertips together as he swiveled slightly in his high-backed desk chair. "And you told him this?"

"Yeah, I did. I don't know who did bring him here, but I don't appreciate the fact that they apparently used me to do it. Don't get me wrong. I think what you and his true benefactor are doing for him is wonderful. He's a terrific kid who deserves a great future, but how did my name get mixed up in it, is what I want to know."

"Well, Mr. Mercy, to be honest, I believe that was young Mr. Flores' assumption. It was certainly not anything I told him. As a matter of fact, when he asked me, I told him I did not know you, and that is a fact, is it not?"

"Yeah," Rick agreed with a nod and a glance at the soft green carpet beneath his feet, recognizing lawyer-speak when he heard it. "We've never met."

"Mr. Mercy, no one here has led your friend to believe you had anything to do with any of the business of this office. It was young Mr. Flores who first mentioned your name. I remember it clearly now. I assured him that was not the case."

A sinking feeling in the pit of his stomach grew stronger.

"That being the case, although I tried to convince him, he did not seem to take my assurances to heart.

I am sorry if this has caused you any amount of distress, but there is really nothing more I can add."

"Then you are telling me it is just a coincidence that of all the banks in Texas, you just happened to set up this account that pays his expenses at TFI, Texas Financial?"

"I am sorry. I don't see the connection. What does that have to do with you?"

"TFI." Rick blinked, far from believing what he was now hearing. "William Joseph Mercy is the president and Chief Financial Officer there."

"Mr. Mercy, the bank president. Of course, I didn't realize.... Most of my dealings have been with a Charles—" Roberto Morales' thoughts were apparently hopscotching faster than his words when he stopped himself abruptly.

"You are related to William Mercy?" A second glance at Rick's T-shirt and worn jeans spoke more than his words.

"He is my father."

"Well, I can see how that would have you wondering, I suppose, and how it might have young José de la Paz, making his assumptions, incorrect as they are. That never occurred to me. I can assure you no one here has deliberately set about to deceive anyone or to use your father's name or institution inappropriately."

The lawyer's piercing gaze flashed across the desk. "To be honest, young Mr. Flores has been overly concerned from the beginning about who his benefactor is. I have tried to assure him that everything that has been done is totally legal and above board and that there will be no extracurricular demands made on him. Even so, he has concerned himself far too much with this particular aspect of the situation. My client has, from the beginning, stated his intent to remain anonymous. It is not unheard of, and it is certainly his right to do so. Maybe it is just the romanticism of it all and its effect on the young. They seem to demand an answer to every question, to resolve every secret at this age. It is difficult for young people to understand there are many things in this world for which there are no answers. Wouldn't you agree?"

Rick contemplated the nervous man in front of him for a long moment. "I came here to try to find some answers for my friend and to try to set the record straight. I have the feeling you have no intention of helping me do either one."

"Exactly what is it you want from me?"

"A name. The name of the person or persons behind Paz's scholarship."

"You must know I am not at liberty to give you that information. José de la Paz is being well taken care of, and there is no reason to believe that will change any time soon. Beyond that, there is also no further need for concern." He stood up, signaling an end to their conversation.

Rick also stood, a wry little smile playing at the corners of his mouth. "Where are you from, Mr. Morales? Originally, I mean, if you do not mind me asking."

The lawyer glanced down, caught off guard by the personal question. "No, I do not object to answering that one. I was born in Cuba. I came here with my parents over twenty years ago in a small boat, fleeing Castro. I was seventeen at the time. Why do you ask?"

Rick answered in Spanish. "Because compared to the situation in El Salvador, the recent history of Cuba has been pretty black and white, Communist or anti-communist, *ya estuvo*."

Roberto Morales seemed more than slightly taken aback, although Rick couldn't tell if it was the reference to Cuba or the fact that he spoke fluent Spanish.

"Under the circumstances," Rick continued, "which includes the tumultuous blood bath that has taken over the country, forcing Paz in a very real sense to stay in this country, I can't blame Paz for wanting to know who is sponsoring him here. I don't think it has anything to do with his age, and I think he's been pretty patient, all things considered. A damned sight more so than I'd have been in his shoes. It's been an education, Mr. Morales. *Muchas gracias*."

He went out quickly, resisting the temptation to slam the door in his anger. He limped past the receptionist's desk and fumbled with his cane as he opened the front door of the suite, losing his grip on both the door and the cane. The latter landed silently on the thick carpet. The door closed as he bent over to retrieve it. He nearly lost his balance as his stiffened hip refused to function. He leaned heavily for a moment against the wall that blocked him from the receptionist's view. He took a deep breath, struggling to regain his composure. The buzz of the receptionist's telephone startled him.

"Yes, Mr. Morales. Yes, I believe he is gone. Did you want me to stop him? Yes, sir. No, sir. I'm sorry he upset you. Mr. Carlos Panameño? Yes, sir. I'll get hold of him immediately."

With a vicious effort, Rick jerked the door wide open.

* * * * *

When he had walked out of the great grey-green glass doors earlier in the morning, Rick never imagined he would be back in the bank before closing that same day. By mid-afternoon, near the end of the business day in the banking business, the lobby had that fatigued, abandoned look curious to places that were normally so full of people in a hurry.

His steps were deliberate this time as he headed straight for his brother-in-law's office. "Don't worry about it, Susan." He dismissed Charles' secretary, who started to rise from her desk as he barged through the closed door.

Charles' feet, crossed and parked on the corner of his oak desk, crashed to the floor at the sudden interruption. Rick heard something about tomorrow's tee time and clubhouse rules upon entering, but Charles' telephone excuse was convincing as he quickly disengaged himself from the conversation and hung up the phone.

"What the hell do you mean, tearing in here like that?" Despite his irritation, his was a hollow attempt to echo his father-in-law's commanding tone. One good look at Rick's face, dark with fury, further undermined his pathetic efforts to appear authoritative. "What's wrong with you?" He asked in a confused state of apprehension.

"I want you to get busy on your computer there," Rick barked as he pointed to the monitor to Charles' left. "Cough up Carlos Panameño's name and address in this city."

Charles looked aghast. "Rick, I can't do that. It's against the bank's policy to access information for personal reasons. You surely know that. Our records are confidential and besides that—"

"Charlie, I'm not asking you for his blessed bank balance or for his sister's number for a date! This is important. Don't start telling me what you can or can't do. I used to work here, remember? I know exactly what you're capable of when it suits you. And I remember a great deal about what you and George, the loan vice-president used to do. Now start that machine, or do you want me to do it for you?" Rick made a move toward the far side of the desk.

"Okay, okay." Charles clicked on the computer and melted backward into his office chair. He began typing the needed access codes. "What's this all about?" He watched Rick pacing back and forth in the limited space afforded by the office walls.

"I can't believe this." Rick seemed to be talking to himself as much as to his brother-in-law. "The more I think about it, the crazier it makes me. All this time, he's had him here. All this time, I could have been there for him and him for me, but no! Carlos Panameño, right there in the middle of it all again!"

"Rick, calm down. What's this all about?" Charles asked again, keeping his voice low, despite his questions, hoping for some sort of rational answers. "Who is this man anyway? Someone from Panama, right? That's not where you were before?"

"Panama? Panameño?" Rick stopped to stare at the man in the bulging three-piece suit as he untangled the confusion in his own mind. "Good grief, Charles. Panameño is the man's last name, not his nationality. Carlos is Salvadoran. He's from El Salvador. That's where I was, with David. It's close to a thousand miles and at least three countries away from Panama. How do you manage to work in this place, anyway?"

"Hey, Rick, what can I tell you? The Hispanics all run together on me. I can't tell the Mexicans from the South Americans from the Puerto Ricans. Who can?" He concentrated on the data beginning to scan across the screen before him.

"Anybody who listens," Rick muttered under his breath.

"What was that?" Charles asked, not really paying attention while fooling with the computer.

"Nothing. I'm sure the Cuban lawyer I just spoke with would be pleased to know in this bank, you don't differentiate between him and Mexican farm laborers and Salvadoran university students seeking political asylum."

"Hey, Rick, don't get touchy—"

"I don't want to get anything, okay?" Rick was still spitting gravel. "I'll just think of you the next time one of the kids coming through the *Casa Oscar Romero* tells me all *norteamericanos* look alike."

Charles shot him a sharp look over his shoulder as Rick moved behind him, reading the numbers slipping across the screen.

"I'm not making it up," Rick laughed, mirthlessly, his hands in the air. "They really do say that."

"You get over there," Charles whined huffily, pointing to the front side of his desk. "I'll get you what you want just to get you out of here, but you're not going to sit here and read client account numbers and balances."

"Fine, but I don't care how much the old guy's worth. Just tell me where I can find him." Rick moved as directed and sat down for the first time since entering the office.

Charles let out a long low whistle. "The man has a dozen different accounts here."

"Why does that not surprise me?"

"What I can't figure out is why I've never heard of him." Charles pushed his glasses higher up his nose.

"Probably because he does little or none of the transactions himself. See if you've got a lawyer named Morales down on some of them. He's probably written in as his business agent."

"Yes, that name is here on several of them, but not all. I remember him. We've spoken a few times."

"I guarantee it's on one, maybe a trust, set up for the benefit of the minor, José de la Paz Flores." Rick leaned back in his chair, letting go of some of his earlier tension.

"Yes, that's here, too. I repeat my question. Who is this man to you?" Charles looked away from the computer screen to squint across the desk at Rick.

"Give me his address, first," Rick barked as he sat up and snatched a pen off the desk.

Charles read it from the screen with a frown. "All we have is an office address. It's care of Centroamericana Imports over in the warehouse district along the shipping channel. Just that and a separate post office box here in the city. I can't believe we don't have any other address listed."

Rick scribbled down the address without further comment and stood up.

"Hey, you were going to tell me what this is all about?" The banker prompted.

"It's a long story, and I doubt you'd care to listen to the whole thing."

"Now wait a minute. You can't just walk out with this when I don't even know what it's about. You said—"

"All right, all right." Rick snapped and leaned his forehead against the edge of the open door frame as he considered a simplified explanation. "Amy said David told you, the reason I took a bullet a few years ago, was over a woman."

Charles nodded. "That's right. I remember Amy insisted at the time, you would never be so foolish. On the other hand, I wasn't so sure." He leaned back in his chair, teasingly, enjoying the moment.

"Well, Panameño was her husband. And I just discovered we've still got one score left to settle."

He left Charles sitting up straight, with his mouth open as he closed the office door quickly.

* * * * *

It was a futile drive to Houston's east side, this late in the day, he was certain, but something, a force he could not name, compelled him to continue. He gripped the black steering wheel of the pickup as he floored the accelerator, his anger rekindling each time his thoughts returned to the deception that had been foisted on him and, most especially, on Paz.

"Forget the ones you have known here." Those words had stayed with him the past four years, echoing in his heart every day since he had left *Las Palomitas*. He had found it impossible—to forget. He had refrained from making any attempts to contact Paz out of fear for the boy's safety, and now he discovered it had all been a farce, some sort of cruel joke.

Paz was in no jeopardy, or at least, he had not been until now. As the truth had come to him, Rick wondered, how long would it take before it dawned on Paz? And what would his reaction be? To abandon everything here, everything he'd worked to learn, and return to his village and God knows what kind of future, if any?

He thought about the ones who came through the center on a daily basis, people who had lost so many loved ones, who had given up everything they had, small plots of land, a house, all their worldly goods—things they had struggled to win bit by bit, their whole lives. Proud people who had walked away, run away because to stay meant certain horrific death, all because they had stood up to those in power. They had dared to try to make life a little better for someone else or simply because they were Christian. He thought about the ones like Juana, who had already lost a husband and had chosen flight rather than sacrifice her children to the cause as well. He thought about the ones who stayed behind, sacrificing everything to send their sons on because to stay as a poor young man in El Salvador often meant choosing between the army or the rebels with no middle ground. Would Paz now end up like Juana or worse, like Simón or his own father? Or would he, upon returning, choose the life of a *muchacho*, a *guerrillero* in the mountains? It was a long way from anything that Imanuel or Mariana had ever envisioned for him, and somehow, despite his best effort, Rick could not imagine his fishing partner-turned-student with an automatic weapon in his hands.

The greater question, however, was why? What was Carlos' purpose? Why had he worked so hard to disguise his involvement in all of this, and why had he denied he and Paz the chance to spend any of the past four years together? That and the answer to a dozen other questions was what he wanted from Carlos.

Rick guided the pickup between the rows of drab warehouses, crammed along a tangle of railroad tracks that lined the edge of the Houston Ship Channel. A few were clearly designated, but many bore no name at all, while others were lettered or numbered in illegible, washed-out legends. His resolve began to weaken until he spied a single bare light bulb burning in the same ludicrous manner as streetlights that come on in the daytime with the approach of an unexpected storm. The small, neatly lettered sign below read *Centroamericana Imports*. Rick jammed the truck into low gear and kicked on the emergency brake before climbing out. He left the cane lying on the seat in the truck cab.

A small dark window in the door at the top of a short set of wooden steps revealed nothing as Rick tried to steal a glance through it before opening the door. Inside, he hesitated for a moment as his eyes adjusted to the dim interior, after the bright afternoon sunlight.

Much of the concrete floor that spread before him was occupied with floor to ceiling stacks of huge cardboard cartons. A handful of workers, all Hispanic, stood to one side, as they talked and smoked, apparently at the end of their shift. One man left the others and walked with a loose, easy gait in Rick's direction.

"Carlos Panameño," was all Rick said.

The man, in a sleeveless tank top and worn work pants, jerked a thumb toward the back of the building. Following the gesture, Rick caught sight of an open metal staircase on the far left, just beyond the knot of idle workmen. It led to a partial second-floor loft, suspended over the back third of the building. As he approached, a man bounded up the stairs to join a few others whom Rick had not noticed at first who were working above. Something about the way he moved tugged at Rick's memory, but he dismissed it, his mind still churning with other issues.

Beneath the steps, Rick discovered a dark narrow hallway, created on the right by the stacks of boxes that led to the rear of the building. Walking by, he saw a box close to the top of one of the stacks with a raggedly torn open side that revealed a tangle of colored rubber sandals, like those he had seen hanging in the *Tienda Guadalupe* years before.

Three doors along the left-hand wall stood closed and unmarked. The first two were locked, but from the last one, Rick heard a familiar deep voice as he turned the knob and walked in on Carlos, seated at a small, cluttered desk. He hung up the telephone as Rick closed the door and leaned against it.

He had been rehearsing this moment in his mind since leaving Roberto Morales' office, considering what he would say, what he would do and now he found all the outrage, all the hostility he was so sure would explode at the very sight of the man, was unavailable to him. As had happened each time their paths had crossed in El Salvador, it was Rick who was keenly aware of being the intruder, the interloper, the one who should be asking this man's permission or even forgiveness, for what he was not even certain now.

Carlos looked almost the same, he noted, the years having changed him little. He was somewhat grayer was all. He looked out of place behind the too-small desk in the dinghy office. Only the window in the far corner of the room offered any relief from the oppressive, gloomy little room. They said nothing, only staring at one another. After a moment, Carlos reached for the phone again.

"Send Angel Sosa back here," was all he said before hanging up.

"You don't need security. I'm not here to do you any harm."

"I heard you saw the boy. I trust you found him well."

"Yeah, well. I guess you could say that. Paz is fine but pretty confused about what's been going on the last few years, and so am I. You are the one who's been sponsoring him, sending him to St. Francis?"

"You must know the answer to that, or you would not have come at all." Carlos' inability to answer a question directly had changed little over the years.

"Yet you've never been to see him?" Rick was not sure what it was about the man's answer that infuriated him so. "You pay for everything, TAKE CARE of everything, and he has no idea who's behind it all. Did you know he thought it was me? I laid eyes on him for the first time today since I climbed into that plane on the beach, and he's thanking me for being his *patrón*. I didn't even know he was in the country."

Carlos folded his hands across his ample stomach like a displaced Buddha as he leaned back slightly in the creaking office chair. "You were the one piece in this puzzle I could not control when it was all over. I knew he thought the money came from you. That was never an issue of importance. The only part that mattered was that he accept the money and the opportunity it offered. And that once here, he would study hard and do a good job. He has done so. Did he tell you that he is the top student in the graduating class this year? No, I did not think so." Carlos continued as he caught the surprised expression on Rick's face. "I receive regular reports. The boy has done well. That is the only important concern."

"But why, Carlos?" Rick could contain himself no longer. "Why this way? Why not tell him the truth? Why did you keep him and me, both of us, in the dark?" He took a step forward.

"Why? You ask me why?" He sat up straight, leaning into the desk, dropping the mild pretense. "Why does anyone do what they do? Why did you climb on that plane to leave *Las Palomitas* when you did not even know where it was going? Because it was the only way out. The same is true for Paz. Why did he accept the chance for a better life when he was unsure who was behind it? Because it was a chance he might not see again, his only way out, and *gracias a Díos*, he was smart enough to take it. A better question might be, why is he happier thinking this comes from you, a foreigner he barely knew, than from one of his own, a citizen of his own country, a man of his own blood?" His fist hit the desk with the last word.

A string of guttural epithets Rick had heard Paz use to describe Carlos while he still lived in *Las Palomitas* raced unbidden through his thoughts. It was true. Paz might have turned down the chance to go to school if he knew Carlos was the source of support.

"Did you know he is considering leaving after graduation and going back to El Salvador, regardless?" was all Rick could think to say.

"I would be surprised if he did not think about it." Carlos stood up and walked toward the one small window. "We all think about that. You, too, I imagine. The day we can go back, unafraid, without the fear of more bloodshed."

It was perhaps the kindest thing he had ever said in Rick's presence, including him as one who cared about the future of El Salvador.

Rick slumped into one of the two old-fashioned armchairs situated in front of the desk. "Carlos, you've got to tell him, all of it. Now that he knows it is not me, he's going to be more insistent about knowing the truth. Surely, if you explain why, he might very well understand. After all, you were doing what she asked you, right? Mariana." He could not believe he had mentioned her name and said it so calmly, as if he did so on a regular basis. She might always be on his mind and his heart, but he rarely spoke her name aloud.

Carlos stayed in front of the window, but he turned back to Rick. "I should have known if you were going to play a part in any of this, it would be as a complication. That has always been your role, yes?"

Rick flushed at the implication, dropping his eyes to the floor.

"You are so anxious for Paz to know the truth, but what about you? Are you certain you are up to it, too? Are you ready to know everything? You best ask yourself and listen carefully to your answer."

"What does that mean?" The uneasiness that had seized him every time he had ever spoken to Carlos in the past was back. How much did he know? It had been worth the risk when Mariana was alive, but now? He shifted in his discomfort in the heavy chair.

A knock on the door granted him a momentary reprieve.

"*Pase adelante*," Carlos barked.

The door swung open, and the worker Rick had seen scramble up the stairs earlier stood in the doorway. He had a gray scraggly beard and mustache and was thinner than the last time Rick had seen him, but there was no mistaking the light of mischief that still glowed in the man's eyes.

"Miguel!" Rick was completely taken aback.

"Don Ricardo," Miguel answered in Spanish as if he and Rick had seen each other only last week on the fishermen's beach at *Las Palomitas*. He grabbed both of Rick's upper arms in half an embrace as he pushed the door shut behind himself with his foot. "I thought that was you earlier when you first came into the warehouse, but I was not sure. You do not walk in the same way, no?"

"No, not exactly," Rick grinned. "What are you doing here?"

"I work here. It is a good thing, yes?"

"Well, yes, sure it is. I heard you were no longer in the village, but Paz says he gets letters from you from San Salvador, but I had no idea—what did he call you? Angel Sosa?" He stopped speaking, glancing over his shoulder.

"Miguel Angel Flores Sosa. Sosa was my mother's name." He shrugged. "It is safer this way, yes?"

"And you work here? For Carlos?"

"Yes, actually, I go back and forth, from here to San Salvador and back again, in the work. I always mail the letters to Paz from there. It makes fewer questions for him to answer, yes?"

"I'm not sure," Rick responded honestly, looking from one to the other of the two men. "Hey, *amigo*, you look good."

"*Sí?*" Miguel raised his eyebrows in question. "Not like an old man?"

"We are all getting a little older. Somedays, I feel a great deal older."

"That is the way of the world, no?" Miguel added with a wink. "It is good to see you, to know with my own eyes that you are well. From what I heard, you did not leave *Las Palomitas* in such a good condition. I was sorry that I did not know until after you were gone."

Their reunion was interrupted by the gruff yet measured voice from the far corner, now speaking in Spanish. "He has seen Paz today, and he says the boy is anxious to know the truth. What do you think?"

Miguel's eyes flitted back and forth between the other two. Sober considerations replaced the joyful countenance, but when he spoke, there was an ease, a change in his manner from the days in the village that Rick could not identify.

Miguel hunched his shoulders forward. "I think we always knew this day would come, yes? We have been lucky that he waited this long."

"I suppose that is true," Carlos sighed. "And this one?" He cocked his head toward Rick.

"This one was also like a son to Imanuel. You know that, even if you do not like to admit it." His face broke into a smile, reminiscent of happier days once again as he reached up and patted the side of Rick's face with a gnarled hand. Something inside of Rick twisted painfully as he was reminded of the similarities between Imanuel and his brother, Miguel.

"You should tell him, Carlos. You should have told him a long time ago. You should have told them both. I told you that, but it was not my decision. I cannot help you with this, *hermano mío*. I will wait outside." He touched his confused friend on the shoulder as he walked toward the door. "Be patient with him, don Ricardo. This will not be easy."

"Wait," Rick called after him as he opened the door. "You called him—"

"I will wait outside," Miguel repeated, pulling the door gently closed behind him.

"What the hell is that all about?" Rick twisted back toward Carlos, a mix of anger and now trepidation threatening to overwhelm him.

Carlos remained resolute, moodily staring out of the window. When he did speak, it was of Mariana. "Men often sought her attention over the years we spent together, once I took her from the village. That was never a surprise. She was a beautiful girl and later, a beautiful woman. But even while they paid attention to her, she never seemed to notice them. Until you came along." He stopped to look at Rick, who remained standing by the door. "You have always been a complication." He was quiet for a moment before asking, "what did she tell you about me?"

"What did she tell me about you?" Rick echoed the question hollowly. "What are you asking? What difference could it possibly make now? If you know—" His voice trailed off as Carlos looked directly at him.

"Is it too much to ask?" There was a deceptively gentle quality to the question. "I cannot believe you spent the time with her that you did, and I was never mentioned."

The vulnerability to his voice lent Rick the courage to attempt an honest answer. "I tried not to ask too much," he began. "The more I learned about her, the more I realized she had dealt with enough pain in her life. The last thing I wanted was to cause her anymore. When she did speak about you, it was respectful, kind, and loving." He faltered over the word and closed his eyes as he remembered. "She said you were a good man and that she would not hurt you deliberately. She said you had saved her life when you took her from the village the first time and that she would always be grateful to you."

"Grateful." Carlos practically snorted the word. "Did you never wonder about me, Richard Mercy? Did you never think about me all that time you were with Mariana? Or did you just think me a fool because I never said or did anything about it?" The power in his voice intensified with each question.

Rick swallowed hard and concentrated on staying on his feet, despite the weakening in his knees. "Did I what?" He stalled for time, trying to determine the best avenue toward any sort of defense.

"Did you never wonder?" he repeated. "In my country, men are killed daily for what you did. *Crimen de pasión*. Crime of passion. No one thinks about it very much. Even in this country, the same thing happens."

Rick said nothing. The only thing he was wondering about was in what condition he might leave this building and when.

"You made her happy." Carlos made it sound more like an accusation than a statement of fact. "I knew it from the evening I found all of you at the restaurant during the *Fiesta de San Rafael*. She had a fight with

Gomez that night. I heard about that later, but more important to her was the dance she had with you."

"She told you?" Rick was incredulous.

"She did not have to. A blind man could see it. She loved you, and you were right. She had more than enough unhappiness in her life. If you could give her some joy, even for a short time, it was not up to me to take it away."

Rick sat back down, daring to breathe a small measure of relief.

"I would love to leave it at that, to let you think I am that generous, but it is not that simple, and it is not the truth. That is what you said you wanted. That is what Miguel spoke of, even now." He put his hands behind his back and pursed his lips.

"You heard what he called me just now?"

"Rick nodded with a frown. "*Hermano mío.* My brother?"

"Because that is what I am, because that is who I am." He took a deep breath before continuing. "There were three brothers, all born in the mountains, far to the north of the place you knew, *Las Palomitas*. You knew two of them, Miguel, the middle one, and Imanuel, the youngest. But the oldest son, Ricardo, became involved with the daughter of a rich man who owned a vacation house there outside their village. It was a foolish thing to do because there was no future for the two of them. He was not wise enough to know that at the time. He was in love and even more incredible, she loved him. It did not matter to her that the young man worked as a gardener and caretaker for her father. They kept their love a secret for a few short months, but when his child began to grow inside of her, they could keep it hidden no longer.

"Her father would not forgive her or the man, and he threw her out and ordered one of his workers to shoot the young man on sight. They were certain they had no choice, and they ran away together. The truth is they had no money and no place to go. Her father was an influential man, but alone, she had nothing. He needed work, and he finally found a job in one of the ports, working on an independent shrimp boat."

He stopped and watched a fly for a moment as it crept across the windowpane. "The work was hard and long, but the worst part was he was not able to stay close to her. There was no money for a doctor, and he worried all the time about leaving her alone. She seemed fine and even laughed when he worried aloud about all that she had given up to be with him. She told him it did not matter, and for a time, he believed her.

"And then the baby came while he was gone, working. They told him later, it happened quickly. The midwife came when the neighbors sent for her but, even she did not know how to help. Paloma died as I held her, just hours after I got off the boat." He closed his eyes.

"You?"

"Yes, me. I was born Ricardo Amado Flores Sosa. I changed my name once I left the mountains to avoid Raúl Gomez and those he hired to pursue me for a time."

"Gomez?" Rick's head was spinning. "Wait a minute. First, you are telling me you're the brother to Miguel and Imanuel. That makes Mariana your niece, for heaven's sakes. And now you tell me, it was Gomez that was after you even then? You and Gomez's daughter?" Rick was back on his feet, but this time there was no fear of reprisals.

"No, she was not my niece. That is what I am trying to tell you. Paloma was the daughter of Raúl Gomez, it is true. And she was everything he was not— open, kind, generous. She died, but her daughter, our daughter, Mariana Paloma, survived. I could not keep her, working on a shrimp boat, so I took her to my youngest brother, Imanuel, and his wife, Ana Guadalupe. Miguel had already moved to *Las Palomitas*, and they were preparing to follow him. They simply told people in their new home that she was their child. Miguel was the only other person who knew any different. He remains outside, even now, if you do not believe me."

"That she was your daughter?" Rick spoke in a hoarse whisper. "Of all the things I ever imagined, whenever I saw you together, I never thought—" He stopped speaking, choking on his own fury as he took a step toward Carlos. "I could kill you myself for what you did to her!"

"And just what is it that you think—? My God, man. I knew who she was! I always knew! I never forgot!" Carlos's detached composure was gone as he shouted.

"Where did it come from then, that she was your wife? Did she know the truth? And how much?" Rick yelled back.

"She knew. She knew it all, and it was her idea that we should be known as a couple," Carlos huffed as he returned to his desk chair. He sat down heavily, and after a couple of deep breaths, he continued.

"She knew none of it until after she herself crossed paths with Gomez. I had heard that he had taken a house at *Las Palomitas* years later, but he did not know about the baby. I did not think he would ever make the connection, and now I know he did not."

"But what about Imanuel? I thought he was her father. Paz still thinks that, doesn't he?"

Carlos studied the surface of the desk before him. "She was safer, more loved in *Las Palomitas* than any place else I could have left her. Imanuel and 'Lupe raised her as their own. Even after 'Lupe died, Imanuel insisted that she stay, that she was a true sister to Paz, and that it would break both their hearts to separate them. He was right, of course. He raised her, and she adored him. Even after she knew the truth, it changed nothing between them."

Rick thought about the gentle jibes she would throw Imanuel's way, calling him an old man and the tears in her eyes, the day he went after Simón's body. Even then, she knew what his fate might be.

"After Paloma died and I left Mariana with Imanuel," Carlos continued his story. "I went back to work on the shrimp boat. I put all my energy, all of my life into the work of pulling shrimp out of the sea. A man has to have some place to put all of his passion when he is in that much pain, or he will lose his mind. The old man who owned the boat, he looked after me, almost like a father. Maybe because he understood the pain of losing the one you love. His wife was dead, and he had no children. Then one day, he died suddenly on the boat, pulling in the nets. Apparently, his heart just stopped. We took the boat in immediately, and I was shocked to discover a few days later that he left the boat to me.

"That's where the name Panameño came from. It was his. I took it after he died as a way of keeping it alive. After that, I worked even harder. And as I slowly built up a little money, I bought a share in another boat, and from there, well, the rest is not important. I went back once or twice to visit Imanuel and Miguel and to look in on Mariana. She was so beautiful, just like her mother. To look at her, it was as if I had nothing to do with creating her. If I committed any sin, it was loving my own child so much, I could never tell her 'no,' even when she wanted to let the world think we were together, rather than the truth.

"When she was hurt, I took her away, to get help for her, as well as to get her away from Gomez. I knew better than most how ruthless he could be."

He sighed. "It was Mariana who devised the business of allowing people to think we were a couple. After what she had been through, she had a profound fear of most men. I told her I did not think it was such a good idea, that it made her look like a young girl interested in an older man for his money. She laughed at that and said it made her feel safer and more secure and that she was not worried about what people thought."

He looked down, amused by the memory. "She liked to tease that it would make people wonder about me, what it was about me that could hold a younger woman's interest."

Rick leaned forward in the chair, his elbows resting on his knees, his head in his hands. "My God, all the time, she let me think, you and her.... why?"

"Because she knew if you thought she was free, you might convince her to leave with you. And she knew, she had already made a choice that made that impractical, if not impossible."

Rick took a steadying breath. "Because of her heart?"

"She told you?"

"I figured it out that last day, after Imanuel's funeral. A lot of little things came together. When I confronted her, she didn't want to tell me, but once she realized I knew—she told me. She said only you and Imanuel knew and that neither of you would have told."

"When she got sick as a child, I took her and Imanuel to see the doctors to find out what was wrong. When they told us she needed to rest, there was no reason to interfere. I took them back to the village, but we never suspected there would be permanent damage to the heart. The truth is, I don't think the doctors knew either."

The room grew silent, both men adrift in their own personal anguish, over a loss no amount of explanation could assuage.

"But how could you let her make a choice like that?" Rick asked as he leaned back, ashen-faced still. "She said you were against it. Surely, if she had stayed in some sort of hospital—" Half-way through, he realized, he did not even know where he was going with the question. It was all too much to take in at once. His eyes brimmed with tears of futility and memories.

A gentle tapping on the door preceded Miguel's entrance. "Are you two still talking?"

"*Pase, pase.*" Carlos waved him in and switched back to Spanish.

"He wants to know why I let Mariana go home instead of making her stay in a hospital." Carlos was back to his normal remote self.

Miguel scoffed with a gentle smile. "Whoever succeeded at making Mariana do anything she did not want to do? She came on the bus that first day because Carlos would not bring her, so she simply came home herself."

Carlos continued. "The doctors told her the only options were to rest, to eat carefully, to stay away from smoking and drinking, and to avoid stress. All the things that doctors always tell people." He waved a hand in the air in dismissal. "She told me once after the doctors' diagnosis that *Las Palomitas* was the only place she might have a chance to do that. She said the stress of living in cities and other places she did not belong was more difficult for her than anything else. I did not take it seriously until the day I came home and found she had left me a note, saying she had taken that damn bus."

"She got more than she expected even on that first bus ride back." Rick found he could think of her with a smile on his face, even if it did little to ease the pain in his heart.

Carlos added. "I suppose the best I can offer is to remind you that if things had happened only a little differently, if she had chosen a hospital, for instance, you would never have met her."

"I've thought of that sometimes," Rick answered. "I've thought about how different my life might have been if I had never gone to El Salvador at all."

"And what answer do you give yourself?"

"That God only knows where I would be by now. I have no reason to believe things would be any better. It has been hard, but I would not trade that time for any other. It changed my life, pushed me in new directions." His thoughts turned to the *Casa Oscar Romero*. "Places I would never have discovered otherwise."

"It is good to know," Miguel added. "And I can tell you, even if he will not, I think she would say the same."

Rick's smile broadened at the kindness in the statement.

"You underestimate me, Miguel Angel. It is true. He gave her happiness in the end. There is no doubt. That is why I never interfered, Mr. Mercy."

"Now we need to convince Paz, no?" Miguel added. "He needs to know that it is his own family that has kept him in school and that when the time is right, when it is safe, he can go back. But it should also be when he has learned enough to have something to offer, yes? That is what his father would have wanted. Of this, I am certain. For his son to be of service, as a teacher, a doctor, a—"

"A priest?" Rick broke in.

"Is that what he is thinking?" Miguel shook his head. "So, just like his father, after all."

Rick nodded.

It was dark when Rick left the warehouse a short time later. Crossing the empty span of concrete floor, he sorely missed his cane, especially at the end of a long day spent mostly on pavement and concrete. He had become pleasantly accustomed to spending a great part of the day walking on the low flat fields around the refugee center. He fell, exhausted, into the driver's seat of the pickup truck.

Carlos and Miguel had agreed that he should discuss what he had learned with Paz since there was a greater possibility of his acceptance if he heard at least a part of it from Rick first. Initially, Rick resisted, not wanting to be perceived in any way as a part of their silent conspiracy, even at this late date. But in the end, he acquiesced, more because of what the end result would mean for Paz than due to their insistence.

His thoughts reeled, lurching from one facet to another, of all that he had learned in a single afternoon. "Are you ready for the truth?" Carlos had asked him.

He knew now, without a doubt, that she had loved him, but as with all of the men in her life, she never trusted him completely. Under the circumstances, he sighed, he really could not blame her. Why, then, did it hurt so, a resurgence of that terrible ache, that overwhelming sense of nothingness that filled the space where his heart was supposed to be? If things had only been a little bit different, if the timing of some part of it had only....

He guided the truck to the side of the highway, where it died almost immediately. He leaned his forehead on his hands against the steering wheel as he struggled to find the balance that would allow him to go on.

"If you are too tired to drive, sir." The voice outside the open driver's window startled him awake. "You should pull off at the next exit."

"What? Oh, Officer, I... I apologize." Rick stared at the Houston policeman standing beside the driver's door. "I had no idea. I didn't intend to fall asleep," Rick stammered, unsure of exactly where he was. "I stopped for just a minute and—"

"It's nearly midnight, sir. Have you been drinking?"

"No, sir. No, that is not the problem, Officer."

The policeman flicked a flashlight across his face, but Rick resisted the temptation to turn away. "This vehicle is registered to an address in the Brownsville area. Is that correct?"

"Yes, that's right. I work there."

"Your license, please."

Rick fished his driver's license from his wallet and handed it over. "Are you planning on driving back to Brownsville tonight?"

"No, I have relatives here in Houston. That's where I'm headed now."

"Very well." The patrolman returned his license. "If you aren't in need of any other assistance, you may proceed but no more sleeping on the side of the road, especially in an unlocked vehicle."

"Yes, sir. Thank you." Rick breathed a sigh of relief as the navy-blue uniformed officer walked back to his own car, topped with flashing revolving lights.

More explanations to be made to Amy and Charles, as well as Paz, was something he did not need right now. The thought made him wince. Tomorrow, he thought, as he parked the truck at the foot of the long driveway leading to his father's house.

'Do not be anxious about tomorrow. Let the day's own trouble be sufficient for the day.' The scripture from Matthew danced through his head. Elena had painted it in Spanish and English, on a small plaque that hung in the kitchen in the center. The thought of it now provided an even stronger support than the cane in his hand as he ambled up the drive with the hope of slipping, unheeded, into bed.

* * * * *

The lush green grounds of St. Francis School for Boys provided an unusual verdant island close to the center of downtown Houston. Strolling across the thick carpet of grass near the campus cathedral, Rick waited for Paz while relishing the patent air of tranquility that seemed to emanate from the buildings and other surroundings of the long-established institution.

He had put off the visit until afternoon, sleeping late into the morning. He had thought of little else since waking, and still, he felt unprepared to share all that needed to be told.

Paz appeared from around the corner of another building, walking on the far side of the quadrangle with a few other boys. He quickly separated and trotted over to Rick.

"They just told me you were here." He greeted his friend with a wide smile of relief, Rick noted. "It is good to see you again." He threw down the book bag he had slung over his shoulder and stretched. "It is good that classes are done for today. For the whole week."

"What are you studying right now?" Rick's effort at benign conversation was strained, but he was still struggling with where to begin.

"We just came from American History class. This country has a very strange history in some cases, yes?"

"I won't deny that. Anything specific?"

"We are studying right now the end of World War I, and although the United States claimed they wanted peace that would last, they would never join the League of Nations. The one that came before the United Nations. Your own president, Woodrow

Wilson, was behind it, and still, they would not join. This is something I do not understand."

"There are a lot of situations like that in life, Paz. Things we do not understand at the time, not until much later. There is a phrase in English about a person being ahead of his time. Maybe that's what the problem was for Woodrow Wilson."

"Maybe," Paz answered. They walked slowly toward the far end of the quadrangle, where Rick sat down on a bench in the late afternoon sunshine. "You seem worried. Is there something wrong?"

"I went to see your friend, Morales, the lawyer, yesterday."

"Yes, and did you learn something more?" Paz dropped to the grass and leaned back, looking up at Rick.

"Yeah, I did. I found out who your sponsor is, and I went to see him."

Paz sat up straight. "And do you know him?"

"Yeah, but before I tell you more, I need for you to tell me a few things. To make everything clear."

"Yes? What do you want to know? I will tell you anything, if I know it. You surely believe that."

"Do you remember the afternoon of the last day, I was in *Las Palomitas*? I surprised you in your house when you thought I'd left. You said you were with Miguel and some of the other fishermen. You came in to get more beer for them, I think. You said something that day about Miguel and Imanuel having another brother. At the time, I did not think much about it, but I just wondered, how much more you know about him?"

"Ricardo? Nothing really. Miguel told me more than my father ever did. He was like that about a few things, things he would not talk about. Miguel, when he drank, would talk a little. He said that Ricardo was older, and from what I understood, he got into trouble with a rich man's daughter. He left their village in the mountains, and they never saw him again. That is all I know. *Por qué?* Why does that have any importance now?"

Rick took a deep breath. "Well, apparently, you have seen him again, many times, you just did not know it. Carlos Panameño, the man we thought of as a friend of your father's, is Ricardo Flores Sosa. The rich man's daughter was Raúl Gomez's daughter, Paloma. They ran away together and had a baby girl, named Mariana—"

"Mariana Paloma," Paz whispered the name as the color drained from his face.

He had done it badly, as he feared he would, running it all together as if to stop for even a moment, he would not be able to continue.

"*Santisima Madre de Díos.* Ricardo, you are telling me that my sister, the one I thought was my sister, was the granddaughter of Raúl Gomez?"

A weak smile tugged at Rick's face. "I can't say that's the first way I thought of it, but yes, it is true. Paloma died after the baby was born, and Ricardo gave her to his brother Imanuel and his wife, Guadalupe, to raise as their own, just as they were moving to *Las Palomitas*. Ricardo changed his name to Carlos Panameño after the name of the man he worked for. He stayed away for many years and never planned to interfere in any way. Gomez did not even know of Mariana's existence, and they all wanted to keep it that way. After what happened between Mariana and Roberto, Gomez's son and her own uncle, Carlos took her away to protect her and to find medical help for her. He said it was her idea to let everyone think they were a couple. It made her feel safer, especially once she knew the truth."

"So why are you telling me all of this now?" Paz climbed to his feet as he began to tremble. "How did you learn all of this? That my sister was really what, my cousin?"

"Because," Rick hesitated a moment longer. "Because it is your father's brother, the man you know as Carlos, who is your sponsor here, your *patron*."

"No!" Paz shouted. "*No puede ser!* That cannot be!"

"Paz, I'm sorry. I know it is not what you wanted to hear, but—"

"Not what I want to hear! It is the worst! Why did you not just tell me it was some relative of Raúl Gomez? That is what I used to worry about, that it was some sort of sick joke. More than once, I thought somehow, they have the wrong boy, and someday, they would find out and then—"

"Paz, calm down." Rick reached up and grabbed hold of Paz's school jersey and pulled him down to sit on the bench beside him. "What are you babbling about?"

"I told you before. It was Carlos who took her away from us, and now you tell me he is the one who took me away from my home. It settles one question quick enough. I am going home where I belong. As fast as I can pack!"

He started to stand, but Rick pulled him back to the bench. "What's wrong with you?"

"What is wrong with me?" Paz's voice cracked as he came close to tears. "Everything! I have been here for years now, living a lie, thinking all this time, that it was you who was doing this incredible thing. Now I find out it is from a man that I always hated. I cannot stay here and continue to live on his money. My whole life has been a lie. My sister was not my sister. A man I hate is my uncle. My father, my mother? Who are they? Do I know? Maybe that is someone else as well!"

"Stop it, Paz!" Rick did not like the position he had been forced into, but he didn't like his young friend's reaction to the whole thing either. "Your father was who he was and nothing more or less. Your father took in his brother's child to love her, raise her, and protect her. You act like it was all done to trick you in some way. Grow up a little, sport. You think you are the only one who got hurt in all of this?"

The sharp tone in Rick's voice cut into Paz's tirade. Rick heaved a weary sigh and continued.

"I won't pretend it is the same because my situation does not have the history that yours does, but believe me, you're not the only one who feels betrayed. I asked Mariana more than once, to leave with me and she always made it sound so impossible. I assumed it was because she was married to Carlos. She wasn't, of course. He was her father, and she knew it. Apparently, he and Imanuel told her the truth sometime after he took her away when she was sixteen. So, all those years, you were blaming him for stealing her away when it was really her idea to act as if they were a married couple. She came back to *Las Palomitas* after her heart began to fail. That's the part she kept from you and from me. Only Carlos and Imanuel knew. She had heart damage from a childhood illness, and when the doctors said she would not live much longer, she decided to go home. She said she had nothing to lose. That's why she could stand her ground with Gomez. She went back because she wanted to die at home, and as it turned out, that is exactly what happened, but not before one other person got involved."

Rick gave the cane a vicious twist into the ground as he finished.

"I'm sorry." Paz was suddenly contrite. "I did not even think how it must make you feel. I know you loved her, too."

"It's not your fault. It's just—"

The bells of the nearby cathedral began to sound a melancholy scale. Rick raised an eyebrow in Paz's direction.

"It is time for vespers. If I do not go..." He let out a ragged breath. "Although *por Díos*, I do not feel like it right now."

A little laugh escaped Rick. "It's all right. Maybe it will help. Come on. I'll go with you."

"But you are not Catholic?"

"My mother was Catholic, and I discovered after she died that she had me baptized, although apparently my father never knew. He was furious when he found the baptismal certificate after her death. See? Many families have their secrets, some big, some small. Since I left *Las Palomitas*, a few things have changed in my life, too. Working for the diocese here in Texas, well... let's say, I have learned 'from whence cometh my help.' I have also learned the fallacy of trying to depend solely on myself or others in this world. Sooner or later, all people will disappoint you, Paz, one way or another. It is not that they mean to, it is simply the way we are made." He stood up and dropped his hand on his friend's shoulder as he gently guided him in the direction of the pealing church bells.

* * * * *

When they came out of the church after the short Mass, a priest, a man of small stature with dark curly hair and dark eyes, stood at the door.

"There are two men who want to speak to you." The priest, speaking with a slight French accent, addressed Paz.

"Father Emil, this is my friend, Ricardo, the one I told you about who once lived in our village in El Salvador."

The Frenchman shook Rick's hand, and Rick began immediately to understand why Paz so admired the man.

"I have heard much about you and your adventures in *Las Palomitas*," he began. "Paz speaks very kindly of you and all that you did there."

Rick responded, as they walked together across the campus toward the main office "I did enjoy life in *Las Palomitas*, just as Paz did."

"Who is it that is waiting? They are here for Ricardo?" Paz asked.

"They asked for the two of you, I think." Father Emil cast a questioning eye in Rick's direction.

"I didn't get a chance to tell you everything earlier," Rick began. "I told you I found Carlos, but I also found Miguel."

"*Mi tío Miguel? Aquí?*" Paz was shocked.

"Yes, he works for Carlos now. I gather he goes back and forth to San Salvador in his export business. I probably would not have believed all that Carlos told me if Miguel had not been with him to back up the whole story."

"But why did he never come to see me?" The agitation was back in Paz's voice. "I do not understand."

"He said it would be safer for you. Fewer questions. I guess they are still afraid of what Gomez might do." Rick hurriedly tried to finish his explanations as they neared the office.

"But Gomez is dead!" Paz hissed under his breath as they followed the priest inside.

Rick felt as if he had hit another wall. "What are you talking about? How do you know?"

"Because it happened just after you left. It was all over the news. Señor Raúl Gomez, the well-known industrialist, killed by *guerrilleros. Los muchachos* got him. I do not know if it was Franco or someone he knew, but he was dead before I left the country."

"Such violence comes with these revolutions, acts of murder even against the children." Father Emil shook his head in sadness as he opened the door for them.

"The government there murders women, children, friends, and relatives of any they judge to be guilty. And then, of course, they also get to decide what constitutes a crime." Rick's answer was unintentionally acidic.

Why is it, he wondered, that all school buildings of a particular era are built so much alike? The same brown poured floor, the same dark brown wooden doors, each with a large window and Venetian blinds, leading off of plaster hallways. A wave of *déjà vu* dread swept over him, as he was suddenly ten years old, walking down the hall of a Midwest grade school on his way to the principal's office.

"Where are we going?" Paz stopped abruptly outside the door Father Emil indicated. "To see Carlos? I do not want to see him. I will not."

"I'm sorry." Rick muscled his way behind him, pushing open the door as he spoke. "You don't have a choice. I still have some questions, and I need answers."

The conference room surprised Rick with its large yellow wood table and soft cushion of mauve carpet. Miguel sat to one side of the head of the long board room table, but Carlos, just as he had in the warehouse, stood stoically staring out the window. Apparently, Rick thought, he had watched their entire approach as they crossed the campus.

"Miguel!" Paz dropped any pretense as he threw his arms around his uncle, who rose to greet his nephew in a similar fashion. Rick thought of the day on the beach when Paz had nearly drowned. Miguel had been the first to speak to him, to put his emotions into words of appreciation.

"It has been too long, boy. Too long!" Miguel roughed up Paz's hair as if he was still a young teen, although now he had to reach above his own head to do so.

"It is true, *Tío*. Rick told me a little bit of what you have been doing. It looks good on you, whatever it is." Paz stepped back and surveyed his uncle from an arm's length.

"It is easier than fishing, that is true." Miguel laughed. "And you? That is what I should say to you. That being a scholar agrees with you, Pazito. You are taller than ever before. They must feed you well here."

"Yes," he replied with his signature smile. "They take very good care of me here." He shot a furtive glance at the man in the far corner.

"I can see that is true. So, tell me, what do you study? What do you learn? You look so—" The old fisherman hesitated, looking for the right word. "So grown up. So educated. You do not look like a barefoot village boy anymore. Your father would be very proud to see you right now." Miguel's gaze dropped to the floor, and he cleared his throat. He dragged the back of his hand quickly across his eyes.

"I will always be a village boy on the inside," Paz replied, a touch of anger creeping into his voice. "Nothing anyone does to the outside of me, nothing that I learn, will change that."

"Oh, I know that," Miguel shrugged, refusing to be drawn into whatever argument Paz was looking for. "I just mean you look good, very much the man now. What do you think, Carlos?"

Carlos spoke without turning around. "I think the staff here has done a good job of guiding a dirty-faced village child onto the proper path to manhood. I think that village child has worked hard to become something his father would indeed be proud of."

An awkward silence hung over them as Paz hesitated, unsure of how to respond.

"Here, sit down, sit down." Miguel took on the nervous air of frenetic activity Rick remembered so well in Imanuel's movements when tension would threaten to take over. "We have much to talk about, yes? I know don Ricardo has explained some things to you, but I am sure you have more questions—"

Rick made no move to join them. "This is family business, really, Miguel. I've done all I can. You all need to work it out from here. I'll just wait outside."

"Don Ricardo, that is not necessary," Miguel began to protest.

"Do not go, Ricardo. I will not stay if you leave." Paz was already leaning toward the door.

"I'm not leaving, Paz. Just going to wait outside the door. I won't be far if you need me."

"How are they doing in there?" Father Emil, still hovering outside the door, asked as Rick joined him.

Rick's heart skipped a beat, startled by the man so close behind him in the hallway.

"I'm sorry," the priest apologized. "I waited. Just to be certain."

"Certain of what?" The question popped out without any forethought.

"Certain of Paz. This is a great deal for him to take in at once." With his head cocked to one side, like an inquisitive, wrinkled little sparrow, Rick could not help but smile at the priest's protective nature.

"Paz has many people who care about him," Father Emil continued as the two of them stood in the hallway, leaning against the wall. "There are the two in there, plus yourself. Even me. Every boy in this school should be so fortunate."

"I imagine that's true. Although from what I hear in there, he is his own worst enemy. In one way, I can't blame him. He feels betrayed by people he trusted to tell him the truth."

The priest's shoulders rose and then fell. "Maybe, but it was done to protect him. It was done out of love. He is a smart boy. We must have hope that when he calms down, he will see that part of it, too."

Rick stole a sideways glance at Emil. "You've known for a long time, haven't you? I mean, about who was keeping him here?"

"Someone had to know. In every family, there is one who keeps the secrets, yes? In the family that we are here at St. Francis, I know most of what is going on, even though these boys think differently."

Rick smiled and shook his head.

"Do you know what is going on in there?"

Rick shrugged. "Not exactly. I only know that it is their fight, not mine."

"But you know what it is that makes them all feel so twisted up inside?"

Rick looked up from the crack on the floor that he had been studying. "Yeah, I know about that, too. It's about losing the ones you love."

"I thought I saw it in you, too, but I was not sure at first. You are not so easy to read."

"Saw what?"

"The guilt. I have heard it called by different names, but the one that describes it best, I think, is survivors' guilt. Paz suffers greatly from this as do the others. I think that is part of the reason he has worked so hard here. Guilt that he is still alive while others, like his father and his sister, have died. What made the difference? Was it something he did or did not do? Was it something the ones who died did differently? One never knows the answer to such questions, of course, but they drive men, just the same. Drive men to do things they would not normally do, like become a great student or sponsor a boy in secret. I think Mr. Carlos Panameño has come through a great many things in his life, but I do not think he believes he is strong enough right now to bear that boy's rejection. His brother believes the same."

Rick examined the face of the man before him. He had no agenda in all of this, he decided. Like Rick, he truly wanted whatever was best for Paz. The raised angry voices from the next room interrupted the two in the hall before Rick could reply.

Inside, they found Paz standing before the table, pointing an accusing finger at Carlos, who remained at his station by the window. Miguel sat with his head in his hands, his elbows resting on the table.

"How could you not know! He worked for you! Did you not know what members of *ORDEN* were doing to us out there in the *campo*, or did you not care? The army, *ORDEN*, the rich ones like Gomez, in truth, like you—they are all the same, working together to wipe out the poor and the Christians! Are you not part of them? They killed my father and my sister! You tell me now that my father was your brother, but why should I believe you? How do I know you are not one of them?"

"Because I'm telling you, that's why!" Carlos lost control of his temper as his voice thundered across the room. "Because I was there when Gomez died. I made it happen for his part in the murder of Imanuel and Mariana. I wanted him to die, for every death he has had a hand in for the last many years. For his own daughter and granddaughter and my brother, too! I only wished to God I had done it sooner!"

The stunned silence was broken only by Father Emil as he pulled the door closed behind him once again. Rick pulled out a chair and collapsed into it as he tried to make sense of what he had just heard.

"What a lie!" Paz scoffed, still on his feet. "Everyone knows the *guerrilleros* killed Gomez. I think it was probably my cousin, don't you, *Tío*? That is what all the newspapers said at the time."

"I have no idea, Paz." Miguel sounded as miserable as he looked. What little family he had left was falling apart right before his eyes. Rick sympathized in silence.

Carlos was gasping for breath as he struggled to regain his composure. "There was a rebel group there that evening, it is true, but they were too late. Gomez and I had already had our little discussion." He snatched another ragged breath.

"I went there with the idea of killing him. I wanted to do it. God knows I'd wanted to do it for years, for what he did to Paloma and me, for pushing us into a corner so tight that she died from as simple a thing as childbirth. For what he put Mariana through. If I had thought it would do any good, I would have told him years ago that she was his granddaughter, but I knew him. He would think only of the part of her that was of *campesino* blood, not the part that was his own."

He swallowed hard before continuing. His manner, as well as his voice, softened at the mention of her name. "All Mariana wanted was a little peace. In the end, she was the one who chose how she wanted to spend the last few months of her life. He had no right to cut that time short or to make her any more miserable than he already had. Oh yes," he said through clenched teeth. "I went to kill him, no mistake there.

"When I reached his gate, it was unlocked, and I knew that meant someone else was already there. I already had the knife in my hand when Fuentes came through the door. He pulled his gun, but he never got the chance to use it. I gave him everything I had been saving for Gomez." Carlos moved away from the window as he spoke. His eyes looked past Paz as if he was seeing it all again.

His voice shifted as he continued. "Fuentes opened his mouth, but he made no sound. His eyes got big and round, and he fell backward. His gun flew across the floor, and Gomez grabbed it, but he just held onto it, pointing it at me. As I came in, I saw that coward Candelario go running out the back.

"There was something strange about the way Gomez held the gun, almost as if he was afraid of it. He stared at it as he held it like it was a snake, something that was going to bite him. I took my knife back and started toward him. After a moment, he quit looking at the gun and looked at me instead."

A weary little smile crossed his face. "I remember I laughed at him. I felt like the spider who was about to feast on the fly, but I wanted him to suffer before he died, and that meant he had to know who it was that was going to kill him and why. I had to tell him who I was. After so many years and changes, he didn't remember the skinny little gardener boy from years before. I reminded him of Paloma, the daughter he had thrown out so long ago. I could see his face change, to crack from the inside out.

"I watched him sink down onto the floor. He kept repeating, two children, two children. I didn't know what he was talking about at first, and then it was two dead children. His two children, a daughter and a son, Paloma and Roberto. I told him I was there to kill him for what he had done to Paloma and her daughter, Mariana, his own granddaughter. That's when he began to scream about how he had never hurt her, only threatened her."

Carlos snorted as if he was coming back to them from wherever it was that he had gone, to be able to tell this last part of the story. "Did you know you cannot kill a crying man? At least, I could not. I went there to kill him but then the moment was gone. He just kept screaming like a mad man. He was going on about how she had been in his house weeks before and had lied about killing Roberto. That's when his own dark secret came out. He and Roberto had been fighting about Roberto's behavior in the village and how he was always brandishing that pistol. The father had accidentally killed the son when he tried to take the pistol away from him. He ran to the beach at first, unsure of what to do, and when he returned, Candelario, who had seen Mariana on the road, was busy telling it that she was the one who had shot Roberto with his own gun. Gomez let the story take its own way after that. She was, he said, part of Roberto's trouble anyway. If she had not lured him into the *mangle* in the first place, none of it would have happened. Can you imagine? He was still blaming her after all that.

"I held the knife close to his face and made sure before I left him that he knew that he was the one who had killed his own daughter, his son, and even his own granddaughter. He was still holding the gun when I left. I waited outside for a few moments, and I saw the *guerrilleros* on the beach. I do not know why they were there, maybe to kidnap him for ransom, but they were too late. I heard one gunshot before they ever entered the house. I went back to see, and Gomez was dead. One shot to the head by his own hand. It was the government who told the story to the news people that he was killed by the guerrillas. It fit very well with their plans, yes?"

Carlos turned toward Rick, calmer now as he finished his bizarre tale. "When I left by the front gate, the rebels were coming in from the beach. I knew what they would find, so I went back to Imanuel's store to put you onto a plane.

"The headline in the newspaper a few days later was about murderous rebels killing a prominent Salvadoran businessman. They went on to say how a brave soldier was killed in his defense and that it was part of the rebels' revenge for the murder of the Archbishop. I knew it was all lies but who was I to tell? I did not want the whole history of our family painted in the newspaper, although I doubt that anyone would have listened or believed. Looking at your faces, I am not even certain you believe me. How could I expect strangers to listen?"

A heavy silence followed before Rick could collect himself well enough to try to put all he was feeling, all he had heard into words. "It is not that I don't believe you, Carlos. I never saw those stories in the news, but then by that time, I was in the hospital. It is all just so...."

"So what?" Carlos snapped. "So *complicado*? I told you once before, no story of El Salvador is ever simple. We are a mixture—those native to the land and Spanish invaders—two peoples who have never mixed well. The violence that hovers over us even now has always been with us. The *Pipil*, the *Leneca*, the people of *Cuscatlán*, were a strong and vibrant people before the Spanish came, but they were not without a fierce and brutal side. Then, the Spanish came and taught the ones on this side of the ocean more about savagery than they could ever have imagined. Today, we are the fruit of both trees, despite the sweet taste outside, the core of both can be bitter. To change that will never be easy, and yet, the people are the only true resource El Salvador has."

Paz had finally taken a seat, a disheartened look covered his face and dominated his sluggish movements.

"But if you knew Gomez and Fuentes were dead, why did you bring Paz here the way you did?" Rick's tormented mind was still trying to find some logic in all that he had heard. "Why keep him in the dark?"

One side of Carlos' face twitched. "There are still as many sides to all of this that you do not understand as there are ones you do, Mr. Mercy. Yes, two of the threats in *Las Palomitas* are dead, but what of the others? It was a long time before I knew what happened to Candelario, a man we all learned too late, could not be trusted. Hernandez remains in the Army, although I am still not certain how much he knew about what was happening in his own command. Like so many with assignments in the *campo*, he was busy running off to San Salvador every chance he could.

"But there are bigger problems than that. How many of our young men are forced to choose between being kidnapped into the army or accused by them of being guerrilla sympathizers for the least little thing, like refusing to join the army because they are needed by their families? They are subversives because they receive the church newsletter or attend Mass regularly or because they have relatives who are involved one way or another. The situation has not improved since you left. Surely you know that. Is it not what you are hearing every day in the kind of work that you do?"

Jolted, Rick met Carlos' gaze. "You know where I work?"

"I made it my business to find out where you were, what you were doing," came the matter-of-fact answer. "You did not answer my question."

"Yes, it's true. The situation is worse, the death toll is higher, and the young men are the most at risk."

"Then you know why I did what I did. And the reason to do it in secret. The answer is plain. Look at his face. I knew he would come if he thought it was you, but not if—if he knew the truth."

All eyes in the room focused on Paz, but Miguel was the first to speak.

"It will take time, Pazito." He reached a gnarled hand across the table. "To accept it all."

Paz pulled back and snapped back to his feet, his anger still alive despite the look of despair. "I do not have to accept anything. I do not understand why the two of you believe him so easily. Why should we?"

"Paz, he is my brother. This I do know. I know what he says is difficult, but it is true."

"Ask yourself what is it you are truly most angry about, boy," Carlos cut short Miguel's consoling words. "Is it me? Or that the money was mine? No, I do not believe that is it. You are still hurting. We all are. Imanuel is dead. Mariana is dead. Do you think we hurt any less than you? He was your father, our brother, his friend. She was my daughter, your sister, his lover." He stumbled over the last word.

When he spoke again, his voice was unnaturally light. "We all loved them, and that is what is killing you, all of us, in a thousand little ways. They should still be alive, just like thousands of others like them. You can walk out that door if you choose, but you are bound to us forever, whether you want to admit it or not. They belonged to us, too. They are gone, but we will always love them. Mariana taught me that. What we felt, what we still feel, will never die." He finished in a whisper.

Rick dared not lift his own wet eyes to face any of the others. Paz stood with his hand on the doorknob, his head bowed low. A sob escaped him, and he made as if to turn toward Miguel but then changed his mind as he yanked open the door and fled down the hall.

Miguel looked helplessly from Carlos to Rick. "I should go after him?"

"No." Rick shook his head. "You were right earlier when you said he needed some time. Let's give him a little." A tortured sigh escaped him. "I have an idea that might help."

* * * * *

The next morning Rick was at the gate of St. Francis at daybreak, his truck packed and ready for his return to the *Casa Oscar Romero*. He had called Elena once again, and this time promised he would be on his way in short order. She had been delighted to hear, however, that he had found Paz. He promised a full explanation upon his arrival.

He caught up to Paz before breakfast and walked him away from the main buildings of the campus. The haggard shadows around Paz's eyes said he had slept little the night before.

"How are you doing?" Rick asked politely.

A shrug was his first answer. "I am sorry I did not say goodbye last night. I hope you know I do not blame you for what has happened. I just cannot accept..." His voice trailed off as his emotions threatened to overwhelm him once again.

"It's all right. I came to say goodbye myself. I've got to get back to the center, back to work. Before I leave, I have a question for you."

"You are leaving today?" Paz looked even more miserable. "It is so soon."

"I know, but I've been gone for some time now, and I really do need to get back. I wanted to ask, what are your plans for spring break? It is coming up soon, in just a couple of weeks, isn't it?"

A blank look crossed Paz's face. "Yes, I suppose it is. During the short breaks, I often stay here. I have gone with one of the priests to visit with them or their families, like a brother or sister or parent. During the long vacations, I have gone to the homes of some of my friends. Father Emil always helps me to arrange something. Now, of course," he sniffed disdainfully. "I know why."

"Well, I've got a plan for you if you are interested. It's an arrangement you can choose to accept or reject all by yourself. Would you like to come and spend a week helping at the *Casa Oscar Romero*? I won't lie to you. It's hard work in some ways, and you'll hear stories that will break your heart. It's a hassle, too in that we're not exactly a favorite with Immigration and the Border Patrol but—"

"Yes, I will come." His answer was low, barely audible.

"Are you sure? I mean, it might be rough on you in some ways, but we can always use another bi-lingual helper."

Paz looked up, his intent unmistakably clear. "I would very much like to come. I think it would be good."

"Great." Rick stretched as if he had just dropped a weight from his own shoulders. "And if you like it, you could even come back for the summer. Now let's see. I bet we could really get some work out of you if you were there for three months."

Paz sat down on a nearby bench. "I had a long talk with Father Emil last night."

Rick said nothing.

"I told him after all I heard, I was ready to leave. That I just had to escape, that it was time for me to go back to El Salvador." He stared down at the spikes of green grass between his feet.

"Aren't you planning on graduating first?"

"Yes, there is that. I would wait until graduation, but then I would go."

"And what did Father Emil say?"

"He told me to consider everything carefully, not just what I learned in the last days. He also told me to pray, not for what I want but for what is best, what will best serve God."

"And..."

"And," Paz gave him half a smile. "Here, you come this morning with a different way to escape, escape to a house named Romero. How can I not say yes?"

"I see your point," Rick nodded.

"Before you go, will you tell me one more thing?" Paz seemed to relax, the more they talked.

"Just now, you tell me all the things about this house, that it is hard work, that you hear such sad stories, and that you are bothered by your own government. With all that, what makes you stay, Ricardo?"

Rick picked a tiny white flower from the grass in front of him and twirled it slowly between his fingers as he considered his answer. "Because I am needed there, in a very real way. It reminds me of you and Imanuel, and of course, Mariana and the way all of you made me feel when I lived in *Las Palomitas*. In each new face I see at the door—worried, haunted, tired faces—I see a little of the haunted ones like Fabiano and Niña Ana. I see the heart-broken ones like Marielos and the sweet ones like her daughters, Isabel and Anita, and even the angry ones like Franco. And in reaching out to each one, I remember your father and how hard he worked, and with each one, I feel a little closer to Mariana and her memory." He concentrated on the flower as he finished in a whisper. "It is the only thing I can do now to be close to her."

Paz put a hand on his friend's shoulder. "*Ya comprendo*," was all he said.

Rick stood up from the bench where he had seated himself next to Paz. "I've got to get going. It's a long drive. A few years ago, we'd have pulled in a net full of fish by this hour." He cast his eyes toward the rising sun.

"It is true," Paz laughed nervously. "We would have much done by this hour."

"So you'll come then? You can ride the bus down if that's okay with you. I'll buy the ticket and send it to you."

Paz nodded.

"Good. There is so much to do, Paz. The threat to so many is worse than ever." He shook Paz's hand and turned toward the front gate of St. Francis School for Boys.

* * * * *

Three men and a woman sat shivering around the gray remains of the campfire from the night before. The children lay sleeping, slightly apart, huddled together under a thin blanket.

The woman looked across the shadowed terrain toward the glowing horizon, where the pale light of dawn would soon give way to the blaze of the rising sun.

"It is almost time," the man spoke softly.

"How much longer, Rafael?" The weariness in the woman's voice threatened to overwhelm her even at this early hour. "How much further? Can we not allow them to sleep a little longer? They are so tired."

He frowned as he answered. "I asked him last night." He tilted his chin toward the taller, nervous man who had walked a short distance away. "I think another three days or so, and we will reach the border. The *Casa Oscar Romero* is not far after that."

"Tell me again," she stared dreamily at the rosy clouds. "Tell me again about where we are going."

He was silent for a moment. "It is as I have told you before. It is a safe place. He told me if anything should happen that I should take you, your brother, your daughters, and the girl, to the *Casa Oscar Romero* in Texas. He told me you would be safe there, and I promised."

She began to rock gently. "It is so hard to believe that they are all gone. When I heard the helicopters that day, I never dreamed they were coming to bomb us."

"Who could have known?" The thin young man at her side reached out, groping along the ground in front of him as he scooped up their few belongings and dropped them into a string bag at his side.

"I will get those. Just wait. Be careful. You will burn your hands if you get too close to the fire."

"I am blind, *hermana mía*," he chided gently, "not stupid. Even I can tell where the fire is."

"No one knew," the man answered the younger man's earlier question. "It was late in the afternoon, and we were not expecting anyone. I think because we had been safe there for so long, we stayed too long. By the time we realized they knew exactly where we were, it was too late. Someone must have told them. By the time we made it to the outside, many were already dead from the stones falling all around us."

The smallest of the children, a little girl around three years old, crawled out from under the blanket and wandered, wide-eyed, toward them. The woman welcomed her with open arms.

Tears slipped down the child's cheeks as she cried without making a sound.

"She still has not spoken a word since that day, has she?" The man whispered.

"No," the woman answered. "She no longer speaks or even makes a sound when she cries."

"She is doing that thing with her fingers again. Look at the way that she moves them. Maybe she is crazy, just like her mother."

"It is all right, *mi amor*." The woman reached out and laid her hand over the child's fluttering fingers. "Yes, it was a fire, a very big fire. You were dreaming, that is all. It is all gone now." She rocked her gently and smoothed the child's long dark blonde tresses from her face, before turning on the man.

"Don't you ever say that again! Her mother was not crazy. Life simply became too much for her to bear. There are days when I understand that very well.

"My daughters were the ones who explained to me. When she makes that sign with her fingers, she is remembering the big fire. She dreams often about the fire on the mountain."

The man snorted. "Big fire, very big fire, indeed. The one the army set to catch any of us who survived. That is their way of doing things, burn down the mountain to kill everything and everyone who is left. Do you remember we heard them joking about it when we crept behind their lines?"

She nodded. "It is such a strange, sad world we live in. It was a fire that gave her life back to her in the first place if you think about it. Was that not the

tale he liked to tell? How he set the little house on
fire to make—"

"*O sí*." The blind boy picked up the story when
she hesitated. "He would tell us all about sneaking
into the village and setting the house on fire where
she was and how he stole her away because they all
thought she was dead."

"Maybe she would have been better off if she had
been dead," the man answered flatly.

"How can you say such a thing?" The woman slid
her hand protectively over the ear of the child that
was not buried in her lap.

"Well, it is true. She was never right in the head
again, was she? Did she ever speak a word to you
or anyone? She just wandered around, like a person
with no mind at all."

"That is not true," the woman continued her
defense. "She was not like everyone else, but she was
not insane."

"How do you know? Tell me one thing that she did
or said," he challenged her.

"She cared for her child, every day, in every way
that mattered."

"I never heard her speak to her own child either."
He stood up as he spoke.

The woman's brother spoke up. "It is true. She did
not speak or seem to be with us in many ways, but
I could feel it when she was beside me. Her soul was
still with us."

"Her soul?" The man snorted. "What do you
know of this? You could not even see her. You have

not seen a thing since that bomb blew up in your face, boy."

"It helps, being blind, to see some things."

"Like what?" There was instant suspicion in his voice.

"I see right now that you are afraid. I do not know of what, but you seem very nervous, and you keep looking around."

"How can you know that I am looking at anything?"

"Every time you look in a different direction, you move your feet. I can hear them moving. What is wrong?"

"You would be worried, too, if you were me. Stuck out here in the middle of God's country, with a blind boy, a woman, and three children, and the *Federales* could be upon us at any minute. I do not like the idea of a Mexican jail any better than a Salvadoran one, and for me, it will be the same, if they catch us. They will send us back, and I do not trust this guide of ours, this *coyote*. I paid him, and he said he would take us, but I don't know."

"He has brought us this far, yes?" she added.

"Yes, it is true, *Niña*, but I will feel safer when we are moving again."

She looked down at the child in her arms. "You asked me how I knew her mother was not crazy. She wrote the word *madrina* in the dirt when we sat inside the cave. She wrote it and then she looked at me and at her daughter, and I knew. I knew she was asking me to be her child's godmother the day she died, and she never had to say a word. She was with my grandmother, drinking tea, and her daughter was with mine. The next thing I knew, the roof caved in on us. I found the two of them together, side by side." She stopped speaking as the words caught in her throat. She smoothed the little girl's hair from her caramel-colored face. "I wonder if her mother remembered the father when she looked at her child."

"Who knows what that woman could remember?"

"She remembered me. Even when I forget about her and shut her out, she never forgot about me. She was my best friend, but she was a better friend to me than I was to her. The only thing I can do now is take care of her daughter for her."

"Well, it is time to wake up her daughter and yours, too. Time to go."

"*Vaya, vaya*. I will wake them." The youth scrambled on all fours across the ground. "I wish he was still here."

"What did you say?" The man whirled around.

"I said, I wished—"

"I know what you said. I wish he was here, too. I wish they were here, and then I would not be doing this all alone!"

"I am sorry." The young man replied in a low, earnest tone. "I did not mean—"

"I know. It means nothing. I am a fighter, not a *niñero*, a caretaker of children. I do not know how to look after all of you so well. That is all."

"You miss them, too, yes? All of them." The young man had the girls up and made his way back to stand beside his nervous companion.

"I miss them, too. It is true." He sighed. "You know, he was a very brave man. He risked his life to save that crazy woman, his own cousin, and in the end, he died up there on the mountain with her, saving all of us."

The woman stood up, placing the still sleeping child at her feet and stretched her back.

"Francisca." She reached out to pick up the child but found she was now standing beside the two men. She smiled at the strange picture they made. She was more accustomed to seeing the larger man gripping an automatic weapon than the hand of a small child.

He stretched out the little one's hand, rubbing his thumb lightly over the scar on the back of her tiny hand. "He said even before they are born, the innocent suffer for the sins of those who come before. Even before she was born, she was marked by a bullet. He kept that bullet for a long time, you know. He said it came out of her mother when her child was born, and he kept it. I saw him hold this little one's hand and touch that mark and cry one night."

"I never knew he cried."

"He said all the children should be free, and that is why she was named Francisca because it means freedom." He was quiet for a moment and then added. "He said he wished she was his child. He loved her and her mother. I think it hurt him very deeply that she was never the same, even after he saved her."

"Look at her." The woman watched the little one walk away with the older two girls. "She is the perfect combination of the two of them—she has her mother's face, those eyes, and her father's hair. He did have beautiful blond hair, no?"

She turned her face into the morning breeze and then bent down to retrieve the last blanket, which she tied into a bundle with the last of their meager belongings and positioned it across her shoulders.

He shook himself loose from the memories that had gathered too close. "Come. We still have a long way to go, but soon you will be free, it is true. All of you."

"And you?"

"I only promised to bring you, not to stay. I will go back."

"Go back?" She was aghast. "But there is nothing to go back to. The army, they destroyed it all."

"It is true that our camp is gone, but there are others who continue to fight. I will join them. That is what I am. A fighter."

"And before? What were you before? I did not even know your name before." A tired little laugh escaped her. "I cannot imagine you were once little, Little Rafael, Rafaelito." She whispered her last word, "Lito."

"*Niña!*" He cautioned. "No names. It is impossible to know who knows who. My name is better known than I would like. The same is true of the others. It is better not to say."

"I am sorry. I am just tired. I did not think."

"We are all tired and hungry. Today, we will find food. I promise, if I have to steal the eggs from beneath the chicken myself. We are getting closer. Another few days, and we can rest in a house named for Monseñor Romero. There will surely be someone there who can help us. Say a prayer for us, Niña Marielos. *Por el amor de los cielos*. Now you have me saying names aloud." He shook his head as he walked ahead.

They began to trail after the others, now walking across the dusty stubble-covered ground.

"I pray that it is true," she sighed. With a last glance at the rising sun, she took a deep breath of the crisp morning air and squared her shoulders with the resolution of one who has no other choice. She followed the others, one dogged step after another.

The smallest one came back to walk with her as the older girls walked one on each side of their blind companion. The woman looked down at the little light-colored hand in her darker one and secretly admired the way this smallest child amongst them followed along without complaint.

"A few more days, Francisca, and we will be free." Her eyes brimmed full of tears, but her voice remained strong. "Free. Free to live."

Uncomprehending, the child found the woman's eyes with her own and gave her a tentative smile as she squeezed her hand.

March 1984. Washington D.C. The Immigration and Naturalization Service (INS) has recently acknowledged that at least 50 Salvadorans deported from the US have been murdered upon their forced repatriation to El Salvador, in response to a report made by the American Civil Liberties Union and the Los Angeles Center for Immigration Rights. The Human Rights Commission of the Catholic Church of El Salvador estimates that 30 percent of returning deportees are killed within two months of their return.

In a related story, according to the INS's own figures, only 71 of the nearly 3,000 Salvadorans who applied for political asylum last year in the United States were granted such status, a rate of 2.4 percent.

March 1984. Washington D.C. In the southwestern states of Texas and Arizona, the Immigration and Naturalization Service (INS) and the US Border Patrol have begun a crackdown on those offering asylum to Central American refugees, especially Salvadorans, despite refugee claims of political persecution in their own country. A handful of Americans associated with church-run assistance programs have been accused, arrested, and charged with transporting illegal aliens. While officials refuse to publicly acknowledge the Salvadorans' plight, some have privately commented that recognition of such claims as legitimate clashes with the [Reagan] Administration's policy of assistance to the government of El Salvador.

Special Thanks

Maria Arnt, former Senior Editor at 2Nimble.
Thank you for your work on this manuscript and
for seeing me through to publishing. You will be
missed by all who have come to know you.
Rest easy, dear friend.

CPSIA information can be obtained
at www.ICGtesting.com
Printed in the USA
LVHW040017051221
705305LV00001B/1